**Peter Haining** has written and edited a number of bestselling books on the supernatural, notably the widely acclaimed *Ghosts: The Illustrated History* (1975) and *A Dictionary of Ghosts* (1982), which has been translated into several languages including French, German, Russian and Japanese. A former journalist and publisher, he lives in a sixteenth-century timber frame house in Suffolk that is haunted by the ghost of a Napoleonic prisoner of war.

*Also available*

The Mammoth Book of Awesome Comic Fantasy
The Mammoth Book of Best New Erotica 3
The Mammoth Book of Best New Horror 14
The Mammoth Book of Climbing Adventures
The Mammoth Book of Comic Crime
The Mammoth Book of Egyptian Whodunnits
The Mammoth Book of Elite Forces
The Mammoth Book of Endurance and Adventure
The Mammoth Book of Explorers
The Mammoth Boom of Eyewitness America
The Mammoth Book of Eyewitness Battles
The Mammoth Book of Eyewitness Everest
The Mammoth Book of Fantasy
The Mammoth Book of Fighter Pilots
The Mammoth Book of Future Cops
The Mammoth Book of Great Detective Stories
The Mammoth Book of Haunted House Stories
The Mammoth Book of Heroes
The Mammoth Book of Heroic and Outrageous Women
The Mammoth Book of Historical Whodunnits
The Mammoth Book of Humor
The Mammoth Book of Illustrated Crime
The Mammoth Book of Journalism
The Mammoth Book of Legal Thrillers
The Mammoth Book of Literary Anecdotes
The Mammoth Book of Locked-Room Mysteries and Impossible Crimes
The Mammoth Book of Maneaters
The Mammoth Book of Men O'War
The Mammoth Book of Mountain Disasters
The Mammoth Book of Murder and Science
The Mammoth Book of Native Americans
The Mammoth Book of Private Eye Stories
The Mammoth Book of Prophecies
The Mammoth Book of Pulp Action
The Mammoth Book of Roaring Twenties Whodunnits
The Mammoth Book of Roman Whodunnits
The Mammoth Book of Science Fiction
The Mammoth Book of Sea Battles
The Mammoth Book of Sex, Drugs and Rock 'n' Roll
The Mammoth Book of Short Erotic Novels
The Mammoth Book of Tales from the Road
The Mammoth Book of the Titanic
The Mammoth Book of UFOs
The Mammoth Book of Vampires
The Mammoth Book of Vampire Stories by Women
The Mammoth Book of War Correspondents
The Mammoth Book of Women Who Kill

# The Mammoth Book of

# HAUNTED HOUSE STORIES

Edited by Peter Haining

CARROLL & GRAF PUBLISHERS
New York

Carroll & Graf Publishers
An imprint of Avalon Publishing Group, Inc.
245 W. 17th Street
New York
NY 10011–5300
www.carrollandgraf.com

First published in the UK by Robinson,
an imprint of Constable & Robinson Ltd 2000

This revised Carroll & Graf edition 2005



ISBN 0-7867-1603-7

Printed and bound in the EU

For my daughter
GEMMA
– who has lived in a haunted house all her life

*"When I was dead, my spirit turned*
*To seek the much-frequented house."*

Christina Rossetti, 1866

*"In general, ghosts are a plus point in marketing a house, either for sale or as a tourist attraction."*

*Daily Telegraph*, 25 June 1994

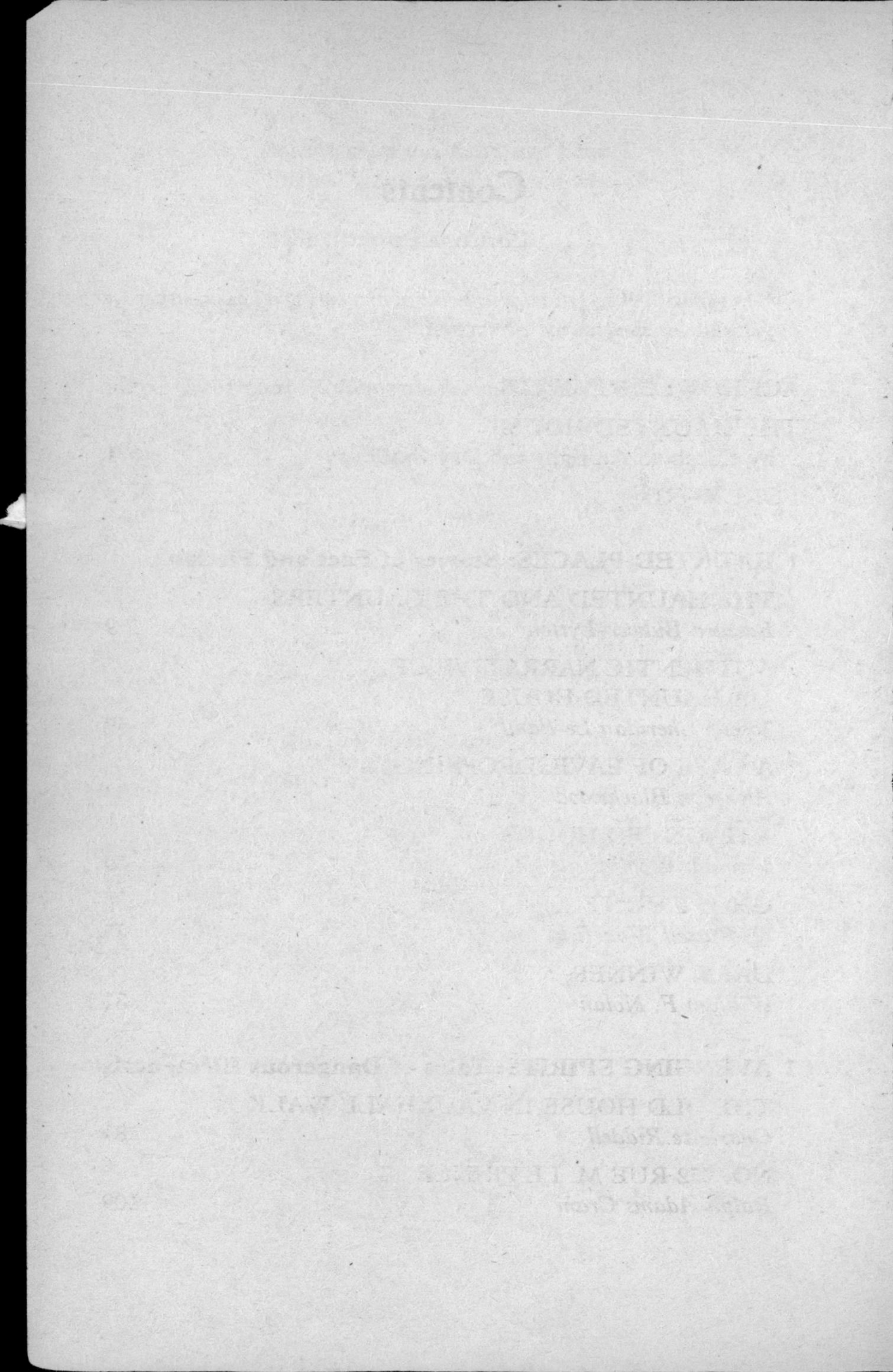

# Contents

ACKNOWLEDGMENTS xiii

THE HAUNTED HOUSE
by Elizabeth Albright and Ray Bradbury 1

FOREWORD 3

1 **HAUNTED PLACES: Stories of Fact and Fiction**

THE HAUNTED AND THE HAUNTERS
*Edward Bulwer-Lytton* 9

AUTHENTIC NARRATIVE OF A HAUNTED HOUSE
*Joseph Sheridan Le Fanu* 39

A CASE OF EAVESDROPPING
*Algernon Blackwood* 53

A HAUNTED HOUSE
*Virginia Woolf* 69

GHOST HUNT
*H. Russell Wakefield* 73

DARK WINNER
*William F. Nolan* 81

2 **AVENGING SPIRITS: Tales of Dangerous Elementals**

THE OLD HOUSE IN VAUXHALL WALK
*Charlotte Riddell* 89

NO. 252 RUE M. LE PRINCE
*Ralph Adams Cram* 109

THE SOUTHWEST CHAMBER
*Mary Eleanor Freeman* 125

THE TOLL-HOUSE
*W. W. Jacobs* 145

FEET FOREMOST
*L. P. Hartley* 157

HAPPY HOUR
*Ian Watson* 191

**3 SHADOWY CORNERS: Accounts of Restless Spirits**

THE ANKARDYNE PEW
*W. F. Harvey* 217

THE REAL AND THE COUNTERFEIT
*Louisa Baldwin* 231

A NIGHT AT A COTTAGE . . .
*Richard Hughes* 249

THE CONSIDERATE HOSTS
*Thorp McClusky* 253

THE GREY HOUSE
*Basil Copper* 265

WATCHING ME, WATCHING YOU
*Fay Weldon* 309

**4 PHANTOM LOVERS: Sex and the Supernatural**

A SPIRIT ELOPEMENT
*Richard Dehan* 329

THE HOUSE OF DUST
*Herbert de Hamel* 339

THE KISSTRUCK BOGIE
*A. E. Coppard* 357

MR EDWARD
*Norah Lofts* 367

HOUSE OF THE HATCHET
*Robert Bloch* 385

NAPIER COURT
*Ramsey Campbell* 403

**5 LITTLE TERRORS: Ghosts and Children**

LOST HEARTS
*M. R. James* 423

THE SHADOWY THIRD
*Ellen Glasgow* 435

A LITTLE GHOST
*Hugh Walpole* 461

THE PATTER OF TINY FEET
*Nigel Kneale* 477

UNINVITED GHOSTS
*Penelope Lively* 489

**6 PSYCHIC PHENOMENA: Signs from the Other Side**

PLAYING WITH FIRE
*Sir Arthur Conan Doyle* 497

THE WHISTLING ROOM
*William Hope Hodgson* 513

BAGNELL TERRACE
*E. F. Benson* 533

THE COMPANION
*Joan Aiken* 547

THE GHOST HUNTER
*James Herbert* 557

COMPUTER SÉANCE
*Ruth Rendell* 563

**7 HOUSES OF HORROR:**
**Terror Visions of the Stars**

IN LETTERS OF FIRE
*Gaston Leroux* 573

THE JUDGE'S HOUSE
*Bram Stoker* 593

THE STORM
*McKnight Malmar* 613

THE WAXWORK
*A. M. Burrage* 627

THE INEXPERIENCED GHOST
*H. G. Wells* 641

SOPHY MASON COMES BACK
*E. M. Delafield* 655

THE BOOGEYMAN
*Stephen King* 669

*APPENDIX: Haunted House Novels: A Listing* 683

# Acknowledgments

Acknowledgment is made to the following authors, agents and publishers for permission to reprint the stories in this collection.

"The Haunted House" © 2000 by Elizabeth Albright and Ray Bradbury. First published in this volume and reprinted by permission of the authors.
"A Case of Eavesdropping" © 1900 by Algernon Blackwood. Originally published in *Pall Mall Magazine*, December 1900. Reprinted by permission of A. P. Watt Ltd.
"A Haunted House" © 1921 by Virginia Woolf. Originally published in *Monday or Tuesday*, Hogarth Press. Reprinted by permission of the Virginia Woolf Estate.
"Ghost Hunt" © 1948 by H. Russell Wakefield. Originally published in *Weird Tales*, 1948. Reprinted by permission of Curtis Brown and the Estate of H. Russell Wakefield.
"Dark Winner" © 1976 by Stuart David Schiff. Originally published in *Whispers* edited by Stuart David Schiff. Reprinted by permission of William F. Nolan.
"The Toll-House" © 1907 by W. W. Jacobs. Originally published in *The Strand*, 1907. Reprinted by permission of the Estate of W. W. Jacobs.
"Feet Foremost" © 1948 by L. P. Hartley. Originally published in *The Travelling Grave & Other Stories*, 1948. Reprinted by permission of Hamish Hamilton Ltd.
"Happy Hour" © 1900 by Ian Watson. First published in *Wheels of Fear* edited by Kathryn Cramer. Reprinted by permission of the author.
"The Ankardyne Pew" © 1928 by W. F. Harvey. First published in *The Beast With Five Fingers*, 1928. Reprinted by permission of Weidenfeld & Nicolson.
"A Night at a Cottage" © 1926 by Richard Hughes. First published in *A Moment in Time*, 1926. Reprinted by permission of David Higham Associates.
"The Grey House" © 1967 by Basil Copper. First published in *Not After Nightfall*, 1967. Reprinted by permission of the author.
"Watching Me, Watching You" © 1980 by Fay Weldon. Commissioned television play in the *Leap in the Dark* series, BBC Bristol 1980, produced by Michael Courcher, directed by Colin Godman. First published in

*Woman's Own* in January 1981 and became the title story of *Watching Me, Watching You*, 1981. Reprinted by permission of Curtis Brown.
"The Kisstruck Bogie" © 1946 by A. E. Coppard. First published in *Fearful Pleasures*, 1946. Reprinted by permission of David Higham Associates.
"Mr Edward" © 1947 by Norah Lofts. First published in *At Close of Eve*, 1947. Reprinted by permission of Hutchinson Ltd.
"House of the Hatchet" © 1941 by Robert Bloch. First published in *Weird Tales*, 1941. Reprinted by permission of A. M. Heath Ltd.
"Napier Court" © 1971 by Ramsey Campbell. First published in *Dark Things* edited by August Derleth, 1971. Reprinted by permission of the author.
"Lost Hearts" © 1895 by M. R. James. First published in *Pall Mall Magazine*, 1895. Reprintd by permission of the M. R. James Estate.
"A Little Ghost" © 1922 by Hugh Walpole. First published in *Red Book Magazine*, 1922. Reprinted by permission of Rupert Hart Davis Ltd.
"The Patter of Tiny Feet" © 1949 by Nigel Kneale. First published in *Tomato Cain*, 1949. Reprinted by permission of The Agency.
"Uninvited Ghosts" © 1984 by Penelope Lively. First published in *Uninvited Ghosts*, 1981. Reprinted by permission of David Higham Associates.
"Bagnell Terrace" © 1928 by E. F. Benson. First published in *Spook Stories*, 1928. Reprinted by permission of A. P. Watt Ltd.
"The Companion" © 1978 by Joan Aiken. First published in *John Creasey's Crime Collection* edited by Herbert Harris, 1978. Reprinted by permission of A. M. Heath Ltd.
"The Ghost Hunter" © 1988 by James Herbert. First published in *Haunted*, 1988. Reprinted by permission of the author and David Higham Associates.
"Computer Séance" © 1997 by Ruth Rendell. First published in *The Oldie*, 1997. Reprinted by permission of Peters, Fraser & Dunlop.
"The Storm" © 1944 by McKnight Malmar. First published in *Good Housekeeping*, February, 1944. Reprinted by permission of Willis King Agency.
"The Waxwork" © 1931 by A. M. Burrage. First published in *Someone in the Room*, 1931. Reprinted by permission of the Estate of A. M. Burrage.
"The Inexperienced Ghost" © 1902 by H. G. Wells. First published in *The Strand*, March, 1902. Reprinted by permission of A. P. Watt Ltd.
"Sophie Mason Comes Back" © 1930 by E. M. Delafield. First published in *Time and Tide*, July 1930. Reprinted by permission of PFD Ltd.
"The Boogeyman" © 1973 by Stephen King. First published in *Cavalier*, March 1973. Reprinted by permission of Ralph M. Vicinanza Ltd.

Every effort has been made to trace the owners of copyright material. The editor would be pleased to hear from anyone if they believe there has been an inadvertent transgression of copyright.

# The Haunted House

By Elizabeth Albright and Ray Bradbury

*This little tale was written to mark Hallowe'en 1999: the last of the twentieth century, but surely not the last to be celebrated. It marks the first appearance in print for eight-year-old Elizabeth and is Ray Bradbury's first collaboration in a career that spans sixty years. Where one writer finished and the other began is a secret – just like the enduring mystery of haunted houses . . .*

Once there was a haunted house where ghosts and goblins lived.
Also The Headless Horseman – Ichabod's ghost – and eerie Jack O'Lanterns.
On the night of Hallowe'en, five kids went to the house.
They had never seen it before.
One of the kids said, "Let's go to the door."
Another kid said, "No! It looks like it is haunted."
The kid who wanted to go in said, "Whoever is with me, say 'I' "
*No-one* said "I" because they were all scared.
The brave kid said, "Fine. *I'll* go by myself."
So he went to the door.
It opened slowly, but no-one was there.
"I'm here" said a voice, "but you can't *see* me!"
"Who are you?" the kids cried.
"I am the man from that famous poem,
*'Last night I saw upon the stair*
*A little man who wasn't there*

*He wasn't there again today,*
*My Gosh, I wish he'd go away.'"*

"So you were *never* here?" the kids cried.
"Never and never *will* be!" said the voice.
"Nice to meet you!" said the kids.
"Even if we really *didn't!*" said the voice.
"Goodbye!" said the kids.
"Hello," said the voice.
And the door shut.

# Foreword

## I Live In A Haunted House

The first sensation was of woodsmoke. A curiously acrid but unmistakable smell that became apparent for a few days in the upper rooms of the house and was experienced by each member of the family. The smoke, which seemed to have no identifiable source and was smelled rather than ever being seen, occurred at a time of the year when there was no longer the need for a fire to be lit in the house. For a while, there seemed to be no logical explanation of the phenomenon – until the night when something quite extraordinary happened to my wife.

Peyton House, where we live, is a sixteenth-century, three-storey timber-frame building which stands in the middle of the picturesque little village of Boxford in Suffolk. It was once the grace-and-favour home of the chief stewards to the Peyton family, the local landowners who lived about a mile away in their Elizabethan manor house, Peyton Hall. For the last twenty years, though, Peyton House has been home to me, my wife Philippa and our three children, Richard, Sean and Gemma. What has happened to us there would seem to have no other explanation than yet another instance of the supernatural at work.

We had been living in the house for a while before we became fully aware of the manifestation that is repeated each year. This realisation came about because of what occurred late one spring evening. It was on a night during the first week of June and Philippa was sitting reading in our bedroom, a high-ceilinged room at the front of the house. On the rear wall of this room there is an interior window which looks out on to the landing. Philippa was engrossed in her book when she was suddenly aware out of the corner of her eye of someone going past the window. She looked up and caught sight of a figure with long hair passing by. A moment later and it was gone.

Philippa's first reaction was that it must have been Gemma going along the landing to the bathroom. Then she realised that our daughter was not in the house. Indeed, the whole place was deserted because everyone *else* had gone out, too. Curiously, though, this realisation did not make her feel afraid. Only the strong conviction that the figure – whoever or whatever it was – was quite benign.

It was to be some months later, and as a result of making a number of enquiries in Boxford, that an explanation for my wife's experience was forthcoming. Tales of a strange visitant in Peyton House were, it seemed, known to a number of the older residents in the village whose parents and grandparents had once worked as servants in the house. Several of these men and women had even lived for a time in the attic rooms. All told of experiencing the ethereal smell, and a few had even seen the long-haired wraith. And all at precisely the same time of year. Even stranger, not one of them had felt there was anything of which to be afraid.

The old house, we were informed, had years ago been surrounded by several acres of land – later sold off for farming and a small housing development long before we arrived – but during the early years of the nineteenth century, at the time of the Napoleonic wars with France, something terrible and tragic had occurred there. A group of French soldiers who had been taken prisoner during the conflict had been billeted at Peyton House, where they were kept in the outbuildings and set to earn their keep by working on the land. This was a common practice during this particular war, and a number of property owners in East Anglia benefited from these gangs of enforced labourers – although there is no evidence that they treated the Frenchmen with anything other than kindness, as long as they worked conscientiously and did not cause any trouble.

Then, one June day, a fire broke out at Peyton House. Fortunately, the blaze was put out before it could do any serious damage to the building, but one of the PoWs was trapped by the flames and perished in a smoke-filled room. There is no record as to whether the man was buried locally or his body returned to

France. Each June thereafter, we were told, a distinct aroma of smoke was evident in the house, growing in intensity until the same specific day when it stopped as dramatically as it had begun.

That day was 6 June – the very day on which Philippa had seen the figure on the landing . . .

This account of the Peyton House ghost, which I entitled "*The Smoke Ghost*", was originally written at the invitation of Stephen Jones for his anthology of true paranormal encounters, *Dancing With The Dark*, published in 1997. The story attracted quite a lot of interest from fellow writers in the supernatural genre, as well as neighbours and friends in Suffolk. All of them, it seemed, had experiences either at first hand, or from people whose integrity they had no reason to doubt, relating to haunted houses. Clearly, interest in house-bound phantoms was as intense now as it has ever been.

I knew at the same time, too, that the theme of haunted houses had been a popular one with authors for the past century and more. Yet amidst the veritable library of collections of ghost stories, very few were solely devoted to this topic. A few day's research confirmed the fact that there was indeed a wealth of material available – and the result is the book now in your hands. Making a selection of tales from so many has not been easy, I must admit, but I do believe that here you will find a *representative* collection covering all the important elements of haunted houses.

An ideal way of setting the mood seemed to me to be with a group of stories – like that of my wife – based on *actual* hauntings. The first of these, "The Haunted and the Haunters" by Edward Bulwer-Lytton may well be the most famous story of its kind and certainly its influence will be evident in all the subsequent tales in the section right up to William F. Nolan's contemporary thriller, "Dark Winner." Nolan's dangerous little protagonist leads neatly into the second section featuring ghosts with a vengeance where again the spirit in Charlotte Riddell's house in Vauxhall Walk is every bit as ancient and malevolent as the evil which haunts the customers in Ian Watson's tale of the Roebuck Public House enjoying a "Happy Hour."

The third section deals with a variety of restless phantoms caught half-way between their world and ours, their stories chillingly recounted by at least two writers, Richard Hughes and Fay Weldon, not generally associated with the supernatural. Whether the spirit world is as obsessed with sex as our own provides the theme for the Phantom Lovers section with Richard Dehan's century-old story indicating that the undead have been interfering with the affairs (if you'll excuse the pun) of men and women for a great many years – and are still doing so according to those excellent modern horror masters, Robert Bloch and Ramsey Campbell.

People begin their love of ghost stories in childhood and it should come as no surprise when considering the number of children who die tragically young that they have featured in a number of haunted house stories. M. R. James, Nigel Kneale and Penelope Lively demonstrate how little darlings can also become little terrors after death. The uncertainty of what lies beyond death has, of course, promoted a continuing interest in the "Other Side" and the penultimate group of stories take the reader through the shadow lands under the guidance of several knowledgeable writers including Sir Arthur Conan Doyle, Joan Aiken and James Herbert.

The final section, "Houses of Horror" has been added to this new edition of the book at the invitation of my publishers. During the almost half a century that I have been editing anthologies of supernatural stories, I have worked on three collections with famous horror film stars – namely Vincent Price, Christopher Lee and Peter Cushing – and researched and written about four other top names, Lon Chaney, Bela Lugosi, Boris Karloff and Robert Englund. All of them proved to be lovers of ghost stories as well as being familiar with supernatural fiction. Amongst these actors' favourite stories, each had one about a haunted house and it is their choices that bring the book to a chilling finale.

For myself, I have continued to live contentedly in my own haunted home, ghost notwithstanding, for over a quarter of a century. I wish you the same enjoyment – and safety – in the ill-omened and often dangerous properties that now await your visit.

Peter Haining
February, 2005

# 1

# HAUNTED PLACES

## *Stories of Fact and Fiction*

No.50, Berkeley Square, London

# The Haunted and the Haunters

## Edward Bulwer-Lytton

### Prospectus

**Address:** 50, Berkeley Square, London W1.

**Property:** *Circa* Eighteenth-century, four-storey town house. Plain fronted with tall windows and a narrow balcony on the second floor. The residence of a former prime minister, George Canning (1770–1827), the house has been much renovated.

**Viewing Date:** August, 1859.

**Agent:** Edward Bulwer-Lytton (1803–1873) was born in London and despite his noble birth was forced to earn his living as a writer, until he inherited the title of Lord Lytton in 1866. In the interim, he had become popular with readers for his historical novels – notably *The Last Days of Pompeii* (1834) – and a number of stories of the occult and supernatural. Highly regarded among these are his novel *A Strange Story* (1861) and short stories, "Glenallan" and "The Haunted and the Haunters", described by H.P. Lovecraft as "one of the best short haunted house tales ever written". It is based on reports Lytton had heard about a building in the heart of London's Mayfair and effectively launched the genre of Haunted House stories.

A friend of mine, who is a man of letters and a philosopher, said to me one day, as if between jest and earnest, "Fancy! since we last met, I have discovered a haunted house in the midst of London."

"Really haunted? – and by what? ghosts?"

"Well, I can't answer that question: all I know is this – six weeks ago my wife and I were in search of a furnished apartment. Passing a quiet street, we saw on the window of one of the houses a bill, 'Apartments Furnished'. The situation suited us; we entered the house – liked the rooms – engaged them by the week – and left them the third day. No power on earth could have reconciled my wife to stay longer; and I don't wonder at it."

"What did you see?"

"Excuse me – I have no desire to be ridiculed as a superstitious dreamer – nor, on the other hand, could I ask you to accept on my affirmation what you would hold to be incredible without the evidence of your own senses. Let me only say this, it was not so much what we saw or heard (in which you might fairly suppose that we were the dupes of our own excited fancy, or the victims of imposture in others) that drove us away, as it was an undefinable terror which seized both of us whenever we passed by the door of a certain unfurnished room, in which we neither saw nor heard anything. And the strangest marvel of all was, that for once in my life I agreed with my wife, silly woman though she be – and allowed, after the third night, that it was impossible to stay a fourth in that house. Accordingly, on the fourth morning I summoned the woman who kept the house and attended on us, and told her that the rooms did not quite suit us, and we would not stay out our week. She said, dryly, "I know why: you have stayed longer than any other lodger. Few ever stayed a second night; none before you a third. But I take it they have been very kind to you."

" 'They – who?' I asked, affecting to smile.

" 'Why, they who haunt the house, whoever they are. I don't mind them; I remember them many years ago, when I lived in this house, not as a servant; but I know they will be the death of me some day. I don't care – I'm old, and must die soon anyhow; and then I shall be with them, and in this house still.' The woman spoke with so dreary a calmness, that really it was a sort of awe that prevented my conversing with her further. I paid for my week, and too happy were my wife and I to get off so cheaply."

"You excite my curiosity," said I; "nothing I should like better than to sleep in a haunted house. Pray give me the address of the one which you left so ignominiously."

My friend gave me the address; and when we parted, I walked straight towards the house thus indicated.

It is situated on the north side of Oxford Street (in a dull but respectable thoroughfare). I found the house shut up – no bill at the window, and no response to my knock. As I was turning away, a beer-boy, collecting pewter pots at the neighboring areas, said to me, "Do you want any one at that house, sir?"

"Yes, I heard it was to be let."

"Let! – why, the woman who kept it is dead – has been dead these three weeks, and no one can be found to stay there, though Mr. J— offered ever so much. He offered Mother, who chars for him, £1 a week just to open and shut the windows, and she would not."

"Would not! – and why?"

"The house is haunted: and the old woman who kept it was found dead in her bed, with her eyes wide open. They say the devil strangled her."

"Pooh! – you speak of Mr. J—. Is he the owner of the house?"

"Yes."

"Where does he live?"

"In G— Street, No.—."

"What is he – in any business?"

"No, sir – nothing particular; a single gentleman."

I gave the pot-boy the gratuity earned by his liberal information, and proceeded to Mr. J—, in G— Street, which was close by the street that boasted the haunted house. I was lucky enough to find Mr. J— at home, an elderly man, with intelligent countenance and prepossessing manners.

I communicated my name and my business frankly. I said I heard the house was considered to be haunted – that I had a strong desire to examine a house with so equivocal a reputation – that I should be greatly obliged if he would allow me to hire it, though only for a night. I was willing to pay for that privilege whatever he might be inclined to ask.

"Sir," said Mr. J—, with great courtesy, "the house is at your service, for as short or as long a time as you please. Rent is out of the question – the obligation will be on my side should you be able to discover the cause of the strange phenomena which at present deprive it of all value. I cannot let it, for I cannot even get a servant to keep it in order or answer the door. Unluckily the house is haunted, if I may use that expression, not only by night, but by day; though at night the disturbances are of a more unpleasant and sometimes of a more alarming character. The poor old woman who died in it three weeks ago was a pauper whom I took out of a workhouse, for in her childhood she had been known to some of my family, and had once been in such good circumstances that she had rented that house of my uncle. She was a woman of superior education and strong mind, and was the only person I could ever induce to remain in the house. Indeed, since her death, which was sudden, and the coroner's inquest, which gave it a notoriety in the neighborhood, I have so despaired of finding any person to take charge of the house, much more a tenant, that I would willingly let it rent-free for a year to any one who would pay its rates and taxes."

"How long is it since the house acquired this sinister character?"

"That I can scarcely tell you, but very many years since. The old woman I spoke of said it was haunted when she rented it between thirty and forty years ago. The fact is, that my life has been spent in the East Indies, and in the civil service of the Company. I returned to England last year, on inheriting the fortune of an uncle, among whose possessions was the house in question. I found it shut up and uninhabited. I was told that it was haunted, that no-one would inhabit it. I smiled at what seemed to me so idle a story. I spent some money in repairing it – added to its old-fashioned furniture a few modern articles – advertised it, and obtained a lodger for a year. He was a colonel retired on half-pay. He came in with his family, a son and a daughter, and four or five servants: they all left the house the next day; and, although each of them declared that he had seen something different from that which had scared the others, a something still was equally terrible to all. I really could not in conscience sue, nor even blame, the colonel for breach of agreement. Then I put in the old woman I have spoken of, and she was empowered to let the house in apartments. I never had one lodger who stayed more than three days. I do not tell you their stories – to no two lodgers have there been exactly the same phenomena repeated. It is better that you should judge for yourself, than enter the house with an imagination influenced by previous narratives; only be prepared to see and to hear something or other, and take whatever precautions you yourself please."

"Have you never had a curiosity yourself to pass a night in that house?"

"Yes. I passed not a night, but three hours in broad daylight alone in that house. My curiosity is not satisfied but it is quenched. I have no desire to renew the experiment. You cannot complain, you see, sir, that I am not sufficiently candid; and unless your interest be exceedingly eager and your nerves unusually strong, I honestly add, that I advise you not to pass a night in that house."

"My interest *is* exceedingly keen," said I, "and though only a coward will boast of his nerves in situations wholly unfamiliar to him, yet my nerves have been seasoned in such variety of danger that I have the right to rely on them – even in a haunted house."

Mr. J— said very little more; he took the keys of the house out of his bureau, gave them to me – and, thanking him cordially for his frankness, and his urbane concession to my wish, I carried off my prize.

Impatient for the experiment, as soon as I reached home, I summoned my confidential servant – a young man of gay spirits, fearless temper, and as free from superstitious prejudices as any one I could think of.

"F—," said I, "you remember in Germany how disappointed we were at not finding a ghost in that old castle, which was said to be haunted by a headless apparition? Well, I have heard of a house in London which, I have reason to hope, is decidedly haunted. I mean to sleep there to-night. From what I hear, there is no doubt that something will allow itself to be seen or to be heard – something, perhaps, excessively horrible. Do you think if I take you with me, I may rely on your presence of mind, whatever may happen?"

"Oh, sir! pray trust me," answered F—, grinning with delight.

"Very well; then here are the keys of the house – this is the address. Go now – select for me any bedroom you please; and since the house has not been inhabited for weeks, make up a good fire – air the bed well – see, of course, that there are candles as well as fuel. Take with you my revolver and my dagger – so much for my weapons – arm yourself equally well; and if we are not a match for a dozen ghosts, we shall be but a sorry couple of Englishmen."

I was engaged for the rest of the day on business so urgent that I had not leisure to think much on the nocturnal adventure to which I had plighted my honor. I dined alone, and very late, and while dining, read, as is my habit. I selected one of the volumes of Macaulay's *Essays*. I thought to myself that I would take the book with me; there was so much of the healthfulness in the style, and practical life in the subjects, that it would serve as an antidote against the influence of superstitious fancy.

Accordingly, about half-past nine, I put the book into my pocket, and strolled leisurely towards the haunted house. I took with me a favorite dog – an exceedingly sharp, bold and vigilant bull-terrier – a dog fond of prowling about strange ghostly corners and passages at night in search of rats – a dog of dogs for a ghost.

It was a summer night, but chilly, the sky somewhat gloomy and overcast. Still there was a moon – faint and sickly, but still a moon – and if the clouds permitted, after midnight it would be brighter.

I reached the house, knocked, and my servant opened with a cheerful smile.

"All right, sir, and very comfortable."

"Oh!" said I, rather disappointed; "have you not seen nor heard anything remarkable?"

"Well, sir, I must own I have heard something queer."

"What – what?"

"The sound of feet pattering behind me; and once or twice small noises like whispers close at my ear – nothing more."

"You are not at all frightened?"

"I! not a bit of it, sir," and the man's bold look reassured me on one point – viz., that happen what might, he would not desert me.

We were in the hall, the street-door closed, and my attention was now drawn to my dog. He had at first run in eagerly enough, but had sneaked back to the door, and was scratching and whining to get out. After patting him on the head, and encouraging him gently, the dog seemed to reconcile himself to the situation, and followed me and F— through the house, but keeping close at my heels instead of hurrying inquisitively in advance, which was his usual and normal habit in all strange places. We first visited the subterranean apartments, the kitchen and other offices, and especially the cellars, in which last there were two or three bottles of wine still left in a bin, covered with cobwebs, and evidently, by their appearance, undisturbed for many years. It was clear that the ghosts were not wine-bibbers. For the rest we discovered nothing of interest. There was a gloomy little backyard with very high walls. The stones of this yard were very damp; and what with the damp, and what with the dust and smoke-grime on the pavement, our feet left a slight impression where we passed.

And now appeared the first strange phenomenon witnessed by myself in this strange abode. I saw, just before me, the print of a foot suddenly form itself, as it were. I stopped, caught hold of my servant, and pointed to it. In advance of that footprint as suddenly dropped another. We both saw it. I advanced quickly to the place; the footprint kept advancing before me, a small footprint – the foot of a child; the impression was too faint thoroughly to distinguish the shape, but it seemed to us both that it was the print of a naked foot. This phenomenon ceased when we arrived at the opposite wall, nor did it repeat itself on returning. We remounted the stairs, and entered the rooms on the ground floor, a dining-parlor, a small back parlor, and a still smaller third room that had been probably appropriated to a footman – all still as death. We then visited the drawing-rooms, which seemed fresh and new. In the front room I seated myself in an armchair. F— placed on the table the candlestick with which he had lighted us. I told him to shut the door. As he turned to do so, a chair opposite to me moved from the wall quickly and noiselessly, and dropped itself about a yard from my own chair, immediately fronting it.

"Why, this is better than the turning tables," said I, with a half-laugh; and as I laughed, my dog put back his head and howled.

F—, coming back, had not observed the movement of the chair. He employed himself now in stilling the dog. I continued to gaze on the chair, and fancied I saw on it a pale blue misty outline of a human figure, but an outline so indistinct that I could only distrust my own vision. The dog now was quiet.

"Put back that chair opposite me," said I to F—; "put it back to the wall."

F— obeyed. "Was that you, sir?" said he, turning abruptly.

"I!—what?"

"Why, something struck me. I felt it sharply on the shoulder – just here."

"No," said I. "But we have jugglers present, and though we may not discover their tricks, we shall catch *them* before they frighten *us*."

We did not stay long in the drawing-rooms – in fact, they felt so damp and so chilly that I was glad to get to the fire upstairs. We locked the doors of the drawing-rooms – a precaution which, I should observe, we had taken with all the rooms we had searched below. The bedroom my servant had selected for me was the best on the floor – a large one, with two windows fronting the street. The four-posted bed, which took up no inconsiderable space, was opposite to the fire, which burnt clear and bright; a door in the wall to the left, between the bed and the window, communicated with the room which my servant appropriated to himself. This last was a small room with a sofa-bed, and had no communication with the landing-place – no other door but that which conducted to the bedroom I was to occupy. On either side of my fireplace was a cupboard, without locks, flush with the wall and covered with the same dull-brown paper. We examined these cupboards – only hooks to suspend female dresses – nothing else; we sounded the walls – evidently solid – the outer walls of the building. Having finished the survey of these apartments, warmed myself a few moments, and lighted my cigar, I then, still accompanied by F—, went forth to complete my reconnoiter. In the landing-place there was another door; it was closed firmly. "Sir," said my servant, in surprise, "I unlocked this door with all the others when I first came; it cannot have got locked from the inside, for—"

Before he had finished his sentence, the door, which neither of us then was touching, opened quietly of itself. We looked at each other a single instant. The same thought seized both – some human agency might be detected here. I rushed in first, my servant followed. A small blank dreary room without furniture – few empty boxes and hampers in a corner – a small window – the shutters closed – not even a fireplace – no other door than that by which we had entered – no carpet on the floor, and the floor seemed very old, uneven, worm-eaten, mended here and there, as was shown by the whiter patches on the wood; but no living being, and no visible place in which a living being could have hidden. As we stood gazing round, the door by which we had entered closed as quietly as it had before opened: we were imprisoned.

For the first time I felt a creep of undefinable horror. Not so my servant. "Why, they don't think to trap us, sir; I could break the trumpery door with a kick of my foot."

"Try first if it will open to your hand," said I, shaking off the vague apprehension that had seized me, "while I unclose the shutters and see what is without."

I unbarred the shutters – the window looked on the little backyard I have before described; there was no ledge without – nothing to break the sheer descent of the wall. No man getting out of that window would have found any footing till he had fallen on the stones below.

F—, meanwhile, was vainly attempting to open the door. He now turned round to me and asked my permission to use force. And I should here state, in justice to the servant, that, far from evincing any superstitious terrors, his nerve, composure, and even gaiety amidst circumstances so extraordinary, compelled my admiration, and made me congratulate myself on having secured a companion in every way fitted to the occasion. I willingly gave him the permission he required. But though he was a remarkably strong man, his force was as idle as his milder efforts; the door did not even shake to his stoutest kick. Breathless and panting, he desisted. I then tried the door myself, equally in vain. As I ceased from the effort, again that creep of horror came over me; but this time it was more cold and stubborn. I felt as if some strange and ghastly exhalation were rising up from the chinks of that rugged floor, and filling the atmosphere with a venomous influence hostile to human life. The door now very slowly and quietly opened as of its own accord. We precipitated ourselves into the landing-place. We both saw a large pale light – as large as the human figure but shapeless and unsubstantial – move before us, and ascend the stairs that led from the landing into the attics. I followed the light, and my servant followed me. It entered, to the right of the landing, a small garret, of which the door stood open. I entered in the same instant. The light then collapsed into a small globule, exceedingly brilliant and vivid; rested a moment on a bed in the corner, quivered, and vanished.

We approached the bed and examined it – a half-tester, such as is commonly found in attics devoted to servants. On the drawers that stood near it we perceived an old faded silk kerchief, with the needle still left in a rent half repaired. The kerchief was covered with dust; probably it had belonged to the old woman who had last died in that house, and this might have been her sleeping room. I had sufficient curiosity to open the drawers: there were a few odds and ends of female dress, and two letters tied round with a narrow ribbon of faded yellow. I took the liberty to possess myself of the letters. We found nothing else in the room worth noticing – nor did the light reappear; but we distinctly heard, as we turned to go, a pattering footfall on the floor – just before us. We went through the other attics (in all four), the footfall still preceding us. Nothing to be seen – nothing but the footfall heard. I had the letters in my hand: just as I was descending the stairs I distinctly felt my wrist seized, and a faint soft effort made to draw the letters from my clasp. I only held them the more tightly, and the effort ceased.

We regained the bedchamber appropriated to myself, and I then remarked that my dog had not followed us when we had left it. He was thrusting himself close to the fire, and trembling. I was impatient to examine the letters; and while I read them, my servant opened a little box in which he had deposited the weapons I had ordered him to bring; took them out, placed them on a table close at my bed-head, and then occupied himself in soothing the dog, who, however, seemed to heed him very little.

The letters were short – they were dated; the dates exactly thirty-five years ago. They were evidently from a lover to his mistress, or a husband to some young wife. Not only the terms of expression, but a distinct reference to a former voyage, indicated the writer to have been a seafarer. The spelling and handwriting were those of a man imperfectly educated, but still the language itself was forcible. In the expressions of endearment there was a kind of rough wild love; but here and there were dark and unintelligible hints at some secret not of love – some secret that seemed of crime. "We ought to love each other," was one of the sentences I remember, "for how every one else would execrate us if all was known." Again: "Don't let any one be in the same room with you at night – you talk in your sleep." And again: "What's done can't be undone; and I tell you there's nothing against us unless the dead could come to life." Here there was underlined in a better handwriting (a female's), "They do!" At the end of the letter latest in date the same female hand had written these words: "Lost at sea the 4th of June, the same day as—."

I put down the letters, and began to muse over their contents.

Fearing, however, that the train of thought into which I fell might unsteady my nerves, I fully determined to keep my mind in a fit state to cope with whatever of marvelous the advancing night might bring forth. I roused myself – laid the letters on the table – stirred up the fire, which was still bright and cheering – and opened my volume of Macaulay. I read quietly enough till about half-past eleven. I then threw myself dressed upon the bed, and told my servant he might retire to his own room, but must keep himself awake. I bade him leave open the door between the two rooms. Thus alone, I kept two candles burning on the table by my bed-head. I placed my watch beside the weapons, and calmly resumed my Macaulay. Opposite to me the fire burned clear; and on the hearthrug, seemingly asleep, lay the dog. In about twenty minutes I felt an exceedingly cold air pass by my cheek, like a sudden draught. I fancied the door to my right, communicating with the landing-place, must have got open; but no – it was closed. I then turned my glance to my left, and saw the flame of the candles violently swayed as by a wind. At the same moment the watch beside the revolver softly slid from the table – softly, softly – no visible hand – it was gone. I sprang up, seizing the revolver with the one hand, the dagger with the other: I was not willing that my weapons should share the fate of the watch. Thus armed, I looked round the floor – no sign of the watch. Three slow, loud, distinct knocks were now heard at the bed-head; my servant called out, "Is that you, sir?"

"No; be on your guard."

The dog now roused himself and sat on his haunches, his ears moving quickly backwards and forwards. He kept his eyes fixed on me with a look so strange that he concentered all my attention on himself. Slowly he rose up, all his hair bristling, and stood perfectly rigid, and with the same wild stare. I had no time, however, to examine the dog. Presently my servant emerged from his room; and if ever I saw horror in the human face, it was then. I should not have recognized him had we met in the street, so altered was every lineament. He passed by me quickly, saying in a whisper that seemed scarcely to come from his lips, "Run – run! it is after me!" He gained the door to the landing, pulled it open, and rushed forth. I followed him into the landing involuntarily, calling him to stop; but, without heeding me, he bounded down the stairs, clinging to the balusters, and taking several steps at a time. I heard, where I stood, the street-door open – heard it again clap to. I was left alone in the haunted house.

It was but for a moment that I remained undecided whether or not to follow my servant; pride and curiosity alike forbade so dastardly a flight. I re-entered my room, closing the door after me, and proceeded cautiously into the interior chamber. I encountered nothing to justify my servant's terror. I again carefully examined the walls, to see if there were any concealed door. I could find no trace of one – not even a seam in the dull-brown paper with which the room was hung. How, then, had the THING, whatever it was, which had so scared him, obtained ingress except through my own chamber?

I returned to my room, shut and locked the door that opened upon the interior one, and stood on the hearth, expectant and prepared. I now perceived that the dog had slunk into an angle of the wall, and was pressing himself close against it, as if literally striving to force his way into it. I approached the animal and spoke to it; the poor brute was evidently beside itself with terror. It showed all its teeth, the slaver dropping from its jaws, and would certainly have bitten me if I had touched it. It did not seem to recognize me. Whoever has seen at the Zoological Gardens a rabbit fascinated by a serpent, cowering in a corner, may form some idea of the anguish which the dog exhibited. Finding all efforts to soothe the animal in vain, and fearing that his bite might be as venomous in that state as in the madness of hydrophobia, I left him alone, placed my weapons on the table beside the fire, seated myself, and recommenced my Macaulay.

Perhaps, in order not to appear seeking credit for a courage, or rather a coolness, which the reader may conceive I exaggerate, I may be pardoned if I pause to indulge in one or two egotistical remarks.

As I hold presence of mind, or what is called courage, to be precisely proportioned to familiarity with the circumstances that lead to it, so I should say that I had been long sufficiently familiar with all experiments that appertain to the Marvelous. I had witnessed many very extraordinary phenomena in various parts of the world – phenomena that would be either totally disbelieved if I stated them, or ascribed to supernatural agencies. Now, my theory is that the Supernatural is the Impossible, and that what is called supernatural is only a something in the laws of nature of which we have been hitherto ignorant. Therefore, if a ghost rise before me, I have not the right to say, "So, then, the supernatural is possible," but rather, "So, then, the apparition of a ghost is, contrary to received opinion, within the laws of nature – *i.e.*, not supernatural."

Now, in all that I had hitherto witnessed, and indeed in all the wonders which the amateurs of mystery in our age record as facts, a material living agency is always required. On the continent you will find still magicians who assert that they can raise spirits. Assume for the moment that they assert truly, still the living material form of the magician is present; and he is the material agency by which, from some constitutional peculiarities, certain strange phenomena are represented to your natural senses.

Accept, again, as truthful, the tales of spirit Manifestation in America – musical or other sounds – writings on paper, produced by no discernible hand – articles of furniture moved without apparent human agency – or the actual sight and touch of hands, to which no bodies seem to belong – still there must be found the MEDIUM or living being, with constitutional peculiarities capable of obtaining these signs. In fine, in all such marvels, supposing even that there is no imposture, there must be a human being like ourselves by whom, or through whom, the effects presented to human beings are produced. It is so with the now familiar phenomena of mesmerism or electro-biology; the mind of the person operated on is affected through a material living agent. Nor, supposing it true that a mesmerized patient can respond to the will or passes of a mesmerizer a hundred miles distant, is the response less occasioned by a material fluid – call it Electric, call it Odic, call it what you will – which has the power of traversing space and passing obstacles, that the material effect is communicated from one to the other. Hence all that I had hitherto witnessed, or expected to witness, in this strange house, I believed to be occasioned through some agency or medium as mortal as myself: and this idea necessarily prevented the awe with which those who regard as supernatural things that are not within the ordinary operations of nature might have been impressed by the adventures of that memorable night.

As, then, it was my conjecture that all that was presented, or would be presented to my senses, must originate in some human being gifted by constitution with the power so to present them, and having some motive so to do, I felt an interest in my theory which, in its way, was rather philosophical than superstitious. And I can sincerely say that I was in as tranquil a temper for observation as any practical experimentalist could be in awaiting the effect of some rare, though perhaps perilous, chemical combination. Of course, the more I kept my mind detached from fancy, the more the temper fitted for observation would be obtained; and I therefore riveted eye and thought on the strong daylight sense in the page of my Macaulay.

I now became aware that something interposed between the page and the light – the page was over-shadowed: I looked up, and I saw what I shall find it very difficult, perhaps impossible, to describe.

It was a Darkness shaping itself forth from the air in very undefined outline. I cannot say it was of a human form, and yet it had more resemblance to a human form, or rather shadow, than to anything else. As it stood, wholly apart and distinct from the air and the light around it, its dimensions seemed gigantic, the summit nearly touching the ceiling. While I gazed, a feeling of intense cold seized me. An iceberg before me could not more have chilled me; nor could the cold of an iceberg have been more purely physical. I feel convinced that it was not the cold caused by fear. As I continued to gaze, I thought – but this I cannot say with precision – that I distinguished two eyes looking down on me from the height. One moment I fancied that I distinguished them clearly, the next they seemed gone; but still two rays of a pale-blue light frequently shot through the darkness, as from the height on which I half believed, half doubted, that I had encountered the eyes.

I strove to speak – my voice utterly failed me; I could only think to myself, "Is this fear? it is *not* fear!" I strove to rise – in vain; I felt as if weighed down by an irresistible force. Indeed, my impression was that of an immense and overwhelming Power opposed to any volition – that sense of utter inadequacy to cope with a force beyond man's, which one may feel *physically* in a storm at sea, in a conflagration, or when confronting some terrible wild beast, or rather, perhaps, the shark of the ocean, I felt *morally*. Opposed to my will was another will, as far superior to its strength as storm, fire, and shark are superior in material force to the force of man.

And now, as this impression grew on me – now came, at last, horror – horror to a degree that no words can convey. Still I retained pride, if not courage; and in my own mind I said, "This is horror, but it is not fear; unless I fear I cannot be harmed; my reason rejects this thing, it is an illusion – I do not fear." With a violent effort I succeeded at last in stretching out my hand towards the weapon on the table; as I did so, on the arm and shoulder I received a strange shock, and my arm fell to my side powerless. And now, to add to my horror, the light began slowly to wane from the candles; they were not, as it were, extinguished, but their flame seemed, very gradually withdrawn; it was the same with the fire – the light was extracted from the fuel; in a few minutes the room was in utter darkness.

The dread that came over me, to be thus in the dark with that dark Thing, whose power was so intensely felt, brought a reaction of nerve. In fact, terror had reached that climax, that either my senses must have deserted me, or I must have burst through the spell. I did burst through it. I found voice, though the voice was a shiek. I remember that I broke forth with words like these – "I do not fear, my soul does not fear"; and at the same time I found the strength to rise. Still in that profound gloom I rushed to one of the windows – tore aside the curtain – flung open the shutters; my first thought was – LIGHT. And when I saw the moon high, clear, and calm, I felt a joy that almost compensated for the previous terror. There was the moon, there was also the light from the gas-lamps in the deserted slumberous street. I turned to look back into the room; the moon penetrated its shadow very palely and partially – but still there was light. The dark Thing, whatever it might be, was gone – except that I could yet see a dim shadow, which seemed the shadow of that shade, against the opposite wall.

My eye now rested on the table, and from under the table (which was without cloth or cover – an old mahogany round table) there rose a hand, visible as far as the wrist. It was a hand, seemingly, as much of flesh and blood as my own, but the hand of an aged person – lean, wrinkled, small, too – a woman's hand. That hand very softly closed on the two letters that lay on the table: hand and letters both vanished. There then came the same three loud measured knocks I heard at the bed-head before this extraordinary drama had commenced.

As those sounds slowly ceased, I felt the whole room vibrate sensibly; and at the far end there rose, as from the floor, sparks or globules like bubbles of light, many-colored – green, yellow, fire-red, azure. Up and down, to and fro, hither, thither, as tiny Will-o'-the-Wisps the sparks moved slow or swift, each at his own caprice. A chair (as in the drawing-room below) was now advanced from the wall without apparent agency, and placed at the opposite side of the table. Suddenly as forth from the chair, there grew a shape – a woman's shape. It was distinct as a shape of life – ghastly as a shape of death. The face was that of youth, with a strange mournful beauty: the throat and shoulders were bare, the rest of the form in a loose robe of cloudy white. It began sleeking its long yellow hair, which fell over its shoulders; its eyes were not turned towards me, but to the door; it seemed listening, watching, waiting. The shadow of the shade in the background grew darker; and again I thought I beheld the eyes gleaming out from the summit of the shadow – eyes fixed upon that shape.

As if from the door, though it did not open, there grew out another shape, equally distinct, equally ghastly – a man's shape – a young man's. It was in the dress of the last century, or rather in a likeness of such dress (for both the male shape and the female, though defined, were evidently unsubstantial, impalpable – simulacra – phantasms); and there was something incongruous, grotesque, yet fearful, in the contrast between the elaborate finery, the courtly precision of that old-fashioned garb, with its ruffles and lace and buckles, and the corpse-like aspect and ghost-like stillness of the flitting wearer. Just as the male shape approached the female, the dark shadow started from the wall, all three for a moment wrapped in darkness. When the pale light returned, the two phantoms were as in the grasp of the shadow that towered between them; and there was a bloodstain on the breast of the female; and the phantom male was leaning on its phantom sword, and blood seemed trickling fast from the ruffles, from the lace; and the darkness of the intermediate Shadow swallowed them up – they were gone. And again the bubbles of light shot, and sailed, and undulated, growing thicker and thicker and thicker and more wildly confused in their movements.

The closet door to the right of the fireplace now opened, and from the aperture there came the form of an aged woman. In her hand she held letters – the very letters over which I had seen *the* Hand close; and behind her I heard a footstep. She turned round as if to listen, and then she opened the letters and seemed to read; and over her shoulder I saw a livid face, the face as of a man long drowned – bloated, bleached, sea-weed tangled in its dripping hair; and at her feet lay a form as of a corpse, and beside the corpse there cowered a child, a miserable squalid child, with famine in its cheeks and fear in its eyes. And as I looked in the old woman's face, the wrinkles and lines vanished and it became a face of youth – hard-eyed, stony, but still youth; and the Shadow darted forth, and darkened over these phantoms as it had darkened over the last.

Nothing now was left but the Shadow, and on that my eyes were intently fixed, till again eyes grew out of the Shadow – malignant, serpent eyes. And the bubbles of light again rose and fell, and in their disorder, irregular, turbulent maze, mingled with the wan moonlight. And now from these globules themselves, as from the shell of an egg, monstrous things burst out; the air grew filled with them; larvæ so bloodless and so hideous that I can in no way describe them except to remind the reader of the swarming life which the solar microscope brings before his eyes in a drop of water – things transparent, supple, agile, chasing each other, devouring each other – forms like nought ever beheld by the naked eye. As the shapes were without symmetry, so their movements were without order. In their very vagrancies there was no sport; they came round me and round, thicker and faster and swifter, swarming over my head, crawling over my right arm, which was outstretched in involuntary command against all evil beings. Sometimes I felt myself touched, but not by them;

invisible hands touched me. Once I felt the clutch as of cold soft fingers at my throat. I was still equally conscious that if I gave way to fear I should be in bodily peril; and I concentrated all my faculties in the single focus of resisting, stubborn will. And I turned my sight from the Shadow – above all, from those strange serpent eyes – eyes that had now become distinctly visible. For there, though in nought else round me, I was aware that there was a WILL, and a will of intense, creative, working evil, which might crush down my own.

The pale atmosphere in the room began now to redden as if in the air of some near conflagration. The larvæ grew lurid as things that live in fire. Again the room vibrated; again were heard the three measured knocks; and again all things were swallowed up in the darkness of the dark Shadow, as if out of that darkness all had come, into that darkness all returned.

As the gloom receded, the Shadow was wholly gone. Slowly as it had been withdrawn, the flame grew again into the candles on the table, again into the fuel in the grate. The whole room came once more calmly, healthfully into sight.

The two doors were still closed, the door communicating with the servant's room still locked. In the corner of the wall into which he had so convulsively niched himself, lay the dog. I called to him – no movement; I approached – the animal was dead; his eyes protruded; his tongue out of his mouth; the froth gathered round his jaws. I took him in my arms; I brought him to the fire, I felt acute grief for the loss of my poor favorite – acute self-reproach; I accused myself of his death; I imagined he had died of fright. But what was my surprise on finding that his neck was actually broken. Had this been done in the dark? – must it not have been by a hand human as mine? – must there not have been a human agency all the while in that room? Good cause to suspect it. I cannot tell. I cannot do more than state the fact fairly; the reader may draw his own inference.

Another surprising circumstance – my watch was restored to the table from which it had been so mysteriously withdrawn; but it had stopped at the very moment it was so withdrawn; nor, despite all the skill of the watchmaker, has it ever gone since – that is, it will go in a strange erratic way for a few hours, and then come to a dead stop – it is worthless.

Nothing more chanced for the rest of the night. Nor, indeed, had I long to wait before the dawn broke. Nor till it was broad daylight did I quit the haunted house. Before I did so, I revisited the little blind room in which my servant and myself had been for a time imprisoned. I had a strong impression – for which I could not account – that from that room had originated the mechanism of the phenomena – if I may use the term – which had been experienced in my chamber. And though I entered it now in the clear day, with the sun peering through the filmy window, I still felt, as I stood on its floor, the creep of the horror which I had first there experienced the night before, and which had been so aggravated by what had passed in my own chamber. I could not, indeed, bear to stay more than half a minute within those walls. I descended the stairs, and again I heard the footfall before me; and when I opened the street door, I thought I could distinguish a very low laugh. I gained my own home, expecting to find my runaway servant there. But he had not presented himself; nor did I hear more of him for three days, when I received a letter from him, dated from Liverpool to this effect:

> "HONORED SIR – I humbly entreat your pardon, though I can scarcely hope that you will think I deserve it, unless – which Heaven forbid – you saw what I did. I feel that it will be years before I can recover myself: and as to being fit for service, it is out of the question. I am therefore going to my brother-in-law at Melbourne. The ship sails tomorrow. Perhaps the long voyage may set me up. I do nothing now but start and tremble, and fancy IT is behind me. I humbly beg you, honored sir, to order my clothes, and whatever wages are due to me, to be sent to my mother's, at Walworth. John knows her address."

The letter ended with additional apologies, somewhat incoherent, and explanatory details as to effects that had been under the writer's charge.

This flight may perhaps warrant a suspicion that the man wished to go to Australia, and had been somehow or other fraudulently mixed up with the events of the night. I say nothing in refutation of that conjecture; rather, I suggest it as one that would seem to many persons the most probable solution of improbable occurrences. My belief in my own theory remained unshaken. I returned in the evening to the house, to bring away in a hack cab the things I had left there, with my poor dog's body. In this task I was not disturbed, nor did any incident worth note befall me, except that still, on ascending and descending the stairs, I heard the same footfall in advance. On leaving the house, I went to Mr. J—'s. He was at home. I returned him the keys, told him that my curiosity was sufficiently gratified, and was about to relate quickly what had passed, when he stopped me, and said, though with much politeness, that he had no longer any interest in a mystery which none had ever solved.

I determined at least to tell him of the two letters I had read, as well as of the extraordinary manner in which they had disappeared, and I then inquired if he thought they had been addressed to the woman who had died in the house, and if there were anything in her early history which could possibly confirm the dark suspicions to which the letters gave rise. Mr. J— seemed startled, and, after musing a few moments, answered, "I am but little acquainted with the woman's earlier history, except, as I before told you, that her family were known to mine. But you revive some vague reminiscences to her prejudice. I will make inquiries, and inform you of their result. Still, even if we could admit the popular superstition that a person who had been either the perpetrator or the victim of dark crimes in life could revisit, as a restless spirit, the scene in which those crimes had been committed, I should observe that the house was infested by strange sights and sounds before the old woman died – you smile – what would you say?"

"I would say this, that I am convinced, if we could get to the bottom of these mysteries, we should find a living human agency."

"What! you believe it is all an imposture? for what object?"

"Not an imposture in the ordinary sense of the word. If suddenly I were to sink into a deep sleep, from which you could not awake me, but in that sleep could answer questions with an accuracy which I could not pretend to when awake – tell you what money you had in your pocket – nay, describe your very thoughts – it is not necessarily an imposture, any more than it is necessarily supernatural. I should be, unconsciously to myself, under a mesmeric influence, conveyed to me from a distance by a human being who had acquired power over me by previous *rapport*."

"But if a mesmerizer could so affect another living being, can you suppose that a mesmerizer could also affect inanimate objects: move chairs – open and shut doors?"

"Or impress our senses with the belief in such effects – we never having been *en rapport* with the person acting on us? No. What is commonly called mesmerism could not do this; but there may be a power akin to mesmerism, and superior to it – the power that in the old days was called Magic. That such a power may extend to all inanimate objects of matter I do not say; but if so, it would not be against nature – it would be only a rare power in nature which might be given to constitutions with certain peculiarities, and cultivated by practice to an extraordinary degree. That such a power might extend over the dead – that is, over certain thoughts and memories that the dead may still retain – and compel, not that which ought properly to be called the SOUL, and which is far beyond human reach, but rather a phantom of what has been most earth-stained on earth, to make itself apparent to our senses – is a very ancient though obsolete theory, upon which I will hazard no opinion. But I do not conceive the power would be supernatural. Let me illustrate what I mean from an experiment which Paracelsus describes as not difficult, and which the author of the *Curiosities of Literature* cites as credible: A flower perishes; you burn it. Whatever were the elements of that flower while it lived are gone, dispersed, you know not wither; you can never discover nor recollect them. But you can, by chemistry, out of the burnt dust of that flower, raise a spectrum of the flower, just as it seemed in life. It may be the same with the human being. The soul has as much escaped you as the essence or elements of the flower. Still you may make a spectrum of it.

"And this phantom, though in the popular superstition it is held to be the soul of the departed, must not be confounded with the true soul; it is but eidolon of the dead form. Hence, like the best attested stories of ghosts or spirits, the thing that most strikes us is the absence of what we hold to be soul; that is, of superior emancipated intelligence. These apparitions come for little or no object – they seldom speak when they do come; if they speak, they utter no ideas above those of an ordinary person on earth. American spirit-seers have published volumes of communications in prose and verse, which they assert to be given in the names of the most illustrious dead – Shakespeare, Bacon – heaven knows whom. Those communications, taking the best, are certainly not a whit of higher order than would be communications from living persons of fair talent and education; they are wondrously inferior to what Bacon, Shakespeare, and Plato said and wrote when on earth. Nor, what is more noticeable, do they ever contain an idea that was not on the earth before. Wonderful, therefore, as such phenomena may be (granting them to be truthful), I see much that philosophy may question, nothing that it is incumbent on philosophy to deny, viz., nothing supernatural. They are but ideas conveyed somehow or other (we have not yet discovered the means) from one mortal brain to another. Whether, in so doing, tables walk of their own accord, or fiend-like shapes appear in a magic circle, or bodyless hands rise and remove material objects, or a Thing of Darkness, such as presented itself to me, freeze our blood – still am I persuaded that these are but agencies conveyed, as if by electric wires, to my own brain from the brain of another. In some constitutions there is a natural chemistry, and these constitutions may produce chemic wonders – in others a natural fluid, call it electricity, and these may produce electric wonders.

"But the wonders differ from Normal Science in this – they are alike objectless, purposeless, puerile, frivolous. They lead on to no grand results; and therefore the world does not heed, and true sages have not cultivated them. But sure I am, that of all I saw or heard, a man, human as myself, was the remote originator; and I believe unconsciously to himself as to the exact effects produced, for this reason: no two persons, you say, have ever told you that they experienced exactly the same thing. Well, observe, no two persons ever experience exactly the same dream. If this were an ordinary imposture, the machinery would be arranged for results that would but little vary; if it were a supernatural agency permitted by the Almighty, it would surely be for some definite end. These phenomena belong to neither class; my persuasion is, that they originate in some brain now far distant; that that brain had no distinct volition in anything that occurred; that what does occur reflects but its devious, motley, ever-shifting, half-formed thoughts; in short, that it has been but the dreams of such a brain put into action and invested with a semi-substance. That this brain is of immense power, that it can set matter into movement, that it is malignant and destructive, I believe; some material force must have killed my dog; the same force might, for aught I know, have sufficed to kill myself, had I been as subjugated by terror as the dog – had my intellect or my spirit given me no countervailing resistance in my will."

"It killed your dog! that is fearful! indeed it is strange that no animal can be induced to stay in that house; not even a cat. Rats and mice are never found in it."

"The instincts of the brute creation detect influences deadly to their existence. Man's reason has a sense less subtle, because it has a resisting power more supreme. But enough; do you comprehend my theory?"

"Yes, though imperfectly – and I accept any crotchet (pardon the word), however odd, rather than embrace at once the notion of ghosts and hobgoblins we imbibed in our nurseries. Still, to my unfortunate house the evil is the same. What on earth can I do with the house?"

"I will tell you what I would do. I am convinced from my own internal feelings that the small unfurnished room at right angles to the door of the bedroom which I occupied, forms a starting point or receptacle for the influences which haunt the house; and I strongly advise you to have the walls opened, the floor removed

– nay, the whole room pulled down. I observe that it is detached from the body of the house, built over the small backyard, and could be removed without injury to the rest of the building."

"And you think, if I did that—".

"You would cut off the telegraph wires. Try it. I am so persuaded that I am right, that I will pay half the expense if you will allow me to direct the operations."

"Nay, I am well able to afford the cost; for the rest, allow me to write to you."

About ten days afterwards I received a letter from Mr. J—, telling me that he had visited the house since I had seen him; that he had found the two letters I had described replaced in the drawer from which I had taken them; that he had read them with misgivings like my own; that he had instituted a cautious inquiry about the woman to whom I rightly conjectured they had been written. It seemed that thirty-six years ago (a year before the date of the letters) she had married, against the wish of her relations, an American of very suspicious character, in fact, he was generally believed to have been a pirate. She herself was the daughter of very respectable tradespeople, and had served in the capacity of nursery governess before her marriage. She had a brother, a widower, who was considered wealthy, and who had one child of about six years old. A month after the marriage, the body of this brother was found in the Thames, near London Bridge; there seemed some marks of violence about his throat, but they were not deemed sufficient to warrant the inquest in any other verdict than that of "found drowned."

The American and his wife took charge of the little boy, the deceased brother having by his will left his sister the guardian of his only child – and in the event of the child's death, the sister inherited. The child died about six months afterwards – it was supposed to have been neglected and ill-treated. The neighbors deposed to have heard it shriek at night. The surgeon who had examined it after death said that it was emaciated as if from want of nourishment, and the body was covered with livid bruises. It seemed that one winter night the child had sought to escape – crept out into the backyard – tried to scale the wall – fallen back exhausted, and been found at morning on the stones in a dying state. But though there was some evidence of cruelty, there was none of murder; and the aunt and her husband had sought to palliate cruelty by alleging the exceeding stubbornness and perversity of the child, who was declared to be half-witted. Be that as it may, at the orphan's death the aunt inherited her brother's fortune. Before the first wedded year was out the American quitted England abruptly, and never returned to it. He obtained a cruising vessel, which was lost in the Atlantic two years afterwards. The window was left in affluence; but reverses of various kinds had befallen her; a bank broke – an investment failed – she went into a small business and became insolvent – then she entered into service, sinking lower and lower, from housekeeper down to maid-of-all work – never long retaining a place, though nothing decided against her character was ever alleged. She was considered sober, honest, and peculiarly quiet in her ways; still nothing prospered with her. And so she had dropped into the workhouse, from which Mr. J— had taken her, to be placed in charge of the very house which she had rented as mistress in the first year of her wedded life.

Mr. J— added that he had passed an hour alone in the unfurnished room which I had urged him to destroy, and that his impressions of dread while there were so great, though he had neither heard nor seen anything, that he was eager to have the walls bared and the floors removed as I had suggested. He had engaged persons for the work, and would commence any day I would name.

The day was accordingly fixed. I repaired to the haunted house – we went into the blind dreary room, took up the skirting, and then the floors. Under the rafters, covered with rubbish, was found a trap-door, quite large enough to admit a man. It was closely nailed down, with clamps and rivets of iron. On removing these we descended into a room below, the existence of which had never been suspected. In this room there had been a window and a flue, but they had been bricked over, evidently for many years. By the help of candles we examined this place; it still retained some mouldering furniture – three chairs, an oak settle, a table –

all of the fashion of about eighty years ago. There was a chest of drawers against the wall, in which we found, half-rotted away, old-fashioned articles of a man's dress, such as might have been worn eighty or a hundred years ago by a gentleman of some rank – costly steel buckles and buttons, like those yet worn in court-dresses, a handsome court sword – in a waistcoat which had once been rich with gold-lace, but which was now blackened and foul with damp, we found five guineas, a few silver coins, and an ivory ticket, probably for some place of entertainment long since passed away. But our main discovery was in a kind of iron safe fixed to the wall, the lock of which it cost us much trouble to get picked.

In this safe were three shelves, and two small drawers. Ranged on the shelves were several small bottles of crystal, hermetically stopped. They contained colorless volatile essences, of the nature of which I shall only say that they were not poisons – phosphor and ammonia entered into some of them. There were also some very curious glass tubes, and a small pointed rod of iron, with a large lump of rock-crystal, and another of amber – also a load-stone of great power.

In one of the drawers we found a miniature portrait set in gold, and retaining the freshness of its colors most remarkably, considering the length of time it had probably been there. The portrait was that of a man who might be somewhat advanced in middle life, perhaps forty-seven or forty-eight.

It was a remarkable face – a most impressive face. If you could fancy some mighty serpent transformed into a man, preserving in the human lineaments the old serpent type, you would have a better idea of that countenance than long descriptions can convey: the width and flatness of frontal – the tapering elegance of contour disguising the strength of the deadly jaw – the long, large, terrible eye, glittering and green as the emerald – and withal a certain ruthless calm, as if from the consciousness of an immense power.

Mechanically I turned round the miniature to examine the back of it, and on the back was engraved a pentacle; in the middle of the pentacle a ladder, and the third step of the ladder was formed by the date 1765. Examining still more minutely, I detected a spring; this, on being pressed, opened the back of the miniature as a lid. Withinside the lid were engraved, "Marianna to thee – be faithful in life and in death to—." Here follows a name that I will not mention, but it was not unfamiliar to me. I had heard it spoken of by old men in my childhood as the name borne by a dazzling charlatan who had made a great sensation in London for a year or so, and had fled the country on the charge of a double murder within his own house – that of his mistress and his rival. I said nothing of this to Mr. J—, to whom reluctantly I resigned the miniature.

We had found no difficulty in opening the first drawer within the iron safe; we found great difficulty in opening the second: it was not locked, but it resisted all efforts, till we inserted in the clinks the edge of a chisel. When we had thus drawn it forth we found a very singular apparatus in the nicest order. Upon a small thin book, or rather tablet, was placed a saucer of crystal: this saucer was filled with a clear liquid – on that liquid floated a kind of compass, with a needle shifting rapidly round; but instead of the usual points of a compass were seven strange characters, not very unlike those used by astrologers to denote the planets.

A peculiar, but not strong nor displeasing odor came from this drawer, which was lined with a wood that we afterwards discovered to be hazel. Whatever the cause of this odor, it produced a material effect on the nerves. We all felt it, even the two workmen who were in the room – a creeping tingling sensation from the tips of the fingers to the roots of the hair. Impatient to examine the tablet, I removed the saucer. As I did so the needle of the compass went round and round with exceeding swiftness, and I felt a shock that ran through my whole frame, so that I dropped the saucer on the floor. The liquid was spilt – the saucer was broken – the compass rolled to the end of the room – and at that instant the walls shook to and fro, as if a giant had swayed and rocked them.

The two workmen were so frightened that they ran up the ladder by which we had descended from the trap-door; but seeing that nothing more happened, they were easily induced to return.

Meanwhile I had opened the tablet: it was bound in plain red leather, with a silver clasp; it contained but one sheet of thick vellum, and on that sheet were inscribed within a double pentacle, words in old monkish Latin, which are literally to be translated thus: "On all that it can reach within these walls – sentient or inanimate, living or dead – as moves the needle, so work my will! Accursed be the house, and restless be the dwellers therein."

We found no more. Mr. J— burnt the tablet and its anathema. He razed to the foundations the part of the building containing the secret room with the chamber over it. He had then the courage to inhabit the house himself for a month, and a quieter, better-conditioned house could not be found in all London. Subsequently he let it to advantage, and his tenant has made no complaints.

# Authentic Narrative of a Haunted House

## Joseph Sheridan Le Fanu

### Prospectus

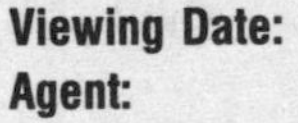

**Address:** Kilkee, Co. Clare, Ireland.

**Property:** Nineteenth-century house facing the Atlantic Ocean. A charming, period property, one of a row of houses, with comfortable rooms for family and servants with stables to the rear. For let fully furnished.

**Viewing Date:** Winter, 1861.

**Agent:** Joseph Sheridan Le Fanu (1814–1873) was born in Dublin, the grandson of the playwright, Richard Brinsley Sheridan, and became a journalist in his native city. He was also fascinated by Irish folk lore, with its tales of ghosts and hauntings, and produced a body of novels and short stories which earned him comparison with Edgar Allan Poe. Haunted houses feature in a number of his novels, including *The House By The Churchyard* (1863) and short stories like "Ghost Stories of the Tiled House", "The Haunted House in Westminster" and "A Haunted House", which he published in 1861 with a modest assurance that "its sole claim to attention is its absolute truth".

Within the last eight years – the precise date I purposely omit. – I was ordered by my physician, my health being in an unsatisfactory state, to change my residence to one upon the sea-coast; and accordingly, I took a house for a year in a fashionable watering-place, at a moderate distance from the city in which I had previously resided, and connected with it by a railway.

Winter was setting in when my removal thither was decided upon; but there was nothing whatever dismal or depressing in the change. The house I had taken was to all appearance, and in point of convenience, too, quite a modern one. It formed one in a cheerful row, with small gardens in front, facing the sea, and commanding sea air and sea views in perfection. In the rear it had coach-house and stable, and between them and the house a considerable grass-plot, with some flower-beds, interposed.

Our family consisted of my wife and myself, with three children, the eldest about nine years old, she and the next in age being girls; and the youngest, between six and seven, a boy. To these were added six servants, whom, although for certain reasons I decline giving their real names, I shall indicate, for the sake of clearness, by arbitrary ones. There was a nurse, Mrs. Southerland; a nursery-maid, Ellen Page; the cook, Mrs. Greenwood; and the housemaid, Ellen Faith; a butler, whom I shall call Smith, and his son, James, about two-and-twenty.

We came out to take possession at about seven o'clock in the evening; every thing was comfortable and cheery; good fires lighted, the rooms neat and airy, and a general air of preparation and comfort, highly conducive to good spirits and pleasant anticipations.

The sitting-rooms were large and cheerful, and they and the bed-rooms more than ordinarily lofty, the kitchen and servants' rooms, on the same level, were well and comfortably furnished, and had, like the rest of the house, an air of recent painting and fitting up, and a completely modern character, which imparted a very cheerful air of cleanliness and convenience.

There had been just enough of the fuss of settling agreeably to occupy us, and to give a pleasant turn to our thoughts after we had retired to our rooms. Being an invalid, I had a small bed to myself – resigning the four-poster to my wife. The candle was extinguished, but a night-light was burning. I was coming up stairs, and she, already in bed, had just dismissed her maid, when we were both startled by a wild scream from her room; I found her in a state of the extremest agitation and terror. She insisted that she had seen an unnaturally tall figure come beside her bed and stand there. The light was too faint to enable her to define any thing respecting this apparition, beyond the fact of her having most distinctly seen such a shape, colourless from the insufficiency of the light to disclose more than its dark outline.

We both endeavoured to re-assure her. The room once more looked so cheerful in the candlelight, that we were quite uninfluenced by the contagion of her terrors. The movements and voices of the servants down stairs still getting things into their places and completing our comfortable arrangements, had also their effect in steeling us against any such influence, and we set the whole thing down as a dream, or an imperfectly-seen outline of the bed-curtains. When, however, we were alone, my wife reiterated, still in great agitation, her clear assertion that she had most positively seen, being at the time as completely awake as ever she was, precisely what she had described to us. And in this conviction she continued perfectly firm.

A day or two after this, it came out that our servants were under an apprehension that, somehow or other, thieves had established a secret mode of access to the lower part of the house. The butler, Smith, had seen an ill-looking woman in his room on the first night of our arrival; and he and other servants constantly saw, for many days subsequently, glimpses of a retreating figure, which corresponded with that so seen by him, passing through a passage which led to a back area in which were some coal-vaults.

This figure was seen always in the act of retreating, its back turned, generally getting round the corner of the passage into the area, in a stealthy and hurried way, and, when closely followed, imperfectly seen again entering one of the coal-vaults, and when pursued into it, nowhere to be found.

The idea of any thing supernatural in the matter had, strange to say, not yet entered the mind of any one of the servants. They had heard some stories of smugglers having secret passages into houses, and using their means of access for purposes of pillage, or with a view to frighten superstitious people out of houses which they needed for their own objects, and a suspicion of similar practices here, caused them extreme uneasiness. The apparent anxiety also manifested by this retreating figure to escape observation, and her always appearing to make her egress at the same point, favoured this romantic hypothesis. The men, however, made a most careful examination of the back area, and of the coal-vaults, with a view to discover some mode of egress, but entirely without success. On the contrary, the result was, so far as it went, subversive of the theory; solid masonry met them on every hand.

I called the man, Smith, up, to hear from his own lips the particulars of what he had seen; and certainly his report was very curious. I give it as literally as my memory enables me:—

His son slept in the same room, and was sound asleep; but he lay awake, as men sometimes will on a change of bed, and having many things on his mind. He was lying with his face towards the wall, but observing a light and some little stir in the room, he turned round in his bed, and saw the figure of a woman, squalid, and ragged in dress; her figure rather low and broad; as well as I recollect, she had something – either a cloak or shawl – on, and wore a bonnet. Her back was turned, and she appeared to be searching or rummaging for something on the floor, and, without appearing to observe him, she turned in doing so towards him. The light, which was more like the intense glow of a coal, as he described it, being of a deep red colour, proceeded from the hollow of her hand, which she held beside her head, and he saw her perfectly distinctly. She appeared middle-aged, was deeply pitted with the smallpox, and blind of one eye. His phrase in describing her general appearance was, that she was "a miserable, poor-looking creature".

He was under the impression that she must be the woman who had been left by the proprietor in charge of the house, and who had that evening, after having given up the keys, remained for some little time with the female servants. He coughed, therefore, to apprize her of his presence, and turned again towards the wall. When he again looked round she and the light were gone; and odd as was her method of lighting herself in her search, the circumstances excited neither uneasiness nor curiosity in his mind, until he discovered next morning that the woman in question had left the house long before he had gone to his bed.

I examined the man very closely as to the appearance of the person who had visited him, and the result was what I have described. It struck me as an odd thing, that even then, considering how prone to superstition persons in his rank of life usually are, he did not seem to suspect any thing supernatural in the occurrence; and, on the contrary, was thoroughly persuaded that his visitant was a living person, who had got into the house by some hidden entrance.

On Sunday, on his return from his place of worship, he told me that, when the service was ended, and the congregation making their way slowly out, he saw the very woman in the crowd, and kept his eye upon her for several minutes, but such was the crush, that all his efforts to reach her were unavailing, and when he got into the open street she was gone. He was quite positive as to his having distinctly seen her, however, for several minutes, and scouted the possibility of any mistake as to identity; and fully impressed with the substantial and living reality of his visitant, he was very much provoked at her having escaped him. He made inquiries also in the neighbourhood, but could procure no information, nor hear of any other persons having seen any woman corresponding with his visitant.

The cook and the housemaid occupied a bedroom on the kitchen floor. It had whitewashed walls, and they were actually terrified by the appearance of the shadow of a woman passing and repassing across the side wall opposite to their beds. They suspected that this had been going on much longer than they were aware, for its presence was discovered by a sort of accident, its movements happening to take a direction in distinct contrariety to theirs.

This shadow always moved upon one particular wall, returning after short intervals, and causing them extreme terror. They placed the candle, as the most obvious specific, so close to the infested wall, that the flame all but touched it; and believed for some time that they had effectually got rid of this annoyance; but one night, notwithstanding this arrangement of the light, the shadow returned, passing and repassing, as heretofore, upon the same wall, although their only candle was burning within an inch of it, and it was obvious that no substance capable of casting such a shadow could have interposed; and, indeed, as they described it, light, and appeared, as I have said, in manifest defiance of the laws of optics.

I ought to mention that the housemaid was a particularly fearless sort of person, as well as a very honest one; and her companion, the cook, a scrupulously religious woman, and both agreed in every particular in their relation of what occurred.

Meanwhile, the nursery was not without its annoyances, though as yet of a comparatively trivial kind. Sometimes, at night, the handle of the door was turned hurriedly as if by a person trying to come in, and at others a knocking was made at it. These sounds occurred after the children had settled to sleep, and while the nurse still remained awake. Whenever she called to know "who is there," the sounds ceased; but several times, and particularly at first, she was under the impression that they were caused by her mistress, who had come to see the children, and thus impressed she had got up and opened the door, expecting to see her, but discovering only darkness, and receiving no answer to her inquiries.

With respect to this nurse, I must mention that I believe no more perfectly trustworthy servant was ever employed in her capacity; and, in addition to her integrity, she was remarkably gifted with sound common sense.

One morning, I think about three or four weeks after our arrival, I was sitting at the parlour window which looked to the front, when I saw the little iron door which admitted into the small garden that lay between the window where I was sitting and the public road, pushed open by a woman who so exactly answered the description given by Smith of the woman who had visited his room on the night of his arrival as instantaneously to impress me with the conviction that she must be the identical person. She was a square, short woman, dressed in soiled and tattered clothes, scarred and pitted with smallpox, and blind of an eye. She stepped hurriedly into the little enclosure, and peered from a distance of a few yards into the room where I was sitting. I felt that now was the moment to clear the matter up; but there was something stealthy in the manner and look of the woman which convinced me that I must not appear to notice her until her retreat was fairly cut off. Unfortunately, I was suffering from a lame foot, and could not reach the bell as quickly as I wished. I made all the haste I could, and rang violently to bring up the servant Smith. In the short interval that intervened, I observed the woman from the window, who having in a leisurely way, and with a kind of scrutiny, looked along the front windows of the house, passed quickly out again, closing the gate after her, and followed a lady who was walking along the footpath at a quick pace, as if with the intention of begging from her. The moment the man entered I told him – "the blind woman you described to me has this instant followed a lady in that direction, try to overtake her." He was, if possible, more eager than I in the chase, but returned in a short time after a vain pursuit, very hot, and utterly disappointed. And, thereafter, we saw her face no more.

All this time, and up to the period of our leaving the house, which was not for two or three months later, there occurred at intervals the only phenomenon in the entire series having any resemblance to what we hear described of "Spiritualism." This was a knocking, like a soft hammering with a wooden mallet, as it seemed in the timbers between the bedroom ceilings and the roof. It had this special peculiarity, that it was always rythmical, and, I think, invariably, the emphasis upon the last stroke. It would sound rapidly "one, two, three, *four* – one, two, three, *four*;" or "one, two, *three* – one, two, *three*," and sometimes "one, *two* – one, *two*," &c., and this, with intervals and resumptions, monotonously for hours at a time.

At first this caused my wife, who was a good deal confined to her bed, much annoyance; and we sent to our neighbours to inquire if any hammering or carpentering was going on in their houses, but were informed that nothing of the sort was taking place. I have myself heard it frequently, always in the same inaccessible part of the house, and with the same monotonous emphasis. One odd thing about it was, that on my wife's calling out, as she used to do when it became more than usually troublesome, "stop that noise", it was invariably arrested for a longer or shorter time.

Of course none of these occurrences were ever mentioned in hearing of the children. They would have been, no doubt, like most children, greatly terrified had they heard any thing of the matter, and known that their elders were unable to account for what was passing; and their fears would have made them wretched and troublesome.

They used to play for some hours every day in the back garden – the house forming one end of this oblong inclosure, the stable and coach-house the other, and two parallel walls of considerable height the sides. Here, as it afforded a perfectly safe playground, they were frequently left quite to themselves; and in talking over their days' adventures, as children will, they happened to mention a woman, or rather the woman, for they had long grown familiar with her appearance, whom they used to see in the garden while they were at play. They assumed that she came in and went out at the stable door, but they never actually saw her enter or depart. They merely saw a figure – that of a very poor woman, soiled and ragged – near the stable wall, stooping over the ground, and apparently grubbing in the loose clay in search of something. She did not disturb, or appear to observe them; and they left her in undisturbed possession of her nook of ground. When seen it was always in the same spot, and similarly occupied; and the description they gave of her general appearance – for they never saw her face – corresponded with that of the one-eyed woman whom Smith, and subsequently as it seemed, I had seen.

The other man, James, who looked after a mare which I had purchased for the purpose of riding exercise, had, like every one else in the house, his little trouble to report, though it was not much. The stall in which, as the most comfortable, it was decided to place her, she peremptorily declined to enter. Though a very docile and gentle little animal, there was no getting her into it. She would snort and rear, and, in fact, do or suffer any thing rather than set her hoof in it. He was fain, therefore, to place her in another. And on several occasions he found her there, exhibiting all the equine symptoms of extreme fear. Like the rest of us, however, this man was not troubled in the particular case with any superstitious qualms. The mare had evidently been frightened; and he was puzzled to find out how, or by whom, for the stable was well-secured, and had, I am nearly certain, a lock-up yard outside.

One morning I was greeted with the intelligence that robbers had certainly got into the house in the night; and that one of them had actually been seen in the nursery. The witness, I found, was my eldest child, then, as I have said, about nine years of age. Having awoke in the night, and lain awake for some time in her bed, she heard the handle of the door turn, and a person whom she distinctly saw – for it was a light night, and the window-shutters unclosed – but whom she had never seen before, stepped in on tiptoe, and with an appearance of great caution. He was a rather small man, with a very red face; he wore an oddly cut frock coat, the collar of which stood up, and trousers, rough and wide, like those of a sailor, turned up at the ankles, and either short boots or clumsy shoes, covered with mud. This man listened beside the nurse's bed, which stood next the door, as if to satisfy himself that she was sleeping soundly; and having done so for some seconds, he began to move cautiously in a diagonal line, across the room to the chimney-piece, where he stood for a while, and so resumed his tiptoe walk, skirting the wall, until he reached a chest of drawers, some of which were open, and into which he looked, and began to rummage in a hurried way, as the child supposed, making search for something worth taking away. He then passed on to the window, where was a dressing-table, at which he also stopped, turning over the things upon it, and standing for some time at the window as if looking out, and then resuming his walk by the side wall opposite to that by which he had moved up to the window, he returned in the same way toward the nurse's bed, so as to reach it at the foot. With its side to the end wall, in which was the door, was placed the little bed in which lay my eldest child, who watched his proceedings with the extremest terror. As he drew near she instinctively moved herself in the bed, with her head and shoulders to the wall, drawing up her feet; but he passed by without appearing to observe, or, at least, to care for her presence. Immediately after the nurse turned in her bed as if about to waken; and when the child, who had drawn the clothes about her head, again ventured to peep out, the man was gone.

The child had no idea of her having seen any thing more formidable than a thief. With the prowling, cautious, and noiseless manner of proceeding common to such marauders, the air and movements of the man whom she had seen entirely corresponded. And on hearing her perfectly distinct and consistent account, I could myself arrive at no other conclusion than that a stranger had actually got into the house. I had, therefore, in the first instance, a most careful examination made to discover any traces of an entrance having been made by any window into the house. The doors had been found barred and locked as usual; but no sign of any thing of the sort was discernible. I then had the various articles – plate, wearing apparel, books, &c., counted; and after having conned over and reckoned up every thing, it became quite clear that nothing whatever had been removed from the house, nor was there the slightest indication of any thing having been so much as disturbed there. I must here state that this child was remarkably clear, intelligent, and observant; and that her description of the man, and of all that had occurred, was most exact, and as detailed as the want of perfect light rendered possible.

I felt assured that an entrance had actually been effected into the house, though for what purpose was not easily to be conjectured. The man, Smith, was equally confident upon this point; and his theory was that the object was simply to frighten us out of the house by making us believe it haunted; and he was more than ever anxious and on the alert to discover the conspirators. It often since appeared to me odd. Every year, indeed, more odd, as this cumulative case of the marvellous becomes to my mind more and more inexplicable – that underlying my sense of mystery and puzzle, was all along the quiet assumption that all these occurrences were one way or another referable to natural causes. I could not account for them, indeed, myself; but during the whole period I inhabited that house, I never once felt, though much alone, and often up very late at night, any of those tremors and thrills which every one has at times experienced when situation and the hour are favourable. Except the cook and housemaid, who were plagued with the shadow I mentioned crossing and recrossing upon the bedroom wall, we all, without exception, experienced the same strange sense of security, and regarded these phenomena rather with a perplexed sort of interest and curiosity, than with any more unpleasant sensations.

The knockings which I have mentioned at the nursery door, preceded generally by the sound of a step on the lobby, meanwhile continued. At that time (for my wife, like myself, was an invalid) two eminent physicians, who came out occasionally by rail, were attending us. These gentlemen were at first only amused, but ultimately interested, and very much puzzled by the occurrences which we described. One of them, at last, recommended that a candle should be kept burning upon the lobby. It was in fact a recurrence to an old woman's recipe against ghosts – of course it might be serviceable, too, against impostors; at all events, seeming, as I have said, very much interested and puzzled, he advised it, and it was tried. We fancied that it was successful; for there was an interval of quiet for, I think, three or four nights. But after that, the noises – the footsteps on the lobby – the knocking at the door, and the turning of the handle recommenced in full force, notwithstanding the light upon the table outside; and these particular phenomena became only more perplexing than ever.

The alarm of robbers and smugglers gradually subsided after a week or two; but we were again to hear news from the nursery. Our second little girl, then between seven and eight years of age, saw in the night time – she alone being awake – a young woman, with black, or very dark hair, which hung loose, and with a black cloak on, standing near the middle of the floor, opposite the hearthstone, and fronting the foot of her bed. She appeared quite unobservant of the children and nurse sleeping in the room. She was very pale, and looked, the child said, both "sorry and frightened," and with something very peculiar and terrible about her eyes, which made the child conclude that she was dead. She was looking, not at, but in the direction of the child's bed, and there was a dark streak across her throat, like a scar with blood upon it. This figure was not motionless; but once or twice turned slowly, and without appearing to be conscious of the presence of the child, or the other occupants of the room, like a person in vacancy or abstraction. There was on this occasion a night-light burning in the chamber; and the child saw, or thought she saw, all these particulars with the most perfect distinctness. She got her head under the bed-clothes; and although a good many years have passed since then, she cannot recall the spectacle without feelings of peculiar horror.

One day, when the children were playing in the back garden, I asked them to point out to me the spot where they were accustomed to see the woman who occasionally showed herself as I have described, near the stable wall. There was no division of opinion as to this precise point, which they indicated in the most distinct and confident way. I suggested that, perhaps, something might be hidden there in the ground; and advised them digging a hole there with their little spades, to try for it. Accordingly, to work they went, and by my return in the evening they had grubbed up a piece of a jawbone, with several teeth in it. The bone was very much decayed, and ready to crumble to pieces, but the teeth were quite sound. I could not tell whether they were human grinders; but I showed the fossil to one of the physicians I have mentioned, who came out the next evening, and he pronounced them human teeth. The same conclusion was come to a day or two later by the other medical man. It appears to me now, on reviewing the whole matter, almost unaccountable that, with such evidence before me, I should not have got in a labourer, and had the spot effectually dug and searched. I can only say, that so it was. I was quite satisfied of the moral truth of every word that had been related to me, and which I have here set down with scrupulous accuracy. But I experienced an apathy, for which neither then nor afterwards did I quite know how to account. I had a vague, but immovable impression that the whole affair was referable to natural agencies. It was not until some time after we had left the house, which, by-the-by, we afterwards found had had the reputation of being haunted before we had come to live in it, that on reconsideration I discovered the serious difficulty of accounting satisfactorily for all that had occurred upon ordinary principles. A great deal we might arbitrarily set down to imagination. But even in so doing there was, *in limine*, the oddity, not to say improbability, of so many different persons having nearly simultaneously suffered from different spectral and other illusions during the short period for which we had occupied that house, who never before, nor so far as we learned, afterwards were troubled by any fears or fancies of the sort. There were other things, too, not to be so accounted for. The odd knockings in the roof I frequently heard myself.

There were also, which I before forgot to mention, in the daytime, rappings at the doors of the sitting-rooms, which constantly deceived us; and it was not till our "come in" was unanswered, and the hall or passage outside the door was discovered to be empty, that we learned that whatever else caused them, human hands did not. All the persons who reported having seen the different persons or appearances here described by me, were just as confident of having literally and distinctly seen them, as I was of having seen the hard-featured woman with the blind eye, so remarkably corresponding with Smith's description.

About a week after the discovery of the teeth, which were found, I think, about two feet under the ground, a friend, much advanced in years, and who remembered the town in which we had now taken up our abode, for a very long time, happened to pay us a visit. He good-humouredly pooh-poohed the whole thing; but at the same time was evidently curious about it. "We might construct a sort of story," said I (I am giving, of course, the substance and purport, not the exact words, of our dialogue), "and assign to each of the three figures who appeared their respective parts in some dreadful tragedy enacted in this house. The male figure represents the murderer; the ill-looking, one-eyed woman his accomplice, who, we will suppose, buried the body where she is now so often seen grubbing in the earth, and where the human teeth and jawbone have so lately been disinterred; and the young woman with dishevelled tresses, and black cloak, and the bloody scar across her throat, their victim. A difficulty, however, which I cannot get over, exists in the cheerfulness, the great publicity, and the evident very recent date of the house." "Why, as to that," said he, "the house is *not* modern; it and those beside it formed an old government store, altered and fitted up recently as you see. I remember it well in my young days, fifty years ago, before the town had grown out in this direction, and a more entirely lonely spot, or one more fitted for the commission of a secret crime, could not have been imagined."

I have nothing to add, for very soon after this my physician pronounced a longer stay unnecessary for my health, and we took our departure for another place of abode. I may add, that although I have resided for considerable periods in many other houses, I never experienced any annoyances of a similar kind elsewhere; neither have I made (stupid dog! you will say), any inquiries respecting either the antecedents or subsequent history of the house in which we made so disturbed a sojourn. I was content with what I knew, and have here related as clearly as I could, and I think it a very pretty puzzle as it stands.

# A Case of Eavesdropping

## Algernon Blackwood

### Prospectus

**Address:** East 21st Street, New York, USA.

**Property:** Former private residence now converted into a boarding house. The rooms are spacious with views to the East River and easy access to Manhattan. Top floor flat to let.

**Viewing Date:** Fall, 1906.

**Agent:** Algernon Blackwood (1869–1951) was born in London, the son of a nobleman. He rebelled against his strict upbringing and in his twenties went to America, where he became a reporter on the *New York Sun*. Here his interest in the supernatural lead him to investigate several haunted houses and start writing the stories that made him famous, in collections such as *The Empty House* (1906), *Incredible Adventures* (1914) and *Strange Stories* (1929). His reputation grew with radio and TV appearances, earning him the epithet "The Ghost Man". There is much of Blackwood in the character of Jim Shorthouse in this story – and he, too, lived in East 21st Street . . .

Jim Shorthouse was the sort of fellow who always made a mess of things. Everything with which his hands or mind came into contact issued from such contact in an unqualified and irremediable state of mess. His college days were a mess: he was twice rusticated. His schooldays were a mess: he went to half a dozen, each passing him on to the next with a worse character and in a more developed state of mess. His early boyhood was the sort of mess that copy-books and dictionaries spell with a big "M", and his babyhood – ugh! was the embodiment of howling, yowling, screaming mess.

At the age of forty, however, there came a change in his troubled life, when he met a girl with half a million in her own right, who consented to marry him, and who very soon succeeded in reducing his most messy existence into a state of comparative order and system.

Certain incidents, important and otherwise, of Jim's life would never have come to be told here but for the fact that in getting into his "messes" and out of them again he succeeded in drawing himself into the atmosphere of peculiar circumstances and strange happenings. He attracted to his path the curious adventures of life as unfailingly as meat attracts flies, and jam wasps. It is to the meat and jam of his life, so to speak, that he owes his experiences; his after-life was all pudding, which attracts nothing but greedy children. With marriage the interest of his life ceased for all but one person, and his path became regular as the sun's instead of erratic as a comet's.

The first experience in order of time that he related to me shows that somewhere latent behind his disarranged nervous system there lay psychic perceptions of an uncommon order. About the age of twenty-two – I think after his second rustication – his father's purse and patience had equally given out, and Jim found himself stranded high and dry in a large American city. High and dry! And the only clothes that had no holes in them safely in the keeping of his uncle's wardrobe.

Careful reflection on a bench in one of the city parks led him to the conclusion that the only thing to do was to persuade the city editor of one of the daily journals that he possessed an observant mind and a ready pen, and that he could "do good work for your paper, sir, as a reporter". This, then, he did, standing at a most unnatural angle between the editor and the window to conceal the whereabouts of the holes.

"Guess we'll have to give you a week's trial," said the editor, who, ever on the lookout for good chance material, took on shoals of men in that way and retained on the average one man per shoal. Anyhow it gave Jim Shorthouse the wherewithal to sew up the holes and relieve his uncle's wardrobe of its burden.

Then he went to find living quarters; and in this proceeding his unique characteristics already referred to – what theosophists would call his Karma – began unmistakably to assert themselves, for it was in the house he eventually selected that this sad tale took place.

There are no "diggings" in American cities. The alternatives for small incomes are grim enough – rooms in a boarding-house where meals are served, or in a room-house where no meals are served – not even breakfast. Rich people live in palaces, of course, but Jim had nothing to do with "sich-like". His horizon was bounded by boarding-houses and room-houses; and, owing to the necessary irregularity of his meals and hours, he took the latter.

It was a large, gaunt-looking place in a side street, with dirty windows and a creaking iron gate, but the rooms were large, and the one he selected and paid for in advance was on the top floor. The landlady looked gaunt and dusty as the house, and quite as old. Her eyes were green and faded, and her features large.

"Waal," she twanged, with her electrifying Western drawl, "that's the room, if you like it, and that's the price I said. Now, if you want it, why, just say so; and if you don't, why, it don't hurt me any."

Jim wanted to shake her, but he feared the clouds of long-accumulated dust in her clothes, and as the price and size of the room suited him, he decided to take it.

"Anyone else on this floor?" he asked.

She looked at him queerly out of her faded eyes before she answered.

"None of my guests ever put such questions to me before," she said; "but I guess you're different. Why, there's no one at all but an old gent that's stayed here every bit of five years. He's over thar," pointing to the end of the passage.

"Ah! I see," said Shorthouse feebly. "So I'm alone up here?"

"Reckon you are, pretty near," she twanged out, ending the conversation abruptly by turning her back on her new "guest", and going slowly and deliberately downstairs.

The newspaper work kept Shorthouse out most of the night. Three times a week he got home at 1 a.m., and three times at 3 a.m. The room proved comfortable enough, and he paid for a second week. His unusual hours had so far prevented his meeting any inmates of the house, and not a sound had been heard from the "old gent" who shared the floor with him. It seemed a very quiet house.

One night, about the middle of the second week, he came home tired after a long day's work. The lamp that usually stood all night in the hall had burned itself out, and he had to stumble upstairs in the dark. He made considerable noise in doing so, but nobody seemed to be disturbed. The whole house was utterly quiet, and probably everybody was asleep. There were no lights under any of the doors. All was in darkness. It was after two o'clock.

After reading some English letters that had come during the day, and dipping for a few minutes into a book, he became drowsy and got ready for bed. Just as he was about to get in between the sheets, he stopped for a moment and listened. There rose in the night, as he did so, the sound of steps somewhere in the house below. Listening attentively, he heard that it was somebody coming upstairs – a heavy tread, and the owner taking no pains to step quietly. On it came up the stairs, tramp, tramp, tramp – evidently the tread of a big man, and one in something of a hurry.

At once thoughts connected somehow with fire and police flashed through Jim's brain, but there were no sounds of voices with the steps, and he reflected in the same moment that it could only be the old gentleman keeping late hours and tumbling upstairs in the darkness. He was in the act of turning out the gas and stepping into bed, when the house resumed its former stillness by the footsteps suddenly coming to a dead stop immediately outside his own room.

With his hand on the gas, Shorthouse paused a moment before turning it out to see if the steps would go on again, when he was startled by a loud knocking on his door. Instantly, in obedience to a curious and unexplained instinct, he turned out the light, leaving himself and the room in total darkness.

He had scarcely taken a step across the room to open the door, when a voice from the other side of the wall, so close it almost sounded in his ear, exclaimed in German, "Is that you, father? Come in."

The speaker was a man in the next room, and the knocking, after all, had not been on his own door, but on that of the adjoining chamber, which he had supposed to be vacant.

Almost before the man in the passage had time to answer in German, "Let me in at once," Jim heard someone cross the floor and unlock the door. Then it was slammed to with a bang, and there was audible the sound of footsteps about the room, and of chairs being drawn up to a table and knocking against furniture on the way. The men seemed wholly regardless of their neighbour's comfort, for they made noise enough to waken the dead.

"Serves me right for taking a room in such a cheap hole," reflected Jim in the darkness. "I wonder whom she's let the room to!"

The two rooms, the landlady had told him, were originally one. She had put up a thin partition – just a row of boards – to increase her income. The doors were adjacent, and only separated by the massive upright beam between them. When one was opened or shut the other rattled.

With utter indifference to the comfort of the other sleepers in the house, the two Germans had meanwhile commenced to talk both at once and at the top of their voices. They talked emphatically, even angrily. The words "Father" and "Otto" were freely used. Shorthouse understood German, but as he stood listening for the first minute or two, an eavesdropper in spite of himself, it was difficult to make head or tail of the talk, for neither would give way to the other, and the jumble of guttural sounds and unfinished sentences was wholly unintelligible. Then, very suddenly, both voices dropped together; and, after a moment's pause, the deep tones of one of them, who seemed to be the "father," said, with the utmost distinctness –

"You mean, Otto, that you refuse to get it?"

There was a sound of someone shuffling in the chair before the answer came. "I mean that I don't know how to get it. It is so much, father. It is *too* much. A part of it—"

"A part of it!" cried the other, with an angry oath, "a part of it, when ruin and disgrace are already in the house, is worse than useless. If you can get half you can get all, you wretched fool. Half-measures only damn all concerned."

"You told me last time—" began the other firmly, but was not allowed to finish. A succession of horrible oaths drowned his sentence, and the father went on, in a voice vibrating with anger –

"You know she will give you anything. You have only been married a few months. If you ask and give a plausible reason you can get all we want and more. You can ask it temporarily. All will be paid back. It will re-establish the firm, and she will never know what was done with it. With that amount, Otto, you know I can recoup all these terrible losses, and in less than a year all will be repaid. But without it . . . You must get it, Otto. Hear me, you must. Am I to be arrested for the misuse of trust moneys? Is our honoured name to be cursed and spat on?" The old man choked and stammered in his anger and desperation.

Shorthouse stood shivering in the darkness and listening in spite of himself. The conversation had carried him along with it, and he had been for some reason afraid to let his neighbourhood be known. But at this point he realised that he had listened too long and that he must inform the two men that they could be overheard to every single syllable. So he coughed loudly, and at the same time rattled the handle of his door. It seemed to have no effect, for the voices continued just as loudly as before, the son protesting and the father growing more and more angry. He coughed again persistently, and also contrived purposely in the darkness to tumble against the partition, feeling the thin boards yield easily under his weight, and making a considerable noise in so doing. But the voices went on unconcernedly, and louder than ever. Could it be possible they had not heard?

By this time Jim was more concerned about his own sleep than the morality of overhearing the private scandals of his neighbours, and he went out into the passage and knocked smartly at their door. Instantly, as if by magic, the sounds ceased. Everything dropped into utter silence. There was no light under the door and not a whisper could be heard within. He knocked again, but received no answer.

"Gentlemen," he began at length, with his lips close to the keyhole and in German, "please do not talk so loud. I can overhear all you say in the next room. Besides, it is very late, and I wish to sleep."

He paused and listened, but no answer was forthcoming. He turned the handle and found the door was locked. Not a sound broke the stillness of the night except the faint swish of the wind over the skylight and the creaking of a board here and there in the house below. The cold air of a very early morning crept down the passage, and made him shiver. The silence of the house began to impress him disagreeably. He looked behind him and about him, hoping, and yet fearing, that something would break the stillness. The voices still seemed to ring on in his ears; but that sudden silence, when he knocked at the door, affected him far more unpleasantly than the voices, and put strange thoughts in his brain – thoughts he did not like or approve.

Moving stealthily from the door, he peered over the banisters into the space below. It was like a deep vault that might conceal in its shadows anything that was not good. It was not difficult to fancy he saw an indistinct moving to-and-fro below him. Was that a figure sitting on the stairs peering up obliquely at him out of hideous eyes? Was that a sound of whispering and shuffling down there in the dark halls and forsaken landings? Was it something more than the inarticulate murmur of the night?

The wind made an effort overhead, singing over the skylight, and the door behind him rattled and made him start. He turned to go back to his room, and the draught closed the door slowly in his face as if there were someone pressing against it from the other side. When he pushed it open and went in, a hundred shadowy forms seemed to dart swiftly and silently back to their corners and hiding-places. But in the adjoining room the sounds had entirely ceased, and Shorthouse soon crept into bed, and left the house with its inmates, waking or sleeping, to take care of themselves, while he entered the region of dreams and silence.

Next day, strong in the common sense that the sunlight brings, he determined to lodge a complaint against the noisy occupants of the next room and make the landlady request them to modify their voices at such late hours of the night and morning. But it so happened that she was not to be seen that day, and when he returned from the office at midnight it was, of course, too late.

Looking under the door as he came up to bed he noticed that there was no light, and concluded that the Germans were not in. So much the better. He went to sleep about one o'clock, fully decided that if they came up later and woke him with their horrible noises he would not rest till he had roused the landlady and made her reprove them with that authoritative twang, in which every word was like the lash of a metallic whip.

However, there proved to be no need for such drastic measures, for Shorthouse slumbered peacefully all night, and his dreams – chiefly of the fields of grain and flocks of sheep on the far-away farms of his father's estate – were permitted to run their fanciful course unbroken.

Two nights later, however, when he came home tired out, after a difficult day, and wet and blown about by one of the wickedest storms he had ever seen, his dreams – always of the fields and sheep – were not destined to be so undisturbed.

He had already dozed off in that delicious glow that follows the removal of wet clothes and the immediate snuggling under warm blankets, when his consciousness, hovering on the borderland between sleep and waking, was vaguely troubled by a sound that rose indistinctly from the depths of the house, and, between the gusts of wind and rain, reached his ears with an accompanying sense of uneasiness and discomfort. It rose on the night air with some pretence of regularity, dying away again in the roar of the wind to reassert itself distantly in the deep, brief hushes of the storm.

For a few minutes Jim's dreams were coloured only – tinged, as it were, by this impression of fear approaching from somewhere insensibly upon him. His consciousness, at first, refused to be drawn back from that enchanted region where it had wandered, and he did not immediately awaken. But the nature of his dreams changed unpleasantly. He saw the sheep suddenly run huddled together, as though frightened by the neighbourhood of an enemy, while the fields of waving corn became agitated as though some monster were moving uncouthly among the crowded stalks. The sky grew dark, and in his dream an awful sound came somewhere from the clouds. It was in reality the sound downstairs growing more distinct.

Shorthouse shifted uneasily across the bed with something like a groan of distress. The next minute he awoke, and found himself sitting straight up in bed – listening. Was it a nightmare? Had he been dreaming evil dreams, that his flesh crawled and the hair stirred on his head?

The room was dark and silent, but outside the wind howled dismally and drove the rain with repeated assaults against the rattling windows. How nice it would be – the thought flashed through his mind – if all winds, like the west wind, went down with the sun! They made such fiendish noises at night, like the crying of angry voices. In the daytime they had such a different sound. If only—

Hark! It was no dream after all, for the sound was momentarily growing louder, and its *cause* was coming up the stairs. He found himself speculating feebly what this cause might be, but the sound was still too indistinct to enable him to arrive at any definite conclusion.

The voice of a church clock striking two made itself heard above the wind. It was just about the hour when the Germans had commenced their performance three nights before. Shorthouse made up his mind that if they began it again he would not put up with it for very long. Yet he was already horribly conscious of the difficulty he would have of getting out of bed. The clothes were so warm and comforting against his back. The sound, still steadily coming nearer, had by this time become differentiated from the confused clamour of the elements, and had resolved itself into the footsteps of one or more persons.

"The Germans, hang 'em!" thought Jim. "But what on earth is the matter with me? I never felt so queer in all my life."

He was trembling all over, and felt as cold as though he were in a freezing atmosphere. His nerves were steady enough, and he felt no diminution of physical courage, but he was conscious of a curious sense of malaise and trepidation, such as even the most vigorous men have been known to experience when in the first grip of some horrible and deadly disease. As the footsteps approached this feeling of weakness increased. He felt a strange lassitude creeping over him, a sort of exhaustion, accompanied by a growing numbness in the extremities, and a sensation of dreaminess in the head, as if perhaps the consciousness were leaving its accustomed seat in the brain and preparing to act on another plane. Yet, strange to say, as the vitality was slowly withdrawn from his body, his senses seemed to grow more acute.

Meanwhile the steps were already on the landing at the top of the stairs, and Shorthouse, still sitting upright in bed, heard a heavy body brush past his door and along the wall outside, almost immediately afterwards the loud knocking of someone's knuckles on the door of the adjoining room.

Instantly, though so far not a sound had proceeded from within, he heard, through the thin partition, a chair pushed back and a man quickly cross the floor and open the door.

"Ah! it's you," he heard in the son's voice. Had the fellow, then, been sitting silently in there all this time, waiting for his father's arrival? To Shorthouse it came not as a pleasant reflection by any means.

There was no answer to this dubious greeting, but the door was closed quickly, and then there was a sound as if a bag or parcel had been thrown on a wooden table and had slid some distance across it before stopping.

"What's that?" asked the son, with anxiety in his tone.

"You may know before I go," returned the other gruffly. Indeed his voice was more than gruff: it betrayed ill-suppressed passion.

Shorthouse was conscious of a strong desire to stop the conversation before it proceeded any further, but somehow or other his will was not equal to the task, and he could not get out of bed.

The conversation went on, every tone and inflexion distinctly audible above the noise of the storm.

In a low voice the father continued. Jim missed some of the words at the beginning of the sentence. It ended with: ". . . but now they've all left, and I've managed to get up to you. You know what I've come for." There was distinct menace in his tone.

"Yes," returned the other; "I have been waiting."

"And the money?" asked the father impatiently.

No answer.

"You've had three days to get it in, and I've contrived to stave off the worst so far – but to-morrow is the end."

No answer.

"Speak, Otto! What have you got for me? Speak, my son; for God's sake, tell me."

There was a moment's silence, during which the old man's vibrating accents seemed to echo through the rooms. Then came in a low voice the answer –

"I have nothing."

"Otto!" cried the other with passion, "nothing!"

"I can get nothing," came almost in a whisper.

"You lie!" cried the other, in a half-stifled voice. "I swear you lie. Give me the money."

A chair was heard scraping along the floor. Evidently the men had been sitting over the table, and one of them had risen. Shorthouse heard the bag or parcel drawn across the table, and then a step as if one of the men was crossing to the door.

"Father, what's in that? I must know," said Otto, with the first signs of determination in his voice. There must have been an effort on the son's part to gain possession of the parcel in question, and on the father's to retain it, for between them it fell to the ground. A curious rattle followed its contact with the floor. Instantly there were sounds of a scuffle. The men were struggling for the possession of the box. The elder man with oaths, and blasphemous imprecations, the other with short gasps that betokened the strength of his efforts. It was of short duration, and the younger man had evidently won, for a minute later was heard his angry exclamation.

"I knew it. Her jewels! You scoundrel, you shall never have them. It is a crime."

The elder man uttered a short, guttural laugh, which froze Jim's blood and made his skin creep. No word was spoken, and for the space of ten seconds there was a living silence. Then the air trembled with the sound of a thud, followed immediately by a groan and the crash of a heavy body falling over on to the table. A second later there was a lurching from the table on to the floor and against the partition that separated the rooms. The bed quivered an instant at the shock, but the unholy spell was lifted from his soul and Jim Shorthouse sprang out of bed and across the floor in a single bound. He knew that ghastly murder had been done – the murder by a father of his son.

With shaking fingers but a determined heart he lit the gas, and the first thing in which his eyes corroborated the evidence of his ears was the horrifying detail that the lower portion of the partition bulged unnaturally into his own room. The glaring paper with which it was covered had cracked under the tension and the boards beneath it bent inwards towards him. What hideous load was behind them, he shuddered to think.

All this he saw in less than a second. Since the final lurch against the wall not a sound had proceeded from the room, not even a groan or a footstep. All was still but the howl of the wind, which to his ears had in it a note of triumphant horror.

Shorthouse was in the act of leaving the room to rouse the house and send for the police – in fact his hand was already on the door-knob – when something in the room arrested his attention. Out of the corner of his eyes he thought he caught sight of something moving. He was sure of it, and turning his eyes in the direction, he found he was not mistaken.

Something was creeping slowly towards him along the floor. It was something dark and serpentine in shape, and it came from the place where the partition bulged. He stooped down to examine it with feelings of intense horror and repugnance, and he discovered that it was moving toward him from the *other side* of the wall. His eyes were fascinated, and for the moment he was unable to move. Silently, slowly, from side to side like a thick worm, it crawled forward into the room beneath his frightened eyes, until at length he could stand it no longer and stretched out his arm to touch it. But at the instant of contact he withdrew his hand with a suppressed scream. It was sluggish – and it was warm! and he saw that his fingers were stained with living crimson.

A second more, and Shorthouse was out in the passage with his hand on the door of the next room. It was locked. He plunged forward with all his weight against it, and, the lock giving way, he fell headlong into a room that was pitch dark and very cold. In a moment he was on his feet again and trying to penetrate the blackness. Not a sound, not a movement. Not even the sense of a presence. It was empty, miserably empty!

Across the room he could trace the outline of a window with rain streaming down the outside, and the blurred lights of the city beyond. But the room was empty, appallingly empty; and so still. He stood there, cold as ice, staring, shivering listening. Suddenly there was a step behind him and a light flashed into the room, and when he turned quickly with his arm up as if to ward off a terrific blow he found himself face to face with the landlady. Instantly the reaction began to set in.

It was nearly three o'clock in the morning, and he was standing there with bare feet and striped pyjamas in a small room, which in the merciful light he perceived to be absolutely empty, carpetless, and without a stick of furniture, or even a window-blind. There he stood staring at the disagreeable landlady. And there she stood too, staring and silent, in a black wrapper, her head almost bald, her face white as chalk, shading a sputtering candle with one bony hand and peering over it at him with her blinking green eyes. She looked positively hideous.

"Waal?" she drawled at length, "I heard yer right enough. Guess you couldn't sleep! Or just prowlin' round a bit – is that it?"

The empty room, the absence of all traces of the recent tragedy, the silence, the hour, his striped pyjamas and bare feet – everything together combined to deprive him momentarily of speech. He stared at her blankly without a word.

"Waal?" clanked the awful voice.

"My dear woman," he burst out finally, "there's been something awful—" So far his desperation took him, but no farther. He positively stuck at the substantive.

"Oh! there hasn't been nothin'," she said slowly still peering at him. "I reckon you've only seen and heard what the others did. I never can keep folks on this floor long. Most of 'em catch on sooner or later – that is, the ones that's kind of quick and sensitive. Only you being an Englishman I thought you wouldn't mind. Nothin' really happens; it's only thinkin' like."

Shorthouse was beside himself. He felt ready to pick her up and drop her over the banisters, candle and all.

"Look there," he said, pointing at her within an inch of her blinking eyes with the fingers that had touched the oozing blood; "look there, my good woman. Is that only thinking?"

She stared a minute, as if not knowing what he meant.

"I guess so," she said at length.

He followed her eyes, and to his amazement saw that his fingers were as white as usual, and quite free from the awful stain that had been there ten minutes before. There was no sign of blood. No amount of staring could bring it back. Had he gone out of his mind? Had his eyes and ears played such tricks with him? Had his senses become false and perverted? He dashed past the landlady, out into the passage, and gained his own room in a couple of strides. Whew! . . . the partition no longer bulged. The paper was not torn. There was no creeping, crawling thing on the faded old carpet.

"It's all over now," drawled the metallic voice behind him. "I'm going to bed again."

He turned and saw the landlady slowly going downstairs again, still shading the candle with her hand and peering up at him from time to time as she moved. A black, ugly, unwholesome object, he thought, as she disappeared into the darkness below, and the last flicker of her candle threw a queer-shaped shadow along the wall and over the ceiling.

Without hesitating a moment, Shorthouse threw himself into his clothes and went out of the house. He preferred the storm to the horrors of that top floor, and he walked the streets till daylight. In the evening he told the landlady he would leave next day, in spite of her assurances that nothing more would happen.

"It never comes back," she said – "that is, not after he's killed."

Shorthouse gasped.

"You gave me a lot for my money," he growled.

"Waal, it aren't my show," she drawled. "I'm no spirit medium. You take chances. Some'll sleep right along and never hear nothin'. Others, like yourself, are different and get the whole thing."

"Who's the old gentleman? – does he hear it?" asked Jim.

"There's no old gentleman at all," she answered coolly. "I just told you that to make you feel easy like in case you did hear anythin'. You were all alone on the floor.

"Say now," she went on, after a pause in which Shorthouse could think of nothing to say but unpublishable things, "say now, do tell, did you feel sort of cold when the show was on, sort of tired and weak, I mean, as if you might be going to die?"

"How can I say?" he answered savagely; "what I felt God only knows."

"Waal, but He won't tell," she drawled out. "Only I was wonderin' how you really did feel, because the man who had that room last was found one morning in bed—"

"In bed?"

"He was dead. He was the one before you. Oh! You don't need to get rattled so. You're all right. And it all really happened, they do say. This house used to be a private residence some twenty-five years ago, and a German family of the name of Steinhardt lived here. They had a big business in Wall Street, and stood 'way up in things."

"Ah!" said her listener.

"Oh yes, they did, right at the top, till one fine day it all bust and the old man skipped with the boodle—"

"Skipped with the boodle?"

"That's so," she said; "got clear away with all the money, and the son was found dead in his house, committed soocide it was thought. Though there was some as said he couldn't have stabbed himself and fallen in that position. They said he was murdered. The father died in prison. They tried to fasten the murder on him, but there was no motive, or no evidence, or no somethin'. I forget now."

"Very pretty," said Shorthouse.

"I'll show you somethin' mighty queer anyways," she drawled, "if you'll come upstairs a minute. I've heard the steps and voices lots of times; they don't pheaze me any. I'd just as lief hear so many dogs barkin'. You'll find the whole story in the newspapers if you look it up – not what goes on here, but the story of the Germans. My house would be ruined if they told all, and I'd sue for damages."

They reached the bedroom, and the woman went in and pulled up the edge of the carpet where Shorthouse had seen the blood soaking in the previous night.

"Look thar, if you feel like it," said the old hag. Stooping down, he saw a dark, dull stain in the boards that corresponded exactly to the shape and position of the blood as he had seen it.

That night he slept in a hotel, and the following day sought new quarters. In the newspapers on file in his office after a long search he found twenty years back the detailed story, substantially as the woman had said, of Steinhardt & Co.'s failure, the absconding and subsequent arrest of the senior partner, and the suicide, or murder, of his son Otto. The landlady's room-house had formerly been their private residence.

# A Haunted House

## Virginia Woolf

### Prospectus

**Address:** Asham House, near Lewes, East Sussex, England.

**Property:** Nineteenth-century, two-storey country home with arched roofs and imposing chimneys. Four bedrooms, dining room and lounge, with attractive floral gardens and two outbuildings.

**Viewing Date:** Summer, 1921.

**Agent:** Virginia Woolf (1882–1941) was born in London and began writing in her teens with the story "A Terrible Tragedy in a Duckpond", which revealed her adolescent perception of death and anticipated her own eventual suicide by drowning in the River Ouse. Brought up in a highly intellectual circle, the Bloomsbury Group, she developed an impressionistic style of writing in her novels *To The Lighthouse* (1927), *The Years* (1937) and *Between The Acts* (1941), as well as in a handful of outre stories including "The Lady in the Looking Glass", "Lappin and Lapinova" and "A Haunted House", which is based on the house where she lived in Sussex.

Whatever hour you woke there was a door shutting. From room to room they went, hand in hand, lifting here, opening there, making sure – a ghostly couple.

"Here we left it," she said. And he added, "Oh, but here too!" "It's upstairs," she murmured. "And in the garden," he whispered. "Quietly," they said, "or we shall wake them."

But it wasn't that you woke us. Oh, no. "They're looking for it; they're drawing the curtain," one might say, and so read on a page or two. "Now they've found it," one would be certain, stopping the pencil on the margin. And then, tired of reading, one might rise and see for oneself, the house all empty, the doors standing open, only the wood pigeons bubbling with content and the hum of the threshing machine sounding from the farm. "What did I come in here for? What did I want to find?" My hands were empty. "Perhaps it's upstairs then?" The apples were in the loft. And so down again, the garden still as ever, only the book had slipped into the grass.

But they had found it in the drawing-room. Not that one could ever see them. The window panes reflected apples, reflected roses; all the leaves were green in the glass. If they moved in the drawing-room, the apple only turned its yellow side. Yet, the moment after, if the door was opened, spread about the floor, hung upon the walls, pendant from the ceiling – what? My hands were empty. The shadow of a thrush crossed the carpet; from the deepest wells of silence the wood pigeon drew its bubble of sound. "Safe, safe, safe," the pulse of the house beat softly. "The treasure buried; the room . . ." the pulse stopped short. Oh, was that the buried treasure?

A moment later the light had faded. Out in the garden then? But the trees spun darkness for a wandering beam of sun. So fine, so rare, coolly sunk beneath the surface the beam I sought always burnt behind the glass. Death was the glass; death was between us; coming to the woman first, hundreds of years ago, leaving the house, sealing all the windows; the rooms were darkened. He left it, left her, went North, went East, saw the stars turned in the Southern sky; sought the house, found it dropped beneath the Downs. "Safe, safe, safe," the pulse of the house beat gladly. "The Treasure yours."

The wind roars up the avenue. Trees stoop and bend this way and that. Moonbeams splash and spill wildly in the rain. But the beam of the lamp falls straight from the window. The candle burns stiff and still. Wandering through the house, opening the windows, whispering not to wake us, the ghostly couple seek their joy.

"Here we slept," she says. And he adds, "Kisses without number." "Waking in the morning –" "Silver between the trees –" "Upstairs –" "In the garden –" "When summer came –" "In winter snowtime –" The doors go shutting far in the distance, gently knocking like the pulse of a heart.

Nearer they come; cease at the doorway. The wind falls, the rain slides silver down the glass. Our eyes darken; we hear no steps beside us; we see no lady spread her ghostly cloak. His hands shield the lantern. "Look," he breathes. "Sound asleep. Love upon their lips."

Stooping, holding their silver lamp above us, long they look and deeply. Long they pause. The wind drives straightly; the flame stoops slightly. Wild beams of moonlight cross both floor and wall, and, meeting, stain the faces bent; the faces pondering; the faces that search the sleepers and seek their hidden joy.

"Safe, safe, safe," the heart of the house beats proudly. "Long years –" he sighs. "Again you found me." "Here," she murmurs, "sleeping; in the garden reading; laughing, rolling apples in the loft. Here we left our treasure –" Stooping, their light lifts the lids upon my eyes. "Safe! safe! safe!" the pulse of the house beats wildly. Waking, I cry "Oh, is this *your* buried treasure? The light in the heart."

# Ghost Hunt

## H. Russell Wakefield

### Prospectus

**Address:** The Grange, near Richmond Bridge, London, England.
**Property:** Georgian-style house in its own grounds with lawns and borders running to the river. A charming, three-storey building with four bedrooms, lounge, dining room and fine reception room.
**Viewing Date:** March, 1938.
**Agent:** Herbert Russell Wakefield (1888–1964) was born in Elham, Kent, took a degree in history and worked for a London publisher when he started writing the ghost stories which today rank him alongside M. R. James. Among his notable collections are *They Return at Evening* (1928), *A Ghostly Company* (1935) and *The Clock Strikes Twelve* (1939). In 1917, he stayed in a period house near Richmond Bridge where a number of suicides had occurred with people throwing themselves into the Thames. He was inspired to write two stories about the place: the much-anthologised "The Red Lodge" (1928) and the equally unnerving "Ghost Hunt" . . .

Well, listeners, this is Tony Weldon speaking. Here we are on the third of our series of Ghost Hunts. Let's hope it will be more successful than the other two. All our preparations have been made and now it is up to the spooks. My colleague tonight is Professor Mignon of Paris. He is the most celebrated investigator of psychic phenomena in the world and I am very proud to be his collaborator.

We are in a medium-sized, three-story Georgian house not far from London. We have chosen it for this reason: it has a truly terrible history. Since it was built, there are records of no less than thirty suicides in or from it and there may well have been more. There have been eight since 1893. Its builder and first occupant was a prosperous city merchant and a very bad hat, it appears: glutton, wine bibber and other undesirable things, including a very bad husband. His wife stood his cruelties and infidelities as long as she could and then hanged herself in the powder closet belonging to the biggest bedroom on the second floor, so initiating a horrible sequence.

I used the expression "suicides in and from it", because while some have shot themselves and some hanged themselves, no less than nine have done a very strange thing. They have risen from their beds during the night and flung themselves to death in the river which runs past the bottom of the garden some hundred yards away. The last one was actually seen to do so at dawn on an autumn morning. He was seen running headlong and heard to be shouting as though to companions running by his side. The owner tells me people simply will not live in the house and the agents will no longer keep it on their books. He will not live in it himself, for very good reasons, he declares. He will not tell us what those reasons are; he wishes us to have an absolutely open mind on the subject, as it were. And he declares that if the professor's verdict is unfavorable, he will pull down the house and rebuild it. One can understand that, for it seems to merit the label, "Death Trap".

Well, that is sufficient introduction. I think I have convinced you it certainly merits investigation, but we cannot guarantee to deliver the goods or the ghosts, which have an awkward habit of taking a night off on these occasions.

And now to business – imagine me seated at a fine satinwood table, not quite in the middle of a big reception room on the ground floor. The rest of the furniture is shrouded in white protective covers. The walls are light oak panels. The electric light in the house has been switched off, so all the illumination I have is a not very powerful electric lamp. I shall remain here with a mike while the professor roams the house in search of what he may find. He will not have a mike, as it distracts him and he has a habit, so he says, of talking to himself while he conducts these investigations. He will return to me as soon as he has anything to report. Is that all clear? Well, then, here is the professor to say a few words to you before he sets forth on his tour of discovery. I may say he speaks English far better than I do. Professor Mignon –

Ladies and gentlemen, this is Professor Mignon. This house is without doubt, how shall I say, impregnated with evil. It affects one profoundly. It is bad, bad, bad! It is soaked in evil and reeking from its wicked past. It must be pulled down, I assure you. I do not think it affects my friend, Mr. Weldon, in the same way, but he is not psychic, not mediumistic, as I am. Now shall we see ghosts, spirits? Ah, that I cannot say! But they are here and they are evil; that is sure. I can feel their presence. There is, maybe, danger. I shall soon know. And now I shall start off with just one electric torch to show me the way. Presently I will come back and tell you what I have seen, or if not seen, felt and perhaps suffered. But remember, though we can summon spirits from the vasty deep, will they come when we call for them? We shall see.

Well, listeners, I'm sure if anyone can, it's the professor. You must have found those few words far more impressive than anything I said. That was an expert speaking on what he knows. Personally, alone here in this big, silent room, they didn't have a very reassuring effect on me. In fact, he wasn't quite correct when he said this place didn't affect me at all. I don't find it a very cheerful spot, by any means. You can be sure of that. I may not be psychic, but I've certainly got a sort of feeling it doesn't want us here, resents us, and would like to see the back of us. *Or else!* I felt that way as soon as I entered the front door. One sort of had to wade through the hostility. I'm not kidding or trying to raise your hopes.

It's very quiet here, listeners. I'm having a look around the room. This lamp casts some queer shadows. There is an odd one near the wall by the door, but I realize now it must be one cast by a big Adams bookcase. I know that's what it is because I peeped under the dust cover when I first came in. It's a very fine piece. It's queer to think of you all listening to me. I shouldn't really mind if I had some of you for company. The owner of the house told us we should probably hear rats and mice in the wainscoting. Well, I can certainly hear them now. Pretty hefty rats, from the sound of them – even you can almost hear them, I should think.

Well, what else is there to tell you about? Nothing very much, except that there's a bat in the room. I think it must be a bat and not a bird. I haven't actually seen it, only its shadow as it flew past the wall just now and then it fanned past my face. I don't know much about bats, but I thought they went to bed in the winter. This one must suffer from insomnia. Ah, there it is again – it actually touched me as it passed.

Now I can hear the professor moving about in the room above. I don't suppose you can – have a try. Now listen carefully –

Hello! Did you hear that? He must have knocked over a chair or something – a heavy chair, from the sound of it. I wonder if he's having any luck. Ah, there's that bat again – it seems to like me. Each time it just touches my face with its wings as it passes. They're smelly things, bats – I don't think they wash often enough. This one smells kind of rotten.

I wonder what the professor knocked over – I can see a small stain forming on the ceiling. Perhaps a flower bowl or something. Hello! Did you hear that sharp crack? I think you must have. The oak panelling stretching, I suppose, but it was almost ear-splitting in here. Something ran across my foot then – a rat, perhaps. I've always loathed rats. Most people do, of course.

That stain on the ceiling has grown quite a lot. I think I'll just go to the door and shout to the professor to make sure he's all right. You'll hear me shout and his answer, I expect –

Professor! – Professor! –

Well, he didn't answer. I believe he's a little bit deaf. But he's sure to be all right. I won't try again just yet, as I know he likes to be undisturbed on these occasions. I'll sit down again for a minute or two. I'm afraid this is rather dull for you, listeners. I'm not finding it so, but then of course – There, I heard him cough. Did you hear that cough, listeners – a sort of very throaty double cough? It seemed to come from – I wonder if he's crept down and is having a little fun with me, because I tell you, listeners, this place is beginning to get on my nerves just a wee little bit, just a bit. I wouldn't live in it for a pension, a very large pension – Get away, you brute! That bat – faugh! It stinks.

Now listen carefully – can you hear those rats? Having a game of Rugger, from the sound of them. I really shall be quite glad to get out of here. I can quite imagine people doing themselves in in this house. Saying to themselves, after all, it isn't much of a life when you think of it – figure it out, is it? Just work and worry and getting old and seeing your friends die. Let's end it all in the river!

I'm not being very cheerful, am I? It's this darned house. Those other two places we investigated didn't worry me a bit, but this – I wonder what the professor's doing, besides coughing. I can't quite make that cough out because – get away, you brute! That bat'll be the death of me! Death of me! Death of me!

I'm glad I've got you to talk to, listeners, but I wish you could answer back. I'm beginning to dislike the sound of my own voice. After a time, if you've been talking in a room alone, you get fanciful. Have you ever noticed that? You sort of think you can hear someone talking back –

There! – No, of course you couldn't have heard it, because it wasn't there, of course. Just in my head. Just subjective, that's the word. That's the word. Very odd. That *was* me laughing, of course. I'm saying "of course" a lot. Of course I am. Well, listeners, I'm afraid this is awfully dull for you. Not for me, though, not for me! No ghosts so far, unless the professor is having better luck –

There! You must have heard that! What a crack that panelling makes! Well, you must have heard that, listeners – better than nothing! Ha, ha! Professor! Professor! Phew, what an echo!

Now, listeners, I'm going to stop talking for a moment. I don't suppose you'll mind. Let's see if we can hear anything –

Did you hear it? I'm not exactly sure what it was. Not sure. I wonder if you heard it? Not exactly, but the house shook a little and the windows rattled. I don't think we'll do that again. I'll go on talking. I wonder how long one could endure the atmosphere of this place. It certainly is inclined to get one down.

Gosh, that stain has grown – the one on the ceiling. It's actually started to drip. I mean form bubbles – they'll start dropping soon. Colored bubbles, apparently. I wonder if the professor is okay? I mean he might have shut himself up in a powder closet or something, and the powder closets in this house aren't particularly – well, you never know, do you?

Now I should have said that shadow had moved. No, I suppose I put the lamp down in a slightly different position. Shadows do make odd patterns, you must have noticed that. This one might be a body lying on its face with its arms stretched out. Cheerful, aren't I? An aunt of mine gassed herself, as a matter of fact – well, I don't know why I told you that. Not quite in the script.

Professor! Professor! Where is that old fuzzy-whiskers? I shall certainly advise the owner to have this place pulled down. Emphatically. Then where'll *you* go! I must go upstairs in a minute or two and see what's happened to the professor. Well, I was telling you about auntie –

D'you know, listeners, I really believe I'd go completely crackers if I stayed here much longer – more or less, anyway, and quite soon, quite soon, quite soon. Absolutely stark, staring! It wears you down. That's exactly it, it wears you down. I can quite understand – well, I won't say all that again. I'm afraid this is all awfully dull for you, listeners. I should switch it off if I were you –

I *should!* What's on the other program? I mean it – switch off! There, what did I tell you – that stain's started to drip drops, drip drops, drip drops, drip drops! I'll go and catch one on my hand –

*Good God!*

Professor! Professor! Professor! Now up those stairs! Which room would it be? Left or right? Left, right, left, right – left has it. In we go –

Well, gentlemen, good evening! What have you done with the professor? I know he's dead – see his blood on my hand? What have you done with him? Make way, please, gentlemen. What have you done with him? D'you want me to sing it – tra-la-la –

Switch off, you fools!

Well, if this isn't too darned funny – ha, ha, ha, ha! Hear me laughing, listeners –

Switch off, you fools!

That can't be him lying there – he hadn't a *red* beard! Don't crowd round me, gentlemen. Don't crowd me, I tell you!

What do you want me to do? You want me to go to the river, don't you? Ha, ha! Now? Will you come with me? Come on, then! To the river! To the river!

# Dark Winner

## William F. Nolan

### Prospectus

**Address:** 3337 Forest Avenue, Kansas City, USA.

**Property:** Twentieth-century, wood-frame house. Situated in a sprawling neighbourhood of predominantly small family homes, the property has three bedrooms, a living room, kitchen and basement. The building is in need of extensive renovation.

**Viewing Date:** July, 1984.

**Agent:** William Francis Nolan (1928–) was born and grew up in Kansas City. He worked as a commercial artist for some years before the success of his novel *Logan's Run* (1967) – written in conjunction with George Clayton Johnson and filmed in 1976 – enabled him to become a full-time author and scriptwriter. He has written a number of stories with Haunted House themes, including "Gibbler's Ghost", "The Party" and "Dark Winner", which Peter Straub found "terribly disturbing". Nolan says the story is based on his first return in twenty years to his childhood home in Kansas City. "I did all the things Frank does when he visits 3337, Forest," he says, "*except* go inside."

**NOTE:** The following is an edited transcript of a taped conversation between Mrs. Franklin Evans, resident of Woodland

Hills, California, and Lt. Harry W. Lyle of the Kansas City Police Department. Transcript is dated 12 July 1984. K.C. Missouri.

LYLE: . . . and if you want us to help you we'll have to know everything. When did you arrive here. Mrs. Evans?

MRS. EVANS: We just got in this morning. A stopover on our trip from New York back to California. We were at the airport when Frank suddenly got this idea about his past.

LYLE: What idea?

MRS. E: About visiting his old neighborhood . . . the school he went to . . . the house where he grew up . . . He hadn't been back here in twenty-five years.

LYLE: So you and your husband planned this . . . nostalgic tour?

MRS. E: Not *planned*. It was very abrupt . . . Frank seemed . . . suddenly . . . *possessed* by the idea.

LYLE: So what happened?

MRS. E: We took a cab out to Flora Avenue . . . to 31st . . . and we visited his old grade school. St. Vincent's Academy. The neighborhood is . . . well, I guess you know it's a slum area now . . . and the school is closed down, locked. But Frank found an open window . . . climbed inside . . .

LYLE: While you waited?

MRS. E: Yes – in the cab. When Frank came out he was all . . . upset . . . Said that he . . . Well, this sounds . . .

LYLE: Go on, please.

MRS. E: He said he felt . . . very *close* to his childhood while he was in there. He was ashen-faced . . . his hands were trembling.

LYLE: What did you do then?

MRS. E: We had the cab take us up 31st to the Isis Theatre. The movie house at 31st and Troost where Frank used to attend those Saturday horror shows they had for kids. Each week a new one . . . "Frankenstein" . . . "Dracula" . . . you know the kind I mean.

LYLE: I know.

MRS. E: It's a porno place now . . . but Frank bought a ticket anyway . . . went inside alone. Said he wanted to go into the balcony, find his old seat . . . see if things had changed . . .

LYLE: And?

MRS. E: He came out looking very shaken . . . saying it had happened again.

LYLE: *What* had happened again?

MRS. E: The feeling about being close to his past . . . to his childhood . . . As if he could –

LYLE: Could what, Mrs. Evans?

MRS. E: . . . step over the line dividing past and present . . . step back into his childhood. That's the feeling he said he had.

LYLE: Where did you go from the Isis?

MRS. E: Frank paid off the cab . . . said he wanted to walk to his old block . . . the one he grew up on . . . 33rd and Forest. So we walked down Troost to 33rd . . . past strip joints and hamburger stands . . . I was nervous . . . we didn't . . . belong here . . . Anyway, we got to 33rd and walked down the hill from Troost to Forest . . . and on the way Frank told me how much he'd hated being small, being a child . . . that he could hardly wait to grow up . . . that to him childhood was a nightmare . . .

LYLE: Then why all the nostalgia?

MRS. E: It wasn't that . . . it was . . . like an *exorcism* . . . Frank said he'd been haunted by his childhood all the years we'd lived in California . . . This was an attempt to get rid of it . . . by facing it . . . seeing that it was really gone . . . that it no longer had any reality . . .

LYLE: What happened on Forest?

MRS. E: We walked down the street to his old address . . . which was just past the middle of the block . . . 3337 it was . . . a small, sagging wooden house . . . in terrible condition . . . but then, *all* the houses were . . . their screens full of holes . . . windows broken, trash in the yards . . . Frank stood in front of his house staring at it for a long time . . . and then he began repeating something . . . over and over.

LYLE: And what was that?

MRS. E: He said it . . . like a litany . . . over and over . . . "I hate you! . . . I hate you!"

LYLE: You mean, he was saying that to *you*?

MRS. E: Oh, no. Not to *me* . . . I asked him what he meant . . . and . . . he said he hated the child he once was, the child who had lived in that house.

LYLE: I see. Go on, Mrs Evans.

MRS. E: Then he said he was going inside . . . that he *had* to go inside the house . . . but that he was afraid.

LYLE: Of what?

MRS. E: He didn't say of what. He just told me to wait out there on the walk. Then he went up on to the small wooden porch . . . knocked on the door. No one answered. Then Frank tried the knob . . . The door was unlocked . . .

LYLE: House was deserted?

MRS. E: That's right. I guess no one had lived there for a long while . . . All the windows were boarded up . . . and the driveway was filled with weeds . . . I started to move towards the porch, but Frank waved me back. Then he kicked the door all the way open with his foot, took a half-step inside, turned . . . and looked around at me . . . There was . . . a terrible fear in his eyes. I got a cold, chilled feeling all through my body – and I started towards him again . . . but he suddenly turned his back and went inside . . . the door closed.

LYLE: What then?

MRS. E: Then I waited. For fifteen . . . twenty minutes . . . a half hour . . . Frank didn't come out. So I went up to the porch and opened the door . . . called to him . . .

LYLE: Any answer?

MRS. E: No. The house was like . . . a hollow cave . . . there were echoes . . . but no answer . . . I went inside . . . walked all through the place . . . into every room . . . but he wasn't there . . . Frank was gone.

LYLE: Out the back, maybe.

MRS. E: No. The back door was nailed shut. Rusted. It hadn't been opened for years.

LYLE: A window then.

MRS. E: They were all boarded over. With thick dust on the sills.

LYLE: Did you check the basement?

MRS. E: Yes, I checked the basement door leading down. It was locked, and the dust hadn't been disturbed around it.
LYLE: Then . . . just where the hell did he *go*?
MRS. E: I don't *know*, Lieutenant! . . . That's why I called you . . . why I came here . . . You've got to find Frank!

**note:** Lt. Lyle did not find Franklin Evans. The case was turned over to Missing Persons – and, a week later, Mrs. Evans returned to her home in California. The first night back she had a dream, a nightmare. It disturbed her severely. She could not eat, could not sleep properly; her nerves were shattered. Mrs. Evans then sought psychiatric help. What follows is an excerpt from a taped session with Dr. Lawrence Redding, a licensed psychiatrist with offices in Beverly Hills, California.

Transcript is dated 3 August 1984. Beverly Hills.

REDDING: And where were you . . .? In the dream, I mean.
MRS. E: My bedroom. In bed, at home. It was as if I'd just been awakened . . . I looked around me – and everything was normal . . . the room exactly as it always is . . . Except for *him* . . . the boy standing next to me.
REDDING: Did you recognize this boy?
MRS. E: No.
REDDING: Describe him to me.
MRS. E: He was . . . nine or ten . . . a *horrible* child . . . with a cold hate in his face, in his eyes . . . He had on a black sweater with holes in each elbow. And knickers . . . the kind that boys used to wear . . . and he had on black tennis shoes . . .
REDDING: Did he speak to you?
MRS. E: Not at first. He just . . . smiled at me . . . and that smile was so . . . so *evil*! . . . And then he said . . . that he wanted me to know he'd won at last . . .
REDDING: Won what?
MRS. E: That's what I asked him . . . calmly, in the dream . . . I asked him what he'd won. And he said . . . oh, My God . . . he said . . .
REDDING: Go on, Mrs. Evans.

MRS. E: . . . that he'd won Frank! . . . that my husband would *never* be coming back . . . that he, the boy, had him now . . . forever! . . . I screamed – and woke up. And, instantly, I remembered something.

REDDING: What did you remember?

MRS. E: Before she died . . . Frank's mother . . . sent us an album she'd saved . . . of his childhood . . . photos . . . old report cards . . . He never wanted to look at it, stuck the album away in a closet . . . After the dream, I got it out, looked through it until I found . . .

REDDING: Yes . . .?

MRS. E: A photo I'd remembered. Of Frank . . . at the age of ten . . . standing in the front yard on Forest . . . He was smiling . . . that same, awful smile . . . and . . . he wore a dark sweater with holes in each elbow . . . knickers . . . and black tennis shoes. It was . . . the *same* boy exactly – the younger self Frank had always hated . . . I *know* what happened in that house now.

REDDING: Then tell me.

MRS. E: The boy was . . . waiting there . . . inside that awful, rotting dead house . . . waiting for Frank to come back . . . all those years . . . waiting there to claim him – because . . . *he* hated the man that Frank had become as much as Frank hated the child he'd once been . . . and the boy was *right*.

REDDING: Right about what, Mrs. Evans?

MRS. E: About winning . . . He took all those years, but . . . He won . . . and . . . Frank lost.

# 2

# AVENGING SPIRITS

## Tales of Dangerous Elementals

# The Old House in Vauxhall Walk

## Charlotte Riddell

### Prospectus

**Address:** Vauxhall Walk, Lambeth, London, England.

**Property:** Large Victorian residence, formerly the property of a wealthy London businessman and his family, now let as single-floor tenements. The building is in need of some renovation.

**Viewing Date:** December, 1882.

**Agent:** Charlotte Riddell (1832–1906) was born in Antrim, Ireland and has been described as the foremost female Victorian writer of supernatural fiction. She became a writer out of necessity when first her father, and then her husband, went bankrupt. Haunted houses were a popular theme in Riddell's work: three novels explore the theme, *The Haunted House at Latchford* (1873), *The Uninhabited House* (1875) and *The Haunted River* (1877) and there are several in the collection, *Weird Stories* (1884), including this story of the ghost of a miserly old woman who haunts a run-down tenement. The writer's own hard life gives an added poignancy to the events it describes . . .

### I

"Houseless – homeless – hopeless!"

Many a one who had before him trodden that same street must

have uttered the same words – the weary, the desolate, the hungry, the forsaken, the waifs and strays of struggling humanity that are always coming and going, cold, starving and miserable, over the pavements of Lambeth Parish; but it is open to question whether they were ever previously spoken with a more thorough conviction of their truth, or with a feeling of keener self-pity, than by the young man who hurried along Vauxhall Walk one rainy winter's night, with no overcoat on his shoulders and no hat on his head.

A strange sentence for one-and-twenty to give expression to – and it was stranger still to come from the lips of a person who looked like and who was a gentleman. He did not appear either to have sunk very far down in the good graces of Fortune. There was no sign or token which would have induced a passer-by to imagine he had been worsted after a long fight with calamity. His boots were not worn down at the heels or broken at the toes, as many, many boots were which dragged and shuffled and scraped along the pavement. His clothes were good and fashionably cut, and innocent of the rents and patches and tatters that slunk wretchedly by, crouched in doorways, and held out a hand mutely appealing for charity. His face was not pinched with famine or lined with wicked wrinkles, or brutalised by drink and debauchery, and yet he said and thought he was hopeless, and almost in his young despair spoke the words aloud.

It was a bad night to be about with such a feeling in one's heart. The rain was cold, pitiless and increasing. A damp, keen wind blew down the cross streets leading from the river. The fumes of the gas works seemed to fall with the rain. The roadway was muddy; the pavement greasy; the lamps burned dimly; and that dreary district of London looked its very gloomiest and worst.

Certainly not an evening to be abroad without a home to go to, or a sixpence in one's pocket, yet this was the position of the young gentleman who, without a hat, strode along Vauxhall Walk, the rain beating on his unprotected head.

Upon the houses, so large and good – once inhabited by well-to-do citizens, now let out for the most part in floors to weekly tenants – he looked enviously. He would have given much to have had a room, or even part of one. He had been walking for a long time, ever since dark in fact, and dark falls soon in December. He was tired and cold and hungry, and he saw no prospect save of pacing the streets all night.

As he passed one of the lamps, the light falling on his face revealed handsome young features, a mobile, sensitive mouth, and that particular formation of the eyebrows – not a frown exactly, but a certain draw of the brows – often considered to bespeak genius, but which more surely accompanies an impulsive organisation easily pleased, easily depressed, capable of suffering very keenly or of enjoying fully. In his short life he had not enjoyed much, and he had suffered a good deal. That night when he walked bareheaded through the rain, affairs had come to a crisis. So far as he in his despair felt able to see or reason, the best thing he could do was to die. The world did not want him; he would be better out of it.

The door of one of the houses stood open, and he could see in the dimly lighted hall some few articles of furniture waiting to be removed. A van stood beside the curb, and two men were lifting a table into it as he, for a second, paused.

"Ah," he thought, "even those poor people have some place to go to, some shelter provided, while I have not a roof to cover my head, or a shilling to get a night's lodging." And he went on fast, as if memory were spurring him, so fast that a man running after had some trouble to overtake him.

"Master Graham! Master Graham!" this man exclaimed, breathlessly; and, thus addressed, the young fellow stopped as if he had been shot.

"Who are you that know me?" he asked, facing round.

"I'm William; don't you remember William, Master Graham? And, Lord's sake, sir, what are you doing out a night like this without your hat?"

"I forgot it," was the answer, "and I did not care to go back and fetch it."

"Then why don't you buy another, sir? You'll catch your death of cold; and besides, you'll excuse me, sir, but it does look odd."

"I know that," said Master Graham grimly, "but I haven't a halfpenny in the world."

"Have you and the Master, then –" began the man, but there he hesitated and stopped.

"Had a quarrel? Yes, and one that will last us our lives," finished the other, with a bitter laugh.

"And where are you going now?"

"Going! Nowhere, except to seek out the softest paving stone, or the shelter of an arch."

"You are joking, sir."

"I don't feel much in a mood for jesting either."

"Will you come back with me, Master Graham? We are just at the last of our moving, but there is a spark of fire still in the grate, and it would be better talking out of this rain. Will you come, sir?"

"Come! Of course I will come," said the young fellow, and, turning, they retraced their steps to the house he had looked into as he passed along.

An old, old house, with long, wide hall, stairs low, easy of ascent, with deep cornices to the ceilings, and oak floorings, and mahogany doors, which still spoke mutely of the wealth and stability of the original owner, who lived before the Tradescants and Ashmoles were thought of, and had been sleeping for longer than they, in St. Mary's churchyard, hard by the archbishop's palace.

"Step upstairs, sir," entreated the departing tenant; "it's cold down here, with the door standing wide."

"Had you the whole house, then, William?" asked Graham Coulton, in some surprise.

"The whole of it, and right sorry I, for one, am to leave it; but nothing else would serve my wife. This room, sir," and with a little conscious pride, William, doing the honours of his late residence, asked his guest into a spacious apartment occupying the full width of the house on the first floor.

Tired though he was, the young man could not repress an exclamation of astonishment.

"Why, we have nothing so large as this at home, William," he said.

"It's a fine house," answered William, raking the embers

together as he spoke and throwing some wood upon them; "but, like many a good family, it has come down in the world."

There were four windows in the room, shuttered close; they had deep, low seats, suggestive of pleasant days gone by; when, well-curtained and well-cushioned, they formed snug retreats for the children, and sometimes for adults also; there was no furniture left, unless an oaken settle beside the hearth, and a large mirror let into the panelling at the opposite end of the apartment, with a black marble console table beneath it, could be so considered; but the very absence of chairs and tables enabled the magnificent proportions of the chamber to be seen to full advantage, and there was nothing to distract the attention from the ornamented ceiling, the panelled walls, the old-world chimney-piece so quaintly carved, and the fire-place lined with tiles, each one of which contained a picture of some scriptural or allegorical subject.

"Had you been staying on here, William," said Coulton, flinging himself wearily on the settee, "I'd have asked you to let me stop where I am for the night."

"If you can make shift, sir, there is nothing as I am aware of to prevent you stopping," answered the man, fanning the wood into a flame. "I shan't take the key back to the landlord till to-morrow, and this would be better for you than the cold streets at any rate."

"Do you really mean what you say?" asked the other eagerly. "I should be thankful to lie here; I feel dead beat."

"Then stay, Master Graham, and welcome. I'll fetch a basket of coals I was going to put in the van, and make up a good fire, so that you can warm yourself; then I must run round to the other house for a minute or two, but it's not far, and I'll be back as soon as ever I can."

"Thank you, William; you were always good to me," said the young man gratefully. "This is delightful," and he stretched his numbed hands over the blazing wood, and looked round the room with a satisfied smile.

"I did not expect to get into such quarters," he remarked, as his friend in need reappeared, carrying a half-bushel basket full of coals, with which he proceeded to make up a roaring fire. "I am sure the last thing I could have imagined was meeting with anyone I knew in Vauxhall Walk."

"Where were you coming from, Master Graham?" asked William curiously.

"From old Melfield's. I was at his school once, you know, and he has now retired, and is living upon the proceeds of years of robbery in Kennington Oval. I thought, perhaps he would lend me a pound, or offer me a night's lodging, or even a glass of wine; but, oh dear, no. He took the moral tone, and observed he could have nothing to say to a son who defied his father's authority. He gave me plenty of advice, but nothing else, and showed me out into the rain with a bland courtesy, for which I could have struck him."

William muttered something under his breath which was not a blessing, and added aloud:

"You are better here, sir, I think, at any rate. I'll be back in less than half an hour."

Left to himself, young Coulton took off his coat, and shifting the settle a little, hung it over the end to dry. With his handkerchief he rubbed some of the wet out of his hair; then, perfectly exhausted, he lay down before the fire and, pillowing his head on his arm, fell fast asleep.

He was awakened nearly an hour afterwards by the sound of someone gently stirring the fire and moving quietly about the room. Starting into a sitting posture, he looked around him, bewildered for a moment, and then, recognising his humble friend, said laughingly:

"I had lost myself; I could not imagine where I was."

"I am sorry to see you here, sir," was the reply; "but still this is better than being out of doors. It has come on a nasty night. I brought a rug round with me that, perhaps, you would wrap yourself in."

"I wish, at the same time, you had brought me something to eat," said the young man, laughing.

"Are you hungry, then, sir?" asked William, in a tone of concern.

"Yes; I have had nothing to eat since breakfast. The governor and I commenced rowing the minute we sat down to luncheon, and I rose and left the table. But hunger does not signify; I am dry and warm, and can forget the other matter in sleep."

"And it's too late now to buy anything," soliloquised the man; "the shops are all shut long ago. Do you think, sir," he added, brightening, "you could manage some bread and cheese?"

"Do I think – I should call it a perfect feast," answered Graham Coulton. "But never mind about food to-night, William; you have had trouble enough, and to spare, already."

William's only answer was to dart to the door and run downstairs. Presently he reappeared, carrying in one hand bread and cheese wrapped up in paper, and in the other a pewter measure full of beer.

"It's the best I could do, sir," he said apologetically. "I had to beg this from the landlady."

"Here's to her good health!" exclaimed the young fellow gaily, taking a long pull at the tankard. "That tastes better than champagne in my father's house."

"Won't he be uneasy about you?" ventured William, who, having by this time emptied the coals, was now seated on the inverted basket, looking wistfully at the relish with which the son of the former master was eating his bread and cheese.

"No," was the decided answer. "When he hears it pouring cats and dogs he will only hope I am out in the deluge, and say a good drenching will cool my pride."

"I do not think you are right there," remarked the man.

"But I am sure I am. My father always hated me, as he hated my mother."

"Begging your pardon, sir; he was over fond of your mother."

"If you had heard what he said about her to-day, you might find reason to alter your opinion. He told me I resembled her in mind as well as body; that I was a coward, a simpleton, and a hypocrite."

"He did not mean it, sir."

"He did, every word. He does think I am a coward, because I– I –" and the young fellow broke into a passion of hysterical tears.

"I don't half like leaving you here alone," said William,

glancing round the room with a quick trouble in his eyes; "but I have no place fit to ask you to stop, and I am forced to go myself, because I am night watchman, and must be on at twelve o'clock."

"I shall be right enough," was the answer. "Only I mustn't talk any more of my father. Tell me about yourself, William. How did you manage to get such a big house, and why are you leaving it?"

"The landlord put me in charge, sir; and it was my wife's fancy not to like it."

"Why did she not like it?"

"She felt desolate alone with the children at night," answered William, turning away his head; then added, next minute; "Now, sir, if you think I can do no more for you, I had best be off. Time's getting on. I'll look round to-morrow morning."

"Good night," said the young fellow, stretching out his hand, which the other took as freely and frankly as it was offered. "What should I have done this evening if I had not chanced to meet you?"

"I don't think there is much chance in the world, Master Graham," was the quiet answer. "I do hope you will rest well, and not be the worse for your wetting."

"No fear of that," was the rejoinder, and the next minute the young man found himself all alone in the Old House in Vauxhall Walk.

## II

Lying on the settle, with the fire burnt out, and the room in total darkness, Graham Coulton dreamed a curious dream. He thought he awoke from deep slumber to find a log smouldering away upon the hearth, and the mirror at the end of the apartment reflecting fitful gleams of light. He could not understand how it came to pass that, far away as he was from the glass, he was able to see everything in it; but he resigned himself to the difficulty without astonishment, as people generally do in dreams.

Neither did he feel surprised when he beheld the outline of a female figure seated beside the fire, engaged in picking something out of her lap and dropping it with a despairing gesture.

He heard the mellow sound of gold, and knew she was lifting and dropping sovereigns. He turned a little so as to see the person engaged in such a singular and meaningless manner, and found that, where there had been no chair on the previous night, there was a chair now, on which was seated an old, wrinkled hag, her clothes poor and ragged, a mob cap barely covering her scant white hair, her cheeks sunken, her nose hooked, her fingers more like talons than aught else as they dived down into the heap of gold, portions of which they lifted but to scatter mournfully.

"Oh! my lost life," she moaned, in a voice of the bitterest anguish. "Oh! my lost life – for one day, for one hour of it again!"

Out of the darkness – out of the corner of the room where the shadows lay deepest – out from the gloom abiding near the door – out from the dreary night, with their sodden feet and the wet dripping from their heads, came the old men and the young children, the worn women and the weary hearts, whose misery that gold might have relieved, but whose wretchedness it mocked.

Round that miser, who once sat gloating as she now sat lamenting, they crowded – all those pale, sad shapes – the aged of days, the infant of hours, the sobbing outcast, honest poverty, repentant vice; but one low cry proceeded from those pale lips – a cry for help she might have given, but which she withheld.

They closed about her, all together, as they had done singly in life; they prayed, they sobbed, they entreated; with haggard eyes the figure regarded the poor she had repulsed, the children against whose cry she had closed her ears, the old people she had suffered to starve and die for want of what would have been the merest trifle to her; then, with a terrible scream, she raised her lean arms above her head, and sank down – down – the gold scattering as it fell out of her lap, and rolling along the floor, till its gleam was lost in the outer darkness beyond.

Then Graham Coulton awoke in good earnest, with the perspiration oozing from every pore, with a fear and an agony upon him such as he had never before felt in all his existence, and with the sound of the heart-rending cry – "Oh! my lost life" – still ringing in his ears.

Mingled with all, too, there seemed to have been some lesson for him which he had forgotten, that, try as he would, eluded his memory, and which, in the very act of waking, glided away.

He lay for a little thinking about all this, and then, still heavy with sleep, retraced his way into dreamland once more.

It was natural, perhaps, that, mingling with the strange fantasies which follow in the train of night and darkness, the former vision should recur, and the young man ere long found himself toiling through scene after scene wherein the figure of the woman he had seen seated beside a dying fire held principal place.

He saw her walking slowly across the floor munching a dry crust – she who could have purchased all the luxuries wealth can command; on the hearth, contemplating her, stood a man of commanding presence, dressed in the fashion of long ago. In his eyes there was a dark look of anger, on his lips a curling smile of disgust, and somehow, even in his sleep, the dreamer understood it was the ancestor to the descendant he beheld – that the house put to mean uses in which he lay had never so far descended from its high estate, as the woman possessed of so pitiful a soul, contaminated with the most despicable and insidious vice poor humanity knows, for all other vices seem to have connection with the flesh, but the greed of the miser eats into the very soul.

Filthy of person, repulsive to look at, hard of heart as she was, he yet beheld another phantom, which, coming into the room, met her almost on the threshold, taking her by the hand, and pleading, as it seemed, for assistance. He could not hear all that passed, but a word now and then fell upon his car. Some talk of former days; some mention of a fair young mother – an appeal, as it seemed, to a time when they were tiny brother and sister, and the accursed greed for gold had not divided them. All in vain; the hag only answered him as she had answered the children, and the young girls, and the old people in his former vision. Her heart was as invulnerable to natural affection as it had proved to human sympathy. He begged, as it appeared, for aid to avert some bitter misfortune or terrible disgrace, and adamant might have been found more yielding to his prayer. Then the figure standing on the hearth changed to an angel, which folded its wings mournfully over its face, and the man, with bowed head, slowly left the room.

Even as he did so the scene changed again; it was night once more, and the miser wended her way upstairs. From below, Graham Coulton fancied he watched her toiling wearily from step to step. She had aged strangely since the previous scenes. She moved with difficulty; it seemed the greatest exertion for her to creep from step to step, her skinny hand traversing the balusters with slow and painful deliberateness. Fascinated, the young man's eyes followed the progress of that feeble, decrepit woman. She was solitary in a desolate house, with a deeper blackness than the darkness of night waiting to engulf her.

It seemed to Graham Coulton that after that he lay for a time in a still, dreamless sleep, upon awakening from which he found himself entering a chamber as sordid and unclean in its appointments as the woman of his previous vision had been in her person. The poorest labourer's wife would have gathered more comforts around her than that room contained. A four-poster bedstead without hangings of any kind – a blind drawn up awry – an old carpet covered with dust, and dirt on the floor – a rickety washstand with all the paint worn off it – an ancient mahogany dressing table, and a cracked glass spotted all over – were all the objects he could at first discern, looking at the room through that dim light which oftentimes obtains in dreams.

By degrees, however, he perceived the outline of someone lying huddled on the bed. Drawing nearer, he found it was that of the person whose dreadful presence seemed to pervade the house. What a terrible sight she looked, with her thin white locks scattered over the pillow, with what were mere remnants of blankets gathered about her shoulders, with her claw-like fingers clutching the clothes, as though even in sleep she was guarding her gold!

An awful and a repulsive spectacle, but not with half the terror in it of that which followed. Even as the young man looked he heard stealthy footsteps on the stairs. Then he saw first one man and then his fellow steal cautiously into the room. Another second, and the pair stood beside the bed, murder in their eyes.

Graham Coulton tried to shout – tried to move, but the

deterrent power which exists in dreams only tied his tongue and paralysed his limbs. He could but hear and look, and what he heard and saw was this: aroused suddenly from sleep, the woman started, only to receive a blow from one of the ruffians, whose fellow followed his lead by plunging a knife into her breast.

Then, with a gurgling scream, she fell back on the bed, and at the same moment, with a cry, Graham Coulton again awoke, to thank heaven it was but an illusion.

## III

"I hope you slept well, sir." It was William, who, coming into the hall with the sunlight of a fine bright morning streaming after him, asked this question: "Had you a good night's rest?"

Graham Coulton laughed, and answered:

"Why, faith, I was somewhat in the case of Paddy, 'who could not slape for dhraming'. I slept well enough, I suppose, but whether it was in consequence of the row with my dad, or the hard bed, or the cheese – most likely the bread and cheese so late at night – I dreamt all the night long, the most extraordinary dreams. Some old woman kept cropping up, and I saw her murdered."

"You don't say that, sir?" said William nervously.

"I do, indeed," was the reply. "However, that is all gone and past. I have been down in the kitchen and had a good wash, and I am as fresh as a daisy, and as hungry as a hunter; and, oh, William, can you get me any breakfast?"

"Certainly, Master Graham, I have brought round a kettle, and I will make the water boil immediately. I suppose, sir" – this tentatively – "you'll be going home to-day?"

"Home!" repeated the young man. "Decidedly not. I'll never go home again till I return with some medal hung to my coat, or a leg or arm cut off. I've thought it all out, William. I'll go and enlist. There's a talk of war; and, living or dead, my father shall have reason to retract his opinion about my being a coward."

"I am sure the admiral never thought you anything of the sort, sir," said William. "Why, you have the pluck of ten!"

"Not before him," answered the young fellow sadly.

"You'll do nothing rash, Master Graham; you won't go 'listing, or aught of that sort, in your anger?"

"If I do not, what is to become of me?" asked the other. "I cannot dig – to beg I am ashamed. Why, but for you, I should not have had a roof over my head last night."

"Not much of a roof, I am afraid, sir."

"Not much of a roof!" repeated the young man. "Why, who could desire a better? What a capital room this is," he went on, looking around the apartment, where William was now kindling a fire; "one might dine twenty people here easily!"

"If you think so well of the place, Master Graham, you might stay here for a while, till you have made up your mind what you are going to do. The landlord won't make any objection, I am very sure."

"Oh! nonsense; he would want a long rent for a house like this."

"I daresay; *if he could get it*," was William's significant answer.

"What do you mean? Won't the place let?"

"No, sir. I did not tell you last night, but there was a murder done here, and people are shy of the house ever since."

"A murder! What sort of a murder? Who was murdered?"

"A woman, Master Graham – the landlord's sister; she lived here all alone, and was supposed to have money. Whether she had or not, she was found dead from a stab in her breast, and if there ever was any money, it must have been taken at the same time, for none ever was found in the house from that day to this."

"Was that the reason your wife would not stop here?" asked the young man, leaning against the mantelshelf, and looking thoughtfully down on William.

"Yes, sir. She could not stand it any longer; she got that thin and nervous no one would have believed it possible; she never saw anything, but she said she heard footsteps and voices, and then when she walked through the hall, or up the staircase, someone always seemed to be following her. We put the children to sleep in that big room you had last night, and they declared they often saw an old woman sitting by the hearth. Nothing ever came my way," finished William, with a laugh; "I was always ready to go to sleep the minute my head touched the pillow."

"Were not the murderers discovered?" asked Graham Coulton.

"No, sir; the landlord, Miss Tynan's brother, had always lain under the suspicion of it – quite wrongfully, I am very sure – but he will never clear himself now. It was known he came and asked her for help a day or two before the murder, and it was also known he was able within a week or two to weather whatever trouble had been harassing him. Then, you see, the money was never found; and, altogether, people scarce knew what to think."

"Humph!" ejaculated Graham Coulton, and he took a few turns up and down the apartment. "Could I go and see this landlord?"

"Surely, sir, if you had a hat," answered William, with such a serious decorum that the young man burst out laughing.

"That is an obstacle, certainly," he remarked, "and I must make a note do instead. I have a pencil in my pocket, so here goes."

Within half an hour from the dispatch of that note William was back again with a sovereign; the landlord's compliments, and he would be much obliged if Mr. Coulton could "step round."

"You'll do nothing rash, sir," entreated William.

"Why, man," answered the young fellow, "one may as well be picked off by a ghost as a bullet. What is there to be afraid of?"

William only shook his head. He did not think his young master was made of the stuff likely to remain alone in a haunted house and solve the mystery it assuredly contained by dint of his own unassisted endeavours. And yet when Graham Coulton came out of the landlord's house he looked more bright and gay than usual, and walked up the Lambeth road to the place where Wiliam awaited his return, humming an air as he paced along.

"We have settled the matter," he said. "And now if the dad wants his son for Christmas, it will trouble him to find him."

"Don't say that, Master Graham, don't," entreated the man, with a shiver; "maybe after all it would have been better if you had never happened to chance upon Vauxhall Walk."

"Don't croak, William," answered the young man; "if it was not the best day's work I ever did for myself I'm a Dutchman."

During the whole of that afternoon, Graham Coulton searched diligently for the missing treasure Mr. Tynan assured him had never been discovered. Youth is confident, and self-opinionated, and this fresh explorer felt satisfied that, though others had failed, he would be successful. On the second floor he found one door locked, but he did not pay much attention to that at the moment, as he believed if there was anything concealed it was more likely to be found in the lower than the upper part of the house. Late into the evening he pursued his researches in the kitchen and cellars and old-fashioned cupboards, of which the basement had an abundance.

It was nearly eleven, when, engaged in poking about amongst the empty bins of a wine cellar as large as a family vault, he suddenly felt a rush of cold air at his back. Moving, his candle was instantly extinguished, and in the very moment of being left in darkness he saw, standing in the doorway, a woman, resembling her who had haunted his dreams overnight.

He rushed with outstretched hands to seize her, but clutched only air. He relit his candle, and closely examined the basement, shutting off communication with the ground floor ere doing so. All in vain. Not a trace could he find of living creature – not a window was open – not a door unbolted.

"It is very odd," he thought, as, after securely fastening the door at the top of the staircase, he searched the whole upper portion of the house, with the exception of the one room mentioned.

"I must get the key of that to-morrow," he decided, standing gloomily with his back to the fire and his eyes wandering about the drawing-room, where he had once again taken up his abode.

Even as the thought passed through his mind, he saw standing in the open doorway a woman with white dishevelled hair, clad in mean garments, ragged and dirty. She lifted her hand and shook it at him with a menacing gesture, and then, just as he was darting towards her, a wonderful thing occurred.

From behind the great mirror there glided a second female

figure, at the sight of which the first turned and fled, uttering piercing shrieks as the other followed her from storey to storey.

Sick almost with terror, Graham Coulton watched the dreadful pair as they fled upstairs past the locked room to the top of the house.

It was a few minutes before he recovered his self-possession. When he did so, and searched the upper apartments, he found them totally empty.

That night, ere lying down before the fire, he carefully locked and bolted the drawing-room door; before he did more he drew the heavy settle in front of it, so that if the lock were forced no entrance could be effected without considerable noise.

For some time he lay awake, then dropped into a deep sleep, from which he was awakened suddenly by a noise as if of something scuffling stealthily behind the wainscot. He raised himself on his elbow and listened, and, to his consternation, beheld seated at the opposite side of the hearth the same woman he had seen before in his dreams, lamenting over her gold.

The fire was not quite out, and at the moment shot up a last tongue of flame. By the light, transient as it was, he saw that the figure pressed a ghostly finger to its lips, and by the turn of his head and the attitude of its body seemed to be listening.

He listened also – indeed, he was too much frightened to do aught else; more and more distinct grew the sounds which had aroused him, a stealthy rustling coming nearer and nearer – up and up it seemed, behind the wainscot.

"It is rats," thought the young man, though, indeed, his teeth were almost chattering in his head with fear. But then in a moment he saw what disabused him of that idea – *the gleam of a candle or lamp through a crack in the panelling*. He tried to rise, he strove to shout – all in vain; and, sinking down, remembered nothing more till he awoke to find the grey light of an early morning stealing through one of the shutters he had left partially unclosed.

For hours after his breakfast, which he scarcely touched, long after William had left him at mid-day, Graham Coulton, having in the morning made a long and close survey of the house, sat thinking before the fire, then, apparently having made up his mind, he put on the hat he had bought, and went out.

When he returned the evening shadows were darkening down, but the pavements were full of people going marketing, for it was Christmas Eve, and all who had money to spend seemed bent on shopping.

It was terribly dreary inside the old house that night. Through the deserted rooms Graham could feel that ghostly semblance was wandering mournfully. When he turned his back he knew she was flitting from the mirror to the fire, from the fire to the mirror; but he was not afraid of her now – he was far more afraid of another matter he had taken in hand that day.

The horror of the silent house grew and grew upon him. He could hear the beating of his own heart in the dead quietude which reigned from garret to cellar.

At last William came; but the young man said nothing to him of what was in his mind. He talked to him cheerfully and hopefully enough – wondered where his father would think he had got to, and hoped Mr. Tynan might send him some Christmas pudding. Then the man said it was time for him to go, and, when Mr. Coulton went downstairs to the hall-door, remarked the key was not in it.

"No," was the answer, "I took it out to-day, to oil it."

"It wanted oiling," agreed William, "for it worked terribly stiff." Having uttered which truism he departed.

Very slowly the young man retraced his way to the drawing-room, where he only paused to lock the door on the outside; then taking off his boots he went up to the top of the house, where, entering the front attic, he waited patiently in darkness and in silence.

It was a long time, or at least it seemed long to him, before he heard the same sound which had aroused him on the previous night – a stealthy rustling – then a rush of cold air – then cautious footsteps – then the quiet opening of a door below.

It did not take as long in action as it has required to tell. In a moment the young man was out on the landing and had closed a portion of the panelling on the wall which stood open; noiselessly he crept back to the attic window, unlatched it, and sprung a rattle, the sound of which echoed far and near through the deserted streets, then rushing down the stairs, he encountered a man who, darting past him, made for the landing above; but perceiving that way of escape closed, fled down again, to find Graham struggling desperately with his fellow.

"Give him the knife – come along," he said savagely; and next instant Graham felt something like a hot iron through his shoulder, and then heard a thud, as one of the men, tripping in his rapid flight, fell from the top of the stairs to the bottom.

At the same moment there came a crash, as if the house was falling, and faint, sick, and bleeding, young Coulton lay insensible on the threshold of the room where Miss Tynan had been murdered.

When he recovered he was in the dining-room, and a doctor was examining his wound.

Near the door a policeman stiffly kept guard. The hall was full of people; all the misery and vagabondism the streets contain at that hour was crowding in to see what had happened.

Through the midst two men were being conveyed to the station-house; one, with his head dreadfully injured, on a stretcher, the other handcuffed, uttering frightful imprecations as he went.

After a time the house was cleared of the rabble, the police took possession of it, and Mr. Tynan was sent for.

"What was that dreadful noise?" asked Graham feebly, now seated on the floor, with his back resting against the wall.

'I do not know. Was there a noise?" said Mr. Tynan, humouring his fancy, as he thought.

"Yes, in the drawing-room, I think; the key is in my pocket."

Still humouring the wounded lad, Mr. Tynan took the key and ran upstairs.

When he unlocked the door, what a sight met his eyes! The mirror had fallen – it was lying all over the floor shivered into a thousand pieces; the console table had been borne down by its weight, and the marble slab was shattered as well. But this was not what chained his attention. Hundreds, thousands of gold pieces were scattered about, and an aperture behind the glass contained boxes filled with securities and deeds and bonds, the possession of which had cost his sister her life.

"Well, Graham, and what do you want?" asked Admiral Coulton that evening as his eldest born appeared before him, looking somewhat pale but otherwise unchanged.

"I want nothing," was the answer, 'but to ask your forgiveness. William has told me all the story I never knew before; and, if you let me, I will try to make it up to you for the trouble you have had. I am provided for," went on the young fellow, with a nervous laugh; 'I have made my fortune since I left you, and another man's fortune as well."

"I think you are out of your senses," said the Admiral shortly.

"No, sir, I have found them," was the answer; "and I mean to strive and make a better thing of my life than I should ever have done had I not gone to the Old House in Vauxhall Walk."

"Vauxhall Walk! What is the lad talking about?"

'I will tell you, sir, if I may sit down," was Graham Coulton's answer, and then he told this story.

# No. 252 Rue M. Le Prince

## Ralph Adams Cram

### Prospectus

**Address:** 252, Rue M. Le Prince, Latin Quarter, Paris, France.

**Property:** Seventeenth-century town house with an unusual facade and black stone archway. Situated close to the Luxembourg Gardens, the property is convenient for the centre of Paris. Requires some restoration.

**Viewing Date:** May, 1886.

**Agent:** Ralph Adams Cram (1863–1942) was born in Hampton Falls, New Hampshire and is best remembered as a distinguished architect, responsible for the revival of Gothic architecture in America in the 1890s and producing a variety of books on the subject, ranging from *Impressions of Japanese Architecture* (1906) to *The Ruined Abbeys of Great Britain* (1928). He was a much travelled man, fascinated by the supernatural, and in 1885 published a collection of ghost stories, *Black Spirits and White*, now rare but regarded as one of the best in the genre. Cram's description of the events which occur in a haunted house in Paris are not for the faint hearted.

When in May, 1886, I found myself at last in Paris, I naturally determined to throw myself on the charity of an old chum of mine, Eugene Marie d'Ardeche, who had forsaken Boston a year or more ago on receiving word of the death of an aunt who had left him such property as she possessed. I fancy this windfall surprised him not a little, for the relations between the aunt and nephew had never been cordial, judging from Eugene's remarks touching the lady, who was, it seems, a more or less wicked and witch-like old person, with a penchant for black magic, at least such was the common report.

Why she should leave all her property to d'Ardeche, no one could tell, unless it was that she felt his rather hobbledehoy tendencies towards Buddhism and occultism might some day lead him to her own unhallowed height of questionable illumination. To be sure d'Ardeche reviled her as a bad old woman, being himself in that state of enthusiastic exaltation which sometimes accompanies a boyish fancy for occultism; but in spite of his distant and repellent attitude, Mlle. Blaye de Tartas made him her sole heir, to the violent wrath of a questionable old party known to infamy as the Sar Torrevieja, the "King of the Sorcerers". This malevolent old portent, whose gray and crafty face was often seen in the Rue M. le Prince during the life of Mlle. de Tartas, had, it seems, fully expected to enjoy her small wealth after her death; and when it appeared that she had left him only the contents of the gloomy old house in the Quartier Latin, giving the house itself and all else of which she died possessed to her nephew in America, the Sar proceeded to remove everything from the place, and then to curse it elaborately and comprehensively, together with all those who should ever dwell therein.

Whereupon he disappeared.

This final episode was the last word I received from Eugene, but I knew the number of the house, 252 Rue M. le Prince. So, after a day or two given to a first cursory survey of Paris, I started across the Seine to find Eugene and compel him to do the honors of the city.

Every one who knows the Latin Quarter knows the Rue M. le Prince, running up the hill towards the Garden of the Luxembourg. It is full of queer houses and odd corners – or was in '86 – and certainly No. 252 was, when I found it, quite as queer as any. It was nothing but a doorway, a black arch of old stone between and under two new houses painted yellow. The effect of this bit of seventeenth century masonry, with its dirty old doors, and rusty broken lantern sticking gaunt and grim out over the narrow sidewalk, was, in its frame of fresh plaster, sinister in the extreme.

I wondered if I had made a mistake in the number; it was quite evident that no one lived behind those cobwebs. I went into the doorway of one of the new hôtels and interviewed the concierge.

No, M. d'Ardeche did not live there, though to be sure he owned the mansion; he himself resided in Meudon, in the country house of the late Mlle. de Tartas. Would Monsieur like the number and the street?

Monsieur would like them extremely, so I took the card that the concierge wrote for me, and forthwith started for the river, in order that I might take a steamboat for Meudon. By one of those coincidences which happen so often, being quite inexplicable, I had not gone twenty paces down the street before I ran directly into the arms of Eugene d'Ardeche. In three minutes we were sitting in the queer little garden of the Chien Bleu, drinking vermouth and absinthe, and talking it all over.

"You do not live in your aunt's house?" I said at last, interrogatively.

"No, but if this sort of thing keeps on I shall have to. I like Meudon much better, and the house is perfect, all furnished, and nothing in it newer than the last century. You must come out with me to-night and see it. I have got a jolly room fixed up for my Buddha. But there is something wrong with this house opposite. I can't keep a tenant in it, – not four days. I have had three, all within six months, but the stories have gone around and a man would as soon think of hiring the Cour des Comptes to live in as No. 252. It is notorious. The fact is, it is haunted the worst way."

I laughed and ordered more vermouth.

"That is all right. It is haunted all the same, or enough to keep it empty, and the funny part is that no one knows *how* it is haunted. Nothing is ever seen, nothing heard. As far as I can find out, people just have the horrors there, and have them so bad they have to go to the hospital afterwards. I have one ex-tenant in the Bicêtre now. So the house stands empty, and as it covers considerable ground and is taxed for a lot, I don't know what to do about it. I think I'll either give it to that child of sin, Torrevieja, or else go and live in it myself. I shouldn't mind the ghosts, I am sure."

"Did you ever stay there?"

"No, but I have always intended to, and in fact I came up here to-day to see a couple of rake-hell fellows I know, Fargeau and Duchesne, doctors in the Clinical Hospital beyond here, up by the Parc Mont Souris. They promised that they would spend the night with me some time in my aunt's house – which is called around here, you must know, 'la Bouche d'Enfer' – and I thought perhaps they would make it this week, if they can get off duty. Come up with me while I see them, and then we can go across the river to Véfour's and have some luncheon, you can get your things at the Chatham, and we will go out to Meudon, where of course you will spend the night with me."

The plan suited me perfectly, so we went up to the hospital, found Fargeau, who declared that he and Duchesne were ready for anything, the nearer the real "bouche d'enfer" the better; that the following Thursday they would both be off duty for the night, and that on that day they would join in an attempt to outwit the devil and clear up the mystery of No. 252.

"Does M. l'Américain go with us?" asked Fargeau.

"Why of course," I replied, "I intend to go, and you must not refuse me, d'Ardeche; I decline to be put off. Here is a chance for you to do the honors of your city in a manner which is faultless. Show me a real live ghost, and I will forgive Paris for having lost the Jardin Mabille."

So it was settled.

Later we went down to Meudon and ate dinner in the terrace room of the villa, which was all that d'Ardeche had said, and more, so utterly was its atmosphere that of the seventeenth century. At dinner Eugene told me more about his late aunt, and the queer goings on in the old house.

Mlle. Blaye lived, it seems, all alone, except for one female servant of her own age; a severe, taciturn creature, with massive Breton features and a Breton tongue, whenever she vouchsafed to use it. No one ever was seen to enter the door of No. 252 except Jeanne the servant and the Sar Torrevieja, the latter coming constantly from none knew whither, and always entering, *never leaving*. Indeed, the neighbors, who for eleven years had watched the old sorcerer sidle crab-wise up to the bell almost every day, declared vociferously that *never* had he been seen to leave the house. Once, when they decided to keep absolute guard, the watcher, none other than Maître Garceau of the Chien Bleu, after keeping his eyes fixed on the door from ten o'clock one morning when the Sar arrived until four in the afternoon, during which time the door was unopened (he knew this, for had he not gummed a ten-centime stamp over the joint and was not the stamp unbroken) nearly fell down when the sinister figure of Torrevieja slid wickedly by him with a dry "Pardon, Monsieur!" and disappeared again through the black doorway.

This was curious, for No. 252 was entirely surrounded by houses, its only windows opening on a courtyard into which no eye could look from the hôtels of the Rue M. le Prince and the Rue de l'Ecole, and the mystery was one of the choice possessions of the Latin Quarter.

Once a year the austerity of the place was broken, and the denizens of the whole quarter stood open-mouthed watching many carriages drive up to No. 252, many of them private, not a few with crests on the door panels, from all of them descending veiled female figures and men with coat collars turned up. Then followed curious sounds of music from within, and those whose houses joined the blank walls of No. 252 became for the moment popular, for by placing the ear against the wall strange music could distinctly be heard, and the sound of monotonous chanting voices now and then. By dawn the last guest would have departed, and for another year the hotel of Mlle. de Tartas was ominously silent.

Eugene declared that he believed it was a celebration of "Walpurgisnacht", and certainly appearances favored such a fancy.

"A queer thing about the whole affair is," he said, "the fact that everyone in the street swears that about a month ago, while I was out in Concarneau for a visit, the music and voices were heard again, just as when my revered aunt was in the flesh. The house was perfectly empty, as I tell you, so it is quite possible that the good people were enjoying an hallucination."

I must acknowledge that these stories did not reassure me; in fact, as Thursday came near, I began to regret a little my determination to spend the night in the house. I was too vain to back down, however, and the perfect coolness of the two doctors, who ran down Tuesday to Meudon to make a few arrangements, caused me to swear that I would die of fright before I would flinch. I suppose I believed more or less in ghosts, I am sure now that I am older I believe in them, there are in fact few things I can *not* believe. Two or three inexplicable things had happened to me, and, although this was before my adventure with Rendel in Pæstum, I had a strong predisposition to believe some things that I could not explain, wherein I was out of sympathy with the age.

Well, to come to the memorable night of the twelfth of June, we had made our preparations and after depositing a big bag inside the doors of No. 252, went across to the Chien Bleu, where Fargeau and Duchesne turned up promptly, and we sat down to the best dinner Père Garceau could create.

I remember I hardly felt that the conversation was in good taste. It began with various stories of Indian fakirs and Oriental jugglery, matters in which Eugene was curiously well read, swerved to the horrors of the great Sepoy mutiny, and thus to reminiscences of the dissecting-room. By this time we had drunk more or less, and Duchesne launched into a photographic and Zolaesque account of the only time (as he said) when he was possessed of the panic of fear; namely, one night many years ago, when he was locked by accident into the dissecting-room of the Loucine, together with several cadavers of a rather unpleasant nature. I ventured to protest mildly against the choice of subjects, the result being a perfect carnival of horrors, so that when we finally drank our last *créme de cacao* and started for "la Bouche d'Enfer", my nerves were in a somewhat rocky condition.

It was just ten o'clock when we came into the street. A hot dead wind drifted in great puffs through the city, and ragged masses of vapor swept the purple sky; an unsavory night altogether, one of those nights of hopeless lassitude when one feels, if one is at home, like doing nothing but drink mint juleps and smoke cigarettes.

Eugene opened the creaking door, and tried to light one of the lanterns; but the gusty wind blew out every match, and we finally had to close the outer doors before we could get a light. At last we had all the lanterns going, and I began to look around curiously. We were in a long, vaulted passage, partly carriageway, partly footpath, perfectly bare but for the street refuse which had drifted in with eddying winds. Beyond lay the courtyard, a curious place rendered more curious still by the fitful moonlight and the flashing of four dark lanterns. The place had evidently been once a most noble palace. Opposite rose the oldest portion, a three-story wall of the time of Francis I, with a great wisteria vine covering half. The wings on either side were more modern, seventeenth century, and ugly, while towards the street was nothing but a flat unbroken wall.

The great bare court, littered with bits of paper blown in by the wind, fragments of packing cases, and straw, mysterious with flashing lights and flaunting shadows, while low masses of torn vapor drifted overhead, hiding, then revealing the stars, and all in absolute silence, not even the sounds of the streets entering this prison-like place, was weird and uncanny in the extreme. I must confess that already I began to feel a slight disposition towards the horrors, but with that curious inconsequence which so often happens in the case of those who are deliberately growing scared, I could think of nothing more reassuring than those delicious verses of Lewis Carroll's:

> "Just the place for a Snark! I have said it twice,
> That alone should encourage the crew.
> Just the place for a Snark! I have said it thrice,
> What I tell you three times is true," –

which kept repeating themselves over and over in my brain with feverish insistence.

Even the medical students had stopped their chaffing, and were studying the surroundings gravely.

"There is one thing certain," said Fargeau, "*anything* might have happened here without the slightest chance of discovery. Did ever you see such a perfect place for lawlessness?"

"And *anything* might happen here now, with the same certainty of impunity," continued Duchesne, lighting his pipe, the snap of the match making us all start. "D'Ardeche, your lamented relative was certainly well fixed; she had full scope here for her traditional experiments in demonology."

"Curse me if I don't believe that those same traditions were more or less founded on fact," said Eugene. "I never saw this court under these conditions before, but I could believe anything now. What's that!"

"Nothing but a door slamming," said Duchesne, loudly.

"Well, I wish doors wouldn't slam in houses that have been empty eleven months."

"It is irritating," and Duchesne slipped his arm through mine; "but we must take things as they come. Remember we have to deal not only with the spectral lumber left here by your scarlet aunt, but as well with the supererogatory curse of that hell-cat Torrevieja. Come on! let's get inside before the hour arrives for the sheeted dead to squeak and gibber in these lonely halls. Light your pipes, your tobacco is a sure protection against 'your whoreson dead bodies'; light up and move on."

We opened the hall door and entered a vaulted stone vestibule, full of dust, and cobwebby.

"There is nothing on this floor," said Eugene, "except servants' rooms and offices, and I don't believe there is anything wrong with them. I never heard that there was, anyway. Let's go up stairs."

So far as we could see, the house was apparently perfectly uninteresting inside, all eighteenth century work, the façade of the main building being, with the vestibule, the only portion of the Francis I work.

"The place was burned during the Terror," said Eugene, "for my great-uncle, from whom Mlle. de Tartas inherited it, was a good and true Royalist; he went to Spain after the Revolution, and did not come back until the accession of Charles X, when he restored the house, and then died, enormously old. This explains why it is all so new."

The old Spanish sorcerer to whom Mlle. de Tartas had left her personal property had done his work thoroughly. The house was absolutely empty, even the wardrobes and bookcases built in had been carried away; we went through room after room, finding all absolutely dismantled, only the windows and doors with their casings, the parquet floors, and the florid Renaissance mantels remaining.

"I feel better," remarked Fargeau. "The house may be haunted, but it don't look it, certainly; it is the most respectable place imaginable."

"Just you wait," replied Eugene. "These are only the state apartments, which my aunt seldom used, except, perhaps, on her annual 'Walpurgisnacht'. Come upstairs and I will show you a better *mise en scène*."

On this floor, the rooms fronting the court, the sleeping-rooms, were quite small, – ("They are the bad rooms all the same," said Eugene) – four of them, all just as ordinary in appearance as those below. A corridor ran behind them connecting with the wing corridor, and from this opened a door, unlike any of the other doors in that it was covered with green baize, somewhat moth-eaten. Eugene selected a key from the bunch he carried, unlocked the door, and with some difficulty forced it to swing inward; it was as heavy as the door of a safe.

"We are now," he said, "on the very threshold of hell itself; these rooms in here were my scarlet aunt's unholy of unholies. I never let them with the rest of the house, but keep them as a curiosity. I only wish Torrevieja had kept out; as it was, he looted them, as he did the rest of the house, and nothing is left but the walls and ceiling and floor. They are something, however, and may suggest what the former condition must have been. Tremble and enter."

The first apartment was a kind of anteroom, a cube of perhaps twenty feet each way, without windows, and with no doors except that by which we entered and another to the right. Walls, floor, and ceiling were covered with a black lacquer, brilliantly polished, that flashed the light of our lanterns in a thousand intricate reflections. It was like the inside of an enormous Japanese box, and about as empty. From this we passed to another room, and here we nearly dropped our lanterns. The room was circular, thirty feet or so in diameter, covered by a hemispherical dome; walls and ceiling were dark blue, spotted with gold stars; and reaching from floor to floor across the dome stretched a colossal figure in red lacquer of a nude woman kneeling, her legs reaching out along the floor on either side, her head touching the lintel of the door through which we had entered, her arms forming its sides, with the fore-arms extended and stretching along the walls until they met the long feet. The most astounding, misshapen, absolutely terrifying thing, I think, I ever saw. From the navel hung a great white object, like the traditional roc's egg of the Arabian Nights. The floor was of red lacquer, and in it was inlaid a pentagram the size of the room, made of wide strips of brass. In the centre of this pentagram was a circular disk of black stone, slightly saucer-shaped, with a small outlet in the middle.

The effect of the room was simply crushing, with this gigantic red figure crouched over it all, the staring eyes fixed on one, no matter what his position. None of us spoke, so oppressive was the whole thing.

The third room was like the first in dimensions, but instead of being black it was entirely sheathed with plates of brass, walls, ceiling, and floor – tarnished now, and turning green, but still brilliant under the lantern light. In the middle stood an oblong altar of porphyry, its longer dimensions on the axis of the suite of rooms, and at one end, opposite the range of doors, a pedestal of black basalt.

This was all. Three rooms, stranger than these, even in their emptiness, it would be hard to imagine. In Egypt, in India, they would not be entirely out of place, but here in Paris, in a commonplace hôtel, in the Rue M. le Prince, they were incredible.

We retraced our steps, Eugene closed the iron door with its

baize covering, and we went into one of the front chambers and sat down, looking at each other.

"Nice party, your aunt," said Fargeau. "Nice old party, with amiable tastes; I am glad we are not to spend the night in *those* rooms."

"What do you suppose she did there?" inquired Duchesne. "I know more or less about black art, but that series of rooms is too much for me."

"My impression is," said d'Ardeche, "that the brazen room was a kind of sanctuary containing some image or other on the basalt base, while the stone in front was really an altar, – what the nature of the sacrifice might be I don't even guess. The round room may have been used for invocations and incantations. The pentagram looks like it. Any way it is all just about as queer and *fin de siécle* as I can well imagine. Look here, it is nearly twelve, let's dispose of ourselves, if we are going to hunt this thing down."

The four chambers on this floor of the old house were those said to be haunted, the wings being quite innocent, and, so far as we knew, the floors below. It was arranged that we should each occupy a room, leaving the doors open with the lights burning, and at the slightest cry or knock we were all to rush at once to the room from which the warning sound might come. There was no communication between the rooms to be sure, but, as the doors all opened into the corridor, every sound was plainly audible.

The last room fell to me, and I looked it over carefully.

It seemed innocent enough, a commonplace, square, rather lofty Parisian sleeping-room, finished in wood painted white, with a small marble mantel, a dusty floor of inlaid maple and cherry, walls hung with an ordinary French paper, apparently quite new, and two deeply embrasured windows looking out on the court.

I opened the swinging sash with some trouble, and sat down in the window seat with my lantern beside me trained on the only door, which gave on the corridor.

The wind had gone down, and it was very still without – still and hot. The masses of luminous vapor were gathering thickly overhead, no longer urged by the gusty wind. The great masses of rank wisteria leaves, with here and there a second blossoming of purple flowers, hung dead over the window in the sluggish air. Across the roofs I could hear the sound of a belated *fiacre* in the streets below. I filled my pipe again and waited.

For a time the voices of the men in the other rooms were a companionship, and at first I shouted to them now and then, but my voice echoed rather unpleasantly through the long corridors, and had a suggestive way of reverberating around the left wing beside me, and coming out at a broken window at its extremity like the voice of another man. I soon gave up my attempts at conversation, and devoted myself to the task of keeping awake.

It was not easy; why did I eat that lettuce salad at Père Garceau's? I should have known better. It was making me irresistibly sleepy, and wakefulness was absolutely necessary. It was certainly gratifying to know that I could sleep, that my courage was by me to that extent, but in the interests of science I must keep awake. But almost never, it seemed, had sleep looked so desirable. Half a hundred times, nearly, I would doze for an instant, only to awake with a start, and find my pipe gone out. Nor did the exertion of relighting it pull me together. I struck my match mechanically, and with the first puff dropped off again. It was most vexing. I got up and walked around the room. It was most annoying. My cramped position had almost put both my legs to sleep. I could hardly stand. I felt numb, as though with cold. There was no longer any sound from the other rooms, nor from without. I sank down in my window seat. How dark it was growing! I turned up the lantern. That pipe again, how obstinately it kept going out! and my last match was gone. The lantern, too, was *that* going out? I lifted my hand to turn it up again. It felt like lead, and fell beside me.

*Then* I awoke – absolutely. I remembered the story of "The Haunters and the Haunted". *This* was the Horror. I tried to rise, to cry out. My body was like lead, my tongue was paralyzed. I could hardly move my eyes. And the light was going out. There was no question about that. Darker and darker yet; little by little the pattern of the paper was swallowed up in the advancing night.

A prickling numbness gathered in every nerve, my right arm slipped without feeling from my lap to my side, and I could not raise it – it swung helpless. A thin, keen humming began in my head, like the cicadas on a hillside in September. The darkness was coming fast.

Yes, this was it. Something was subjecting me, body and mind, to slow paralysis. Physically I was already dead. If I could only hold my mind, my consciousness, I might still be safe, but could I? Could I resist the mad horror of this silence, the deepening dark, the creeping numbness? I knew that, like the man in the ghost story, my only safety lay here.

It had come at last. My body was dead, I could no longer move my eyes. They were fixed in that last look on the place where the door had been, now only a deepening of the dark.

Utter night: the last flicker of the lantern was gone. I sat and waited; my mind was still keen, but how long would it last? There was a limit even to the endurance of the utter panic of fear.

Then the end began. In the velvet blackness came two white eyes, milky, opalescent, small, far away – awful eyes, like a dead dream. More beautiful than I can describe, the flakes of white flame moving from the perimeter inward, disappearing in the centre, like a never ending flow of opal water into a circular tunnel. I could not have moved my eyes had I possessed the power: they devoured the fearful, beautiful things that grew slowly, slowly larger, fixed on me, advancing, growing more beautiful, the white flakes of light sweeping more swiftly into the blazing vortices, the awful fascination deepening in its insane intensity as the white, vibrating eyes grew nearer, larger.

Like a hideous and implacable engine of death the eyes of the unknown Horror swelled and expanded until they were close before me, enormous, terrible, and I felt a slow, cold, wet breath propelled with mechanical regularity against my face, enveloping me in its fetid mist, in its charnel-house deadliness.

With ordinary fear goes always a physical terror, but with me in the presence of this unspeakable Thing was only the utter and awful terror of the mind, the mad fear of a prolonged and ghostly nightmare. Again and again I tried to shriek, to make some nose, but physically I was utterly dead. I could only feel myself go mad with the terror of hideous death. The eyes were close on me – their movement so swift that they seemed to be but palpitating flames, the dead breath was around me like the depths of the deepest sea.

Suddenly a wet, icy mouth, like that of a dead cuttle-fish, shapeless, jelly-like, fell over mine. The horror began slowly to draw my life from me, but, as enormous and shuddering folds of palpitating jelly swept sinuously around me, my will came back, my body awoke with the reaction of final fear, and I closed with the nameless death that enfolded me.

What was it that I was fighting? My arms sunk through the unresisting mass that was turning me to ice. Moment by moment new folds of cold jelly swept round me, crushing me with the force of Titans. I fought to wrest my mouth from this awful Thing that sealed it, but, if ever I succeeded and caught a single breath, the wet, sucking mass closed over my face again before I could cry out. I think I fought for hours, desperately, insanely, in a silence that was more hideous than any sound – fought until I felt final death at hand, until the memory of all my life rushed over me like a flood, until I no longer had strength to wrench my face from that hellish succubus, until with a last mechanical struggle I fell and yielded to death.

Then I heard a voice say, "If he is dead, I can never forgive myself; I was to blame."

Another replied, "He is not dead, I know we can save him if only we reach the hospital in time. Drive like hell, *cocher!* twenty francs for you, if you get there in three minutes."

Then there was night again, and nothingness, until I suddenly awoke and stared around. I lay in a hospital ward, very white and sunny, some yellow *fleurs-de-lis* stood beside the head of the pallet, and a tall sister of mercy sat by my side.

To tell the story in a few words, I was in the Hôtel Dieu, where the men had taken me that fearful night of the twelfth of June. I asked for Fargeau or Duchesne, and by and by the latter came, and sitting beside the bed told me all that I did not know.

It seems that they had sat, each in his room, hour after hour, hearing nothing, very much bored, and disappointed. Soon after two o'clock Fargeau, who was in the next room, called to me to ask if I was awake. I gave no reply, and, after shouting once or twice, he took his lantern and came to investigate. The door was locked on the inside! He instantly called d'Ardeche and Duchesne, and together they hurled themselves against the door. It resisted. Within they could hear irregular footsteps dashing here and there, with heavy breathing. Although frozen with terror, they fought to destroy the door and finally succeeded by using a great slab of marble that formed the shelf of the mantel in Fargeau's room. As the door crashed in, they were suddenly hurled back against the walls of the corridor, as though by an explosion, the lanterns were extinguished, and they found themselves in utter silence and darkness.

As soon as they recovered from the shock, they leaped into the room and fell over my body in the middle of the floor. They lighted one of the lanterns, and saw the strangest sight that can be imagined. The floor and walls to the height of about six feet were running with something that seemed like stagnant water, thick, glutinous, sickening. As for me, I was drenched with the same cursed liquid. The odor of musk was nauseating. They dragged me away, stripped off my clothing, wrapped me in their coats, and hurried to the hospital, thinking me perhaps dead. Soon after sunrise d'Ardeche left the hospital, being assured that I was in a fair way to recovery, with time, and with Fargeau went up to examine by daylight the traces of the adventure that was so nearly fatal. They were too late. Fire engines were coming down the street as they passed the Académie. A neighbor rushed up to d'Ardeche: "O Monsieur! what misfortune, yet what fortune! It is true *la Bouche d'Enfer* – I beg pardon, the residence of the lamented Mlle. de Tartas – was burned, but not wholly, only the ancient building. The wings were saved, and for that great credit is due the brave firemen. Monsieur will remember them, no doubt."

It was quite true. Whether a forgotten lantern, overturned in the excitement, had done the work, or whether the origin of the fire was more supernatural, it was certain that "the Mouth of Hell" was no more. A last engine was pumping slowly as d'Ardeche came up; half a dozen limp, and one distended, hose stretched through the *porte cochère*, and within only the façade of Francis I remained, draped still with the black stems of the wisteria. Beyond lay a great vacancy, where thin smoke was rising slowly. Every floor was gone, and the strange halls of Mlle. Blaye de Tartas were only a memory.

With d'Ardeche I visited the place last year, but in the stead of the ancient walls was then only a new and ordinary building, fresh and respectable; yet the wonderful stories of the old *Bouche d'Enfer* still lingered in the Quarter, and will hold there, I do not doubt, until the Day of Judgment.

# The Southwest Chamber

## Mary Eleanor Freeman

### Prospectus

**Address:** Ackley Mansion, near Acton, New England, USA.

**Property:** *Circa* nineteenth-century house. Large, vaunted rooms, with fine bay windows and decorated in exquisite style. A new chamber extension offers additional accommodation.

**Viewing Date:** Summer, 1903.

**Agent:** Mary Eleanor Freeman (1852–1930) was born in Randolph, Massachusetts, and while working as secretary to the author and physician, Oliver Wendell Holmes, began writing poetry and novels with a strong New England regional flavour. When the supernatural caught her interest, the result was a group of short stories which combined domestic realism with supernaturalism and these have proved very influential. Several of the tales are about the persistence of strong emotions in supernatural terms – such as "The Shadow on the Wall" and "The Lost Ghost" – but none are more dramatic than "The Southwest Chamber" about the ghost of a grim old aunt whose viciousness and hatred manifests itself as a force of evil.

"That school-teacher from Acton is coming to-day," said Miss Sophia Gill. "I have decided to put her in the southwest chamber."

Amanda looked at her sister with an expression of mingled doubt and terror. "You don't suppose she would—" she began hesitatingly.

"Would what!" demanded Sophia sharply. Both were below the medium height and stout, but Sophia was firm where Amanda was flabby. Amanda wore a baggy old muslin (it was a hot day), and Sophia was uncompromisingly hooked up in a starched and boned cambric over her high shelving figure.

"I didn't know but she would object to sleeping in that room, as long as Aunt Harriet died there such a little while ago," faltered Amanda.

"Well," said Sophia, "of all the silly notions! If you are going to pick out rooms where nobody has died you'll have your hands full. I don't believe there's a room or a bed in this house that somebody hasn't passed away in."

"Well, I suppose I am silly to think of it, and she'd better go in there," said Amanda.

"I know she had. Now I guess you'd better go and see if any dust has settled on anything since it was cleaned, and open the west windows and let the sun in, while I see to that cake."

Amanda went to her task in the southwest chamber.

Nobody knew how this elderly woman with the untrammelled imagination of a child dreaded to enter the southwest chamber, and yet she could not have told why she had the dread. She had occupied rooms which had been once tenanted by persons now dead. But this was different. She entered and her heart beat thickly in her ears. Her hands were cold. The room was a very large one. The four windows were closed, the blinds also. The room was in a film of green gloom. The furniture loomed out vaguely. The white counterpane on the bed showed like a blank page.

Amanda crossed the room, opened one of the windows, and threw back the blind. Then the room revealed itself an apartment full of an aged and worn, but no less valid state. Pieces of old mahogany swelled forth; a peacock-patterned chintz draped the bedstead. The closet door stood ajar. There was a glimpse of purple drapery floating from a peg inside. Amanda went across and took down the garment hanging there. She wondered how her sister had happened to leave it when she cleaned the room. It was an old loose gown which had belonged to her aunt. She took it down shuddering, and closed the closet door after a fearful glance into its dark depths. It was a long closet with a strong odor of lovage. Aunt Harriet had had a habit of eating lovage and had carried it constantly in her pocket.

Amanda received the odor with a start as if before an actual presence. She was always conscious of this fragrance of lovage as she tidied the room. She spread fresh towels over the washstand and the bureau; she made the bed. Then she thought to take the purple gown from the easy chair where she had just thrown it and carry it to the garret and put it in the trunk with the other articles of the dead woman's wardrobe which had been packed away there; *but the purple gown was not on the chair!*

Amanda Gill was not a woman of strong convictions even as to her own actions. She directly thought that possibly she had been mistaken and had not removed it from the closet. She glanced at the closet door and saw with surprise that it was open, and she had thought she had closed it, but she instantly was not sure of that. So she entered the closet and looked for the purple gown. *It was not there!*

Amanda Gill went feebly out of the closet and looked at the easy chair again. The purple gown was not there! She looked wildly around the room. She went down on her trembling knees and peered under the bed, she opened the bureau drawers, she looked again in the closet. Then she stood in the middle of the floor and fairly wrung her hands.

There is a limit at which self-refutation must stop in any sane person. Amanda Gill had reached it. She knew that she had seen that purple gown in that closet; she knew that she had removed it and put it on the easy chair. She also knew that she had not taken it out of the room.

Then the thought occurred to her that possibly her sister Sophia might have entered the room unobserved while her back was turned and removed the dress. A sensation of relief came over her. Her blood seemed to flow back into its usual channels; the tension of her nerves relaxed.

"How silly I am!" she said aloud.

She hurried out and downstairs into the kitchen where Sophia was making cake, stirring with splendid circular sweeps of a wooden spoon a creamy yellow mass. Sophia looked up as her sister entered.

"Have you got it done?" said she.

"Yes," replied Amanda. Then she hesitated. A sudden terror overcame her. It did not seem as if it were at all probable that Sophia had left that foamy cake mixture a second to go to Aunt Harriet's chamber and remove that purple gown.

"Did you come up in Aunt Harriet's room while I was there?" she asked weakly.

"Of course I didn't. Why?"

"Nothing," replied Amanda.

Suddenly she realized that she could not tell her sister what had happened. She knew what Sophia would say if she told her. She dropped into a chair and began shelling the beans with nerveless fingers.

For the next hour or two the women were very busy. They kept no servant. When they had come into possession of this fine old place by the death of their aunt it had seemed a doubtful blessing. There was not a cent with which to pay for repairs and taxes and insurance. There had been a division in the old Ackley family years before. One of the daughters had married against her mother's wish, and had been disinherited. She had married a poor man by the name of Gill, and shared his humble lot in sight of her former home and her sister and mother living in prosperity, until she had borne three daughters; then she died, worn out with overwork and worry.

The mother and the elder sister had been pitiless to the last. Neither had ever spoken to her since she left her home the night of her marriage. They were hard women.

The three daughters of the disinherited sister had lived quiet and poor but not actually needy lives. Jane, the middle daughter, had married, and died in less than a year. Amanda and Sophia had taken the girl baby she left when the father married again. Sophia had taught a primary school for many years; she had saved enough to buy the little house in which they lived. Amanda had crocheted lace, and embroidered flannel, and made tidies and pincushions, and now in their late middle life had come the death of the aunt to whom they had never spoken, although they had often seen her, who had lived in solitary state in the old Ackley mansion until she was more than eighty. There had been no will, and they were the only heirs, with the exception of young Flora Scott, the daughter of the dead sister.

Sophia had promptly decided what was to be done. The small house was to be sold, and they were to move into the old Ackley house and take boarders to pay for its keeping. She scouted the idea of selling it. She had an enormous family pride.

Sophia and Amanda Gill had been living in the old Ackley house a fortnight, and they had three boarders: an elderly widow with a comfortable income, a young Congregationalist clergyman, and the middle-aged single woman who had charge of the village library. Now the school-teacher from Acton, Miss Louisa Stark, was expected for the summer.

Flora, their niece, was a very gentle girl, rather pretty, with large, serious blue eyes, a seldom smiling mouth, and smooth flaxen hair. She was delicate and very young – sixteen on her next birthday.

She came home soon now with her parcels of sugar and tea from the grocer's. She entered the kitchen gravely and deposited them on the table by which her Aunt Amanda was seated stringing beans. Flora wore an obsolete turban-shaped hat of black straw which had belonged to the dead aunt; it set high like a crown, revealing her forehead. Her dress was an ancient purple-and-white print, too long and too large, except over the chest, where it held her like a straight waistcoat.

"Flora," said Sophia, "you go up to the room that was your Greataunt Harriet's and take the water-pitcher off the washstand and fill it with water."

"In *that* chamber?" asked Flora. Her face changed a little.

"Yes, in that chamber," returned her Aunt Sophia sharply. "Go right along."

Flora went. Very soon she returned with the blue-and-white water-pitcher and filled it carefully at the kitchen sink.

"Now be careful and not spill it," said Sophia as she went out of the room carrying it gingerly.

Then the village stage-coach was seen driving round to the front of the house. The house stood on a corner.

"Here, Amanda, you look better than I do, you go and meet her," said Sophia. "Show her right up to her room."

Amanda removed her apron hastily and obeyed. Sophia hurried with her cake. She had just put it in the oven, when the door opened and Flora entered carrying the blue water-pitcher.

"What are you bringing down that pitcher again for?" asked Sophia.

"She wants some water, and Aunt Amanda sent me," replied Flora.

"For the land sake! She hasn't used all that great pitcher full of water so quick?"

"There wasn't any water in it," replied Flora.

Her high, childish forehead was contracted slightly with a puzzled frown as she looked at her aunt.

"Didn't I see you filling the pitcher with water not ten minutes ago, I want to know?"

"Yes, ma'am."

"Let me see that pitcher." Sophia examined the pitcher. It was not only perfectly dry from top to bottom, but even a little dusty. She turned severely on the young girl. "That shows," said she, "you did not fill the pitcher at all. You let the water run at the side because you didn't want to carry it upstairs. I am ashamed of you. It's bad enough to be lazy, but when it comes to not telling the truth!"

The young girl's face broke up suddenly into piteous confusion and her blue eyes became filmy with tears.

"I did fill the pitcher, honest," she faltered. "You ask Aunt Amanda."

"I'll ask nobody. The pitcher is proof enough. Water don't go off and leave the pitcher dusty on the inside if it was put in ten minutes ago. Now you fill that pitcher quick, and carry it upstairs, and if you spill a drop there'll be something besides talk."

Flora filled the pitcher, with the tears falling over her cheeks. She snivelled softly as she went out, balancing it carefully against her slender hip. Sophia followed her up the stairs to the chamber where Miss Louisa Stark was waiting for the water to remove the soil of travel.

Louisa Stark was stout and solidly built. She was a masterly woman inured to command from years of school-teaching. She carried her swelling bulk with majesty; even her face, moist and red with the heat, lost nothing of its dignity of expression.

She was standing in the middle of the floor with an air which gave the effect of her standing upon an elevation. She turned when Sophia and Flora, carrying the water-pitcher, entered.

"This is my sister Sophia," said Amanda, tremulously.

Sophia advanced, shook hands with Miss Louisa Stark and bade her welcome and hoped she would like her room. Then she moved toward the closet. "There is a nice large closet in this room –" she said, then she stopped short.

The closet door was ajar, and a purple garment seemed suddenly to swing into view as if impelled by some wind.

"Why, here is something left in this closet," Sophia said in a mortified tone.

She pulled down the garment with a jerk, and as she did so Amanda passed her in a weak rush for the door.

"I am afraid your sister is not well," said the school-teacher from Acton. "She may be going to faint."

"She is not subject to fainting spells," replied Sophia, but she followed Amanda.

She found her in the room which they occupied together, lying on the bed, very pale and gasping. She leaned over her.

"Amanda, what is the matter? Don't you feel well?" she asked.

"I feel a little faint."

Sophia got a camphor bottle and began rubbing her sister's forehead.

"Do you feel better?" she asked.

Amanda nodded.

"I guess if you feel better I'll just get that dress of Aunt Harriet's and take it up garret."

Sophia hurried out, but soon returned.

"I want to know," she said, looking sharply and quickly around, "if I brought that purple dress in here? It isn't in that chamber, nor the closet. You aren't lying on it, are you?"

"I lay down before you came in," replied Amanda.

"So you did. Well, I'll go and look again."

Presently Amanda heard her sister's heavy step on the garret stairs. Then she returned with a queer defiant expression on her face.

"I carried it up garret after all and put it in the trunk," said she. "I declare, I forgot it. I suppose your being faint sort of put it out of my head."

Sophia's mouth was set; her eyes upon her sister's scared, agitated face were full of hard challenge.

"I must go right down and see to that cake," said she, going out of the room. "If you don't feel well, you pound on the floor with the umbrella."

Amanda looked after her. She knew that Sophia had not put that purple dress of her dead Aunt Harriet's in the trunk in the garret.

Meantime Miss Louisa Stark was settling herself in the south-west chamber. She unpacked her trunk and hung her dresses carefully in the closet. She was a very punctilious woman. She put on a black India silk dress with purple flowers. She pinned her lace at her throat with a brooch, very handsome, although somewhat obsolete – a bunch of pearl grapes on black onyx, set in gold filigree.

As she surveyed herself in the little swing-mirror surmounting the old-fashioned mahogany bureau she suddenly bent forward and looked closely at the brooch. Instead of the familiar bunch of pearl grapes on the black onyx, she saw a knot of blond-and-black hair under glass surrounded by a border of twisted gold. She felt a thrill of horror. She unpinned the brooch, and it was her own familiar one, the pearl grapes and the onyx. "How very foolish I am," she thought. She thrust the pin in the lace at her throat, and again looked at herself in the glass, and there it was again – the knot of blond-and-black hair and twisted gold.

Louisa Stark looked at her own large, firm face above the brooch and it was full of terror and dismay which were new to it. She straightway began to wonder if there could be anything wrong with her mind. She remembered that an aunt of her mother's had been insane. A sort of fury with herself possessed her. She stared at the brooch in the glass with eyes at once angry and terrified. Then she removed it again and there was her own old brooch. Finally she thrust the gold pin through the lace again, fastened, it, and, turning a defiant back on the glass, went down to supper.

At the supper table she met the other boarders. She viewed the elderly widow with reserve, the clergyman with respect, the middle-aged librarian with suspicion. The latter wore a very youthful shirt-waist, and her hair in a girlish fashion, which the school-teacher, who twisted hers severely from the straining roots at the nape of the neck to the small, smooth coil at the top, condemned as straining after effects no longer hers by right.

The librarian, who had a quick alertness of manner, addressed her.

"What room are you in, Miss Stark?" said she.

"I am at a loss how to designate the room," replied Miss Stark stiffly.

The librarian, whose name was Eliza Lippincott, turned abruptly to Miss Amanda Gill, over whose delicate face a curious color compounded of flush and pallor was stealing.

"What room did your aunt die in, Miss Amanda?" asked she abruptly.

Amanda cast a terrified glance at her sister, who was serving a second plate of pudding for the minister.

"That room," she replied feebly.

"That's what I thought," said the librarian with a certain triumph. "I calculated that must be the room she died in, for it's the best room in the house, and you haven't put anybody in it before. Somehow the room that anybody has died in lately is generally the last room anybody is put in."

The young minister looked up from his pudding. He was very spiritual, but he had had poor picking in his previous boarding place, and he could not help a certain abstract enjoyment over Miss Gill's cooking.

"You certainly, Miss Lippincott," he remarked with his gentle, almost caressing inflection of tone, "do not for a minute believe that a higher power would allow any manifestation on the part of a disembodied spirit – who we trust is in her heavenly home – to harm one of His servants?"

"Oh, Mr. Dunn, of course not," replied Eliza Lippincott with a blush. "Of course not. I never meant to imply—"

"Of course dear Miss Harriet Gill was a professing Christian," remarked the widow, "and I don't suppose a professing Christian would come back and scare folks if she could. I wouldn't be a mite afraid to sleep in the room; I'd rather have it than the one I've got." Then she turned to Miss Stark. "Any time you feel timid in that room, I'm ready and willing to change with you," said she.

"Thank you. I have no desire to change. I am perfectly satisfied with my room," replied Miss Stark with freezing dignity, which was thrown away upon the widow.

Miss Louisa Stark did not sit down in the parlor with the other boarders after dinner. She went straight to her room. She felt tired after her journey, and meditated a loose wrapper and writing a few letters quietly before she went to bed. When she entered the southwest chamber she saw against the wall paper directly facing the door the waist of her best black satin dress hung over a picture.

"That is very strange," she said to herself, and a thrill of vague horror came over her. She knew or thought she knew, that she had put that black satin dress waist away nicely folded between towels in her trunk.

She took down the black waist and laid it on the bed preparatory to folding it, but when she attempted to do so she discovered that the two sleeves were firmly sewed together. Louisa Stark stared at the sewed sleeves. "What does this mean?" she asked herself. She examined the sewing carefully; the stitches were small, and even, and firm, of black silk.

She moved toward the door. For a moment she thought that this was something legitimate, about which she might demand information; then she became doubtful. Suppose she herself had done this absurd thing, or suppose that she had not, what was to hinder the others from thinking so – what was to hinder a doubt being cast upon her own memory and reasoning powers?

Louisa Stark had been on the verge of a nervous breakdown in spite of her iron constitution and her great will power. No woman can teach school for forty years with absolute impunity. She was more credulous as to her own possible failings than she had ever been in her whole life. She was cold with horror and terror, and yet not so much horror and terror of the supernatural as of her own self. The weakness of belief in the supernatural was nearly impossible for this strong nature. She could more easily believe in her own failing powers.

She started toward the mirror to unfasten her dress, then she remembered the strange circumstance of the brooch, and stopped short. Then she straightened herself defiantly and marched up to the bureau and looked in the glass. She saw reflected therein, fastening the lace at her throat, the old-fashioned thing of a large oval, a knot of fair and black hair under the glass, set in a rim of twisted gold. She unfastened it with trembling fingers and looked at it. It was her own brooch, the cluster of pearl grapes on black onyx. Louisa Stark placed the trinket in its little box on the nest of pink cotton and put it away in the bureau drawer. Only death could disturb her habit of order.

Her fingers were so cold they felt fairly numb as she unfastened her dress; she staggered when she slipped it over her head. She went to the closet to hang it up and recoiled. A strong smell of lovage came to her nostrils, a purple gown near the door swung softly against her face as if impelled by some wind from within. All the pegs were filled with garments not her own, mostly of somber black.

Suddenly Louisa Stark recovered her nerve. This, she told herself, was something distinctly tangible. Somebody had been taking liberties with her wardrobe. Somebody had been hanging some one else's clothes in her closet. She hastily slipped on her dress again and marched straight down stairs.

She found Sophia Gill standing by the kitchen table kneading dough with dignity.

"Miss Gill," said Miss Ctark, with her utmost school-teacher manner, "I wish to inquire why you have had my clothes removed from the closet in my room and others substituted?"

Sophia Gill stood, with her hand fast in the dough, regarding her. Her own face paled slowly and reluctantly, her mouth stiffened.

"I'll go upstairs with you, Miss Stark," said she, "and see what the trouble is." She spoke stiffly, with constrained civility.

Sophia and Louisa Stark went up to the southwest chamber. The closet door was shut. Sophia threw it open, then she looked at Miss Stark. On the pegs hung the school-teacher's own garments in orderly array.

"I can't see that there is anything wrong," remarked Sophia grimly.

Miss Stark sank down on the nearest chair. She saw her own clothes in the closet. She knew there had been no time for any human being to remove those which she thought she had seen and put hers in their places. She knew it was impossible. Again the awful horror of herself overwhelmed her.

She muttered something, she scarcely knew what. Sophia then went out of the room. In the morning Miss Stark did not go down to breakfast, and left before noon.

Directly the widow, Mrs. Elvira Simmons, knew that the school-teacher had gone, and the southwest room was vacant, she begged to have it in exchange for her own. Sophia hesitated a moment.

"I have no objections, Mrs. Simmons," said she, "if—"

"If what?" asked the widow.

"If you have common sense enough not to keep fussing because the room happens to be the one my aunt died in," said Sophia bluntly.

"Fiddlesticks!" said the widow.

That very afternoon she moved into the southwest chamber.

The widow was openly triumphant over her new room. She talked a deal about it at the dinner-table.

"You are sure you don't feel afraid of ghosts?" said the librarian. "I wouldn't sleep in that room after –" she checked herself with an eye on the minister.

"After what?" asked the widow.

"Nothing," replied Eliza Lippincott in an embarrassed fashion.

"You did see or hear something – now what was it, I want to know?" said the widow that evening when they were alone in the parlor. The minister had gone to make a call.

"Well," said Eliza hesitatingly, "if you'll promise not to tell."

"Yes, I promise; what was it?"

"Well, one day last week just before the school-teacher came, I went into that room to see if there were any clouds. I wanted to wear my gray dress, and I was afraid it was going to rain, so I wanted to look at the sky at all points, and – You know that chintz over the bed, and the valance? What pattern should you say it was?"

"Why, peacocks on a blue ground. Good land, I shouldn't think any one who had ever seen that would forget it."

"Well, when I went in there that afternoon it was not peacocks on a blue ground; it was great red roses on a yellow ground."

"Did Miss Sophia have it changed?"

"No. I went in there again an hour later and the peacocks were there."

The widow stared at her a moment, then she began to laugh rather hysterically.

"Well," said she, "I guess I shan't give up my nice room for any such tomfoolery as that. I guess I would just as soon have red roses on a yellow ground as peacocks on a blue; but there's no use talking, you couldn't have seen straight. How could such a a thing have happened?"

"I don't know," said Eliza Lippincott, "but I know I wouldn't sleep in that room if you'd give me a thousand dollars."

When Mrs. Simmons went to the southwest chamber that night, she cast a glance at the bed-hanging. There were the peacocks on the blue ground. She gave a contemptuous thought of Eliza Lippincott.

But just before Mrs. Simmons was ready to get into bed she looked again at the hangings, and there were the red roses on the yellow ground instead of the peacocks on blue. She looked long and sharply. Then she crossed the room, turned her back to the bed, and looked out at the night from the east window. It was clear, and the full moon had just risen. She watched it a moment sailing over the dark blue in its nimbus of gold. Then she looked around at the bed hangings. She still saw the red roses on the yellow ground.

Mrs. Simmons was struck in the most vulnerable point. This apparent contradiction of the reasonable as manifested in such a commonplace thing as the chintz of a bed-hanging affected this ordinary, unimaginative woman as no ghostly appearance could have done. Those red roses on the yellow ground were to her much more ghastly than any strange figure clad in the white robes of the grave entering the room.

She took a step toward the door, then she turned with a resolute air. "As for going downstairs and owning up I'm scared and having that Lippincott girl crowing over me, I won't for any red roses instead of peacocks. I guess they can't hurt me, and as long as we've both of us seen 'em I guess we can't both be getting loony," she said.

Mrs. Elvira Simmons blew out her light and got into bed. After a little she fell asleep.

But she was awakened about midnight by a strange sensation in her throat. She had dreamed that some one with long white fingers was strangling her, and she saw bending over her the face of an old woman in a white cap. When she waked there was no old woman, the room was almost as light as day in the full moonlight, and looked very peaceful; but the strangling sensation continued, and besides that, her face and ears felt muffled. She put up her hand and felt that her head was covered with a ruffled nightcap tied under her chin so tightly that it was exceedingly uncomfortable. A great qualm of horror shot over her. She tore the thing off frantically and flung it from her with a convulsive effort as if it had been a spider. She sprang out of bed and was going toward the door when she stopped.

It suddenly occurred to her that Eliza Lippincott might have entered the room and tied on the cap while she was asleep. Then she tried to open the door, but to her astonishment found that it was bolted on the inside. "I must have locked it after all," she reflected with wonder, for she never locked her door.

She went toward the spot where she had thrown the cap – she had stepped over it on her way to the door – but it was not there. She searched the whole room, lighting the lamp, but she could not find the cap. Finally she gave it up. She extinguished her lamp and went back to bed. She fell asleep again, to be again awakened in the same fashion. That time she tore off the cap as before, but she did not fling it on the floor. Instead, she held to it with a fierce grip. Her blood was up.

Holding fast to the flimsy white thing, she sprang out of bed, ran to the window which was open, slipped the screen, and flung it out; but a sudden gust of wind, though the night was calm, arose and it floated back in her face. She clutched at it. It eluded her clutching fingers. Then she did not see it at all. She examined the floor, she lighted her lamp again and searched, but there was no sign of it.

Mrs. Simmons was then in such a rage that all terror had disappeared for the time. To be baffled like this and resisted by something which was nothing to her straining senses filled her with intensest resentment.

Finally she got back into bed again; she did not go to sleep. She felt strangely drowsy, but she fought against it. She was wide awake, staring at the moonlight, when she suddenly felt the soft white strings of the thing tighten round her throat and realized that her enemy was again upon her. She seized the strings, untied them, twitched off the cap, ran with it to the table where her scissors lay and furiously cut it into small bits. She cut and tore, feeling an insane fury of gratification.

She tossed the bits of muslin into a basket and went back to bed. Almost immediately she felt the soft strings tighten round her throat. Then at last she yielded, vanquished. This new refutal of all the laws of reason by which she had learned, as it were, to spell her theory of life was too much for her equilibrium. She pulled off the clinging strings feebly, drew the thing from her head, slid weakly out of bed, caught up her wrapper and hastened out of the room. She went noiselessly along the hall to her own old room, entered it, got into her familiar bed, and lay there the rest of the night shuddering and listening, and if she dozed, waking with a start at the feeling of the pressure upon her throat – to find that it was not there, yet still unable to shake off entirely the horror.

She went down to breakfast the next morning with an imperturbable face. When asked by Eliza Lippincott how she had slept, she replied with an appearance of calmness which was bewildering that she had not slept very well. She never did sleep very well in a new bed, and she thought she would go back to her old room.

Eliza Lippincott was not deceived, however, neither were the Gill sisters, nor the young girl Flora. Eliza Lippincott spoke out bluntly.

"You needn't talk to me about sleeping well," said she. "I know something queer happened in that room last night by the way you act."

They all looked at Mrs. Simmons inquiringly – the librarian with malicious curiosity and triumph, the minister with sad incredulity, Sophia Gill with fear and indignation, Amanda and the young girl with unmixed terror. The widow bore herself with dignity.

"I saw nothing nor heard nothing which I trust could not have been accounted for in some rational manner," said she.

"What was it?" persisted Eliza Lippincott.

"I do not wish to discuss the matter any further," replied Mrs. Simmons shortly. Then she passed her plate for more creamed potato. She felt that she would die before she confessed to the ghastly absurdity of that nightcap, or to having been disturbed by the flight of peacocks off a blue field of chintz. She left the whole matter so vague that in a fashion she came off the mistress of the situation.

That afternoon the young minister, John Dunn, went to Sophia Gill and requested permission to occupy the southwest chamber that night.

"I don't ask to have my effects moved there," said he, "for I could scarcely afford a room so much superior to the one I now occupy, but I should like, if you please, to sleep there to-night for the purpose of refuting in my own person any unfortunate superstition which may have obtained root here."

Sophia Gill thanked the minister gratefully and eagerly accepted his offer.

That night about twelve o'clock the Reverend John Dunn essayed to go to his nightly slumber in the southwest chamber. He had been sitting up until that hour preparing his sermon.

He traversed the hall with a little night-lamp in his hand; he opened the door of the southwest chamber and essayed to enter. He might as well have essayed to enter the solid side of a house. He could look into the room full of soft lights and shadows under the moonlight which streamed in at the windows. He could see the bed in which he had expected to pass the night, but he could not enter. Whenever he strove to do so, he had a curious sensation as if he were trying to press against an invisible person who met him with a force of opposition impossible to overcome. The minister was not an athletic man, yet he had considerable strength. He squared his elbows, set his mouth hard, and strove to push his way through into the room. The opposition which he met was as sternly and mutely terrible as the rocky fastness of a mountain in his way.

For a half-hour John Dunn, doubting, raging, overwhelmed with spiritual agony as to the state of his own soul rather than fear, strove to enter the southwest chamber. He was simply powerless against this uncanny obstacle. Finally a great horror as of evil itself came over him. He was a nervous man and very young. He fairly fled to his own chamber and locked himself in like a terror-stricken girl.

The next morning he went to Miss Gill and told her frankly what had happened.

"What it is I know not, Miss Sophia," said he, "but I firmly believe, against my will, that there is in that room some accursed evil power at work of which modern faith and modern science know nothing."

Miss Sophia Gill listened with grimly lowering face.

"I think I will sleep in that room myself to-night," she said, when the minister had finished.

There were occasions when Miss Sophia Gill could put on a manner of majesty, and she did now.

It was ten o'clock that night when Sophia Gill entered the southwest chamber. She had told her sister what she intended doing and had been proof against her tearful entreaties. Amanda was charged not to tell the young girl, Flora.

"There is no use in frightening that child over nothing," said Sophia.

Sophia, when she entered the southwest chamber, set the lamp which she carried on the bureau, and began moving about the room, pulling down the curtains, taking the nice white counterpane off the bed, and preparing generally for the night.

As she did so, moving with great coolness and deliberation, she became conscious that she was thinking some thoughts that were foreign to her. She began remembering what she could not have remembered, since she was not then born: the trouble over her mother's marriage, the bitter opposition, the shutting the door upon her, the ostracizing her from heart and home. She became aware of a most singular sensation of bitter resentment, and not against the mother and sister who had so treated her own mother, but against her own mother herself, and then she became aware of a like bitterness extended to her own self. She felt malignant toward her mother as a young girl whom she remembered, though she could not have remembered, and she felt malignant toward her own self, and her sister Amanda, and Flora. Evil suggestions surged in her brain – suggestions which turned her heart to stone and which still fascinated her. And all the time by a sort of double consciousness she knew that what she thought was strange and not due to her own volition. She knew that she was thinking the thoughts of some other person, and she knew who. She felt herself possessed.

But there was tremendous strength in the woman's nature. She had inherited strength for good and righteous self-assertion from the evil strength of her ancestors. They had turned their own weapons against themselves. She made an effort which seemed more than human, and was conscious that the hideous thing was gone from her. She thought her own thoughts. Then she scouted to herself the idea of anything supernatural about the terrific experience. "I am imagining everything," she told herself.

She went on with her preparations; she went to the bureau to take down her hair. She looked in the glass and saw, instead of her own face, middle-aged and good to see, with its expression of a life of honesty and good-will to others and patience under trials, the face of a very old woman scowling forever with unceasing hatred and misery at herself and all others, at life and death, at that which had been and that which was to come. She saw, instead of her own face in the glass, the face of her dead Aunt Harriet, topping her own shoulders in her own well-known dress!

Sophia Gill left the room. She went into the one which she shared with her sister Amanda. Amanda looked up and saw her standing there with her handkerchief pressed to her face.

"Oh, Sophia, let me call in somebody. Is your face hurt? Sophia, what is the matter with your face?" fairly shrieked Amanda.

Suddenly Sophia took the handkerchief from her face.

"Look at me, Amanda Gill," she said.

Amanda looked, shrinking.

"What is it? Oh, what is it? You don't look hurt. What is it, Sophia?"

"What do you see?"

"Why, I see you."

"Me?"

"Yes, you. What did you think I would see?"

Sophia Gill looked at her sister.

"Never as long as I live will I tell you what I thought you would see, and you must never ask me," said she. "I am going to sell this house."

# The Toll-House

## W. W. Jacobs

### Prospectus

**Address:** The Toll-House, Wapping, London, England.

**Property:** Early nineteenth-century lodge house. Situated not far from the River Thames, the building has a number of large rooms on three floors and a stylish hallway and stairs. The property is surrounded by a substantial garden. To be let unfurnished.

**Viewing Date:** Autumn, 1909.

**Agent:** William Wymark Jacobs (1863–1943) was born in London and spread his literary talent widely as a journalist, humourist, dramatist and novelist. He became popular with readers for a series of tales about the lives of seamen, but in 1902 wrote "The Monkey's Paw" a horror story which has been filmed, adapted for radio and television, and is probably one of the most anthologised stories in English fiction. Haunted buildings feature in several of his tales, including "Jerry Bundler", "The Three Sisters" and "The Toll-House", the story of a fearsome ghost who takes his toll of visitors. It has deservedly been ranked the equal of "The Monkey's Paw".

"It's all nonsense," said Jack Barnes. "Of course people have died in the house; people die in every house. As for the noises –

wind in the chimney and rats in the wainscot are very convincing to a nervous man. Give me another cup of tea, Meagle."

"Lester and White are first," said Meagle, who was presiding at the tea-table of the Three Feathers Inn. "You've had two."

Lester and White finished their cups with irritating slowness, pausing between sips to sniff the aroma, and to discover the sex and dates of arrival of the "strangers" which floated in some numbers in the beverage. Mr. Meagle served them to the brim, and then, turning to the grimly expectant Mr. Barnes, blandly requested him to ring for hot water.

"We'll try and keep your nerves in their present healthy condition," he remarked. "For my part I have a sort of half-and-half belief in the supernatural."

"All sensible people have," said Lester. "An aunt of mine saw a ghost once."

White nodded.

"I had an uncle that saw one," he said.

"It always is somebody else that sees them," said Barnes.

"Well, there is the house," said Meagle, "a large house at an absurdly low rent, and nobody will take it. It has taken toll of at least one life of every family that has lived there – however short the time – and since it has stood empty caretaker after caretaker has died there. The last caretaker died fifteen years ago."

"Exactly," said Barnes. "Long enough ago for legends to accumulate."

"I'll bet you a sovereign you won't spend the night there alone, for all your talk," said White suddenly.

"And I," said Lester.

"No," said Barnes slowly. "I don't believe in ghosts nor in any supernatural things whatever; all the same, I admit that I should not care to pass a night there alone."

"But why not?" inquired White.

"Wind in the chimney," said Meagle, with a grin.

"Rats in the wainscot," chimed in Lester.

"As you like," said Barnes, colouring.

"Suppose we all go?" said Meagle. "Start after supper, and get there about eleven? We have been walking for ten days now without an adventure – except Barnes's discovery that ditch-water smells longest. It will be a novelty, at any rate, and, if we break the spell by all surviving, the grateful owner ought to come down handsome."

"Let's see what the landlord has to say about it first," said Lester. "There is no fun in passing a night in an ordinary empty house. Let us make sure that it is haunted."

He rang the bell, and, sending for the landlord, appealed to him in the name of our common humanity not to let them waste a night watching in a house in which spectres and hobgoblins had no part. The reply was more than reassuring, and the landlord, after describing with considerable art the exact appearance of a head which had been seen hanging out of a window in the moonlight, wound up with a polite but urgent request that they would settle his bill before they went.

"It's all very well for you young gentlemen to have your fun," he said indulgently; "but, supposing as how you are all found dead in the morning, what about me? It ain't called the Toll-House for nothing, you know."

"Who died there last?" inquired Barnes, with an air of polite derision.

"A tramp," was the reply. "He went there for the sake of half-a-crown, and they found him next morning hanging from the balusters, dead."

"Suicide," said Barnes. "Unsound mind."

The landlord nodded. "That's what the jury brought it in," he said slowly; "but his mind was sound enough when he went in there. I'd known him, off and on, for years. I'm a poor man, but I wouldn't spend the night in that house for a hundred pounds."

He repeated this remark as they started on their expedition a few hours later. They left as the inn was closing for the night; bolts shot noisily behind them, and, as the regular customers trudged slowly homewards, they set off at a brisk pace in the direction of the house. Most of the cottages were already in darkness, and lights in others went out as they passed.

"It seems rather hard that we have got to lose a night's rest in order to convince Barnes of the existence of ghosts," said White.

"It's in a good cause," said Meagle. "A most worthy object; and something seems to tell me that we shall succeed. You didn't forget the candles, Lester?"

"I have brought two," was the reply; "all the old man could spare."

There was but little moon, and the night was cloudy. The road between high hedges was dark, and in one place, where it ran through a wood, so black that they twice stumbled in the uneven ground at the side of it.

"Fancy leaving our comfortable beds for this!" said White again. "Let me see; this desirable residential sepulchre lies to the right, doesn't it?"

"Farther on," said Meagle.

They walked on for some time in silence, broken only by White's tribute to the softness, the cleanliness, and the comfort of the bed which was receding farther and farther into the distance. Under Meagle's guidance they turned off at last to the right, and, after a walk of a quarter of a mile, saw the gates of the house before them.

The lodge was almost hidden by over-grown shrubs and the drive was choked with rank growths. Meagle leading, they pushed through it until the dark pile of the house loomed above them.

"There is a window at the back where we can get in, so the landlord says," said Lester, as they stood before the hall door.

"Window?" said Meagle. "Nonsense. Let's do the thing properly. Where's the knocker?"

He felt for it in the darkness and gave a thundering rat-tat-tat at the door.

"Don't play the fool," said Barnes crossly.

"Ghostly servants are all asleep," said Meagle gravely, "but *I'll* wake them up before I've done with them. It's scandalous keeping us out here in the dark."

He plied the knocker again, and the noise volleyed in the emptiness beyond. Then with a sudden exclamation he put out his hands and stumbled forward.

"Why, it was open all the time," he said, with an odd catch in his voice. "Come on."

"I don't believe it was open," said Lester, hanging back. "Somebody is playing us a trick."

"Nonsense," said Meagle sharply. "Give me a candle. Thanks. Who's got a match?"

Barnes produced a box and struck one, and Meagle, shielding the candle with his hand, led the way forward to the foot of the stairs. "Shut the door, somebody," he said; "there's too much draught."

"It is shut," said White, glancing behind him.

Meagle fingered his chin. "Who shut it?" he inquired, looking from one to the other. "Who came in last?"

"I did," said Lester, "but I don't remember shutting it – perhaps I did, though."

Meagle, about to speak, thought better of it, and, still carefully guarding the flame, began to explore the house, with the others close behind. Shadows danced on the walls and lurked in the corners as they proceeded. At the end of the passage they found a second staircase, and ascending it slowly gained the first floor.

"Careful!" said Meagle, as they gained the landing.

He held the candle forward and showed where the balusters had broken away. Then he peered curiously into the void beneath.

"This is where the tramp hanged himself, I suppose," he said thoughtfully.

"You've got an unwholesome mind," said White, as they walked on. "This place is quite creepy enough without you remembering that. Now let's find a comfortable room and have a little nip of whisky apiece and a pipe. How will this do?"

He opened a door at the end of the passage and revealed a small square room. Meagle led the way with the candle, and, first melting a drop or two of tallow, stuck it on the mantelpiece. The others seated themselves on the floor and watched pleasantly as White drew from his pocket a small bottle of whisky and a tin cup.

"H'm! I've forgotten the water," he exclaimed.

"I'll soon get some," said Meagle.

He tugged violently at the bell-handle, and the rusty jangling of a bell sounded from a distant kitchen. He rang again.

"Don't play the fool," said Barnes roughly.

Meagle laughed. "I only wanted to convince you," he said kindly. "There ought to be, at any rate, one ghost in the servants' hall."

Barnes held up his hand for silence.

"Yes?" said Meagle, with a grin at the other two. "Is anybody coming?"

"Suppose we drop this game and go back," said Barnes suddenly. "I don't believe in spirits, but nerves are outside anybody's command. You may laugh as you like, but it really seemed to me that I heard a door open below and steps on the stairs."

His voice was drowned in a roar of laughter.

"He is coming round," said Meagle, with a smirk. "By the time I have done with him he will be a confirmed believer. Well, who will go and get some water? Will, you, Barnes?"

"No," was the reply.

"If there is any it might not be safe to drink after all these years," said Lester. "We must do without it."

Meagle nodded, and taking a seat on the floor held out his hand for the cup. Pipes were lit, and the clean, wholesome smell of tobacco filled the room. White produced a pack of cards; talk and laughter rang through the room and died away reluctantly in distant corridors.

"Empty rooms always delude me into the belief that I possess a deep voice," said Meagle. "To-morrow I—"

He started up with a smothered exclamation as the light went out suddenly and something struck him on the head. The others sprang to their feet. Then Meagle laughed.

"It's the candle," he exclaimed. "I didn't stick it enough."

Barnes struck a match, and re-lighting the candle, stuck it on the mantelpiece, and sitting down took up his cards again.

"What was I going to say?" said Meagle. "Oh, I know; to-morrow I—"

"Listen!" said White, laying his hand on the other's sleeve. "Upon my word I really thought I heard a laugh."

"Look here!" said Barnes. "What do you say to going back?

I've had enough of this. I keep fancying that I hear things too; sounds of something moving about in the passage outside. I know it's only fancy, but it's uncomfortable."

"You go if you want to," said Meagle, "and we will play dummy. Or you might ask the tramp to take your hand for you, as you go downstairs."

Barnes shivered and exclaimed angrily. He got up, and, walking to the half-closed door, listened.

"Go outside," said Meagle, winking at the other two. "I'll dare you to go down to the hall door and back by yourself."

Barnes came back, and, bending forward, lit his pipe at the candle.

"I am nervous, but rational," he said, blowing out a thin cloud of smoke. "My nerves tell me that there is something prowling up and down the long passage outside; my reason tells me that that is all nonsense. Where are my cards?"

He sat down again, and, taking up his hand, looked through it carefully and led.

"Your play, White," he said, after a pause.

White made no sign.

"Why, he is asleep," said Meagle. "Wake up, old man. Wake up and play."

Lester, who was sitting next to him, took the sleeping man by the arm and shook him, gently at first and then with some roughness; but White, with his back against the wall and his head bowed, made no sign. Meagle bawled in his ear, and then turned a puzzled face to the others.

"He sleeps like the dead," he said, grimacing. "Well, there are still three of us to keep each other company."

"Yes," said Lester, nodding. "Unless—Good Lord! suppose—"

He broke off, and eyed them, trembling.

"Suppose what?" inquired Meagle.

"Nothing," stammered Lester. "Let's wake him. Try him again. *White*! WHITE!"

"It's no good," said Meagle seriously; "there's something wrong about that sleep."

"That's what I meant," said Lester; "and if *he* goes to sleep like that, why shouldn't—"

Meagle sprang to his feet. "Nonsense," he said roughly. "He's tired out; that's all. Still, let's take him up and clear out. You take his legs and Barnes will lead the way with the candle. *Yes? Who's that?*"

He looked up quickly towards the door.

"Thought I heard somebody tap," he said, with a shamefaced laugh. "Now, Lester, up with him. One, two – *Lester! Lester!*"

He sprang forward too late; Lester, with his face buried in his arms, had rolled over on the floor fast asleep, and his utmost efforts failed to awake him.

"He – is – asleep," he stammered. "Asleep!"

Barnes, who had taken the candle from the mantelpiece, stood peering at the sleepers in silence and dropping tallow over the floor.

"We must get out of this," said Meagle. "Quick!"

Barnes hesitated. "We can't leave them here—" he began.

"We must," said Meagle, in strident tones. "If you go to sleep I shall go – Quick! Come!"

He seized the other by the arm and strove to drag him to the door. Barnes shook him off, and, putting the candle back on the mantelpiece, tried again to arouse the sleepers.

"It's no good," he said at last, and, turning from them, watched Meagle. "Don't you go to sleep," he said anxiously.

Meagle shook his head, and they stood for some time in uneasy silence. "May as well shut the door," said Barnes at last.

He crossed over and closed it gently. Then at a scuffling noise behind him he turned and saw Meagle in a heap on the hearth-stone.

With a sharp catch in his breath he stood motionless. Inside the room the candle, fluttering in the draught, showed dimly the grotesque attitudes of the sleepers. Beyond the door there seemed to his overwrought imagination a strange and stealthy unrest. He tried to whistle, but his lips were parched, and in a mechanical fashion he stooped, and began to pick up the cards which littered the floor.

He stopped once or twice and stood with bent head listening. The unrest outside seemed to increase; a loud creaking sounded from the stairs.

"Who is there?" he cried loudly.

The creaking ceased. He crossed to the door, and, flinging it open, strode out into the corridor. As he walked his fears left him suddenly.

"Come on!" he cried, with a low laugh. "All of you! All of you! Show your faces – your infernal ugly faces! Don't skulk!"

He laughed again and walked on; and the heap in the fireplace put out its head tortoise fashion and listened in horror to the retreating footsteps. Not until they had become inaudible in the distance did the listener's features relax.

"Good Lord, Lester, we've driven him mad," he said, in a frightened whisper. "We must go after him."

There was no reply. Meagle sprang to his feet.

"Do you hear?" he cried. "Stop your fooling now; this is serious. *White! Lester!* Do you hear?"

He bent and surveyed them in angry bewilderment. "All right," he said, in a trembling voice. "You won't frighten me, you know."

He turned away and walked with exaggerated carelessness in the direction of the door. He even went outside and peeped through the crack, but the sleepers did not stir. He glanced into the blackness behind, and then came hastily into the room again.

He stood for a few seconds regarding them. The stillness in the house was horrible; he could not even hear them breathe. With a sudden resolution he snatched the candle from the mantelpiece and held the flame to White's finger. Then as he reeled back stupefied, the footsteps again became audible.

He stood with the candle in his shaking hand, listening. He heard them ascending the farther staircase, but they stopped suddenly as he went to the door. He walked a little way along the passage, and they went scurrying down the stairs and then at a jog-trot along the corridor below. He went back to the main staircase, and they ceased again.

For a time he hung over the balusters, listening and trying to pierce the blackness below; then slowly, step by step, he made his way downstairs, and, holding the candle above his head, peered about him.

"Barnes!" he called. "Where are you?"

Shaking with fright, he made his way along the passage, and summoning up all his courage, pushed open doors and gazed fearfully into empty rooms. Then, quite suddenly, he heard the footsteps in front of him.

He followed slowly for fear of extinguishing the candle, until they led him at last into a vast bare kitchen, with damp walls and a broken floor. In front of him a door leading into an inside room had just closed. He ran towards it and flung it open, and a cold air blew out the candle. He stood aghast.

"Barnes!" he cried again. "Don't be afraid! It is I – Meagle!"

There was no answer. He stood gazing into the darkness, and all the time the idea of something close at hand watching was upon him. Then suddenly the steps broke out overhead again.

He drew back hastily, and passing through the kitchen groped his way along the narrow passages. He could now see better in the darkness, and finding himself at last at the foot of the staircase, began to ascend it noiselessly. He reached the landing just in time to see a figure disappear round the angle of a wall. Still careful to make no noise, he followed the sound of the steps until they led him to the top floor, and he cornered the chase at the end of a short passage.

"Barnes!" he whispered. "Barnes!"

Something stirred in the darkness. A small circular window at the end of the passage just softened the blackness and revealed the dim outlines of a motionless figure. Meagle, in place of advancing, stood almost as still as a sudden horrible doubt took possession of him. With his eyes fixed on the shape in front he fell back slowly, and, as it advanced upon him, burst into a terrible cry.

"Barnes! For God's sake! Is it *you?*"

The echoes of his voice left the air quivering, but the figure before him paid no heed. For a moment he tried to brace his courage up to endure its approach, then with a smothered cry he turned and fled.

The passages wound like a maze, and he threaded them blindly in a vain search for the stairs. If he could get down and open the hall door –

He caught his breath in a sob; the steps had begun again. At a lumbering trot they clattered up and down the bare passages, in and out, up and down, as though in search of him. He stood appalled, and then as they drew near entered a small room and stood behind the door as they rushed by. He came out and ran swiftly and noiselessly in the other direction, and in a moment the steps were after him. He found the long corridor and raced along it at top speed. The stairs he knew were at the end, and with the steps close behind he descended them in blind haste. The steps gained on him, and he shrank to the side to let them pass, still continuing his headlong flight. Then suddenly he seemed to slip off the earth into space.

Lester awoke in the morning to find the sunshine streaming into the room, and White sitting up and regarding with some perplexity a badly-blistered finger.

"Where are the others?" inquired Lester.

"Gone, I suppose," said White. "We must have been asleep."

Lester arose, and stretching his stiffened limbs, dusted his clothes with his hands and went out into the corridor. White followed. At the noise of their approach a figure which had been lying asleep at the other end sat up and revealed the face of Barnes. "Why, I've been asleep," he said, in surprise. "I don't remember coming here. How did I get here?"

'Nice place to come for a nap," said Lester severely, as he pointed to the gap in the balusters. "Look there! Another yard and where would you have been?"

He walked carelessly to the edge and looked over. In response to his startled cry the others drew near, and all three stood staring at the dead man below.

# Feet Foremost

## L. P. Hartley

### Prospectus

**Address:** Low Threshold Hall, north Suffolk, England.

**Property:** Queen Anne style building, elegant low frontage with square, castellated tower at north end. Surrounded by lush lawns and borders running down to a stream. Recently renovated to a very high standard.

**Viewing Date:** August, 1938.

**Agent:** Leslie Poles Hartley (1895–1972) was born in Whittlesea, Cambridge, and became famous as a novelist of country life and morals as exemplified in *The Go-Between* (1953) which has been filmed and adapted for television. He has also been credited with writing some of the most sophisticated ghost stories in the English language, and was quoted as saying that this type of story was "if not the highest, certainly the most exacting form of literary art". The best of Hartley's work is to be found in *Night Fears* (1924), *The Killing Bottle* (1932) and *The Travelling Grave* (1948). "Feet Foremost" is one of several of his supernatural stories set in elegant country houses and features the continuing malevolence of a spirit dead for 400 years.

The house-warming at Low Threshold Hall was not an event that affected many people. The local newspaper, however, had half a column about it, and one or two daily papers supplemented the usual August dearth of topics with pictures of the house. They were all taken from the same angle, and showed a long, low building in the Queen Anne style flowing away from a square tower on the left which was castellated and obviously of much earlier date, the whole structure giving somewhat the impression to a casual glance of a domesticated church, or even of a small railway train that had stopped dead on finding itself in a park. Beneath the photograph was written something like "Suffolk Manor House re-occupied after a hundred and fifty years," and, in one instance, "Inset, (L.) Mr. Charles Ampleforth, owner of Low Threshold Hall; (R.) Sir George Willings, the architect responsible for the restoration of this interesting mediaeval relic." Mr. Ampleforth's handsome, slightly Disraelian head, nearly spiked on his own flagpole, smiled congratulations at the grey hair and rounded features of Sir George Willings who, suspended like a bubble above the Queen Anne wing, discreetly smiled back.

To judge from the photograph, time had dealt gently with Low Threshold Hall. Only a trained observer could have told how much of the original fabric had been renewed. The tower looked particularly convincing. While as for the gardens sloping down to the stream which bounded the foreground of the picture – they had that old-world air which gardens so quickly acquire. To see those lush lawns and borders as a meadow, that mellow brickwork under scaffolding, needed a strong effort of the imagination.

But the guests assembled in Mr Ampleforth's drawing-room after dinner and listening to their host as, not for the first time, he enlarged upon the obstacles faced and overcome in the work of restoration, found it just as hard to believe that the house was old. Most of them had been taken to see it, at one time or another, in process of reconstruction; yet even within a few days of its completion, how unfinished a house looks! Its habitability seems determined in the last few hours. Magdalen Winthrop, whose beautiful, expressive face still (to her hostess' sentimental eye) bore traces of the slight disappointment she had suffered earlier in the evening, felt as if she were in an Aladdin's palace. Her glance wandered appreciatively from the Samarcand rugs to the pale green walls, and dwelt with pleasure on the high shallow arch, flanked by slender columns, the delicate lines of which were emphasised by the darkness of the hall behind them. It all seemed so perfect and so new; not only every sign of decay but the very sense of age had been banished. How absurd not to be able to find a single grey hair, so to speak, in a house that had stood empty for a hundred and fifty years! Her eyes, still puzzled, came to rest on the company, ranged in an irregular circle round the open fireplace.

"What's the matter, Maggie?" said a man at her side, obviously glad to turn the conversation away from bricks and mortar. "Looking for something?"

Mrs. Ampleforth, whose still lovely skin under the abundant white hair made her face look like a rose in snow, bent forward over the cream-coloured satin bedspread she was embroidering and smiled. "I was only thinking," said Maggie, turning to her host whose recital had paused but not died upon his lips, "how surprised the owls and bats would be if they could come in and see the change in their old home."

"Oh, I do hope they won't," cried a high female voice from the depths of a chair whose generous proportions obscured the speaker.

"Don't be such a baby, Eileen," said Maggie's neighbour in tones that only a husband could have used. "Wait till you see the family ghost."

"Ronald, please! Have pity on my poor nerves!" The upper half of a tiny, childish, imploring face peered like a crescent moon over the rim of the chair.

"If there is a ghost," said Maggie, afraid that her original remark might be construed as a criticism, "I envy him his beautiful surroundings. I would willingly take his place."

"Hear, hear," agreed Ronald. "A very happy haunting-ground. Is there a ghost, Charles?"

There was a pause. They all looked at their host.

"Well," said Mr Ampleforth, who rarely spoke except after a pause and never without a slight impressiveness of manner, "there is and there isn't."

The silence grew even more respectful.

"The ghost of Low Threshold Hall," Mr. Ampleforth continued, "is no ordinary ghost."

"It wouldn't be," muttered Ronald in an aside Maggie feared might be audible.

"It is, for one thing," Mr. Ampleforth pursued, "exceedingly considerate."

"Oh, how?" exclaimed two or three voices.

"It only comes by invitation."

"Can anyone invite it?"

"Yes, anyone."

There was nothing Mr. Ampleforth liked better than answering questions; he was evidently enjoying himself now.

"How is the invitation delivered?" Ronald asked. "Does one telephone, or does one send a card: 'Mrs. Ampleforth requests the pleasure of Mr. Ghost's company on – well – what is tomorrow? – the eighteenth August, Moaning and Groaning and Chain Rattling. R.S.V.P.'?"

"That would be a sad solecism," said Mr. Ampleforth. "The ghost of Low Threshold Hall is a lady."

"Oh," cried Eileen's affected little voice. "I'm so thankful. I should be much less frightened of a female phantom."

"She hasn't attained years of discretion," Mr. Ampleforth said. "She was only sixteen when—"

"Then she's not 'out'?"

"Not in the sense you mean. I hope she's not 'out' in any sense," said Mr. Ampleforth, with grim facetiousness.

There was a general shudder.

"Well, I'm glad we can't ask her to an evening party," observed Ronald. "A ghost at tea-time is much less alarming. Is she what is called a 'popular girl'?"

"I'm afraid not."

"Then why do people invite her?"

"They don't realise what they're doing."

"A kind of pig in a poke business, what? But you haven't told us yet how we're to get hold of the little lady."

"That's quite simple," said Mr. Ampleforth readily. "She comes to the door."

The drawing-room clock began to strike eleven, and no one spoke till it had finished.

"She comes to the door," said Ronald with an air of deliberation, "and then – don't interrupt, Eileen, I'm in charge of the cross-examination – she – she hangs about—"

"She waits to be asked inside."

"I suppose there is a time-honoured formula of invitation: 'Sweet Ermyntrude, in the name of the master of the house I bid thee welcome to Low Threshold Hall. There's no step, so you can walk straight in.' Charles, much as I admire your house, I do think it's incomplete without a doorstep. A ghost could just sail in."

"There you make a mistake," said Mr. Ampleforth impressively. "Our ghost cannot enter the house unless she is lifted across the threshold."

"Like a bride," exclaimed Magdalen.

"Yes," said Mr. Ampleforth. "Because she came as a bride." He looked round at his guests with an enigmatic smile.

They did not disappoint him. "Now, Charlie, don't be so mysterious! Do tell us! Tell us the whole story."

Mr. Ampleforth settled himself into his chair. "There's very little to tell," he said, with the reassuring manner of someone who intends to tell a great deal, "but this is the tale. In the time of the Wars of the Roses the owner of Low Threshold Hall (I need not tell you his name was not Ampleforth) married *en troisièmes noces* the daughter of a neighbouring baron much less powerful than he. Lady Elinor Stortford was sixteen when she came and she did not live to see her seventeenth birthday. Her husband was a bad hat (I'm sorry to have to say so of a predecessor of mine), a very bad hat. He ill-treated her, drove her mad with terror, and finally killed her."

The narrator paused dramatically but the guests felt slightly disappointed. They had heard so many stories of that kind.

"Poor thing," said Magdalen, feeling that some comment was necessary, however flat. "So now she haunts the place. I suppose it's the nature of ghosts to linger where they've suffered, but it seems illogical to me. I should want to go somewhere else."

"The Lady Elinor would agree with you. The first thing she does when she gets into the house is make plans for getting out. Her visits, as far as I can gather, have generally been brief."

"Then why does she come?" asked Eileen.

"She comes for vengeance," Mr. Ampleforth's voice dropped at the word. "And apparently she gets it. Within a short time of her appearance, someone in the house always dies."

"Nasty spiteful little girl," said Ronald, concealing a yawn. "Then how long is she in residence?"

"Until her object is accomplished."

"Does she make a dramatic departure – in a thunder-storm or something?"

"No, she is just carried out."

"Who carries her this time?"

"The undertaker's men. She goes out with the corpse. Though some say—"

"Oh, Charlie, do stop!" Mrs. Ampleforth interrupted, bending down to gather up the corners of her bedspread. "Eileen will never sleep. Let's go to bed."

"No! No!" shouted Ronald. "He can't leave off like that. I must hear the rest. My flesh was just beginning to creep."

Mr. Ampleforth looked at his wife.

"I've had my orders."

"Well, well," said Ronald, resigned. "Anyhow, remember what I said. A decent fall of rain, and you'll have a foot of water under the tower there, unless you put in a doorstep."

Mr. Ampleforth looked grave. "Oh no, I couldn't do that. That would be to invite er – er – trouble. The absence of a step was a precaution. That's how the house got its name."

"A precaution against what?"

"Against Lady Elinor."

"But how? I should have thought a draw-bridge would have been more effective."

"Lord Deadham's immediate heirs thought the same. According to the story they put every material obstacle they could to bar the lady's path. You can still see in the tower the grooves which contained the portcullis. And there was a flight of stairs so steep and dangerous they couldn't be used without risk to life and limb. But that only made it easier for Lady Elinor."

"How did it?"

"Why, don't you see, everyone who came to the house, friends and strangers alike, had to be helped over the threshold! There was no way of distinguishing between them. At last when so many members of the family had been killed off that it was threatened with extinction, someone conceived a brilliant idea. Can you guess what it was, Maggie?"

"They removed all the barriers and levelled the threshold, so that any stranger who came to the door and asked to be helped into the house was refused admittance."

"Exactly. And the plan seems to have worked remarkably well."

"But the family did die out in the end," observed Maggie.

"Yes," said Mr. Ampleforth, "soon after the middle of the eighteenth century. The best human plans are fallible, and Lady Elinor was very persistent."

He held the company with his glittering raconteur's eye.

But Mrs. Ampleforth was standing up. "Now, now," she said, "I gave you twenty minutes" grace. It will soon be midnight. Come along, Maggie, you must be tired after your journey. Let me light you a candle." She took the girl's arm and piloted her into the comparative darkness of the hall. "I think they must be on this table," she said, her fingers groping; "I don't know the house myself yet. We ought to have had a light put here. But it's one of Charlie's little economies to have as few lights as possible. I'll tell him about it. But it takes so long to get anything done in this out-of-the-way spot. My dear, nearly three miles to the nearest clergyman, four to the nearest doctor! Ah, here we are, I'll light some for the others. Charlie is still holding forth about Lady Elinor. You didn't mind that long recital?" she added, as, accompanied by their shadows, they walked up the stairs. "Charlie does so love an audience. And you don't feel uncomfortable or anything? I am always so sorry for Lady Elinor, poor soul, if she ever existed. Oh, and I wanted to say we were so disappointed about Antony. I feel we got you down to-day on false pretences.

Something at the office kept him. But he's coming to-morrow. When is the wedding to be, dearest?"

"In the middle of September."

"Quite soon now. I can't tell you how excited I am about it. I think he's such a dear. You both are. Now which is your way, left, right, or middle? I'm ashamed to say I've forgotten."

Maggie considered. "I remember; it's to the left."

"In that black abyss? Oh, darling, I forgot; do you feel equal to going on the picnic to-morrow? We shan't get back till five. It'll be a long day: I'll stay at home with you if you like – I'm tired of ruins."

"I'd love to go."

"Good-night, then."

"Good-night."

In the space of ten minutes the two men, left to themselves, had succeeded in transforming the elegant Queen Anne drawing-room into something that looked and smelt like a bar-parlour.

"Well," observed Ronald who, more than his host, had been responsible for the room's deterioration, "time to turn in. I have a rendezvous with Lady Elinor. By the way, Charles," he went on, "have you given the servants instructions in anti-Elinor technique – told them only to admit visitors who can enter the house under their own steam, so to speak?"

"Mildred thought it wisest, and I agree with her," said Mr. Ampleforth, "to tell the servants nothing at all. It might unsettle them, and we shall have hard work to keep them as it is."

"Perhaps you're right," said Ronald. "Anyhow it's no part of their duty to show the poor lady out. Charles, what were you going to say that wasn't fit for ears polite when Mildred stopped you?"

Mr. Ampleforth reflected. "I wasn't aware—"

"Oh, yes, she nipped your smoking-room story in the bud. I asked 'Who carries Lady Elinor out?' and you said 'The undertaker's men; she goes out with the corpse,' and you were going to say something else when you were called to order."

"Oh, I remember," said Mr. Ampleforth. 'It was such a small point, I couldn't imagine why Mildred objected. According to one story, she doesn't go out *with* the corpse, she goes out in it."

Ronald pondered. "Don't see much difference, do you?"

"I can't honestly say I do."

"Women are odd creatures," Ronald said. "So long."

The cat stood by the library door, miaowing. Its intention was perfectly plain. First it had wanted to go out; then it strolled up and down outside the window, demanding to come in; now it wanted to go out again. For the third time in half an hour Antony Fairfield rose from his comfortable chair to do its bidding. He opened the door gently – all his movements were gentle; but the cat scuttled ignominiously out, as though he had kicked it. Antony looked round. How could he defend himself from disturbance without curtailing the cat's liberty of movement? He might leave the window and the door open, to give the animal freedom of exit and entrance; though he hated sitting in a room with the door open, he was prepared to make the sacrifice. But he couldn't leave the window open because the rain would come in and spoil Mrs. Ampleforth's beautiful silk cushions. Heavens, how it rained! Too bad for the farmers, thought Antony, whose mind was always busying itself with other people's misfortunes. The crops had been looking so well as he drove in the sunshine from the station, and now this sudden storm would beat everything down. He arranged his chair so that he could see the window and not keep the cat waiting if she felt like paying him another visit. The pattering of the rain soothed him. Half an hour and they would be back – Maggie would be back. He tried to visualise their faces, all so well known to him: but the experiment was not successful. Maggie's image kept ousting the others; it even appeared, somewhat grotesquely, on the top of Ronald's well-tailored shoulders. They mustn't find me asleep, thought Antony; I should look too middle-aged. So he picked up the newspaper from the floor and turned to the cross-word puzzle. "Nine points of the law" in nine – ten letters. That was a very easy one: "Possession." Possession, thought Antony; I must put that down. But as he had no pencil and was too sleepy to get one, he repeated the word over and over again: Possession, Possession. It worked like a charm. He fell asleep and dreamed.

In his dream he was still in the library, but it was night and somehow his chair had got turned around so that he no longer faced the window, but he knew that the cat was there, asking to come in; only someone – Maggie – was trying to persuade him not to let it in. "It's not a cat at all," she kept saying; "it's a Possession. I can see its nine points, and they're very sharp." But he knew that she was mistaken, and really meant nine lives, which all cats have: so he thrust her aside and ran to the window and opened it. It was too dark to see so he put out his hand where he thought the cat's body would be, expecting to feel the warm fur; but what met his hand was not warm, nor was it fur . . . He woke with a start to see the butler standing in front of him. The room was flooded with sunshine.

"Oh, Rundle," he cried, "I was asleep. Are they back?"

The butler smiled.

"No, sir, but I expect them every minute now."

"But you wanted me?"

"Well, sir, there's a young lady called, and I said the master was out, but she said could she speak to the gentleman in the library? She must have seen you, sir, as she passed the window."

"How very odd. Does she know me?"

"That was what she said, sir. She talks rather funny."

"All right, I'll come."

Antony followed the butler down the long corridor. When they reached the tower their footsteps rang on the paved floor. A considerable pool of water, the result of the recent heavy shower, had formed on the flagstones near the doorway. The door stood open, letting in a flood of light; but of the caller there was no sign.

"She was here a moment ago," the butler said.

"Ah, I see her," cried Antony. "At least, isn't that her reflected in the water? She must be leaning against the door-post."

"That's right," said Rundle. "Mind the puddle, sir. Let me give you a hand. I'll have this all cleared up before they come back."

* * *

Five minutes later two cars, closely following each other, pulled up at the door, and the picnic party tumbled out.

"Dear me, how wet!" cried Mrs. Ampleforth, standing in the doorway. "What has happened, Rundle? Has there been a flood?"

"It was much worse before you arrived, madam," said the butler, disappointed that his exertions with mop, floorcloth, scrubbing-brush, and pail were being so scantily recognised. "You could have sailed a boat on it. Mr. Antony he—"

"Oh, has he arrived? Antony's here, isn't that splendid?"

"Antony!" they all shouted. "Come out! Come down! Where are you?"

"I bet he's asleep, the lazy devil," remarked Ronald.

"No, sir," said the butler, at last able to make himself heard. "Mr. Antony's in the drawing-room with a lady."

Mrs. Ampleforth's voice broke the silence that succeeded this announcement.

"With a lady, Rundle? Are you sure?"

"Well, madam, she's hardly more than a girl."

"I always thought Antony was that sort of man," observed Ronald. "Maggie, you'd better—"

"It's too odd," interposed Mrs. Ampleforth hastily, 'Who in the world can she be?"

"I don't see there's anything odd in someone calling on us," said Mr. Ampleforth. "What's her name, Rundle?"

"She didn't give a name, sir."

"That is rather extraordinary. Antony is so impulsive and kindhearted. I hope – ah, here he is."

Antony came towards them along the passage, smiling and waving his hands. When the welcoming and hand-shaking were over:

"We were told you had a visitor," said Mrs. Ampleforth.

"Yes," said Ronald. "I'm afraid we arrived at the wrong moment."

Antony laughed and then looked puzzled. "Believe me, you didn't," he said. "You almost saved my life. She speaks such a queer dialect when she speaks at all, and I had reached the end of my small talk. But she's rather interesting. Do come along and see her: I left her in the library." They followed Antony down the passage. When they reached the door he said to Mrs. Ampleforth:

"Shall I go in first? She may be shy at meeting so many people."

He went in. A moment later they heard his voice raised in excitement.

"Mildred! I can't find her! She's gone!"

Tea had been cleared away, but Antony's strange visitor was still the topic of conversation. "I can't understand it," he was saying, not for the first time. "The windows were shut, and if she'd gone by the door we must have seen her."

"Now, Antony," said Ronald severely, "let's hear the whole story again. Remember, you are accused of smuggling into the house a female of doubtful reputation. Furthermore the prosecution alleges that when you heard us call (we were shouting ourselves hoarse, but he didn't come at once, you remember) you popped her out of that window and came out to meet us, smiling sheepishly, and feebly gesticulating. What do you say?"

"I've told you everything," said Antony. "I went to the door and found her leaning against the stonework. Her eyes were shut. She didn't move and I thought she must be ill. So I said, 'Is anything the matter?' and she looked up and said, 'My leg hurts.' Then I saw by the way she was standing that her hip must have been broken once and never properly set. I asked her where she lived, and she didn't seem to understand me; so I changed the form of the question, as one does on the telephone, and asked where she came from, and she said, 'A little further down,' meaning down the hill, I suppose."

"Probably from one of the men's cottages," said Mr. Ampleforth.

"I asked if it was far, and she said 'No', which was obvious, otherwise her clothes would have been wet and they weren't, only a little muddy. She even had some mud on her mediaeval bridesmaid's head-dress (I can't describe her clothes again, Mildred; you know how bad I am at that). So I asked if she'd had a fall, and she said, 'No, she got dirty coming up,' or so I understood her. It wasn't easy to understand her; I suppose she talked the dialect of these parts. I concluded (you all say you would have known long before) that she was a little mad, but I didn't like to leave her looking so rotten, so I said, 'Won't you come in and rest a minute?' Then I wished I hadn't".

"Because she looked so pleased?"

"Oh, much more than pleased. And she said, 'I hope you won't live to regret it,' rather as though she hoped I should. And then I only meant just to take her hand, because of the water, you know, and she was lame—"

"And instead she flung herself into the poor fellow's arms—"

"Well, it amounted to that. I had no option! So I carried her across and put her down and she followed me here, walking better than I expected. A minute later you arrived. I asked her to wait and she didn't. That's all."

"I should like to have seen Antony doing the St. Christopher act!" said Ronald. "Was she heavy, old boy?"

Antony shifted in his chair. "Oh, no," he said, "not at all. Not at all heavy." Unconsciously he stretched his arms out in front of him, as though testing an imaginary weight. "I see my hands are grubby," he said with an expression of distaste. "I must go and wash them. I won't be a moment, Maggie."

That night, after dinner, there was some animated conversation in the servants' hall.

"Did you hear any more, Mr. Rundle?" asked a housemaid of the butler, who had returned from performing his final office at the dinner-table.

"I did," said Rundle, "but I don't know that I ought to tell you."

"It won't make an difference, Mr. Rundle, whether you do or don't. I'm going to give in my notice to-morrow. I won't stay in a haunted house. We've been lured here. We ought to have been warned."

"They certainly meant to keep it from us," said Rundle. "I myself had put two and two together after seeing Lady Elinor; what Wilkins said when he came in for his tea only confirmed my suspicions. No gardener can ever keep a still tongue in his head. It's a pity."

"Wouldn't you have told us yourself, Mr. Rundle?" asked the cook.

"I should have used my discretion," the butler replied. "When I informed Mr. Ampleforth that I was no longer in ignorance, he said, 'I rely on you, Rundle, not to say anything which might alarm the staff.'"

"Mean, I call it," exclaimed the kitchen-maid indignantly. "They want to have all the fun and leave us to die like rats in a trap."

Rundle ignored the interruption.

"I told Mr. Ampleforth that Wilkins had been tale-bearing and would he excuse it in an outdoor servant, but unfortunately we were now in possession of the facts."

"That's why they talked about it at dinner," said the maid who helped Rundle to wait.

"They didn't really throw the mask off till after you'd gone, Lizzie," said the butler. "Then I began to take part in the conversation."

He paused for a moment.

"Mr. Ampleforth asked me whether anything was missing from the house, and I was able to reply, 'No, everything was in order.'"

"What else did you say?" inquired the cook.

"I made the remark that the library window wasn't fastened, as they thought, but only closed, and Mrs. Turnbull laughed and said, 'Perhaps it's only a thief, after all,' but the others didn't think she could have got through the window, unless her lameness was all put on. And then I told them what the police had said about looking out for a suspicious character."

"Did they seem frightened?" asked the cook.

"Not noticeably," replied the butler. "Mrs. Turnbull said she hoped the gentleman wouldn't stay long over their port. Mr. Ampleforth said, 'No, they had had a full day, and would be glad to go to bed.' Mrs. Ampleforth asked Miss Winthrop if she wanted to change her bedroom, but she said she didn't. Then

Mr. Fairfield asked if he could have some iodine for his hand, and Miss Winthrop said she would fetch some. She wanted to bring it after dinner, but he said, 'Oh, to-morrow morning will do, darling.' He seemed rather quiet."

"What's he done to his hand?"

"I saw the mark when he took his coffee. It was like a burn."

"They didn't say they were going to shut the house up, or anything?"

"Oh, Lord, no. There's going to be a party next week. They'll all have to stay for that."

"I never knew such people," said the kitchen-maid. "They'd rather die, and us too, than miss their pleasures. I wouldn't stay another day if I wasn't forced. When you think she may be here in this very room, listening to us!" She shuddered.

"Don't you worry, my girl," said Rundle, rising from his chair with a gesture of dismissal. "She won't waste her time listening to you."

"We really might be described as a set of crocks," said Mr. Ampleforth to Maggie after luncheon the following day. "You, poor dear, with your headache; Eileen with her nerves; I with – well – a touch of rheumatism; Antony with his bad arm."

Maggie looked troubled.

"My headache is nothing, but I'm afraid Antony isn't very well."

"He's gone to lie down, hasn't he?"

"Yes."

"The best thing. I telephoned for the doctor to come this evening. He can have a look at all of us, ha! ha! Meanwhile, where will you spend the afternoon? I think the library's the coolest place on a stuffy day like this; and I want you to see my collection of books about Low Threshold – my Thresholdiana, I call them."

Maggie followed him into the library.

"Here they are. Most of them are nineteenth-century books, publications of the Society of Antiquaries, and so on; but some are older. I got a little man in Charing Cross Road to hunt them out for me; I haven't had time to read them all myself."

Maggie took a book at random from the shelves.

"Now I'll leave you," said her host. "And later in the afternoon I know that Eileen would appreciate a little visit. Ronald says it's nothing, just a little nervous upset, stomach trouble. Between ourselves, I fear Lady Elinor is to blame."

Maggie opened the book. It was called *An Enquiry into the Recent Tragicall Happenings at Low Threshold Hall in the County of Suffolk, with some Animadversions on the Barbarous Customs of our Ancestors*. It opened with a rather tedious account of the semi-mythical origins of the Deadham family. Maggie longed to skip this, but she might have to discuss the book with Mr. Ampleforth, so she ploughed on. Her persistence was rewarded by a highly coloured picture of Lady Elinor's husband and an account of the cruelties he practised on her. The story would have been too painful to read had not the author (Maggie felt) so obviously drawn upon a very vivid imagination. But suddenly her eyes narrowed. What was this? "Once in a Drunken Fitt he so mishandled her that her thigh was broken near the hip, and her screames were so loud they were heard by the servants through three closed doores; and yet he would not summon a Chirurgeon, for (quoth he)" – Lord Deadham's reason was coarse in the extreme; Maggie hastened on.

"And in consequence of these Barbarities her nature which was soft and yielding at the first was greatly changed, and those who sawe her now (but Pitie seal'd their lips) would have said she had a Bad Hearte."

No wonder, thought Maggie, reading with a new and painful interest how the murdered woman avenged herself on various descendants, direct and collateral, of her persecutor. "And it hath been generally supposed by the vulgar that her vengeance was directed only against members of that family from which she had taken so many Causeless Hurtes; and the depraved, defective, counterfeit records of those times have lent colour to this Opinion. Whereas the truth is as I now state it, having had access to those death-bed and testamentary depositions which, preserved in ink however faint, do greater service to verity than the relations of Pot-House Historians, enlarged by Memory and confused by

Ale. Yet it is on such Testimonies that rash and sceptical Heads rely when they assert that the Lady Elinor had no hand in the late Horrid Occurrence at Low Threshold Hall, which I shall presently describe, thinking that a meer visitor and no blood relation could not be the object of her vengeance, notwithstanding the evidence of two serving-maids, one at the door and one craning her neck from an upper casement, who saw him beare her in: The truth being that she maketh no distinction between persons, but whoso admits her, on him doth her vengeance fall. Seven times she hath brought death to Low Threshold Hall; Three, it is true, being members of the family, but the remaining four indifferent Persons and not connected with them, having in common only this piece of folie, that they, likewise, let her in. And in each case she hath used the same manner of attack, as those who have beheld her first a room's length, then no further than a Lovers Embrace, from her victim have *in articulo mortis* delivered. And the moment when she is no longer seen, which to the watchers seems the Clarion and Reveille of their hopes, is in reality the knell; for she hath not withdrawn further, but approached nearer, she hath not gone out but entered in; and from her dreadful Citadel within the body rejoices, doubtless, to see the tears and hear the groanes, of those who with Comfortable Faces (albeit with sinking Hearts), would soothe the passage of the parting Soul. Their Lacrimatory Effusions are balm to her wicked Minde; the sad gale and ventilation of their sighs a pleasing Zephyre to her vindictive spirit."

Maggie put down the book for a moment and stared in front of her. Then she began again to read.

"Once only hath she been cheated of her Prey, and it happened thus. His Bodie was already swollen with the malignant Humours she had stirred up in him and his life despaired of when a kitchen-wench was taken with an Imposthume that bled inwardly. She being of small account and but lately arrived they did only lay her in the Strawe, charging the Physician (and he nothing loth, expecting no Glory or Profit from attendance on such a Wretched creature) not to Divide his Efforts but use all his skill to save their Cousin (afterwards the twelfth Lord). Notwithstanding which precaution he did hourly get worse until sodainely a change came and he began to amend. Whereat was such rejoicing (including an Ox roasted whole) that the night was spent before they heard the serving-maid was dead. In their Revels they gave small heed to this Event, not realising that they owed His life to Hers; for a fellow-servant who tended the maid (out of charity) declared that her death and the cousin's recovery followed as quickly as a clock striking Two. And the Physician said it was well, for she would have died in any case.

"Whereby we must conclude that the Lady Elinor, like other Apparitions, is subject to certain Lawes. One, to abandon her Victim and seeking another tenement to transfer her vengeance, should its path be crossed by a Body yet nearer Dissolution: and another is, she cannot possess or haunt the corpse after it has received Christian Buriall. As witness the fact that the day after the Interment of the tenth Lord she again appeared at the Doore and being recognised by her inability to make the Transit was turned away and pelted. And another thing I myself believe but have no proof of is: That her power is circumscribed by the wall of the House; those victims of her Malignitie could have been saved but for the dreadful swiftnesse of the disease and the doctors unwillingness to move a Sicke man; otherwise how could the Termes of her Curse that she pronounced be fulfilled: 'They shall be carried out Feet Foremost'?"

Maggie read no more. She walked out of the library with the book under her arm. Before going to see how Antony was she would put it in her bedroom where no one could find it. Troubled and oppressed she paused at the head of the stairs. Her way lay straight ahead, but her glance automatically travelled to the right where, at the far end of the passage, Antony's bedroom lay. She looked again; the door, which she could only just see, was shut now. But she could swear it had closed upon a woman. There was nothing odd in that; Mildred might have gone in, or Muriel, or a servant. But all the same she could not rest. Hurriedly she changed her dress and went to Antony's room. Pausing at the door she listened and distinctly heard his voice, speaking rapidly and in a low tone; but no one seemed to reply. She got no answer to her knock, so, mustering her courage, she walked in.

The blind was down and the room half dark, and the talking continued, which increased her uneasiness. Then, as her eyes got used to the darkness, she realised, with a sense of relief, that he was talking in his sleep. She pulled up the blind a little, so that she might see his hand. The brown mark had spread, she thought, and looked rather puffy, as though coffee had been injected under the skin. She felt concerned for him. He would never have gone properly to bed like that, in his pyjamas, if he hadn't felt ill, and he tossed about restlessly. Maggie bent over him. Perhaps he had been eating a biscuit: there was some gritty stuff on the pillow. She tried to scoop it up but it eluded her. She could make no sense of his mutterings, but the word "light" came in a good deal. Perhaps he was only half asleep and wanted the blind down. At last her ears caught the sentence that was running on his lips: "She was so light." Light? A light woman? Browning. The words conveyed nothing to her, and not wishing to wake him she tiptoed from the room.

"The doctor doesn't seem to think seriously of any of us, Maggie, you'll be glad to hear," said Mr. Ampleforth, coming into the drawing-room about six o'clock. "Eileen's coming down to dinner. I am to drink less port – I didn't need a doctor, alas! to tell me that. Antony's the only casualty: he's got a slight temperature, and had better stay where he is until to-morrow. The doctor thinks it is one of those damnable horse-flies: his arm is a bit swollen, that's all."

"Has he gone?" asked Maggie quickly.

"Who, Antony?"

"No, no, the doctor."

"Oh, I'd forgotten your poor head. No, you'll just catch him. His car's on the terrace."

The doctor, a kindly, harassed middle-aged man, listened patiently to Maggie's questions.

"The brown mark? Oh, that's partly the inflammation, partly the iodine – he's been applying it pretty liberally, you know, amateur physicians are all alike; feel they can't have too much of a good thing."

"You don't think the water here's responsible? I wondered if he ought to go away."

"The water? Oh no. No, it's a bite all right, though I confess I can't see the place where the devil got his beak in. I'll come tomorrow, if you like, but there's really no need."

The next morning, returning from his bath, Ronald marched into Antony's room. The blind went up with a whizz and a smack, and Antony opened his eyes.

"Good morning, old man," said Ronald cheerfully. "Thought I'd look in and see you. How goes the blood-poisoning? Better?"

Antony drew up his sleeve and hastily replaced it. The arm beneath was chocolate-coloured to the elbow.

"I feel pretty rotten," he said.

"I say, that's bad luck. What's this?" added Ronald, coming nearer. "Have you been sleeping in both beds?"

"Not to my knowledge," murmured Antony.

"You have, though," said Ronald. "If this bed hasn't been slept in, it's been slept on, or lain on. That I can swear. Only a head, my boy, could have put that dent in the pillow, and only a pair of muddy – hullo! The pillow's got it, too."

"Got what?" asked Antony drowsily.

"Well, if you ask me, it's common garden mould."

"I'm not surprised. I feel pretty mouldy, too."

"Well, Antony; to save your good name with the servants, I'll remove the traces."

With characteristic vigour Ronald swept and smoothed the bed.

"Now you'll be able to look Rundle in the face."

There was a knock on the door.

"If this is Maggie," said Ronald, "I'm going."

It was, and he suited the action to the word.

"You needn't trouble to tell me, dearest," she said, "that you are feeling much better, because I can see that you aren't."

Antony moved his head uneasily on the pillow.

"I don't feel very flourishing, to tell you the honest truth."

"Listen" – Maggie tried to make her voice sound casual – "I don't believe this is a very healthy place. Don't laugh, Antony;

we're all of us more or less under the weather. I think you ought to go away."

"My dear, don't be hysterical. One often feels rotten when one wakes up. I shall be all right in a day or two."

"Of course you will. But all the same if you were in Sussex Square you could call in Fosbrook – and, well, I should be more comfortable."

"But you'd be here!"

"I could stay at Pamela's."

"But, darling, that would break up the party. I couldn't do it; and it wouldn't be fair to Mildred."

"My angel, you're no good to the party, lying here in bed. And as long as you're here, let me warn you they won't see much of me."

A look of irritation Maggie had never noticed before came into his face as he said, almost spitefully:

"Supposing the doctor won't allow you to come in? It may be catching, you know."

Maggie concealed the hurt she felt.

"All the more reason for you to be out of the house."

He pulled up the bedclothes with a gesture of annoyance and turned away.

"Oh, Maggie, don't keep nagging at me. You ought to be called Naggie, not Maggie."

This was an allusion to an incident in Maggie's childhood. Her too great solicitude for a younger brother's safety had provoked the gibe. It had always wounded her, but never so much as coming from Antony's lips. She rose to go.

"Do put the bed straight," said Antony, still with face averted. "Otherwise they'll think you've been sleeping here."

"What?"

"Well, Ronald said something about it."

Maggie closed the door softly behind her. Antony was ill, of course, she must remember that. But he had been ill before, and was always an angelic patient. She went down to breakfast feeling miserable.

* * *

After breakfast, at which everyone else had been unusually cheerful, she thought of a plan. It did not prove so easy of execution as she hoped.

"But, dearest Maggie," said Mildred, "the village is nearly three miles away. And there's nothing to see there."

"I love country post-offices," said Maggie; "they always have such amusing things."

"There is a post-office," admitted Mildred. "But are you sure it isn't something we could do from here? Telephone, telegraph?"

"Perhaps there'd be a picture-postcard of the house," said Maggie feebly.

"Oh, but Charlie had such nice ones," Mildred protested. "He's so house-proud, you could trust him for that. Don't leave us for two hours just to get postcards. We shall miss you so much, and think of poor Antony left alone all the morning."

Maggie had been thinking of him.

"He'll get on all right without me," she said lightly.

"Well, wait till the afternoon when the chauffeur or Ronald can run you over in a car. He and Charlie have gone into Norwich and won't be back till lunch."

"I think I'll walk," said Maggie. "It'll do me good."

"I managed that very clumsily," she thought, "so how shall I persuade Antony to tell me the address of his firm?"

To her surprise his room was empty. He must have gone away in the middle of writing a letter, for there were sheets lying about on the writing-table and, what luck! an envelope addressed to Higgins & Stukeley, 312 Paternoster Row. A glance was all she really needed to memorise the address; but her eyes wandered to the litter on the table. What a mess! There were several pages of notepaper covered with figures. Antony had been making calculations and, as his habit was, decorating them with marginal illustrations. He was good at drawing faces, and he had a gift for catching a likeness. Maggie had often seen, and been gratified to see, slips of paper embellished with portraits of herself – full-face, side-face, three-quarter-face. But this face that looked out from among the figures and seemed to avoid her glance, was not hers. It was the face of a woman she had never seen before but whom she felt she would recognise anywhere, so consistent and vivid were the likeness. Scattered among the loose leaves were the contents of Antony's pocket-book. She knew he always carried her photograph. Where was it? Seized by an impulse, she began to rummage among the papers. Ah, here it was. But it was no longer hers! With a few strokes Antony had transformed her oval face, unlined and soft of feature, into a totally different one, a pinched face with high cheekbones, hollow cheeks, and bright hard eyes, from whose corners a sheaf of fine wrinkles spread like a fan: a face with which she was already too familiar.

Unable to look at it she turned away and saw Antony standing behind her. He seemed to have come from the bath for he carried a towel and was wearing his dressing-gown.

"Well," he said. "Do you think it's an improvement?"

She could not answer him, but walked over to the washstand and took up the thermometer that was lying on it.

"Ought you to be walking about like that," she said at last, "with a temperature of a hundred?"

"Perhaps not," he replied, making two or three goat-like skips towards the bed. "But I feel rather full of beans this morning."

Maggie edged away from his smile towards the door.

"There isn't anything I can do for you?"

"Not to-day, my darling."

The term of endearment struck her like a blow.

Maggie sent off her telegram and turned into the village street. The fact of being able to do something had relieved her mind: already in imagination she saw Antony being packed into the Ampleforths' Daimler with rugs and hotwater bottles, and herself, perhaps, seated by the driver. They were endlessly kind, and would make no bones about motoring him to London. But though her spirits were rising her body felt tired; the day was sultry, and she had hurried. Another bad night like last night, she thought, and I shall be a wreck. There was a chemist's shop over the way, and she walked in.

"Can I have some sal volatile?"

"Certainly, madam."

She drank it and felt better.

"Oh, and have you anything in the way of a sleeping draught?"

"We have some allodanol tablets, madam."

"I'll take them."

"Have you a doctor's prescription?"

"No."

"Then I'm afraid you'll have to sign the poison book. Just a matter of form."

Maggie recorded her name, idly wondering what J. Bates, her predecessor on the list, meant to do with his cyanide of potassium.

"We must try not to worry," said Mrs. Ampleforth, handing Maggie her tea, 'but I must say I'm glad the doctor has come. It relieves one of responsibility, doesn't it? Not that I feel disturbed about Antony – he was quite bright when I went to see him just before lunch. And he's been sleeping since. But I quite see what Maggie means. He doesn't seem himself. Perhaps it would be a good plan, as she suggests, to send him to London. He would have better advice there."

Rundle came in.

"A telegram for Mr. Fairfield, madam."

"It's been telephoned: "Your presence urgently required Tuesday morning – Higgins & Stukeley." Tuesday, that's to-morrow. Everything seems to point to his going, doesn't it, Charles?"

Maggie was delighted, but a little surprised, that Mrs. Ampleforth had fallen in so quickly with the plan of sending Antony home.

"Could he go to-day?" she asked.

"To-morrow would be too late, wouldn't it?" said Mr. Ampleforth drily. "The car's at his disposal: he can go whenever he likes."

Through her relief Maggie felt a little stab of pain that they were both so ready to see the last of Antony. He was generally such a popular guest.

"I could go with him," she said.

Instantly they were up in arms, Ronald the most vehement of

all. "I'm sure Antony wouldn't want you to. You know what I mean, Maggie, it's such a long drive, in a closed car on a stuffy evening. Charlie says he'll send a man, if necessary."

Mr. Ampleforth nodded.

"But if he were ill!" cried Maggie.

The entrance of the doctor cut her short. He looked rather grave.

"I wish I could say I was satisfied with Mr. Fairfield's progress," he said, "but I can't. The inflammation has spread up the arm as far as the shoulder, and there's some fever. His manner is odd, too, excitable and apathetic by turns." He paused. "I should like a second opinion."

Mr. Ampleforth glanced at his wife.

"In that case wouldn't it be better to send him to London? As a matter of fact, his firm has telegraphed for him. He could go quite comfortably in the car."

The doctor answered immediately:

"I wouldn't advise such a course. I think it would be most unwise to move him. His firm – you must excuse me – will have to do without him for a day or two."

"Perhaps," suggested Maggie trembling, "it's a matter that could be arranged at his house. They could send over someone from the office. I know they make a fuss about having him on the spot," she concluded lamely.

"Or doctor," said Mr. Ampleforth, "could you do us a very great kindness and go with him? We could telephone to his doctor to meet you, and the car would get you home by midnight."

The doctor squared his shoulders: he was clearly one of those men whose resolution stiffens under opposition.

"I consider it would be the height of folly," he said, "to move him out of the house. I dare not do it on my responsibility. I will get a colleague over from Ipswich to-morrow morning. In the meantime, with your permission, I will arrange for a trained nurse to be sent to-night."

Amid a subdued murmur of final instructions, the doctor left.

As Maggie, rather late, was walking upstairs to dress for dinner she met Rundle. He looked anxious.

"Excuse me, miss," he said. "but have you seen Mr. Fairfield. I've asked everyone else, and they haven't. I took him up his supper half an hour ago, and he wasn't in his room. He'd got his dress clothes out, but they were all on the bed except his stiff shirt."

"Have you been to look since?" asked Maggie.

"No, miss."

"I'll go and see."

She tiptoed along the passage to Antony's door. A medley of sounds, footsteps, drawers being opened and shut, met her ears.

She walked back to Rundle. "He's in there all right," she said. "Now I must make haste and dress."

A few minutes later a bell rang in the kitchen.

"Who's that?"

"Miss Winthrop's room," said the cook. "Hurry up, Lettice, or you'll have Rundle on your track – he'll be back in a minute."

"I don't want to go," said Lettice. "I tell you I feel that nervous—"

"Nonsense, child," said the cook. "Run along with you."

No sooner had the maid gone than Rundle appeared.

"I've had a bit of trouble with Master Antony," he said. "He's got it into his head that he wants to come down to dinner. 'Rundle,' he said to me, confidentially, 'do you think it would matter us being seven? I want them to meet my new friend.' 'What friend, Mr. Fairfield?' I said. 'Oh," he said, 'haven't you seen her? She's always about with me now.' Poor chap, he used to be the pick of the bunch, and now I'm afraid he's going potty."

"Do you think he'll really come down to dinner?" asked the cook, but before Rundle could answer Lettice rushed into the room.

"Oh," she cried, "I knew it would be something horrid! I knew it would be! And now she wants a floor cloth and a pail! She says they mustn't know anything about it! But I won't go again – I won't bring it down, I won't even touch it!"

"What won't you touch?"

"The waste-paper basket."

"Why, what's the matter with it?"

"It's . . . it's all bloody!"

When the word was out she grew calmer, and even seemed anxious to relate her experience.

"I went upstairs directly she rang" ("That's an untruth to start with," said the cook) "and she opened the door a little way and said, 'Oh, Lettice, I've been so scared!' And I said, 'What's the matter, miss?' And she said, 'There's a cat in here.' Well, I didn't think that was much to be frightened of, so I said, 'Shall I come in and catch him, miss?' and she said (deceitful-like, as it turned out), 'I should be so grateful.' Then I went in but I couldn't see the cat anywhere, so I said, 'Where is he?' At which she pointed to the waste-paper basket away by the dressing-table, and said, 'In that waste-paper basket.' I said, 'Why, that makes it easier, miss, if he'll stay there.' She said, 'Oh, he'll stay there all right.' Of course I took her meaning in a moment, because I know cats do choose queer, out-of-the-way places to die in, so I said, 'You mean the poor creature's dead, miss?' and I was just going across to get him because ordinarily I don't mind the body of an animal when she said (I will do her that justice), 'Stop a minute, Lettice, he isn't dead; he's been murdered.' I saw she was all trembling, and that made me tremble, too. And when I looked in the basket – well—"

She paused, partly perhaps to enjoy the dramatic effect of her announcement. "Well, if wasn't our Thomas! Only you couldn't have recognised him, poor beast, his head was bashed in that cruel."

"Thomas!" said the cook. "Why he was here only an hour ago."

"That's what I said to Miss Winthrop. 'Why, he was in the kitchen only an hour ago,' and then I came over funny, and when she asked me to help her clean the mess up I couldn't not if my life depended on it. But I don't feel like that now," she ended inconsequently. "I'll go back and do it!" She collected her traps and departed.

"Thomas!" muttered Rundle. "Who could have wished the poor beast any harm? Now I remember, Mr. Fairfield did ask me to get him out a clean shirt . . . I'd better go up and ask him."

He found Antony in evening dress seated at the writing-table. He had stripped it of writing material and the light from two candles gleamed on its polished surface. Opposite to him on the other side of the table was an empty chair. He was sitting with his back to the room; his face, when he turned it at Rundle's entrance, was blotchy and looked terribly tired.

"I decided to dine here after all, Rundle," he said. Rundle saw that the Bovril was still untouched in his cup.

"Why, your supper'll get cold, Mr. Fairfield," he said.

"Mind your own business," said Antony. "I'm waiting."

The Empire clock on the drawing-room chimney-piece began to strike, breaking into a conversation which neither at dinner nor afterwards had been more than desultory.

"Eleven," said Mr. Ampleforth. "The nurse will be here any time now. She ought to be grateful to you, Ronald, for getting him into bed."

"I didn't enjoy treating Antony like that," said Ronald.

There was a silence.

"What was that?" asked Maggie suddenly.

"It sounded like the motor."

"Might have been," said Mr. Ampleforth. "You can't tell from here."

They strained their ears, but the rushing sound had already died away. "Eileen's gone to bed, Maggie," said Mrs. Ampleforth. "Why don't you? We'll wait up for the nurse, and tell you when she comes."

Rather reluctantly Maggie agreed to go.

She had been in her bedroom about ten minutes, and was feeling too tired to take her clothes off, when there came a knock at the door. It was Eileen.

"Maggie," she said, "the nurse has arrived. I thought you'd like to know."

"Oh, how kind of you," said Maggie. "They were going to tell me, but I expect they forgot. Where is she?"

"In Antony's room. I was coming from the bath and his door was open."

"Did she look nice?"

"I only saw her back."

"I think I'll go along and speak to her," said Maggie.

"Yes, do. I don't think I'll go with you."

As she walked along the passage Maggie wondered what she would say to the nurse. She didn't mean to offer her professional advice. But even nurses are human, and Maggie didn't want this stranger to imagine that Antony was, well, always like that – the spoilt, tiresome, unreasonable creature of the last few hours. She could find no harsher epithets for him, even after all his deliberate unkindness. The woman would probably have heard that Maggie was his fiancée; Maggie would try to show her that she was proud of the relationship and felt it an honour.

The door was still open so she knocked and walked in. But the figure that uncoiled itself from Antony's pillow and darted at her a look of malevolent triumph was not a nurse, nor was her face strange to Maggie; Maggie could see, so intense was her vision at that moment, just what strokes Antony had used to transform her own portrait into Lady Elinor's. She was terrified, but she could not bear to see Antony's rather long hair nearly touching the floor nor the creature's thin hand on his labouring throat. She advanced, resolved at whatever cost to break up this dreadful tableau. She approached near enough to realise that what seemed a strangle-hold was probably a caress, when Antony's eyes rolled up at her and words, frothy and toneless like a chain of bursting bubbles, came popping from the corner of his swollen mouth: "Get out, damn you!" At the same moment she heard the stir of presences behind her and a voice saying, "Here is the patient, nurse; I'm afraid he's half out of bed, and here's Maggie, too. What *have* you been doing to him, Maggie?" Dazed, she turned about. "Can't you see?" she cried; but she might have asked the question of herself, for when she looked back she could only see the tumbled bed, the vacant pillow, and Antony's hair trailing the floor.

* * *

The nurse was a sensible woman. Fortified by tea, she soon bundled everybody out of the room. A deeper quiet than night ordinarily brings invaded the house. The reign of illness had begun.

A special embargo was laid on Maggie's visits. The nurse said she had noticed that Miss Winthrop's presence agitated the patient. But Maggie extracted a promise that she should be called if Antony got worse. She was too tired and worried to sleep, even if she had tried to, so she sat up fully dressed in a chair, every now and then trying to allay her anxiety by furtive visits to Antony's bedroom door.

The hours passed on leaden feet. She tried to distract herself by reading the light literature with which her hostess had provided her. Though she could not keep her attention on the books, she continued to turn their pages, for only so could she kept at bay the conviction that had long been forming at the back of her mind and that now threatened to engulf her whole consciousness: the conviction that the legend about Low Threshold was true. She was neither hysterical nor superstitious, and for a moment she had managed to persuade herself that what she had seen in Antony's room was an hallucination. The passing hours robbed her of that solace. Antony was the victim of Lady Elinor's vengeance. Everything pointed to it: the circumstances of her appearance, the nature of Antony's illness, the horrible deterioration in his character – to say nothing of the drawings, and the cat.

There were only two ways of saving him. One was to get him out of the house; she had tried that and failed; if she tried again she would fail more signally than before. But there remained the other way.

The old book about *The Tragicall Happenings at Low Threshold Hall* still reposed in a drawer; for the sake of her peace of mind Maggie had vowed not to take it out, and till now she had kept her vow. But as the sky began to pale with the promise of dawn and her conviction of Antony's mortal danger grew apace, her resolution broke down.

"Whereby we must conclude," she read, "that the Lady Elinor, like other Apparitions, is subject to certain Lawes.

One, to abandon her Victim and seeking another tenement enter into it and transfer her vengeance, should its path be crossed by a Body yet nearer Dissolution . . ."

A knock that had been twice repeated, startled her out of her reverie.

"Come in!"

"Miss Winthrop," said the nurse, "I'm sorry to tell you the patient is weaker. I think the doctor had better be telephoned for."

"I'll go and get someone," said Maggie. "Is he much worse?"

"Very much, I'm afraid."

Maggie had no difficulty in finding Rundle; he was already up.

"What time is it, Rundle?" she asked. "I've lost count."

"Half-past four, miss." He looked very sorry for her.

"When will the doctor be here?"

"In about an hour, miss, not more."

Suddenly she had an idea. "I'm so tired, Rundle, I think I shall try to get some sleep. Tell them not to call me unless . . . unless . . ."

"Yes, miss," said Rundle. "You look altogether done up."

About an hour! So she had plenty of time. She took up the book again. "Transfer her vengeance . . . seeking another tenement . . . a Body nearer Dissolution." Her idle thoughts turned with compassion to the poor servant girl whose death had spelt recovery to Lord Deadham's cousin but been so little regarded: "the night was spent" before they heard that she was dead. Well, this night was spent already. Maggie shivered. "I shall die in my sleep," she thought. "But shall I feel her come?" Her tired body sickened with nausea at the idea of such a loathsome violation. But the thought still nagged at her. "Shall I realise even for a moment that I'm changing into . . . into?" Her mind refused to frame the possibility. "Should I have time to do anyone an injury?" she wondered. "I could tie my feet together with a handkerchief; that would prevent me from walking." Walking . . . walking . . . The word let loose on her mind a new flood of terrors. She could not do it! She could not lay herself open for ever to this horrible occupation! Her tormented imagination began to busy itself with the details of her funeral; she saw mourners following her coffin into the church. But Antony was not amongst them; he was better but too ill to be there. He could not understand why she had killed herself, for the note she had left gave no hint of the real reason, referred only to continual sleeplessness and nervous depression. So she would not have his company when her body was committed to the ground. But that was a mistake; it would not be her body, it would belong to that other woman and be hers to return to by the right of possession.

All at once the screen which had recorded such vivid images to her mind's eye went blank; and her physical eye, released, roamed wildly about the room. It rested on the book she was still holding. "She cannot possess or haunt the corpse," she read, "after it has received Christian Buriall." Here was a ray of comfort. But (her fears warned her) being a suicide she might not be allowed Christian burial. How then? Instead of the churchyard she saw a cross-roads, with a slanting signpost on which the words could no longer be read; only two or three people were there; they kept looking furtively about them and the grave-digger had thrown his spade aside and was holding a stake . . .

She pulled herself together with a jerk. "These are all fancies," she thought. "It wasn't fancy when I signed the poison book." She took up the little glass cylinder; there were eighteen tablets and the dose was one or two. Daylight was broadening apace; she must hurry. She took some notepaper and wrote for five minutes. She had reached the words "No one is to blame" when suddenly her ears were assailed by a tremendous tearing, whirring sound: it grew louder and louder until the whole room vibrated. In the midst of the deafening din something flashed past the window, for a fraction of a second blotting out the daylight. Then there was a crash such as she had never heard in her life.

All else forgotten, Maggie ran to the window. An indescribable scene of wreckage met her eyes. The aeroplane had been travelling at a terrific pace: it was smashed to atoms. To right and left the lawn was littered with fragments, some of which had made great gashes in the grass, exposing the earth. The pilot had been flung clear; she could just see his legs sticking out from a flower-bed under the wall of the house. They did not move and she thought he must be dead.

While she was wondering what to do she heard voices underneath the window.

"We don't seem to be very lucky here just now, Rundle," said Mr. Ampleforth.

"No, sir."

There was a pause. Then Mr. Ampleforth spoke again.

"He's still breathing, I think."

"Yes, sir, he is, just."

"You take his head and I'll take his feet, and we'll get him into the house."

Something began to stir in Maggie's mind. Rundle replied:

"If you'll pardon my saying so, sir, I don't think we ought to move him. I was told once by a doctor that if a man's had a fall or anything it's best to leave him lying."

"I don't think it'll matter if we're careful."

"Really, sir, if you'll take my advice—"

There was a note of obstinacy in Rundle's voice. Maggie, almost beside herself with agitation, longed to fling open the window and cry "Bring him in! Bring him in!" But her hand seemed paralysed and her throat could not form the words.

Presently Mr. Ampleforth said:

"You know we can't let him stay here. It's beginning to rain."

(Bring him in! Bring him in!)

"Well, sir, it's your responsibility . . ."

Maggie's heart almost stopped beating.

"Naturally I don't want to do anything to hurt the poor chap."

(Oh, bring him in! Bring him in!)

The rain began to patter on the pane.

"Look here, Rundle, we must get him under cover."

"I'll fetch that bit of wing, sir, and put over him."

(Bring him in! Bring him in!)

Maggie heard Rundle pulling something that grated on the gravel path. The sound ceased and Mr. Ampleforth said:

"The very thing for a stretcher, Rundle! The earth's so soft, we can slide it under him. Careful, careful!" Both men were breathing hard. "Have you got your end? Right." Their heavy, measured footfalls grew fainter and fainter.

The next thing Maggie heard was the motor-car returning with the doctor. Not daring to go out, and unable to sit down, she stood, how long she did not know, holding her bedroom door ajar. At last she saw the nurse coming towards her.

"The patient's a little better, Miss Winthrop. The doctor thinks he'll pull through now."

"Which patient?"

"Oh, there was never any hope for the other poor fellow."

Maggie closed her eyes.

"Can I see Antony?" she said at last.

"Well, you may just peep at him."

Antony smiled at her feebly from the bed.

# Happy Hour

## Ian Watson

### Prospectus

**Address:** The Roebuck Public House, near Stony Stratford, Buckinghamshire, England.

**Property:** Elizabethan building with authentic low-beamed ceilings, comfortable furnishings and restaurant annex. Ample living accommodation. A popular local venue with substantial catchment area.

**Viewing Date:** Summer, 1990.

**Agent:** Ian Watson (1943–) was born on Tyneside and was a teacher in Tanzania and Tokyo for some years before returning to England to become one of the first lecturers in Future Studies. He has written an impressive variety of award-winning science fiction and supernatural novels – including *The Embedding* (1973), *The Gardens of Delight* (1980) and *The Fire Worm* (1988) – and has been described as the "natural successor to H.G. Wells". Watson is a master of short stories dealing with the nature of perception, as he demonstrates in "Happy Hour", which is about an ancient evil mixed up with modern technology. The setting, he says, is based on a *real* pub.

With an abrupt loud clatter the steel slats of the exhaust fan exploded open, making our hearts lurch. Martin mimed quick pistol shots at it.

"Pung! Pung! Gotcha."

That fan was set just beneath the bowed, beamed ceiling of the bar in the Roebuck. The contraption was at least twenty years out of date. It didn't purr softly like a modern fan. It exploded open, showing its teeth, and gulped at the atmosphere. One of the historic stones of this pub – built in the reign of Good Queen Bess, so a sign on the wall boasted – had been removed so that the thing could be inserted. The actual mechanism was hidden inside the wall. When the fan was in repose, all that showed was a slatted cream panel one foot square lying flush with the cream plaster-work. You hardly noticed it, forgot all about it – until suddenly the Xtractall opened its mouth as if by its own volition; until the flat panel became a dozen razor lips spaced an inch apart, through which fuggy air was sucked into its throat.

The fan throbbed lustily, sucking Charlotte's cigarette smoke and my own cigar smoke into it.

"Does it have a built-in smoke detector?" I wondered.

"We could ask what's-his-name. Our host." Jenny nodded toward the deserted bar counter.

"Host" was somewhat of a misnomer. The landlord was a quiet, wispy chap with little by way of personality. He smiled amiably, but he was no conversationalist; and frankly we liked it this way. Right now he would be round in the restaurant annex neatening the array of silver and wineglasses on the tables. The Roebuck was one of those few country pubs that opened fairly promptly at six of an evening, but it relied for its main trade on the gourmet menu from about half-past seven till ten. It wasn't much of a hangout for locals and yokels.

To be sure, now that the licensing hours had been liberalized, the place could have stayed open all day long. Yet what rural pub would bother to? We were lucky to have found the Roebuck.

Jenny and I, Charlotte and Martin, and Alice (who was special) all commuted to London and back by way of big, glassy Milton Keynes Station. Charlotte and Martin had bought a sizable thatched cottage in a couple of acres this side of Buckingham. Jenny and I were based in a different little village outside of Stony Stratford, in a barn conversion. Alice lived . . . somewhere in the vicinity. Alone? Or otherwise? Alice was our delicious enigma. Apparently she was in publishing. Webster-Freeman: art and oriental-wisdom volumes, shading into the outright occult. I sometimes fantasized her dancing naked around a bonfire or homemade altar along with other like spirits, firelight or candlelight winking between her legs. If such was the case, she had never tried to recruit us (and, curiously, my fantasies along these lines never provoked an erection). We were merely one slice of her life on Friday evenings: a slice lasting an hour – twice as long when we all dined at the Roebuck once a month.

Why had we been so honored by Alice? Perhaps she was lonely under her capable, gorgeous facade. Perhaps we were neutrals with whom she could be friends without obligations or ties.

I myself worked for an oil company and was in charge of Butadiene, a gas used as fuel and also in the manufacture of synthetic rubbers. Since I was on the contracts rather than the chemistry side, the job called for some foreign travel – quick trips to Eastern Europe, Mexico, Japan, from which I returned tired out – but otherwise my career was ho-hum. I assumed I would be with the same mob for the rest of my working life, slowly advancing. In our company salaries were somewhat pinched to start with (and indeed to continue with!) until the final five years, when suddenly you were rolling in money and could practically write yourself cheques. Thus my masters assured staff loyalty.

My wife, Jenny, was office manager for an airline, which gave us free tickets once a year to hot, exotic places where I didn't need to sit haggling in an office. Jenny was a short, trim blonde who wore smartly tailored suits and lavish bows like big silken napkins tucked into her neckline.

Burly, early-balding Martin was an architect, and his spouse, Charlotte, willowy and auburn, was a senior secretary to an export-import firm called, uninventively, Exportim, which managed to sound like some Soviet trade bureau.

And Alice was . . . Alice.

Weekdays (except Fridays) Martin and Charlotte and Jenny and I all drove our own cars to MK Station, since we might need to work late and catch different trains home. Every Friday, however, my wife and I shared a car; so did Martin and his wife. On that day nothing would make us miss the same return train and our wind-down drink with Alice at the Roebuck. Needless to say, our minor contribution toward car-sharing in no way relieved the parking pressure at MK. By seven-fifteen in the morning every weekday the station car parks were full up, and the central reservations and traffic islands were becoming crowded with vehicles. The new city in the Buckinghamshire countryside boasted a fine network of roads, but where parking was concerned, the planners had cocked up. Pressure, pressure. No wonder we looked forward to our Friday evenings. Or our once-a-month dinner.

I screwed my cigar butt into one ashtray at the exact moment when Charlotte stubbed out her Marlboro in another – as if she and I had been reproached by the extractor fan for our filthy habits. We glanced at one another and burst out laughing. The fan thumped shut.

"I heard this in Hungary," I said. "There's a new Russian wristwatch on the market, triumph of Soviet technology. It'll do absolutely everything: time zones, phases of the moon, built-in calculator. It only weighs a few ounces. 'So what's the snag?' asks this fellow. 'Oh,' says his informant, 'it's just the two suitcases of batteries you need to carry round with it . . .' "

Then Alice told a dirty joke.

"This British couple went for a holiday in the States to tour the national parks. Well, in the first park they made friends with a skunk. They adored the skunk so much they took it with them in their trailer to the next park, then the next. Come the end of their holiday, they could hardly bear to be parted from the animal. 'I wish we could take it home,' said the husband, 'but how could we avoid the quarantine laws?' 'I know,' said his wife, 'I'll stick the skunk inside my knickers, and we'll smuggle it in that way.' 'Great idea,' agreed her husband, 'but, um, what about the smell?' The wife shrugged and sighed. 'If it dies, it dies.' "

Alice was good that way. She was incredibly desirable – tall, slim, long legs, wonderful figure, that mass of raven hair, olive skin, dark broody eyes – but she easily defused any sexual tensions that might have undermined our little group. Lust from the men; or jealousy from the ladies. Charlotte had first fallen into conversation with Alice on the homeward train, and introduced her to the rest of us at journey's end. We rarely sat together on the train itself. Such a rush to catch it. Carriages would be crowded; and we all had work to keep us busy.

Alice refrained from letting us know her home address or phone number – perhaps wisely, in case Martin or I tried to see her privately. Nor, in fact, had she ever asked about our own homes. A tacit agreement prevailed, not to know. Meanwhile, she certainly made our Friday evening group react together. She was our catalyst. Without her, we would have been just two everyday couples. With her, we felt special: a new sort of unit, a sparkling fivesome.

Gleefully Martin took over the baton of joke-telling.

"The mother superior of this convent school invited a Battle of Britain hero to address her girls," he said with relish. "The flying ace told them, 'I was at eight thousand feet in my Spitfire. I saw a fokker to the left of me. There was another fokker to the right of me. I looked up, and the sky was full of fokkers.' 'I should explain, girls,' interrupted the mother superior, 'that the Fokker-Wolf was a Second World War German fighter plane.' 'That's quite right, Mother,' said the airman, 'but these fokkers were flying Messerschmidts.' "

Though the jokes themselves might have seemed silly – it's the way they're told, isn't it? – we excelled ourselves in wit and amity that evening . . . until the pub cat came a-calling on us. This mog was a scruffy ginger specimen, which I had seen the landlord shooing outdoors on a couple of occasions. With the unerring instinct of pussies, it made straight for Alice, to rub against her leg. She drew away.

"I loathe cats. I'm allergic."

"Gid away!" Martin flapped and clapped his hands. The mog retreated a little, not particularly deterred.

So much, I thought wryly, for Alice being any kind of spare-time witch; and to my scanty store of information about her I added the knowledge that there were no felines in her home.

She shifted uncomfortably. "I can't bear to touch them. I really don't like them." This was the first sour note in any of our evenings.

"Derrick," Jenny said to me, "for heaven's sake grab it and shove it out of the door."

"It's their hair," murmured Alice. "It would give me a terrible rash. I hope they don't let it sleep in here at night. Sprawling on these seats, rubbing fur off all the time. If they do let it, and I knew that, well . . ."

The end of our Friday fivesome. Panic. We would never find another suitable pub.

"I'm sure it's an outdoor cat," Martin assured her. I was shoving my chair back quietly prior to attempting to collar the beast, when that fan on the wall went *click-clack*. It simply opened its slats for a moment, then shut them again as if a strong buffet of wind had surged through from outside – though the weather had been clement when we drove up.

The cat skedaddled as if a bucket of water had been dumped on it.

"That's scuttled him. Thanks, fan. Must be turning blowy outside."

"We should go," said Alice.

"Till next week?" Anxious me.

"Oh yes," she promised. We all rose.

But outside the night was perfectly still. Not even a breeze.

The following Friday our trio of vehicles all arrived at almost the same time at the Roebuck. Under the bare chestnut tree standing sentinel by the car park, Charlotte inhaled.

"Is that your perfume, Alice? It's glorious."

It was indeed: rich, musky, wild, yet subtle nevertheless, like some treasure forever unattainable, unownable.

"A friend of mine runs a perfumery down in the Cotswolds," Alice told her. "This is a new creation."

"Could you possibly get me –?" began Charlotte. "No, don't. Never mind. It doesn't matter."

Of course not. If Charlotte wore that ravishing scent, what might Martin imagine? Alice didn't press her.

"I'm trying to give up smoking," added Charlotte as we headed through the November chill toward the door. "Tonight I think I'll do without."

This seeming nonsequitur was actually an intimate confidence between the two women; indeed between all of us. We mustn't pollute Alice's fragrance. The onus now lay on me to refrain from lighting up any of my slim panatelas.

I rechecked our host's name painted over the lintel of the door – John Chalmers, of course – though I needn't have bothered. I had to tinkle the bell on the counter several times before he came, seeming too preoccupied even to greet us beyond a few nods. As soon as I had extracted a couple of pints of Adnam's for Martin and me, a gin for Jenny, and a lowland single malt for Alice, Chalmers withdrew. Alice was a connoisseur of scotches; another grace note in her favor.

"I'd like to sit under the fan tonight," she announced.

So as to minimize her own fragrance diplomatically, symbolically? We sat at a table different from our usual one. Scarcely a couple of minutes passed before – *clunk-clack* – the slats of the fan sprang open, and the machinery sucked air.

"How odd," said Martin. "None of us is smoking, and it switches on."

"Maybe," I said recklessly to Alice, "it's breathing your scent in. Maybe it's in love with you."

Jenny darted me a dubious glance. The fan continued operating without ceasing, throbbing away, never shutting down.

Unaccountably John Chalmers kept wandering into the body of the bar, dusting ashtrays, adjusting the hang of hunting prints on the walls.

"What's up, man?" Martin asked the landlord during his third incursion.

"Tiger's gone missing. Our cat."

"Aaah," breathed Alice. "I meant to ask: Do you let that cat roam these rooms during the night?"

"The whole place gets a thorough vacuuming every morning," said our house-proud host.

Alice pursed her lips. "An old building. Nooks and crannies. Mice?"

"I have never found any dead vermin inside. Outside, I've found Tiger's trophies. What do you expect? Not in here, never. If there's any mice, he scares 'em off."

Alice continued gazing at him till he took umbrage. "Health inspector gave us a pat on the back last month. He's more interested in kitchens, but he said this was the most spick-and-span bar he'd seen in all the county." Chalmers wandered off, restaurantward.

When he had gone off, Martin pointed up at the busy Xtractall. "*There's* a tiny bit that isn't spick." A russet something – barely noticeable – had lodged between the edge of one slat and the housing.

"What is it?" Alice asked, in a need-to-know tone. Martin had to take off his shoes and clamber onto an upholstered chair, handkerchief in hand.

"Just you be careful of those fingers!" Charlotte called.

"S'all right. Safety grille inside. Stops idiots from mincing themselves." He pried with the hanky and stepped down. "Bit of ginger fur. Ugh, skin? Dried blood?" Hastily he folded the hanky over and plunged it deep in his pocket. I glanced anxiously at Alice, but she was smiling up at the fan.

Presently Charlotte started kidding Alice gently about the arty occult books published by Webster-Freeman. Charlotte had popped into a bookshop to buy new pages of her personal organizer, had happened upon a display of those volumes, and had skimmed through a few out of curiosity.

"What's the use of it all nowadays?" she asked. "Is it a spiritual thread in a material world? Gurus, psychedelics . . . But the sixties are gone forever."

Alice mused. "For a while it seemed as if the world would change. As if a new age were coming: of joy, the flesh, the mind, old values in a new incarnation. Instead, what came was plastic people making plastic money."

Was she criticizing us? We got on so *well* together. Yet there was always the edge of wondrous difference, as if Alice came from . . . elsewhere, outside of our ken.

"You could only have been a little girl in the sixties," protested Charlotte.

"Could I?" Alice craned her lovely neck to look at the Xtrac-tall. "I suppose that's a piece of the sixties. Soon it'll be replaced by some silent faceless box controlled by a microchip . . ."

"High time too," said Martin. "Can't imagine why Chalmers hangs on to the thing."

"He doesn't know why," said Alice. "He's one of the most neutral people I've ever seen. Till the usual restaurant crowd turn up, prattling about barn conversions and BMWs, this place is limbo. Imagine if the past could grow angry – bitter, like a disillusioned parent . . . yet still somehow hopeful and radiant too. In a schizophrenic way! Trying to keep the old faiths alive . . . And what if earlier epochs feel the same way about, say, the whole twentieth century? If those epochs still try to intrude and guide their offspring who have changed out of recognition? To keep the old flames alive. Smilingly, yet bitterly too."

"Er, how can the past keep watch on the present?" Martin asked with a grin. He thought a joke was due, but Alice stared at him quite seriously.

"The collective unconscious, which is timeless. The imprint of memory on material objects. Don't you think this is what angels and devils may be all about? Affirmative vibrations from the past – and negative, angry, twisted ones?"

"Beats me," said Martin. He laughed. "I always design vibrations out of buildings, mount 'em on shock absorbers, that sort of thing. Make sure there are no resonances likely to set people's teeth on edge."

My teeth were on edge. I felt that Alice was on the brink of revealing herself . . . to us, the chosen few. She was the joyous, positive spirit of an older world – and I wondered how old she really was. She liked us. She hoped for us. Yet for the most part the old world hated us?

She said to Charlotte, "I suppose Webster-Freeman's wisdom books must basically be about power, a power that has grown weak but still lingers on." I had the momentary weird impression that Alice herself had only leafed through those volumes, as casually as Charlotte had. "Power today is money, property, investments, plastic. Empty, dead power. Zombie power. Yet so vigorous. The world's soul is dying . . . of hunger. The plastic body thrives. That fan," she added, "may well be a creature of the sixties."

"Time to replace it," Martin said stoutly.

"And what did it replace? An ancient stone, a hungry old stone. Well," and she smiled sweetly, "must dash home in a few minutes and microwave some goodies. Mustn't we all?"

Was that what she would really do at home, wherever home was?

Before departing, Alice told a ridiculous joke about how to circumcise a whale. How? You use four skin divers. After booking a table in the restaurant for the following Friday, to sample the oysters and partridge, we left contented.

"Alice was in an odd mood tonight," Jenny remarked after we got home. "She *was* just kidding, don't you think?"

"I think that was the real Alice. But I don't know if Alice is real, the way we are."

Jenny giggled. "Do we imagine her every Friday? Is she the soul that's missing from our lives?"

"Not exactly. We're her hope . . . for something. Some . . . rekindling." I thought of flames, and a naked woman dancing, leaping the fire, singeing her public hair. "And yet . . . we don't matter too much to her. That place matters more. Chalmers's pub. The limbo pub, at that empty hour. That's what binds us together."

"*You* aren't hoping for something from her, are you?" she asked archly.

"No, You know that would ruin—" I had been about to say "the magic." I said instead, "The happy hour. Maybe," I added, "without us it's difficult for her to make contact with the modern world."

"Come off it! Charlotte met her on the train from Euston. Alice is in publishing. In business."

*Is she?* I wondered. Alice spoke as if she had been at home in the sixties . . . not just a little girl back then, but herself as now.

And I suspected, crazily, that she had existed in earlier times too.

Charlotte had met Alice on the train, Had any of us bumped into Alice *again*, either on the London-bound train or the return one? I knew I hadn't. I had glimpsed Alice coming out of MK Station, and also cruising for parking in her Saab; yet I had never seen her anywhere on the platform at Euston. Given the rush and the crowding, that wasn't totally odd in itself – unless none of us had ever coincided with Alice after that first occasion. Certainly Jenny had never mentioned doing so.

I refrained from asking. We microwaved duck *à l'orange*, went to bed, and made love the same way we usually made love on a Friday night. When Jen and I were making love, I never thought about Alice, never visualized her – as if I were forbidden to, as if Alice could reach out and control me. Only afterwards did I lie awake wondering about angels and demons – contrasting values in the same equation – as messages, vibrations from the past intent on charming or savaging the present day, but not widely so, only marginally, except where a magical intersection of persons and places occurred.

On Monday I had some hard talking to do to some visiting Hungarians, though I mustn't be too stringent. I enjoyed the hospitality in Hungary.

Next Friday, in the Roebuck, we had already scrutinized the menu through in the bar, and ordered. Jenny and Charlotte went off together to the ladies' room. I myself was overcome by an urgent need to piss. So, apparently, was Martin. Martin and I both apologized simultaneously to Alice and fled to relieve ourselves, leaving her alone. Until then the fan had remained tight-lipped. *Clunk-clack*, I heard as we retreated.

It was a long, strong piss for both of us. Martin and I left one urinal basin untenanted between us: a kind of ceramic sword laid not between knight and lady but between squire and squire, both of us being chaste, faithful squires of Alice. Let us get up to no monkey business together. It's odd that women can waltz off together to the ladies' as a sort of social event, whereas chaps should do no such thing, as if mutual urination is a queer sign. Have the boys gone off together to compare their organs? In this case, need dictated.

As we were walking back, bladders emptied out, I heard the fan shut off and close itself. The bar proved to be deserted. We assumed that Alice had followed our wives to the powder room. We chatted about the innovative design of a new office block currently soaring near Euston Station. People were christening it "the totem pole." Then our ladies returned without sight of Alice.

In case Chalmers had summoned us and Alice had gone ahead to the restaurant, I checked there, in vain. Chalmers's wife ducked out from the kitchen to remark that I was a little early. I checked the car park, where Alice's Saab sat in darkness.

"Can't find her anywhere, folks!" I spotted Alice's silvery purse lying on the carpet. Before I could go to retrieve it, Martin hurried to my side and gripped my arm.

"Look at the fan," he whispered fiercely.

The slats of the Xtractall were moving in and out gently one by one, top to bottom, in an undulating fashion. I thought of someone sucking their teeth. The edge of each slat was streaked crimson, thin lines that faded, even as I watched, as if being absorbed or licked away atom by atom.

"Are my eyes playing tricks?"

"What do *you* think, Derrick?"

"You aren't suggesting—?"

"I bloody well am. I've been doing some stiff thinking about Alice since her spiel last week—"

"*Stiff* thinking?"

He looked exasperated. "I never get a hard-on thinking about her. Fact is, I can't seem to, whatever Charlotte may imagine."

"Me neither."

"She's an enchantress. Supernatural. I mean it, old son. Haven't you suspected?"

I nodded cautiously. This wasn't *quite* the thing to admit to one another.

"I thought she might be a modern-day witch," I said. "Despite commuting to Euston and driving a Saab. Type of books she publishes, you know?" I was only telling him a quarter of the truth. Since last weekend I had thought ever more about "angels" and "devils" – for want of better names! – about benign and angry vibrations from a past that had been disenfranchised, in a kind of time-crossed disinheritance: the plastic children forsaking the memory of the parent. Alice was more than any latter-day witch – and less, because she wasn't of our time at all, in spite of her modern gear and jokes.

"Not a witch, Derrick. A *lamia*. As in Keats's poem. Had to read that at school. A female spirit who preys on travelers."

"She never preyed on us."

"Just so. She was being a good girl with us. Friday evening was her leisure time, her friendly hour. She *stopped* us from feeling, well, lustful."

"What are you two arguing about?" asked Charlotte. She and Jenny couldn't see the fan without turning. "Did one of you say something to Alice that you shouldn't? Something to offend her?"

"No, damn it," swore Martin.

"But something did go wrong," I insisted, "and she melted away."

"No!" He grabbed and shook me. Jenny started up, fearing that we were about to have a brawl – about Alice, right in front of our wives. "You don't get it, do you?" His face leered into mine. "The fan ate her. It fell in love with her just like you said – and it consumed her. It sucked her into itself."

"It—?"

"The bloody fan!"

By now the slats of the Xtractall were quite clean, and no longer made that munching motion.

Charlotte also leapt up. "You're mad!"

"Get away from under that fan, love," begged Martin. "Remember the cat that went missing? Remember how Alice hated cats? The fan ate the cat up for her – we found that scrap of bloody fur up there, right? – and Alice knew; she knew."

I recalled Alice's smile, directed at the fan.

"One night last week the fan extracted poor old Tiger," he went on. "Remember what Alice said about how the fan replaced a hungry old stone? Something up there is kin to her."

A demon, I thought – to her angel. But both of them aspects of the past, still wooing the present weakly, in friendly or venomous guise.

"That thing's much more powerful than Alice guessed," insisted Martin. "When we all went off to the toilets – and who sent us, her or the fan? – it sucked her in because it wanted her."

What Charlotte did next was either quite stupid or remarkably brave. Of course, she did not see Alice the way we fellows saw her. Maybe women couldn't. She kicked off her shoes, burrowed in her own bag for a neglected pack of cigarettes, lit one, and mounted a chair.

"That's impossible," she said. "Physically impossible – leaving aside the wild idea of an extractor fan falling in love." Charlotte puffed smoke at the blank face of the fan.

"The cat fur," Martin protested.

*Clunk-clack*: The fan opened up. The mechanism whirred. Smoke disappeared. Charlotte never flinched. She flicked her lighter for illumination. Daringly she teased two long fingernails between the slats and tugged. Several strong black strands of hair came free.

"Oh," she said, and jumped down. "Is this some joke the two of you cooked up with Alice? Is she waiting outside the door stifling her giggles?"

Martin crossed his heart like a child. And Charlotte faltered. I was wrong: Each in our way we must have been thinking along similar lines about Alice. Our ladies had both been resisting such conclusions.

"It's still impossible," Charlotte said, "unless the fan leads somewhere else than just to the ordinary outside. And unless it changes what it takes. Unless it etherializes stuff instead of merely making mincemeat! Maybe it does. What was the landlord saying about never finding any mice? How can that be a magic fan? How?"

By now Jenny was caught up in our conviction. "We can't call the police. They would think we were insane. We don't even know Alice's surname, let alone where she—"

I had remembered the purse and swooped. I emptied it on a table over the beer mats. Car keys. Cosmetics. Tiny bottle of perfume. Ten- and twenty-pound notes, but no loose change. A tarnished old medallion. No driver's license, no cheque book, no hint of her full name or where she lived.

"At least we have the car keys," said Martin.

"There'll be no clues in her car," I told him. "She isn't any ordinary human being."

"Oh, we know that already, Derrick darling." My wife's tone was somewhat spiced with irony.

"She's a supernatural being. Didn't we know it all along?" I was echoing Martin, but those had been my sentiments anyway.

Charlotte didn't disagree with my assessment, however sceptical she may have seemed before. "And she's our friend," she reminded me. "*Was*, at any rate! So two supernatural forces have collided here—"

"Or come together. Like the poles of a magnet, like anode and cathode."

"What do you suppose our landlord knows about that fan?"

I laughed. "Our Mr. Chalmers doesn't realize the fan's possessed. He thinks Tiger was a demon mouser. I doubt he knows much about the stone that was drilled to dust to make space for the fan. The ancient stone, the sacrifice stone." A hard pain in my left hand alerted me to the fact that I was clutching that medallion from Alice's purse. As I opened my palm, the pain numbed to a cold tingling.

"Carry on." Charlotte eyed the metal disc intently, an amulet from some ancient time.

Words struggled to the surface like flotsam from a shipwreck. Don't hold them down. Relax. Let them bob up.

"The vibrations of the sacred stone imbued that space up there. When the stone was destroyed, the force possessed the fan that replaced it. At least a fan could *do* something, unlike a block of stone. It could open up a channel – to somewhere – a feeding channel. No one had fed the stone for centuries. It lay neglected, inert. Some Elizabethan builder picked it up and used it as part of the pub wall. It stayed inert. It was hungry, weak. It was the demon side of . . . the angry past. But it was kin to Alice."

I was holding Alice's medallion out blatantly, like a compass. The disc was so worn that its face was almost smooth; I could barely make out faint symbols unknown to me. A coin from the realm of magic, I thought, from the domain of lamias and hungry spirits. The inscription was well-nigh erased. How had Alice kept her vitality so long? By connecting with people such as us? Preying on some, befriending others?

Jenny touched the piece of metal and recoiled as if stung. "It's freezing."

"That space up there is dangerous," said Charlotte, who had so boldly shone a light into it. "Still, it didn't bite my fingers off. It only reacts to some stimuli – Alice being the biggest stimulus of all, eh, fellows?"

"It took her by surprise," I said. "It was playing possum till we went to the toilet; till the vibrations tickled our bladders. Or maybe that was Alice's doing. She wanted to be alone with it. It overwhelmed her."

She had been well aware of it, must have sensed its true nature when we first brought her here. She was flesh; it was an object – her malign counterpart, which nevertheless yearned for her. She wanted to commune with a kindred force, but imagined she was stronger.

"We want her back, don't we?" Charlotte went on. "This is the machine age, right? We know machines. That thing's out of synch with the age."

"What are you driving at?" Martin asked his wife.

"You're a dab hand at fixing things, aren't you?" She jerked a thumb at the leaded window behind the bar counter. A NO VACANCIES sign hung facing us. Consequently anyone approaching from outside would read the alternative invitation, VACANCIES. "We'll spend the night here. You have a tool box in the car. When all's completely quiet, we'll sneak down, do a spot of dismantling, and reverse those damned fan blades so that the air blows into this room, not out. Air, and whatever else."

"Cigarette and cigar smoke is like foul incense to it," I found myself saying.

"She'll come back minced," muttered Jenny. "Spread all over the floor, sticking to the walls."

"Why should she? If it can take her apart, it can put her back together! We must try," insisted Charlotte.

We were blunderers. We were the opposite of stone-age man placed cold before the instrument panel of a Saab or Jaguar. We were techno-man faced with the stone and blood controls of some old, alternative world of spirit forces.

Chalmers appeared, and announced, "Your table's ready. If you'd like to come through?"

"I'm afraid there'll only be four of us," said Martin.

"Did the other lady leave? This *is* the time you booked for."

"I know. She was called away. A friend came for her. She had to leave her car. We'll see to that tomorrow."

Chalmers raised an eyebrow.

"Fact is," blustered Martin, "we'd like to enjoy a bit of a celebration. Special occasion! Do you have two double rooms free for the night? Don't want the police stopping us afterward. Breathalyzing us. Can't risk that."

The landlord brightened. "We do, as it happens."

"We'll take them."

"Mr. Chalmers," said Charlotte, "out of curiosity, why did you mount that fan in that particular position?"

"Had to put it somewhere didn't we? That was the first year we came here, oh . . . a long while ago. As I recall, the plaster up there was prone to staining. Dark damp stains. The stone behind was . . ." He wrinkled his nose. "Oozy." Changing the subject, he waved at the counter. "If you get thirsty during the night," he joked, "help yourselves. You're regulars. Guests can drink anytime. Just leave a note for me to tot up."

Charlotte beamed at him. "Thank you very much, Mr. Chalmers."

Yes, I thought, we're all raving insomniacs. We'll certainly be holding a quiet party down here at two in the morning.

"My pleasure. Will you come this way?"

If we were supposed to be celebrating, Chalmers and his wife and the pair of waitresses from the village must have decided that the Roebuck's cuisine wasn't our pleasure that evening, to judge from how we picked at it. Or else we were engaged in a peculiar silent quarrel about the choice of fare. However, we did sink some wine, almost a bottle apiece. As we toyed with our food, the restaurant began to fill up with local subgentry enjoying a night out. When we returned to the other room for coffee, the place was crowded and the fan was busily sucking smoke out. Incense of drugful death, I thought, wondering whether this might be a phrase from Keats.

Jenny and I lay stiffly on top of the bedspread, never quite sinking below the surface of sleep. Eventually our wristwatch alarms roused us. Soon Charlotte tapped at our door. She had a torch. We tiptoed down creaky though carpet-muffled stairs to rendezvous with Martin, who had switched on the dim wall lamps in the bar and was up on a chair, scrutinizing the surface of the Xtractall with a powerful torch beam. Before we went up to our separate bedrooms, he had fetched his tool kit – nonchalantly, as though the metal box was a suitcase containing our absent pajamas and nighties.

"Charlotte," he said, "nip behind the counter and find the switch for the fan. It's bound to be labelled. Make sure that it's off. Not that being off might make much difference!"

"Why not?"

"How do mice get sucked into it overnight?"

"*If* they do," I said. I should have followed this thought through. I should have pursued this possibility. I should have!

"Fan's off," she stage-whispered.

"Right. Up on a chair, Derrick. Hold the torch."

I complied, and Martin unscrewed the housing, then removed the safety grille.

"'Course, it mightn't be possible to reverse the action . . ." Perspiration beaded his brow. He wasn't looking forward to plunging his hands into the works. "Hold the beam steady. Ye-ssss. The mounting unfastens here, and here. Slide it out. Turn it round. Bob's your uncle."

He worked away. Presently he withdrew the inner assembly gingerly, reversed it, slid it back inside.

"I keep imagining Alice walking in," said Jenny. "What silly jokers we would seem. What a studenty sort of prank, gimmicking a fan so that cold and smoke blow *into* the pub!"

Martin unclenched his teeth. "If Alice tried to come through the front door now, she'd probably set off a burglar alarm . . . There we are! Pass the grille up, Jenny, will you? Now the slats. It's got to be just the way it was before . . ."

We both stepped down and cleared the chairs away, then hauled a table aside to clear a space, as if Alice would simply float down from that little opening above, her feet coming to rest lightly on the carpet.

"Switch the power on, Charlotte. Got a cigar handy, Derrick?"

When I shook my head, Charlotte brought a pack from behind the counter, stripping the cellophane wrapper with her nails. Lighting a panatela, I didn't merely let the smoke uncurl. I sucked and blew out powerfully.

"Let's all hold hands and wish," suggested Jenny.

We did so. Me, puffing away like a chimney, Jenny, Martin, and Charlotte. What silly jokers.

*Clunk-clack.* The slat opened and the fan whirred, blowing a dusty breeze down at our faces. The noise of the mechanism altered. Without actually becoming louder, the fan seemed to rev up as if a furious turbine were spinning inside the wall almost beyond the pitch of our ears. Our chorus line retreated. Then it happened.

Matter gushed through the slats of the fan – bubbling, convulsing substances, brown and white and crimson, blobs of yellow, strands of ginger and black – which all coalesced into a surging column of confusion struggling to reassemble itself before our eyes.

"Alice!" squealed Jenny.

The thing before us was Alice, and it wasn't Alice. It was her, and it was a cat, and it was mice and iridescent black beetles and spiders and flies, whatever the fan had swallowed. The shape was human, and most of the mass was Alice, but the rest was fur and wings and tiny legs and all else, melted together, interwoven with scraps of clothing, black hair growing out at random. I was too appalled to scream.

The Alice-creature jerked brown lips apart as if tearing a hole in its head, and *it* might have wanted to shriek. The noise that emerged was a coughing, strangled growl. Facetted eyes ranged the room. And us; and us.

"We're sorry!" babbled Martin. "We're so sorry. Tell us what to do!"

Unbidden, I knew. Terrified, I snatched from my pocket the medallion and the keys to the Saab and tossed these onto the table nearest to the half-human creature.

Her fingers seized the keys. Her legs took her to the front door. Her hand unlatched and unbolted the door – so she was still intelligent. Tearing the front door open, she fled into darkness.

A few moments later an engine roared, headlamps stabbed the night, tyres gouged gravel. Her Saab slewed its way onto the road. It was Martin who shut the door and relocked it – he had been wrong about burglar alarms. There were none.

"What have we done?" moaned Jenny.

"Maybe we saved her from something worse," I said. "Maybe she knows how to heal herself. She left her medallion . . . why would she do that?"

Martin groaned and sat down heavily. "You don't need fucking jewelry when your body's glistening with bits of beetles."

I gathered the worn, cryptic medal up. "This is much more than jewelry. We'd better keep it."

"No," mumbled my wife, as I dropped the disc into my jacket pocket.

"It would be terrible not to have it to give to her if she comes back."

"It could *lead* that thing to us, Derrick."

"What's going on?" John Chalmers had come down-stairs, attired in a paisley dressing gown and, God help us, a nightcap with dangling tassel. He seemed to be holding something behind his back – a cudgel, a shotgun? He moved in behind the counter and laid down whatever it was.

"Our friend came back for her car," Charlotte attempted to explain. "We're sorry we woke you."

"You're all fully dressed. You weren't intending to . . . depart?"

"You said we could partake of a late drink if we wished, Mr. Chalmers."

"Mm. Screwdrivers?"

For one stupid moment I imagined he was offering to fix cocktails for us. However, he was eyeing Martin's tools, still lying in view.

Charlotte was quick on the uptake. "Our friend's car needed fixing. That's why she had to leave it earlier."

Chalmers shook his head skeptically.

"I'd like a brandy, please," she told him. Her hand was straying automatically to the shoulder bag she had brought down with her, hunting in it . . .

"Don't smoke, love!" Martin said urgently. "If you have any, don't light up! Make that two brandies, will you? Doubles."

"Same for us," I said.

As Chalmers busied himself, Martin nodded significantly at the fan. It was still set to blow, not suck. Could anything else emerge from between those slats? Or was the eerie zone beyond its blades, the zone of the past, empty now? Where the hell had my panatela gone? I was dimly aware of discarding it when the fan began to gush. Ah – it was lying in an ashtray. Gone out, by the look of it. Nevertheless, I crushed the cigar into extinction. How could we put the fan to rights? Chalmers would be on the alert till daybreak. We couldn't. We would have to abandon the Roebuck in the morning, abandon and never come back. We gulped our brandies and trooped upstairs.

Next morning, haggard and exhausted, we ate bacon and eggs in the restaurant, paid our bills, and went out to the two cars. The day was bright and crisp; frost lingered.

"So, no more Fridays for us," Martin said dully. "Get rid of that medallion, will you, Derrick?"

"Alice may need it," I said.

"She may need us, she may need you," said Charlotte, "but not in the same way as before."

We parted and drove off from the Roebuck through the dead, cold countryside.

Jenny worked on me all weekend about that wretched medallion until I did promise to dispose of it. On Monday morning, walking through London to work, I dropped the worn disc down a sewer grating.

That night I dreamed about Alice, the Alice we had known before. This time she beckoned me lasciviously toward a doorway. She dropped her clothing. Naked, she invited me.

On Tuesday, prior to a meeting with some Japanese about supplies of Butadiene, Martin phoned me at the office.

"A car followed me home last night, Derrick. It hung well back, but when I was passing through—" – he mentioned a village with some decent street lighting – "I'm sure it was a Saab. Thought I'd better tip you off, eh? I've been thinking . . ." He sounded furtive. "I've been thinking about Alice. She never knew where we lived, did she?"

"I'm not sure she wanted to know."

"She knows now, so far as I'm concerned." He rang off.

Martin didn't phone again – though I made a call, to Webster-Freeman, publishers. They had never heard of an Alice. I wasn't surprised.

It's Friday night, and I'm driving home on my own, listening to Vivaldi's *Four Seasons*. It's the time that should be the happy hour. Jenny and I both took our cars to MK today. Headlights are following me, always keeping the same distance behind whether I speed up or slow down. If Alice comes calling, what do I give to her now?

Since Monday I've been increasingly haunted by mental snapshots of the old Alice. The other day I heard on the radio how the average male thinks about sex eight times an hour; that's how often Alice crosses my mind.

I realize that I've fallen in love – or in lust – with her. Does Martin secretly feel the same way – for his "lamia"? These feelings overpower me as surely as I was possessed in the pub that night by an urge to piss, the need to release myself. Even after what happened, maybe Alice left that medallion behind to protect us – from the altered lamia? Now that token no longer does so.

Ahead there's a lay-by where a caravan is parked permanently: Sally's Café, serving breakfast to truck drivers all day long – but not by night, when it's locked up, shuttered, abandoned.

I'm pulling in, and braking fifty yards past the caravan. Will the car in my mirror overshoot, pass by? No. It pulls in too. It parks abreast of Sally's Café, douses its lights. A Saab, I'd say.

The driver's door swings open. Soon I may understand all about Alice and her domain, which we first denied, then stupidly desecrated. Has the past's love of us all turned sour now? Grown vicious?

A dark, amorphous figure emerges from the Saab, and rushes toward me. I'll let her in. The Alice we knew always appreciated jokes. The final joke is: I've become an almighty fan of hers. Will I have time to tell her? To hear her laugh – or shriek? I open the door. I can't help myself.

# 3

# SHADOWY CORNERS

## Accounts of Restless Spirits

# The Ankardyne Pew

## W. F. Harvey

### Prospectus

**Address:** Ankardyne House, Garvington, Worcestershire, England.

**Property:** Early eighteenth-century gentlemen's residence. Imposing building with numerous rooms and servants' quarters. It has exceptional views across the neighbouring fens. The house is also linked to the local church by an underground flagged passageway.

**Viewing Date:** February 1890.

**Agent:** William Fryer Harvey (1885–1937) was born in Yorkshire, educated at Balliol College Oxford, and won a medal for gallantry during World War I. He is best remembered for a single, much anthologised and filmed horror story, "The Beast with Five Fingers" – despite having written numerous other weird stories, collected in *The Beast With Five Fingers* (1928), *Midnight Tales* (1946) and *The Arm of Mrs. Egan* (1952). Houses and inns disturbed by ghosts occur in several of his tales, notably "The Heart of the Fire", "Midnight House" and "The Ankardyne Pew", which describes the events at an old mansion haunted by the most ominous noises and sounds.

The following narrative of the occurrences that took place at Ankardyne House in February 1890, is made up chiefly of extracts from letters written by my friend, the Rev. Thomas Prendergast, to his wife, immediately before taking up residence at the vicarage, together with transcripts from the diary which I kept at the time. The names throughout are, of course, fictitious.

*February 9th.* I am sorry that I had no opportunity yesterday of getting over to the vicarage, so your questions – I have not lost the list – must remain unanswered. It is almost a quarter of a mile away from the church, in the village. You see, the church, unfortunately, is in the grounds of the park, and there is a flagged passage, cold and horribly draughty, that leads from Ankardyne House to the great loose box of the Ankardyne pew. The squires in the old days could come in late and go out early, or even stay away altogether, without any one being the wiser. The whole situation of the church is bad and typically English – the House of God in the squire's pocket. Why should he have right of secret access? I haven't had time to examine the interior – early eighteenth-century, I should guess – but as we drove up last evening in the dusk, the tall gloomy façade of Ankardyne House, with the elegant little church – a Wren's nest – adjoining it, made me think of a wicked uncle, setting off for a walk in the woods with one of the babes. The picture is really rather apt, as you will agree, when you see the place. It's partly a question of the height of the two buildings, partly a question of the shape of the windows, those of the one square, deep-set, and grim; of the other round – the raised eyebrows of startled innocence.

We were quite wrong about Miss Ankardyne. She is a charming little lady, not a trace of Lady Catherine de Bourgh, and is really looking forward to having you as her nearest neighbour. I will write more of her to-morrow, but the stable clock has struck eleven and my candle is burning low.

*February 10th.* I measured the rooms as you asked me to. They are, of course, larger than ours at Garvington, and will swallow all our furniture and carpets. But you will like the vicarage. It, at least, is a cheerful house; faces south, and isn't, like this place, surrounded by woods. I suppose familiarity with the skies and wide horizons of the fens accounts for the shut-in feeling one gets here. But I have never seen such cedars!

And now to describe Miss Ankardyne. She is perhaps seventy-five, *petite* and bird-like, with the graceful, alert poise of a bird. I should say that sight and hearing are abnormally acute and have helped to keep her young. She is a good talker, well read, and interested in affairs, and a still better listener. Parson's pride! you will exclaim; since we are only two, and if she listens, I must talk. But I mean what I say. All that the archdeacon told us is true; you are conscious in her presence of a living spirit of peace. By the way, she is an interesting example of your theory that there are some people for whom animals have an instinctive dislike – indeed, the best example I have met. For Miss Ankardyne tells me that, though since childhood she has had a fondness for all living creatures, especially for birds, it is one which is not at first reciprocated. She can, after assiduous, continuous persevering, win their affection; her spaniel, her parrot, and Karkar, the tortoiseshell cat, are obviously attached to her. But strange dogs snarl, if she attempts to fondle them; and she tells me that, when she goes to the farm to feed the fowls, the birds seem to sense her coming and *run from the scattered corn.* I have heard of cows showing this antipathy to individuals, but never before of birds. There is an excellent library here, that badly needs cataloguing. The old vicar, had, I believe, begun the task at the time of his fatal seizure.

I have been inside the church. Anything less like dear old Garvington it would be impossible to find. Architecturally, it has its points, but the unity of design, on which everything here depends, is broken by the Ankardyne pew. Its privacy is an abomination. Even from the pulpit it is impossible to see inside, and I can well believe the stories of the dicing squires and their Sunday play. Miss Ankardyne refuses to use it. The glass is crude and uninteresting; but there is an uncommon chancel screen of Spanish workmanship, which somehow seems in keeping with the place. I wish it didn't.

We shall miss the old familiar monuments. There is no snub-nosed crusader here, no worthy Elizabethan knight, like our Sir John Parkington, kneeling in supplication, with those nicely balanced families on right and left. The tombs are nearly all

Ankardyne tombs – urns, weeping charities, disconsolate relicts, and all the cold Christian virtues. You know the sort. The Ten Commandments are painted on oak panels on either side of the altar. From the Ankardyne pew I doubt if you can see them.

*February 11th.* You ask about my neuritis. It is better, despite the fact that I have been sleeping badly. I wake up in the morning, sometimes during the night, with a burning headache and a curious tingling feeling about the tongue, which I can only attribute to indigestion. I am trying the effect of a glass of hot water before retiring. When we move into the vicarage, we shall at least be spared the attention of the owls, which make the nights so dismal here. The place is far too shut in by trees, and I suppose, too, that the disused outbuildings give them shelter. Cats are bad enough, but I prefer the sound of night-walkers to night-fliers. It won't be long now before we meet. They are getting on splendidly with the vicarage. The painters have already started work; the new kitchen range has come, and is only waiting for the plumbers to put it in. Miss Ankardyne is leaving for a visit to friends in a few days' time. It seems that she always goes away about this season of the year – wise woman! – so I shall be alone next week. She said Dr. Hulse would be glad to put me up, if I find the solitude oppressive, but I shan't trouble him. You would like the old butler. His name is Mason, and his wife – a Scotchwoman – acts as housekeeper. The three maids are sisters. They have been with Miss Ankardyne for thirty years, and are everything that maids should be. They belong to the Peculiar People. I cannot desire that they should be orthodox. If I could be sure that Dr. Hulse was as well served . . .

*February 13th.* I had an experience last night which moved me strangely. I hardly know what to make of it. I went to bed at half-past ten after a quiet evening with Miss Ankardyne. I thought she seemed in rather poor spirits, and tried to cheer her by reading aloud. She chose a chapter from *The Vicar of Wakefield.* I awoke soon after one with an intolerable feeling of oppression, almost of dread. I was conscious, too – and in some way my alarm was associated with this – of a burning, tingling, piercing pain in my tongue. I got up from bed and was about to pour myself out a glass of water, when I heard the sound of someone speaking. The voice was low and continuous, and seemed to come from an adjoining room. I slipped on my dressing-gown and, candle in hand, went out into the corridor. For a moment I stood in silence. Frankly, I was afraid. The voice proceeded from a room two doors away from mine. As I listened, I recognized it as Miss Ankardyne's. She was repeating the Benedicite.

There were such depths of sadness, so much of the weariness of defeat in this song of triumph of the Three Children saved from the furnace of fire, that I felt I could not leave her. I should have spoken before knocking, for I could almost feel that gasp of fear. "Oh, no!" she said, "Oh, no! Not now!" and then, as if bracing herself for a great effort: "Who is it?"

I told her and she bade me enter. The poor little woman had risen from her knees and was trembling from head to foot. I spent about an hour with her and left her sleeping peacefully. I did not wish to rouse the house, but I managed to find the Masons' room and arranged for Mrs. Mason to sit by the old lady.

I can't say what happened in that hour we spent together in talk and in prayer. There is something very horrible about this house, that Miss Ankardyne is dimly aware of. Something connected with pain and fire and a bird, and something that was human too. I was shaken to the very depths of my being. I don't think I ever felt the need for prayer and the power of prayer as I did last night. The stable clock has just struck five.

*February 14th.* I have arranged for Miss Ankardyne to go away to-morrow. She is fit to travel, and is hardly fit to stay. I had a long talk with her this morning. I think she is the most courageous woman I know. All her life she has felt that the house is haunted, and all her life she has felt pity for that which haunts it. She says that she is sure that she is living it down; that the house is better than it was; but that at this season of the year it is almost too much for her. She is anxious that I should stay with Dr. Hulse. I feel, however, that I must see this business through. She then suggested that I should invite a friend to stay with me. I thought of Pellow. You remember how we were obliged to postpone his visit last September. I had a letter from him only last Friday. He is living in this part of the world and could probably run over for a day or two.

The extracts from Mr. Prendergast's letters end here. The following are excerpts from my diary:

*February 16th.* Arrived at Ankardyne House at midday. Prendergast had meant to meet me at the station, but had been suddenly called away to visit a dying parishioner. I had in consequence a couple of hours by myself in which to form an impression of the place. The house dates from the early eighteenth century. It is dignified though sombre, and is closely surrounded on three sides by shrubberies of rhododendrons and laurel, that merge into thick woods. The cedars in the park must be older than any of the buildings. Miss Ankardyne, I gather, has lived here all her life, and the house gives you the impression of having been lived in, a slightly sinister mansion, well aired by a kindly soul. There is a library that should be well worth exploring. The family portraits are in the dining-room. None are of outstanding interest. The most unusual feature of the house is its connection with the church, which has many of the characteristics of a private chapel. It does not actually abut on the building, but is joined to it by a low, curved façade, unpierced by windows. A corridor, lighted from above, runs behind the façade and gives a private entry from the house to the church. The door into this corridor opens into the spacious hall of Ankardyne House; but there is a second mode of access (of which Prendergast seemed unaware) from Miss Ankardyne's bed-chamber down a narrow stair. This door is kept locked and has never been opened, as far as Mason, the butler, can recollect. The church, with the curved façade connecting it to the house, is balanced on the other side by the coach-house and stables, which can be approached in a similar manner from the kitchens. The architect has certainly succeeded in conveying the idea that religion and horseflesh can be made elegant adjuncts to the life of a country gentleman. Prendergast came in just before luncheon. He does not look well, and was obviously glad to see me and to unburden himself. In the afternoon I had a long talk with Mason, the butler, a very level-headed man.

From what Prendergast tells me I gather that Miss Ankardyne's experiences have been both auditory and visual. They are certainly vague.

*Auditory*. The cry of a bird – sometimes she thinks it is an owl, sometimes a cock – sometimes a human cry with something bird-like in it. This she has heard almost as long as she can remember, both outside the house and inside her room, but most frequently in the direction of the corridor that leads to the church. The cry is chiefly heard at night, hardly ever before dusk. (This would point to an owl.) It has become less frequent of recent years, but at this particular season is most persistent. Mason confirms this. He doesn't like the sound, and doesn't know what to make of it. The maids believe that it is an evil spirit; but, as it can have no power over them – they belong to the Peculiar People – they take no notice of it.

*Visual and Sensory*. From time to time – less frequently, again, of recent years – Miss Ankardyne wakes up "with her eyes balls of fire." She can distinguish nothing clearly for several minutes. Then the red spheres slowly contract to pin-pricks; there is a moment of sharp pain; and normal vision is restored. At other times she is aroused from sleep by a sharp, piercing pain in her tongue. She has consulted several oculists, who find that her sight is perfectly normal. I believe she has never known a day's illness. Prendergast seems to have had a similar, though less vivid, experience; he used the term "burning" headache.

I have elicited from Mason the statement that animals dislike the house, with the exception of Karkar, Miss Ankardyne's cat, who seems entirely unaffected. The spaniel refuses to sleep in Miss Ankardyne's bedroom; and on one occasion, when the parrot's cage was brought up there, the bird "fell into such a screaming fit, that it nearly brought the house down." This I believe, for I tried the experiment myself with the reluctant consent of Mrs. Mason. The feathers of the bird lay back flat on its head and neck with rage, and then it began to shriek in a really horrible way.

All this, of course, is very vague. We have no real evidence of anything supernatural. What impresses me most is the influence of the house on a woman of Miss Ankardyne's high character and courage.

*February 18th.* Certainly an interesting night. After a long walk with Prendergast in the afternoon I went to bed early with a volume of Trollope and a long candle. I did what I have never done before – fell asleep with the candle burning. When I awoke, it was within an inch of the socket; the fire had settled into a dull glow. Close to the candlestick on the table by my bedside stood a carafe of water. As I lay in bed, too sleepy to move, I was conscious of the hypnotic effect induced by gazing into a crystal. Slowly the surface of the glass grew dim and then gradually cleared from the centre. I was looking into the interior of a building, which I at once recognized as Ankardyne church. I could make out the screen and the Ankardyne pew. It seemed to be night, though I could see more clearly than if it had been night – the monuments in the aisle, for example. There were not as many as there are now. Presently the door of the Ankardyne pew opened and a man stepped out. He was dressed in black coat and knee-breeches, such as a clergyman might have worn a century or more ago. In one hand he held a lighted candle, the flame of which he sheltered with the other. I judged him to be of middle age. His face wore an expression of extreme apprehension. He crossed the church, casting backward glances as he went, and stopped before one of the mural monuments in the south aisle. Then, placing his candle on the ground, he drew from his pocket a hammer and some tools and, kneeling on the ground, began to work feverishly at the base of the inscription. When he had finished, and the task was not long, he seemed to moisten a finger and, running it along the floor, rubbed the dust into the newly cut stone. He then picked up his tools and began to retrace his steps. But the wind seemed to have risen; he had difficulty in shielding the flame of the candle, and just before he regained the door of the Ankardyne pew, it went out.

That was all that I saw in the crystal. I was now wide awake. I got out of bed, put fresh fuel on the fire, and wrote this account in my diary, while the picture was still vivid.

*February 19th.* Slept splendidly, despite the fact that I was prepared to spend a wakeful night. After a late breakfast I went with Prendergast into the church and had no difficulty in identifying the monument. It is in the east end of the south aisle, immediately opposite the Ankardyne pew and partly hidden by the American organ. The inscription reads:

> IN MEMORY OF FRANCIS ANKARDYNE, ESQUIRE, of Ankardyne Hall, in the County of Worcester, late Captain in His Majesty's 42nd Regiment of Foot.
> He departed this life 27th February 1781.
> Rev. xiv. 12, 13.

I brought the Bible from the lectern. "Here are lives," said Prendergast, "which can fitly be commemorated by such verses: 'Here is the patience of the saints; here are they that keep the commandments of God.' Miss Ankardyne's is one. And I suppose,' he added, "that there may be some of whom the eleventh verse is true." He read it out to me: "And the smoke of their torment ascendeth for ever and ever; and they have no rest day nor night, who worship the beast and his image, and whosever receiveth the mark of his name."

I thought at first that he was right; that the 12 might originally have been engraved as 11. But closer scrutiny showed that, though some of the figures had certainly been tampered with, it was not either the 2 or the 3. Prendergast hit on what I believe is the right solution. "The R," he said, "has been superimposed on an L, and the I was originally 5. The reference is to Leviticus xiv. 52, 53." If he is correct, we have still far to go. I have read and reread those verses so often during the day, that I can write them down from memory:

"And he shall cleanse the house with the blood of the bird, and with the running water, and with the living bird, and with the cedar wood, and with the hyssop, and with the scarlet:

"But he shall let go the living bird out of the city into the open fields, and make an atonement for the house; and it shall be clean."

Miss Ankardyne told Prendergast that she was dimly aware of something connected with pain and fire and a bird. It is at least a curious coincidence.

Mason knows nothing about Francis Ankardyne except his name. He tells me that the Ankardyne squires of a hundred years ago had a reputation for evil living; in that, of course, they were not peculiar.

Spent the afternoon in the library in a rather fruitless search for clues. I found two books with the name "Francis Ankardyne" written on the fly-leaf. It was perhaps just as well that they should be tucked away on one of the upper shelves. One was inscribed as the gift of his cousin, Cotter Crawley. Query: Who is Crawley, and can he be identified with my man in black?

I tried to reproduce the crystal-gazing under conditions similar to those of the other night, but without success. I have twice heard the bird. It might be either an owl or a cock. The sound seemed to come from outside the house, and was not pleasant.

*February 19th.* To-morrow Prendergast moves into the vicarage and I return home. Miss Ankardyne prolongs her stay at Malvern for another fortnight, and is then to visit friends on the south coast. I should like to have seen and questioned her, and so have discovered something more of the family history. Both Prendergast and I are disappointed. It seemed as if we were on the point of solving the mystery, and now it is as dark as ever. This new society in which Myers is interested should investigate the place.

So ends my diary, but not the story. Some four months after the events narrated I managed to secure through a second-hand book dealer four bound volumes of the *Gentleman's Magazine*. They had belonged to a Rev. Charles Phipson, once Fellow of Brasenose College and incumbent of Norton-on-the-Wolds. One evening, as I was glancing through them at my leisure, I came upon the following passage, under the date April 1789:

> At Tottenham, John Ardenoif, Esq., a young man of large fortune and in the splendour of his carriages and horses rivalled by few country gentlemen. His table was that of hospitality, where, it may be said, he sacrificed too much to conviviality; but if he had his foibles, he had his merits also, that far outweighed them. Mr. A. was very fond of cock-fighting and had a favourite cock upon which he won many profitable matches. The last bet he laid upon this cock he lost, which so enraged him that he had the bird tied to a spit and roasted alive before a large fire. The screams of the miserable bird were so affecting, that some gentlemen who were present attempted to interfere, which so enraged Mr. A. that he seized a poker and with the most furious vehemence declared that he would kill the first man who interposed; but in the midst of his passionate asseverations, he fell down dead upon the spot. Such, we are assured, were the circumstances which attended the death of this great pillar of humanity.

Beneath was written: 'see also the narrative of Mr. C— at the end of this volume.'

I give the story as I found it, inscribed in minute hand-writing on the terminal fly-leaves:

> During his last illness the Rev. Mr. C—gave me the following account of a similar instance of Divine Judgment. Mr. A— of A— House, in the county of W—, was notorious for his open practice of infidelity. He was an ardent votary of the chase, a reckless gamester, and was an enthusiast in his love of cock-fighting. After carousing one evening with a boon companion, he proposed that they should then and there match the birds which they had entered for a contest on the morrow. His friend declaring that his bird should fight only in a cockpit, Mr. A— announced that he had one adjoining the very room in which they were. The birds were brought, lights called for, and Mr. A— opening the door,

> led his guest down a flight of stairs and along a corridor to what he at first supposed were the stables. It was only after the match had begun, that he realized to his horror that they were in the family pew of A— church, to which A— House had private access. His expostulations only enraged his host, who commenced to blaspheme, wagering his very soul on the success of his bird, the victor of fifty fights. On this occasion the cock was defeated. Beside himself with frenzy, Mr. A— rushed back to his bed-chamber and, declaring that the Judgment Day had come and that the bird should never crow again, thrust a wire into the embers, burned out its eyes, and bored through its tongue. He then fell down in some form of apoplectic fit. He recovered and continued his frenzied course of living for some years. It was noticed, however, that he had an impediment in his speech, especially remarkable when he was enraged, the effect of which was to make him utter a sound like the crowing of a cock. It became a cant phrase in the neighbourhood: "When A— crows, honest men must move." Two years after this awful occurrence, his sight began to fail. He was killed in the hunting field. His horse took fright and, bolting, carried him for over a mile across bad country to break his neck in an attempt to leap a ten-foot wall. At each obstacle they encountered, Mr. A— called out, but the noise that came from his throat only seemed to terrify his horse the more. Mr. C— vouches for the truth of the story, having had personal acquaintance with both the parties.

The supposition that the Rev. Mr. C— was none other than the boon companion of Francis Ankardyne did not seem to occur to the mind of the worthy Mr. Phipson. That such was the case, I have no doubt. I saw him once in a glass darkly; and I saw later at Ankardyne House a silhouette of Cotter Crawley in an old album, and recognized the weak, foolish profile.

Who it was who drew up the wording of the monument in Ankardyne church, I do not know. Probably the trustees of the heir, a distant kinsman and a mere boy. Perhaps the mason mistook the R for an L, the 1 for a 5. Perhaps he was a grim jester; perhaps the dead man guided the chisel. But I can picture the horror of Cotter Crawley in being confronted with those suggestive verses. I see him stealing from the house, which after years of absence he has brought himself to revisit, at night. I see him at work, cold, yet feverish, on the tell-tale stone. I see him stricken by remorse and praying, as the publican prayed, without in the shadow.

Part of this story Prendergast and I told to Miss Ankardyne. The family pew is pulled down, and of the passage that connected the church with the house, only the façade is left. The house itself is quieter than it has been for years. A nephew of Miss Ankardyne from India is coming to live there soon. He has children, but I do not think there is anything of which they need be afraid. As I wrote before, it has been well aired by a kindly soul.

# The Real and the Counterfeit

## Louisa Baldwin

### Prospectus

**Address:** Stonecroft House, near Garthside, Northumberland, England.

**Property:** *Circa* seventeenth-century country house. Built of stone with spacious rooms and a magnificent oak panelled hall. Historically important property erected on the site of a Cistercian Monastery destroyed during the Reformation.

**Viewing Date:** December, 1895.

**Agent:** Louisa Baldwin (1845–1925) was born in Cambridge and got her inspiration to become a novelist and poet from being related to Rudyard Kipling, She enjoyed considerable popularity with Victorian readers for her trio of "society" novels, *The Story of a Marriage* (1880), *Where Town and Country Meet* (1885) and *Richard Dare* (1890). Her interest in the supernatural prompted her to write ghost stories for the Christmas issues of several magazines and these were later collected as *The Shadow on the Blind* in 1895. "The Real and the Counterfeit" is one of the best, recounting the terrible fate that awaits a practical joker who masquerades as a ghost in a haunted house.

Will Musgrave determined that he would neither keep Christmas alone, nor spend it again with his parents and sisters in the south of France.

The Musgrave family annually migrated southward from their home in Northumberland, and Will as regularly followed them to spend a month with them in the Riviera, till he had almost forgotten what Christmas was like in England. He rebelled at having to leave the country at a time when, if the weather was mild, he should be hunting, or if it was severe, skating, and he had no real or imaginary need to winter in the south. His chest was of iron and his lungs of brass. A raking east wind that drove his parents into their thickest furs, and taught them the number of their teeth by enabling them to count a separate and well-defined ache for each, only brought a deeper colour into the cheek, and a brighter light into the eye of the weather-proof youth. Decidedly he would not go to Cannes, though it was no use annoying his father and mother, and disappointing his sisters, by telling them beforehand of his determination.

Will knew very well how to write a letter to his mother in which his defection should appear as an event brought about by the overmastering power of circumstances, to which the sons of Adam must submit. No doubt that a prospect of hunting or skating, as the fates might decree, influenced his decision. But he had also long promised himself the pleasure of a visit from two of his college friends, Hugh Armitage and Horace Lawley, and he asked that they might spend a fortnight with him at Stonecroft, as a little relaxation had been positively ordered for him by his tutor.

"Bless him," said his mother fondly, when she had read his letter, "I will write to the dear boy and tell him how pleased I am with his firmness and determination." But Mr. Musgrave muttered inarticulate sounds as he listened to his wife, expressive of incredulity rather than of acquiescence, and when he spoke it was to say, "Devil of a row three young fellows will kick up alone at Stonecroft! We shall find the stables full of broken-kneed horses when we go home again."

Will Musgrave spent Christmas day with the Armitages at their place near Ripon. And the following night they gave a dance at which he enjoyed himself as only a very young man can do, who has not yet had his fill of dancing, and who would like nothing better than to waltz through life with his arm round his pretty partner's waist. The following day, Musgrave and Armitage left for Stonecroft, picking up Lawley on the way, and arriving at their destination late in the evening, in the highest spirits and with the keenest appetites. Stonecroft was a delightful haven of refuge at the end of a long journey across country in bitter weather, when the east wind was driving the light dry snow into every nook and cranny. The wide, hospitable front door opened into an oak panelled hall with a great open, fire burning cheerily, and lighted by lamps from overhead that effectually dispelled all gloomy shadows. As soon as Musgrave had entered the house he seized his friends, and before they had time to shake the snow from their coats, kissed them both under the misletoe bough and set the servants tittering in the background.

"You're miserable substitutes for your betters," he said, laughing and pushing them from him, "but it's awfully unlucky not to use the misletoe. Barker, I hope supper's ready, and that it is something very hot and plenty of it, for we've travelled on empty stomachs and brought them with us," and he led his guests upstairs to their rooms.

"What a jolly gallery!" said Lawley enthusiastically as they entered a long wide corridor, with many doors and several windows in it, and hung with pictures and trophies of arms.

"Yes, it's our one distinguishing feature at Stonecroft," said Musgrave. "It runs the whole length of the house, from the modern end of it to the back, which is very old, and built on the foundations of a Cistercian monastery which once stood on this spot. The gallery's wide enough to drive a carriage and pair down it, and it's the main thoroughfare of the house. My mother takes a constitutional here in bad weather, as though it were the open air, and does it with her bonnet on to aid the delusion."

Armitage's attention was attracted by the pictures on the walls, and especially by the lifesize portrait of a young man in a blue coat, with powdered hair, sitting under a tree with a staghound lying at his feet.

"An ancestor of yours?" he said, pointing at the picture.

"Oh, they're all one's ancestors, and a motley crew they are, I must say for them. It may amuse you and Lawley to find from which of them I derive my good looks. That pretty youth whom you seem to admire is my great-great-grandfather. He died at twenty-two, a preposterous age for an ancestor. But come along Armitage, you'll have plenty of time to do justice to the pictures by daylight, and I want to show you your rooms. I see everything is arranged comfortably, we are close together. Our pleasantest rooms are on the gallery, and here we are nearly at the end of it. Your rooms are opposite to mine, and open into Lawley's in case you should be nervous in the night and feel lonely so far from home, my dear children."

And Musgrave bade his friends make haste, and hurried away whistling cheerfully to his own room.

The following morning the friends rose to a white world. Six inches of fine snow, dry as salt, lay everywhere, the sky overhead a leaden lid, and all the signs of a deep fall yet to come.

"Cheerful this, very," said Lawley, as he stood with his hands in his pockets, looking out of the window after breakfast. "The snow will have spoilt the ice for skating."

"But it won't prevent wild duck shooting," said Armitage, "and I say, Musgrave, we'll rig up a toboggan out there. I see a slope that might have been made on purpose for it. If we get some tobogganing, it may snow day and night for all I care, we shall be masters of the situation any way."

"Well thought of Armitage," said Musgrave, jumping at the idea.

"Yes, but you need two slopes and a little valley between for real good tobogganing," objected Lawley, "otherwise you only rush down the hillock like you do from the Mount Church to Funchal, and then have to retrace your steps as you do there, carrying your car on your back. Which lessens the fun considerably."

"Well, we can only work with the material at hand," said Armitage; "let's go and see if we can't find a better place for our toboggan, and something that will do for a car to slide in."

"That's easily found – empty wine cases are the thing, and stout sticks to steer with," and away rushed the young men into the open air, followed by half a dozen dogs barking joyfully.

"By Jove! if the snow keeps firm, we'll put runners on strong chairs and walk over to see the Harradines at Garthside, and ask the girls to come out sledging, and we'll push them," shouted Musgrave to Lawley and Armitage, who had outrun him in the vain attempt to keep up with a deer-hound that headed the party. After a long and careful search they found a piece of land exactly suited to their purpose, and it would have amused their friends to see how hard the young men worked under the beguiling name of pleasure. For four hours they worked like navvies making a toboggan slide. They shovelled away the snow, then with pickaxe and spade, levelled the ground, so that when a carpet of fresh snow was spread over it, their improvised car would run down a steep incline and be carried by the impetus up another, till it came to a standstill in a snow drift.

"If we can only get this bit of engineering done to-day," said Lawley, chucking a spadeful of earth aside as he spoke, "the slide will be in perfect order for to-morrow."

"Yes, and when once it's done, it's done for ever," said Armitage, working away cheerfully with his pick where the ground was frozen hard and full of stones, and cleverly keeping his balance on the slope as he did so. "Good work lasts no end of a time, and posterity will bless us for leaving them this magnificent slide."

"Posterity may, my dear fellow, but hardly our progenitors if my father should happen to slip down it," said Musgrave.

When their task was finished, and the friends were transformed in appearance from navvies into gentlemen, they set out through thick falling snow to walk to Garthside to call on their neighbours the Harradines. They had earned their pleasant tea and lively talk, their blood was still aglow from their exhilarating work, and their spirits at the highest point. They did not return to Stonecroft till they had compelled the girls to name a time when they would come with their brothers and be launched down the scientifically prepared slide, in wine cases well padded with cushions for the occasion.

Late that night the young men sat smoking and chatting together in the library. They had played billiards till they were tired, and Lawley had sung sentimental songs, accompanying himself on the banjo, till even he was weary, to say nothing of what his listeners might be. Armitage sat leaning his light curly head back in the chair, gently puffing out a cloud of tobacco smoke. And he was the first to break the silence that had fallen on the little company.

"Musgrave," he said suddenly, "an old house is not complete unless it is haunted. You ought to have a ghost of your own at Stonecroft."

Musgrave threw down the yellow-backed novel he had just picked up, and became all attention.

"So we have, my dear fellow. Only it has not been seen by any of us since my grandfather's time. It is the desire of my life to become personally acquainted with our family ghost."

Armitage laughed. But Lawley said, "You would not say that if you really believed in ghosts."

"I believe in them most devoutly, but I naturally wish to have my faith confirmed by sight. You believe in them too, I can see."

"Then you see what does not exist, and so far you are in a fair way to see ghosts. No, my state of mind is this," continued Lawley, "I neither believe, nor entirely disbelieve in ghosts. I am open to conviction on the subject. Many men of sound judgment believe in them, and others of equally good mental capacity don't believe in them. I merely regard the case of the bogies as not proven. They may, or may not exist, but till their existence is plainly demonstrated, I decline to add such an uncomfortable article to my creed as a belief in bogies."

Musgrave did not reply, but Armitage laughed a strident laugh.

"I'm one against two, I'm in an overwhelming minority," he said. "Musgrave frankly confesses his belief in ghosts, and you are neutral, neither believing nor disbelieving, but open to conviction. Now I'm a complete unbeliever in the supernatural, root and branch. People's nerves no doubt play them queer tricks, and will continue to do so to the end of the chapter, and if I were so fortunate as to see Musgrave's family ghost to-night, I should no more believe in it than I do now. By the way, Musgrave, is the ghost a lady or a gentleman?" he asked flippantly.

"I don't think you deserve to be told."

"Don't you know that a ghost is neither he nor she?" said Lawley. "Like a corpse, it is always *it*."

"That is a piece of very definite information from a man who neither believes nor disbelieves in ghosts. How do you come by it, Lawley?" asked Armitage.

"Mayn't a man be well informed on a subject although he suspends his judgment about it? I think I have the only logical mind among us. Musgrave believes in ghosts though he has never seen one, you don't believe in them, and say that you would not be convinced if you saw one, which is not wise, it seems to me."

"It is not necessary to my peace of mind to have a definite opinion on the subject. After all, it is only a matter of patience, for if ghosts really exist we shall each be one in the course of time, and then, if we've nothing better to do, and are allowed to play such unworthy pranks, we may appear again on the scene, and impartially scare our credulous and incredulous surviving friends."

"Then I shall try to be beforehand with you, Lawley, and turn bogie first; it would suit me better to scare than to be scared. But, Musgrave, do tell me about your family ghost; I'm really interested in it, and I'm quite respectful now."

"Well, mind you are, and I shall have no objection to tell you what I know about it, which is briefly this:– Stonecroft, as I told you, is built on the site of an old Cistercian Monastery destroyed at the time of the Reformation. The back part of the house rests on the old foundations, and its walls are built with the stones that were once part and parcel of the monastery. The ghost that has been seen by members of the Musgrave family for three centuries past, is that of a Cistercian monk, dressed in the white habit of his order. Who he was, or why he has haunted the scenes of his earthly life so long, there is no tradition to enlighten us. The ghost has usually been seen once or twice in each generation. But as I said, it has not visited us since my grandfather's time, so, like a comet, it should be due again presently."

"How you must regret that was before your time," said Armitage.

"Of course I do, but I don't despair of seeing it yet. At least I know where to look for it. It has always made its appearance in the gallery, and I have my bedroom close to the spot where it was last seen, in the hope that if I open my door suddenly some moonlight night I may find the monk standing there."

"Standing where?" asked the incredulous Armitage.

"In the gallery, to be sure, midway between your two doors and mine. That is where my grandfather last saw it. He was waked in the dead of night by the sound of a heavy door shutting. He ran into the gallery where the noise came from, and, standing opposite the door of the room I occupy, was the white figure of the Cistercian monk. As he looked, it glided the length of the gallery and melted like mist into the wall. The spot where he disappeared is on the old foundations of the monastery, so that he was evidently returning to his own quarters."

"And your grandfather believed that he saw a ghost?" asked Armitage disdainfully.

"Could he doubt the evidence of his senses? He saw the thing as clearly as we see each other now, and it disappeared like a thin vapour against the wall."

"My dear fellow, don't you think that it sounds more like an anecdote of your grandmother than of your grandfather?" remarked Armitage. He did not intend to be rude, though he succeeded in being so, as he was instantly aware by the expression of cold reserve that came over Musgrave's frank face.

"Forgive me, but I never can take a ghost story seriously," he said. "But this much I will concede – they may have existed long ago in what were literally the dark ages, when rushlights and sputtering dip candles could not keep the shadows at bay. But in this latter part of the nineteenth century, when gas and the electric light have turned night into day, you have destroyed the very conditions that produced the ghost – or rather the belief in it, which is the same thing. Darkness has always been bad for human nerves. I can't explain why, but so it is. My mother was in advance of the age on the subject, and always insisted on having a good light burning in the night nursery, so that when as a child I woke from a bad dream I was never frightened by the darkness.

And in consequence I have grown up a complete unbeliever in ghosts, spectres, wraiths, apparitions, dopplegängers, and the whole bogie crew of them," and Armitage looked round calmly and complacently.

"Perhaps I might have felt as you do if I had not begun life with the knowledge that our house was haunted," replied Musgrave with visible pride in the ancestral ghost. "I only wish that I could convince you of the existence of the supernatural from my own personal experience. I always feel it to be the weak point in a ghost-story, that it is never told in the first person. It is a friend, or a friend of one's friend, who was the lucky man, and actually saw the ghost." And Armitage registered a vow to himself, that within a week from that time Musgrave should see his family ghost with his own eyes, and ever after be able to speak with his enemy in the gate.

Several ingenious schemes occurred to his inventive mind for producing the desired apparition. But he had to keep them burning in his breast. Lawley was the last man to aid and abet him in playing a practical joke on their host, and he feared he should have to work without an ally. And though he would have enjoyed his help and sympathy, it struck him that it would be a double triumph achieved, if both his friends should see the Cistercian monk. Musgrave already believed in ghosts, and was prepared to meet one more than half way, and Lawley, though he pretended to a judicial and impartial mind concerning them, was not unwilling to be convinced of their existence, if it could be visibly demonstrated to him.

Armitage became more cheerful than usual as circumstances favoured his impious plot. The weather was propitious for the attempt he meditated, as the moon rose late and was approaching the full. On consulting the almanac he saw with delight that three nights hence she would rise at 2 A.M., and an hour later the end of the gallery nearest Musgrave's room would be flooded with her light. Though Armitage could not have an accomplice under the roof, he needed one within reach, who could use needle and thread, to run up a specious imitation of the white robe and hood of a Cistercian monk. And the next day, when they went to the

Harradines to take the girls out in their improvised sledges, it fell to his lot to take charge of the youngest Miss Harradine. As he pushed the low chair on runners over the hard snow, nothing was easier than to bend forward and whisper to Kate, "I am going to take you as fast as I can, so that no one can hear what we are saying. I want you to be very kind, and help me to play a perfectly harmless practical joke on Musgrave. Will you promise to keep my secret for a couple of days, when we shall all enjoy a laugh over it together?"

"O yes, I'll help you with pleasure, but make haste and tell me what your practical joke is to be."

"I want to play ancestral ghost to Musgrave, and make him believe that he has seen the Cistercian monk in his white robe and cowl, that was last seen by his respected credulous grandpapa."

"What a good idea! I know he is always longing to see the ghost, and takes it as a personal affront that it has never appeared to him. But might it not startle him more than you intend?" and Kate turned her glowing face towards him, and Armitage involuntarily stopped the little sledge, "for it is one thing to wish to see a ghost, you know, and quite another to think that you see it."

"Oh, you need not fear for Musgrave! We shall be conferring a positive favour on him, in helping him to see what he's so wishful to see. I'm arranging it so that Lawley shall have the benefit of the show as well, and see the ghost at the same time with him. And if two strong men are not a match for one bogie, leave alone a home-made counterfeit one, it's a pity."

"Well, if you think it's a safe trick to play, no doubt you are right. But how can I help you? With the monk's habit, I suppose?"

"Exactly. I shall be so grateful to you if you will run up some sort of garment, that will look passably like a white Cistercian habit to a couple of men, who I don't think will be in a critical frame of mind during the short time they are allowed to see it. I really wouldn't trouble you if I were anything of a sempster (is that the masculine of sempstress?) myself, but I'm not. A thimble bothers me very much, and at college, when I have to sew on a button, I push the needle through on one side with a threepenny bit, and pull it out on the other with my teeth, and it's a laborious process."

Kate laughed merrily. "Oh, I can easily make something or other out of a white dressing gown, fit for a ghost to wear, and fasten a hood to it."

Armitage then told her the details of his deeply laid scheme, how he would go to his room when Musgrave and Lawley went to theirs on the eventful night, and sit up till he was sure that they were fast asleep. Then when the moon had risen, and if her light was obscured by clouds he would be obliged to postpone the entertainment till he could be sure of her aid, he would dress himself as the ghostly monk, put out the candles, softly open the door and look into the gallery to see that all was ready. "Then I shall slam the door with an awful bang, for that was the noise that heralded the ghost's last appearance, and it will wake Musgrave and Lawley, and bring them both out of their rooms like a shot. Lawley's door is next to mine, and Musgrave's opposite, so that each will command a magnificent view of the monk at the same instant, and they can compare notes afterwards at their leisure."

"But what shall you do if they find you out at once?"

"Oh, they won't do that! The cowl will be drawn over my face, and I shall stand with my back to the moonlight. My private belief is, that in spite of Musgrave's yearnings after a ghost, he won't like it when he thinks he sees it. Nor will Lawley, and I expect they'll dart back into their rooms and lock themselves in as soon as they catch sight of the monk. That would give me time to whip back into my room, turn the key, strip off my finery, hide it, and be roused with difficulty from a deep sleep when they come knocking at my door to tell me what a horrible thing has happened. And one more ghost story will be added to those already in circulation," and Armitage laughed aloud in anticipation of the fun.

"It is to be hoped that everything will happen just as you have planned it, and then we shall all be pleased. And now will you turn the sledge round and let us join the others, we have done conspiring for the present. If we are seen talking so exclusively to each other, they will suspect that we are brewing some mischief together. Oh, how cold the wind is! I like to hear it whistle in my hair!" said Kate as Armitage deftly swung the little sledge round and drove it quickly before him, facing the keen north wind, as she buried her chin in her warm furs.

Armitage found an opportunity to arrange with Kate, that he would meet her half way between Stonecraft and her home, on the afternoon of the next day but one, when she would give him a parcel containing the monk's habit. The Harradines and their house party were coming on Thursday afternoon to try the toboggan slide at Stonecraft. But Kate and Armitage were willing to sacrifice their pleasure to the business they had in hand.

There was no other way but for the conspirators to give their friends the slip for a couple of hours, when the important parcel would be safely given to Armitage, secretly conveyed by him to his own room, and locked up till he should want it in the small hours of the morning.

When the young people arrived at Stonecroft Miss Harradine apologised for her younger sister's absence, occasioned, she said, by a severe headache. Armitage's heart beat rapidly when he heard the excuse, and he thought how convenient it was for the inscrutable sex to be able to turn on a headache at will, as one turns on hot or cold water from a tap.

After luncheon, as there were more gentlemen than ladies, and Armitage's services were not necessary at the toboggan slide, he elected to take the dogs for a walk, and set off in the gayest spirits to keep his appointment with Kate. Much as he enjoyed maturing his ghost plot, he enjoyed still more the confidential talks with Kate that had sprung out of it, and he was sorry that this was to be the last of them. But the moon in heaven could not be stayed for the performance of his little comedy, and her light was necessary to its due performance. The ghost must be seen at three o'clock next morning, at the time and place arranged, when the proper illumination for its display would be forthcoming.

As Armitage walked swiftly over the hard snow, he caught sight of Kate at a distance. She waved her hand gaily and pointed smiling to the rather large parcel she was carrying. The red glow of the winter sun shone full upon her, bringing out the warm tints in her chestnut hair, and filling her brown eyes with soft lustre, and Armitage looked at her with undisguised admiration.

"It's awfully good of you to help me so kindly," he said as he took the parcel from her, "and I shall come round to-morrow to tell you the result of our practical joke. But how is the headache?" he asked smiling, "you look so unlike aches or pains of any kind, I was forgetting to enquire about it."

"Thank you, it is better. It was not altogether a made-up headache, though it happened opportunely. I was awake in the night, not in the least repenting that I was helping you, of course, but wishing it was all well over. One has heard of this kind of trick sometimes proving too successful, of people being frightened out of their wits by a make-believe ghost, and I should never forgive myself if Mr. Musgrave or Mr. Lawley were seriously alarmed."

"Really, Miss Harradine, I don't think that you need give yourself a moment's anxiety about the nerves of a couple of burly young men. If you are afraid for anyone, let it be for me. If they find me out, they will fall upon me and rend me limb from limb on the spot. I can assure you I am the only one for whom there is anything to fear," and the transient gravity passed like a cloud from Kate's bright face. And she admitted that it was rather absurd to be uneasy about two stalwart young men compounded more of muscle than of nerves. And they parted, Kate hastening home as the early twilight fell, and Armitage, after watching her out of sight, retracing his steps with the precious parcel under his arm.

He entered the house unobserved, and reaching the gallery by a back staircase, felt his way in the dark to his room. He deposited his treasure in the wardrobe, locked it up, and attracted by the sound of laughter, ran downstairs to the drawing-room. Will Musgrave and his friends, after a couple of hours of glowing exercise, had been driven indoors by the darkness, nothing loath to partake of tea and hot cakes, while they talked and laughed over the adventures of the afternoon.

"Wherever have you been, old fellow?" said Musgrave as Armitage entered the room. "I believe you've a private toboggan of your own somewhere that you keep quiet. If only the moon rose at a decent time, instead of at some unearthly hour in the night, when it's not of the slightest use to anyone, we would have gone out looking for you."

"You wouldn't have had far to seek, you'd have met me on the turnpike road."

"But why this subdued and chastened taste? Imagine preferring a constitutional on the high road when you might have been tobogganning with us! My poor friend, I'm afraid you are not feeling well!" said Musgrave with an affectation of sympathy that ended in boyish laughter and a wrestling match between the two young men, in the course of which Lawley more than once saved the tea table from being violently overthrown.

Presently, when the cakes and toast had disappeared before the youthful appetites, lanterns were lighted, and Musgrave and his friends, and the Harradine brothers, set out as a bodyguard to take the young ladies home. Armitage was in riotous spirits, and finding that Musgrave and Lawley had appropriated the two prettiest girls in the company, waltzed untrammelled along the road before them lantern in hand, like a very will-o'-the-Wisp.

The young people did not part till they had planned fresh pleasures for the morrow, and Musgrave, Lawley, and Armitage returned to Stonecroft to dinner, making the thin air ring to the jovial songs with which they beguiled the homeward journey.

Late in the evening, when the young men were sitting in the library, Musgrave suddenly exclaimed, as he reached down a book from an upper shelf, "Hallo! I've come on my grandfather's diary! Here's his own account of how he saw the white monk in the gallery. Lawley, you may read it if you like, but it shan't be wasted on an unbeliever like Armitage. By Jove! what an odd coincidence! It's forty years this very night, the thirtieth of December, since he saw the ghost," and he handed the book to Lawley, who read Mr Musgrave's narrative with close attention.

"Is it a case of 'almost thou persuadest me'?" asked Armitage, looking at his intent and knitted brow.

"I hardly know what I think. Nothing positive either way at

any rate." And he dropped the subject, for he saw Musgrave did not wish to discuss the family ghost in Armitage's unsympathetic presence.

They retired late, and the hour that Armitage had so gleefully anticipated drew near. "Goodnight both of you," said Musgrave as he entered his room, "I shall be asleep in five minutes. All this exercise in the open air makes a man absurdly sleepy at night," and the young men closed their doors, and silence settled down upon Stonecroft Hall. Armitage and Lawley's rooms were next to each other, and in less than a quarter of an hour Lawley shouted a cheery good-night, which was loudly returned by his friend. Then Armitage felt somewhat mean and stealthy. Musgrave and Lawley were both confidingly asleep, while he sat up alert and vigilant maturing a mischievous plot that had for its object the awakening and scaring of both the innocent sleepers. He dared not smoke to pass the tedious time, lest the tell-tale fumes should penetrate into the next room through the keyhole, and inform Lawley if he woke for an instant that his friend was awake too, and behaving as though it were high noon.

Armitage spread the monk's white habit on the bed, and smiled as he touched it to think that Kate's pretty fingers had been so recently at work upon it. He need not put it on for a couple of hours yet, and to occupy the time he sat down to write. He would have liked to take a nap. But he knew that if he once yielded to sleep, nothing would wake him till he was called at eight o'clock in the morning. As he bent over his desk the big clock in the hall struck one, so suddenly and sharply it was like a blow on the head, and he started violently. "What a swinish sleep Lawley must be in that he can't hear a noise like that!" he thought, as snoring became audible from the next room. Then he drew the candles nearer to him, and settled once more to his writing, and a pile of letters testified to his industry, when again the clock struck. But this time he expected it, and it did not startle him, only the cold made him shiver. "If I hadn't made up my mind to go through with this confounded piece of folly, I'd go to bed now," he thought, "but I can't break faith with Kate. She's made the robe and I've got to wear it, worse luck," and with a great yawn he threw down his pen, and rose to look out of the window. It was a clear frosty night. At the edge of the dark sky, sprinkled with stars, a faint band of cold light heralded the rising moon. How different from the grey light of dawn, that ushers in the cheerful day, is the solemn rising of the moon in the depth of a winter night. Her light is not to rouse a sleeping world and lead men forth to their labour, it falls on the closed eyes of the weary, and silvers the graves of those whose rest shall be broken no more. Armitage was not easily impressed by the sombre aspect of nature, though he was quick to feel her gay and cheerful influence, but he would be glad when the farce was over, and he no longer obliged to watch the rise and spread of the pale light, solemn as the dawn of the last day.

He turned from the window, and proceeded to make himself into the best imitation of a Cistercian monk that he could contrive. He slipt the white habit over all his clothing, that he might seem of portly size, and marked dark circles round his eyes, and thickly powdered his face a ghastly white.

Armitage silently laughed at his reflection in the glass, and wished that Kate could see him now. Then he softly opened the door and looked into the gallery. The moonlight was shimmering duskily on the end window to the right of his door and Lawley's. It would soon be where he wanted it, and neither too light nor too dark for the success of his plan. He stepped silently back again to wait, and a feeling as much akin to nervousness as he had ever known came over him. His heart beat rapidly, he started like a timid girl when the silence was suddenly broken by the hooting of an owl. He no longer cared to look at himself in the glass. He had taken fright at the mortal pallor of his powdered face. "Hang it all! I wish Lawley hadn't left off snoring. It was quite companionable to hear him." And again he looked into the gallery, and now the moon shed her cold beams where he intended to stand. He put out the light and opened the door wide, and stepping into the gallery threw it to with an echoing slam that only caused Musgrave and Lawley to start and turn on their pillows. Armitage stood dressed as the ghostly monk of Stonecroft, in the pale moonlight in the middle of the gallery, waiting for the door on either side to fly open and reveal the terrified faces of his friends.

He had time to curse the ill-luck that made them sleep so heavily that night of all nights, and to fear lest the servants had heard the noise their master had been deaf to, and would come hurrying to the spot and spoil the sport. But no one came, and as Armitage stood, the objects in the long gallery became clearer every moment, as his sight accommodated itself to the dim light. "I never noticed before that there was a mirror at the end of the gallery! I should not have believed the moonlight was bright enough for me to see my own reflection so far off, only white stands out so in the dark. But is it my own reflection? Confound it all, the thing's moving and I'm standing still! I know what it is! It's Musgrave dressed up to try to give me a fright, and Lawley's helping him. They've forestalled me, that's why they didn't come out of their rooms when I made a noise fit to wake the dead. Odd we're both playing the same practical joke at the same moment! Come on, my counterfeit bogie, and we'll see which of us turns white-livered first!"

But to Armitage's surprise, that rapidly became terror, the white figure that he believed to be Musgrave disguised, and like himself playing ghost, advanced towards him, slowly gliding over the floor which its feet did not touch. Armitage's courage was high, and he determined to hold his ground against the something ingeniously contrived by Musgrave and Lawley to terrify him into belief in the supernatural. But a feeling was creeping over the strong young man that he had never known before. He opened his dry mouth as the thing floated towards him, and there issued a hoarse inarticulate cry, that woke Musgrave and Lawley and brought them to their doors in a moment, not knowing by what strange fright they had been startled out of their sleep. Do not think them cowards that they shrank back appalled form the ghostly forms the moonlight revealed to them in the gallery. But as Armitage vehemently repelled the horror that drifted nearer and nearer to him, the cowl slipped from his head, and his friends recognised his white face, distorted by fear, and, springing towards him as he staggered, supported him in their arms.

The Cistercian monk passed them like a white mist that sank into the wall, and Musgrave and Lawley were alone with the dead body of their friend, whose masquerading dress had become his shroud.

# A Night at a Cottage . . .

## Richard Hughes

### Prospectus

**Address:** Farm-labourer's cottage, near Bromyard, Worcestershire, England.

**Property:** Nineteenth-century thatched cottage with its own small garden, set back from the road to the nearby village. Unoccupied forsome years, the property is sound but requires some restoration work.

**Viewing Date:** Autumn, 1926.

**Agent:** Richard Hughes (1900–1976) was born in Wales and the country is featured in a number of his short stories and novels. Educated at Oxford, he worked in the theatre for some years before achieving fame with his one-act play, *The Sister's Tragedy* (1922), following this with several best-selling novels of high adventure, including *A High Wind in Jamaica* (1929), *In Hazard* (1938) and *The Wooden Shepherdess* (1972). In his younger days, Richard Hughes spent a considerable time on the road in England and Europe, which gives an added *frisson* to this story of one man's terrifying encounter in an old, deserted cottage.

On the evening that I am considering I passed by some ten or twenty cosy barns and sheds without finding one to my liking; for Worcestershire lanes are devious and muddy, and it was nearly dark when I found an empty cottage set back from the road in a little bedraggled garden. There had been heavy rain earlier in the day, and the straggling fruit-trees still wept over it.

But the roof looked sound, there seemed no reason why it should not be fairly dry inside – as dry, at any rate, as I was likely to find anywhere.

I decided; and with a long look up the road, and a long look down the road, I drew an iron bar from the lining of my coat and forced the door, which was held only by a padlock and two staples. Inside, the darkness was damp and heavy; I struck a match, and with its haloed light I saw the black mouth of a passage somewhere ahead of me; and then it spluttered out. So I closed the door carefully, though I had little reason to fear passers-by at such a dismal hour and in so remote a lane; and lighting another match, I crept down this passage to a little room at the far end, where the air was a bit clearer, for all that the window was boarded across. Moreover, there was a little rusted stove in this room; and thinking it too dark for any to see the smoke, I ripped up part of the wainscot with my knife, and soon was boiling my tea over a bright, small fire, and drying some of the day's rain out of my steamy clothes. Presently I piled the stove with wood to its top bar, and setting my boots where they would best dry, I stretched my body out to sleep.

I cannot have slept very long, for when I woke the fire was still burning brightly. It is not easy to sleep for long, anyhow, on the level boards of a floor, for the limbs grow numb, and any movement wakes. I turned over, and was about to go again to sleep when I was startled to hear steps in the passage. As I have said, the window was boarded, and there was no other door from the little room – no cupboard even – in which to hide. It occurred to me rather grimly that there was nothing to do but to sit up and face the music, and that would probably mean being hauled back to Worcester Jail, which I had left two bare days before, and where, for various reasons, I had no anxiety to be seen again.

The stranger did not hurry himself, but presently walked slowly down the passage, attracted by the light of the fire; and when he came in he did not seem to notice me where I lay huddled in a corner, but walked straight over to the stove and warmed his hands at it. He was dripping wet – wetter than I should have thought it possible for a man to get, even on such a rainy night, and his clothes were old and worn. The water dripped from him on to the floor; he wore no hat, and the straight hair over his eyes dripped water that sizzled spitefully on the embers.

It occurred to me at once that he was no lawful citizen, but another wanderer like myself: a gentleman of the road; so I gave him some sort of greeting, and we were presently in conversation. He complained much of the cold and the wet, and huddled himself over the fire, his teeth chattering and his face an ill white.

"No," I said, "it is no decent weather for the road, this. But I wonder this cottage isn't more frequented, for it's a tidy little bit of a cottage."

Outside, the pale dead sunflowers and giant weeds stirred in the rain.

"Time was," he answered, "there wasn't a tighter little cot in the co-anty, nor a purtier garden. A regular little parlour, she was. But now no folk'll live in it, and there's very few tramps will stop here either."

There were none of the rags and tins and broken food about that you find in a place where many beggars are used to stay.

"Why's that?" I asked.

He gave a very troubled sigh before answering.

"Gho-asts," he said; "gho-asts. Him that lived here. It is a mighty sad tale, and I'll not tell it to you; but the upshot of it was that he drownded himself, down to the mill-pond. All slimy, he was, and floating, when they pulled him out of it. There are fo-aks have seen un floating on the pond, and fo-aks have seen un set round the corner of the school, waiting for his childer. Seems as if he had forgotten, like how they were all gone dead, and the why he drownded hisself. But there are some say he walks up and down this cottage, up and down; like when the smallpox had 'em, and they couldn't sleep but if they heard his feet going up and down by their do-ars. Drownded hisself down to the pond, he did; and now he Walks."

The stranger sighed again, and I could hear the water squelch in his boots as he moved himself.

"But it doesn't do for the like of us to get superstitious," I answered. "It wouldn't do for us to get seeing ghosts, or many's the wet night we'd be lying in the roadway."

"No," he said; "no, it wouldn't do at all. I never had belief in Walks myself."

I laughed.

"Nor I that," I said. "I never see ghosts, whoever may."

He looked at me again in his queer melancholy fashion.

"No," he said. "'Spect you don't ever. Some folk do-ant. It's hard enough for poor fellows to have no money to their lodging, apart from gho-asts sceering them."

"It's the coppers, not spooks, make me sleep uneasy," said I. "What with coppers, and meddlesome-minded folk, it isn't easy to get a night's rest nowadays."

The water was still oozing from his clothes all about the floor, and a dank smell went up from him.

"God, man!" I cried, "can't you *never* get dry?"

"Dry?" He made a little coughing laughter. "Dry? I shan't never be dry . . . 'Tisn't the likes of us that ever get dry, be it wet *or* fine, winter *or* summer. See that!"

He thrust his muddy hands up to the wrist in the fire, glowering over it fiercely and madly. But I caught up my two boots and ran crying out into the night.

# The Considerate Hosts

## Thorp McClusky

### Prospectus

**Address:** Felders, near Little Rock Falls, Arkansas, USA.

**Property:** Clapboard rural house with grey, weather-beaten exterior. The building is screened by mature trees and it has a small garden. Located on a back road to Little Rock.

**Viewing Date:** December, 1939.

**Agent:** Thorp McClusky (1906–?) was born in Arkansas and worked as a clerk while augmenting his income with items for the famous US pulp magazine, *Weird Tales*, to which he contributed one of the magazine's best-remembered stories, "The Crawling Horror" in November 1936. "The Considerate Hosts" was also first published in the magazine and selected by the famous American editor, Bennett Cerf, as one of the all-time best supernatural tales for his collection, *Famous Ghost Stories* (1944). Although the concept of a traveller lost in a storm may not be new, what the hero of this story discovers when he crosses the threshold of the old house *certainly is* . . .

Midnight.

It was raining, abysmally. Not the kind of rain in which people sometimes fondly say they like to walk, but rain that was heavy and pitiless, like the rain that fell in France during the war. The road, unrolling slowly beneath Marvin's headlights, glistened like the flank of a great backsnake; almost Marvin expected it to writhe out from beneath the wheels of his car. Marvin's small coupé was the only man-made thing that moved through the seething night.

Within the car, however, it was like a snug little cave. Marvin might almost have been in a theater, unconcernedly watching some somber drama in which he could revel without really being touched. His sensation was almost one of creepiness; it was incredible that he could be so close to the rain and still so warm and dry. He hoped devoutly that he would not have a flat tire on a night like this!

Ahead a tiny red pinpoint appeared at the side of the road, grew swiftly, then faded in the car's glare to the bull's-eye of a lantern, swinging in the gloved fist of a big man in a streaming rubber coat. Marvin automatically braked the car and rolled the right-hand window down a little way as he saw the big man come splashing toward him.

"Bridge's washed away," the big man said. "Where you going, Mister?"

"Felders, damn it!"

"You'll have to go around by Little Rock Falls. Take your left up that road. It's a county road, but it's passable. Take your right after you cross Little Rock Falls bridge. It'll bring you into Felders."

Marvin swore. The trooper's face, black behind the ribbons of water dripping from his hat, laughed.

"It's a bad night, Mister."

"Gosh, yes! Isn't it!"

Well, if he must detour, he must detour. What a night to crawl for miles along a rutty back road!

Rutty was no word for it. Every few feet Marvin's car plunged into water-filled holes, gouged out from beneath by the settling of the light roadbed. The sharp, cutting sound of loose stone against the tires was audible even above the hiss of the rain.

Four miles, and Marvin's motor began to sputter and cough, Another mile, and it surrendered entirely. The ignition was soaked; the car would not budge.

Marvin peered through the moisture-streaked windows, and, vaguely, like blacker masses beyond the road, he sensed the presence of thickly clustered trees. The car had stopped in the middle of a little patch of woods. "Judas!" Marvin thought disgustedly. "What a swell place to get stalled!" He switched off the lights to save the battery.

He saw the glimmer then, through the intervening trees, indistinct in the depths of rain.

Where there was a light there was certainly a house, and perhaps a telephone. Marvin pulled his hat tightly down upon his head, clasped his coat collar up around his ears, got out of the car, pushed the small coupé over on the shoulder of the road, and ran for the light.

The house stood perhaps twenty feet back from the road, and the light shone from a front-room window. As he plowed through the muddy yard – there was no sidewalk – Marvin noticed a second stalled car – a big sedan – standing black and deserted a little way down the road.

The rain was beating him, soaking him to the skin; he pounded on the house door like an impatient sheriff. Almost instantly the door swung open, and Marvin saw a man and a woman standing just inside, in a little hallway that led directly into a well-lighted living-room.

The hallway itself was quite dark. And the man and woman were standing close together, almost as though they might be endeavoring to hide something behind them. But Marvin, wholly preoccupied with his own plight, failed to observe how unusual it must be for these two rural people to be up and about, fully dressed, long after midnight.

Partly shielded from the rain by the little overhang above the door, Marvin took off his dripping hat and urgently explained his plight.

"My car. Won't go. Wires wet, I guess. I wonder if you'd let me use your phone? I might be able to get somebody to come out from Little Rock Falls. I'm sorry that I had to—"

"That's all right," the man said. "Come inside. When you knocked at the door you startled us. We – we really hadn't – well, you know how it is, in the middle of the night and all. But come in."

"We'll have to think this out differently, John," the woman said suddenly.

Think what out differently? thought Marvin absently.

Marvin muttered something about you never can be too careful about strangers, what with so many hold-ups and all. And, oddly, he sensed that in the half darkness the man and woman smiled briefly at each other, as though they shared some secret that made any conception of physical danger to themselves quietly, mildly amusing.

"We weren't thinking of you in that way," the man reassured Marvin. "Come into the living-room."

The living-room of that house was – just ordinary. Two overstuffed chairs, a davenport, a bookcase. Nothing particularly modern about the room. Not elaborate, but adequate.

In the brighter light Marvin looked at his hosts. The man was around forty years of age, the woman considerably younger, twenty-eight, or perhaps thirty. And there was something definitely attractive about them. It was not their appearance so much, for in appearance they were merely ordinary people; the woman was almost painfully plain. But they moved and talked with a curious singleness of purpose. They reminded Marvin of a pair of gray doves.

Marvin looked around the room until he saw the telephone in a corner, and he noticed with some surprise that it was one of the old-style, coffee-grinder affairs. The man was watching him with peculiar intentness.

"We haven't tried to use the telephone tonight," he told Marvin abruptly, "but I'm afraid it won't work."

"I don't see how it *can* work," the woman added.

Marvin took the receiver off the hook and rotated the little crank. No answer from Central. He tried again, several times, but the line remained dead.

The man nodded his head slowly. "I didn't think it would work," he said, then.

"Wires down or something, I suppose," Marvin hazarded.

"Funny thing, I haven't seen one of those old-style phones in years. Didn't think they used 'em any more."

"You're out in the sticks now," the man laughed. He glanced from the window at the almost opaque sheets of rain falling outside.

"You might as well stay here a little while. While you're with us you'll have the illusion, at least, that you're in a comfortable house."

What on earth is he talking about? Marvin asked himself. Is he just a little bit off, maybe? That last sounded like nonsense.

Suddenly the woman spoke.

"He'd better go, John. He can't stay here too long, you know. It would be horrible if someone took his license number and people – jumped to conclusions afterward. No one should know that he stopped here."

The man looked thoughtfully at Marvin.

"Yes, dear, you're right. I hadn't thought that far ahead. I'm afraid, sir, that you'll have to leave," he told Marvin. "Something extremely strange—"

Marvin bristled angrily, and buttoned his coat with an air of affronted dignity.

"I'll go," he said shortly. "I realize perfectly that I'm an intruder. You should not have let me in. After you let me in I began to expect ordinary human courtesy from you. I was mistaken. Good night."

The man stopped him. He seemed very much distressed.

"Just a moment. Don't go until we explain. We have never been considered discourteous before. But tonight – tonight . . .

"I must introduce myself. I am John Reed, and this is my wife, Grace."

He paused significantly, as though that explained everything, but Marvin merely shook his head. "My name's Marvin Phelps, but that's nothing to you. All this talk seems pretty needless."

The man coughed nervously. "Please understand. We're only asking you to go for your own good."

"Oh, sure," Marvin said. "Sure. I understand perfectly. Good night."

The man hesitated. "You see," he said slowly, "things aren't as they seem. We're really ghosts."

"You don't say!"

"My husband is quite right," the woman said loyally. "We've been dead twenty-one years."

"Twenty-two years next October," the man added, after a moment's calculation. "It's a long time."

"Well, I never heard such hooey!" Marvin babbled. "Kindly step away from that door, Mister, and let me out of here before I swing from the heels."

"I know it sounds odd," the man admitted, without moving, "and I hope that you will realize that it's from no choosing of mine that I have to explain. Nevertheless, I was electrocuted, twenty-one years ago, for the murder of the Chairman of the School Board, over in Little Rock Falls. Notice how my head is shaved, and my split trouser-leg? The fact is, that whenever we materialize we have to appear exactly as we were in our last moment of life. It's a restriction on us."

Screwy, certainly screwy. And yet Marvin hazily remembered that School Board affair. Yes, the murderer *had* been a fellow named Reed. The wife had committed suicide a few days after burial of her husband's body.

It was such an odd insanity. Why, they *both* believed it. They even dressed the part. That odd dress the woman was wearing. 'Way out of date. And the man's slit trouser-leg. The screwy cluck had even shaved a little patch on his head, too, and his shirt was open at the throat.

They didn't look dangerous, but you never can tell. Better humor them, and get out of here as quick as I can.

Marvin cleared his throat.

"If I were you – why, say, I'd have lots of fun materializing. I'd be at it every night. Build up a reputation for myself."

The man looked disgusted. "I should kick you out of doors," he remarked bitterly. "I'm trying to give you a decent explanation, and you keep making fun of me."

"Don't bother with him, John," the wife exclaimed. "It's getting late."

"Mr. Phelps," the self-styled ghost doggedly persisted, ignoring the woman's interruption, "perhaps you noticed a car stalled on the side of the road as you came into our yard. Well, that car, Mr. Phelps, belongs to Lieutenant-Governor Lyons, of Felders, who prosecuted me for that murder and won a conviction, although he knew that I was innocent. Of course he wasn't Lieutenant-Governor then; he was only County Prosecutor . . .

"That was a political murder, and Lyons knew it. But at that time he still had his way to make in the world – and circumstances pointed toward me. For example, the body of the slain man was found in the ditch just beyond my house. The body had been robbed. The murderer had thrown the victim's pocketbook and watch under our front steps. Lyons said that I had *hidden* them there – though obviously I'd never have done a suicidal thing like that, had I really been the murderer. Lyons knew that, too – but he had to burn somebody.

"What really convicted me was the fact that my contract to teach had not been renewed that spring. It gave Lyons a ready-made motive to pin on me.

"So he framed me. They tried, sentenced, and electrocuted me, all very neatly and legally. Three days after I was buried, my wife committed suicide."

Though Marvin was a trifle afraid, he was nevertheless beginning to enjoy himself. Boy, what a story to tell the gang! If only they'd believe him!

"I can't understand," he pointed out slyly, "how you can be so free with this house if, as you say, you've been dead twentyone years or so. Don't the present owners or occupants object? If I lived here I certainly wouldn't turn the place over to a couple of ghosts – especially on a night like this!"

The man answered readily, "I told you that things are not as they seem. This house has not been lived in since Grace died. It's not a very modern house, anyway – and people have natural prejudices. At this very moment you are standing in an empty room. Those windows are broken. The wallpaper has peeled away, and half the plaster has fallen off the walls. There is really no light in the house. If things appeared to you as they really are you could not see your hand in front of your face."

Marvin felt in his pocket for his cigarettes. "Well," he said, "you seem to know all the answers. Have a cigarette. Or don't ghosts smoke?"

The man extended his hand. "Thanks," he replied. "This is an unexpected pleasure. You'll notice that although there are ash-trays about the room there are no cigarettes or tobacco. Grace never smoked, and when they took me to jail she brought all my tobacco there to me. Of course, as I pointed out before, you see this room exactly as it was at the time she killed herself. She's wearing the same dress, for example. There's a certain form about these things, you know."

Marvin lit the cigarettes. "Well!" he exclaimed. "Brother, you certainly seem to think of everything! Though I can't understand, even yet, why you want me to get out of here. I should think that after you've gone to all this trouble, arranging your effects and so on, you'd want somebody to haunt."

The woman laughed dryly.

"Oh, you're not the man we want to haunt, Mr. Phelps. You came along quite by accident; we hadn't counted on you at all. No, Mr. Lyons is the man we're interested in."

"He's out in the hall now," the man said suddenly. He jerked his head toward the door through which Marvin had come. And all at once all this didn't seem half so funny to Marvin as it had seemed a moment before.

"You see," the woman went on quickly, "this house of ours is on a back road. Nobody ever travels this way. We've been trying for years to – to haunt Mr. Lyons, but we've had very little success. He lives in Felders, and we're pitifully weak when we go to Felders. We're strongest when we're in this house, perhaps because we lived here so long.

"But tonight, when the bridge went out, we knew that our opportunity had arrived. We knew that Mr. Lyons was not in Felders, and we knew that he would have to take this detour in order to get home.

"We felt very strongly that Mr. Lyons would be unable to pass this house tonight.

"It turned out as we had hoped. Mr. Lyons had trouble with his car, exactly as you did, and he came straight to this house to ask if he might use the telephone. Perhaps he had forgotten us, years ago – twenty-one years is a long time. Perhaps he was confused by the rain, and didn't know exactly where he was.

"He fainted, Mr. Phelps, the instant he recognized us. We have known for a long time that his heart is weak, and we had hoped that seeing us would frighten him to death, but he is still alive. Of course while he is unconscious we can do nothing more. Actually, we're almost impalpable. If you weren't so convinced that we are real you could pass your hand right through us.

"We decided to wait until Mr. Lyons regained consciousness and then to frighten him again. We even discussed beating him to death with one of those non-existent chairs you think you see. You understand, his body would be unmarked; he would really die of terror. We were still discussing what to do when you came along.

"We realized at once how embarrassing it might prove for you if Mr. Lyons' body were found in this house tomorrow and the police learned that you were also in the house. That's why we want you to go."

"Well," Marvin said bluntly, "I don't see how I can get my car away from here. It won't run, and if I walk to Little Rock Falls and get somebody to come back here with me the damage'll be done."

"Yes," the man admitted thoughtfully. "It's a problem."

For several minutes they stood like a tableau, without speaking. Marvin was uneasily wondering: Did these people really have old Lyons tied up in the hallway; were they really planning to murder the man? The big car standing out beside the road belonged to *somebody* . . .

Marvin coughed discreetly.

"Well, it seems to me, my dear shades," he said, "that unless you are perfectly willing to put me into what might turn out to be a very unpleasant position you'll have to let your vengeance ride, for tonight, anyway."

"There'll never be another opportunity like this," the man pointed out. "That bridge won't go again in ten lifetimes."

"We don't want the young man to suffer though, John."

"It seems to me," Marvin suggested, "as though this revenge idea of yours is overdone, anyway. Murdering Lyons won't really do you any good, you know."

"It's the customary thing when a wrong has been done," the man protested.

"Well, maybe," Marvin argued, and all the time he was wondering whether he were really facing a madman who might be dangerous or whether he were at home dreaming in bed; "but I'm not so sure about that. Hauntings are pretty infrequent, you must admit. I'd say that shows that a lot of ghosts really don't care much about the vengeance angle, despite all you say. I think that if you check on it carefully you'll find that a great many ghosts realize that revenge isn't so much. It's really the thinking about revenge, and the planning it, that's all the fun. Now, for the sake of argument, what good would it do you to put old Lyons away? Why, you'd hardly have any incentive to be ghosts any more. But if you let him go, why, say, any time you wanted to, you could start to scheme up a good scare for him, and begin to calculate how it would work, and time would fly like everything. And on top of all that, if anything happened to me on account of tonight, it would be just too bad for you. *You'd* be haunted, really. It's a bad rule that doesn't work two ways."

The woman looked at her husband. "He's right, John," she said tremulously. "We'd better let Lyons go."

The man nodded. He looked worried.

He spoke very stiffly to Marvin. "I don't agree entirely with all you've said," he pointed out, "but I admit that in order to protect you we'll have to let Lyons go. If you'll give me a hand we'll carry him out and put him in his car."

"Actually, I suppose, I'll be doing all the work."

"Yes," the man agreed, "you will."

They went into the little hall, and there, to Marvin's complete astonishment, crumpled on the floor lay old Lyons. Marvin recognized him easily from the newspaper photographs he had seen.

"Hard-looking duffer, isn't he?" Marvin said, trying to stifle a tremor in his voice.

The man nodded without speaking.

Together, Marvin watching the man narrowly, they carried the lax body out through the rain and put it into the big sedan. When the job was done the man stood silently for a moment, looking up into the black invisible clouds.

"It's clearing," he said matter-of-factly. "In an hour it'll be over."

"My wife'll kill me when I get home," Marvin said.

The man made a little clucking sound. "Maybe if you wiped your ignition now your car'd start. It's had a chance to dry a little."

"I'll try it," Marvin said. He opened the hood and wiped the distributor cap and points and around the spark plugs with his handkerchief. He got in the car and stepped on the starter, and the motor caught almost immediately.

The man stepped toward the door, and Marvin doubled his right fist, ready for anything. But then the man stopped.

"Well, I suppose you'd better be going along," he said. "Good night."

"Good night," Marvin said. "And thanks. I'll stop by one of these days and say hello."

"You wouldn't find us in," the man said simply.

By Heaven, he *is* nuts, Marvin thought. "Listen, brother," he said earnestly, "you aren't going to do anything funny to old Lyons after I'm gone?"

The other shook his head. "No. Don't worry."

Marvin let in the clutch and stepped on the gas. He wanted to get out of there as quickly as possible.

In Little Rock Falls he went into an all-night lunch and telephoned the police that there was an unconscious man sitting in a car three or four miles back on the detour. Then he drove home.

Early the next morning, on his way to work, he drove back over the detour.

He kept watching for the little house, and when it came in sight he recognized it easily from the contour of the rooms and the spacing of the windows and the little overhang above the door.

But as he came closer he saw that it was deserted. The windows were out, the steps had fallen in. The clapboards were gray and weather-beaten, and naked rafters showed through holes in the roof.

Marvin stopped his car and sat there beside the road for a little while, his face oddly pale. Finally he got out of the car and walked over to the house and went inside.

There was not one single stick of furniture in the rooms. Jagged scars showed in the ceilings where the electric fixtures had been torn away. The house had been wrecked years before by vandals, by neglect, by the merciless wearing of the sun and the rain.

In shape alone were the hallway and living-room as Marvin remembered them. "*There*," he thought, "is where the bookcases were. The table was *there* – the davenport *there*."

Suddenly he stooped, and stared at the dusty boards and underfoot.

On the naked floor lay the butt of a cigarette. And, a half-dozen feet away, lay another cigarette that had not been smoked – that had not even been lighted!

Marvin turned around blindly, and, like an automaton, walked out of that house.

Three days later he read in the newspapers that Lieutenant-Governor Lyons was dead. The Lieutenant-Governor had collapsed, the item continued, while driving his own car home from the state capital the night the Felders bridge was washed out. The death was attributed to heart disease . . .

After all, Lyons was not a young man.

So Marvin Phelps knew that, even though his considerate ghostly hosts had voluntarily relinquished their vengeance, blind, impartial nature had meted out justice. And, in a strange way, he felt glad that that was so, glad that Grace and John Reed had left to Fate the punishment they had planned to impose with their own ghostly hands . . .

# The Grey House

## Basil Copper

### Prospectus

**Address:** The Grey House, near Burgundy, France.

**Property:** Eighteenth-century stone house in beautiful countryside position. The property has a red-tiled roof, round-capped turret, plus unique classical Great Hall and terrace overlooking garden. In need of complete restoration.

**Viewing Date:** Summer, 1967.

**Agent:** Basil Copper (1924–) was born in London and worked as a journalist and editor while developing his skill as one of Britain's pre-eminent writers of macabre fiction. Haunted houses have featured in his novels *The Curse of the Fleers* (1976) and *The House of the Wolf* (1983), plus several short stories, including "Dust to Dust", "Wish You Were Here" and "The Grey House." Many people have dreamt of converting an old ruin into a new home, and it was after coming across one in a remote region of France that Copper was inspired to write this story. As he shows, though, it is as well to know *all* about any old building before undertaking such a task.

### 1

To Angele, standing in the sunlight of a late summer afternoon, The Grey House, as they came to call it, had an air of chill desolation that was at variance with the brightness and warmth of the day. It was uninhabited and had evidently been so for many years. But Philip was delighted with the place; he clapped his hands like a child of five and then strolled around, his arms folded, lost in silent admiration. He needs and must have it and wouldn't rest until he had rooted out the local agent and made an offer for the house.

Philip, her husband, was a writer; apart from a series of successful detective stories which brought him the larger part of his income, he was the author of a number of striking tales of mystery and the macabre. The Grey House would give him inspiration, he chuckled: Angele, stifling her doubts, didn't like to dampen her husband's enthusiasm and trailed round behind him and the estate agent with growing dislike.

They had spotted the place after a long day's drive in the older parts of Burgundy. Then in early afternoon, they had stopped for a late lunch in the small mediaeval city which nestled among the blue haze of the surrounding mountains. The view was enchanting and after lunch they spent a pleasant hour on the ramparts, tracing out the path of a small river which wound its way foaming between great boulders and woods of dark pines.

It was Philip who first sighted The Grey House. It was down a narrow lane and the path to it was long choked with nettles. It was the last house, separated from its neighbours by several hundreds of yards of rough cartway and trees, over-grown shrubbery and bushes. It was unquestionably a ruin. The place looked something like a barn or stable.

It was largely constructed of great blocks of grey stone, which decided them on its name, with one round-capped turret hanging at an insane angle over the big front door, large as a church. There was a round tower at one side, immensely old and covered in lichen. The roof, of red crab tiles, sagged ominously and would obviously need a lot of repairs.

The big old wooden door was locked but Philip led the way with enthusiasm, cutting a swathe through breast-high nettles for his wife. They followed the great frowning wall down the lane until the property obviously came to an end. The rest of the lane was an impenetrable mass of brambles. But Philip had seen enough. Through the trees below the bluff he could see the rusted iron railings of a balcony and there were even some out-buildings and what looked like an old water mill.

"We could get this place for a song," he told his wife gleefully. "It would want a lot of doing up of course, but the terrace would be ideal for my writing and what a view!"

Against such enthusiasm Angele could find no valid argument; so half an hour later found them back in the city square, at the office of M. Gasion, the principal of the main firm of agents in the area.

M. Gasion, a short broad-shouldered man of cheerful aspect and obviously addicted to the grape was shattered at the prospect of such a sale. The property had been on his books for more than forty years, over twenty years before he acquired the firm. Therefore, he was a little hazy about the antecedents of the estate. Yes, it would need a lot of doing up, he agreed; he did not think monsieur need worry about the price.

It would not be heavy and as they would see, though it needed a great deal of renovation, it had possibilities, distinct possibilities. He positively purred with enthusiasm and Angele could not help smiling to herself. A purchaser like Philip would hardly happen more than once in a lifetime; no wonder M. Gasion was pleased.

It was absurdly cheap, she had to agree. The asking price was £300, which included the main building and tower, the terrace, out-buildings and mill house, together with a short strip of orchard below the bluff on which the terrace was set. Nothing would do but that Philip must conclude the deal then and there. This called for a great deal of bustle and the notaire was sent for, while Angele, Philip and the agent went on a tour of the building. There was further delay while the key was hunted up but at last the small procession set off.

The big door gave back with a creak after M. Gasion's repeated applications and the first ray of sunshine for something like forty years found difficulty in penetrating the interior. The unusual activity round the old building had not passed notice among the local people who lived higher up the lane and Angele had seen the curious glances they cast towards her, though Philip, as usual, was too absorbed in talk with the agent to notice anything.

Angele glanced over her shoulder as they went in the main door and was not surprised to see a small knot of gawping householders standing at the last bend in the lane in front of the house. Surprisingly, the house was wired for electricity but the main switchboard inside the door, fixed by great bolts directly into the ancient stone, was bare except for fragments of rusted wire and fittings covered with verdigris. The electricity had been cut off in the twenties, when the last tenants left, explained M. Gasion.

He carried a powerful electric lantern, despite the brightness of the afternoon. The house had formerly belonged to the de Menevals, the great landed proprietors who had now died out. They had owned a chateau which formerly stood in a vast park on the mountain opposite. The building had burned down in a great fire and explosion over a hundred years earlier and now only the stones remained. The last de Meneval, Gaston, had died a violent death, said M. Gasion with relish. He was apparently a great one for the ladies and had kept The Grey House for entertaining his girl friends.

"*Une maison d'assignation*," he explained to Philip with a smile, man to man. Philip returned the smile with a grin and the trio went into the house. Angele could not repress a shudder at the interior and wondered what deeds the old house had seen. She and Philip had visited the ruins of the old chateau earlier the same afternoon; it was one of the sights of the district. The park was now kept as a public pleasaunce, and the guide had told the stories of blood and violence with distinct enthusiasm.

But one did not need even that to picture dark scenes of lust centuries before, as they gazed at the ruined and distorted remains of the house, which even now bore traces of charring on ancient beams and on the undersides of blackened stones. She was disquieted to hear that The Grey House had belonged to the de Menevals too, and her own French ancestry – her mother had come from these very parts – with its heightened sensibilities, rang a little bell somewhere back in her brain.

When the door swung open even the agent was not prepared for the long undisturbed foetor which met them; it was so strong that it seemed almost to darken the sunlight and they were forced to open the main door and remain outside for a few minutes before they could enter.

"Faugh!" said M. Gasion, with unrestrained disgust but even this did not seem to dampen Philip's ardour.

"Loads of atmosphere, eh?" he said, turning to Angele with a smile. After a minute they descended some broad stone steps. The smell was still strong but not so offensive and Angele had to admit that it was probably due to vegetable decay. To her surprise, the light of the agent's torch, supplemented by small windows high up, disclosed a vast stone hall. There was a fireplace to one side in which an ox could have been roasted and the remains of an old gallery which had collapsed with age and woodworm.

But the floor was covered with an indescribable medley of old rubbish. It was impossible to do more than look hurriedly around and be careful where one trod. Many of the massive roof beams would need replacing and Philip's face became more thoughtful as the tour continued. The house would evidently need a great deal more renovation than he had bargained for. However, he brightened as they went through into the other rooms. The stones of the house were sound and would merely need replastering and painting. There were two more large reception rooms, though nothing on the scale of the old hall, which was partly subterranean; another room was used as a kitchen.

On the top floor, under vast, sagging roof beams, through which the sky could be seen, was another huge room over the Great Hall below. This could be partitioned and would make a corridor with bathroom, and three large bedrooms, said Philip. Or he could make a study and leave one spare bedroom for guests. The open mass of the tower spread out from one end room of this large upper storey and Philip could find no place for that at the moment, in his readymade scheme of things.

They had saved the best for last; off the kitchen, whose door was finally forced with screaming protest, they came upon the glory of The Grey House. It was nothing more or less than a large tiled terrace, but it gave the place a cachet that finally clinched the deal in Philip's mind, weighing the cost, as he was, against the utility and suitability of the house for his writing purposes.

The rusty iron railings which enclosed the terrace, had evidently been of great elegance, and would no doubt be so again; Philip was already confiding to M. Gasion that he would have them painted pale blue. He could have his writing table *comme ça* and they could eat dinner under electric light at night *sur le balcon*. Even the agent was momentarily impressed by his enthusiasm.

For the view was magnificent; that could not be gainsaid. Below the balcony, the terrain dropped sheer for forty feet or so over a stone outcrop, to the small strip of orchard which was part of the purchase. A thick belt of leafy trees blotted out the immediate view, but above them were wooded hills and valleys, with the stream trickling between until the eye was arrested by the mountain opposite surmounted by the ruins of the old chateau. Angele was surprised to see how the white of the stones stood out against the dark blue haze, even at that distance. Just below and to the left was the small stone building of the old water mill, through which the stream meandered beyond the orchard.

When they tore themselves away from the unearthly beauties of that sylvan view, dusk was already falling and the tinkle of the water in the mill house had assumed a melancholy that it had lacked in the sunlight of the earlier afternoon. A thin mist was already rising above the belt of dark trees which abutted the orchard. Angele pointed this out to Philip as perhaps being undesirable, unhealthy.

"Oh, no," said Philip with a short laugh. "Bound to get a mist with water at this time of the year, especially after the heat of the day. We're too high up for it to affect us in any case." But nevertheless, even as he spoke, the mist, white and clammy, almost like thick smoke, drifted up over the trees and already the farthest branches were wavering in its tendrils.

No more was said; the party went back indoors, led by M. Gasion's enormous torch and once outside, the door was firmly locked and secured by double padlocks. The trio were silent on the way back to the town and, after a little reflection, M. Gasion spoke to Angele. Philip had gone to get something from the car and they were alone for a moment in the office.

"You do not like the house, madame?"

Angele was noncommittal. She did not want to spoil Philip's evident delight in the property, but at the same time she had many reservations of her own about the dark, silent grey pile above the water mill, which sounded so eerily in the dusk. Instead, she stammered some words about the property being so derelict and the enormous expense she was afraid her husband would be put to.

The agent's face cleared as though it had been sponged. If that was all that was worrying madame, he was prepared to lower the price.

Quite frankly, he had been rather taken aback by the degree of decay; he would be quite happy to take the equivalent of £250 to effect a quick sale. Philip had just returned from the car at this moment and was delighted with the news; so Angele had unwittingly been the means of sealing the bargain.

The notaire also, a lean, vulpine man named Morceau, had just arrived, cross at being disturbed at his favourite cafe. Introductions were made, M. Gasion produced a bottle and some glasses and over much agreeable smacking of lips and handing round of delectable little biscuits, the details of the sale were worked out.

An hour later Philip and Angele left the office, potential owners of The Grey House. They were to stay at a hotel in the city for a few days until the legal niceties had been gone into; that would take time, but there was nothing to stop monsieur from having the property surveyed or putting work in hand, for the remainder of the proceedings were a formality. So Philip signed a paper, handed over a cheque, wired his literary agent in London that he was staying on and would write, and worked himself into an agreeable enthusiasm over the possibilities of The Grey House.

It was decided between him and Angele that they would return to London for a couple of weeks, to wind up their immediate affairs and then return to Burgundy for the autumn. They would occupy themselves during that time by working on the house, assisted by local labour and then decide, with the assistance of a local architect, just what major repairs and alterations would be necessary. They would go back to London in November and keep in touch with the work through the architect. Then they intended to return to The Grey House in the spring to supervise the final stages and arrange for a house-warming.

By next summer Philip hoped they would be fully installed for a six-month season of prolific and profitable writing for him and a period of pleasure and entertaining for her. He was determined that they would make the old house a show place, a necessary pilgrimage for their London friends; and all that night, long after the rest of the hotel was asleep, he kept Angele awake with plans and possibilities. Angele had her reservations but kept her own counsel. She felt that she might be mistaken in her intuitions and after all, carpenters and builders could make a magnificent job of the old house. She would wait and see what transpired.

## 2

A month later The Grey House was already under siege. Philip had engaged a local builder and he, two assistants and Philip and Angele in their oldest clothes, were in a frenzy of demolition and renovation. Philip had decided that they would tackle the Great Hall first. It was mainly of stone and once they had got rid of the loathsome accumulation which littered the floor, they would rid the house of that putrescent smell. But first there was one set-back.

Pierre, the builder they had engaged, was a stolid, good-looking man, broad as a barrel, in his early fifties; as was the custom he worked with his hands with his assistants, taking his share of the heavy work as well as directing operations. He was surprised, as were all the local people, that The Grey House was to be re-opened and lived in after all this time, but he was quite glad of the job.

But the first afternoon, there was a short consultation among his two workmen and they drew the builder to one side. Philip, who had been down the lane returned at that moment and Pierre asked to speak to him. He seemed embarrassed and eventually said that nothing could be done until the electric light was in operation; his point was that the loathsome conditions underfoot in the Great Hall made good lighting essential.

This was understandable enough but Angele thought she could discern odd expressions in the eyes of the two workmen. Despite herself, she was convinced that they had other reasons for their request. Fortunately, a modern water supply was already laid on to the house, and Philip had merely to request the local electricity company to restore the current. Like many English people he was naive about local conditions and Angele had laughingly assured him that it would take a month or more before anything would be done about it.

Philip told the assembled workmen that the current would be turned on that afternoon. There was a general air of disbelief but Philip said he had an appointment with the electricity people at two o'clock and sat down upon an upturned box in front of the house to wait. Pierre and his workmen chatted among themselves. Philip was the only person present to believe the statement.

When half-past three came with not a stroke of work done it became obvious even to Philip that the electricity would not be connected. He jumped up angrily and drove off in his car. He was unable to achieve any satisfaction and found the company office locked; no doubt the official in charge was in one of the local cafes.

Incensed at this lack of efficiency Philip phoned M. Gasion who presently came down to the house himself. He assured Philip that he had sorted out the misunderstanding and that the workmen would be at The Grey House without fail the following day. Mollified, Philip announced that they could still get some work done while daylight lasted. It was not half past four, so, lighting a couple of lanterns, the party of five – M. Gasion having returned to his office – set off through the gloomy reception rooms to the terrace. Here, restored by the bright sunlight and the atmosphere of open countryside, the workmen unloaded their tools and set about clearing the area, amid jokes and laughter.

The whole terrace seemed to be covered with lichen and here and there fungoid growths; two of the workmen started scraping this off to reveal the intricately patterned tiles beneath, while Pierre, Philip and Angele busied themselves with clearing the area of brushwood, fallen branches and other debris which had accumulated over the years. This they threw off the balcony into the orchard below; it made loud crashing noises in the brittle branches of dead trees and for some reason gave Angele considerable uneasiness.

She looked sharply down to the water mill and the dark trees at the orchard end, but nothing moved and she attributed her feelings to nerves and the thin tinkle of falling water. In an hour, good progress had been made and when repeated applications with buckets of water had been carried out to the considerable area of tiling cleared by the workmen, it was seen that the whole terrace was one of considerable elegance and beauty.

Philip had recovered his good humour when he saw what an excellent start it was and how pleasantly and efficiently the workmen had carried out their task.

It was evident that with this team the house would be in good hands and Philip was obviously in a great hurry to complete the preliminaries and get to grips with the major problems. He spoke with Pierre of the work to be done to the main roof and the sagging turret; this would have to be a priority and needed to be started well before the winter. Pierre told him that work on this would commence within a fortnight, once working arrangements had been achieved inside.

It was in this atmosphere of mutual satisfaction that the day's work ended. Dusk was falling and the lanterns had been carried on to the terrace to complete the clearing of the tiles. Another of the workmen was already chipping rust from the great sweep of the balcony. It made an ugly sound in the dusk and was re-echoed from the dark woods below. As they finished and carried the tools back into the house for the night, there was a faint rustling in the underbrush at the back of the house down by the water mill. Angele was the only one to hear it; she strained her eyes down to the orchard below and thought she could see the faintest shadow slip into the darker shade of the old trees at the end of the orchard.

Probably a cat. There were lots of them haunting the lanes down near The Grey House. Big, grey brutes they were, and sometimes she heard them howling sadly in the dusk when she and Philip went out. The big door of the house shrieked, as though annoyed at the intrusion into the long silence of forty years, when they left. Outside, on the small terrace in front of The Grey House, where Philip intended to lay tiles and build a small garage later, the employer and the employed congratulated one another and there was much shaking of hands.

Then Philip insisted on buying everyone a drink at the first cafe they came across. All parted with mutual expressions of goodwill and it was quite dark when Philip and Angele had got back to their hotel. He was resolved to make a good start the next day and had asked the electricity people to come in at nine o'clock. The workmen would arrive at twelve and with luck and sufficient illumination they could make a good start on clearing the Great Hall.

The following morning the electricity employees surprisingly arrived almost at the specified hour; The Grey House was opened again and around midday a jubilant Philip was allowed to pull the master switch and the Great Hall was flooded with light. Much of the house would need re-wiring and Philip had many special schemes for heating and outdoor floodlighting, but that would come later.

For the moment, naked bulbs and trailing lengths of flex were draped all over the house in order to give the workmen good light to work by. Philip hoped also to have two great picture windows opened up in the stonework of the Great Hall to let light into the building during daytime.

This, and a number of other anomalies puzzled him and he resolved to look up the history of the de Menevals in the great historical library in the City Museum, when time would afford. That opportunity did not arise until the next year; in the meantime Philip and his wife, with their team of workmen, followed by the interest of M. Gasion, M. Morceau and later, the architect, went at the work of restoration with enthusiasm.

But strangely, the progress of the first day wasn't repeated. One of the workmen went sick the second afternoon and, assuredly, the stench from the floor of the Great Hall was such as to turn a strong stomach; Philip got round that with buckets of hot water and disinfectant and after a while they cleared some of the miasma which seemed to hang around the old foundations.

Lorry load after lorry load of malodorous rubbish left for the city tip and even the sick workman, who returned to duty the next day, had to admit there had been a great improvement. But there was something which made Angele vaguely uneasy, though Philip seemed as blind to the atmosphere of the place as ever. He was puzzled at the inordinate number of lights and flex positions the workmen were obliged to insist on, especially when working among the noisesome rafters and complained that the cost of electricity and bulbs would soon gross the total cost of the house if things went on that way.

Yet Angele understood perfectly the feelings of the workmen and marvelled again at the insensitivity of her husband to the atmosphere; especially as his name as an author had been largely made through the description of just such situations. About a week after the renovation of the house had begun the workmen were still clearing the upper storey and Pierre expected an early start to the roof repairs; Philip had been delighted with some unusual finds among the debris of centuries. A curiously marked ring, evidently belonging to a man of rank; a sword hilt, a tankard with a strange inscription in the Latin tongue and some porcelain jars and containers for which none of them could assign any known use.

Philip took them back to his hotel for cleaning and said he would use them for decorating the house when restoration was complete. One afternoon one of the workmen came to Philip with a bizarre object he had found in one of the upper rooms. It was a long instrument with a spike of very old metal on one end of it; the other end was a sort of whip or switch. The thongs were made of wire, stained with the rust of centuries.

A learned Abbe from the City University, with whom Philip had become great friends, was visiting the Grey House on the afternoon in question. Monsignor Joffroy turned quite pale, Angele noticed.

"May I see?" he asked, taking the whip from Philip with unseemly haste. He drew him on to one side. The good Abbe looked worried.

"I do not wish to alarm you, my friend, but this is an unclean thing," he said, almost fiercely.

"See." He pointed out an inscribed tablet on the shaft of the instrument. "These are the arms of the de Menevals. We have a locked room of the Musee d'Antiquités at the University, devoted to such relics of the sadistic de Menevals. If you would permit me, I will see it is deposited for safe keeping. It is not fit that such mementoes should be allowed in the outside world."

He crossed himself and Angele could not repress a shudder. Though inclined to be amused, Philip could not but be impressed by the earnestness and deadly seriousness of Monsignor Joffroy's manner and he readily assented to his friend's request.

"I should like to hear something of the history of the de Menevals from you, some time," he said. "It would make good material for some of my books."

The Abbe laid his hand on Philip's arm and looked steadily into his eyes.

"Believe me, my friend, such things are not for books – or rather for books of your sort. Your essays in the macabre, admirable and successful as they are, are children's nursery tales compared with the things that went on in the chateau above – now no more, praise be to God."

A few minutes later the Monsignor excused himself, made his farewells to Angele and returned to the university; he left behind him a somewhat thoughtful Philip and a thoroughly disturbed Angele. Sensibly, Philip said nothing to Pierre and the workmen; and to M. Gasion, whom he met for an occasional glass of cassis at the latter's home, he was guarded; he made no comment on the curious whip, but discussed some of the other finds which the workmen had made. He did learn one thing about the de Menevals from the inscription on the tankard, but of this he said nothing, even to Angele.

She herself had one more unusual experience on the afternoon of the same day as Monsignor Joffroy's visit. She was alone on the terrace at dusk; she was no longer afraid of the low tinkling of water, to which she had become accustomed and even the mist did not affect her with uneasiness. She was trimming branches of an old tree which overhung the balcony.

This was now almost complete, wanting only a few final touches and, with an electric light above the glazed double doors, was taking on an unaccustomed elegance. She had gone down to Philip to ask him about something and when she came back the last glow of the fading sun was sinking behind the mountain. She was overcome by the melancholy of the scene and had remained seated while her gaze played over the terrain spread out so enticingly before her. It was while she was so occupied that she felt rather than saw a faint, dark shadow steal out from one orchard tree and disappear behind another.

Why she did the next thing she was not quite sure; but on some obscure impulse she suddenly stooped, picked up a large bundle of chopped branches from the tree, stepped noiselessly to the edge of the balcony and hurled the mass of wood and foliage through the air into the orchard below. The bundle fell where she had aimed, quite by chance, and with a sharp, almost frightening crash into the tree beneath which the shape had melted.

More branches fell to the ground and from the midst of the splintered wood something dark and long launched itself like a streak through the orchard; the creature poised and jumped up on to the edge of an outbuilding of the water mill. As far as she could judge, Angele saw a huge, grey cat. It had enormous yellow eyes that flickered with anger in the dusk. It looked back over its shoulder at her reproachfully and then disappeared into the bushes.

A moment later she heard a stealthy swish as it vanished and was evidently making its way through the dark trees at the back of the orchard. More startled than alarmed she left the terrace rather hurriedly for the welcome shelter of the house, which now blazed with lights from every room.

The next day Monsignor Joffroy was dining with them on the terrace of their hotel and Angele mentioned the cat. It was the first time she had spoken of it. Philip seemed only mildly interested but the effect on the Abbe was electric. His hand twitched and his glass of cognac soaked the table cloth. There was a flurry of apologies and in the midst of mopping up, Angele felt the Abbe's eyes fixed on her.

"There is no such animal, madame," he said with a terrible emphasis.

"Oh, come now, Monsignor," Philip laughed good-naturedly. "There's nothing so remarkable about that. There are dozens of cats around the lanes leading to The Grey House. I've seen 'em myself."

The Abbe continued to look at the girl. "Nevertheless, I must insist, there is no such animal. A trick of the light . . ."

Angele did not press the point and a moment or two later the conversation passed on to other topics. But she felt the Abbe's eyes on her from time to time during the evening, and she read concern in their friend's eyes.

The house was making excellent progress. As the autumn colours deepened and the melancholy around The Grey House gradually gave way to orderliness and a more modern atmosphere, Angele's unease subsided. The couple had arranged to leave for England in November as planned and would return in April, when the main architectural changes would be made and Philip would be on hand to supervise and give advice. They were due to depart on the following Tuesday, and in the meantime wandered about the house, idly watching the workmen and planning even more grandiose effects for the spring.

The architect they had finally engaged, Roget Frey, was thoroughly in accord with Philip's ideas and he had been enthusiastic about the designs the gifted young man had produced. Philip knew he could trust him to realise the effect he wanted. The house was to be a blend of ancient and modern, with every comfort, yet the mediaeval atmosphere was to be retained, particularly in the Great Hall and in the rooms above it.

The roof was more than half finished and two great picture

windows had been punched into the ancient stonework high up in the eastern wall of the Great Hall, more than thirty feet above the fireplace.

Philip had ideas about these windows and he didn't want to reveal his special plans to Angele or the workmen until their return; Roget had worked out a fine design for his piece de resistance and he was convinced his house would be a show place for his friends if the final result was only half as spectacular as his designs.

The work to be done in the winter would be long and arduous and Philip was glad they would be in the comfort of their London flat; there was no heating in the Grey House as yet and the wind and rain on that exposed ledge would find them totally unprepared. Pierre had promised that all would be up to schedule by spring, and in the warmer weather he and Angele could work out the elegant details, the central heating and style of radiators, the furnishing, the curtains and the hundred and one other things that would make The Grey House a masterful blend of old and new.

In the meantime Pierre and his men were to finish the roof; prepare and glaze new windows; install the central heating plant; build a garage and terrace in front of the house; scrape and plaster the interior walls and line the Great Hall with oak panelling. Philip could imagine the stupendous effect the whole thing would have when it was finished; he strolled around the house in a delighted daze, noting the fine new staircases, the cedar handrails in the modern parts of the house and the start already made in creating a streamlined kitchen for Angele.

The whole of the upper storey had yet to be converted into several rooms; there was much to be done. But he was glad he had given his confidence to Pierre and Roget. They would see that the work had a quality seldom seen nowadays. The men had already made a start on the interior of the Great Hall and their scaffolding and lights lined the walls at a dizzy height from the flagged floor; another gang was at work on the roof outside and the place resembled a great, humming factory.

In striking contrast to the mist-haunted ambience of their first sight of the place, Philip was pacing about on the terrace, smoking a pipe, and picturing himself writing a new series of novels of the macabre in this evocative atmosphere. He had two novels coming out shortly, but he would have to get down to some hard work in England in the coming winter. Then he would return to The Grey House and by late summer would be well back in his stride.

His publisher was pleased with the consistency of his output and he had no doubt that the quiet surroundings here would contribute a great deal to his writing. If only Angele liked the place a little better . . . Still, she had seemed more pleased with the house lately and he felt that, when she saw the new kitchen and all the latest gadgets he proposed to install for her, she would be as delighted with the Grey House as he.

His musings were suddenly interrupted by a startled cry.

It came from the direction of the Great Hall and in a few moments more he heard the sharp noise of running footsteps on the stone floor. It was Pierre.

"Monsieur!" There was a hard excitement in the voice, but no alarm. He quickened his own steps towards the builder. The couple met at the entrance of the Great Hall and in instant later Philip was sharing Pierre's excitement.

The workmen had been scraping down the wall of the Great Hall over the fireplace, preparatory to re-plastering; Philip had long pondered a centerpiece which would provide a striking point for the eye in this chamber and now he had the answer. Beneath the layers of old plaster on the surface of the ancient wall, a painting had begun to reveal itself.

When Philip arrived, two workmen were engrossed in clearing away an area which appeared to depict a man's blue waistcoat with gold gilt buttons. Philip joined them on the scaffolding and studied the painting, as it began to appear with mounting excitement. Pierre seized a paint brush and a can of water and started clearing another area; the four men worked on.

The rest of the house was silent, Angele and Monsignor Joffroy having gone for a walk and the men on the roof having a temporary break from their labours.

After an hour, a painting of unique and demoniac nature had emerged; viewing it from the floor of the Great Hall by the brilliant electric light which the workmen held to illuminate it, Philip was jubilantly aware of having found his centrepiece – remarkably appropriate in view of his profession as a novelist of the macabre – and yet at the same time he could not help having serious doubts as to the effect it might have on his visitors.

The radiant colours were unblurred by their long sojourn under the whitewash of an earlier age and the painting really stood out remarkably. It depicted a singularly sinister old man, in a grey tricorn hat and blue coat with gold buttons. His knee breeches were caught in with gold cords and his black shoes had silver gilt buckles. He was pushing his way through some sort of dark, wet undergrowth with concentrated ferocity. In his arms and hanging head downwards as he dragged her into the darkling bushes was a young girl.

She was stark naked, her pink body, depicted with pitiless detail by the unknown painter of obvious genius, streaked with gouts of blood where the brambles had gashed her. Her eyes were closed, either in death or a faint, it was impossible to tell, and her long gold hair dragged through the wet grass. It was difficult to convey the hideous effect this painting of diabolical brilliance had upon the viewer.

In the old man's left hand, held towards the observer, was the curious spiked whip which Philip had seen in this very house not so many weeks before. The workmen were still busy washing away the covering whitewash from the bottom righthand corner of the picture and their backs obscured the details from Philip's view. He strode about the floor of the hall, trying to get a better perspective.

At the very bottom of the painting was an enamelled coat of arms with a Latin inscription underneath, which he would have translated later. He was no scholar and would ask Monsignor Joffroy what he made of it. As the workmen again began their interminable hammering upon the roof above his head, the footsteps of the Abbe himself were heard upon the entrance stair.

His face was pale in the light of the electric lamps and he

seemed to stagger and made a warding off gesture with his hand, as he caught sight of the painting, which the workmen had now finished uncovering.

"For the love of God, Monsieur," he cried harshly. "Not this horror . . ."

Amazed, Philip ran to meet him but a startled shriek from the stairhead above interrupted the projected dialogue. Monsignor Joffroy, remarkably agile for his late middle-age, was even before Philip on the stair. The two men were just in time to save Angele as she fell fainting to the stone floor.

"Let us get her out of this hall," the priest whispered, his head close to Philip's, as they began to lift her. He waved off the alarmed workmen who were swarming down the scaffolding. "Nothing, nothing at all. Just a fainting fit – madame was merely startled by the painting . . ."

Half an hour later, Philip re-entered the hall. Angele, pale and distraught, had returned to the hotel, driven by Roget Frey, who had called to see the work in progress. Finally calm, she had refused to say what was the cause of her alarm and had attributed it to the shock of seeing the painting in such vivid detail.

Viewed from the top of the stairs, it did strike one with terrific effect, Philip had to admit, pausing at the spot where Angele had stood. But even his stolid materialism had begun to crack with what he had learned in the past few minutes. Monsignor Joffroy, before leaving to comfort Angele, had advised him to have the painting effaced; or bricked over.

"No good can come of it," he insisted, but he would not, or could not, explain anything further. He had, however, confirmed what Philip had already guessed. The arms beneath the strange picture were those of the de Menevals. The motto beneath the escutcheon was the old and terrible one by which the de Menevals had lived: "Do as thou wilt."

But the thing which disturbed Philip most of all was the painting's final detail, which the workmen had uncovered last of all. Upon this point Monsignor Joffroy had persisted in a stubborn silence.

Philip looked at the picture again and certain words of the

Abbe's came to mind. Following behind the dreadful couple and gazing with sardonic expression at the viewer was a terrible cat, three times larger than any ever seen in this mortal life. A great, grey cat, with blazing yellow eyes.

## 3

In London, Angele and Philip resumed the interrupted round of their life. The events of the previous autumn seemed blurred and far away and their strangeness something of the imagining, rather than reality. Their friends constantly chaffed them about their old grey house and their preferring to live in such a remote place, rather than to enjoy London life and all the privileges of a successful novelist there.

Philip, however, never tired of telling his friends what a fascinating gem he had unearthed and in truth he had a most interesting way of relating his stories so that his listeners were more than half convinced, even the most hidebound and desk-bound of their acquaintances. A good dozen or more couples accepted invitations to visit them the following summer, seduced by the lilt of Philip's voice, for his narration of the tale of the Grey House was almost as fascinating as his printed work.

Angele was, perhaps, pleased at this success and now that she was back in her own familiar atmosphere, the events at The Grey House seemed trivial and commonplace. She supposed it was something that could have happened to anybody. And environment could do many things. The Grey House had an undeniable ambience that spoke of matters best forgotten, but electric light and modern fittings would dispel them.

She should have been the novelist; Philip often teased her and said she was the one with all the imagination. It was true in a way, too; as she thought this, she looked over at him in a corner of the lounge, pipe in mouth and a pint tankard in one hand. He looked young and supple at forty-five, not a grey hair in his glossy black head; she was proud of him and the success they had made of life and their marriage.

It was silly to worry so about The Grey House and a ridiculous atmosphere; it was all the same in old houses. Come to that, she had exactly the same sensation in the Paris Conciergerie, with all its terrible associations with the Comite de Salut Public and Marie Antoinette. She dismissed the thoughts from her mind and listened with an interest that was not feigned when Philip read her the latest progress reports from Roget Frey or M. Gasion.

Sometimes, too, the Abbe would write them little notes in his scholarly handwriting, but he never referred to The Grey House, save in the most general way, or the painting. Particularly not the painting. Angele herself had seen it again since her stupid fainting fit on the staircase; she had to admit that in the daylight and with her husband and friends around her, it no longer frightened her.

It was a diabolical subject and he was a disgusting old man – the painter had caught a most sinister expression on his face, which left the viewer feeling uneasy – but that was all. Even the cat wasn't the same as the one she had fancied in the orchard; the one in the picture was at least the size of a bloodhound, but the eyes and face were different.

They even laughed at it, she and Philip and Roget; Philip had said it might have had nine lives but even a cat as big as that could hardly have lived for two hundred years into the late twentieth century. No, that no longer worried her. But what did worry her then, if the cause of the worry – the sight of a cat in an orchard; the atmosphere of an old house; the discovery of a painting – had no fear for her?

She was hard put to it to define a reason and eventually forgot all about it as her normal London life went on. Philip's two books were published, one in December, one in early spring, and achieved an even greater success than before. They had money in abundance and life seemed to hold great promise.

The progress reports on the house were satisfactory and as late spring advanced, Philip began to tear his thoughts away from his life in England and his mind flew to The Grey House, waiting for him to give it the final touches. A flurry of invitations went out from him and Angele and then the couple found themselves with only two weeks to go before they were off again.

The regular letters told Philip that the roof had been completed; all the domestic arrangements were in the final stages; the panelling of the Great Hall and its picture windows had gone smoothly; the electric lighting was functioning satisfactorily. Roget Frey said that the surprise he and Philip had planned was also going to schedule; he had the work carried out in sections and the structure would be erected whenever Philip chose. The garage and the front terrace too, were nearly complete; the remainder of the work, including the reconstruction of the upper storey would await Philip's supervision in the spring.

The author was more than pleased; indeed, judging by the excellent photographs Roget had sent him, the house seemed even more impressive than he had envisaged when he started out on his elaborate scheme of renovation. The terrace overlooking the water mill also looked superb and he hoped to erect a glass marquee on one side so that they could eat in the open in summer even when it rained.

Much against the Abbe's advice, he had decided to keep the painting as the centerpiece of the Great Hall; from his researches he had considered that it represented the old Vicomte Hector de Meneval, one of the most debauched and sadistic of the line. It was no doubt how the old boy liked to see himself, in an obscene and allegorical situation, representing the black arts.

So he had instructed Frey to have the painting framed in oak and preserved under glass. In deference to Angele, the Abbe and other friends of more tender nerves, he had decided to have a plain sliding panel in the modern Swedish style erected over the work. In that way he could have his cake and eat it, he reflected. And at the touch of a button the old rogue would be revealed, to shock his friends on a cold winter's night.

The two weeks drew to an end at last; Philip attended a dinner given in his honour by his publisher, extended the last of his invitations, drank through his farewell party and in the first week in May – rather later than he had intended – he and Angele with the car set off on the cross-Channel ferry. They stopped at Fontainebleau for the night and next day made an uneventful journey south.

They had decided to camp out in the house temporarily, as the greater part was habitable; from what Roget had said, the bathroom was partly in order, the working parts of the kitchen completely so. They could extemporise and superintend the final arrangements themselves. But even so, both liked comfort and rather than arrive late in the afternoon with inadequate provision for food, they had booked in at their old hotel for two nights before deciding to launch themselves completely on to the facilities of The Grey House.

Their telegrams had preceded them and their old friends M. Gasion, Roget and the Abbe presented themselves punctually for dinner. It was a time of laughter and jokes shared, which Philip always remembered; and, when the builder Pierre put in an appearance just as they had given him up, the evening seemed complete. Afterwards, they sat out on the balcony, smoking, drinking their cognac and looking over the lights of the quiet city.

All was well at the house, the couple learned; things had gone even better than expected and Pierre and Roget Frey were obviously bubbling with enthusiasm. If they could decently have done so, they would have dragged Philip and Angele into the car that night and over to the house, late as it was.

Roget Frey and Philip chaffed the Abbe over what they called the "boxing in" of the painting, but though he good-humouredly smiled at their sallies, it was obvious that his eyes had a serious and thoughtful look. The party broke up late and Philip never had a chance to speak to any of his friends alone. The pair rose late the next morning.

It was after midday before Frey, the builder Pierre and M. Gasion arrived at the hotel to escort their friends in triumph to their new home. There had certainly been an extraordinary change in The Grey House. In front of the house was a terrace of pink tiles, the great entrance door sparkled with pale yellow paint and boxes of flowers garlanded the façade, with more flowers hanging in baskets on hooks suspended from the walls.

On the roof, new red tiles caught the sunshine and the straightened turrent must have looked as it did in the eighteenth century. On one side, a new garage was nearing completion, needing but a final coat of paint, while white balustrades edging the terrace gave the last touch in a notable and inspired piece of restoration.

The ancient and the modern blended in perfect harmony and even Angele could not resist a gasp of pleasure. With congratulations on all sides, architect, builder and agent passed inside the great door to show the couple the wonders of the interior. It was a happy afternoon and Philip was well pleased, not only with his choice of restorers but in his own ability to choose good men.

When the mutual congratulations were over, the party stayed on for a convivial dinner; and while the majority remained in the dining room, chatting over coffee and cognac, served by a local domestic, Philip and Roget Frey retired to the Great Hall to discuss the next stages of the work. Even the Abbe, when he put in an appearance around nine o'clock in the evening, had to admit that the house now had great charm and style; if he had any reservations he, at any rate, was wise enough to keep them to himself.

He glanced up at the space over the fireplace when he entered the Great Hall and appeared relieved to see nothing but a smooth wooden panel where the painting was formerly visible. During the next few days Philip and Angele settled down into a more or less stable routine. They had two small portable beds installed in one of the half-completed rooms on the first floor and ate in the kitchen or on the terrace.

This was in order to avoid inconvenience and extra trouble for the workmen, who were now proceeding with the later stages of the work under Pierre and Roget's direction. Philip was already writing and the steady clack of his typewriter could be heard from the terrace several hours each day. Roget was in and out several times a day, the work went well; all in all, it was a busy time for the couple. Some evenings they would drive into the city for a meal or a drink with their friends; and, several afternoons a week, Angele would go shopping, either alone or with Philip.

She was busy ordering furniture, domestic utensils, hangings and the many hundreds of individual items which the house would need. Surprisingly, the renovation of The Grey House was not costing as much as they had budgeted for, despite the extensive nature of the work; this was mainly due to Roget's goodness in the matter of fees and to the builder's reasonable rates and friendly attitude.

This meant that Angele had more to spend on furnishings and she wanted to make sure that her side of the decorating measured up to the high standards set by her husband. Angele was not troubled by any more disturbing thoughts and she had grown used to the tinkling of thc water mill. The mist was now rising thickly from the area of trees at the bottom of the orchard, due to the extremely hot weather, but she paid no more attention to that either.

About the third week in July, the first of their friends from London arrived to inspect the progress of the house. Doreen and Charles Hendry were a jolly couple and they were delighted with The Grey House as they first saw it from their sports car one afternoon. But for some reason their enthusiasm evaporated after their first raptures. One of the guest rooms was now ready for occupation, though still unpainted. It overlooked, from a higher point, the orchard and the grove of trees at the foot of the terrace and it was this room which Doreen and Charles occupied their first night at The Grey House.

The next morning, at breakfast on the terrace, Angele could not help noticing that Doreen looked drawn and tired. Even Philip sensed this, for he asked, "Sleep well?"

Charles looked embarrassed. He glanced round the breakfast table and said with a short laugh, "Well, as a matter of fact we didn't sleep a wink. There was such a howling of cats all night, that we were awake most of the time. Never heard anything like it. One great brute was in the orchard. I got up to sling some water at it. It had burning yellow eyes – gave me quite a turn."

"Sorry about that," said Philip. "Yes, there are a lot of cats round here, now that you come to mention it, but I can't say they've bothered us to that extent. Have you heard them, dear?" he said, turning to Angele.

His wife had turned quite white. She stammered some casual remark and quickly excused herself. There was nothing else of moment during the Hendrys' short stay. And short it was. They had originally intended to remain for two weeks but after a few days Charles pleaded urgent business which necessitated his return to England. As their sports car headed up the lane and Angele and Philip waved them off, Angele could have sworn there was relief in Doreen's eyes as they drove away from The Grey House.

Imagined or not, there was no doubt that Charles' business was a pretext, for Philip ran into him in one of the main squares of the city a couple of afternoons later, to their mutual embarrassment. On the Friday of the same week Philip made a startling discovery which did something to disturb the peace of his mind, while the effect on Angele was deeply felt. Philip returned from a walk with Roget and asked Pierre, "I say, did you know there was an old graveyard at the end of the lane?"

Pierre shrugged and answered that he believed that was so; but it was a good way from the house, well screened by trees. He could not see that it was of any importance. In face of this indifference Philip had to agree that the affair seemed of little moment. But the way of its discovery had been a shock to him, though he was loath to admit it.

He and Roget had been out surveying the extent of the property; Philip had wanted to have a closer look at the orchard and the water mill building and there was also the question of repair of walls and fences. When they had gone some way towards their boundary, forcing their way through breast-high nettles in places, Philip was surprised to see a large area of rusted iron railings and the white gleam of marble through the trees.

Roget was almost as surprised as he. The two men, impelled by some curiosity, the source of which was obscure, were soon confronted by an elaborate ironwork gate with a rusted metal scroll, whose hieroglyphs seemed familiar; the stone pillars on either side were covered with lichens and moss and the stone ball on one column had long fallen into the grass.

The gate was ajar and after some hesitation, the two men pushed it open and went on into the cemetery. Its extent was quite small but there was a frightful mouldering stench emanating from the ancient tombs with which they were surrounded, and the long, echoing screech the gate made as it went back on its age-old hinges, set their teeth on edge.

There seemed to be about thirty tombs in the cemetery and it was evident that a hundred years or more had passed since the latest occupant was laid to rest. As they gazed round, Roget said with a nervous catch in his breath, "This must be the old de Meneval graveyard. They were brought here from the chateau above. They had to be laid in this place, far from the town, because of the public outcry. I seem to remember in the old histories that the townspeople said they were an accursed strain and there was a great ecclesiastical debate over their being interred in the municipal cemetery. So the Bishop of the province had this private *cimetíere* set aside for the use of the family."

Philip could not hold back a shiver at these words, reinforced by the melancholy scene around him. He saw now that the dark grove of trees below the orchard had screened the graveyard from view, as no doubt it was meant to do. There was no doubt, however, as to the reason for the dank mist which rose over the orchard and surroundings at night. The place was unhealthy and Philip would have to seek the advice of the health authorities.

The pair had been traversing the small avenues which bisected the old graveyard and now found themselves in front of an imposing monument which stood in the most secluded part; overgrow hedges of laurel surrounded it and the lower part of the tomb was effaced by the encroachment of brambles and tangled grasses. Philip noticed with interest that the mausoleum was in the form of a great marble portico, in the style of a Greek temple, which evidently covered a vault of considerable proportions below.

On the face of the portico was repeated the escutcheon which appeared below the painting in the Great Hall of The Grey House; he was the name of Hector de Meneval and others of his house, the dates of birth and death obliterated with time. But as he looked closer, he saw that he had been mistaken; the dates of birth were clearly given, but the remainder of the legend was left blank after each name – there was not even the customary dash. This was decidedly curious.

Roget had left his side for a moment and was puzzling out a massive Latin inscription which extended along the side of the mausoleum. Roughly translated it ran, "Mighty are they, great joy is theirs; they shall taste of Life Everlasting." Somehow, this inscription left a vaguely unpleasant impression on Philip's mind and he could not help remembering, for the first time, the sly and cunning expression of the old man in the painting.

He was about to retrace his steps towards the gate when there was a sharp exclamation from Roget. He joined his friend and saw, following the line of Roget's somewhat unsteady finger, that one side of the tomb had collapsed, after long years of erosion by wind and rain. The earth had fallen in, carrying with it fragments of marble and through the gaping hole in the side of the mausoleum could be seen part of the interior of the vault.

There were dark steps and even what looked like part of a catafalque some distance below. A faint miasma exuded from this charnel place and seemed to poison the air around the tomb. A little farther off, Philip noted another curious feature. The grass around the hole in the marble seemed crushed and torn, as though something heavy had been dragged along; the trail continued for some distance into the dark and sombre bushes which bordered the cemetery gate.

Neither man liked the idea of following that trail and after a few moments, by mutual, unspoken consent they hurried away to the healthy sanity of the upper lanes which led to the house. The gate shrieked mockingly behind them. Philip did not mention their visit to the old cemetery in any detail and after her first shock of alarm, Angele gave the matter no more thought. And the following week there was a minor celebration, culminating in the unveiling of Philip's surprise.

The principal of Philip's publishing firm was to be in Burgundy for a few days and had promised to spend a day with them and inspect their new quarters. Philip had laid on a party in his honour and the climax was to be the architectural coup he had planned for the Great Hall. This chamber had been barred to all members of the household and friends for three days beforehand and the noise of hammering and sawing echoed throughout the house all day long; Roget and Philip were in conference behind the locked doors and workmen carrying heavy baulks of timber and elaborately carved beams in and out, smilingly, disclaimed all knowledge of the nature of the affair.

The party was a big success and the unlocking of the Great Hall set the seal on a momentous occasion; tables laden with wine and food were set down the middle, an epic fire blazed in the hearth, for the stone hall was a cold place even in summer, despite the wooden panelling; and lights blazed from half a hundred metal wall fittings. But what enchanted the guests was the architectural feature on which Philip and Roget had worked for such a long time.

Completely surrounding the upper part of the hall, like a minstrel gallery, ran an airy balcony which continued over the fireplace round to a point above the huge door. Each side of the entrance, beautifully carved oak balustrades ran up to the balcony, encasing polished oak staircases. The whole length of the balconies themselves, except where the two great picture windows pierced the wall, were a blaze of colour; thousands of books, the cream of Philip's collection, lined the walls in finely fitted mahogany bookcases. The whole thing was a triumph and the guests could not resist audible murmurs of admiration.

A few minutes later, ascending the first staircase, hand in hand with Philip, Angele had to admit that the idea was the crown of the Great Hall. Thirty feet above the flagged pavement she looked down on the shimmering dazzle of faces and the babble of guests' conversation rose like the noise of the sea above the clink of glasses. On the balconies themselves visitors could browse among the books set out row on row, spreading from wall to wall; the views from the picture windows were magnificent and with the stout railing at her back, Angele could see across mile after mile of hazy blue mountain.

The balcony ran across and dipped a little below the great central panel of the fireplace and this was the only unfortunate feature of the affair from her point of view; for whenever the panel was unrolled it must bring the viewer on the balcony in close proximity to the disturbing painting, even though it were still a good half dozen feet above.

It was this which caused the only disruptive element of the party for Angele. She and Philip were admiring the setting from this point when Roget or another friend in the hall below decided to demonstrate the ingenious panel for an intrigued guest. The button was pressed, the panel slid silently back and there, not two yards away, Angele saw with a shock the same hideous scene. The sight was so unexpected that she gave a gasp and reeled back against the railing.

Philip was beside her in an instant, his face wrinkled with worry.

"What is it?" he asked, looking round him swiftly, in a manner she had never seen before.

"Nothing," she said. "I just feel faint, that's all. It must be the height."

As Philip led her below, a girl who had never had a qualm on even the loftiest mountain top, she looked again at the picture but she did not see repeated the optical illusion which had so unnerved her. That it must be an optical illusion, she did not doubt. But she could have sworn that the baleful eye of the old Vicomte had closed, for just the faintest fraction, in an obscene wink. The effect must be one of the texture of the paint, combined with the light on the glass above it. But she could not recapture the sensation, though she tried again as they went downstairs; and a few minutes later the panel closed again over it, to the wondering murmur of the assembled guests.

## 4

It was now again turning towards late summer. Philip was beginning to get in his stride with writing, Roget came seldom to the house, the remaining one or two workmen were pottering amiably on the sunny days, putting the finishing touches to the decor. Angele had been too busy to spare any thoughts for morbid imaginings, and she was well satisfied with the effect of the furniture and hangings she was arranging with such competent art.

But the Abbe came more often to the house than ever. Angele was glad of his company; and his benign eye, in which there shone such wisdom and benevolence, gave her a solid feeling of comfort and safety. Monsignor Joffroy spoke little of the matters which so deeply troubled him, but with humorous and interesting discourse kept the little dinner parties gay with laughter, as the night moths fluttered round the lamps as they took their evening ease on the balcony, whose magnificent views never ceased to delight them.

The couple had on two or three occasions been the guests of the Abbe at his quarters in the old university, and had duly marvelled at the extent and antiquity of the great library which was its proudest boast. It was on one of these occasions that Philip asked the old man if he could consult one of the rare and unexpurgated histories of the de Meneval family.

Monsignor Joffroy was reluctant to do this, but assented at last and eventually left Philip alone in his study with a great brass-bound book which had four locks. Translating the crabbed Latin was a long and tiresome task but Philip eventually unravelled a sickening story which explained much that was dark and horrifying about the de Menevals. He replaced the book on the shelf and sat pondering; for the first time he had some doubts about the wisdom of his purchase of The Grey House.

He afterwards refused to speak of what he had seen in the locked book, but he did hint to Roget Frey something of the practices of the old de Menevals which had led the people of the city a hundred years before to lay siege to the chateau and burn it about the ears of the atrocious occupants. The events which led the citizenry to this extreme measure had concerned the abduction of young girls from the neighbourhood, which the de Menevals were in the habit of procuring for their unspeakable rites.

Philip could not go on – the details were too blasphemous and appalling to contemplate, even in the Latin, but it did explain the curious content of the painting in the Great Hall. Philip was now convinced that the study depicted a literal subject and not an allegorical one and this caused him great disquiet. When he left the Abbe's library, the old man refused to discuss the subject with him. But Monsignor Joffroy looked him in the eye with great intensity and said with emphasis, "Take care of your wife, monsieur!"

For some days afterwards Philip was seen to wander about The Grey House with an odd and abstracted air, but he gradually recovered his spirits as the warm and sunny days went by. He had been to see the sanitary authorities regarding the old graveyard and had been promised that the thing would be looked into. But, as is the way in rural France, no action was immediately forthcoming, the weeks went by and Philip eventually forgot about it.

It was in early September, on a day of golden and benevolent splendour, that Angele had an odd experience. She had been standing on the balcony drinking in the beauty of the wild scene, against the backcloth of the far mountains. There was a hush, broken only by the faint tinkle of water. Philip had gone into town to see about some business with Roget and the only other thing which disturbed the silence was the occasional chink of china as Gisele, the hired girl, washed up the crockery from lunch.

She was thinking about nothing in particular, except possibly what they would be having for dinner. As she lowered her gaze from the distant mountain peaks and the white stones of the chateau on the heights above, her eye was arrested by the early leaves of autumn which fell like faint flakes of snow on to the golden foliage of the old orchard. She then heard a faint rustling sound and presently noticed the figure of a man.

He was standing in the far corner of the orchard, near the water mill, and she could not see him at all clearly. He wore a blue coat, like most French workmen wear, and he seemed to be shading his eyes against the sun. She was not at all alarmed, and as she cast her eyes on him, he gave her a long, piercing glance back over his shoulder, but owing to the intervening foliage she was not able to see his features with any detail. The gesture reminded her of something, though she could not for the moment place it, and when she looked again the man had gone.

She mentioned the matter to Philip when he arrived home and he only said with studied casualness, "Oh, I expect the sanitary people have got around to doing that work I asked them about."

This view was reinforced the following day when Pierre and Philip had occasion to go down the far lane on a matter connected with the outfall of the drainage. Philip pointed out to Pierre a long swathe which had been forced through the nettles.

The trail, which was in a different place from the route taken by Philip and Roget on the occasion of their visit, appeared to run from the old graveyard to a point by an ancient, broken-down fence, and then through the orchard below the house. Pierre said nothing but gave Philip a very curious look. The two men made no further reference to the matter.

It was when they were turning to go back that Philip asked Pierre whether they might not visit the orchard. He had never been there since his original inspection of the water mill, but his curiosity had been aroused by the tracks and he wanted to see if the municipal authorities had taken action. Pierre seemed strangely reluctant and mentioned the lateness of the hour; the setting sun was already casting long shadows and a faint swathe of mist could be seen faintly outlining the farthest trees.

Both men were by now rather disturbed by the atmosphere and Philip started when the long drawn-out yowl of a cat sounded from far away. They stood listening for a moment at the entrance of the orchard but the noise was not repeated. Then Philip went boldly crunching his way through a tangle of brush into the old place, more for his own peace of mind than to impress the builder with his English phlegm.

There was nothing out of the way in the orchard. The trail gave out in the centre. There were only a few rusted agricultural implements, half-hidden in the grass. But Philip was surprised to see that a long iron ladder, wreathed in a tangle of branches and mossy lichen, was stapled to the wall below The Grey House. It led up to a point just below the balcony. This was something he felt he ought to look into.

A few minutes later the two men were back in the sunlit uplands of the inhabited lanes leading to the town and were able to forget the strange, brooding atmosphere of the orchard area. Pierre shook his head when Philip mentioned the matter of the ladder. He imagined it would have been placed there in case of fire. For some reason this gave Philip an enormous peace of mind. He expanded in the glow of the sun and insisted that Pierre accompany him to a cafe for an aperitif.

When he arrived back at the house, he found Angele setting the table on the terrace, with Gisele prattling commonplaces as she bustled to and from the kitchen. On pretext of admiring the view, he looked eagerly for the ladder. Yes, there it was, in a rather different position from what he had imagined below. It must be the foreshortening. He did not know why, but he was disturbed to find that anyone coming from below could gain the balcony by this means, old and rusty as the ladder was. Though this in itself was illogical, for the ladder was surely designed to ensure that people from the house could gain the orchard in case of fire.

This again puzzled him, for the ladder ended about three feet from the balcony, in a tangle of brambles and bushes. He saw something else too, which disturbed him more than he cared to admit. The edges of the ladder were covered with lichen and moss. On all the rungs which he could see, the green of years had been torn away, as though by ascending feet.

Philip slept badly that night, but as day succeeded day and the calm of the Indian summer brought with it nothing but blue skies and contentment, he warmed again to The Grey House.

Angele was in good spirits and the couple made their usual visits. Though the work on the house was finished, their local friends were as before; Pierre, Roget, M. Gasion and the Abbe.

Philip was writing better than ever in the more peaceful atmosphere. A book of demoniac tales which he had finished shortly after arrival in Burgundy in May was having a sensational sale in England and the Continental and American rights were being negotiated. He had reason to feel satisfied. And though the Abbe had attempted to dissuade them from the idea, he had started on his most ambitious novel of the macabre to date, a history based loosely on that of the de Menevals. He had quite recovered his spirits and the odd events which earlier had set his mind on strange and sombre paths, now provided much the same material for his book.

His enthusiasm blazed up as day after day found him hunched over his typewriter and Angele could hear the machine clacking on into the long hours of the night. He preferred to work on the balcony even when the nights began to turn cold in early October. Angele remonstrated with him about this, but he laughed at her and her old wives' remedies for colds, and told her not to worry. He had a good sweater on and his pipe for company.

The days of October continued scorching hot, though the nights were cool and Philip was pleased with his progress on the book; he had five chapters finished and another three shaped out in the rough. He began to talk of finishing before the end of November so that he could get an early draft to the publishers before the new year.

Angele was pleased for his sake but troubled at his appearance. Philip had begun to get pale with overwork and his eyes had deep hollows under them which she had never seen before. She had hoped that they would be away to England before the winter set in, but to her alarm Philip had begun to talk of staying at The Grey House the whole winter round. It was all very well for him, with all his work to occupy him, but it would be a dull existence for her once the long, dark wet days of the Burgundy winter set in.

They had left the matter open, without quarrelling over it, and Angele had Philip's promise that if the book was finished within the next month, as well it might be, then they would go back to London and he would deliver the manuscript to the publishers himself. He would not show her the material, for fear of spoiling the effect.

"It's the best thing I've ever done," he said, biting hard on his pipe in his enthusiasm. "I've never known a book come along so well. It's almost as though it's writing itself."

Angele shot him a sharp look, but said nothing.

"It's a curious thing," he went on, after a bit, his brows wrinkled over the mass of typed sheets before him. "There's some of this stuff I don't even remember writing. There's a bit here which gets the mediaeval atmosphere exactly . . . no, perhaps you'd better not read it now. Wait until the end. It spoils it to take it out of context."

Angele continued to watch her husband's progress on the novel with mounting alarm; she had never seen him like this, but consoled herself with the thought that it would do no good to interfere and at the rate he was going they would soon be away to England for the winter.

A few days later, Philip announced in triumph that the last chapter was in progress and that he would revise and re-shape the book in England. Angele greeted the news with unconcealed relief. Philip looked at her in surprise. His face was white and his eyes looked wild with his long hours of composition. Then he put down his pipe and took her in his arms.

"I know it hasn't been much fun for you, darling," he said. "But it will only be a few days more now and then we're off home. I can promise you that the book will be the biggest thing I've ever done. I'm sure you will agree with me that it has all been worthwhile."

Husband and wife, both pleased at the turn of events, occupied themselves with planning their departure and in the evenings Philip pressed on at fever heat with the final pages of the book. They were to leave on the following Wednesday and some of their effects were already packed. The car was to go in for servicing the following day and Angele felt strangely content with her life, with her relationship with Philip and even with The Grey House. She supposed that by next year she would be quite used to its strange atmosphere.

On the Saturday evening Philip finished his work early. He had been at the book hard all afternoon but the climax he was shaping had finally eluded him. He had got up from the table on the terrace with an exclamation of disgust and carried the typewriter and the thick bundle of manuscript through into the dining room. She remembered him putting a fresh sheet of paper into the machine and then they went up to bed.

It was in the middle of the night when she awoke. At first she half drifted back into sleep but then came wide awake, her mind puzzled by a series of sharp, scratching noises. Then she turned, her mind at ease, as she realised Philip must be working again. He had evidently gone back to the novel he had discarded. But then a great fear came into her mind as her arm came into contact with her husband's body at her side and she heard his steady breathing. The scratching noise, loud in the still night, went on from the dining room, arousing a thousand fears in her confused brain.

By a great effort of will-power, for she was a brave woman, she steeled herself to get out of bed without waking her husband. Not bothering to put on a dressing gown, she tip-toed out of the room and down the short flight of stairs; she did not heed the chill of the night air on her skin or notice the coldness of the flagstones on her bare feet.

When she had closed the door of the bedroom behind her, she switched on the light. The blaze of yellow radiance on familiar things steadied her and left her with a core of hard anger; she went down the remaining stairs with a firm step. The scratching which had aroused her attention went on. As she advanced, she threw switch after switch and as light sprang up beneath her hand so her courage rose. When she was about ten yards away from the dining room a board suddenly creaked under her feet. The scratching immediately stopped and she heard an odd scrabbling noise on the floor.

As she pushed open the door with a furiously thudding heart and threw the switch, the sudden glare of light showed her that the room was empty. All was in its place, the whole house now silent, except for the faint tapping of the night wind against the balcony outside. As she thought of this, she set the great lights of the terrace aflame in the gloom but nothing moved in all the expanse of tile and wrought iron.

She forced herself to look at the table. Several sheets of new paper were laid on top of the typewriter ready for copying. The last sheet was in French, in painfully formed handwriting, covering half the page. She read, "And the flesh of virgins is desirable above all others and whosoever acquire this tenderest of all meat shall find the Everlasting Life. And the fairest of all the married women shall be taken to bride by the Whore-Master and the tomb shall flame forth brighter than the wedding-bower . . ." The words ended there, in mid-sentence, the ink still wet.

Angele, shaking and sick, as she backed away from the table, still had time to notice something on the cloth by the machine. It was a small piece of green lichen.

## 5

On the Tuesday, Philip and Angele had invited their friends to a farewell dinner and Philip was to read them portions of his novel. The remainder of the previous week-end was occupied in packing and on Monday afternoon Philip rushed in to Angele, jubilant. The book was finished and he waved the thick mass of manuscript over his head in triumph. Angele had not mentioned to him the events of Saturday evening; something dark hung over the house and she knew in her heart that whatever she could say would make no difference. She was only glad that she would soon be gone without the winter to face; in the meantime she shared Philip's joy in his completed work – on the surface at any event.

The pair spent the mid-afternoon talking over future plans and after an early tea, Philip left for Roget's house; he had arranged to have a drink with his friend and discuss some business. He had plans for the orchard and he proposed to have a big stone wall built to block off the old graveyard – a scheme with which Angele fervently agreed. Gisele was to stay with Angele and Philip intended to return about nine o'clock so that they could get in an early night.

They had to prepare for the party the following day and there would be much to do. It had been a hot day again and Gisele and her mistress sat chatting on the balcony; the steepening sun dyed the opposite mountains a deep carmine and as the rays dipped below the hills it left the valley in deep shadow. It began to be cold, the tinkle of water from the old mill house sounded oddly loud in the silence and thick swathes of mist billowed silently across the orchard.

The cats in the lane below the house seemed to be noisy tonight and Angele abruptly got up and went to fetch a woolly sweater. After a while, she and Gisele moved into the kitchen to continue their conversation but they kept the terrace lights on. Philip had left his thick bundle of manuscript to read; she had promised to give him her opinion on it when he returned, though she felt sure it would take her more than the three hours she had allowed herself.

From time to time, as the two girls were talking, Angele turned to look at the great pile of paper which stood on the typing table in the corner of the terrace where Philip usually worked. Presently she excused herself; Gisele had some cleaning to do and went to get out her vacuum cleaner. Angele took a cup of coffee on to the terrace and sat down at the table. She did not know why she did this, but she felt that Philip's novel had to be read on the terrace, where most of it had been written. The title page was headed: IN THE VALE OF CROTH.

She read on, fascinated. It was the most extraordinary thing Philip had ever written. She did not know how she could have found the ideas in it revolting; perhaps she had started at the wrong page. Taken out of context such a book could give the wrong impression. An hour must have passed, an hour in which the silence was broken only by the measured rustle of turning pages or the faint noises of Gisele's cleaning operations. Her cup of coffee grew cold, untasted.

Presently, she looked up, startled. Her eyes were shining and had an intense expression. Strangely, too, the terrace had suddenly grown oppressively hot. She knew she had to be properly prepared for the final part of the book. She had too many clothes on for this heat – she had to be prepared. When she emerged from her bedroom ten minutes later she had a strange sly look on her face but her cheeks were burning and her eyes bright with longing. She was naked except for a flimsy night-gown which revealed every detail of her figure.

Her hair was freshly combed and she crept almost furtively past the room where Gisele was dusting. Once on the terrace she flung herself on the book and began to devour the pages with her eyes. Eight o'clock fled past and there were only a few dozen pages left. There was a lustful expression on her face and her whole body had begun to tremble. She paid no attention to the thin mist which had begun to envelope the balcony. She strained her eyes to learn the unmentionable secret revealed in the last page of the novel.

Her eyes glazed as she read what no woman was meant to read; something aeons old called through the pages to her. She thought of the whip with the spike and her flesh quivered with delicious terror. As she reached the last sentence of the book there was a rustling on the balcony, which did not distract her.

Her eyes took in the last words on the pages before her, "Nude thou shalt be, naked thou shalt be, unashamed thou shalt be; Prepare thou then to do thy Master's will. Prepare thou, BRIDE OF CROTH."

Angele was already on her feet; her eyes were closed, her tongue lolled out of her mouth, a bead of moisture rolled from under one eyelid.

"Take me, Master," she breathed. Something slit the thin silk of her night-gown, exposing her breasts to the chill air. An unutterable stench was in her nostrils, but she smiled happily as ancient arms lifted her from the balcony.

## 6

Philip returned happily from Roget's house a little after nine, but his casual homecoming soon changed into bewilderment, then terror. The maid, Gisele, sunk into an unnaturally deep sleep on a divan in the dining room, when aroused, expressed only astonishment; the last thing she remembered, she had been dusting the room. Philip went through the house calling his wife's name.

He found the floor of their bedroom littered with every last stitch of his wife's clothing. But it was on the balcony that stark fear leapt out at him for the first time. It was not the overturned coffee cup, the jumble of typed paper littered across the terrace or even the green lichenous mould. But something had forced its way through the mass of brambles from the old ladder below the balcony; it was this, and the strands of his wife's blonde hair caught on the thorns which sent him almost out of his mind.

Seizing a powerful electric searchlight from the garage, he set out down the steep, nettle-grown lane, calling his wife's name. His voice echoed back eerily and once again he caught the loathsome stench of putrescence which seemed to emanate from the mist which swirled about these lower parts. His heart leaped in his throat as the beam of his lamp picked out something white in the gloom. It was then, he thinks, that he gave up hope of seeing Angele again; in the darkest moment of his life idiot fear babbled out at him as the probing beam caught Angele's pathetic, torn, blood-stained scrap of nightgown fast on a patch of nettles as the unnamable thing had carried her through the night.

Philip's knees gave under him and he trembled violently; for the path through the nettles led directly to the old grave-yard and he knew that, much as he loved his wife, he dare not go there alone at night to face such forces. It was a nightmare journey as he stumbled back up the lane; falling, hacking his shins on outcrops of rock, cutting his face with brambles. He looked an appalling sight as he staggered into a cafe on the edge of the town and made his pathetic telephone plea to Roget Frey.

The young architect not only came in his car at once, but collected Monsignor Joffroy from the university on his way over. The couple were with the demented Philip in a quarter of an hour. His appearance shocked them both but a few words only told the old Abbe all he had suspected and feared from the first.

He had come fully prepared. Round his neck he had an ornate silver crucifix; he carried a prayer book in one hand and, curiously, a crowbar. Roget Frey had also armed himself with a revolver and in the back of his car were two enormous electric lamps, like car headlights.

"Courage, *mon pauvre ami*," said Monsignor Joffroy, helping Philip into a seat beside him. "What must be done, must be done. I fear it is too late to save your dear wife, but we must do all we can to destroy this evil being in order to save her soul." Horrified, half dazed, understanding only a quarter of what he was told, Philip clutched the Monsignor's arm as Roget's sports car leapt like a demented thing down the narrow lane at suicidal speed.

At the bottom Frey drove straight at the wall of brambles and stinging nettles as far as he could. The headlights shone a brilliant radiance right down towards the cemetery gates. Frey left the lights on and the engine running.

"To remind us of normality," he said with great emphasis.

"This will do," said Monsignor Joffroy, making a great sign of the cross in the air before him. "The rest is in God's hands."

Roget handed a long crowbar to Philip, the prelate carried one searchlight and the other crowbar, and Roget had his revolver in one hand and the second searchlight in his left. The three men walked abreast through the wet grass, making no attempt at concealment. Philip put down his own flashlight at the cemetery entrance, which lit up a considerable part of the graveyard; he had recovered his courage now and led the way towards the de Meneval tomb.

Their feet echoed hollowly over the gravel and Philip dropped to one knee as a thing with great flaming eyes drove at them from the top of a gravestone. Frey's revolver roared twice, with deafening impact, and a broken-backed, yowling creature that had been the great cat went whimpering to die in the bushes. Monsignor Joffroy had jumped up instantly and without swerving set off at a run towards the de Meneval tomb. The others followed, trembling from the sudden shock of the revolver shots.

Philip could never forget that charnel house scene. Like a tableau out of Goya, it ever haunted his life. The nude body of Angele, quite dead, splashed with gouts of blood, but with an expression of diabolical happiness on her face, was clutched fast in the arms of a thing which lay on its side at the entrance of the tomb, as though exhausted. It was dressed in a frayed and faded blue coat and the abomination had apparently broken one of its old and brittle legs as it dropped from the balcony. This had accounted for its slow progress to the malodorous lair beneath the old de Meneval mausoleum.

But the worst horror was to come. In one withered and grey, parchment-like paw was clutched a whip-and-spike instrument dabbled with fresh young blood. The face, half-eaten away and with the broken bones portruding from the split, rotted skin, was turned towards them. Something moved and the eyes, which were still alive, gazed balefully at the three men. Old de Meneval was malevolent to the last.

Monsignor Joffroy hesitated not an instant. Pronouncing the name of the Father, the Son and the Holy Ghost in a voice like thunder, he held aloft the cross. Then, handing it to Philip, he brought down the great crowbar again and again on the brittle ancient blasphemy that had once been a man. Teeth and hair flew in all directions, old bones cracked and split and dust and putrefaction rose in the still air. At length, all was quiet.

Panting, the Monsignor led the two men away. "This is all we can do for tonight," he said. "Much remains to be done in the morning, but this abomination will never walk again."

He sprinkled holy water from a bottle over the remains of Angele and covered it with a blanket from the car. To Philip's anguished protests over his wife, he remained adamant.

"We must not move her," he insisted. "She is no longer your wife, my poor friend. She belongs to them. For her own sake and for her immortal soul we must do what has to be done."

Little remains to be told, though the city will remember for many a long year the horrors which were found in the old de Meneval tomb. Monsignor Joffroy obtained a special dispensation from the Bishop that same night and the very next morning, at first light, a battalion of the Infanterie Coloniale were called in to work under the Abbe's directions.

These soldiers, hardened and toughened on the forge of war as they were, saw sights which made them act like frightened children when the vault below was opened. Monsignor Joffroy, calm and strong, prevented a panic and bore himself like a true man of the church that day. Indeed, many said that the sights he saw and the things he had to do hastened the good man's own end.

The body of Angele was taken to a hastily prepared pyre behind the canvas shelter in the old cemetery and burned while priests conducted a service. In the vault of the de Menevals a stupefying sight awaited the intruders, priest and soldier alike. Some say that there were more than thirty bodies, de Menevals and the naked corpses of fresh young girls, as undecayed as the day they were abducted from the neighbourhood upwards of two hundred years before.

The searchers also found vast passages and chambers under the earth, equipped as for the living, where the undead dead still held obscene and blasphemous rites. Be that as it may, and no one can now say for certain that all this is true, the Bishop himself with Monsignor Joffroy as his chaplain held a service of exorcism and afterwards the troops went in with flame guns and destroyed every last one of those horrors as they lay.

The underground chambers were blown up by Army engineers and the whole of the area cauterised and purified. Later, by order of the Bishop the field was concreted over and from that day to this the people of the city have remained unmolested, neither does mist appear in the orchard by the mill house.

The Grey House still stands, now fast falling to ruin and deserted. M. Gasion, greyer now, has retired and gone to live in a villa in Normandy; Monsignor Joffroy is dead; and Roget Frey is a successful architect, practising in Paris.

## 7

Philip is still a successful novelist. He lives in London, with a very young wife, who is not serious at all, and is content with what she calls the simple things of life. He seldom goes abroad, very occasionally to France, and never to Burgundy. His stories now, while very popular in the English-speaking world, are not what they were.

They are mainly comedies and light pieces, with an occasional political drama. Though he is still a year or so short of fifty, his hair is quite white and his face that of an old man. It is only when one looks closely into his eyes that one can see the fires of the pit.

Two small footnotes. Afterwards, in The Grey House, Roget Frey found a great pile of grey ash in a circular stone jar on the terrace.

In the Great Hall, the painting of the old man and the girl had disappeared; the whole wall had been gouged out from the balcony and the solid stone pitted as though with a pickaxe.

He did not make any inquiries and he had no theories, so the mysteries remain.

# Watching Me, Watching You

## Fay Weldon

### Prospectus

**Address:** 66, Aldermans Drive, Bristol, Somerset, England.

**Property:** Nineteenth-century terraced house in residential area of the city. Spacious rooms on two floors with a basement offering additional space. The house is prime for redevelopment in an area destined to become fashionable.

**Viewing Date:** Winter, 1980.

**Agent:** Fay Weldon (1931– ) was born in Worcester and educated at the University of St Andrews, where she began to write. She has subsequently become a champion of women's rights and novels like *The Fat Woman's Joke* (1967), *Down Among The Women* (1971) and *Female Friends* (1975) have played a major role in the development of female consciousness. Weldon has also written a number of excellent ghost stories, including "Angel, All Innocence", "Breakages", "Spirit of the House" and "Watching Me, Watching You", in which the ghost *itself* is the guide to a haunted house that is typical of those in which millions of people live.

The ghost liked the stairs best, where people passed quickly and occasionally, holding their feelings in suspense between the closing of one door and the opening of another. Mostly, the ghost slept. He preferred sleep. But sometimes the sense of something important happening, some crystallization of the past or omen for the future, would wake him, and he would slither off the stair and into one room or another of the house to see what was going on. Presently, he wore an easy path of transition into a particular room on the first floor – as sheep will wear an easy path in the turf by constant trotting to and fro. Here, as the seasons passed, a plane tree pressed closer and closer against the window, keeping out light and warmth. The various cats which lived out their lives in the house seldom went into this small damp back room, and seemed to feel the need to race up and down that portion of the stairs the ghost favoured, though sitting happily enough at the bottom of the stairs, or on the top landing.

Many houses contain ghosts. (It would be strange if they didn't.) Mostly they sleep, or wake so seldom their presence is not noticed, let alone minded. If a glass falls off a shelf in 1940, and a door opens by itself in 1963, and a sense of oppression is felt in 1971, and knocking sounds are heard on Christmas Day, 1980 – who wants to make anything of that? Four inexplicable happenings in a week call for exorcism – the same number spread over forty years call for nothing more than a shrug and a stiff drink.

66 Aldermans Drive, Bristol. The house had stood for a hundred and thirty years, and the ghost had slept and occasionally sighed and slithered sideways, and otherwise done little else but puff out a curtain on a still day for all but ten of those. He entered the house on the shoulders of a parlour-maid. She had been to a seance in the hope of raising her dead lover, but had raised something altogether more elusive, if at least sleepier, instead. The maid had stayed in the house until she died, driving her mistress to suicide and marrying the master the while, and the ghost had stayed too, long after all were dead, and the house empty, with paper peeling off the walls, and the banisters broken,

and carpets rotting on the floors, and dust and silence everywhere.

The ghost slept, and woke again to the sound of movement, and different voices. The new people were numerous: they warmed gnarled winter hands before gas-fires, and the smell of boiled cabbage and sweat wafted up the stairs, and exhaustion and indifference prevailed. In the back room on the first floor, presently, a girl gave birth to a baby. The ghost sighed and puffed out the curtains. In this room, earlier, the maid's mistress had hanged herself, making a swinging shadow against the wall in the gas-light shining from the stairs. The ghost had a sense of justice, or at any rate balance. He slept again.

The house emptied. Rain came through broken tiles into the back room. A man with a probe came and pierced into the rotten beams of roof and floor, and shook his head and laughed. The tree thrust a branch through the window, and a sparrow flew in, and couldn't get out, and died, and after mice and insects and flies had finished with it, was nothing more than two slender white bones, placed crosswise.

It was 1965. The front door opened and a man and a woman entered, and such was their natures that the ghost was alert at once. The man's name was Maurice: he was burly and warm-skinned; his hands were thick and crude; labourer's hands, but clean and soft. His hair was pale and tightly curled; he was bearded; his eyes were large and heavily hooded. He looked at the house as if he were already its master: as if he cared nothing for its rotten beams and its leaking roof.

"We'll have it," he said. She laughed. It was a nervous laugh, which she used when she was frightened. She had a small cross face half-lost in a mass of coarse red hair. She was tiny waisted, big-bosomed and long-legged; her limbs lean and freckly. Her fingers were long and fragile. "But it's falling down," said Vanessa. "How can we afford it?"

"Look at the detail on the cornices!" was all he said. "I'm sure they're original."

"I expect we can make something of it," she said.

She loved him. She would do what she could for him. The ghost sensed cruelty, somewhere: he bustled around, stirring the air.

"It's very draughty," she complained.

They looked into the small back room on the first floor and even he shivered.

"I'll never make anything of this room," she said.

"Vanessa," he said. "I trust you to do something wonderful with everything."

"Then I'll make it beautiful," she said, loud and clear, marking out her future. "Even this, for you."

The plane tree rubbed against the window pane.

"It's just a question of lopping a branch or two," he said.

One night, after dark, when builders' trestles were everywhere, and the sour smell of damp lime plaster was on the stairs. Maurice spread a blanket for Vanessa in the little back room.

"Not here," she said.

"It's the only place that isn't dusty," he said.

He made love to her, his broad, white body covering her narrow, freckled one altogether.

"Today the divorce came through," he said.

Other passions split the air. The ghost felt them. Outside in the alley which ran behind the house, beneath the plane tree, stood another woman. Her face was round and sweet, her hair was short and mousy, her eyes bright, bitter and wet. In the house the girl cried out and the man groaned; and the watcher's face became empty, drained of sweetness, left expressionless, a vacuum into which something had to flow. The ghost left with her, on her shoulders.

* * *

"I have fibrositis now," said Anne, "as well as everything else." She said it to herself, into the mirror, when she was back home in the basement of the house in Upton Park, where once she and Maurice had lived and built their life. She had to say it to herself, because there was no one else to say it to, except their child Wendy, and Wendy was only four and lay asleep in a pile of blankets on the floor, her face and hands sticky and unwashed. Anne threw an ashtray at the mirror and cracked it, and Wendy woke and cried. "Seven years bad luck," said Anne. "Well, who's counting!"

Sweetness had run out: sourness took its place: she too had marked out her future.

The ghost found a space against the wall between the barred windows of the room, and took up residence there, and drowsed, waking sometimes to accompany Anne on her midnight vigils to 66 Aldermans Drive. Presently he wore an easy route for himself, slipping and slithering between the two places, and no longer needed her for the journey. Sometimes he was here, sometimes there.

In Aldermans Drive he found a painted stairwell and a mended banister, but stairs which were still uncarpeted, and a cat which howled and shot upstairs. The ghost moved in to the small back room and the door pushed open in his path and shadows swung and shifted against the wall.

Vanessa was wearing jeans. She and Maurice were papering the room with bright patterned paper. They were laughing: she had glue in her hair.

"When we're rich," she was saying, "I'll never do this kind of thing again. We'll always have professionals in to do it."

"When we're rich!" He yearned for it.

"Of course we'll be rich. You'll write a bestseller; you're far better than anyone else. Genius will out!"

* * *

If he felt she misunderstood the nature of genius, or was insensitive to what he knew by instinct, that popularity and art are at odds, he said nothing. He indulged her. He kissed her. He loved her.

"What are those shadows on the wall?" she asked.

"We always get those in here," he said. "It's the tree against the window."

"We'll have to get it lopped," she said.

"It seems a pity," he said. "Such a wonderful old tree."

He trimmed another length of paper.

"How can the tree be casting shadows?" she asked. "The sun isn't out."

"Some trick of reflected light," said Maurice. The knife in his hand slipped, and he swore.

"It doesn't matter," said Vanessa, looking at the torn paper, "it doesn't have to be perfect. It's only Wendy's room. And then only for weekends. It's not as if she was going to be here all the time."

"Perhaps you and I should have this room," said Maurice, "and Wendy could have the one next door. It overlooks the crescent. It has a view, and a balcony. She'll love it."

"So would I," said Vanessa.

"I don't want Wendy to feel second-best," said Maurice. "Not after all we've put her through."

"All that's happened to her," corrected Vanessa, tight lipped.

"And don't say 'only Wendy'," he rebuked her. "She is my child, after all."

"It isn't fair! Why couldn't you be like other people? Why do you have to have a past?"

They worked in silence for a little, and the ghost writhed palely in the anger in the air, and then Vanessa relented and smiled and said. "Don't let's quarrel," and he said, "you know I love you," and the fine front room was Wendy's and the small back room was to house their marriage bed.

"I'm sure I closed the door," said Vanessa presently, "but now it's open."

"The catch is weak," said Maurice. "I'll mend it when I can. There's just so much to do in a home this size," and he sighed and the sigh exhaled out of the open window into the street.

"Goodbye," said Vanessa.

"Why did you say goodbye?" asked Maurice.

"Because the net curtains flapped and whoever came in through the door was clearly going out by the window," said Vanessa, thinking she was joking, too young and beautiful and far from death to mind an unseen visitor or so. The ghost whirled away on the remnant of Maurice's sigh, over the roof-tops and the brow of the hill, and down into Upton Park, where it was winter, no longer summer, and little Wendy was six, and getting out of bed, bare cold toes on chilly lino.

The ghost's observations were now from outside time. So a man might stand on a station overpass and watch a train go through beneath. Such a man could see, if he chose, any point along the train – in front of him the future, behind him the past, directly beneath him, changing always from past to future, his main rumbling, noisy perception of the present. The ghost keeps his gaze steadily forward.

The clock says five to nine; Anne is asleep in bed. Wendy shakes her awake.

"My feet are cold," says the little girl.

"Then put on your slippers," mourns the mother, out of sleep. It has been an uneasy, unsatisfying slumber. Once she lay next to Maurice and fancied she drew her strength out of his slumbering body, hot beside her, like some spiritual water-bottle. She clings to the fancy in her mind: she refuses to sleep as she did when a child, composed and decent in solitude, providing her own warmth well enough.

"Won't I be late for school?" asks Wendy.

"No," says Anne, in the face of all evidence to the contrary.

"It is ever so cold," says Wendy. "Can I light the gas-fire?"

"No you can't," says Anne. "We can't afford it."

"Daddy will pay the bill," says Wendy, hopefully. But her mother just laughs.

"I'm frightened," says Wendy, all else having failed. "The curtains are waving about and the window isn't even open. Can I get into your bed?"

Anne moves over and the child gets in.

An egg teeters on the edge of the table, amidst the remnants of last night's chips and tomato sauce, and falls and smashes. Anne sits up in bed, startled into reaction. "How did that happen?" she asks, aloud. But there is no one to reply, for Wendy has fallen asleep, and the ghost is spinning and spinning, nothing but a whirl of air in the corner of the eye, and no one listens to him, anyway.

Further forward still, and there's Vanessa, sitting up in bed, bouncy brown-nippled breasts half covered by fawn lace. It is a brass bed, finely filigreed. Maurice wears black silk pyjamas. He sits on the edge of the bed, while Vanessa sips fresh orange juice, and opens his letters.

"Any cheques?" asks Vanessa.

"Not today," he says. Maurice is a writer. Cheques bounce through the letter box with erratic energy: bills come in with a calm, steady beat. It is a tortoise and hare situation, and the tortoise always wins.

"Perhaps you should change your profession," she suggests. "Be an engineer or go into advertising. I hate all this worry about money."

A mirror slips upon its string on the wall, hangs sidewise. Neither notice.

"Is that a letter from Anne?" asks Vanessa. "What does she want now?"

"It's her electricity bill," he says.

"She's supposed to pay that out of her monthly cheque. She only sends you these demands to make you feel unhappy and guilty. She's jealous of us. How I despise jealousy! What a bitch she is!"

"She has a child to look after," says Maurice. "My child."

"If I had your child, would you treat me better?" she asks.

"I treat you perfectly well," he says, pulling the bedclothes back, rubbing black silk against beige lace, and the mirror falls off the wall altogether, startling them, stopping them. "This whole room will have to be stripped out," complains Vanessa. "The plaster is rotten. I'll get arthritis from the damp." Vanessa notices, sometimes, as she walks up and down the stairs, that her knees ache.

Wendy is ten. Anne's room has been painted white, and there are cushions on the chairs, and dirty washing is put in the basket, not left on the floor, and times are a little better. A little. There is passion in the air.

"Vanessa says I can stay all week not just weekends, and go to school from Aldermans Drive!" says Wendy. "Live with Dad, and not with you."

"What did you say?" asks Anne, trying to sound casual.

"I said no thank you," says Wendy. "There's no peace over there. They always have the builders in. Bang, bang, bang! And Dad's always shut away in a room, writing. I prefer it here, in spite of everything. Damp and draughts and all."

The damp on the wall between the barred windows is worse. It makes a strange shape on the wall; it seems to change from day to day. The house belongs to Maurice. He will not have the roof over their heads mended. He says he cannot afford to. In the rooms above live tenants, protected by law, who pay next to nothing in rent. How can he spare the money needed to keep the house in good order – and why, according to Vanessa, should he?

* * *

"We're just the rejects of the world," says Anne to Wendy, and Wendy believes her, and her mouth grows tight and pouty instead of firm and generous, as it could have been, and her looks are spoiled. Anne is right, that's the trouble of it. Rejects!

"How my shoulder hurts," say Anne. She should have stayed at home, never crossed the city to stand beneath the plane-tree in the alley behind Aldermans Drive, allowed herself her paroxysms of jealousy, grief, and solitary sexual frenzy. She has had fibrositis ever since. But she felt what she felt. You can help what you do, but not what you feel.

The ghost looks further forward to Aldermans Drive and finds the bed gone in the small back room, and a dining table in its place, and candles lit, and guests, and smooth mushroom soup being served. The candles throw shadows on to the wall: this way, that way. One of the guests tries to make sense of them, but can't. She has wild blonde hair and a fair skin and a laughing mouth, unlike Maurice's other women. Her name is Audrey. She is an actress. Maurice's hair is falling out. His temples are quite bare, and he has a moustache now instead of a beard, and he seems distinguished, rather than aspiring. His hand smoothes Audrey's little one, and Vanessa sees. Maurice defies her jealousy: he smiles blandly, cruelly, at his wife.

He turns to Audrey's husband, who is eighteen years older than Audrey, and says, "Ah youth, youth!" and offers back Audrey's hand, closing the husband's fingers over the wife's so that nobody could possibly take offence, and Vanessa feels puzzled at her own distress, and her glass of red wine tips over on its own account.

"Vanessa! Clumsy!" reproaches Maurice.

"But I didn't!" she says. No one believes her. Why should they? They pour white wine on the stain to neutralize the red, and it works, and looking at the tablecloth, presently, no one would have known anything untoward had happened at all.

* * *

"We must have security," Vanessa weeps from time to time.

"I can't stand the uncertainty of it all! You must stop being a writer. Or write something different. Stop writing novels. Write for television instead."

"No, you must stop spending the money," he shouts. "Stop doing up this house. Changing this, changing that."

"But I want it to be nice. We must have a nursery. I can't keep the baby in a drawer."

Vanessa is pregnant.

"Why not? It's what Anne had to do, thanks to you."

"Anne! Can't you ever forget Anne?" she shrieks. "Does she have to be on our backs for ever? She has ruined our lives."

But their lives aren't ruined. The small back room becomes a nursery. The baby sleeps there. He is a boy, his name is Jonathan. he sleeps badly and cries a lot and is hard to love. His eyes follow the shadows on the wall, this way, that way.

"There's nothing wrong with his eyes," says the doctor, visiting, puzzled at the mother's fears. "But his chest is bad."

Vanessa sits by the cot and rocks her feverish child.

"For you and I—" she sings, as she sings when she is nervous, driving away fear with melody –

"–have a guardian angel – on high with nothing to do –

–but to give to you and to give – to me –

–love for ever – true—".

Maurice is in the room. Vanessa is crying.

"But why won't you go back to work?" he demands. "It would take the pressure off me. I could write what I want to write, not what I have to write."

"I want to look after my baby myself," she weeps. "It's a man's job to support his family. And you're not exactly William Shakespeare. Why don't you write films? That's where the money is."

The baby coughs. The doctor says the room is too damp for its good. "I never liked this room," says Vanessa, as she and

Maurice carry out the cot. "And you and I always quarrel in it. The quarrelling room. I hate it. But I love you."

"I love you," he says, crossing his fingers.

The ghost looks forward. Aldermans Drive has become one of the most desirable streets in Bristol, all new paint and French kitchenware and Welsh dressers seen through lighted windows. The property is in Maurice's name, as seems reasonable, since he earns the money. He writes films, for Hollywood.

Anne's bed turns into a foam settee by day: she has a cooker instead of a gas ring: the window bars have gone: the panes are made of reinforced glass. She has had a telephone installed. Wendy has platform heels and puts cream on her spots.

The ghost looks further forward, and Anne has a boyfriend. A man sits opposite her in a freshly covered armchair. Broken springs have been taped flat. Sometimes she lets him into her bed, but his flesh is cool and none too firm, and she remembers Maurice's body, hot-water bottle in her bed, and won't forget. Won't. Can't.

"Is it wrong to hate people?" asks Anne. "I hate Vanessa, and with reason. She is a thief. Why do people ask her into their houses? Is it that they don't realize, or just that they don't care? She stole my husband: she tried to steal my child. Maurice has never been happy with her. He never wanted to leave me. She seduced him. She thought he'd be famous one day; how wrong she was! He's sold out, you know! One day he'll come back to me, what's left of him, and I'll be expected to pick up the bits."

"But he's married to her. They have a child. How can he come back to you?" He is a nice man, a salesman, thoughtful and kind.

"So was I married to him. So do I have his child."

How stubborn she is!

"You're obsessive." He is beginning to be angry. Well, he has been angry often enough before, and still stayed around for more.

"While you take Maurice's money," he says, "you will never be free of him."

"Those few miserable pennies! What difference can they make? I live in penury, while she lives in style. He is Wendy's father; he has an obligation to support us. He was the guilty party, after all."

"The law no longer says guilty or not guilty, in matter of divorce."

"Well, it should!" She is passionate. "He should pay for what he did to me and Wendy. He destroyed our lives."

The ghost is lulled by the turning wheel of her thoughts, so steady on its axis: he drowses; responds to a spasm of despair, an act of decision on the man's part, one morning, as he leaves Anne's unsatisfactory bed. He dresses silently: he means to go: never to come back. He looks in the mirror to straighten his tie and sees Anne's face instead of his own.

He cries out and Anne wakes.

"I'm sorry," she says. "Don't go."

But he does, and he doesn't come back.

The gap between what could be, and what is, defeats him.

Anne has a job as a waitress. It is a humiliation. Maurice does not know she is earning. Anne keeps it a secret, for Vanessa would surely love an excuse to reduce Anne's alimony, already whittled away by inflation.

The decorators are back in Aldermans Drive. The smell of fresh plaster has the ghost alert. Paper is being stripped from walls: doors driven through here: walls dismantled there. The cat runs before the ghost, like a leaf before wind, looking for escape; finding none, cornered in the small back room, where animals never go if they can help it, and the shadows swing to and fro, and the tiny crossed bones from a dead sparrow are lodged beneath the wainscot.

* * *

"Get out of here, cat!" cries Vanessa. "I hate cats, don't you? Maurice loves them. But they don't like me: for ever trying to trip me on the stairs, when I had to go to the baby, in the night."

"I expect they were jealous," says the man with her. He is young and handsome, with shrewd, insincere eyes and a lecher's mouth. He is a decorator. He looks at the room with dislike, and at Vanessa, speculatively.

"The worst room in the house," she laments. "It's been bedroom, dining room, nursery. It never works! I hope it's better as a bathroom."

He moves his hand to the back of her neck but she laughs and sidesteps.

"The plaster's shockingly damp," he says, and as if to prove his opinion the curtain rail falls off the wall altogether, making a terrible clatter and clash, and the cat yowls and Vanessa shrieks, and Maurice strides up the stairs to see what is happening, and what was in the air between Vanessa and Toby evaporates. The ghost is on Anne's side – if ghosts take sides.

How grand and boring the house is now! There is a faint scent of chlorine in the air; it comes from the swimming pool in the basement. The stair walls are mirrored: a maid polishes away at the first landing but it's always a little misery. She marvels at how long the flowers last, when placed on the little Georgian stair-table brought by Vanessa for Maurice on his fifty-second birthday. The maid is in love with Maurice, but Maurice has other fish to fry.

Further forward still: something's happening in the bathroom! The bath is deep blue and the taps are gold, and the wallpaper rose, but still the shadows swing to and fro, against the wall.

Audrey has spilt red wine upon her dress. She is more beautiful than she was. She is intelligent. She is no longer married or an actress: she is a solicitor. Maurice admires that very much. He thinks women should be useful, not like Vanessa. He is tired of girls who have young flesh and liquid eyes and love his bed but despise him in their hearts. Audrey does not despise him. Vanessa has forgotten how.

Maurice is helping Audrey sponge down her dress. His hand strays here and there. She is accustomed to it: she does not mind.

"What are those shadows on the wall?" she asks.

"Some trick of the light," he says.

"Perhaps we should use white wine to remove the red," she says. "Remember that night so long ago? It was in this room, wasn't it! Vanessa had it as a dining room, then. I think I fell in love with you that night."

"And I with you," he says.

Is it true? – He can hardly remember.

"What a lot of time we've wasted," he laments, and this for both of them is true enough. They love each other.

"Dear Maurice," she says, "I can't bear to see you so unhappy. It's all Vanessa's doing. She stopped you writing. You would be a great writer if it wasn't for her, not just a Hollywood hack! You still could be!"

He laughs, but he is moved. He thinks it might be true. If it were not for Vanessa he would not just be rich and successful, he would be rich, successful, and renowned as well.

"Vanessa says this room is haunted," he says, seeing the shadows himself, almost defined at last, a body hanging from a noose: a woman destroyed, or self-destroyed. What's the difference? Love does it. Love and ghosts.

"What's the matter?" Audrey asks. He's pale.

"We could leave here," he says. "Leave this house. You and me."

A shrewd light gleams in her intelligent, passionate eyes. How he loves her!

"A pity to waste all this," says Audrey. "It is your home, after all, Vanessa's never liked it. If anyone leaves, it should be her."

The flowers on the landing are still fresh and sweet a week later. Maurice will keep the table they stand upon – a gift from Vanessa to him, after all. If you give someone something, it's theirs for ever. That is the law, says Audrey.

Vanessa moves her belongings from the bathroom shelf. She wants nothing of his, nothing. Just a few personal things – toothbrush, paste, cleansing cream. She will take her child and go. She cannot remain under the same roof, and he won't leave.

"You must see it's for the best, Vanessa," says Maurice, awkwardly. "We haven't really been together for years, you and I."

"All that bed-sharing?" she enquires. "That wasn't together? The meals, the holidays, the friends, the house? The child? Not together?"

"No," he says. "Not together the way I feel with Audrey." She can hardly believe it. So far she is shocked, rather than distressed. presently, distress will set in: but not yet.

"I'll provide for you, of course," he says, "You and the child. I always looked after Anne, didn't I? Anne and Wendy." Vanessa turns to stare at him, and over his shoulder sees a dead woman hanging from a rope, but who is to say where dreams begin and reality ends? At the moment she is certainly in a nightmare. She looks back to Maurice, and sees the horror of her own life, and the swinging body fades, if indeed it was ever there. The door opens, by itself.

"You never did fix the catch," she says.

"No," he replies. "I never got round to it."

The train beneath the overpass was nearly through. The past had caught up with the present and the present was dissolving into the future, and the future was all but out of sight.

It was 1980. The two women, Anne and Vanessa, sat together in the room in Upton Park. The damp patch was back again, but hidden by one of the numerous posters which lined the walls calling on women to live, to be free, to protest, to re-claim the right, demand wages for housework, to do anything in the world but love. The personal, they proclaimed, was the political. Other women came and went in the room.

"However good the present is," said Anne, "the past cannot be undone. I wasted so much of my life. I look back and see scenes I would rather not remember. Little things; silly things, even. Wendy being late for school, a lover looking in a mirror. Damp on a wall. I used to think this room was haunted."

"I used to think the same of Aldermans Drive," said Vanessa, "but now I realize what it was. What I sensed was myself now, looking back; me now watching me then, myself remembering me with sorrow for what I was and need never have been."

They talked about Audrey.

"They say she's unfaithful to him," said Anne. "Well, he's nearly sixty and she's thirty-five. What did he expect?"

"Love," said Vanessa, "like the rest of us."

# 4

# PHANTOM LOVERS

## Sex and the Supernatural

# A Spirit Elopement

## Richard Dehan

### Prospectus

**Address:** Mon Desir, Guernsey, Channel Islands.

**Property:** Eighteenth-century mansion house standing in its own spacious grounds, screened by lofty red-brick walls, with a wrought iron gate entranceway. Tastefully decorated in yellow-white.

**Viewing Date:** April, 1915.

**Agent:** "Richard Dehan" was the pseudonym of Clotilde Mary Graves (1863–1932), who was born in County Cork, Ireland and became popular with readers on both sides of the Atlantic for her humorous novels and stories of witchcraft and pagan religions, including *Under The Hermes* (1917) and *The Eve of Pascua* (1920). She also travelled a great deal and wrote short stories on a variety of themes from the Boer War to Eskimo folklore. Graves resided in the Channel Islands for several years, which were the inspiration for this story.

When I exchanged my maiden name for better or worse, and dearest Vavasour and I, at the conclusion of the speeches – I was married in a travelling-dress of Bluefern's – descended the steps of mamma's house in Ebury Street – the Belgravian, *not* the Pimlican end – and, amid a hurricane of farewells and a hailstorm of pink and yellow and white *confetti*, stepped into the brougham that was to convey us to Waterloo Station, *en route* for Southampton – our honeymoon was to be spent in Guernsey – we were perfectly well satisfied with ourselves and each other. This state of mind is not uncommon at the outset of wedded life. You may have heard the horrid story of the newly-wedded cannibal chief, who remarked that he had never yet known a young bride to disagree with her husband in the early stages of the honeymoon. I believe if dearest Vavasour had seriously proposed to chop me into *cotêlettes* and eat me, with or without sauce, I should have taken it for granted that the powers that he had destined me to the high end of supplying one of the noblest of created beings with an *entrée* dish.

We were idiotically blissful for two or three days. It was flowery April, and Guernsey was looking her loveliest. No horrid hotel or boarding-house sheltered our lawful endearments. Some old friends of papa's had lent us an ancient mansion standing in a wild garden, now one pink riot of almond-blossom, screened behind lofty walls of lichened red brick and weather-worn, wrought-iron gates, painted yellow-white like all the other iron and wood work about the house.

"Mon Désir" the place was called, and the fragrance of potpourri yet hung about the old panelled salons. Vavasour wrote a sonnet – I have omitted to speak before of my husband's poetic gifts – all about the breath of new Passion stirring the fragrant dust of dead old Love, and the kisses of lips long mouldered that mingled with ours. It was a lovely sonnet, but crawly, as the poetical compositions of the Modern School are apt to be. And Vavasour was an enthusiastic convert to, and follower of, the Modern School. He had often told me that, had not his father heartlessly thrown him into his brewery business at the outset of his career – Sim's Mild and Bitter Ales being the foundation upon which the family fortunes were originally reared – he, Vavasour, would have been, ere the time of speaking, known to Fame, not only as a Minor Poet, but a Minor Decadent Poet – which trisyllabic addition, I believe, makes as advantageous a difference as the word "native" when attached to an oyster, or the guarantee "new laid" when employed with reference to an egg.

Dear Vavasour's temperament and tastes having a decided bias towards the gloomy and mystic, he had, before his great discovery of his latent poetical gifts, and in the intervals of freedom from the brain-carking and soul-stultifying cares of business, made several excursions into the regions of the Unknown. He had had some sort of intercourse with the Swedenborgians, and had mingled with the Muggletonians; he had coquetted with the Christian Scientists, and had been, until Theosophic Buddhism opened a wider field to his researches, an enthusiastic Spiritualist. But our engagement somewhat cooled his passion for psychic research, and when questioned by me with regard to table-rappings, manifestations, and materialisations, I could not but be conscious of a reticence in his manner of responding to my innocent desire for information. The reflection that he probably, like Canning's knife-grinder, had no story to tell, soon induced me to abandon the subject. I myself am somewhat reserved at this day in my method of dealing with the subject of spooks. But my silence does not proceed from ignorance.

Knowledge came to me after this fashion. Though the April sun shone bright and warm upon Guernsey, the island nights were chill. Waking by dear Vavasour's side – the novelty of this experience has since been blunted by the usage of years – somewhere between one and two o'clock towards break of the fourth day following our marriage, it occurred to me that a faint cold draught, with a suggestion of dampness about it, was blowing against my right cheek. One of the windows upon that side – our room possessed a rather unbecoming cross-light – had probably been left open. Dear Vavasour, who occupied the right side of our couch, would wake with toothache in the morning, or, perhaps, with mumps! Shuddering, as much at the latter idea as with cold, I opened my eyes, and sat up in bed with a definite intention of getting out of it and shutting the offending casement. Then I saw Katie for the first time.

She was sitting on the right side of the bed, close to dear Vavasour's pillow; in fact, almost hanging over it. From the first moment I knew that which I looked upon to be no creature of flesh and blood, but the mere apparition of a woman. It was not only that her face, which struck me as both pert and plain; her hands; her hair, which she wore dressed in an old-fashioned ringletty mode – in fact, her whole personality was faintly luminous, and surrounded by a halo of bluish phosphorescent light. It was not only that she was transparent, so that I saw the pattern of the old-fashioned, striped, dimity bed-curtain, in the shelter of which she sat, quite plainly through her. The consciousness was further conveyed to me by a voice – or the toneless, flat, faded impression of a voice – speaking faintly and clearly, not at my outer, but at my inner ear.

"Lie down again, and don't fuss. It's only Katie!" she said.

"Only Katie!" I liked that!

"I dare say you don't," she said tartly, replying as she had spoken, and I wondered that a ghost should exhibit such want of breeding. "But you have got to put up with me!"

"How dare you intrude here – and at such an hour!" I exclaimed mentally, for there was no need to wake dear Vavasour by talking aloud when my thoughts were read at sight by the ghostly creature who sat so familiarly beside him.

"I knew your husband before you did," responded Katie, with a faint phosphorescent sneer. "We became acquainted at a *séance* in North-West London soon after his conversion to Spiritualism, and have seen a great deal of each other from time to time." She tossed her shadowy curls with a possessive air that annoyed me horribly. "He was constantly materialising me in order to ask questions about Shakespeare. It is a standing joke in our Spirit world that, from the best educated spook in our society down to the most illiterate astral that ever knocked out 'rapport' with one 'p,' we are all expected to know whether Shakespeare wrote his own plays, or whether they were done by another person of the same name."

"And which way was it?" I asked, yielding to a momentary twinge of curiosity.

Katie laughed mockingly. "There you go!" she said, with silent contempt.

"I wish *you* would!" I snapped back mentally. "It seems to me that you manifest a great lack of refinement in coming here!"

"I cannot go until Vavasour has finished," said Katie pertly. "Don't you see that he has materialised me by dreaming about me? And as there exists *at present*" – she placed an annoying stress upon the last two words – "a strong sympathy between you, so it comes about that I, as your husband's spiritual affinity, am visible to your waking perceptions. All the rest of the time I am hovering about you, though unseen."

"I call it detestable!" I retorted indignantly. Then I gripped my sleeping husband by the shoulder. "Wake up! wake up!" I cried aloud, wrath lending power to my grasp and a penetrative quality to my voice. "Wake up and leave off dreaming! I cannot and will not endure the presence of this creature another moment!"

"*Whaa—*" muttered my husband, with the almost inebriate incoherency of slumber, "*whasamaramydarling*?"

"Stop dreaming about that creature," I cried, "or I shall go home to Mamma!"

"Creature?" my husband echoed, and as he sat up I had the satisfaction of seeing Katie's misty, luminous form fade slowly into nothingness.

"You know who I mean!" I sobbed. "Katie – your spiritual affinity, as she calls herself!"

"You don't mean," shouted Vavasour, now thoroughly roused, "that you have seen *her*?"

"I do mean it," I mourned. "Oh, if I had only known of your having an entanglement with any creature of the kind, I would never have married you – never!"

"Hang her!" burst out Vavasour. Then he controlled himself, and said soothingly: "After all, dearest, there is nothing to be jealous of—"

"I jealous! And of that—" I was beginning, but Vavasour went on:

"After all, she is only a disembodied astral entity with whom I became acquainted – through my fifth principle, which is usually well developed – in the days when I moved in Spiritualistic society. She was, when living – for she died long before I was born – a young lady of very good family. I believe her father was a clergyman . . . and I will not deny that I encouraged her visits."

"Discourage them from this day!" I said firmly. "Neither think of her nor dream of her again, or I will have a separation."

"I will keep her, as much as possible, out of my waking thoughts," said poor Vavasour, trying to soothe me; "but a man cannot control his dreams, and she pervades mine in a manner which, even before our engagement, my pet, I began to find annoying. However, if she really is, as she has told me, a lady by birth and breeding, she will understand" – he raised his voice as though she were there and he intended her to hear – "that I am now a married man, and from this moment desire to have no further communication with her. Any suitable provision it is in my power to make—"

He ceased, probably feeling the difficulty he would have in explaining the matter to his lawyers; and it seemed to me that a faint mocking sniggle, or rather the auricular impression of it, echoed his words. Then, after some more desultory conversation, we fell soundly asleep. An hour may have passed when the same chilly sensation as of a damp draught blowing across the bed roused me. I rubbed my cheek and opened my eyes. They met the pale, impertinent smile of the hateful Katie, who was installed in her old post beside Vavasour's end of the bolster.

"You see," she said, in the same soundless way, and with a knowing little nod of triumph, "it is no use. He is dreaming of me again!"

"Wake up!" I screamed, snatching the pillow from under my husband's head and madly hurling it at the shameless intruder. This time Vavasour was almost snappish at being disturbed. Daylight surprised us in the middle of our first connubial quarrel. The following night brought a repetition of the whole thing, and so on, *da capo*, until it became plain to us, to our mutual disgust, that the more Vavasour strove to banish Katie from his dreams, the more persistently she cropped up in them. She was the most ill-bred and obstinate of astrals – Vavasour and I the most miserable of newly-married people. A dozen times in a night I would be roused by that cold draught upon my cheek, would open my eyes and see that pale, phosphorescent, outline perched by Vavasour's pillow – nine times out of the dozen would be driven to frenzy by the possessive air and cynical smile of the spook. And although Vavasour's former regard for her was now converted into hatred, he found the thought of her continually invading his waking mind at the most unwelcome seasons. She had begun to appear to both of us *by day as well as by night* when our poisoned honeymoon came to an end, and we returned to town to occupy the house which Vavasour had taken and furnished in Sloane Street. I need only mention that Katie accompanied us.

Insufficient sleep and mental worry had by this time thoroughly soured my temper no less than Vavasour's. When I charged him with secretly encouraging the presence I had learned to hate, he rudely told me to think as I liked! He implored my pardon for this brutality afterwards upon his knees, and with the passage of time I learned to endure the presence of his attendant shade with patience. When she nocturnally hovered by the side of my sleeping spouse, or in constituence no less filmy than a whiff of cigarette-smoke, appeared at his elbow in the face of day, I saw her plainly, and at these moments she would favour me with a significant contraction of the eyelid, which was, to say the least of it, unbecoming in a spirit who had been a clergyman's daughter. After one of these experiences it was that the idea which I afterwards carried into execution occurred to me.

I began by taking in a few numbers of a psychological publication entitled *The Spirit-Lamp*. Then I formed the acquaintance of Madame Blavant, the renowned Professoress of Spiritualism and Theosophy. Everybody has heard of Madame, many people have read her works, some have heard her lecture. I had heard her lecture. She was a lady with a strong determined voice and strong determined features. She wore her plentiful grey hair piled in sibylline coils on the top of her head, and – when she lectured – appeared in a white Oriental silk robe that fell around her tall gaunt figure in imposing folds. This robe was replaced by one of black satin when she held her *séances*. At other times, in the seclusion of her study, she was draped in an ample gown of Indian chintz innocent of cut, but yet imposing. She smiled upon my new-born desire for psychic instruction, and when I had subscribed for a course of ten private *séances* at so many guineas apiece she smiled more.

Madame lived in a furtive, retiring house, situated behind high walls in Endor's Grove, N.W. A long glass tunnel led from the garden gate to the street door, for the convenience of Mahatmas and other persons who preferred privacy. I was one of those persons, for not for spirit worlds would I have had Vavasour know of my repeated visits to Endor's Grove. Before these were over I had grown quite indifferent to supernatural manifestations, banjos and accordions that were thrummed by invisible performers, blood-red writing on mediums' wrists, mysterious characters in slate-pencil, Planchette, and the Table Alphabet. And I had made and improved upon acquaintance with Simon.

Simon was a spirit who found me attractive. He tried in his way to make himself agreeable, and, with my secret motive in view – let me admit without a blush – I encouraged him. When I knew I had him thoroughly in hand, I attended no more *séances* at Endor's Grove. My purpose was accomplished upon a certain night, when, feeling my shoulder violently shaken, I opened the eyes which had been closed in simulated slumber to meet the indignant glare of my husband. I glanced over his shoulder. Katie did not occupy her usual place. I turned my glance towards the arm-chair which stood at my side of the bed. It was not vacant. As I guessed, it was occupied by Simon. There he sat, the luminously transparent appearance of a weak-chinned, mild-looking young clergyman, dressed in the obsolete costume of eighty years previously. He gave me a bow in which respect mingled with some degree of complacency, and glanced at Vavasour.

"I have been explaining matters to your husband," he said, in that soundless spirit-voice with which Katie had first made me acquainted. "He understands that I am a clergyman and a reputable spirit, drawn into your life-orbit by the irresistible attraction which your mediumistic organisation exercises over my—"

"There, you hear what he says!" I interrupted, nodding confirmatively at Vavasour. "Do let me go to sleep!"

"What, with that intrusive beast sitting beside you?" shouted Vavasour indignantly. "Never!"

"Think how many months I have put up with the presence of Katie!" said I. "After all, it's only tit for tat!" And the ghost of a twinkle in Simon's pale eye seemed to convey that he enjoyed the retort.

Vavasour grunted sulkily, and resumed his recumbent position. But several times that night he awakened me with renewed objurgations of Simon, who with unflinching resolution maintained his post. Later on I started from sleep to find Katie's usual seat occupied. She looked less pert and confident than usual, I thought, and rather humbled and fagged, as though she had had some trouble in squeezing her way into Vavasour's sleeping thoughts. By day, after that night, she seldom appeared. My husband's brain was too much occupied with Simon, who assiduously haunted me. And it was now my turn to twit Vavasour with unreasonable jealousy. Yet though I gloried in the success of my stratagem, the continual presence of that couple of spooks was an unremitting strain upon my nerves.

But at length an extraordinary conviction dawned on my mind, and became stronger with each successive night. Between Simon and Katie an acquaintance had sprung up. I would awaken, or Vavasour would arouse, to find them gazing across the barrier of the bolster which divided them with their pale negatives of eyes, and chatting in still, spirit voices. Once I started from sleep to find myself enveloped in a kind of mosquito-tent of chilly, filmy vapour, and the conviction rushed upon me that He and She had leaned across our couch and exchanged an intangible embrace. Katie was the leading spirit in this, I feel convinced – there was no effrontery about Simon. Upon the next night I, waking, overheard a fragment of conversation between them which plainly revealed how matters stood.

"We should never have met upon the same plane," remarked Simon silently, "but for the mediumistic intervention of these people. Of the man" – he glanced slightingly towards Vavasour –

"I cannot truthfully say I think much. The lady" – he bowed in my direction – "is everything that a lady should be!"

"You are infatuated with her, it is plain!" snapped Katie, "and the sooner you are removed from her sphere of influence the better."

"Her power with me is weakening," said Simon, "as Vavasour's is with you. Our outlines are no longer so clear as they used to be, which proves that our astral individualities are less strongly impressed upon the brains of our earthly sponsors than they were. We are still materialised; but how long this will continue—" He sighed and shrugged his shoulders.

"Don't let us wait for a formal dismissal, then," said Katie boldly. "Let us throw up our respective situations."

"I remember enough of the Marriage Service to make our union, if not regular, at least respectable," said Simon.

"And I know quite a fashionable place on the Outside Edge of Things, where we could settle down," said Katie, "and live practically on nothing."

I blinked at that moment. When I saw the room again clearly, the chairs beside our respective pillows were empty.

Years have passed, and neither Vavasour nor myself has ever had a glimpse of the spirits whom we were the means of introducing to one another. We are quite content to know ourselves deprived for ever of their company. Yet sometimes, when I look at our three babies, I wonder whether that establishment of Simon's and Katie's on the Outside Edge of Things includes a nursery.

# The House of Dust

## Herbert de Hamel

### Prospectus

**Address:** The Square, Brevolt, Belgium.
**Property:** Nineteenth-century town house located in a quiet square adjacent to the mayor's residence. Ornately and stylishly decorated, the property ensures privacy in the heart of the town.
**Viewing Date:** Autumn, 1917.
**Agent:** Herbert de Hamel (*c.* 1888–1939) was born in Reading, Berkshire and after several nondescript jobs, turned to writing and became a notable author and dramatist, with several of his plays produced successfully on the London stage. Among his most popular books were *The Unnecessary Undoing of Mr. Purgle* (1927), *The Mills of Hell* (1935) and *Many Thanks – Ben Hassett* (1936) which was reprinted several times. "The House of Dust", first published in 1934, was attacked as being in bad taste because of its portrayal of a wartime sexual encounter between a German officer and a young female – a girl whose identity provides the chilling climax to the story.

I

Captain Kurt Von Unserbach was bored. He was bored from the duelling scar on the top of his close-cropped head to the corns on his tightly shod feet.

The ends of his wide mouth drooped; his eyes, opened wide beneath his raised brows, stared unseeingly ahead; his back maintained its pose of stiffness, rather from habit than from any volition on the part of its owner. Never before had unkind Fortune cast his little strutting steps in a town where the women were so plain of face and so flat of figure. Even their very virtue repelled him.

And yet a poet or an artist might have asked no happier fate than to be quartered in such surroundings. Brevolt had its history; not, perhaps, to be found in the dry pages of books, but written for all time in its own winding streets and mossy squares.

The moonlight fell upon the mouldering spires, upon high-pitched tiles pierced by dormer windows, and upon glistening patchworks of leaded panes. It struggled down the quaint house-fronts with their mullioned windows till it reached the massive iron-studded doors, frowning beneath their gothic arches. It silvered once again the old stone shields: sable shadows on a ground argent, a device older by far than the proud hatchments in gules and azure and vert which had long since peeled from the crumbling surfaces.

But Kurt von Unserbach cursed savagely at the cobble stones. His cavalry boots had hurt him even on the pavements of his loved Berlin. He cursed, too, at the impulse which had urged him to leave his overheated rooms and wander forth into the night air. It did not occur to him to turn back.

He crossed the market square, noting, without a single glance of admiration, the spire-decked Town Hall where the burghers had feasted Van Arteveldt on his return from Crècy. Unheedingly he passed the city wall, looming black and imposing even in its ruined state, where the women of Brevolt had beaten back the fierce assaults of Alva. After marching some fifty paces down the country road he stopped, removed his busby, and gazed about him. A smile of genuine pleasure lit up his face. On either side of him an orderly row of poplars stretched away to some unseen vanishing point. Their perspective was faultless. Their tidiness and method reminded him of the Fatherland. So Brevolt had something beautiful in it after all. But those awful women! Ach! – those awful women!

It was told of him, in the mess of the Blue Hussars, that, on being asked by his colonel if he had found Naples as beautiful as it was reputed, he had replied: "Beautiful! Beautiful! – and eyes of so dark a brown."

In his native country such favours had been showered on him as may come only to one who is grotesquely ugly and is clad in a dashing uniform of pale blue and silver. Moreover, so highly well born was he that his marriage was an affair of state. He could not wed, however much he might become entangled, without the consent of his emperor. Many a fair German had sobbed, with the sentimental abandon of her race, when he had gently but very firmly shattered all hope of a future that should redeem a too happy past with him. "This can go no further. I am, in honour, bound to tell you that my marriage to you will not be permitted."

And never did the honour of Kurt von Unserbach shine forth so brightly as when the charms of white arms and red lips had begun to cloy.

He rubbed the middle finger of his right hand reflectively up and down one large outstanding ear and wrinkled his short nose. He wished that the army in front would make more progress towards Calais. He desired above all things to be quartered in England – as an exponent of martial law. English women had invariably laughed at him when he manufactured love for their benefit. They were treacherous, like all their race. They would trust themselves alone with him and then box his ears when he tried to kiss them. There was a Miss Smith who had called him Dan Lenobach.

And he was tied by the leg in Brevolt! And the women of Brevolt –! *Ach, himmel!*

"Pardon, monsieur."

Kurt von Unserbach jumped as though he had been touched with a spur. He had fancied himself to be entirely alone with his thoughts. By his side stood two women. One of them was of medium height and broad. The other was tall and graceful. Both were heavily veiled.

"Pardon, monsieur," repeated the taller of the two, in a tone so silvery and clear, and in a voice so well modulated, as to convince the cavalryman that he was addressed by no Flemish peasant. "My mother and I," she continued, "have been out to see one who was wounded. We were delayed till after nightfall and we are now afraid to pass the soldiers at the gate. They were insulting to me once, and since then we have kept indoors."

She spoke in French, a language with which he was imperfectly acquainted; and yet, to his surprise, he had understood her every word. Her voice thrilled him and held him spellbound. He was convinced, entirely without reason, that such delicate tones and inflections could only come from the most beautiful of women.

"They are Saxon Landsturm," he replied with a contempt that could only have been equalled by a Saxon saying, "They are Prussians."

"But you are a Prussian officer," continued the voice, "and we should be quite safe with you, if you would have the great kindness to escort us past the guard-room."

Captain von Unserbach hastily clapped his busby onto his head. Then, properly dressed, he clicked his heels together and bowed stiffly from his hips. "Once you are seen with me you can go anywhere in safety, at any time," he remarked gravely.

He wished that she would draw her veil aside. If the mere sound of her voice had the power to send his blood thumping through his heart, what effect might not the sight of her face have upon him? He pondered deeply as they walked slowly back towards the ancient gateway. "The intelligence which never deserts the Prussian officer." This impartial remark, made by his favourite Prussian general, repeated itself again and again with silent persistence till they had reached the great block of masonry. Then came the inspiration: as brilliant and subtle as any that had ever been granted to him.

"Pardon," he remarked, through the elaborate machinery of another bow, "but if, upon my responsibility, you are enabled to pass the guard without examination, it is a mere formality that you should allow me to see your faces."

The elder woman at once uncovered her face. He barely

glanced in her direction. He acknowledged her action by a curt nod and turned again to her companion.

The baffling lace no longer hid her features, but lent its dark folds to outline the oval of her face. Her hair, black as the shadow of the gateway on the road, was drawn to each side over her low forehead and threw into vivid relief the ivory gleam of her skin. Her lips were parted slightly to show the white daintiness of her teeth. But it was her eyes that held the glance of Kurt von Unserbach – eyes that shone with the strangest of lights in the full rays of the moon – eyes that gripped him and fascinated him – that drew him from himself and sent him swirling and spinning up into the clouds – intoxicated and delirious.

"Are you satisfied, Herr Kapitan?"

His body bowed automatically, and then stood erect to receive him as he swooped back to earth.

"You know my rank?" he inquired, grasping at any conversational straw in the raging waters of his confusion.

"I have seen you so often from my window – and—"

"And—?"

"And have—" the dark eyes wavered for a second and then looked fearlessly and steadily into his own. "And have admired you so."

"Ach, so!" Her eyes still held his own – and he was reduced almost to incoherence. "So good and so beautiful!" he murmured.

"No woman is good – who really loves," she whispered.

He averted his eyes from a sense of physical pain, caused by the intensity of her gaze, and the curious eerie effect of the moonlight.

"Ach – yes! Yes! Yes!" he exclaimed vehemently; which was strange, since her previous remark accorded entirely with his own sentiments concerning women. "Whatever you did must be good and beautiful!"

He glanced hastily towards her. Her eyes were still fixed upon him.

"Let us be going in," said the other woman. "It is becoming chilly."

A sudden cold wind swept hushing through the trees and swirled the dead leaves round his feet.

He drew his cloak about him and turned towards the gateway. A light flashed in his face, followed by the crash of rifle-butts as the guard sprang to attention. He was proud that his companions should witness this tribute to his rank.

"I will accompany you to your house," he explained with elaborate subtlety. "Lest there might perhaps be some drunken soldiers in the street. If you are with me then you will be quite safe."

His spurs jingled joyously as he crossed the market place, and the cobbles no longer hurt his feet.

"Is it not beautiful?" said his companion.

He looked about him with interest, as though the quaint gables and turrets were stage scenery erected but a few moments before. "Very beautiful," he agreed. "It would make a very beautiful background for a statue." He regarded the square with increased favour. "There would be room for at least twenty statues."

"Perhaps one of them would be that of Captain Kurt von Unserbach?"

There was no trace of levity in her tone – nor would it have occurred to him to seek for one. "I have done nothing as yet to deserve a statue," he replied. "There is a statue of my father in our village. It is of the most costly marble and the best workmanship. But one can have only one father to honour." He walked some twenty paces in silence and then added, with genuine sadness and regret: "I have no child – to raise a statue to me when I am dead."

Neither did he wonder that she should know his name. He was the only Prussian officer in that little Flemish town.

For the rest of the journey he was too occupied to make any further remarks. Carefully and methodically he noted every architectural detail that might serve as a guide on future visits to his unknown destination. Occasionally the roughness of the cobbles swayed him towards his companion and for a brief moment their shoulders would touch and, once, the filmy lace veil caressed his cheek.

Once, also, his little eyes glared and snapped arrogantly at a passing infantry officer whose gaze betokened too lively admiration.

Some fifty paces farther, a gently detaining hand was laid upon his arm – and he followed his escort through a narrow passage between two overhanging buildings. This alley led them into a small square which was well known to him. On the far side stood the *préfecture of police*, while on his right hand he could discern the familiar outline of the late mayor's private residence.

Opposite a broad double door, studded with large square-headed nails, the party halted. He noticed the details with the greatest care. The wood was dark chestnut or oak, polished with age. In the left half, as he stood facing it, was a small but heavily barred iron grid, painted black. From the solid stone lintel projected a curiously wrought lantern-bracket. The moulding of the jambs on either side was ornamented with a series of small stone shields and bugles arranged alternately.

The younger woman opened a narrow door that was contained in the right-hand half of the large one and passed within.

"We are most grateful to you for the trouble which you have taken on our behalf," said her mother. "It is a pleasure to find a Prussian officer who can be courteous to two lonely and friendless women."

As she turned and went through the doorway a warm glow lit up the hall beyond. "Good night," she said, her hand upon the latch, "and again our sincere thanks. We must not detain you any longer."

Kurt von Unserbach had no intention of allowing the matter to end there. He placed his foot in such a position that the door could not be closed. "I am not on duty to-night," he explained firmly. "There is no reason why I should hurry back."

His natural courtesy and sense of chivalry bade him wait for an invitation before attempting to force his way in.

The younger woman laughed, and his skin bristled to the bulging nape of his neck. He pressed his foot more firmly against the woodwork.

"We could not very well ask you in at this hour, Herr Kapitan," she explained. "But if you – as an officer of the invading army – insist on coming in – the responsibility lies with you alone."

The little gurgle of merriment which followed affected him as no laughter had ever done. He thrilled again as though a skeleton hand were playing scales up and down his spine. He appreciated the mocking note: she was laughing at herself – at the conventions – and at her mother.

"I will accept the full responsibility," he replied gravely, "but I should appreciate the mere formality of an invitation."

"Will you not come in, then, after your great kindness?" Her tone this time defied all his attempts at analysis. "Our dinner is a cold one, but I think you will agree that there is no chef living that can equal the artist who prepared it."

"Thank you extremely," he replied; and a moment later the well-oiled latch had clicked behind him.

The large open hall felt pleasantly warm after the chilly draughts of the street, and he was conscious of a faint and subtle perfume which appealed to all that was sensual in his nature. He approved of the scent very strongly, and wondered whether it came from the masses of cut flowers which glowed and gleamed wherever there was a ledge on which the great glass bowls could stand. Then his eye was attracted by the life-size frescoes which adorned the side walls. He screwed his small eyeglass into his eye and studied them with interest. They were literal translations in colour of various classical incidents which are not usually translated literally in print. The drawing and the colouring were obviously the work of a master hand, strong and vigorous and almost alive. Yet although they were devoid of all vulgarity and indecency, they were the very incarnation of suggestiveness. They resembled those books which threaten always to be improper on the next page.

"Good!" exclaimed the visitor. "Very good. They might almost have been painted by a German artist."

"Shall we go upstairs?" said his hostess. "We do not live in the ground floor rooms. They are too dark and dismal."

"I will look at those pictures again by daylight and perhaps I will photograph them," he said, as he crossed the tiled floor and followed her up the stairs. As he climbed, he stroked the broad flat top of the old bannister-rail with his hand, delighting in the smoothness of its time-worn surface.

So richly were the stairs carpeted that his spurred heels made no sound.

The dining-room was a large apartment with heavily curtained windows. Down the centre ran a massive refectory table, covered with a damask cloth and sparkling with glass and silver. Across one end of the room stood a similar table, which did duty as a sideboard. In one amazed and comprehensive glance he realized that it was laden with those delicacies most dear to a famished German heart and stomach. Amongst the dishes there stood, or lay in small baskets, bottles fat and thin, bottles whose corks were covered with silver, with gilt, with red or white or green.

Captain Kurt von Unserbach moistened his lips, wrenched his unwilling glance from the end table, and turned to make a complimentary speech to his hostess. To his surprise he found that he was alone. He had not heard her leave the room.

The next five minutes he spent, to his complete satisfaction, in studying the various dishes and in apportioning to each delicacy its relative weight in terms, not of appetite, but of capacity.

"My mother is very tired after her walk."

Captain von Unserbach started guiltily and removed his finger from his mouth. These thick carpets were delightful to walk upon, but they were devilish inconvenient at times.

"She has retired to bed and hopes that you will excuse her."

Kurt von Unserbach clicked his heels and excused her with all the good will in the world. Then he raised his eyes and forgot even the good things upon the table.

Many a heart has been lost in the moonlight to be recovered instantly in the more mellow glow of lamps. But this woman was even more bewitchingly beautiful now that he could see the full glory of her coiled black hair. No trace of a warmer tint stained the smooth ivory of her skin. Her eyes, he realized, were not dark brown but were almost black with a little emerald green sparkle in their depths.

He looked up at the ceiling to see if there was a green shade to any of the lamps. There was not. Wherefore he looked into her eyes again – and his glance was gripped and held till he prayed that her lids might close for one brief second. When at last they fell, he sank back into a chair and breathed fast.

One thing he vowed silently: that, Emperor or no Emperor, he could never love any woman but this. He no longer wished to go to England. Miss Smith–! He broke in upon his own thoughts with a sudden shout of laughter. What did ten thousand Misses Smith weight in the balance against one smile of this woman.

"Come; you must be famished after your onerous duties as *chevalier aux dames*," she laughed. "See; I will wait upon you by way of repaying the debt."

Whereupon, the Captain tucked one corner of his napkin into the collar of his uniform and fell more deeply in love than ever. She served him with never too much of this and with never too little of that. He could not have helped himself with more delicate accuracy. Moreover, she ate practically nothing, a novelty which appealed to his æsthetic sense.

And the wines! Were there ever such wines! Each one in its turn seemed to have gained an added delicacy of flavour from the memory of its predecessor. It would have been a pleasure even to sip them – it was paradise to swallow them by the glassful. An Englishman would have slipped silently beneath the table, but Kurt von Unserbach merely leant back on a roseate cloud and twiddled his feet at the prosaic world below.

The banquet ended with a coffee liqueur under a film of fresh cream, and with one of his own cigars.

"You are a German," he exclaimed ecstatically. "You must be a German. You are a Prussian of the Prussians."

"I am of no nationality," she replied. "I was once an Alsacienne – but now I belong to no nation."

"Then you were half a German," he exclaimed in triumph, "and I will make you entirely a Prussian."

"But your marriage is an affair of state. Your emperor would never agree that you should marry me."

Captain von Unserbach settled himself more comfortably back

on his rosette cloud and twiddled his feet at the Emperor. "I am *von und zu*," he declared haughtily, "and if he refuses his consent I will threaten to kill myself."

From the expression in her eyes he gathered that this would be an even greater blow to her than to the Emperor. He hastened to assure her that he would not carry this threat to the extreme of fulfilling it.

"And – tell me," she changed the subject, "were you in that first great advance into Belgium?"

"My regiment was one of the first that rode ahead past the fortress of Liège," he answered proudly. "But why talk of other women when I have you here with me?"

But she encouraged him to speak of his doings, and her eyes mastered his as the fumes of the wine loosened his tongue. And as he told her tale after tale of those hideous days, the green lights in the depths of her eyes shone steadily – and coldly.

"That is from your point of view," she said. "But supposing your army had found it a military necessity to sack this town. Supposing that your triumphant soldiers had already broken into this house before I had met you?"

Von Unserbach shuddered and winced. "Ach – don't! It is unthinkable!" He deliberately evaded her meaning. "All these beautiful things would then have been destroyed."

"And for me? Do you care nothing then for me?"

For one second he stared back at her, and then he sprang to his feet. His chair fell to the floor unheeded. "God in Heaven!" he shouted. "Care for you! I love you more than anything!"

He strode towards her and took her into his arms.

## II

At five o'clock the following morning Captain Kurt von Unserbach let himself out silently by the narrow door. His face wore an expression of rapturous ecstasy. He drew his cloak tightly round him, and set out at a brisk strut for the barracks. It was certainly a cruel stroke of fate which had torn him from paradise at such an hour; but he reflected that the same fate which had selected him for early morning duties on that particular day had also thrown him in the path of this wonderful happiness. But for Fate he would never had met his– ? "Thousand devils!" he laughed. "Why, I don't even know her name."

He felt in his pocket for his cigar case and then remembered suddenly that he had left it on the mantelshelf in the bedroom. He paused for a moment and then turned again towards the barracks. He would not have time to go back, and it would be safe enough in her keeping. If her mother found it . . . ? He shrugged his shoulders. She could always say that she had taken it in there to keep it safe.

That morning was all seconds, and every second seemed like an hour. Moreover he was ravenously hungry, in spite of the heavy meal he had devoured such a short time before. His subordinates suffered even more than was usual. His only other gleam of consolation was the glance of unconcealed envy cast upon him by the infantry officer he had passed on the previous night.

As soon as he was off duty and had swallowed a hasty but ample lunch he hurried to the square. At first he was unable to locate the house, which had a strangely different appearance in the light of day. The door jambs with their shields and bugles he had found easily enough; but what, in the moonlight, had appeared to be a door of polished wood with a painted grid in it, was shabby in the extreme. The grid was red with rust. Blistered and dirty paint hung in tattered strips from the woodwork. He tugged at the remains of an iron handle, and in the distance sounded the metallic bleat of a broken bell. He rang again and listened. There was an echo which resembled those to be found only in an empty house. He stepped back into the roadway and looked up at the windows. Those which were not broken were covered with grime. He then noticed that there was no wrought iron lantern-bracket over the door. He heaved a sigh of relief. It could not be the same house.

He crossed the square to the police station and marched straight into the Prefect's private room. "Can you tell me where I can find a house with a pattern of shields and bugles on the supports of the stone door-frame?"

"I can," replied the Prefect wearily, placing his pen carefully in the tray of his inkstand.

"A house with a door of some dark wood with a painted grid in it, and a lantern bracket over it."

"I cannot. There is no such house in Brevolt."

"Rubbish. I dined there last night."

The Prefect bowed in silence. It is not wise to contradict Prussian officers. Otherwise he might not now have been acting as mayor in addition to his police duties.

"Well?" demanded Captain von Unserbach.

"There is only one house in Brevolt with a pattern on its lintels such as you describe, and that is the one at which you have just been ringing. There was once a lantern-bracket such as you describe, but it fell down five years ago. The door was painted for the first and last time some forty years ago. The house is to let; but it has a bad name."

"Why?"

"Its last owners were not altogether desirable people."

"I am not asking about its last owners. Who lives there now?"

"Nobody."

"You had better be careful as to how you tell me lies. I know perfectly well that a lady and her daughter are residing in that house. I do not know what your reasons for denying that fact may be, but you need have no fear that I intend them the slightest harm."

The Prefect crossed the room and opened a locker. He selected a bundle of documents, untied the string, and extracted a pencil drawing. "Is that the lady you are seeking?" he asked.

"Yes!" Von Unserbach shouted. "Thousand devils! Why have you been wasting all my time with your lies. Empty house – you blockhead! Do you mean to tell me that two ladies and their household and ten vans of furniture could move in under your very nose and you not know it! You shall hear more about this!"

"And what is it you wish?"

"Wish! Why to get in there of course!"

The Prefect held out his hand for the pencil sketch. "It belongs to the police records," he explained.

"It belongs to me," replied the Prussian.

The police officer took a large key from the locker, and returned the remainder of the documents. Captain von Unserbach followed him across the square and, as soon as the narrow door had groaned and grated open, he pushed past him into the hall.

The Prefect heard the guttural oath of astonishment which followed, and smiled drily behind his pointed grey beard.

Kurt von Unserbach stood on the threshold – staring straight ahead of him – rigid with horror and amazement.

The hall was empty. There was no trace of furniture, nor of the glass vases of flowers, nor of the rich stair-carpet. The dust lay half an inch thick over the tiled floor, over the stairs, over the bannisters, over everything.

"Are you looking for the frescoes?" inquired the Prefect politely. "They were painted out over thirty years ago. They were scarcely of a nature to attract respectable tenants."

But it was not the invisibility of the frescoes, it was not the absence of the furniture, which had terrified the soldier. There were fingermarks trailing through the dust on the bannister rail. There were footmarks in the dust on the floor, footmarks which led past the walls where the frescoes had been, and showed upon the stairs. And the marks on the bannister rail had been made by his own fingers, and the marks on the floor had been trodden out by his own cavalry boots. And besides these there were no other marks in the dust.

"Now that we are here it is a pity that you should not see over the house once again," suggested the police officer. "The owners would sell it for a mere trifle. But it would interest me very much to know how you got in last night? The keyhole was clogged with dust."

Kurt von Unserbach followed him up the stairs in silence. His brain was numbed. It was capable of nothing save obedience to outside suggestions.

The door to the dining-room resisted the efforts of the Prefect to open it. The bolt of the lock had rusted and the handle refused to turn. The Prussian pushed him aside and wrenched and tugged and twisted. Then he put his shoulder to the door and burst it open.

The room was empty. The massive tables and the solid chairs had vanished. There was now no carpet on the floor save a carpet of thick dust patterned with marks of his own boots. In the centre of the room and by the end wall, where the tables had stood, the dust lay smooth and untrodden. He saw clearly the marks where he had paced up and down beside the sumptuous dishes while waiting for– ? For– ? Waiting for– ? With an effort he resumed control of his brain. He snatched the pencil sketch from his pocket and thrust it towards the Prefect. "Who is she?" he demanded. "Who is that?"

"Your pardon, one moment; but is that your cigar end, and cigar ash, over there in the grate?"

"Who is that – please?" He spoke civilly – almost coaxingly. He was no longer merely a Prussian officer. He was a man, striving to fight down the fear that was growing in him.

"She came from Alsace with her mother, after the great war of 1870. A Prussian officer made their house his headquarters."

"Ach!" The tone was one of comprehension, disgust, and fury.

"Ah – how she hated the Prussians! They were too vile even for her. She vowed that she would never return to France while a single one of that breed grunted through it unharmed. She was a bad woman – but she loved her country passionately. She continued her profession here for three years."

"What profession?"

"In 1870 there was only one profession open to women," replied the Prefect drily.

"But – the furniture! The furniture! How could it have been taken away in the night – and the dust not disturbed! In the night –? I tell you it was here at five o'clock this morning!"

"It was sold to pay off their debts. The table that was in the centre of the room has stood in the Mayor's house for the last forty years. It is the one across which you fired at him. The chairs were purchased by the late Burgomaster and the other table" – he indicated the end wall – "was purchased by my father."

"When?" Von Unserbach asked the question with an effort, and scarcely dared listen for the reply.

"The great oaken bed with the hangings of crimson velvet worked with golden fleurs-de-lys," the old man continued in a tone of professional interest, "was broken up for firewood. No one would bid for it, by reason of the murder."

"Broken up!" Kurt von Unserbach almost screamed the words. His forehead was damp. The colour had left his florid cheeks.

"Your pardon! You asked me when they were sold. It was in August 1874. I remember the date because it was exactly a month after the two women were executed. They cannot have been altogether bad, because they loved their country."

Captain von Unserbach spoke rapidly in whispers. His words were inaudible. His lower lip hung loosely.

"Since that date the house has been closed," added the Prefect after a polite pause. "You have doubtless noticed how thick the dust is."

But Kurt von Unserbach was cursing his way through a half-forgotten prayer. He turned suddenly, with military precision, and strutted down the passage to the next room. He did not dare to go slowly, lest the remnant of his courage should fail him. He threw back the door and halted with a sharp click of his heels.

On the mantel-shelf lay his cigar case, exactly as he had left it.

The thick dust on the floor was undisturbed save for the imprints of his own bare feet.

He stared at the bare corner where, that very morning had stood the semblance of a great oaken bed – with hangings of crimson velvet worked with golden fleurs-de-lys. It was the space of a full minute before his eyes no longer focused on the patch of smooth dust. He turned – clicked his heels – and fell headlong on to the floor.

## III

Captain Kurt von Unserbach is now an inmate of the great military asylum in the Koenigstrasse. He is not violent. He struts up and down his cell, clicking his heels when he turns. He sleeps only in the daytime, and then always upon the floor. Between the hours of eleven o'clock at night and five o'clock in the morning he is subject to strange fits of terror – and it is then only that he speaks – crying out always the same five words.

# The Kisstruck Bogie

## A. E. Coppard

### Prospectus

**Address:** Kisstruck House, near Westbury, Wiltshire, England.

**Property:** *Circa* eighteenth-century country house with fine balcony, recently completely restored and neatly renovated. Situated in extensive parkland, with its own lake, and screened by mature trees.

**Viewing Date:** Summer, 1923.

**Agent:** Alfred Edgar Coppard (1978–1957) was born in Folkestone, Kent and his unique stories of fantasy and the supernatural – often with sly sexual connotations – are today acknowledged as classics of their kind. Trained originally as an accountant, he became a full-time writer after the success of his first book, *Adam and Eve and Pinch Me* (1921), and thereafter produced a series of collections of short tales all notable for their style, originality and wry humour. "The Kisstruck Bogie" is the ghost of a man who committed suicide and now haunts an old mansion until the chance of redemption arrives in the form of a pretty female ghost . . .

Kisstruck told me this horrible tale. I do not believe a word of it, but I write it out, because it was vouched for by Kisstruck whose integrity I respect; his quick humour and pleasant intelligence (for a bachelor) are not easily beguiled. All the same I do not believe it, he has fooled me before now with notions just as outlandish as his name – for Kisstruck *is* a curious name. American, I fancy, or something equally peculiar. For if there were such things as ghosts one ought to be able, when all is said and done and seen and noted, one ought to be able to establish some yardstick of proof. I take my stand upon that, and that is how I put it to Kisstruck.

He sighed and said: "Well, I have only told you what I know."

And I said: "Nonsense, you do *not* know it, you only told me what you *heard*, and to be quite frank with you I think you only think you heard it."

He sighed again, morosely: "Then I claim that I think I heard it, but for *me* – don't you see? – that is knowledge. To believe only in what you see is to ignore . . . O, the universe! It's no better than seeing only what you want to believe in, like a bishop."

That's as far as I could get towards demolishing his belief in this episode. Because he certainly *has* a belief, with perhaps some private intimations of which I am unaware, or intuitions to which I have no clue. For myself I have not the faintest belief in it, having been born a sceptic; to this day, if it is possible to be sceptical about anything I become, *ipso facto*, uncontrollably sceptical.

He once bought – this was years ago, remember – he bought a tumbledown ruin of a house in a country neighbourhood that must have been the very personification of solitude. I never gathered exactly where this was, Kisstruck declined to tell me, but I have a hunch that if you took a reading of a line between the spire of the cathedral at Salisbury and the town hall of Bath, crossed by another line from Wells to St. Paul's (I mean the one in London), the place would be found somewhere at the intersection: but it does not matter very much for the house was burnt to the ground long since. He gave me a nice-description of the house as it was after he had repaired it, an old-fashioned dwelling with a balcony, screened by trees in a place that seemed to be a sort of a park. There was a dull leaden lake close by. Quite solitary, I never saw the place, he having lived there before, I made his acquaintance, and, as I told you, it is now gone for ever. Apparently it had been empty for many years owing to a strange death or murder that occurred there, though nobody seemed to know what, as it was said to be haunted in consequence, though nobody seemed to know how.

"When I bought the house," Kisstruck said, "the vendors did not mention anything about a murder or a ghost."

"Naturally!" I couldn't help sneering.

"O, perhaps they didn't know," he said, "and anyhow it wouldn't have deterred me for I am pretty thick-skinned. Barring a daily domestic help I lived there alone. I hope I am not an unfriendly creature, but I really do enjoy that sort of existence. I soon got to hear some rumour of haunting and, of course, I scoffed at the notion."

"Isn't it amazing, Kisstruck," I said, "the infernal credence still given to common superstitious bosh! Makes one despair of human nature."

"Yes, I laughed at it," Kisstruck said.

"The way it persists!"

"Yes, the way it persists."

"All gas and my old grandmother!"

"Just what I thought and said. And yet, you know," Kisstruck scratched his poll in a comical forlorn manner – "I had to modify my opinion all the same."

Gracious heaven, at that hint of compromise I flew at Kisstruck – argumentatively, of course, and a priori. I tried to floor him on the simple question of clothes. In any spook tale there is generally some emphasis upon what the thing is supposed to be wearing. That's to authenticate the madness.

"Kisstruck," I said, "listen. I'll allow you for the moment the postulate of ghost. Here we go, then. A man dies, is laid out, shrouded and coffined, and put in his grave with a ton of earth on top of him. Now, out he comes, generally dressed as he was known in life. *Dressed*, Kisstruck! How *could* a ghost have clothes? Or wear them? And why? Are they real clothes? No, he must be wearing the ghosts of his clothing, see! His coat and his collar, or his armour and chains, must have spiritual essences, his boots and braces are informed with ghostly being. How can anybody accept that foolery?"

"No," Kisstruck agreed. "Still, you never can tell how such a thing may turn out. You remember, don't you:

"'*There are more things in heaven and earth, Horatio, than are dreamt of in your philosophy.*'?"

"Yes, yes, but the ghost in that case, too,

"*Was armed at point, exactly, cap-a-pie.*"

"What spiritual foundation reposes in a beaver and sword and buckler, tell me that, Kisstruck? Do you believe there's a spirit confined in a hat, or that there's a hereafter for a pair of trousers? No bunkum, now. Ghosts, at the very least, should be naked, shouldn't they? Always!"

"Naked," mused Kisstruck. "What a suggestion for some of those Freudians to handle!"

"Noise, too!" I went on. "How the deuce do you obtain noise from an incorporeal thing?"

"Seems impossible, and that's what I said," Kisstruck answered.

"And so it couldn't even speak."

"No. I told him that, too, but he did all the same."

"Him?" I asked.

"This ghost," said Kisstruck.

"Yah!" I snorted, "Don't try to stuff me with any of your bogies!" I took a good stare at my friend. He didn't flinch.

"I can only tell you what happened, actually happened, and to me of all people." said he. "Believe it or not, just as you please."

"O, all right," I said. "Go on with you. I'll buy it!"

And this is what he told me.

"For the first week after I got into that house I saw no mortal soul except the woman who came in the morning to do domestic work. If I remember rightly her name was Yiggle. As you know, I'm not an unsociable being, but I enjoy such solitude. I did in those days at any rate. Not so much now, I confess, but in a small measure I still do, and it can't be mere egotism, otherwise I'd be more expansive, I suppose. The weather was kind and it became my custom to lounge of an evening on the balcony – there was a nice iron-railed balcony, did I mention that? – a very agreeable balcony, smoking my pipe and reading or thinking poetic thoughts until the stars came out. This balcony was so narrow that I had to place my lounge chair sideways to the rail and sit facing the trellis work at the end; behind me was just the opposite trellis hung with some creeping vine. On a particular evening I sat a good while longer than usual, sprawled out, feeling superbly alone, king of all that congenial solitude, until it grew quite late and darkness hemmed all around me. Through the balcony railing I could see stars reflected below me in the lake's dull water; the surrounding trees, whose bulging tops I could easily make out against the starred sky, were masses of whispering gloom. For the first time it became a wee bit eerie, not unpleasant to a stable mind, but rather stirring to imagine night-black panthers stealing velvet-toed under the trees, or aerial serpents writhing in combat up among the branches.

"There had been no intimation of any other presence near me, I understood there was no other soul living within a mile of the place, so there was nothing to prepare me for the sudden shock of a voice at my shoulder. I was momentarily paralysed. Somebody or something was there behind me. I didn't believe in ghosts. I didn't think of a ghost, but I was remotely alone, it was pretty dark, and a stranger moving in marvellous silence had crept up there behind me; I tell you, my blessed heart absolutely rattled in my ribs. 'Mother of holy heaven!' I gasped – though why such a phrase should escape me I can't think; I have no religious element in my being, so why should I make that particular exclamation? Can you explain that?"

"O never mind your elements, Kisstruck, get on with the story, do!"

" 'Mother of holy heaven!' I said. I was petrified. I was unable to rise or even turn my head. I . . . could . . . not! I was held stiff and breathless, with a feeling of horror in my very hair that seemed to be making little corkscrew spirals. There may have been a waft of iciness, some chill of the grave, but I couldn't have felt it with my whole body seething in a sweat of apprehension. I wasn't frightened. You may laugh, but I know you can be horrified without feeling fear. In a moment or two I got grip of myself and leapt up out of the chair and faced around."

Kisstruck startled me by jumping up and striking an attitude to illustrate this. He stood poised and silent so long that I had to say, "Well, what then?"

He relaxed and resumed his seat.

"There was nothing there, nobody – and yet that voice spoke to me again. 'Where are you?' I said, pretty sharply too! 'Who are you? What do you want? Come out of it!' And the voice answered, and I listened, and I understood. It said: 'I am sorry to startle you, I can't help it; don't be alarmed, I don't mean any harm.' Obviously a man's voice. 'But where are you?' I shouted. It replied, 'I'm here. Can't you see me? Here I am.' 'I can't see anything,' I said. The voice answered: 'I can see you plainly.' Quite close to me, only a foot or two away. And then it seemed to get excited and anxious, and said: 'But you must! Here I am. See now?' And it was closer still. 'No, nothing at all,' I said. There was a brief silence, until I asked: 'Are you there?' for you know it was remarkably like telephoning, 'Are you there?' And that voice answered and said: 'You do not believe in me.' I asked: 'What do you mean?' 'You are sceptical,' it said. I asked: 'What about?' and it said: 'Ghosts!' 'Yes,' I said, 'I certainly am.' 'Pity,' it said sadly, 'I happen to be one.'"

At this point Kisstruck turned to that exasperating business of getting out his tobacco pouch and preparing his pipe, during which operation he suspended his narrative. Of course I pounded at him with question after question.

"What was he like, this . . . this creature?"

"I keep telling you, old chap, I could not see him. I could hear him and I could understand him, that's all."

"Not see anything?"

"There was nothing there to see."

"Quite invisible?"

"Absolutely."

"And yet he could see you?"

"So he said, and indeed he could for he told me of my own appearance, clothes and so forth – will you believe that?"

"No, Kisstruck. You may think me horridly incredulous and uncivil but I emphatically don't believe it."

"It sounds ridiculous to me now, I know, I know, but you have my word for it, honour bright you have. A ghost was there right enough; I could hear him and understand him, but nothing could I see although it was not so dark as all that implies and my eyesight is excellent, quite a high standard as eyesights go nowadays with all these confounded opticians prowling around. And I never *did* see him, although I had many contacts with him afterwards. Yes, I did. You are quite right on one point about them, real ghosts *are* invisible and you never see them at all, let alone see through them. I got to know this one very well, he was a friendly fellow, none of the vampire nuisance about him, nothing to shake the very core of one's being, as they say, but an amiable creature in spite of his history. He got into the habit of joining me of an evening on the balcony, always there, never elsewhere, or at any other time; he was very obliging about that and I welcomed the visits. He, too, was so obviously – if I may use that word – obviously glad of the chance to discourse with someone after being cut off from all contacts and all possibilities of haunting anybody for so many years, all those years the house had been empty. It must have been a dreary time for him; could anything be more devitalising than the task of haunting a house that is, as it were, unhauntable through the absence of human contacts? He had grown despondent in those years, time was getting on, he had his career – such as it might be – to think of, and was anxious about his position, his status, for no spook likes to be made a fool of or to feel neglected or ignored. Also he feared he might get stale and lose his form through sheer inactivity.

"Well, now, I think I had better tell you the story, as I learned it direct from him and not from any idle rumour, of the crime which brought him low and made a wraith of him. He was – that is to say he had been – a country gentleman of small means, his family having declined from an estate of importance in the county. A queer thing is that it never once occurred to me to ask him his name, and as he never volunteered it I have not been able to verify any history of his forbears. I did ask him, more than once, what he had been like to look at, who or what he had resembled, but he – I mean the voice – would not respond to that enquiry and I concluded that it was in some way out of his power to do so.

"He had married somewhat late in life, at about the age of forty, and brought his bride to that house. She was some ten years his junior, and although he did not betray any such opinion of her I cannot think she was a very nice creature. I fancy she was one of those ladies who not being a real lady aspire to be adopted in some way by a real gentleman. Anyway, he married her and took her to the house with the balcony, the one I've been telling you about. The marriage turned out a failure. Within a year his wife eloped with some merchant and my poor friend, who was fatally fond of her, suffered in consequence an incurable melancholy, a sort of mania. Everything he did then, everything he saw then, he felt he was seeing or doing for the very last time. In travelling about, as he did for a while in quest of distraction from his unremitting grief, he would gaze at any well-known view and bemoan to himself: 'This is not beautiful at all and it has no pleasant associations for me, but – I shall never see it again!' And that would make him weep. Stupid, but uncontrollable. If he were sawing up a log or planting a flower border the same thought arose, 'I shall never do this again' – and much weeping. Soon it got round to immediate things like putting on his gloves or his boots, even eating his meals. It is a bad state for any man to get into; as soon as you begin to imagine you won't see such things again you are likely to see things you never began to imagine. The end was inevitable. He found himself developing what he called 'extinctive tendencies,' by which I understood he had a craving to shed blood, terribly wanted to, dreamed constantly of killing people – nobody in particular, just anybody – and the desire became so insistent that in terrible fear of surrendering to indiscriminate blood-lust and the slaughter of unoffending mortals he shot *himself*. 'Just here in my temple, see that hole!' he said to me. I had to remind him that he was invisible to me; in the eagerness of his telling he had forgotten it. It was really rather funny, that! So there's the story as I had it from him. Is there anything really incredible in it?"

"Certainly, Kisstruck! I'm waiting to hear how he became a ghost."

"Ah that! My dear chap I cannot tell. I'm afraid we shall never know now."

"And why should he haunt that house?"

"My dear chap! Isn't that what a ghost is for? It was where he had shot himself, on that balcony. What else could you expect?"

That is a ripe instance of the logic of my friend Kisstruck. How strange to have had all that stupendous experience, to know so much, and yet understand so little! But still, I am quite fond of him although he infuriates me so often.

"Mr. Kisstruck," I said sternly, "will you oblige me by getting to the end of this legend."

"O, it's not legend," he protested, "and there's nothing much to follow; his real-life story was what interested me, the other side of him lost its thrill after a while. For a few weeks we were friendly enough, in a sort of way, then his appearance began to drop off, because he had at least established contact with a human being – me! – and that appears to be a difficult thing for them to do; having done it he qualified for the privilege of coming and going and ranging elsewhere. He wasn't my type, you know, he hadn't the sort of mind I could make pleasant exchanges with, in fact he became rather vulgar-minded and servile and ingratiating, called me sir, and so on. It affected me unpleasantly, suggesting some taint in his character: he would hint coarsely and leeringly at things I do not care to hear about. The truth was that in his enlarged peregrinations he had been having an affair with another ghost, a young lady spook who had an interest in some fishmonger's establishment – I don't know what, and it was a long way off. I gathered there had been some impropriety on her part, and that he had succumbed, with the . . . er . . . the usual consequences, and so they . . . er . . . they had to get married."

"O, Kisstruck! Damn you!"

"Yes, listen! By special licence, it seems they have a system."

Of course I was stunned. I glared at Kisstruck in exasperation and had a hot desire to kick him. "Went and got married, you say! To another ghost, eh!"

He got up and paced about, deliberating, then said: "That's what I understood from him, I hope it's true, because later there was, you know . . . a little encumbrance."

Well, Well! Where do we go from here! My friend was unquestionably serious about it.

"Kisstruck!" I yelled – I had to yell – "Are you demented; are you, Kisstruck, are you?"

"Tut, tut," he said mildly. "And they both came to see me before the house burnt down, they came together – only the once, though."

"Only once, eh! And you saw them?"

"No, of course not."

"And what did they have to say, Mr. Kisstruck?"

"She, unfortunately, nothing. She seemed to be dumb as well as invisible."

"Ho, ho, Mr. Kisstruck. Now I've got you! If you neither saw nor heard her how the devil do you know she was there?"

"He told me she was with him then," Kisstruck said. "Besides, I noticed a curious thing that night. It was moonlight, and on the white wall of the balcony – what do you think? I saw she was casting a faint misty shadow. And by and by, old chap, you are quite right, they do not appear to wear any clothes. There was her shadow, a most elegant outline on the wall, and it was clear she had nothing on, nothing at all."

# Mr Edward

## Norah Lofts

### Prospectus

**Address:** Bidstone Place, Buckinghamshire, England.

**Property:** Fine Georgian house situated in the centre of the village of Bidstone. Built of mellow bricks with a mature garden, the property is within easy travelling distance of adjacent town.

**Viewing Date:** July, 1947.

**Agent:** Norah Lofts (1904–1983) was born in Shipdham, Norfolk and trained as a teacher before turning to writing and becoming one of Britain's most popular romantic novelists. Her ability to mix love, drama and history was evident from her first novel, *I Met A Gypsy* (1935), and her fascination with old buildings can be seen in several of her books, including *The Town House* (1959), *The House at Sunset* (1962) and, especially, *Haunted House* (1978). Norah Lofts lived in a Georgian mansion in Suffolk not unlike the one in the curious story of Mr. Edward, featuring a lecherous old ghost who has an eye on the latest tenant of a haunted house.

Three half-blown rosebuds, a crimson, a pink and a cream, with reddish thornless stems and glossy leaves, lay beside the battered silver hand-mirror on Mrs. Amery's dressing-table. She picked them up in her work-worn fingers and sniffed their dewy fragrance, then, feeling the prick of imminent tears, laid them down again and snatched up her comb, running it swiftly through the wayes of her hair, which, though fading now, and thinner, still grew attractively from her broad-lined forehead and clung in close natural curls at the back of her head.

A feeling of grateful happiness swept over her. She had so much dreaded this holiday-time, shrinking from the demands it would make, fearing that Roger would resent the plan, that she would not have time to spare for him and that the process of growing away from her, begun at St. Aubyn's, where he was one of sixty pupils and she the mere matron-housekeeper and cook-at-odd-times, would be accelerated. But her fears had been groundless; the house was friendly, the work the reverse of onerous, and surely here, in this little flowery token, was proof that Roger, under the new casualness, the schoolboy slang, the greed and general twelve-year-old untouchability, was her own boy still.

As she moved about the room tidying it and stripping the bed and then moving on to repeat the process in Roger's room her mind was busy, recalling, in this new light of thankfulness, the chance events which had brought her to spend the eight weeks of the summer vacation at Bidstone Place. For three years now, the three years of widowhood, she had been in charge of the domestic side of St. Aubyn's, a select and prosperous little school run by another widow, Mrs. Bigmore. It was an arrangement advantageous to both sides, for by taking Roger Amery as a pupil Mrs. Bigmore had gained an enviable hold over Mrs. Amery, and Mrs. Amery, by accepting her servitude, had won release, temporarily, at least, from the problem of how a woman, skilled in no art or trade, could house and feed and educate her son.

But during the Easter holiday of her third year Mrs. Amery, in the midst of a bout of house-cleaning which she never thought of blaming, had been taken ill. The school doctor called her inability to concentrate, her loss of memory and her tendency to weep over her state "nervous prostration", and Mrs. Bigmore, a little frightened, had bundled her into a nursing home, kept by yet another widowed friend, where, in return for much meticulous mending, the arranging of several thousand flowers, the cooking of occasional meals and the entertainment of more wealthy patients, Mrs. Amery was given her breakfast in bed, a sleeping draught at bedtime and the privilege of an infrequent visit from the regular physician.

That, too, was a fortunate arrangement, but it left Mrs. Amery at the end of the term practically penniless, since she had for three months earned nothing but her keep, and the problem of what she was to do about the holiday was responsible for many of the symptoms which the physician of the nursing home regarded so gloomily. And yet, just a week before the end of term, that problem had been solved too. For Mrs. Stanhope, one of Mrs. Bigmore's dearest friends, and a very wealthy woman, had scented War in the air, and bethought herself of her hitherto despised country residence in the wilds of Buckinghamshire, and considered how pleasant it would be to make this place – an unwanted legacy from old Uncle Edward – into a comfortable, safe retreat, complete with every modern convenience. Uncle Edward had lived and died as a staunch Victorian, and Bidstone Place, which Mrs. Stanhope had sometimes let and sometimes loaned and generally avoided, needed a great deal of attention before it could be fit for what she called human habitation. Only, she confided sadly to Mrs. Bigmore, it did seem that if the War was imminent one should spend one last summer on the Continent, and if one did, how would the alterations get done?

Mrs. Bigmore had pondered the problem for about ten minutes and then said grandly, "My Mrs. Amery." And my Mrs. Amery, offered a holiday home, her keep and the boy's and the generous sum of twenty pounds, had battled with her diffidence and her nervousness and the lethargy which was the legacy of her illness and accepted the offer with a willingness that was more feigned than real. Desperately she wished that she could have gone, as usual, to the crowded boarding-house at Felixstowe where Roger always had such a good time; abjectly she had feared the interviews with electricians and plumbers and painters; neurotically she had pictured Bidstone Place as a vast Gothic mansion; in the depths of depression she had accepted from Mrs. Stanhope's hand the list of the "absolute minimum", the notes to the tradespeople of the neighbouring town, the money for necessary expenses, such as the wages of women to scrub, and finally her own cheque.

She had explained the position to Roger, who had said, with twelve-year-old shrewdness, two cogent things. "Old Jigsaw's usefully good at finding jobs for other people. That comes from keeping a school. School-teachers always think you're up to mischief unless you're sweating about something." And when Mrs. Amery had pointed out that the arrangement was made out of Mrs. Bigmore's kindness, he had almost snarled and said, "It'd have been a lot kinder if she'd paid you for last term, and then we could have gone to Felixstowe as usual."

Yet, despite this unpromising beginning, the holiday was being a happy one. Bidstone Place was neither enormous, Gothic, nor intimidating. In fact Mrs. Amery could not remember feeling such a sense of welcome from any house since the moment when she entered, as a bride, the peculiar establishment which her husband had prepared for her in far-away Kenya. And it was not isolated; it stood, a gracious building of mellow Georgian brick, in the very centre of a pleasant village, and there was an excellent bus service to the town. Roger had instantly struck up a friendship with two boys named Fenton who lived about a mile away and who had ponies and a boating lake and a tennis court which they seemed only too anxious to share. And Mrs. Amery had found, to her utter relief, that in the town the very mention of Mrs. Stanhope's name was sufficient to win not only prompt and eager service, but civility as well. On this morning, as she picked the roses from her dressing-table and carried them down as she went to prepare breakfast, she was as happy as she had been at any moment since the death of Roger's father.

She served Roger with a cup of steaming coffee and a plateful of bacon, egg, fried bread and tomato, and then said: "Thank you for the roses, darling. It was a lovely thought."

Roger, a sturdy, fair-haired boy with a brown face and a peculiarly deliberate manner, looked up from his breakfast and said, "Are you being sarky?"

"Of course not. Why? These roses" – she touched the three buds where they stood in a little vase in the centre of the table – "that you put on my dressing-table."

The dust of freckles on Roger's face was lost in a wave of dusky colour. "I didn't put them there." There was a note of surliness in his voice. And Mrs. Amery thought, "How odd boys are – to do a thing like that and then deny it."

"Then I must have done it myself," she said frivolously. "There's no one else in the house."

"Well, you do forget things, don't you?" said Roger, more comfortably. "I say, though, I am glad you'll be back next term. That other woman couldn't manage anything. In fact Brooks Major said that if you weren't there next term he'd get his people to take him away, him and Minor too. I wonder what the Jigsaw'd say to *that*."

"She'd survive, I expect," said Mrs. Amery coolly, beginning to spread her toast. Yet the subject of the rose-buds, thus lightly dismissed, nagged at her mind. Two explanations were possible, and neither of them was completely acceptable. Either Roger had picked them and was now ashamed of the gesture – and if that were so it suggested a psychological problem – or else she had, in a moment of complete aberration, gone down to the garden, cut three flowers, put them on the dressing-table in her own bedroom and then, with a sense of pleasure and surprise, discovered them there. And if that were so she was still ill.

After breakfast she went upstairs and carefully inspected the soles of her slippers; they bore no traces of a visit to a dewy garden.

Throughout the day she was too busy to give much thought to the matter. She had been in the house for well over a week now and the work was going forward; cheerful, casual young men knelt or reached about with lengths of electric wiring in their fingers, and from the corners of their months – they were chain-smokers to a man – talked to one another in a language which might have been Hindustani for all Mrs. Amery understood of it. Other men followed, closely and sometimes impatiently, with pots of paint and distemper and long strips of writhing, sticky paper.

All day the house hummed with activity. And Mrs. Amery was busy, inspecting colours to see if they matched, consulting Mrs. Stanhope's lists, telephoning for some article which was suddenly indispensable, trying to keep a clear path, as she called it, in front of and behind a number of busy men, each intent upon his own little job. Already she could see that, should War come, Mrs. Stanhope would be sure of a very pleasant, comfortable retreat.

And yet, as the dull warm colours gave way to white and duck-egg and primrose, as the curves and scrolls were banished in favour of straight lines, when the creeper that clustered about the windows fell away and the daylight poured into the rooms, when a flick of the finger could banish the darkness from every corner of the house at any moment, Mrs. Amery was conscious of a feeling which was not exactly of regret, but something nearer nostalgia. The friendly shabbiness, the almost diffident old-fashionedness, of the house was being banished, a richness and a warmth was oozing away under every stroke of the workmen's hammers, every sweep of their paint-filled brushes.

The painters and the plumbers and the electricians were fetched by a truck which called for them every afternoon at half past five. Roger usually came home tired, dirty and hungry at about seven, and in the interval Mrs. Amery, after washing and changing her dress, devoted herself to the preparation of supper, expending thought and ingenuity in her effort to offer the child at the same time what he liked and what she considered good for him. But on the evening of the day when she had found the rose-buds she did not expect Roger until eight, and at six o'clock, after her daily round of tidying, she sat down in the small room which she had taken for a sitting-room, put her feet up on the sofa, took a book in her hand and prepared for an hour's rest.

She never opened the book. For at first, with a faint frown on her broad forehead and a rather worried expression in her child-ish blue eyes, she reverted to the problem of the flowers. Could it really be that she had gathered them herself and so utterly have forgotten having done so? If so she trembled for her sanity; and not for the first time she remembered her Great-aunt Vinny, who had died in a private lunatic asylum.

It was a warm afternoon, sultry with the heat of late July, and the window behind Mrs. Amery's head was wide open. Suddenly, as she reclined on the sofa, thinking her uncomfortable thoughts and yet trying not to worry because she had been warned that worry was the one thing she must avoid, she felt a sharp cold draught on the back of her neck, as though a wet bandage had been pressed against her curls.

She looked at the door to see whether it had swung open and caused a through current of air. But the door was closed, and a glance at the window showed her that the shabby net curtains – doomed for the rag-bag – hung motionless. Yet the sharp draught continued and it was chilly enough to send a shudder down her spine. Springing to her feet, she slammed down the window. Then, returning to the sofa, she sat down again and inserted one finger in the book.

But the queer feeling at the back of her neck persisted, and now, as well as the sense of cold there was a sense of movement, as though a very cold hand were gently lifting and caressing the curls of her hair. Instinctively she put up her hand, felt it warm against her own warm neck, and in the same instant felt the cold touch run over her shoulder, over the short sleeve of her dress, down on to the bare flesh of her arm and finally fasten on her hand. It was, save for its coldness, exactly the gesture and touch that a lover might use.

But in that terrible moment Mrs. Amery was too panic-stricken to recognize the caressing quality of the touch. She sat quite still, even her breathing stopped by the force of her fear. Then, gasping, like a woman who has just been dragged back from drowning in icy water, she shook her hand violently and the cold clasp loosened – as a warm human hand might, finding itself unwelcome, relax its hold – and Mrs. Amery, on legs that shook so violently that they only just bore her weight, stumbled towards the door. As she did so she heard, beyond all question of doubt or argument, the sound of a sigh, heavy with longing, wistful, frustrated.

A few staggering steps carried her into the kitchen, mundane and modern, with its recently connected electric stove and purring refrigerator. A few more brought her outside the back door and to the tradesmen's entrance. Here, in the warm sunshine, amid the scent of new paint and freshly sawn wood, she paused for a moment, drawing deep steadying breaths and leaning her hand on the kitchen window-sill. She was still shuddering violently and her face and hands were wet with perspiration. But she had recovered sufficiently to begin to take stock of her position. And awkward enough she found it. A glance at her watch told her that it was only just quarter past six, and Roger would not be back until eight. She knew that she would never dare to re-enter the house alone; and the supper was not even started.

She drew out her handkerchief and dried her face and hands, walked round to the front of the house and down to the wrought-iron railings which divided the front lawn from the village street. Almost opposite the proprietor of the little general shop was leisurely putting up his shutters; two late shoppers stood in the doorway gossiping. A dog lay on the path, lazily scratching his fleas. Away to the right two little girls turned a rope while a third skipped inexpertly. The complete normality of the scene made Mrs. Amery, who was given to self-derision, feel very foolish. Suppose anyone asked why she was standing here when she should be in the kitchen making a macaroni cheese. And suppose she replied that she had felt cold all down her arm and on her hand, and had heard a sigh. How they would laugh . . . those women, and the shopkeeper putting up his shutters, and the children; why, even the dog would laugh and point out that after hard exercise one did cool off suddenly. And the sigh? Why, her own breathing, a gasp of foolish, imaginative fear.

She stood there until the church clock at the end of the street chimed the half hour, and the women shoppers, each with a start of surprise, darted away in opposite directions. And by that time she had almost convinced herself that her imagination or her state of health was responsible for her experience. Almost, but not quite. Had she been quite convinced she would, being a conscientious little woman, have turned and re-entered the house and put on the macaroni. Instead, she turned towards the direction of the Fentons' house, and walked, with slow deliberation, almost counting each step, to meet Roger. At the imposing gateway, which she recognized from her son's laconic description, she paused. She was too diffident to inflict her company uninvited, and the Fentons sounded rather lordly. So she sat on a bank near the gateway until she heard Roger's footsteps – unmistakable to the ear of love – and then rose up and pretended that she had reached the gateway just as he did.

Roger's sole comment was: "You shouldn't have come so far, Mum. It's the hell of a walk." His after-thought, "I wish I'd got a bike," set Mrs. Amery to her familiar occupation of counting pennies.

She dreaded the night. Suppose, she thought (just as she had, earlier, supposed an argument in the opposite direction), suppose that she had not imagined that moment in the little sitting-room; if such a thing could happen in the clear light of late afternoon, what might not the night bring? She longed, with a longing as keen as that of a thirsty man for water, to suggest to Roger that the door between their bedrooms should stand open. But she dared not do it. She was certain by this time that she was a sick woman, the victim of an inflamed imagination, and she was really terrified lest some germ of her malaise might infect the child. She was always – had been for three long years – morbidly conscious that a boy without a father suffers a severe disadvantage, she shrank from the thought that she might try to make Roger take his father's place in her life, and at the same time she shrank from pampering him unduly, or making him precocious, or timid. So she allowed him to chatter his way into his own room and shut the door, and decorations have been awarded for less courage than went into her last "good night".

She lay down, with every nerve tense, and, keeping her light burning, read, with vagrant attention, her book, until from sheer exhaustion she fell asleep and woke to find Roger by her bedside. In one hand he carried a cup of scalding tea and in the other two very full-blown roses. The expression on his face was very queer; half shamed, and yet reminiscent of himself at four years old before self-consciousness dawned. He thrust the cup into her hand and laid the flowers on the bed-cover. "Thought it'd save you getting them yourself," he muttered, with a smile which redeemed the sentence from gruffness. Her heart melted in a wave of adoration and understanding. Of course, he was shy. All nice boys were; they dreaded committing themselves; had a horror of being thought "soft". Sniffing her roses, sipping her tea, remembering, self-derisively, her overnight fears, Mrs. Amery was happy again.

Yet when, at half past five, the truck roared away, leaving a vacuum of silence behind it, Mrs. Amery, although by this time self-convinced that her fears of yesterday were groundless, avoided the little sitting-room and stayed in the kitchen. After she had prepared the supper she sat down on a chair by the window and began to darn one of Roger's socks. Deliberately she held her thoughts in rein, pondering the differences in the ways boys had of wearing out their hose, some at the toe, others at the heel, others again at the ball of the foot. Yet it was with less surprise than with a sense of foredooming that she became aware after a few moments of the onset of fear. The silence of the house, the expanse of its emptiness, the mere fact of her own physical isolation, began to bear in upon her like enemies.

She fought the pressure, darning madly, counting the thrusts of her needle until a voice in her mind said, clearly and accusingly, "You're counting because you're afraid, you're afraid, you're afraid." And at that Mrs. Amery halted her needle and sat quite still, bringing everything that was in her, sense, reason, self-scorn and courage, to the business of meeting and withstanding her fear. She was still trying to mock herself into sanity when the half-finished sock was lifted gently from her hand and laid in her lap. And as she stared at the moving sock with incredulous, terror-filled eyes, she became conscious of a scent which, later on, she identified as that of hair-oil.

Her stumbling, staggering exit was a repetition of that of the day before; but, being already in the kitchen, she was nearer the blessed sanctuary of the open air. Yet today she was more deeply frightened and took longer to recover herself. She felt an urgent need for human company, and stood for a while looking up and down the village street, wishing that there were some house where her sudden arrival would be welcome and unquestioned. But there was none, for she had made no friends.

Then suddenly she remembered a name and an address which she had glanced at, unthinking and unnoticing, which had somehow become photographed on her mind. It was the name and address of a woman whom Mrs. Stanhope had selected as a possible scrubber. It was a legitimate errand, and, controlling herself with an effort, Mrs. Amery went in search of the woman. She was an old woman, with gnarled hands and stooping shoulders. But within their network of wrinkles her eyes were lively and intelligent. She would be glad, she said, to do any amount of scrubbing, and having said that, she embarked, almost as though she detected in Mrs. Amery a willing listener, upon a tangled maze of reminiscences, her own life-story, her memories of Mrs. Stanhope and the work she had done for her at various times, and, most potent memory of all, Mr. Edward.

"A rare one for the ladies was Mr. Edward; right down to the time he died. Making love to his nurse, they say he was when the last seizure come on him. Holding her hand, he was." The bright old eyes sparkled with the suggestion that, in their time, they too had had their share of Mr. Edward's attention. There flashed through Mrs. Amery's facile imagination a vision of a neat, black-eyed, smiling, bestreamered maid-servant lingering in the passage or on the stairs of the house from which she herself had just fled. Had that touch . . . ah, but it would have been warm and human then! . . . fallen upon that shoulder, now so bowed, rested on that hand, now so gnarled?

With mechanical politeness and the smile which was almost automatic, Mrs. Amery took leave of the crone and walked away between the bright borders of the cottage garden. She felt a little dizzy, so rapidly was her mind working. One small nodule of incredulous common sense was trying to reject the fantastic conclusions which nervous dread, romanticism and remembered experience were forcing upon her. After all, misers haunted the sites of their buried hoards, murderers walked by the scenes of their crimes; why should not an inveterate philanderer be earthbound too? Earthbound! Terrible word. Terrible in its implications, terrible even in itself if repeated.

She walked rapidly, trying to outstrip her fear; but Roger met her before she was half way to the Fentons'; he too was hurrying, sweating slightly.

"Thought I'd start early and save you a bit of a walk," he explained.

"What made you think I'd come?" She was pleased to hear her voice so light and normal.

"Just guessed," he said. He linked his arm with hers, as he did sometimes when they were alone, and chattered on, describing his day's exploits. She walked alongside him, wishing with all her heart that they were going to the station, going to take a room in the village, going anywhere rather than back into that haunted house. The idea of retreating without putting up a further struggle hung tantalizingly in her mind; but she had the twenty pounds to earn; and over her there hung not only the idea of the money, and of Mrs. Stanhope's wrath, but behind that, Mrs. Bigmore. If she should let down Mrs. Bigmore's favourite friend, bring one of that masterful woman's plans to ridicule . . . why finish the thought? It was an unthinkable hypothesis.

But on that night she cajoled Roger into making the final round of doors and windows with her; and then, almost sick with self-contempt, and trying desperately to keep the note of pleading out of her voice, arranged for the communicating doors between their rooms to stay open, giving the heat as an excuse. Nothing untoward happened; but once, as she lay miserably watchful and wakeful, the child called, "Whassa matter, Mum?" in a voice thick with sleep. She called back, "Nothing. Why?" He muttered indistinguishably and in the morning denied any memory of the moment.

For two days and nights she managed, by little ruses and craftinesses, to avoid being in the house alone for a moment. But they were two days of misery. She was conscious now, in a way which was new, of being watched, reproachfully and with an increasing malevolence. It was as though some actual suitor, finding himself constantly rebuffed, were feeling love turn to hatred. And at the same time she knew that there were human eyes watching her too. Those big blue eyes of Roger's, capable of such frankness and at the same time of such secretiveness, were beginning to dwell upon her with a kind of furtive interest. He was not blind, she felt, to her loss of interest in food, or to the ravages which broken sleep can inflict upon a face no longer young. Once he asked if her head ached. And on each afternoon, just before the truck drove away, he had arrived home, breathless and hot, giving some excuse for his early arrival and yet, it seemed, rather out of temper.

Then, suddenly, he began to ask questions. Were they to spend the whole holiday here? Well, she countered, until the work was finished, at least. And how long would that be? Couldn't the chaps hurry a bit? She fenced with other questions. Wasn't he happy here? Was he tired of the Fentons? She added, unwisely: "You needn't spend so long here, you know. I can always come and meet you."

He stared, and she stumbled on: "I mean, I don't see much of you all day. I like to make our evenings seem long."

A new worry came to prey upon her. Suppose Roger guessed that she was afraid of the house and susceptible to something uncanny about it; suppose he saw through her pathetic subterfuges to gain company; suppose he became frightened too. He was, after all, her child; he was very young, and already his life, she thought with self-reproach, was unnatural enough. He had a precocious knowledge of ways and means . . . and this ghastly holiday plan might result in some morbid complex which would remain with him for the rest of his childhood at the least. It was all her fault, too. Probably the whole thing was the fabric of an inflamed imagination.

Thinking like this through the long hours of daylight, she almost convinced herself, and just before dusk, instead of angling for Roger's company on her evening round, she said – and the effort cost her dear – "I'll just do the doors and windows before supper, dear. You go on reading."

She sped round the house in a blind mad manner, as though the whole place was afire and she running to escape the flames. And nothing happened until she reached the drawing-room, which she had left till last because it was near the sitting-room, where Roger was reading. The tall wide windows were open to help the new paint to dry and to disperse the odour. She had a moment of her ever-ready self-reproach that she should be closing them so early. But as she rattled down the last window and stood on tiptoe to fasten the catch, she became aware, through all the smell of paint, of the fragrance of macassar oil, and in the same second, that cold clasp was all about her, holding her motionless, stopping her very blood. Her hands froze to the window-catch, her face froze in a grimace of terror, her heels stayed poised away from the floor and her involuntary cry of horror passed soundless through her stiff throat and ice-bound lips.

Roger's heavy nailed shoes clinked on the stone floor of the hall and Roger's voice, blessedly human, struck her frozen ears. "Shall I turn on the griller?"

The cold clasp melted; and as it did so Mrs. Amery heard the sigh again. It was no longer wistful. This time its frustration had a furious, exasperated note.

"You do look odd," said Roger.

"I strained myself, I think, reaching to fasten the window."

She was afraid to sleep. She lay with her mind going round in a circle, like a circus pony. She would not stay in the house another day; she would forfeit the twenty pounds and Mrs. Bigmore's esteem and risk her job – for the headmistress's displeasure would be far-reaching, she knew. And yet . . . and yet . . . it meant Roger's schooling, and so much else – little things, down to the very football boots which she had promised him for next term. So, round and round, one decision after another, until the window grew grey with the blessed daylight, and courage came back and the twenty pounds regained its value and Mrs. Bigmore her importance; and for the hundredth time Mrs. Amery was sure that she was the victim of her own imagination, or still ill, or going mad like poor Great-aunt Vinny, and that therefore it was most important that she should try to make friends for Roger while she still could.

Half way through breakfast Roger, who had been uncommonly silent, said, rather crossly:

"I wish you'd speak if you must come into a chap's room in the night."

"I . . . I . . ." she said, setting down her cup with a jerk that spilled coffee into the saucer. "Oh . . . it was only that I turned cold myself and wondered whether you'd like your eiderdown pulled over."

"I was all right till you came. But your hand was like ice and then I woke up and didn't get warm again for ages. Why didn't you pull it up when you were there?"

"You seemed warm enough."

She was sick with a new fear. So now it was Roger who was threatened. And she could see the deadly, the truly awful, logic of that.

She thought: "Maybe I am mad . . . but he isn't. And though I might be able to save him from my fear, I can't save him from his own."

She picked up the half-cup of coffee and drained it. Then she said, steadily, without emotion:

"Roger, would you like to go to Felixstowe after all, for the rest of the holiday?" There flashed into that inward eye which she would have been the last to call, with the poet, "the bliss of solitude", the notices that spattered the shop windows, "Cook wanted", "Waitresses required". Surely there was something she could find.

The child's brown face lightened and she realized suddenly that she had been missing that carefree look. But it dimmed again, and he said stubbornly:

"Not unless you come, too."

"Oh, I meant us both. Would you like to get your things together while I go and send some telegrams?"

In the train, the feeling which had begun to assail her in the post-office reached an agonizing pitch. Remorse and self-contempt attacked her until she felt physically ill. She had thrown away a job, risked another, lost twenty pounds which she needed and was about to spend money which she hadn't yet earned . . . and for what? Why? She was ready to answer, "Because I imagine things." She looked at her son, sitting opposite, lost to the world in some schoolboy paper or other and thought, Poor Roger; his father is dead and his mother is mad.

Roger folded the paper. He studied his mother carefully for some seconds and then asked:

"I say, will you ever go back to that place . . . Bidstone I mean?"

"No. I shan't go back."

"Then I'll tell you something. I don't know whether you spotted it or not . . . but, gosh, there was something very queer there."

"Queer, darling? In what way?"

"Well . . ." he paused, choosing his words. "Did you notice that I always got back pretty early? Did you notice I always sort of stuck close in the evening? I was sort of scared you'd guess why. Well, gosh, Mum, that place was spooky. I don't mean spies or smugglers pretending to be spooks. This was a real one. Honest, Mum. I saw it. I was afraid you might, too."

"No," said Mrs. Amery truthfully, "I never saw anything."

"Gosh, I'm glad of that. Say, that was why I sort of kept on about getting away, you know. I saw the thing dozens of times."

"It's imagination," said Mrs. Amery, more from habit than from intention.

"This wasn't. I saw him as plain as I'm seeing you. Old, he was, in a plum-coloured velvet coat and sort of tight long trousers. And a lot of hair and whiskers. I tell you, Mum, I didn't like it at all."

"I think . . ." said Mrs. Amery, feeling sick and dizzy, "I think you'd better try to forget about it, darling."

"Forget it!" he exclaimed, aghast at such misunderstanding. "Forget it! I should think not. Why, think what a tale it'll be to tell the chaps after Lights Out. Gosh, I'll make their flesh creep. A real live ghost, seen with my very own eyes. Gosh, if you hadn't been there, Mum, I'd have found out what he was looking for, buried treasure or a lost will or something. He had a kind of . . . well . . . more of a hungry look."

"Roger," said Mrs. Amery, "you're making *my* flesh creep. I believe you're making up the whole thing on purpose."

And then she began to wonder – as was her wont – whether she was handling *this* affair properly.

# House of the Hatchet

## Robert Bloch

### Prospectus

**Address:** Kluva Mansion, Prentiss Road, Los Angeles, USA.
**Property:** Nineteenth-century, two-storey tenement building. Restored as a tourist attraction named "The House of Terror", it is billed as "A Genuine Authentic Haunted House".
**Viewing Date:** May, 1955.
**Agent:** Robert Bloch (1917–1994) was born in Chicago and began his career in advertising, writing stories in his spare-time for the legendary pulp magazine, *Weird Tales*, until the success of his novel, *Psycho* (1959), filmed by Alfred Hitchcock, turned him into a household name. His fiendish imagination and gallows humour made Bloch's stories unique in fantasy fiction, especially those using the Haunted House motif, such as "The Curse of the House", "The Hungry House" and "House of the Hatchet", reprinted here. In this, an old mansion where a notorious axe murderer killed his wife – now a tourist attraction – has the most appalling effect on one visitor . . .

Daisy and I were enjoying one of our usual quarrels. It started over the insurance policy this time, but after we threshed that out we went into the regular routine. Both of us had our cues down perfectly.

"Why don't you go out and get a job like other men instead of sitting around the house pounding a typewriter all day?"

"You knew I was a writer when I married you. If you were so hot to hitch up with a professional man you ought to have married that broken-down intern you ran around with. You'd know where he was all day; out practising surgery by dissecting hamburgers in that chili parlor down the street."

"Oh, you needn't be so sarcastic. At least George would do his best to be a good provider."

"I'll say he would. He provided me with a lot of laughs ever since I met him."

"That's the trouble with you – you and your superior attitude! Think you're better than anybody else. Here we are, practically starving, and you have to pay instalments on a new car just to show it off to your movie friends. And on top of that you go and take out a big policy on me just to be able to brag about how you're protecting your family. I wish I *had* married George – at least he'd bring home some of that hamburger to eat when he finished work. What do you expect me to live on, used carbon paper and old typewriter ribbons?"

"Well, how the devil can I help it if the stuff doesn't sell? I figured on that contract deal but it fell through. You're the one that's always beefing about money – who do you think I am, the goose that laid the golden egg?"

"You've been laying plenty of eggs with those last stories you sent out."

"Funny. Very funny. But I'm getting just a little tired of your second-act dialogue, Daisy."

"So I've noticed. You'd like to change partners and dance, I suppose. Perhaps you'd rather exchange a little sparkling repartee with that Jeanne Corey. Oh, I've noticed the way you hung around her that night over at Ed's place. You couldn't have got much closer without turning into a corset."

"Now listen, you leave Jeanne's name out of this."

"Oh, I'm supposed to leave Jeanne's name out of it, eh? Your wife mustn't take the name of your girlfriend in vain. Well, darling, I always knew you were a swift worker, but I didn't think it had gone that far. Have you told her that she's your inspiration yet?"

"Damn it, Daisy, why must you go twisting around everything I say—"

"Why don't you insure her, too? Bigamy insurance – you could probably get a policy issued by Brigham Young."

"Oh, turn it off, will you? A fine act to headline our anniversary, I must say."

"Anniversary?"

"Today's May 18th, isn't it?"

"May 18th—"

"Yeah. Here, shrew."

"Why – honey, it's a necklace—"

"Yeah. Just a little dividend on the bonds of matrimony."

"Honey – you bought this for me? – with all our bills and—"

"Never mind that. And quit gasping in my ear, will you? You sound like Little Eva before they hoist her up with the ropes."

"Darling, it's so beautiful. Here."

"Aw, Daisy. Now see what you've done. Made me forget where we left off quarreling. Oh, well."

"Our anniversary. And to think I forgot!"

"Well, I didn't. Daisy."

"Yes?"

"I've been thinking – that is, well, I'm just a sentimental cuss at heart, and I was sort of wondering if you'd like to hop in the car and take a run out along the Prentiss Road."

"You mean like that day we – eloped?"

"Um hum."

"Of course, darling. I'd love to. Oh, honey, where *did* you get this necklace?"

That's how it was. Just one of those things. Daisy and I, holding our daily sparring match. Usually it kept us in trim. Today, though, I began to get the feeling that we had overtrained. We'd quarrelled that way for months, on and off. I don't know why; I wouldn't be able to define "incompatibility" if I saw it on my divorce-papers. I was broke, and Daisy was a shrew. Let it go at that.

But I felt pretty clever when I dragged out my violin for the *Hearts and Flowers*. Anniversary, necklace, re-tracing the honeymoon route; it all added up. I'd found a way to keep Daisy quiet without stuffing a mop into her mouth.

She was sentimentally happy and I was self-congratulatory as we climbed into the car and headed up Wilshire towards Prentiss Road. We still had a lot to say to each other, but in repetition it would be merely nauseating. When Daisy felt good she went in for baby-talk – which struck me as being out of character.

But for a while we were both happy. I began to kid myself that it was just like old times; we really were the same two kids running away on our crazy elopement. Daisy had just "gotten off" from the beauty parlor and I'd just sold my script series to the agency, and we were running down to Valos to get married. It was the same spring weather, the same road, and Daisy snuggled close to me in the same old way.

But it wasn't the same. Daisy wasn't a kid any more; there were no lines in her face, but there was a rasp in her voice. She hadn't taken on any weight, but she'd taken on a load of querulous ideas. I was different, too. Those first few radio sales had set the pace; I began to run around with the big-shots, and that costs money. Only lately I hadn't made any sales, and the damned expenses kept piling up, and everytime I tried to get any work done at the house there was Daisy nagging away. Why did we have to buy a new car? Why did we have to pay so much rent? Why such an insurance policy? Why did I buy three suits?

So I buy her a necklace and she shuts up. There's a woman's logic for you.

Oh well, I figured, today I'll forget it. Forget the bills, forget her nagging, forget Jeanne – though that last was going to be hard. Jeanne was quiet, and she had a private income, and she thought baby-talk was silly. Oh well.

We drove on to Prentiss Road and took the old familiar route. I stopped my little stream-of-consciousness act and tried to get into the mood. Daisy *was* happy; no doubt of that. We'd packed an overnight bag, and without mentioning it we both knew we'd stay at the hotel in Valos, just as we had three years ago when we were married.

Three years of drab, nagging monotony –

But I wasn't going to think about that. Better to think about Daisy's pretty blond curls gleaming in the afternoon sunshine; to think about the pretty green hills doing ditto in the afternoon ditto. It was spring, the spring of three years ago, and all life lay before us – down the white concrete road that curved across the hills to strange heights of achievement beyond.

So we drove on, blithely enough. She pointed out the signs and I nodded or grunted or said "Uh-uh" and the first thing I knew we were four hours on the road and it was getting past afternoon and I wanted to get out and stretch my legs and besides –

There it lay. I couldn't have missed the banner. And even if I did, there was Daisy, squealing in my ear.

"Oh, honey – look."

CAN YOU TAKE IT?
THE HOUSE OF TERROR
VISIT A GENUINE, AUTHENTIC HAUNTED HOUSE

And in smaller lettering, beneath, further enticements were listed.

"See the Kluva Mansion! Visit the Haunted Chamber – see the Axe used by the Mad Killer! DO THE DEAD RETURN? Visit the HOUSE OF TERROR – only genuine attraction of its kind. ADMISSION–25¢"

Of course I didn't read all this while slashing by at 60 m.p.h. We pulled up as Daisy tugged my shoulder, and while she read, I looked at the large, rambling frame building. It looked like dozens of others we passed on the road; houses occupied by "swamis" and "mediums" and "Yogi Psychologists." For this was the lunatic fringe where the quacks fed on the tourist trade. But here was a fellow with a little novelty. He had something a bit different. That's what I thought.

But Daisy evidently thought a lot more.

"Ooh, honey, let's go in."

"What?"

"I'm so stiff from all this driving, and besides, maybe they sell hot dogs inside or something, and I'm hungry."

Well. That was Daisy. Daisy the sadist. Daisy the horror-movie fan. She didn't fool me for a minute. I knew all about my wife's pretty little tastes. She was a thrill-addict. Shortly after our marriage she'd let down the bars and started reading the more lurid murder trial news aloud to me at breakfast. She began to leave ghastly magazines around the house. Pretty soon she was dragging me to all the mystery-pictures. Just another one of her annoying habits – I could close my eyes at any time and conjure up the drone of her voice, tense with latent excitement, as she read about the Cleveland torso slayings, or the latest hatchet-killing.

Evidently nothing was too synthetic for her tastes. Here was an old shack that in its palmiest days was no better than a tenement house for goats; a dump with a lurid side-show banner flung in front of the porch – and still she had to go in. "Haunted House" got her going. Maybe that's what had happened to our marriage. I would have pleased her better by going around the house in a black mask, purring like Bela Lugosi with bronchitis, and caressing her with a hatchet.

I attempted to convey some of the pathos of my thoughts in the way I replied, "What the blazes?" but it was a losing battle. Daisy had her hand on the car door. There was a smile on her face – a smile that did queer things to her lips. I used to see that smile when she read the murder-news; it reminded me, unpleasantly, of a hungry cat's expression while creeping up on a robin. She was a shrew and she was a sadist.

But what of it? This was a second honeymoon; no time to spoil things just when I'd fixed matters up. Kill half an hour here and then on to the hotel in Valos.

"Come *on!*"

I jerked out of my musings to find Daisy halfway up the porch. I locked the car, pocketed the keys, joined her before the dingy door. It was getting misty in the late afternoon and the clouds rolled over the sun. Daisy knocked impatiently. The door opened slowly, after a long pause in the best haunted-house tradition. This was the cue for a sinister face to poke itself out and emit a greasy chuckle. Daisy was just itching for that, I knew.

Instead she got W. C. Fields.

Well, not quite. The proboscis was smaller, and not so red. The cheeks were thinner, too. But the checked suit, the squint, the jowls, and above all that "step right up gentlemen" voice were all in the tradition.

"Ah. Come in, come in. Welcome to Kluva Mansion, my friends, welcome." The cigar fingered us forward. "Twenty-five cents, please. Thank you."

There we were in the dark hallway. It really was dark, and there certainly was a musty enough odor, but I knew damned well the house wasn't haunted by anything but cockroaches. Our comic friend would have to do some pretty loud talking to convince me; but then, this was Daisy's show.

"It's a little late, but I guess I've got time to show you around. Just took a party through about fifteen minutes ago – big party from San Diego. They drove all the way up just to see the Kluva Mansion, so I can assure you you're getting your money's worth."

All right buddy, cut out the assuring, and let's get this over with. Trot out your zombies, give Daisy a good shock with an electric battery or something, and we'll get out of here.

"Just what is this haunted house and how did you happen to come by it?" asked Daisy. One of those original questions she was always thinking up. She was brilliant like that all the time. Just full of surprises.

"Well, it's like this, lady. Lots of folks ask me that and I'm only too glad to tell them. This house was built by Ivan Kluva – don't know if you remember him or not – Russian movie director, came over here about '23 in the old silent days, right after DeMille began to get popular with his spectacle pictures. Kluva was an 'epic' man; had quite a European reputation, so they gave him a contract. He put up this place, lived here with his wife. Aren't many folks left in the movie colony that remember old Ivan Kluva; he never really got to direct anything either.

"First thing he did was to mix himself up with a lot of foreign cults. This was way back, remember; Hollywood had some queer birds then. Prohibition, and a lot of wild parties; dope addicts, all kinds of scandals, and some stuff that never did get out. There was a bunch of devil-worshippers and mystics, too – not like these fakes down the road; genuine article. Kluva got in with them.

"I guess he was a little crazy, or got that way. Because one night, after some kind of gathering here, he murdered his wife. In the upstairs room, on a kind of an altar he rigged up. He just took a hatchet to her and hacked off her head. Then he disappeared. The police looked in a couple of days later; they found her, of course, but they never did locate Kluva. Maybe he jumped off the cliffs behind the house. Maybe – I've heard stories – he killed her as a sort of sacrifice so he could *go away*. Some of the cult members were grilled, and they had a lot of wild stories about worshipping things or beings that granted boons to those who gave them human sacrifices; such boons as *going away* from Earth. Oh, it was crazy enough, I guess, but the police did find a damned funny statue behind the altar that they didn't like and never showed around, and they burned a lot of books and things they got hold of here. Also they chased that cult out of California."

All this corny chatter rolled out in a drone and I winced. Now I'm only a two-bit gag-writer, myself, but I was thinking that if I went in for such things I could improvise a better story than this poorly-told yarn and I could ad-lib it more effectively than this bird seemed able to do with daily practice. It sounded so stale, so flat, so unconvincing. The rottenest "thriller plot" in the world.

Or –

It struck me then. Perhaps the story was true. Maybe this was the solution. After all, there were no supernatural elements yet. Just a dizzy Russian devil-worshipper murdering his wife with a hatchet. It happens once in a while; psychopathology is full of such records. And why not? Our comic friend merely bought the house after the murder, cooked up his "haunt" yarn, and capitalized.

Evidently my guess was correct, because old Bugle-beak sounded off again.

"And so, my friends, the deserted Kluva Mansion remained, alone and untenanted. Not utterly untenanted, though. There was the ghost. Yes, the ghost of Mrs. Kluva – the Lady in White."

Phooey! Always it has to be the Lady in White. Why not in pink, for a change, or green? Lady in White – sounds like a burlesque headliner. And so did our spieler. He was trying to push his voice down into his fat stomach and make it impressive.

"Every night she walks the upper corridor to the murder chamber. Her slit throat shines in the moonlight as she lays her head once again on the blood-stained block, again receives the fatal blow, and with a groan of torment, disappears into thin air."

Hot air, you mean, buddy.

"Oooh," said Daisy. "She would."

"I say the house was deserted for years. But there were tramps, vagrants, who broke in from time to time to stay the night. They stayed the night – and longer. Because in the morning they were always found – on the murder block, with their throats chopped by the murder axe."

I wanted to say "Axe-ually?" but then, I have my better side. Daisy was enjoying this so; her tongue was almost hanging out.

"After a while nobody would come here; even the tramps shunned the spot. The real estate people couldn't sell it. Then I rented. I knew the story would attract visitors, and frankly, I'm a business man."

Thanks for telling me, brother. I thought you were a fake.

"And now, you'd like to see the murder chamber? Just follow me, please. Up the stairs, right this way. I've kept everything just as it always was, and I'm sure you'll be more than interested in—"

Daisy pinched me on the dark stairway. "Ooh, sugar, aren't you thrilled?"

I don't like to be called "sugar." And the idea of Daisy actually finding something "thrilling" in this utterly ridiculous farce was almost nauseating. For a moment I could have murdered her myself. Maybe Kluva had something there at that.

The stairs creaked, and the dusty windows allowed a sepulchral light to creep across the mouldy floor as we followed the waddling showman down the black hallway. A wind seemed to have sprung up outside, and the house shook before it, groaning in torment.

Daisy giggled nervously. In the movie-show she always twisted my lapel-buttons off when the monster came into the room where the girl was sleeping. She was like that now – hysterical.

I felt as excited as a stuffed herring in a pawnshop.

W. C. opened a door down the hall and fumbled around inside. A moment later he reappeared carrying a candle and beckoned us to enter the room. Well, that was a little better. Showed some imagination, anyway. The candle was effective in the gathering darkness; it cast blotches of shadow over the walls and caused shapes to creep in the corners.

"Here we are," he almost whispered.

And there we were.

Now I'm not psychic. I'm not even highly imaginative. When Orson Welles is yammering on the radio I'm down at the hamburger stand listening to the latest swing music. But when I entered that room I *knew* that it, at least, wasn't a fake. The air reeked of murder. The shadows ruled over a domain of death. It was cold in here, cold as a charnel-house. And the candle-light fell on the great bed in the corner, then moved to the center of the room and covered a monstrous bulk. The murder block.

It was something like an altar, at that. There was a niche in the wall behind it, and I could almost imagine a statue being placed there. What kind of a statue? A black bat, inverted and crucified? Devil-worshippers used that, didn't they? Or was it another and more horrible kind of idol? The police had destroyed it. But the block was still there, and in the candle-light I saw the stains. They trickled over the rough sides.

Daisy moved closer to me and I could feel her tremble.

Kluva's chamber. A man with an axe, holding a terrified woman across the block; the strength of inspired madness in his eyes, and in his hands, an axe –

"It was here, on the night of January twelfth, nineteen twenty-four, that Ivan Kluva murdered his wife with—"

The fat man stood by the door, chanting out his listless refrain. But for some reason I listened to every word. Here in this room, those words were real. They weren't scareheads on a sideshow banner; here in the darkness they had meaning. A man and his wife, and murder. Death is just a word you read in the newspaper. But some day it becomes real; dreadfully real. Something the worms whisper in your ears as they chew. Murder is a word, too. It is the power of death, and sometimes there are men who exercise that power, like gods. Men who kill are like gods. They take away life. There is something cosmically obscene about the thought. A shot fired in drunken frenzy, a blow struck in anger, a bayonet plunged in the madness of war, an accident, a car-crash – these things are part of life. But a man, any man, who lives with the thought of Death; who thinks and plans a deliberate, cold-blooded murder –

To sit there at the supper table, looking at his wife, and saying, "Twelve o'clock. You have five more hours to live, my dear. Five more hours. Nobody knows that. Your friends don't know it. Even you don't know it. No one knows – except myself. Myself, and Death, I am Death. Yes, I am Death to you. I shall numb your body and your brain, I shall be your lord and master. You were born, you have lived, only for this single supreme moment; that I shall command your fate. You exist only that I may kill you."

Yes, it was obscene. And then, this block, and a hatchet.

"Come upstairs, dear." And his thoughts, grinning behind the words. Up the dark stairs to the dark room, where the block and hatchet waited.

I wondered if he hated her. No, I suppose not. If the story was true, he had sacrificed her for a purpose. She was just the most handy, the most convenient person to sacrifice. He must have had blood like the water under the polar peaks.

It was the room that did it, not the story. I could feel him in the room, and I could feel *her*.

Yes, that was funny. Now I could feel *her*. Not as a being, not as a tangible presence, but as a force. A restless force. Something that stirred in back of me before I turned my head. Something hiding in the deeper shadows. Something in the blood-stained block. A chained spirit.

"Here I died. I ended here. One minute I was alive, unsuspecting. The next found me gripped by the ultimate horror of Death. The hatchet came down across my throat, so full of life, and sliced it out. Now I wait. I wait for others, for there is nothing left to me but revenge. I am not a person any longer, nor a spirit. I am merely a force – a force created as I felt my life slip away from my throat. For at that moment I knew but one feeling with my entire dying being; a feeling of utter, cosmic hatred. Hatred at the sudden injustice of what had happened to me. The force was born then when I died; it is all that is left of me. Hatred. Now I wait, and sometimes I have a chance to let the hatred escape. By killing another I can feel the hatred rise, wax, grow strong. Then for a brief moment I rise, wax, grow strong; feel real again, touch the hem of life's robe, which once I wore. Only by surrendering to my dark hate can I survive in death. And so I lurk; lurk here in this room. Stay too long and I shall return. Then, in the darkness, I seek your throat and the blade bites and I taste again the ecstasy of reality."

The old drizzle-puss was elaborating his story, but I couldn't hear him for my thoughts. Then all at once he flashed something out across my line of vision; something that was like a stark shadow against the candle-light.

It was a hatchet.

I felt, rather than heard, when Daisy went "Ooooh!" beside me. Looking down I stared into two blue mirrors of terror that were her eyes. I had thought plenty, and what her imaginings had been I could guess. The old bird was stolid enough, but he brandished that hatchet, that hatchet with the rusty blade, and it got so I couldn't look at anything else but the jagged edge of the hatchet. I couldn't hear or see or think anything; there was that hatchet, the symbol of Death. There was the real crux of the story; not in the man or the woman, but in that tiny razor-edge line. That razor-edge was really Death. That razor-edge spelled doom to all living things. Nothing in the world was greater than that razor-edge. No brain, no power, no love, no hate could withstand it.

And it swooped out in the man's hands and I tore my eyes away and looked at Daisy, at anything, just to keep the black thought down. And I saw Daisy, her face that of a tortured Medusa.

Then she slumped.

I caught her. Bugle-beak looked up with genuine surprise.

"My wife's fainted," I said.

He just blinked. Didn't know what the score was, at first. And a minute later I could swear he was just a little bit pleased. He thought his story had done it, I suppose.

Well, this changed all plans. No Valos, no drive before supper.

"Any place around here where she can lie down?" I asked. "No, not in this room."

"My wife's bedroom is down the hall," said Bugle-beak.

His wife's bedroom, eh? But no one stayed here after dark, he had said – the damned old fake!

This was no time for quibbling. I carried Daisy into the room down the hall, chafed her wrists.

"Shall I send my wife up to take care of her?" asked the now solicitous showman.

"No, don't bother. Let me handle her; she gets these thing every so often – hysteria, you know. But she'll have to rest a while."

He shuffled down the hall, and I sat there cursing. Damn the woman, it was just like her! But too late to alter circumstances now. I decided to let her sleep it off.

I went downstairs in the darkness, groping my way. And I was only halfway down when I heard a familiar pattering strike the roof. Sure enough – a typical West Coast heavy dew was falling. Fine thing, too; dark as pitch outside.

Well, there was the set-up. Splendid melodrama background. I'd been dragged to movies for years and it was always the same as this.

The young couple caught in a haunted house by a thunderstorm. The mysterious evil caretaker. (Well, maybe he wasn't, but he'd have to do until a better one came along.) The haunted room. The fainting girl, asleep and helpless in the bedroom. Enter Boris Karloff dressed in three pounds of nose-putty.

"Grrrrrr!" says Boris. "Eeeeeeeh!" says the girl. "What's that?" shouts Inspector Toozefuddy from downstairs. And then a mad chase. "Bang! Bang!" And Boris Karloff falls down into an open manhole. Girl gets frightened. Boy gets girl. Formula.

I thought I was pretty clever when I turned on the burlesque thought pattern, but when I got down to the foot of the stairs I knew that I was playing hide-and-go-seek with my thoughts. Something dark and cold was creeping around in my brain, and I was trying hard to avoid it. Something to do with Ivan Kluva and his wife and the haunted room and the hatchet. Suppose there was a ghost and Daisy was lying up there alone and –

"Ham and eggs?"

"What the—" I turned around. There was Bugle-beak at the foot of the stairs.

"I said, would you care for some ham and eggs? Looks pretty bad outside and so long as the Missus is resting I thought maybe you'd like to join the wife and me in a little supper."

I could have kissed him, nose and all.

We went into the back. Mrs. was just what you'd expect; thin woman in her middle forties, wearing a patient look. The place was quite cosy, though; she had fixed up several rooms as living quarters. I began to have a little more respect for Bugle-beak. Poor showman though he was, he seemed to be making a living in a rather novel way. And his wife was an excellent cook.

The rain thundered down. Something about a little lighted room in the middle of a storm that makes you feel good inside. Confidential. Mrs. Keenan – Bugle-beak introduced himself as Homer Keenan – suggested that I might take a little brandy up to Daisy. I demurred, but Keenan perked up his ears – and nose – at the mention of brandy and suggested we have a little. The *little* proved to be a half-gallon jug of fair peach-brandy, and we filled our glasses. As the meal progressed we filled them again. And again. The liquor helped to chase that dark thought away, or almost away. But it still bothered me. And so I got Homer Keenan into talking. Better a boring conversation than a boring thought – boring little black beetle of thought, chewing away in your brain.

"So after the carny folded I got out from under. Put over a little deal in Tia and cleaned up but the Missus kind of wanted to settle down. Tent business in this country all shot to blazes anyway. Well, I knew this Feingerber from the old days, like I say – and he put me up to this house. Yeah, sure, that part is genuine enough. There was an Ivan Kluva and he did kill his wife here. Block and axe genuine too; I got a state permit to keep 'em. Museum, this is. But the ghost story, of course that's just a fake. Gets them in, though. Some week-ends we play to capacity crowds ten hours a day. Makes a nice thing of it. We live here – say, let's have another nip of this brandy, whaddy say? Come on, it won't hurt you. Get it from a Mex down the road a ways."

Fire. Fire in the blood. What did he mean the ghost story was fake? When I went into that room I smelled murder. I thought *his* thoughts. And then I had thought *hers*. Her hate was in that room; and if it wasn't a ghost, what was it? Somehow it all tied in with that black thought I had buzzing in my head; that damned black thought all mixed up with the axe and hate, and poor Daisy lying up there helpless. Fire in my head. Brandy fire. But not enough. I could still think of Daisy, and all at once something blind gripped me and I was afraid and I trembled all over, and I couldn't wait. Thinking of her like that, all alone in the storm, near the murder-room and the block and the hatchet – I knew I must go to her. I couldn't stand the horrid suspicion.

I got up like a fool, mumbled something about looking after her, and ran up the black staircase. I was trembling, trembling, until I reached her bedside and saw how peacefully she lay there. Her sleep was quite untroubled. She was even smilling. She didn't know. She wasn't afraid of ghosts and hatchets. Looking at her I felt utterly ridiculous, but I did stare down at her for a long time until I regained control of myself once again . . . .

When I went downstairs the liquor had hit me and I felt drunk. The thought was gone from my brain now, and I was beginning to experience relief.

Keenan had refilled my glass for me, and when I gulped it down he followed suit and immediately poured again. This time we sat down to a real gab-fest.

I began to talk. I felt like an unwinding top. Everything began to spin out of my throat. I told about my life; my "career," such as it was; my romance with Daisy, even. Just felt like it. The liquor.

Before you know it I was pulling a True Confession of my own, with all the trimmings. How things stood with Daisy and me. Our foolish quarrels. Her nagging. Her touchiness about things like our car, and the insurance, and Jeanne Corey. I was maudlin enough to be petty. I picked on her habits. Then I began to talk about this trip of ours, and my plans for a second honeymoon, and it was only instinct that shut me up before becoming actually disgusting.

Keenan adopted an older "man-of-the-world" attitude, but he finally broke down enough to mention a few of his wife's salient deficiencies. What I told him about Daisy's love for the horrors prompted him to tease his wife concerning her own timidity. It developed that while she knew the story was a fake, she still shied away from venturing upstairs after nightfall – just as though the ghost were real.

Mrs. Keenan bridled. She denied everything. Why she'd go upstairs any time at all. Any time at all.

"How about now? It's almost midnight. Why not go up and take a cup of coffee to that poor sick woman?" Keenan sounded like somebody advising Little Red Riding-Hood to go see her grandmother.

"Don't bother,'" I assured him. "The rain's dying down. I'll go up and get her and we'll be on our way. We've got to get to Valos, you know."

"Think I'm afraid, eh?" Mrs. Keenan was already doing things with the coffee pot. Rather dizzily, but she managed.

"You men, always talking about your wives. I'll show you!" She took the cup, then arched her back eloquently as she passed Keenan and disappeared in the hallway.

I got an urge.

Sobriety rushed to my head.

"Keenan," I whispered.

"Whazzat?"

"Keenan, we must stop her!"

"What for?"

"You ever gone upstairs at night?"

"Course not. Why sh'd I? All dusty up there, mus' keep it tha'way for cust'mers. Never go up."

"Then how do you know the story isn't true?" I talked fast. Very.

"What?"

"I say perhaps there *is* a ghost."

"Aw, go on!"

"Keenan, I tell you I felt something up there. You're so used to the place you didn't notice, but I *felt* it. A woman's hate, Keenan. A woman's hate!" I was almost screaming; I dragged him from his chair and tried to push him into the hall. I had to stop her somehow. I was afraid.

"That room is filled with menace." Quickly I explained my thoughts of the afternoon concerning the dead woman – surprised and slain, so that she died only with a great hate forming as life left her; a hate that endured, that thrived on death alone. A hate, embodied, that would take up the murder hatchet and slay –

"Stop your wife, Keenan," I screamed. "Stop her!"

"What about your wife?" chuckled the showman. "Besides," and he leered, drunkenly, "I'll tell you somethin' I wasn't gonna tell. It's *all* a fake." He winked. I still pushed him towards the staircase.

"All a fake," he wheezed. "Not only ghost part. But – there never was a Ivan Kluva, never was no wife. Never was no killing. Jus' old butcher's block. Hatchet's my hatchet. No murder, no ghost, nothin' to be afraid of. Good joke, make myself hones' dollar. All a fake!"

"Come on!" I screamed, and the black thought came back and it sang in my brain and I tried to drag him up the stairs, knowing it was too late, but still I had to do something –

And then *she* screamed.

I heard it. She was running out of the room, down the hall. And at the head of the stairs she screamed again, but the scream turned into a gurgle. It was black up there, but out of the blackness tottered her silhouette. Down the stairs she rolled; bump, bump, bump. Same sound as a rubber ball. But she was a woman, and she ended up at the bottom of the stairs with the axe still stuck in her throat.

Right there I should have turned and run, but that thing inside my head wouldn't let me. I just stood there as Keenan looked down at the body of his wife, and I babbled it all out again.

"I hated her – you don't understand how those little things count – and Jeanne waiting – there was the insurance – if I did it at Valos no one would ever know – here was accident, but better."

"There is no ghost," Keenan mumbled. He didn't even hear me. "There is no ghost," I stared at the slashed throat.

"When I saw the hatchet and she fainted, it came over me. I could get you drunk, carry her out, and you'd never know—"

"What killed my wife?" he whispered. "There is no ghost."

I thought again of my theory of a woman's hate surviving death and existing thereafter only with an urge to slay. I thought of that hate, embodied, grabbing up a hatchet and slaying, saw Mrs. Keenan fall, then glanced up at the darkness of the hall as the grinning song in my brain rose, forcing me to speak.

"There is a ghost now," I whispered. "You see, the second time I went up to see Daisy, I killed her with this hatchet."

# Napier Court

## Ramsey Campbell

### Prospectus

**Address:** Napier Court, Lower Brichester, England.

**Property:** Twentieth-century spacious town house. Well appointed living room, dining room, kitchen and several bedrooms, with tasteful fixtures and fittings which make it an ideal family residence.

**Viewing Date:** Autumn, 1971.

**Agent:** Ramsey Campbell (1946– ) was born in Liverpool and after working as a tax officer and librarian, has become one of the pre-eminent figures in modern fantasy and horror fiction with his stories that are a unique mixture of his influences – M. R. James and Algernon Blackwood – and the horrors of contemporary society. Since his debut with "The Church in the High Street" (1962), he has written a series of novels and stories on the themes of possession and the supernatural, notably *Needing Ghosts* (1990) and *Strange Things and Stranger Places* (1993), as well as menacing short stories like this one about a young girl and the ill-omened building that is her home.

Alma Napier sat up in bed. Five minutes ago she'd lain down *Victimes de Devoir* to cough, then stared round her bedroom heavy-eyed; the partly open door reflected panels of cold October sunlight, which glanced from the flowered wall-paper, glared from the glass-fronted bookcase, but left the metronome on top in shadow and failed to reach the corner where her music-stand was standing. She'd thought she had heard footsteps on the stairs. Beyond the brilliant panel she could see the darker landing; she waited for someone to appear. Her clock, displayed within its glass tube, showed 11:30. It must be Maureen. Then she thought: could it be her parents? Had they decided to give up their holiday after all? She had looked forward to being left alone for a fortnight when her cold had confined her to the house; she wanted time to prove herself, to make her own way – she felt a stab of misery as she listened. Couldn't they leave her alone for two weeks? Didn't they trust her? The silence thickened; the darkness on the landing seemed to move. "Who's there? Is that you, Maureen?" she called and coughed. The darkness moved again. Of course it didn't, she said, willing her hands to unclench. She held up one; the little finger twitched. Don't be childish, she told herself, where's your strength? She slid out of the cocoon of warmth, slipped on her slippers and dressing-gown, and went downstairs.

The house was empty. "You see?" she said aloud. What else had she expected? She entered the kitchen. On the window-sill sat the medicine her mother had bought. "I don't like to leave you alone," she'd said two hours ago. "Promise you'll take this and stay in bed until you're better. I've asked Maureen to buy anything you need while she's shopping." "Mother," Alma had protested, "I could have asked her. After all, she is *my* friend." "I know I'm being over-protective, I know I can't expect to be liked for it any more" and oh God, Alma thought, all the strain of calming her down, of parting friends; there was no longer any question of love. As her mother was leaving the bedroom while her father bumped the last case down to the car, she'd said: "Alma, I don't want to talk about Peter, as you well know, but you did promise—" "I've told you," Alma had replied somewhat sharply, "I shan't be seeing him again." That was all over. She wished everything was over, all this possessiveness which threatened to erase her completely; she wished she could be left alone with her music. But that was not to be, not for two years. There was the medicine-bottle, incarnating her mother's continued influence in the house. Taking medicine for a cold was a sign of weakness, in Alma's opinion. But her chest hurt terribly when she coughed; after all, her mother wasn't imposing it on her, if she took it that was her own decision. She measured a spoonful and gulped it down. Then she padded determinedly through the hall, past the living-room (her father's desk reflected in one mirror), the dining-room (her mother's flower arrangements preserved under glass in another), and upstairs, past her mother's Victorian valentines framed above the ornate banister. Now, she ordered herself, to bed, and another chapter of *Victimes de Devoir* before Maureen arrived. She'd never make the Brichester French Circle if she carried on like this.

But as soon as she climbed into bed, trying to preserve its bag of warmth, she was troubled by something she remembered having seen. In the hall – what had been wrong? She caught it: as she'd mounted the stairs she'd seen a shape in the hall mirror. Maureen's coat hanging on the coat-stand – but Maureen wasn't here. Certainly something pale had stood against the front-door panes. About to investigate, she addressed herself: the house was empty, there could be nothing there. All right, she'd asked Maureen to check the story of the house in the library's files of the *Brichester Herald* – but that didn't mean she believed the hints she'd heard in the corner shop that day before her mother had intervened with "Now, Alma, don't upset yourself" and to the shopkeeper: "Haunted, indeed! I'm afraid we grew out of that sort of thing in Severnford!" If she had seemed to glimpse a figure in the hall it merely meant she was delirious. She'd asked Maureen to check purely because she wanted to face up to the house, to come to terms with it. She was determined to stop thinking of her room as her refuge, where she was protected by her music. Before she left the house she wanted to make it a step towards maturity.

The darkness shifted on the landing. Tired eyes, she explained – yet her room enfolded her. She reached out and removed her flute from its case; she admired its length, its shine, the perfection of its measurements as they fitted to her fingers. She couldn't play it now – each time she tried she coughed – but it seemed charged with beauty. Her appreciation over, she laid the instrument to rest in its long black box.

"You retreat into your room and your music." Peter had said that, but he'd been speaking of a retreat from Hiroshima, from the conditions in Lower Brichester, from all the horrid things he'd insisted she confront. That was over, she said quickly, and the house was empty. Yet her eyes strayed from *Victimes de Devoir*.

Footsteps on the stairs again. This time she recognized Maureen's. The others – which she hadn't heard, of course – had been indeterminate, even sexless. She though she'd ask Maureen whether she'd left her coat in the hall; she might have entered while Alma had slept, with the key she'd borrowed. The door opened and the panel of sunlight fled, darkening the room. No, thought Alma; to enquire into possible delusions would be an admission of weakness.

Maureen dropped her carrier and sneezed. "I think I've got your cold," she said indistinctly.

"Oh dear." Alma's mood had darkened with the room, with her decision not to speak. She searched for conversation in which to lose herself. "Have you heard yet when you're going to library school?" she asked.

"It's not settled yet. I don't know, the idea of a spinster career is beginning to depress me. I'm glad you're not faced with that."

"You shouldn't brood," Alma advised, restlessly stacking her books on the bedspread.

Maureen examined the titles. "*Victimes de Devoir, Thérèse Desqueyroux*. In the original French, good Lord. Why are you grappling with these?"

"So that I'll be an interesting young woman," Alma replied instantly. "I'm sure I've told you I feel guilty doing nothing. I can't practise, not with this cold. I only hope it's past before the Camside concert. Which reminds me, do you think I could borrow your transistor during the day? For the music programme. To give me peace."

"All right. I can't today, I start work at one. Though I think – no, it doesn't matter."

"Go on."

"Well, I agree with Peter, you know that. You can't have peace and beauty without closing your eyes to the world. Didn't he say that to seek peace in music was to seek complete absence of sensation, of awareness?"

"He said that and you know my answer." Alma unwillingly remembered; he had been here in her room, taking in the music in the bookcase, the polished gramophone – she'd sensed his disapproval and felt miserable; why couldn't he stay the strong forthright man she'd come to admire and love? "Really, darling, this is an immature attitude," he'd said. "I can't help feeling you want to abdicate from the human race and its suffering." Her eyes embraced the room. This was security, apart from the external chaos, the horrid part of life. "Even you appreciate the beauty of the museum exhibits," she told Maureen.

"I suppose that's why you work there. I admire them, yes, but in many cases by ignoring their history of cruelty."

"Why must you and Peter always look for the horrid things? What about this house? There are beautiful things here. That gramophone – you can look at it and imagine all the craftsmanship it took. Doesn't that seem to you fulfilling?"

"You know we leftists have a functional aesthetic. Anyway—" Maureen paused. "If that's your view of the house you'd best not know what I found out about it."

"Go on, I want to hear."

"If you insist. The *Brichester Herald* was useless – they reported the death of the owner and that was all – but I came across a chapter in Pamela Jones' book on local hauntings which gives the details. The last owner of the house lost a fortune in the stock market – I don't know how exactly, of course it's not my field – and he became a recluse in this house. There's worse to come, are you sure you want –? Well, he went mad. Things started disappearing, so he said, and he accused something he thought was living in the house, something that used to stand behind him or mock him from the empty rooms. I can imagine how he started having hallucinations, looking at this view—"

Alma joined her at the window. "Why?" she disagreed. "I think it's beautiful." She admired the court before the house, the stone pillars framing the iron flourish of the gates; then a stooped woman passed across the picture, heaving a pram from which overflowed a huge cloth bag of washing. Alma felt depressed again; the scene was spoilt.

"Sorry, Alma," Maureen said; her cold hand touched Alma's fingers. Alma frowned slightly and insinuated herself between the sheets. ". . . Sorry," Maureen said again. "Do you want to hear the rest? It's conventional, really. He gassed himself. The Jones book has something about a note he wrote – insane, of course; he said he wanted to 'fade into the house, the one possession left to me', whatever that meant. Afterwards the stories started; people used to see someone very tall and thin standing at the front door on moonlit nights, and one man saw a figure at an upstairs window with its head turning back and forth like clockwork. Yes, and one of the neighbours used to dream that the house was 'screaming for help' – the book explained that, but not to me I'm afraid. I shouldn't be telling you all this, you'll be alone until tonight."

"Don't worry, Maureen. It's just enjoyably creepy."

"A perceptive comment. It blinds you to what really happened. To think of him in this house, possessing the rooms, eating, sleeping – you forget he lived once, he was *real*. I wonder which room—?"

"You don't have to harp on it," Alma said. "You sound like Peter."

"Poor Peter, you *are* attacking him today. He'll be here to protect you tonight, after all."

"He won't, because we've parted."

"You could have stopped me talking about him, then. But how for God's sake did it happen?"

"Oh, on Friday. I don't want to talk about it." Walking hand in hand to the front door and as always kissing as Peter turned the key; her father waiting in the hall: "Now listen, Peter, this can't go on" – prompted by her mother, Alma knew, her father was too weak to act independently. She'd pulled Peter into the kitchen – "Go, darling, I'll try and calm them down" she'd said desperately – but her mother was waiting, immediately animated, like a fairground puppet by a penny: "You know you've broken my heart, Alma, marrying beneath you." Alma had slumped into a chair, but Peter leaned against the dresser, facing them all, her mother's prepared speech: "Peter, I will not have you marrying Alma – you're uneducated, you'll get nowhere at the library, you're obsessed with politics and you don't care how much they distress Alma—" and on and on. If only he'd come to her instead of standing pugnaciously apart! She'd looked up at him finally, tearful, and he'd said: "Well, darling, I'll answer any point of your mother's you feel is not already answered" – and suddenly everything had been too much; she'd run sobbing to her room. Below the back door had closed. She'd wrenched open the window; Peter was crossing the garden beneath the rain. "Peter!" she'd cried out. "Whatever happens I still love you—" but her mother was before her, pushing her away from the window, shouting down: "Go back to your kennel!" . . . "What?" she asked Maureen, distracted back.

"I said I don't believe it was your decision. It must have been your mother."

"That's irrelevant. I broke it off finally." Her letter: "It would be impossible to continue when my parents refuse to receive you but anyway I don't want to any more, I want to study hard and become a musician" – she'd posted it on Saturday after a sleepless sobbing night, and immediately she'd felt released, at peace. Then the thought disturbed her: it must have reached Peter by now; surely he wouldn't try to see her? But he wouldn't be able to get in; she was safe.

"You can't tell me you love your mother more than Peter. You're simply taking refuge again."

"Surely you don't think I love her now. But I still feel I must be loyal. Is there a difference between love and loyalty?"

"Never having had either, I wouldn't know. Good God, Alma, stop barricading yourself with pseudo-philosophy!"

"If you must know, Maureen, I shall be leaving them as soon as I've paid for my flute. They gave it me for my twenty-first and now they're threatening to take it back. It'll take me two years, but I shall pay."

"And you'll be twenty-five. God Almighty, why? Bowing down to private ownership?"

"You wouldn't understand any more than Peter would."

"You've returned the ring, of course."

"No." Alma shifted *Victimes de Devoir*. "Once I asked Peter if I could keep it if we broke up." Two weeks before their separation; she'd felt the pressures – her parents' crush, his horrors – misshaping her, callous as thumbs on plasticine, And he'd replied that there'd be no question of their breaking up, which she'd taken for assent.

"And Peter's feelings?" Maureen let the question resonate, but it was muffled by the music.

"Maureen, I just want to remember the happy times!"

"I don't understand that remark. At least, perhaps I do, but I don't like it."

"You don't approve."

"I do not." Maureen brandished her watch; from her motion she might have been about to slap Alma. "I can't discuss it with you. I'll be late." She buttoned herself into her coat on the landing. "I suppose I'll see Peter later," she said, and clumped downstairs.

With the slam Alma was alone. Her hot-water bottle chilled her toes; she thrust it to the foot of the bed. The room was darker; rain patted the pane. The metronome stood stolid in the shadow as if stilled for ever. Maureen might well see Peter later; they both worked at Brichester Central Library. What if Maureen should attempt to heal the breach, to lend Peter her key? It was the sort of thing Maureen might well do, particularly as she liked Peter. Alma recalled suggesting once that they take Maureen out – "she does seem lonely, Peter" – only to find the two of them ideologically united against her; the most difficult two hours she'd spent with either of them, listening to their agreement on Vietnam and the rest across the cocktail-bar table: horrid. Later she'd go down and bolt the door. But now – she turned restlessly and *Victimes de Devoir* toppled to the floor. She felt guilty not to be reading on – but she yearned to fill herself with music.

The shadows weighed on her eyes; she pulled the cord for light. Spray laced the window like cobwebs on a misty morning; outside the world was slate. The needle on her gramophone was dulled, but she selected the first record, Britten's *Nocturne* ("Finnegan's Half-Awake" Peter had commented; she'd never understood what he meant). She placed the needle and let the music expand through her, flowing into troubled crevices. The beauty of Peter Pears' voice. Peter. Suddenly she was listening to the words: sickly light, huge sea-worms – She picked off the needle; she didn't want it to wear away the beauty. Usually Britten could transmute all to beauty. Had Peter's pitiless vision thrown the horrid part into such relief? Once she'd taken him to a concert of the *War Requiem* and in the interval he'd commented: "I agree with you – Britten succeeds completely in beautifying war, which is precisely my objection." And later he'd admitted that for the last half-hour he'd been pitying the poor cymbal-player, bobbing up and down on cue as if in church. That was his trouble: he couldn't achieve peace.

Suppose he came to the house? she thought again. Her gaze flew to the bedroom door, the massed dark on the landing. For a moment she was sure that Peter was out there; wasn't someone watching her from the stairs? She coughed jaggedly; it recalled her. Deliberately she lifted her flute from its case and rippled a scale before the next cough came. Later she'd practise, no matter how she coughed; her breathing exercises might cure her lungs. "I find all these exercises a little terrifying," said Peter: "a little robotic." She frowned miserably; he seemed to wait wherever she sought peace. But thoughts of him carried her to the dressing-table drawer, to her ring; she didn't have to remember, the diamond itself crystallized beauty. She turned the jewel but it refused to sparkle beneath the heavy sky. Had he been uneducated? Well, he'd known nothing about music, he'd never known what a cadenza was – "what's the point of your academic analysis, where does it touch life?" Enough. She snapped the lid on the ring and restored it to its drawer. From now on she'd allow herself no time for disturbing memories: down-stairs for soup – she must eat – then her flute exercises followed by *Victimes de Devoir* until she needed sleep.

The staircase merged into the hall, vaguely defined beneath her drowsiness; the Victorian valentines seemed dusty in the dusk, neglected in the depths of an antique shop. As Alma passed the living-room a stray light was caught in the mirror and a memory was trapped: herself and Peter on the couch, separating instantly, tongues retreating guiltily into mouths, each time the opening door flashed in the mirror: towards the end Peter would clutch her rebelliously, but she couldn't let her parents come on them embracing, not after their own marriage had been drained of love. "We'll be each other's peace," she'd once told Peter, secretly aware as she spoke that she was terrified of sex. Once they were engaged she'd felt a duty to give in – but she'd panted uncontrollably, her mouth gulping over his, shaming her. One dreadful night Peter had rested his head on her shoulder and she'd known that he was consulting his watch behind her back. And suddenly, weeks later, it had come right; she was at peace, soothed, her fears almost engulfed – which was precisely when her parents had shattered the calm, the door thrown open, jarring the mirror: "Peter, this is a respectable house, I won't have you keeping us all up like this until God knows what hour, even if you are used to that sort of thing—" and then that final confrontation – Quickly, Alma told herself, onward. She thrust the memories back into the darkness of the two dead rooms to be crushed by her father's desk, choked by her mother's flowers.

On the kitchen windowsill the medicine was black against the back garden, the grey grass plastered down by rain: it loomed like a poison bottle in a Hitchcock film. What was Peter doing at this moment? Where would he be tonight? She fumbled sleepily with the tin of tomato soup and watched it gush into the pan. Where would he be tonight? With someone else? If only he would try to contact her, to show her he still cared – Nonsense. She turned up the gas. No doubt he'd be at the cinema; he'd tried to force films on her, past her music. Such as the film they'd seen on the afternoon of their parting, the afternoon they'd taken off work together, *Hurry Sundown*; it hadn't been the theme of racism which had seemed so horrid, but those scenes with Michael Caine sublimating his sex-drive through his saxophone – she'd brushed her hair against Peter's cheek, hopefully, desperately, but he was intent on the screen, and she could only guess his thoughts, too accurately. Perhaps he and Maureen would find each other; Alma hoped so – then she could forget about them both. The soup bubbled and she poured it into a dish. Gas sweetened the air; she checked the control, but it seemed turned tight. The dresser – there he had stood, pugnaciously apart, watching her. She set the medicine before her on the table; she'd take it upstairs with her – she didn't want to come downstairs again. In her mind she overcame the suffocating shadow of the rooms, thick with years of tobacco-smoke in one, with lavender-water in another, by her shining flute, the sheets of music brightly turning.

A dim thin figure moved down the hall towards the kitchen; it hadn't entered by the front door – rather had it emerged from the twin vista in the hall mirror. Alma sipped her soup, not tasting it but warmed. The figure fingered the twined flowers, sat at her father's desk. Alma bent her head over the plate. The figure stood outside the kitchen door, one hand on the doorknob. Alma stood; her chair screeched; she saw herself pulled erect by panic in the familiar kitchen like a child in darkness, and willed herself to sit. The figure climbed the stairs, entered her room, padded through the shadows, examining her music, breathing on her flute. Alma's spoon tipped and the soup drained back into its disc. Then, determinedly, she dipped again.

She had to fasten her thoughts on something as she mounted the stairs, medicine in hand; she thought of the Camside orchestral concert next week – thank God she wouldn't be faced with Peter chewing gum amid the ranks of placid tufted eggs. She felt for her bedroom light switch. Behind the bookcase shadows sprang back into hiding and were defined. She smiled at the room and at herself; then carefully she closed the door. After the soup she felt a little hot, light-headed. She moved to the window and admired the court set back from the bare street; above the roofs the sky was diluted lime-and-lemon beneath clouds like wads of stuffing. " 'Napier Court' – I see the point, but don't you think that naming houses is a bit pretentious?" Alma slid her feet through the cold sheets, recoiling from the frigid bottle. She'd fill it later; now she needed rest. She set aside *Victimes de Devoir* and lay back on the pillow.

Alma awoke. Someone was outside on the landing. At once she knew: Peter had borrowed Maureen's key. He came into the room, and as he did so her mother appeared from behind the door and drove the music-stand into his face. Alma awoke. She was swaddled in blankets, breathing through them. For a moment she lay inert; one hand was limp between her legs, her ear pressed on the pillow; these two parts of her felt miles distant, and something vast throbbed silently against her eardrums. She catalogued herself: slight delirium, a yearning for the toilet. She drifted with the bed; she disliked to emerge, to be oriented by the cold.

Nonsense, don't indulge your weakness, she told herself, and poked her head out. Surely she'd left the light on? Darkness blindfolded her, warm as the blankets. She reached for the cord, and the blue window blackened as the room appeared. The furniture felt padded by delirium. Alma burned. She struggled into her dressing-gown and saw the clock: 12:05. Past midnight and Maureen hadn't come? Then she realized: the clock had stopped – it must have been around the time of Maureen's departure. Of course Maureen wouldn't return; she'd been repelled by disapproval. Which meant that Alma would have no transistor, no means of discovering the time. She felt as if she floated, bodiless, disoriented, robbed of sensation, and went to the window for some indication; the street was deserted, as it might be at any hour soon after dark.

Turning from the pane she pivoted in the mirror; behind her the bed stood at her left. That wasn't right; right was where it stood. Or did it reverse in the reflection? She turned to look but froze; if she faced round she'd meet a figure waiting, hands outstretched, one side of its face incomplete, like those photographs from Vietnam Peter had insisted she confront – The thought released her; she turned to an empty room. So much for her delirium. Deliberately she switched out the light and padded down the landing.

On her way back she passed her mother's room; she felt compelled to enter. Between the twin beds shelves displayed the Betjemans, the books on Greece, histories of the Severn Valley. On the beds the sheets were stretched taut as one finds them on first entering a hotel room. When Peter had stayed for weekends her father had moved back into this room. Her father – out every night to the pub with his friends; he hadn't been vindictive to her mother, just unfeeling and unable to adjust to her domestic rhythm. When her mother had accused Alma of "marrying beneath her" she'd spoken of herself. Deceptively freed by their absence, Alma began to understand her mother's hostility to Peter. "You're a handsome bugger," her mother had once told him; Alma had pinpointed that as the genesis of her hostility – it had preyed on her mother's mind, this lowering herself to say what she thought he'd like only to realize that the potential of this vulgarity lurked within herself. Now Alma saw the truth; once more sleeping in the same room as her husband, she'd had the failure of her marriage forced upon her; she'd projected it on Alma's love for Peter. Alma felt released; she had understood them, perhaps she could even come once more to love them, just as eventually she'd understood that buying Napier Court had fulfilled her father's ambition to own a house in Brichester – her father, trying to talk to Peter who never communicated to him (he might have been unable, but this was no longer important), finally walking away from Peter whistling "Release Me" which he'd reprised the day after the separation, somewhat unfeelingly she thought. Even this she could understand. To seal her understanding, she turned out the light and closed the door.

Immediately a figure rose before her mother's mirror, combing long fingers through its hair. Alma managed not to shudder; she strode to her own door, opened it on blackness, and crossed to her bed. She reached out to it and fell on her knees; it was not there.

As she knelt trembling, the house rearranged itself round her; the dark corridors and rooms, perhaps not empty as she prayed, watched pitilessly, came to bear upon her. She staggered to her feet and clutched the cord, almost touching a gaping face, which was not there when the light came on. Her bed was inches from her knees, where it had been when she left it, she insisted. Yet this failed to calm her. There was more than darkness in the house; she was no longer comfortingly alone in her warm and welcoming home. Had Peter borrowed Maureen's key? All at once she hoped he had; then she'd be in his arms, admitting that her promise to her mother had been desperate; she yearned for his protection – strengthened by it she believed she might confront horrors if he demanded them.

She watched for Peter from the window. One night while he was staying Peter had come to her room – She focused on the court; it seemed cut off from the world, imprisoning. Eclipsed by the gatepost, a pedestrian crossing's beacons exchanged signals without meaning; she thought of others flashing far into the night on cold lonely country roads, and shivered. He had come into her room; they'd caressed furtively and whispered so as not to wake her parents, though now she suspected that her mother had lain awake, listening through her father's snores. "Take me," she'd pleaded – but in the end she couldn't; the wall was too attentive. Now she squirmed at her remembered endearments: "my nice Peter" – "my handsome Peter" – "my lovely Peter" – and at last her halting praise of his body, the painful search for new phrases. She no longer cared to recall; she sloughed off the memories with an epileptic shudder.

Suddenly a man appeared in the gateway of the court. Alma stiffened. The figure passed; she relaxed, but only for a moment; had there not been something strange about its long loping strides, its trailing shadow? This was childish, she rebuked herself; she'd no more need to become obsessed with someone hastening to a date than with Peter, who was no longer in a position to protect her. She turned from the window before the figure should form behind her, and picked up her flute. Half-an-hour of exercises, then sleep. She opened the case. It was empty.

It was as if her mother had returned and taken back the flute; she felt the house again rise up round her. She grasped an explanation; last time she'd fingered her flute – when had that been? Time had slipped away – she hadn't replaced it in its case. She threw the sheets back from the bed; only the dead bottle was exposed. She knelt again and peered beneath the bed. Something bent above her, waiting, grinning. No, the flute hadn't rolled. She stood up and the figure moved behind her. "Don't!" she whimpered. At that moment she saw that the dressing-table drawer was open. She took one step towards it, to her ring, but could not look into it, knowing what was there – a face peering up at her from the drawer, its eyes opening, infinitely slowly, the lashes parting stickily – Delirium again? It didn't matter. Alma's lips trembled. She could still escape. She went to the wardrobe – but nothing could have made her open it; instead she caught up her clothes from the chair at the foot of the bed and dressed clumsily, dragging her skirt round to reach the zip. The room was silent; her music had fled, but any minute something else would take its place.

Since she had to face the darkened house, she did so. She trembled only once. The Victorian valentines hung immobile; the mirrors extended the darkness, strengthened its power. The house waited. Alma fell into the court; from the cobblestones, the erect gateposts, the street beyond, she drew courage. Two years and she'd be far from here, a complete person. Freed from fear, she left the front door open. But she shivered; the night air knifed through the dangerous warmth of her cold. She must go – where? To Maureen's, she decided; that was not too far, and she knew Maureen to be kind. She'd forget her disapproval if she saw Alma like this. Alma strode towards the orange fan which flared from the beacon behind the gatepost, and stopped.

Resting against the beacon was a white bag, half as high as Alma. She'd seen such bags before, full of laundry. Yet she could not force herself to pull back the gates and pass. Suddenly the gates were her protection against the shapeless mass, for deep within herself she suppressed a horror that the bag might move towards her, flapping. It couldn't be what it appeared, who would have left it there at this time of night? A car hissed past on the glittering tarmac. Alma choked a scream for help. Screaming in the middle of the street – what would her mother have thought? Musicians didn't do that sort of thing. Besides, why shouldn't someone have left a bag of washing at the crossing while she went for help to heft it to the laundry? Alma touched the gates and withdrew, chilled; here she was, risking pneumonia in the night, and for what? The panic of delirium. As a child she'd screamed hoarsely through her cold that a man was bending over her; she was too old for that. Back to bed – no, to find her flute, and then to bed, to purge herself of these horrid visions. Ironically she thought: Peter would be proud of her if he knew. Her flute – must the two years any longer be meaningful? Still touched by understanding, she couldn't think that her parents would hold to their threat, made after all before she'd written to Peter. What must have been a night-breeze moved the bag. Forcing her footsteps not to drag, Alma left the orange radiance and closed the door behind her; her last test.

In the hall the thing she had thought was Maureen's coat shifted wakefully. Alma ignored it, but her flesh crept hot and cold. At the far end of the hall mirror, a figure approached, arms extended as if blindly. Alma smiled; it was too like a childish fear to frighten her: "enjoyably creepy" – she tried to recapture her mood of the morning, but every organ of her body felt hot and pounding. She broke and ran to her room; the light, oddly, was still on.

In the rooms below, her father's desk creaked; the flower arrangements writhed. Did it matter? Alma argued desperately. There was no lock on her door, but she refused to barricade it; there was nothing solid abroad in the house, nothing to harm her but the lure of her own fears. Her flute – she wouldn't play it once she found it; she'd go to bed with its protection. She moved round the bed and saw the flute, overlaid by *Victimes de Devoir*. The flute was bent in half.

One tear pressed from Alma's eyes before she realized the full horror. As she whirled, completely disoriented, a mirror crashed below. Something shrieked towards her through the corridors. She sank onto the bed, defenceless, wishing all were over. Music blasted from the record-player, the *Nocturne*; Alma leapt up and screamed. "In roaring he shall rise," the voice bawled, "and on the surface—" A music-stand was hurled to the floor. "– *die!*" The needle scraped across the record and clicked off. The walls seemed on the point of tearing, bulging inwards. Alma no longer cared. She'd screamed once; she could do no more. Now she waited.

When the figure formed deep in the mirror she knew that all was over. She faced it, drained of feeling. It grew closer, arms stretched out, its face inflated grey by gas. Alma wept; it was horrid. She knew who it was; a shaft of truth had pierced the suffocating warmth of her delirium. The suicide had possessed the house, was the house; he had waited for someone like her. "Go on," she sobbed at him, "take me!" The bloated cheeks moved in a swollen grin; the arms stretched out for her and vanished.

The house was empty. Alma was surrounded by a vacuum into which something must rush. She stood up shaking and fell into the vacuum; her sight was torn away. She tried to move; there was no longer any muscle to respond. She felt nothing, but utter horror closed her in. Somewhere she sensed her body, moving happily on her bedroom carpet, picking up her ruined flute, breathing a hideous note into it. She tried to scream. Impossible.

Only in dreams can houses scream for help.

5

# LITTLE TERRORS

## Ghosts and Children

# Lost Hearts

## M. R. James

### Prospectus

**Address:** Aswarby Hall, Lincolnshire, England.

**Property:** Early eighteenth-century mansion. A tall, red-brick building, with classical, stone-pillared porch and wings housing the stables and offices of the hall. Set amidst well-maintained parkland with oak and fir trees.

**Viewing Date:** September, 1811.

**Agent:** Montague Rhodes James (1862–1936) was born in Goodnestone, Kent, but grew up in East Anglia before becoming a scholar at King's College, Cambridge, and later Provost of Eton. He began writing ghost stories as a Christmas amusement for friends and pupils, but the publication of these in collections like *Ghost Stories of an Antiquary* (1904), *More Ghost Stories of an Antiquary* (1911) and *A Warning to the Curious* (1925) established him as one of the greats of supernatural fiction. In "Lost Hearts", he combines his knowledge of young people and ghosts in the tale of a little boy in danger from occult powers who finds supernatural forces coming to his aid . . .

It was, as far as I can ascertain, in September of the year 1811 that a post-chaise drew up before the door of Aswarby Hall, in the heart of Lincolnshire. The little boy who was the only passenger in the chaise, and who jumped out as soon as it had stopped, looked about him with the keenest curiosity during the short interval that elapsed between the ringing of the bell and the opening of the hall door. He saw a tall, square, red-brick house, built in the reign of Anne; a stone-pillared porch had been added in the purer classical style of 1790; the windows of the house were many, tall and narrow, with small panes and thick white woodwork. A pediment, pierced with a round window, crowned the front. There were wings to right and left, connected by curious glazed galleries, supported by colonnades, with the central block. These wings plainly contained the stables and offices of the house. Each was surmounted by an ornamental cupola with a gilded vane.

An evening light shone on the building, making the window-panes glow like so many fires. Away from the Hall in front stretched a flat park studded with oaks and fringed with firs, which stood out against the sky. The clock in the church-tower, buried in trees on the edge of the park, only its golden weather-cock catching the light, was striking six, and the sound came gently beating down the wind. It was altogether a pleasant impression, though tinged with the sort of melancholy appropriate to an evening in early autumn, that was conveyed to the mind of the boy who was standing in the porch waiting for the door to open to him.

The post-chaise had brought him from Warwickshire, where, some six months before, he had been left an orphan. Now, owing to the generous offer of his elderly cousin, Mr. Abney, he had come to live at Aswarby. The offer was unexpected, because all who knew anything of Mr. Abney looked upon him as a somewhat austere recluse, into whose steady-going household the advent of a small boy would import a new and, it seemed, incongruous element. The truth is that very little was known of Mr. Abney's pursuits or temper. The Professor of Greek at Cambridge had been heard to say that no one knew more of the religious beliefs of the later pagans than did the owner of Aswarby. Certainly his library contained all the then available books bearing on the Mysteries, the Orphic poems, the worship of Mithras, and the Neo-Platonists. In the marble-paved hall stood a fine group of Mithras slaying a bull, which had been imported from the Levant at great expense by the owner. He had contributed a description of it to the *Gentleman's Magazine*, and he had written a remarkable series of articles in the *Critical Museum* on the superstitions of the Romans of the Lower Empire. He was looked upon, in fine, as a man wrapped up in his books, and it was a matter of great surprise among his neighbours that he should even have heard of his orphan cousin, Stephen Elliott, much more that he should have volunteered to make him an inmate of Aswarby Hall.

Whatever may have been expected by his neighbours, it is certain that Mr. Abney – the tall, the thin, the austere – seemed inclined to give his young cousin a kindly reception. The moment the front door was opened he darted out of his study, rubbing his hands with delight.

"How are you, my boy? – how are you? How old are you?" said he – "that is, you are not too much tired, I hope, by your journey to eat your supper?"

"No, thank you, sir," said Master Elliott; "I am pretty well."

"That's a good lad," said Mr. Abney. "And how old are you, my boy?"

It seemed a little odd that he should have asked the question twice in the first two minutes of their acquaintance.

"I'm twelve years old next birthday, sir," said Stephen.

"And when is your birthday, my dear boy? Eleventh of September, eh? That's well – that's very well. Nearly a year hence, isn't it? I like – ha, ha! – I like to get these things down in my book. Sure it's twelve? Certain?"

"Yes, quite sure, sir."

"Well, well! Take him to Mrs. Bunch's room, Parkes, and let him have his tea – supper – whatever it is."

"Yes, sir," answered the staid Mr. Parkes; and conducted Stephen to the lower regions.

Mrs. Bunch was the most comfortable and human person whom Stephen had as yet met in Aswarby. She made him completely at home; they were great friends in a quarter of an hour: and great friends they remained. Mrs. Bunch had been born in the neighbourhood some fifty-five years before the date of Stephen's arrival, and her residence at the Hall was of twenty years' standing. Consequently, if anyone knew the ins and outs of the house and the district, Mrs. Bunch knew them; and she was by no means disinclined to communicate her information.

Certainly there were plenty of things about the Hall and the Hall gardens which Stephen, who was of an adventurous and inquiring turn, was anxious to have explained to him. "Who built the temple at the end of the laurel walk? Who was the old man whose picture hung on the staircase, sitting at a table, with a skull under his hand?" These and many similar points were cleared up by the resources of Mrs. Bunch's powerful intellect. There were others, however, of which the explanations furnished were less satisfactory.

One November evening Stephen was sitting by the fire in the housekeeper's room reflecting on his surroundings.

"Is Mr. Abney a good man, and will he go to heaven?" he suddenly asked, with the peculiar confidence which children possess in the ability of their elders to settle these questions, the decision of which is believed to be reserved for other tribunals.

"Good? – bless the child!" said Mrs. Bunch. "Master's as kind a soul as ever I see! Didn't I never tell you of the little boy as he took in out of the street, as you may say, this seven years back? and the little girl, two years after I first come here?"

"No. Do tell me all about them, Mrs. Bunch – now this minute!"

"Well," said Mrs. Bunch, "the little girl I don't seem to recollect so much about. I know master brought her back with him from his walk one day, and give orders to Mrs. Ellis, as was housekeeper then, as she should be took every care with. And the pore child hadn't no one belonging to her – she telled me so her own self – and here she lived with us a matter of three weeks it might be; and then, whether she were somethink of a gipsy in her blood or what not, but one morning she out of her bed afore any of us had opened a eye, and neither track nor yet trace of her have

I set eyes on since. Master was wonderful put about, and had all the ponds dragged; but it's my belief she was had away by them gipsies, for there was singing round the house for as much as an hour the night she went, and Parkes, he declare as he heard them a-calling in the woods all that afternoon. Dear, dear! a hodd child she was, so silent in her ways and all, but I was wonderful taken up with her, so domesticated she was – surprising."

"And what about the little boy?" said Stephen.

"Ah, that pore boy!" sighed Mrs. Bunch. "He were a foreigner – Jevanny he called hisself – and he come a-tweaking his 'urdy-gurdy round and about the drive one winter day, and master 'ad him in that minute, and ast all about where he came from, and how old he was, and how he made his way, and where was his relatives, and all as kind as heart could wish. But it went the same way with him. They're a hunruly lot, them foreign nations, I do suppose, and he was off one fine morning just the same as the girl. Why he went and what he done was our question for as much as a year after; for he never took his 'urdy-gurdy, and there it lays on the shelf."

The remainder of the evening was spent by Stephen in miscellaneous cross-examination of Mrs. Bunch and in efforts to extract a tune from the hurdy-gurdy.

That night he had a curious dream. At the end of the passage at the top of the house, in which his bedroom was situated, there was an old disused bathroom. It was kept locked, but the upper half of the door was glazed, and, since the muslin curtains which used to hang there had long been gone, you could look in and see the lead-lined bath affixed to the wall on the right hand, with its head towards the window.

On the night of which I am speaking, Stephen Elliott found himself, as he thought, looking through the glazed door. The moon was shining through the window, and he was gazing at a figure which lay in the bath.

His description of what he saw reminds me of what I once beheld myself in the famous vaults of St. Michan's Church in Dublin, which possess the horrid property of preserving corpses from decay for centuries. A figure inexpressibly thin and pathetic, of a dusty leaden colour, enveloped in a shroud-like garment, the thin lips crooked into a faint and dreadful smile, the hands pressed tightly over the region of the heart.

As he looked upon it, a distant, almost inaudible moan seemed to issue from its lips, and the arms began to stir. The terror of the sight forced Stephen backwards, and he awoke to the fact that he was indeed standing on the cold boarded floor of the passage in the full light of the moon. With a courage which I do not think can be common among boys of his age, he went to the door of the bathroom to ascertain if the figure of his dream were really there. It was not, and he went back to bed.

Mrs. Bunch was much impressed next morning by his story, and went so far as to replace the muslin curtain over the glazed door of the bathroom. Mr. Abney, moreover, to whom he confided his experiences at breakfast, was greatly interested, and made notes of the matter in what he called "his book".

The spring equinox was approaching, as Mr. Abney frequently reminded his cousin, adding that this had been always considered by the ancients to be a critical time for the young: that Stephen would do well to take care of himself, and to shut his bedroom window at night; and that Censorinus had some valuable remarks on the subject. Two incidents that occurred about this time made an impression upon Stephen's mind.

The first was after an unusually uneasy and oppressed night that he had passed – though he could not recall any particular dream that he had had.

The following evening Mrs. Bunch was occupying herself in mending his nightgown.

"Gracious me, Master Stephen!" she broke forth rather irritably, "how do you manage to tear your nightdress all to flinders this way? Look here, sir, what trouble you do give to poor servants that have to darn and mend after you!"

There was indeed a most destructive and apparently wanton series, of slits or scorings in the garment, which would undoubtedly require a skilful needle to make good. They were confined to the left side of the chest – long, parallel slits, about six inches in length, some of them not quite piercing the texture of the linen.

Stephen could only express his entire ignorance of their origin: he was sure they were not there the night before.

"But," he said, "Mrs. Bunch, they are just the same as the scratches on the outside of my bedroom door; and I'm sure I never had anything to do with making *them*."

Mrs. Bunch gazed at him open-mouthed, then snatched up a candle, departed hastily from the room, and was heard making her way upstairs. In a few minutes she came down.

"Well," she said, "Master Stephen, it's a funny thing to me how them marks and scratches can 'a' come there – too high up for any cat or dog to 'ave made 'em, much less a rat: for all the world like a Chinaman's finger-nails, as my uncle in the tea-trade used to tell us of when we was girls together. I wouldn't say nothing to master, not if I was you, Master Stephen, my dear; and just turn the key of the door when you go to your bed."

"I always do, Mrs. Bunch, as soon as I've said my prayers."

"Ah, that's a good child: always say your prayers, and then no-one can't hurt you."

Herewith Mrs. Bunch addressed herself to mending the injured nightgown, with intervals of meditation, until bed-time. This was on a Friday night in March, 1812.

On the following evening the usual duet of Stephen and Mrs. Bunch was augmented by the sudden arrival of Mr. Parkes, the butler, who as a rule kept himself rather *to* himself in his own pantry. He did not see that Stephen was there: he was, moreover, flustered, and less slow of speech than was his wont.

"Master may get up his own wine, if he likes, of an evening," was his first remark. "Either I do it in the daytime or not at all, Mrs. Bunch. I don't know what it may be: very like it's the rats, or the wind got into the cellars; but I'm not so young as I was, and I can't go through with it as I have done."

"Well, Mr. Parkes, you know it is a surprising place for the rats, is the Hall."

"I'm not denying that, Mrs. Bunch; and, to be sure, many a time I've heard the tale from the men in the shipyards about the rat that could speak. I never laid no confidence in that before; but to-night, if I'd demeaned myself to lay my ear to the door of the further bin, I could pretty much have heard what they was saying."

"Oh, there, Mr. Parkes, I've no patience with your fancies! Rats talking in the wine-cellar indeed!"

"Well, Mrs. Bunch, I've no wish to argue with you: all I say is, if you choose to go to the far bin, and lay your ear to the door, you may prove my words this minute."

"What nonsense you do talk, Mr. Parkes – not fit for children to listen to! Why, you'll be frightening Master Stephen there out of his wits."

"What! Master Stephen?" said Parkes, awaking to the consciousness of the boy's presence. "Master Stephen knows well enough when I'm a-playing a joke with you, Mrs. Bunch."

In fact, Master Stephen knew much too well to suppose that Mr. Parkes had in the first instance intended a joke. He was interested, not altogether pleasantly, in the situation; but all his questions were unsuccessful in inducing the butler to give any more detailed account of his experiences in the wine-cellar.

We have now arrived at March 24, 1812. It was a day of curious experiences for Stephen: a windy, noisy day, which filled the house and the gardens with a restless impression. As Stephen stood by the fence of the grounds, and looked out into the park, he felt as if an endless procession of unseen people were sweeping past him on the wind, borne on resistlessly and aimlessly, vainly striving to stop themselves, to catch at something that might arrest their flight and bring them once again into contact with the living world of which they had formed a part. After luncheon that day Mr. Abney said:

"Stephen, my boy, do you think you could manage to come to me to-night as late as eleven o'clock in my study? I shall be busy until that time, and I wish to show you something connected with your future life which it is most important that you should know. You are not to mention this matter to Mrs. Bunch nor to anyone else in the house; and you had better go to your room at the usual time."

Here was a new excitement added to life: Stephen eagerly

grasped at the opportunity of sitting up till eleven o'clock. He looked in at the library door on his way upstairs that evening, and saw a brazier, which he had often noticed in the corner of the room, moved out before the fire; an old silver-gilt cup stood on the table, filled with red wine, and some written sheets of paper lay near it. Mr. Abney was sprinkling some incense on the brazier from a round silver box as Stephen passed, but did not seem to notice his step.

The wind had fallen, and there was a still night and a full moon. At about ten o'clock Stephen was standing at the open window of his bedroom, looking out over the country. Still as the night was, the mysterious population of the distant moonlit woods was not yet lulled to rest. From time to time strange cries as of lost and despairing wanderers sounded from across the mere. They might be the notes of owls or water-birds, yet they did not quite resemble either sound. Were not they coming nearer? Now they sounded from the nearer side of the water, and in a few moments they seemed to be floating about among the shrubberies. Then they ceased; but just as Stephen was thinking of shutting the window and resuming his reading of *Robinson Crusoe*, he caught sight of two figures standing on the gravelled terrace that ran along the garden side of the Hall – the figures of a boy and girl, as it seemed; they stood side by side, looking up at the windows. Something in the form of the girl recalled irresistibly his dream of the figure in the bath. The boy inspired him with more acute fear.

Whilst the girl stood still, half smiling, with her hands clasped over her heart, the boy, a thin shape, with black hair and ragged clothing, raised his arms in the air with an appearance of menace and of unappeasable hunger and longing. The moon shone upon his almost transparent hands, and Stephen saw that the nails were fearfully long and that the light shone through them. As he stood with his arms thus raised, he disclosed a terrifying spectacle. On the left side of his chest there opened a black and gaping rent; and there fell upon Stephen's brain, rather than upon his ear, the impression of one of those hungry and desolate cries that he had heard resounding over the woods of Aswarby all that evening. In another moment this dreadful pair had moved swiftly and noiselessly over the dry gravel, and he saw them no more.

Inexpressibly frightened as he was, he determined to take his candle and go down to Mr. Abney's study, for the hour appointed for their meeting was near at hand. The study or library opened out of the front hall on one side, and Stephen, urged on by his terrors, did not take long in getting there. To effect an entrance was not so easy. The door was not locked, he felt sure, for the key was on the outside of it as usual. His repeated knocks produced no answer. Mr. Abney was engaged: he was speaking. What! why did he try to cry out? and why was the cry choked in his throat? Had he, too, seen the mysterious children? But now everything was quiet, and the door yielded to Stephen's terrified and frantic pushing.

On the table in Mr. Abney's study certain papers were found which explained the situation to Stephen Elliott when he was of an age to understand them. The most important sentences were as follows:

"It was a belief very strongly and generally held by the ancients – of whose wisdom in these matters I have had such experience as induces me to place confidence in their assertions – that by enacting certain processes, which to us moderns have something of a barbaric complexion, a very remarkable enlightenment of the spiritual faculties in man may be attained: that, for example, by absorbing the personalities of a certain number of his fellow-creatures, an individual may gain a complete ascendancy over those orders of spiritual beings which control the elemental forces of our universe.

"It is recorded of Simon Magus that he was able to fly in the air, to become invisible, or to assume any form he pleased, by the agency of the soul of a boy whom, to use the libellous phrase employed by the author of the *Clementine Recognitions*, he had 'murdered.' I find it set down, moreover, with considerable detail in the writings of Hermes Trismegistus, that similar happy results may be produced by the absorption of the hearts of not less than three human beings below the age of twenty-one years.

To the testing of the truth of this receipt I have devoted the greater part of the last twenty years, selecting as the *corpora vilia* of my experiment such persons as could conveniently be removed without occasioning a sensible gap in society. The first step I effected by the removal of one Phœbe Stanley, a girl of gipsy extraction, on March 24, 1792. The second, by the removal of a wandering Italian lad, named Giovanni Paoli, on the night of March 23, 1805. The final 'victim' – to employ a word repugnant in the highest degree to my feelings – must be my cousin, Stephen Elliott. His day must be this March 24, 1812.

"The best means of effecting the required absorption is to remove the heart from the *living* subject, to reduce it to ashes, and to mingle them with about a pint of some red wine, preferably port. The remains of the first two subjects, at least, it will be well to conceal: a disused bathroom or wine-cellar will be found convenient for such a purpose. Some annoyance may be experienced from the psychic portion of the subjects, which popular language dignifies with the name of ghosts. But the man of philosophic temperament – to whom alone the experiment is appropriate – will be little prone to attach importance to the feeble efforts of these beings to wreak their vengeance on him. I contemplate with the liveliest satisfaction the enlarged and emancipated existence which the experiment, if successful, will confer on me; not only placing me beyond the reach of human justice (so-called), but eliminating to a great extent the prospect of death itself."

Mr. Abney was found in his chair, his head thrown back, his face stamped with an expression of rage, fright, and mortal pain. In his left side was a terrible lacerated wound, exposing the heart. There was no blood on his hands, and a long knife that lay on the table was perfectly clean. A savage wild-cat might have inflicted the injuries. The window of the study was open, and it was the opinion of the coroner that Mr. Abney had met his death by the agency of some wild creature. But Stephen Elliott's study of the papers I have quoted led him to a very different conclusion.

# The Shadowy Third

## Ellen Glasgow

### Prospectus

**Address:** Lower Fifth Avenue, New York, USA.

**Property:** Early nineteenth-century family house, less fashionable than when built, but distinguished by iron railings, stylish windows and a fanlight above the doorway. The property contains a fine drawing room and pleasant study.

**Viewing Date:** December, 1916.

**Agent:** Ellen Glasgow (1874–1945) was born in Richmond, Virginia and established her reputation as a writer of regional novels set in the American south, especially with *The Miller of Old Church* (1911), *The Romantic Comedians* (1926) and *The Sheltered Life* (1932), which earned her a Pulitzer Prize in 1941. She also wrote a number of highly praised ghost stories with strong emotional undertones, the best of which were collected as *The Shadowy Third* in 1923. The title story, about the ghost of a dead baby intervening in a vile husband's plot to drive his wife insane, is acknowledged as a landmark in the development of the psychological supernatural tale.

When the call came I remember that I turned from the telephone in a romantic flutter. Though I had spoken only once to the great surgeon, Roland Maradick, I felt on that December afternoon that to speak to him only once – to watch him in the operating-room for a single hour – was an adventure which drained the color and the excitement from the rest of life. After all these years of work on typhoid and pneumonia cases, I can still feel the delicious tremor of my young pulses; I can still see the winter sunshine slanting through the hospital windows over the white uniforms of the nurses.

"He didn't mention me by name. Can there be a mistake?" I stood, incredulous yet ecstatic, before the superintendent of the hospital.

"No, there isn't a mistake. I was talking to him before you came down." Miss Hemphill's strong face softened while she looked at me. She was a big, resolute woman, a distant Canadian relative of my mother's and the kind of nurse, I had discovered in the month since I had come up from Richmond, that Northern hospital boards, if not Northern patients, appear instinctively to select. From the first, in spite of her hardness, she had taken a liking – I hesitate to use the word "fancy" for a preference so impersonal – to her Virginia cousin. After all, it isn't every Southern nurse, just out of training, who can boast a kinswoman in the superintendent of a New York hospital. If experience was what I needed, Miss Hemphill, I judged, was abundantly prepared to supply it.

"And he made you understand positively that he meant me?" The thing was so wonderful that I simply couldn't believe it.

"He asked particularly for the nurse who was with Miss Hudson last week when he operated. I think he didn't even remember that you had a name – this isn't the South, you know, where people still regard nurses as human, not as automata. When I asked if he meant Miss Randolph, he repeated that he wanted the nurse who had been with Miss Hudson. She was small, he said, and cheerful-looking. This, of course, might apply to one or two others, but none of these was with Miss Hudson. Miss Maupin, the only nurse, except you, who went near her, is large and heavy."

"Then I suppose it is really true?" My pulses were tingling. "And I am to be there at six o'clock?"

"Not a minute later. The day nurse goes off duty at that hour, and Mrs. Maradick is never left by herself for an instant."

"It is her mind, isn't it? And that makes it all the stranger that he should select me, for I have had so few mental cases."

"So few cases of any kind." Miss Hemphill was smiling, and when she smiled I wondered if the other nurses would know her. "By the time you have gone through the treadmill in New York, Margaret, you will have lost a good many things besides your inexperience. I wonder how long you will keep your sympathy and your imagination? After all, wouldn't you have made a better novelist than a nurse?"

"I can't help putting myself into my cases. I suppose one ought not to?"

"It isn't a question of what one ought to do, but of what one must. When you are drained of every bit of sympathy and enthusiasm and have got nothing in return for it, not even thanks, you will understand why I try to keep you from wasting yourself."

"But surely in a case like this – for Doctor Maradick?"

"Oh, well, of course – for Doctor Maradick?" She must have seen that I implored her confidence, for, after a minute, she let fall almost carelessly a gleam of light on the situation. "It is a very sad case when you think what a charming man and a great surgeon Doctor Maradick is."

Above the starched collar of my uniform I felt the blood leap in bounds to my cheeks. "I have spoken to him only once," I murmured, "but he is charming, and, oh, so kind and handsome, isn't he?"

"His patients adore him."

"Oh, yes, I've seen that. Every one hangs on his visits." Like the patients and the other nurses, I, also had come by delightful, if imperceptible, degrees to hang on the daily visits of Doctor Maradick. He was, I suppose, born to be a hero to women. Fate had selected him for the rôle, and it would have been sheer impertinence for a mortal to cross wills with the invisible Powers. From my first day in his hospital, from the moment when I watched, through closed shutters, while he stepped out of his car,

I have never doubted that he was assigned to the great part in the play. If I had been ignorant of his spell – of the charm he exercised over his hospital – I should have felt it in the waiting hush, like a drawn breath, which followed his ring at the door and preceded his imperious footstep on the stairs. My first impression of him, even after the terrible events of the next year, records a memory that is both careless and splendid. At that moment, when, gazing through the chinks in the shutters, I watched him, in his coat of dark fur, cross the pavement over the pale streaks of sunshine, I knew beyond any doubt – I knew with a sort of infallible prescience – that my fate was irretrievably bound with his in the future. I knew this, I repeat, though Miss Hemphill would still insist that my foreknowledge was merely a sentimental gleaning from indiscriminate novels. But it wasn't only first love, impressionable as my kinswoman believed me to be. It wasn't only the way he looked, handsome as he was. Even more than his appearance – more than the shining dark of his eyes, the silvery brown of his hair, the dusky glow in his face – even more than his charm and his magnificence, I think, the beauty and sympathy in his voice won my heart. It was a voice, I heard some one say afterward, that ought always to speak poetry.

So you will see why – if you do not understand at the beginning, I can never hope to make you believe impossible things! – so you will see why I accepted the call when it came as an imperative summons. I couldn't have stayed away after he sent for me. However much I may have tried not to go, I know that in the end I must have gone. In those days, while I was still hoping to write novels, I used to talk a great deal about "destiny" (I have learned since then how silly all such talk is), and I suppose it was my "destiny" to be caught in the web of Roland Maradick's personality. But I am not the first nurse to grow love-sick about a doctor who never gave her a thought.

"I am glad you got the call, Margaret. It may mean a great deal to you. Only try not to be too emotional about it." I remember that Miss Hemphill was holding a bit of rose-geranium in her hand while she spoke – one of the patients had given it to her from a pot she kept in her room, and the scent of the flower is still in my nostrils – or my memory. Since then – oh, long since then – I have wondered if she also had been caught in the web.

"I wish I knew more about the case." I was clearly pressing for light. "Have you ever seen Mrs. Maradick?"

"Oh, dear, yes. They have been married only a little over a year, and in the beginning she used to come sometimes to the hospital and wait outside while the doctor made his visits. She was a very sweet-looking woman then – not exactly pretty, but fair and slight, with the loveliest smile, I think, I have ever seen. In those first months she was so much in love that we used to laugh about it among ourselves. To see her face light up when the doctor came out of the hospital and crossed the pavement to his car, was as good as a play. We never got tired watching her – I wasn't superintendent then, so I had more time to look out of the window while I was on day duty. Once or twice she brought her little girl in to see one of the patients. The child was so much like her that you would have known them anywhere for mother and daughter."

I had heard that Mrs. Maradick was a widow, with one child, when she first met the doctor, and I asked now, still seeking an illumination I had not found: "There was a great deal of money, wasn't there?"

"A great fortune. If she hadn't been so attractive, people would have said, I suppose, that Doctor Maradick married her for her money. Only," she appeared to make an effort of memory, "I believe I've heard somehow that it was all left in trust away from Mrs. Maradick if she married again. I can't, to save my life, remember just how it was; but it was a queer will, I know, and Mrs. Maradick wasn't to come into the money unless the child didn't live to grow up. The pity of it—"

A young nurse came into the office to ask for something – the keys, I think, of the operating-room, and Miss Hemphill broke off inconclusively as she hurried out of the door. I was sorry that she left off just when she did. Poor Mrs. Maradick! Perhaps I was too emotional, but even before I saw her I had begun to feel her pathos and her strangeness.

My preparations took only a few minutes. In those days I

always kept a suitcase packed and ready for sudden calls; and it was not yet six o'clock when I turned from 10th Street into Fifth Avenue, and stopped for a minute, before ascending the steps, to look at the house in which Doctor Maradick lived. A fine rain was falling, and I remember thinking, as I turned the corner, how depressing the weather must be for Mrs. Maradick. It was an old house, with damp-looking walls (though that may have been because of the rain) and a spindle-shaped iron railing which ran up the stone steps to the black door, where I noticed a dim flicker through the old-fashioned fan-light. Afterward I discovered that Mrs. Maradick had been born in the house – her maiden name was Calloran – and that she had never wanted to live anywhere else. She was a woman – this I found out when I knew her better – of strong attachments to both persons and places; and though Doctor Maradick had tried to persuade her to move up-town after her marriage, she had clung, against his wishes, to the old house in lower Fifth Avenue. I dare say she was obstinate about it in spite of her gentleness and her passion for the doctor. Those sweet, soft women, especially when they have always been rich, are sometimes amazingly obstinate. I have nursed so many of them since – women with strong affections and weak intellects – that I have come to recognize the type as soon as I set eyes upon it.

My ring at the bell was answered after a little delay, and when I entered the house I saw that the hall was quite dark except for the waning glow from an open fire which burned in the library. When I gave my name, and added that I was the night nurse, the servant appeared to think my humble presence unworthy of illumination. He was an old Negro butler, inherited perhaps from Mrs. Maradick's mother, who, I learned afterward, had been from South Carolina; and while he passed me on his way up the staircase, I heard him vaguely muttering that he "wan't gwinter tu'n on dem lights twel de chile had done playin'."

To the right of the hall, the soft glow drew me into the library, and crossing the threshold timidly I stooped to dry my wet coat by the fire. As I bent there, meaning to start up at the first sound of a footstep, I thought how cosy the room was after the damp walls outside to which some bared creepers were clinging; and I was watching pleasantly the strange shapes and patterns the firelight made on the old Persian rug, when the lamps of a slowly turning motor flashed on me through the white shades at the window. Still dazzled by the glare, I looked round in the dimness and saw a child's ball of red and blue rubber roll toward me out of the gloom of one of the adjoining rooms. A moment later, while I made a vain attempt to capture the toy as it spun past me, a little girl darted airily, with peculiar lightness and grace, through the doorway, and stopped quickly, as if in surprise at the sight of a stranger. She was a small child – so small and slight that her footsteps made no sound on the polished floor of the threshold; and I remember thinking while I looked at her that she had the gravest and sweetest face I had ever seen. She couldn't – I decided this afterward – have been more than six or seven, yet she stood there with a curious prim dignity, like the dignity of a very old person, and gazed up at me with enigmatical eyes. She was dressed in Scotch plaid, with a bit of red ribbon in her hair, which was cut in a fringe over her forehead and hung very straight to her shoulders. Charming as she was, from her uncurled brown hair to the white socks and black slippers on her little feet, I recall most vividly the singular look in her eyes, which appeared in the shifting light to be of an indeterminate color. For the odd thing about this look was that it was not the look of childhood at all. It was the look of profound experience, of bitter knowledge.

"Have you come for your ball?" I asked; but while the friendly question was still on my lips, I heard the servant returning. Even in my haste I made a second ineffectual grasp at the plaything, which rolled, with increased speed, away from me into the dusk of the drawing-room. Then, as I raised my head, I saw that the child also had slipped from the room; and without looking after her I followed the old Negro into the pleasant study above, where the great surgeon awaited me.

Ten years ago, before hard nursing had taken so much out of me, I blushed very easily, and I was aware at the moment when I crossed Doctor Maradick's study that my cheeks were the color of peonies. Of course, I was a fool – no one knows this better than I do – but I had never been alone, even for an instant, with him before, and the man was more than a hero to me, he was – there isn't any reason now why I should blush over the confession – almost a god. At that age I was mad about the wonders of surgery, and Roland Maradick in the operating-room was magician enough to have turned an older and more sensible head than mine. Added to his great reputation and his marvellous skill, he was, I am sure of this, the most splendid-looking man, even at forty-five, that one could imagine. Had he been ungracious – had he been positively rude to me, I should still have adored him, but when he held out his hand, and greeted me in the charming way he had with women, I felt that I would have died for him. It is no wonder that a saying went about the hospital that every woman he operated on fell in love with him. As for the nurses – well, there wasn't a single one of them who had escaped his spell – not even Miss Hemphill, who could scarcely have been a day under fifty.

"I am glad you could come, Miss Randolph. You were with Miss Hudson last week when I operated?"

I bowed. To save my life I couldn't have spoken without blushing the redder.

"I noticed your bright face at the time. Brightness, I think, is what Mrs. Maradick needs. She finds her day nurse depressing." His eyes rested so kindly upon me that I have suspected since that he was not entirely unaware of my worship. It was a small thing, heaven knows, to flatter his vanity – a nurse just out of a training-school – but to some men no tribute is too insignificant to give pleasure.

"You will do your best, I am sure." He hesitated an instant – just long enough for me to perceive the anxiety beneath the genial smile on his face – and then added gravely: "We wish to avoid, if possible, having to send her away for treatment."

I could only murmur in response, and after a few carefully chosen words about his wife's illness, he rang the bell and directed the maid to take me upstairs to my room. Not until I was ascending the stairs to the third story did it occur to me that he had really told me nothing. I was as perplexed about the nature of Mrs. Maradick's malady as I had been when I entered the house.

I found my room pleasant enough. It had been arranged – by Doctor Maradick's request, I think – that I was to sleep in the house, and after my austere little bed at the hospital I was agreeably surprised by the cheerful look of the apartment into which the maid led me. The walls were papered in roses, and there were curtains of flowered chintz at the window, which looked down on a small formal garden at the rear of the house. This the maid told me, for it was too dark for me to distinguish more than a marble fountain and a fir-tree, which looked old, though I afterward learned that it was replanted almost every season.

In ten minutes I had slipped into my uniform and was ready to go to my patient; but for some reason – to this day I have never found out what it was that turned her against me at the start – Mrs. Maradick refused to receive me. While I stood outside her door I heard the day nurse trying to persuade her to let me come in. It wasn't any use, however, and in the end I was obliged to go back to my room and wait until the poor lady got over her whim and consented to see me. That was long after dinner – it must have been nearer eleven than ten o'clock – and Miss Peterson was quite worn out by the time she came to fetch me.

"I'm afraid you'll have a bad night," she said as we went downstairs together. That was her way, I soon saw, to expect the worst of everything and everybody.

"Does she often keep you up like this?"

"Oh, no, she is usually very considerate. I never knew a sweeter character. But she still has this hallucination—"

Here again, as in the scene with Doctor Maradick, I felt that the explanation had only deepened the mystery. Mrs. Maradick's hallucination, whatever form it assumed, was evidently a subject for evasion and subterfuge in the household. It was on the tip of my tongue to ask, "What is her hallucination?" – but before I could get the words past my lips we had reached Mrs. Maradick's door, and Miss Peterson motioned me to be silent. As the door opened a little way to admit me, I saw that Mrs. Maradick was already in bed, and that the lights were out except for a night-lamp burning on a candle-stand beside a book and a carafe of water.

"I won't go in with you," said Miss Peterson in a whisper; and I was on the point of stepping over the threshold when I saw the little girl, in the dress of Scotch plaid, slip by me from the dusk of the room into the electric light of the hall. She held a doll in her arms, and as she went by she dropped a doll's work-basket in the doorway. Miss Peterson must have picked up the toy, for when I turned in a minute to look for it I found that it was gone. I remember thinking that it was late for a child to be up – she looked delicate, too – but, after all, it was no business of mine, and four years in a hospital had taught me never to meddle in affairs that do not concern me. There is nothing a nurse learns quicker than not to try to put the world to rights in a day.

When I crossed the floor to the chair by Mrs. Maradick's bed, she turned over on her side and looked at me with the sweetest and saddest smile.

"You are the new night nurse," she said in a gentle voice; and from the moment she spoke I knew that there was nothing hysterical or violent about her mania – or hallucination, as they called it. "They told me your name, but I have forgotten it."

"Randolph – Margaret Randolph." I liked her from the start, and I think she must have seen it.

"You look very young, Miss Randolph."

"I am twenty-two, but I suppose I don't look quite my age. People usually think I am younger."

For a minute she was silent, and while I settled myself in the chair by the bed I thought how strikingly she resembled the little girl I had seen first in the afternoon, and then leaving her room a few moments ago. They had the same small, heart-shaped faces, colored ever so faintly; the same straight, soft hair, between brown and flaxen; and the same large, grave eyes, set very far apart under arched eyebrows. What surprised me most, however, was that they both looked at me with that enigmatical and vaguely wondering expression – only in Mrs. Maradick's face the vagueness seemed to change now and then to a definite fear – a flash, I had almost said, of startled horror.

I sat quite still in my chair, and until the time came for Mrs. Maradick to take her medicine not a word passed between us. Then, when I bent over her with the glass in my hand, she raised her head from the pillow and said in a whisper of suppressed intensity:

"You look kind. I wonder if you could have seen my little girl?"

As I slipped my arm under the pillow I tried to smile cheerfully down on her. "Yes, I've seen her twice. I'd know her anywhere by her likeness to you."

A glow shone in her eyes, and I thought how pretty she must have been before illness took the life and animation out of her features. "Then I know you're good." Her voice was so strained and low that I could barely hear it. "If you weren't good you couldn't have seen her."

I thought this queer enough, but all I answered was: "She looked delicate to be sitting up so late."

A quiver passed over her thin features, and for a minute I thought she was going to burst into tears. As she had taken the medicine, I put the glass back on the candle-stand and, bending over the bed, smoothed the straight brown hair, which was as fine and soft as spun silk, back from her forehead. There was something about her – I don't know what it was – that made you love her as soon as she looked at you.

"She always had that light and airy way, though she was never sick a day in her life," she answered calmly after a pause. Then, groping for my hand, she whispered passionately: "You must not tell him – you must not tell any one that you have seen her!"

"I mustn't tell any one?" Again I had the impression that had come to me first in Doctor Maradick's study, and afterward with Miss Peterson on the staircase, that I was seeking a gleam of light in the midst of obscurity.

"Are you sure there isn't any one listening – that there isn't any one at the door?" she asked, pushing aside my arm and sitting up among the pillows.

"Quite, quite sure. They have put out the lights in the hall."

"And you will not tell him? Promise me that you will not tell him." The startled horror flashed from the vague wonder of her expression. "He doesn't like her to come back, because he killed her."

"Because he killed her!" Then it was that light burst on me in a blaze. So this was Mrs. Maradick's hallucination! She believed that her child was dead – the little girl I had seen with my own eyes leaving her room; and she believed that her husband – the great surgeon we worshipped in the hospital – had murdered her. No wonder they veiled the dreadful obsession in mystery! No wonder that even Miss Peterson had not dared to drag the horrid thing out into the light! It was the kind of hallucination one simply couldn't stand having to face.

"There is no use telling people things that nobody believes," she resumed slowly, still holding my hand in a grasp that would have hurt me if her fingers had not been so fragile. "Nobody believes that he killed her. Nobody believes that she comes back every day to the house. Nobody believes – and yet you saw her—"

"Yes, I saw her – but why should your husband have killed her?" I spoke soothingly, as one would speak to a person who was quite mad; yet she was not mad, I could have sworn this while I looked at her.

For a moment she moaned inarticulately, as if the horror of her thought were too great to pass into speech. Then she flung out her thin, bare arm with a wild gesture.

"Because he never loved me!" she said. "He never loved me!"

"But he married you," I urged gently after a moment in which I stroked her hair. "If he hadn't loved you, why should he have married you?"

"He wanted the money – my little girl's money. It all goes to him when I die."

"But he is rich himself. He must make a fortune from his profession."

"It isn't enough. He wanted millions." She had grown stern and tragic. "No, he never loved me. He loved someone else from the beginning – before I knew him."

It was quite useless, I saw, to reason with her. If she wasn't mad, she was in a state of terror and despondency so black that it had almost crossed the borderline into madness. I thought once of going up-stairs and bringing the child down from her nursery; but, after a moment's thought, I realized that Miss Peterson and Doctor Maradick must have long ago tried all these measures. Clearly, there was nothing to do except soothe and quiet her as much as I could; and this I did until she dropped into a light sleep which lasted well into the morning.

By seven o'clock I was worn out – not from work, but from the strain on my sympathy – and I was glad, indeed, when one of the maids came in to bring me an early cup of coffee. Mrs. Maradick was still sleeping – it was a mixture of bromide and chloral I had given her – and she did not wake until Miss Peterson came on duty an hour or two later. Then, when I went down-stairs, I found the dining-room deserted except for the old housekeeper, who was looking over the silver. Doctor Maradick, she explained to me presently, had his breakfast served in the morning-room on the other side of the house.

"And the little girl? Does she take her meals in the nursery?"

She threw me a startled glance. Was it, I questioned afterward, one of distrust or apprehension?

"There isn't any little girl. Haven't you heard?"

"Heard? No. Why, I saw her only yesterday."

The look she gave me – I was sure of it now – was full of alarm.

"The little girl – she was the sweetest child I ever saw – died just two months ago of pneumonia."

"But she couldn't have died." I was a fool to let this out, but the shock had completely unnerved me. "I tell you I saw her yesterday."

The alarm in her face deepened. "That is Mrs. Maradick's trouble. She believes that she still sees her."

"But don't you see her?" I drove the question home bluntly.

"No." She set her lips tightly. "I never see anything."

So I had been wrong, after all, and the explanation, when it came, only accentuated the terror. The child was dead – she had died of pneumonia two months ago – and yet I had seen her, with my own eyes, playing ball in the library; I had seen her slipping out of her mother's room, with her doll in her arms.

"Is there another child in the house? Could there be a child belonging to one of the servants?" A gleam had shot through the fog in which I was groping.

"No, there isn't any other. The doctors tried bringing one once, but it threw the poor lady into such a state she almost died of it. Besides, there wouldn't be any other child as quiet and sweet-looking as Dorothea. To see her skipping along in her dress of Scotch plaid used to make me think of a fairy, though they say that fairies wear nothing but white or green."

"Has any one else seen her – the child, I mean – any of the servants?"

"Only old Gabriel, the colored butler, who came with Mrs. Maradick's mother from South Carolina. I've heard that negroes often have a kind of second sight – though I don't know that that is just what you would call it. But they seem to believe in the supernatural by instinct, and Gabriel is so old and doty – he does no work except answer the door-bell and clean the silver – that nobody pays much attention to anything that he sees—"

"Is the child's nursery kept as it used to be?"

"Oh, no. The doctor had all the toys sent to the children's hospital. That was a great grief to Mrs. Maradick; but Doctor Brandon thought, and all the nurses agreed with him, that it was best for her not to be allowed to keep the room as it was when Dorothea was living."

"Dorothea? Was that the child's name?"

"Yes, it means the gift of God, doesn't it? She was named after the mother of Mrs. Maradick's first husband, Mr. Ballard. He was the grave, quiet kind – not the least like the doctor."

I wondered if the other dreadful obsession of Mrs. Maradick's had drifted down through the nurses or the servants to the housekeeper; but she said nothing about it, and since she was, I suspected, a garrulous person, I thought it wiser to assume that the gossip had not reached her.

A little later, when breakfast was over and I had not yet gone up-stairs to my room, I had my first interview with Doctor Brandon, the famous alienist who was in charge of the case. I had never seen him before, but from the first moment that I looked at him I took his measure, almost by intuition. He was, I suppose, honest enough – I have always granted him that, bitterly as I have felt toward him. It wasn't his fault that he lacked red blood in his brain, or that he had formed the habit, from long association with abnormal phenomena, of regarding all life as a disease. He was the sort of physician – every nurse will understand what I mean – who deals instinctively with groups instead of with individuals. He was long and solemn and very round in the face; and I hadn't talked to him ten minutes before I knew he had been educated in Germany, and that he had learned over there to treat every emotion as a pathological manifestation. I used to wonder what he got out of life – what any one got out of life who had analyzed away everything except the bare structure.

When I reached my room at last, I was so tired that I could barely remember either the questions Doctor Brandon had asked or the directions he had given me. I fell asleep, I know, almost as soon as my head touched the pillow; and the maid who came to inquire if I wanted luncheon decided to let me finish my nap. In the afternoon, when she returned with a cup of tea, she found me still heavy and drowsy. Though I was used to night nursing, I felt as if I had danced from sunset to daybreak. It was fortunate, I reflected, while I drank my tea, that every case didn't wear on one's sympathies as acutely as Mrs. Maradick's hallucination had worn on mine.

Through the day, of course, I did not see Doctor Maradick, but at seven o'clock, when I came up from my early dinner on my way to take the place of Miss Peterson, who had kept on duty an hour later than usual, he met me in the hall and asked me to come into his study. I thought him handsomer than ever in his evening clothes, with a white flower in his buttonhole. He was going to some public dinner, the housekeeper told me, but, then, he was always going somewhere. I believe he didn't dine at home a single evening that winter.

"Did Mrs. Maradick have a good night?" He had closed the door after us, and, turning now with the question, he smiled kindly, as if he wished to put me at ease in the beginning.

"She slept very well after she took the medicine. I gave her that at eleven o'clock."

For a minute he regarded me silently, and I was aware that his personality – his charm – had been focused upon me. It was almost as if I stood in the centre of converging rays of light, so vivid was my impression of him.

"Did she allude in any way to her – to her hallucination?" he asked.

How the warning reached me – what invisible waves of sense-perception transmitted the message – I have never known; but while I stood there, facing the splendor of the doctor's presence, every intuition cautioned me that the time had come when I must take sides in the household. While I stayed there I must stand either with Mrs. Maradick or against her.

"She talked quite rationally," I replied after a moment.

"What did she say?"

"She told me how she was feeling, that she missed her child, and that she walked a little every day about her room."

His face changed – how, I could not at first determine.

"Have you seen Doctor Brandon?"

"He came this morning to give me his directions."

"He thought her less well to-day. He has even advised me to send her to Rosedale."

I have never, even in secret, tried to account for Doctor Maradick. He may have been sincere. I tell only what I know – not what I believe or imagine – and the human is sometimes as inscrutable, as inexplicable, as the supernatural.

While he watched me I was conscious of an inner struggle, as if opposing angels warred somewhere in the depths of my being. When at last I made my decision, I was acting less from reason, I knew, than in obedience to the pressure of some secret current of thought. Heaven knows, even then, the man held me captive while I defied him.

"Doctor Maradick," I lifted my eyes for the first time frankly to his, "I believe that your wife is as sane as I am – or as you are."

He started. "Then she did not talk freely to you?"

"She may be mistaken, unstrung, piteously distressed in mind" – I brought this out with emphasis – "but she is not – I am willing to stake my future on it – a fit subject for an asylum. It would be foolish – it would be cruel to send her to Rosedale."

"Cruel, you say?" A troubled look crossed his face, and his voice grew very gentle. "You do not imagine that I could be cruel to her?"

"No, I do not think that." My voice also had softened.

"We will let things go on as they are. Perhaps Doctor Brandon may have some other suggestion to make." He drew out his watch and compared it with the clock – nervously, I observed, as if his action were a screen for his discomfiture or his perplexity. "I must be going now. We will speak of this again in the morning."

But in the morning we did not speak of it, and during the month that I nursed Mrs. Maradick I was not called again into her husband's study. When I met him in the hall or on the staircase, which was seldom, he was as charming as ever; yet, in spite of his courtesy, I had a persistent feeling that he had taken my measure on that evening, and that he had no further use for me.

As the days went by Mrs. Maradick seemed to grow stronger. Never, after our first night together, had she mentioned the child to me; never had she alluded by so much as a word to her dreadful charge against her husband. She was like any other woman recovering from a great sorrow, except that she was sweeter and gentler. It is no wonder that every one who came near her loved her; for there was a mysterious loveliness about her like the mystery of light, not of darkness. She was, I have always thought, as much of an angel as it is possible for a woman to be on this earth. And yet, angelic as she was, there were times when it seemed to me that she both hated and feared her husband. Though he never entered her room while I was there, and I never heard his name on her lips until an hour before the end, still I could tell by the look of terror in her face whenever his step passed down the hall that her very soul shivered at his approach.

During the whole month I did not see the child again, though one night, when I came suddenly into Mrs. Maradick's room, I found a little garden, such as children make out of pebbles and bits of box, on the window-sill. I did not mention it to Mrs.

Maradick, and a little later, as the maid lowered the shades, I noticed that the garden had vanished. Since then I have often wondered if the child were invisible only to the rest of us, and if her mother still saw her. But there was no way of finding out except by questioning, and Mrs. Maradick was so well and patient that I hadn't the heart to question. Things couldn't have been better with her than they were, and I was beginning to tell myself that she might soon go out for an airing, when the end came suddenly.

It was a mild January day – the kind of day that brings the foretaste of spring in the middle of winter, and when I came down-stairs in the afternoon, I stopped a minute by the window at the end of the hall to look down on the box maze in the garden. There was an old fountain, bearing two laughing boys in marble, in the centre of the gravelled walk, and the water, which had been turned on that morning for Mrs. Maradick's pleasure, sparkled now like silver as the sunlight splashed over it. I had never before felt the air quite so soft and springlike in January; and I thought, as I gazed down on the garden, that it would be a good idea for Mrs. Maradick to go out and bask for an hour or so in the sunshine. It seemed strange to me that she was never allowed to get any fresh air except the air that came through her windows.

When I went into her room, however, I found that she had no wish to go out. She was sitting, wrapped in shawls, by the open window, which looked down on the fountain; and as I entered she glanced up from a little book she was reading. A pot of daffodils stood on the window-sill – she was very fond of flowers and we tried always to keep some growing in her room.

"Do you know what I was reading, Miss Randolph?" she asked in her soft voice; and then she read aloud a verse while I went over to the candle-stand to measure out a dose of medicine.

" 'If thou hast two loaves of bread, sell one and buy daffodils, for bread nourisheth the body, but daffodils delight the soul.' That is very beautiful, don't you think so?"

I said "Yes," that it was beautiful; and then I asked her if she wouldn't go downstairs and walk about in the garden?

"He wouldn't like it," she answered; and it was the first time she had mentioned her husband to me since the night I came to her. "He doesn't want me to go out."

I tried to laugh her out of the idea; but it was no use, and after a few minutes I gave up and began talking of other things. Even then it did not occur to me that her fear of Doctor Maradick was anything but a fancy. I could see, of course, that she wasn't out of her head; but sane persons, I knew, sometimes have unaccountable prejudices, and I accepted her dislike as a mere whim or aversion. I did not understand then, and – I may as well confess this before the end comes – I do not understand any better to-day. I am writing down the things I actually saw, and I repeat that I have never had the slightest twist in the direction of the miraculous.

The afternoon slipped away while we talked – she talked brightly when any subject came up that interested her – and it was the last hour of day – that grave, still hour when the movement of life seems to droop and falter for a few precious minutes – that brought us the thing I had dreaded silently since my first night in the house. I remember that I had risen to close the window, and was leaning out for a breath of the mild air, when there was the sound of steps, consciously softened in the hall outside, and Doctor Brandon's usual knock fell on my ears. Then, before I could cross the room, the door opened, and the doctor entered with Miss Peterson. The day nurse, I knew, was a stupid woman; but she had never appeared to me so stupid, so armored and incased in her professional manner, as she did at that moment.

"I am glad to see that you have been taking the air." As Doctor Brandon came over to the window, I wondered maliciously what devil of contradictions had made him a distinguished specialist in nervous diseases.

"Who was the other doctor you brought this morning?" asked Mrs. Maradick gravely; and that was all I ever heard about the visit of the second alienist.

"Someone who is anxious to cure you." He dropped into a chair beside her and patted her hand with his long, pale fingers. "We are so anxious to cure you that we want to send you away to the country for a fortnight or so. Miss Peterson has come to help you get ready, and I've kept my car waiting for you. There couldn't be a nicer day for a little trip, could there?"

The moment had come at last. I knew at once what he meant, and so did Mrs. Maradick. A wave of color flowed and ebbed in her thin cheeks, and I felt her body quiver when I moved from the window and put my arms on her shoulders. I was aware again, as I had been aware that evening in Doctor Maradick's study, of a current of thought that beat from the air around into my brain. Though it cost me my career as a nurse and my reputation for sanity, I knew that I must obey that invisible warning.

"You are going to take me to an asylum," said Mrs. Maradick.

He made some foolish denial or evasion; but before he had finished I turned from Mrs. Maradick and faced him impulsively. In a nurse this was flagrant rebellion, and I realized that the act wrecked my professional future. Yet I did not care – I did not hesitate. Something stronger than I was driving me on.

"Doctor Brandon," I said, "I beg you – I implore you to wait until to-morrow. There are things I must tell you."

A queer look came into his face, and I understood, even in my excitement, that he was mentally deciding in which group he should place me – to which class of morbid manifestations I must belong.

"Very well, very well, we will hear everything," he replied soothingly; but I saw him glance at Miss Peterson, and she went over to the wardrobe for Mrs. Maradick's fur coat and hat.

Suddenly, without warning, Mrs. Maradick threw the shawls away from her, and stood up. "If you send me away." she said, "I shall never come back. I shall never live to come back."

The gray of twilight was just beginning, and while she stood there, in the dusk of the room, her face shone out as pale and flower-like as the daffodils on the windowsill. "I cannot go away!" she cried in a sharper voice. "I cannot go away from my child!"

I saw her face clearly; I heard her voice; and then – the horror of the scene sweeps back over me! – I saw the door slowly open and the little girl run across the room to her mother. I saw her lift her little arms, and I saw the mother stoop and gather her to her bosom. So closely locked were they in that passionate embrace that their forms seemed to mingle in the gloom that enveloped them.

"After this can you doubt?" I threw out the words almost savagely – and then, when I turned from the mother and child to Doctor Brandon and Miss Peterson, I knew breathlessly – oh, there was a shock in the discovery! – that they were blind to the child. Their blank faces revealed the consternation of ignorance, not of conviction. They had seen nothing except the vacant arms of the mother and the swift, erratic gesture with which she stooped to embrace some phantasmal presence. Only my vision – and I have asked myself since if the power of sympathy enabled me to penetrate the web of material fact and see the spiritual form of the child – only my vision was not blinded by the clay through which I looked.

"After this can you doubt?" Doctor Brandon had flung my words back to me. Was it his fault, poor man, if life had granted him only the eyes of flesh? Was it his fault if he could see only half of the thing there before him?

But they couldn't see, and since they couldn't see I realized that it was useless to tell them. Within an hour they took Mrs. Maradick to the asylum; and she went quietly, though when the time came for parting from me she showed some faint trace of feeling. I remember that at the last, while we stood on the pavement, she lifted her black veil, which she wore for the child, and said: "Stay with her, Miss Randolph, as long as you can. I shall never come back."

Then she got into the car and was driven off, while I stood looking after her with a sob in my throat. Dreadful as I felt it to be, I didn't, of course, realize the full horror of it, or I couldn't have stood there quietly on the pavement. I didn't realize it, indeed, until several months afterward when word came that she had died in the asylum. I never knew what her illness was, though I vaguely recall that something was said about "heart failure" – a loose enough term. My own belief is that she died simply of the terror of life.

To my surprise Doctor Maradick asked me to stay on as his office nurse after his wife went to Rosedale; and when the news of her death came there was no suggestion of my leaving. I don't know to this day why he wanted me in the house. Perhaps he thought I should have less opportunity to gossip if I stayed under his roof; perhaps he still wished to test the power of his charm over me. His vanity was incredible in so great a man. I have seen him flush with pleasure when people turned to look at him in the street, and I know that he was not above playing on the sentimental weaknesses of his patients. But he was magnificent, heaven knows! Few men, I imagine, have been the objects of so many foolish infatuations.

The next summer Doctor Maradick went abroad for two months, and while he was away I took my vacation in Virginia. When we came back the work was heavier than ever – his reputation by this time was tremendous – and my days were so crowded with appointments, and hurried fittings to emergency cases, that I had scarcely a minute left in which to remember poor Mrs. Maradick. Since the afternoon when she went to the asylum the child had not been seen in the house; and at last I was beginning to persuade myself that the little figure had been an optical illusion – the effect of shifting lights in the gloom of the old rooms – not the apparition I had once believed it to be. It does not take long for a phantom to fade from the memory – especially when one leads the active and methodical life I was forced into that winter. Perhaps – who knows? – (I remember telling myself) the doctors may have been right, after all, and the poor lady may have actually been out of her mind. With this view of the past, my judgment of Doctor Maradick insensibly altered. It ended, I think, in my acquitting him altogether. And then, just as he stood clear and splendid in my verdict of him, the reversal came so precipitately that I grow breathless now whenever I try to live it over again. The violence of the next turn in affairs left me, I often fancy, with a perpetual dizziness of the imagination.

It was in May that we heard of Mrs. Maradick's death, and exactly a year later, on a mild and fragrant afternoon, when the daffodils were blooming in patches around the old fountain in the garden, the housekeeper came into the office, where I lingered over some accounts, to bring me news of the doctor's approaching marriage.

"It is no more than we might have expected," she concluded rationally. "The house must be lonely for him – he is such a sociable man. But I can't help feeling," she brought out slowly after a pause in which I felt a shiver pass over me, "I can't help feeling that it is hard for that other woman to have all the money poor Mrs. Maradick's first husband left her."

"There is a great deal of money, then?" I asked curiously.

"A great deal." She waved her hand, as if words were futile to express the sum. "Millions and millions!"

"They will give up this house, of course?"

"That's done already, my dear. There won't be a brick left of it by this time next year. It's to be pulled down and an apartment-house built on the ground."

Again the shiver passed over me. I couldn't bear to think of Mrs. Maradick's old home falling to pieces.

"You didn't tell me the name of the bride," I said. "Is she some one he met while he was in Europe?"

"Dear me, no! She is the very lady he was engaged to before he married Mrs. Maradick, only she threw him over, so people said, because he wasn't rich enough. Then she married some lord or prince from over the water; but there was a divorce, and now she has turned again to her old lover. He is rich enough now, I guess, even for her!"

It was all perfectly true, I suppose; it sounded as plausible as a story out of a newspaper; and yet while she told me I was aware of a sinister, an impalpable hush in the atmosphere. I was nervous, no doubt; I was shaken by the suddenness with which the housekeeper had sprung her news on me; but as I sat there I had quite vividly an impression that the old house was listening – that there was a real, if invisible, presence somewhere in the room or the garden. Yet, when an instant afterward I glanced through the long window which opened down to the brick terrace, I saw only the faint sunshine over the deserted garden, with its maze of box, its marble fountain, and its patches of daffodils.

The housekeeper had gone – one of the servants, I think, came for her – and I was sitting at my desk when the words of Mrs. Maradick on that last evening floated into my mind. The daffodils brought her back to me; for I thought, as I watched them growing, so still and golden in the sunshine, how she would have enjoyed them. Almost unconsciously I repeated the verse she had read to me.

"If thou hast two loaves of bread, sell one and buy daffodils" – and it was at that very instant, while the words were on my lips, that I turned my eyes to the box maze and saw the child's skipping rope along the gravelled path to the fountain. Quite distinctly, as clear as day, I saw her come, with what children call the dancing step, between the low box borders to the place where the daffodils bloomed by the fountain. From her straight brown hair to her frock of Scotch plaid and her little feet, which twinkled in white socks and black slippers over the turning rope, she was as real to me as the ground on which she trod or the laughing marble boys under the splashing water. Starting up from my chair, I made a single step to the terrace. If I could only reach her – only speak to her – I felt that I might at last solve the mystery. But with my first call, with the first flutter of my dress on the terrace, the airy little form melted into the dusk of the maze. Not a breath stirred the daffodils, not a shadow passed over the sparkling flow of the water; yet, weak and shaken in every nerve, I sat down on the brick step of the terrace and burst into tears. I must have known that something terrible would happen before they pulled down Mrs. Maradick's home.

The doctor dined out that night. He was with the lady he was going to marry, the housekeeper told me; and it must have been almost midnight when I heard him come in and go upstairs to his room. I was downstairs because I had been unable to sleep, and the book I wanted to finish I had left that afternoon in the office. The book – I can't remember what it was – had seemed to me very exciting when I began it in the morning; but after the visit of the child I found the romantic novel as dull as a treatise on nursing. It was impossible for me to follow the lines, and I was on the point of giving up and going to bed, when Doctor Maradick opened the front door with his latch-key and went up the staircase. "There can't be a bit of truth in it." I thought over and over again as I listened to his even step ascending the stairs. "There can't be a bit of truth in it." And yet, though I assured myself that "there couldn't be a bit of truth in it," I shrank, with a creepy sensation, from going through the house to my room in the third story. I was tired out after a hard day, and my nerves must have reacted morbidly to the silence and the darkness. For the first time in my life I knew what it was to be afraid of the unknown, of the invisible; and while I bent over my book, in the glare of the electric light, I became conscious presently that I was straining my senses for some sound in the spacious emptiness of the rooms overhead. The noise of a passing motor-car in the street jerked me back from the intense hush of expectancy; and I can recall the wave of relief that swept over me as I turned to my book again and tried to fix my distracted mind on its pages.

I was still sitting there when the telephone on my desk rang, with what seemed to my overwrought nerves a startling abruptness, and the voice of the superintendent told me hurriedly that Doctor Maradick was needed at the hospital. I had become so accustomed to these emergency calls in the night that I felt reassured when I had rung up the doctor in his room and had heard the hearty sound of his response. He had not yet undressed, he said, and would come down immediately while I ordered back his car, which must just have reached the garage.

"I'll be with you in five minutes!" he called as cheerfully as if I had summoned him to his wedding.

I heard him cross the floor of his room; and before he could reach the head of the staircase, I opened the door and went out into the hall in order that I might turn on the light and have his hat and coat waiting. The electric button was at the end of the hall, and as I moved toward it, guided by the glimmer that fell from the landing above, I instinctively lifted my eyes to the staircase, which climbed dimly, with its slender mahogany balustrade, as far as the third story. Then it was, at the very moment when the doctor, humming gayly, began his quick descent of the steps, that I distinctly saw – I will swear to this on my death-bed –

a child's skipping-rope lying loosely coiled, as if it had dropped from a careless little hand, in the bend of the staircase. With a spring I had reached the electric button, flooding the hall with light; but as I did so, while my arm was still outstretched behind me, I heard the humming voice change to a cry of surprise or terror, and the figure on the staircase tripped heavily and stumbled with groping hands into emptiness. The scream of warning died in my throat while I watched him pitch forward down the long flight of stairs to the floor at my feet. Even before I bent over him, before I wiped the blood from his brow and felt for his silent heart, I knew that he was dead.

Something – it may have been, as the world believes, a misstep in the dimness, or it may have been, as I am ready to bear witness, a phantasmal judgment – something had killed him at the very moment when he most wanted to live.

# A Little Ghost

## Hugh Walpole

### Prospectus

**Address:** Baldwin House, Drymouth, Cornwall, England.

**Property:** Eighteenth-century country house in close proximity to the sea. Spacious and comfortable rooms. A feature of the property is an underground passageway to the beach reputedly used in the past by smugglers.

**Viewing Date:** December, 1922.

**Agent:** Hugh Seymour Walpole (1884–1941) was born in Auckland, New Zealand, but grew up in Cornwall and after a period as a teacher became famous as a novelist of country life, in particular for his Lakeland saga, *The Herries Chronicle* (1930–33). As a descendant of the "father" of the Gothic novel, Horace Walpole, author of *The Castle of Otranto* (1764), and a master of the atmospheric tale, it is perhaps not surprising that he wrote a number of ghost stories, including three acknowledged classics, "Mrs Lunt", "The Tarn" and "A Little Ghost", the memorable account of a small girl ghost in an old house who befriends the troubled narrator of the story.

1

Ghosts? I looked across the table at Truscott and had a sudden desire to impress him. Truscott has, before now, invited confidences in just that same way, with his flat impassivity, his air of not caring whether you say anything to him or no, his determined indifference to your drama and your pathos. On this particular evening he had been less impassive. He had himself turned the conversation towards Spiritualism, séances, and all that world of humbug, as he believed it to be, and suddenly I saw, or fancied that I saw, a real invitation in his eyes, something that made me say to myself: "Well, hang it all, I've known Truscott for nearly twenty years; I've never shown him the least little bit of my real self; he thinks me a writing money-machine, with no thought in the world beside my brazen serial stories and the yacht that I purchased out of them."

So I told him this story, and I will do him the justice to say that he listened to every word of it most attentively, although it was far into the evening before I had finished. He didn't seem impatient with all the little details that I gave. Of course, in a ghost story, details are more important than anything else. But was it a ghost story? Was it a story at all? Was it true even in its material background? Now, as I try to tell it again, I can't be sure. Truscott is the only other person who has ever heard it, and at the end of it he made no comment whatever.

It happened long ago, long before the War, when I had been married for about five years, and was an exceedingly prosperous journalist, with a nice little house and two children, in Wimbledon.

I lost suddenly my greatest friend. That may mean little or much as friendship is commonly held, but I believe that most Britishers, most Americans, most Scandinavians, know before they die one friendship at least that changes their whole life experience by its depth and colour. Very few Frenchmen, Italians or Spaniards, very few Southern people at all, understand these things.

The curious part of it in my particular case was that I had known this friend only four or five years before his death, that I had made many friendships both before and since that have endured over much longer periods, and yet this particular friendship had a quality of intensity and happiness that I have never found elsewhere.

Another curious thing was that I met Bond only a few months before my marriage, when I was deeply in love with my wife, and so intensely preoccupied with my engagement that I could think of nothing else. I met Bond quite casually at someone's house. He was a large-boned, broad-shouldered, slow-smiling man with close-cropped hair turning slightly grey, and our meeting was casual; the ripening of our friendship was casual; indeed, the whole affair may be said to have been casual to the very last. It was, in fact, my wife who said to me one day, when we had been married about a year or so: "Why, I believe you care more for Charlie Bond than for anyone else in the world." She said it in that sudden, disconcerting, perceptive way that some women have. I was entirely astonished. Of course I laughed at the idea. I saw Bond frequently. He often came to the house. My wife, wiser than many wives, encouraged all my friendships, and she herself liked Charlie immensely. I don't suppose that anyone disliked him. Some men were jealous of him; some men, the merest acquaintances, called him conceited; women were sometimes irritated by him because so clearly he could get on very easily without them; but he had, I think, no real enemy.

How could he have had? His good nature, his freedom from all jealousy, his naturalness, his sense of fun, the absence of all pettiness, his common sense, his manliness, and at the same time his broad-minded intelligence, all these things made him a most charming personality. I don't know that he shone very much in ordinary society. He was very quiet and his wit and humour came out best with his intimates.

I was the showy one, and he always played up to me, and I think I patronized him a little and thought deep down in my subconscious self that it was lucky for him to have such a brilliant friend, but he never gave a sign of resentment. I believe now that he knew me, with all my faults and vanities and absurdities, far better than anyone else, even my wife, did, and that is one of the reasons, to the day of my death, why I shall always miss him so desperately.

However, it was not until his death that I realized how close we had been. One November day he came back to his flat, wet and chilled, didn't change his clothes, caught a cold, which developed into pneumonia, and after three days was dead. It happened that that week I was in Paris, and I returned to be told on the doorstep by my wife of what had occurred. At first I refused to believe it. When I had seen him a week before he had been in splendid health; with his tanned, rather rough and clumsy face, his clear eyes, no fat about him anywhere, he had looked as though he would live to a thousand, and then when I realized that it was indeed true I did not during the first week or two grasp my loss.

I missed him, of course; was vaguely unhappy and discontented; railed against life, wondering why it was always the best people who were taken and the others left; but I was not actually aware that for the rest of my days things would be different, and that that day of my return from Paris was a crisis in my human experience. Suddenly one morning, walking down Fleet Street, I had a flashing, almost blinding, need of Bond that was like a revelation. From that moment I knew no peace. Everyone seemed to me dull, profitless and empty. Even my wife was a long way away from me, and my children, whom I dearly loved, counted nothing to me at all. I didn't, after that, know what was the matter with me. I lost my appetite, I couldn't sleep, I was grumpy and nervous. I didn't myself connect it with Bond at all. I thought that I was overworked, and when my wife suggested a holiday, I agreed, got a fortnight's leave from my newspaper, and went down to Glebeshire.

Early December is not a bad time for Glebeshire. It is just then the best spot in the British Isles. I knew a little village beyond St. Mary's Moor, that I had not seen for ten years, but always remembered with romantic gratitude, and I felt that that was the place for me now.

I changed trains at Polchester and found myself at last in a little jingle driving out to sea. The air, the wide open moor, the smell of the sea delighted me, and when I reached my little village, with its sandy cove and the boats drawn up in two rows in front of a high rocky cave, and when I ate my eggs and bacon in the little parlour of the inn overlooking the sea, I felt happier than I had done for weeks past; but my happiness did not last long. Night after night

I could not sleep. I began to feel acute loneliness and knew at last in full truth that it was my friend whom I was missing, and that it was not solitude I needed, but his company. Easy enough to talk about having his company, but I only truly knew, down here in this little village, sitting on the edge of the green cliff, looking over into limitless sea, that I was indeed never to have his company again. There followed after that a wild, impatient regret that I had not made more of my time with him. I saw myself, in a sudden vision, as I had really been with him, patronizing, indulgent, a little contemptuous of his good-natured ideas. Had I only a week with him now, how eagerly I would show him that I was the fool and not he, that I was the lucky one every time!

One connects with one's own grief the place where one feels it, and before many days had passed I had grown to loathe the little village, to dread, beyond words, the long, soughing groan of the sea as it drew back down the slanting beach, the melancholy wail of the seagull, the chattering women under my little window. I couldn't stand it. I ought to go back to London, and yet from that, too, I shrank. Memories of Bond lingered there as they did in no other placc, and it was hardly fair to my wife and family to give them the company of the dreary, discontented man that I just then was.

And then, just in the way that such things always happen, I found on my breakfast-table one fine morning a forwarded letter. It was from a certain Mrs. Baldwin, and, to my surprise, I saw that it came from Glebeshire, but from the top of the county and not its southern end.

John Baldwin was a Stock Exchange friend of my brother's, a rough diamond, but kindly and generous, and not, I believed, very well off. Mrs. Baldwin I had always liked, and I think she always liked me. We had not met for some little time and I had no idea what had happened to them. Now in her letter she told me that they had taken an old eighteenth-century house on the north coast of Glebeshire, not very far from Drymouth, that they were enjoying it very much indeed, that Jack was fitter than he had been for years, and that they would be delighted, were I ever in that part of the country, to have me as their guest. This suddenly seemed to me the very thing. The Baldwins had never known Charlie Bond, and they would have, therefore, for me no association with his memory. They were jolly, noisy people, with a jolly, noisy family, and Jack Baldwin's personality was so robust that it would surely shake me out of my gloomy mood. I sent a telegram at once to Mrs. Baldwin, asking her whether she could have me for a week, and before the day was over I received the warmest of invitations.

Next day I left my little fishing village and experienced one of those strange, crooked, in-and-out little journeys that you must undergo if you are to find your way from one obscure Glebeshire village to another.

About midday, a lovely, cold, blue December midday, I discovered myself in Polchester with an hour to wait for my next train. I went down into the town, climbed the High Street to the magnificent cathedral, stood beneath the famous Arden Gate, looked at the still more famous tomb of the Black Bishop, and it was there, as the sunlight, slanting through the great east window, danced and sparkled about the wonderful blue stone of which that tomb is made, that I had a sudden sense of having been through all this before, of having stood just there in some earlier time, weighed down by some earlier grief, and that nothing that I was experiencing was unexpected. I had a curious sense, too, of comfort and condolence, that horrible grey loneliness that I had felt in the fishing village suddenly fell from me, and for the first time since Bond's death, I was happy. I walked away from the cathedral, down the busy street, and through the dear old market-place, expecting I know not what. All that I knew was that I was intending to go to the Baldwins and that I would be happy there.

The December afternoon fell quickly, and during the last part of my journey I was travelling in a ridiculous little train, through dusk, and the little train went so slowly and so casually that one was always hearing the murmurs of streams beyond one's window, and lakes of grey water suddenly stretched like plates of glass to thick woods, black as ink, against a faint sky. I got out at my little wayside station, shaped like a rabbit-hutch, and found a motor waiting for me. The drive was not long, and suddenly I was outside the old eighteenth-century house and Baldwin's stout butler was conveying me into the hall with that careful, kindly patronage, rather as though I were a box of eggs that might very easily be broken.

It was a spacious hall, with a large open fireplace, in front of which they were all having tea. I say "all" advisedly, because the place seemed to be full of people, grown-ups and children, but mostly children. There were so many of these last that I was not, to the end of my stay, to be able to name most of them individually.

Mrs. Baldwin came forward to greet me, introduced me to one or two people, sat me down and gave me my tea, told me that I wasn't looking at all well, and needed feeding up, and explained that Jack was out shooting something, but would soon be back.

My entrance had made a brief lull, but immediately everyone recovered and the noise was terrific. There is a lot to be said for the freedom of the modern child. There is a lot to be said against it, too. I soon found that in this party, at any rate, the elders were completely disregarded and of no account. Children rushed about the hall, knocked one another down, shouted and screamed, fell over grown-ups as though they were pieces of furniture, and paid no attention at all to the mild "Now children" of a plain, elderly lady who was, I supposed, a governess. I fancy that I was tired with my criss-cross journey, and I soon found a chance to ask Mrs. Baldwin if I could go up to my room. She said: "I expect you find these children noisy. Poor little things. They must have their fun. Jack always says that one can only be young once, and I do so agree with him."

I wasn't myself feeling very young that evening (I was really about nine hundred years old), so that I agreed with her and eagerly left youth to its own appropriate pleasures. Mrs. Baldwin took me up the fine broad staircase. She was a stout, short woman, dressed in bright colours, with what is known, I believe, as an infectious laugh. Tonight, although I was fond of her, and knew very well her good, generous heart, she irritated me, and for some reason that I could not quite define. Perhaps I felt at once that she was out of place there and that the house resented her, but in all this account, I am puzzled by the question as to whether I imagine now, on looking back, all sorts of feelings that were not really there at all, but come to me now because I know of what happened afterwards. But I am so anxious to tell the truth, the whole truth, and nothing but the truth, and there is nothing in the world so difficult to do as that.

We went through a number of dark passages, up and down little pieces of staircase that seemed to have no beginning, no end, and no reason for their existence, and she left me at last in my bedroom, said that she hoped I would be comfortable, and that Jack would come and see me when he came in, and then paused for a moment, looking at me. "You really don't look well," she said. "You've been overdoing it. You're too conscientious. I always said so. You shall have a real rest here. And the children will see that you're not dull."

Her last two sentences seemed scarcely to go together. I could not tell her about my loss. I realized suddenly, as I had never realized in our older acquaintance, that I should never be able to speak to her about anything that really mattered.

She smiled, laughed and left me. I looked at my room and loved it at once. Broad and low-ceilinged, it contained very little furniture, an old four-poster, charming hangings of some old rose-coloured damask, an old gold mirror, an oak cabinet, some high-backed chairs, and then, for comfort, a large armchair with high elbows, a little quaintly shaped sofa dressed in the same rose colour as the bed, a bright crackling fire, and a grandfather clock. The walls, faded primrose, had no pictures, but on one of them, opposite my bed, was a gay sampler worked in bright colours of crimson and yellow and framed in oak.

I liked it, I loved it, and drew the armchair in front of the fire, nestled down into it, and before I knew, I was fast asleep. How long I slept I don't know, but I suddenly woke with a sense of comfort and well-being which was nothing less than exquisite. I belonged to it, that room, as though I had been in it all my days. I had a curious sense of companionship that was exactly what I had been needing during these last weeks. The house was very still, no voices of children came to me, no sound anywhere, save the sharp crackle of the fire and the friendly ticking of the old clock. Suddenly I thought that there was someone in the room with me, a rustle of something that might have been the fire and yet was not.

I got up and looked about me, half smiling, as though I expected to see a familiar face. There was no-one there, of course, and yet I had just that consciousness of companionship that one has when someone whom one loves very dearly and knows very intimately is sitting with one in the same room. I even went to the other side of the four-poster and looked around me, pulled for a moment at the silver-coloured curtains, and of course saw no-one. Then the door suddenly opened and Jack Baldwin came in, and I remember having a curious feeling of irritation as though I had been interrupted. His large, breezy, knickerbockered figure filled the room. "Hullo!" he said, "delighted to see you. Bit of luck your being down this way. Have you got everything you want?"

## II

That was a wonderful old house. I am not going to attempt to describe it, although I have stayed there quite recently. Yes, I stayed there on many occasions since that first of which I am now speaking. It has never been quite the same to me since that first time. You may say, if you like, that the Baldwins fought a battle with it and defeated it. It is certainly now more Baldwin than – well, whatever it was before they rented it. They are not the kind of people to be defeated by atmosphere. Their chief duty in this world, I gather, is to make things Baldwin, and very good for the world too; but when I first went down to them the house was still challenging them. "A wee bit creepy," Mrs. Baldwin confided to me on the second day of my visit. "What exactly do you mean by that?" I asked her. "Ghosts?"

"Oh, there are those, of course," she answered. "There's an underground passage, you know, that runs from here to the sea, and one of the wickedest of the smugglers was killed in it, and his ghost still haunts the celler. At least that's what we were told by our first butler, here; and then, of course, we found that it was the butler, not the smuggler, who was haunting the cellar, and since his departure the smuggler hasn't been visible." She laughed. "All the same, it isn't a comfortable place. I'm going to wake up some of those old rooms. We're going to put in some more windows. And then there are the children," she added.

Yes, there were the children. Surely the noisiest in all the world. They had reverence for nothing. They were the wildest savages, and especially those from nine to thirteen, the cruellest and most uncivilized age for children. There were two little boys, twins I should think, who were nothing less than devils, and regarded their elders with cold, watching eyes, said nothing in protest when scolded, but evolved plots afterwards that fitted precisely the chastiser. To do my host and hostess justice, all the children were not Baldwins, and I fancy that the Baldwin contingent was the quietest.

Nevertheless, from early morning until ten at night, the noise was terrific and you were never sure how early in the morning it would recommence. I don't know that I personally minded the noise very greatly. It took me out of myself and gave me something better to think of, but, in some obscure and unanalysed way, I felt that the house minded it. One knows how the poets have written about old walls and rafters rejoicing in the happy, careless laughter of children. I do not think this house rejoiced at all, and it was queer how consistently I, who am not supposed to be an imaginative person, thought about the house.

But it was not until my third evening that something really happened. I say "happened", but did anything really happen? You shall judge for yourself.

I was sitting in my comfortable armchair in my bedroom, enjoying that delightful half-hour before one dresses for dinner.

There was a terrible racket up and down the passages, the children being persuaded, I gathered, to go into the schoolroom and have their supper, when the noise died down and there was nothing but the feathery whisper of the snow – snow had been falling all day – against my window-pane. My thoughts suddenly turned to Bond, directed to him as actually and precipitately as though he had suddenly sprung before me. I did not want to think of him. I had been fighting his memory these last days, because I had thought that the wisest thing to do, but now he was too much for me.

I luxuriated in my memories of him, turning over and over all sorts of times that we had had together, seeing his smile, watching his mouth that turned up at the corners when he was amused, and wondering finally why he should obsess me the way that he did, when I had lost so many other friends for whom I had thought I cared much more, who, nevertheless, never bothered my memory at all. I sighed, and it seemed to me that my sigh was very gently repeated behind me. I turned sharply round. The curtains had not been drawn. You know the strange, milky pallor that reflected snow throws over objects, and although three lighted candles shone in the room, moon-white shadows seemed to hang over the bed and across the floor. Of course there was no-one there, and yet I stared and stared about me as though I were convinced that I was not alone. And then I looked especially at one part of the room, a distant corner beyond the four-poster, and it seemed to me that someone was there. And yet no-one was there. But whether it was that my mind had been distracted, or that the beauty of the old snow-lit room enchanted me, I don't know, but my thoughts of my friend were happy and reassured. I had not lost him, I seemed to say to myself. Indeed, at that special moment he seemed to be closer to me than he had been while he was alive.

From that evening a curious thing occurred. I only seemed to be close to my friend when I was in my own room – and I felt more than that. When my door was closed and I was sitting in my armchair, I fancied that our new companionship was not only Bond's, but was something more as well. I would wake in the middle of the night or in the early morning and feel quite sure that I was not alone; so sure that I did not even want to investigate it further, but just took the companionship for granted and was happy.

Outside that room, however, I felt increasing discomfort. I hated the way in which the house was treated. A quite unreasonable anger rose within me as I heard the Baldwins discussing the improvements that they were going to make, and yet they were so kind to me, and so patently unaware of doing anything that would not generally be commended, that it was quite impossible for me to show my anger. Nevertheless, Mrs. Baldwin noticed something. "I am afraid the children are worrying you," she said one morning, half interrogatively. "In a way it will be a rest when they go back to school, but the Christmas holidays is their time, isn't it? I do like to see them happy. Poor little dears."

The poor little dears were at that moment being Red Indians all over the hall.

"No, of course, I like children," I answered her. "The only thing is that they don't – I hope you won't think me foolish – somehow quite fit in with the house."

"Oh, I think it's so good for old places like this," said Mrs. Baldwin briskly, "to be woken up a little. I'm sure if the old people who used to live here came back they'd love to hear all the noise and laughter."

I wasn't so sure myself, but I wouldn't disturb Mrs. Baldwin's contentment for anything.

That evening in my room I was so convinced of companionship that I spoke.

"If there's anyone here," I said aloud, "I'd like them to know that I'm aware of it and am glad of it."

Then, when I caught myself speaking aloud, I was suddenly terrified. Was I really going crazy? Wasn't that the first step towards insanity when you talked to yourself? Nevertheless, a moment later I was reassured. There *was* someone there.

That night I woke, looked at my luminous watch and saw that it was a quarter past three. The room was so dark that I could not even distinguish the posters of my bed, but – there was a very faint glow from the fire, now nearly dead. Opposite my bed there seemed to me to be something white. Not white in the accepted sense of a tall, ghostly figure; but, sitting up and staring, it seemed to me that the shadow was very small, hardly reaching above the edge of the bed.

"Is there anyone there?" I asked. "Because, if there is, do speak to me. I'm not frightened. I know that someone has been here all this last week, and I am glad of it."

Very faintly then, and so faintly that I cannot to this day be sure that I saw anything at all, the figure of a child seemed to me to be visible.

We all know how we have at one time and another fancied that we have seen visions and figures, and then have discovered that it was something in the room, the chance hanging of a coat, the reflection of a glass, a trick of moonlight that has fired our imagination. I was quite prepared for that in this case, but it seemed to me then that as I watched the shadow moved directly in front of the dying fire, and delicate as the leaf of a silver birch, like the trailing rim of some evening cloud, the figure of a child hovered in front of me.

Curiously enough the dress, which seemed to be of some silver tissue, was clearer than anything else. I did not, in fact, see the face at all, and yet I could swear in the morning that I had seen it, that I knew large, black, wide-open eyes, a little mouth very faintly parted in a timid smile, and that, beyond anything else, I had realized in the expression of that face fear and bewilderment and a longing for some comfort.

## III

After that night the affair moved very quickly to its little climax.

I am not a very imaginative man, nor have I any sympathy with the modern craze for spooks and specters. I have never seen, nor fancied that I had seen, anything of a supernatural kind since that visit, but then I have never known since that time such a desperate need of companionship and comfort, and is it not perhaps because we do not want things badly enough in this life that we do not get more of them? However that may be, I was sure on this occasion that I had some companionship that was born of a need greater than mine. I suddenly took the most frantic and unreasonable dislike of the children in that house. It was exactly as though I had discovered somewhere in a deserted part of the building some child who had been left behind by mistake by the last occupants and was terrified by the noisy exuberance and ruthless selfishness of the new family.

For a week I had no more definite manifestation of my little friend, but I was as sure of her presence there in my room as I was of my own clothes and the armchair in which I used to sit.

It was time for me to go back to London, but I could not go. I asked everyone I met as to legends and stories connected with the old house, but I never found anything to do with a little child. I looked forward all day to my hour in my room before dinner, the time when I felt the companionship closest. I sometimes woke in the night and was conscious of its presence, but, as I have said, I never saw anything.

One evening the older children obtained leave to stay up later. It was somebody's birthday. The house seemed to be full of people, and the presence of the children led after dinner to a perfect riot of noise and confusion. We were to play hide-and-seek all over the house. Everybody was to dress up. There was, for that night at least, to be no privacy anywhere. We were all, as Mrs. Baldwin said, to be ten years old again. I hadn't the least desire to be ten years old, but I found myself caught into the game, and had, in sheer self-defence, to run up and down the passages and hide behind doors. The noise was terrific. It grew and grew in volume. People got hysterical. The smaller children jumped out of bed and ran about the passages. Somebody kept blowing a motor-horn. Somebody else turned on the gramophone.

Suddenly I was sick of the whole thing, retreated into my room, lit one candle and locked the door. I had scarcely sat down in my chair when I was aware that my little friend had come. She was standing near to the bed, staring at me, terror in her eyes. I have never seen anyone so frightened. Her little breasts panting beneath her silver gown, her very fair hair falling about her shoulders, her little hands clenched. Just as I saw her, there were loud knocks on the door, many voices shouting to be admitted, a perfect babel of noise and laughter. The little figure moved, and then – how can I give any idea of it? – I was conscious of having something to protect and comfort. I saw nothing, physically I felt nothing, and yet I was murmuring, "There, there, don't mind. They shan't come in. I'll see that no one touches you. I understand. I understand." For how long I sat like that I don't know. The noises died away, voices murmured at intervals, and then were silent. The house slept. All night I think I stayed there comforting and being comforted.

I fancy now – but how much of it may not be fancy? – that I knew that the child loved the house, had stayed so long as was possible, at last was driven away, and that that was her farewell, not only to me, but all that she most loved in this world and the next.

I do not know – I could swear to nothing. Of what I am sure is that my sense of loss in my friend was removed from that night and never returned. Did I argue with myself that the child companionship included also my friend? Again, I do not know. But of one thing I am now sure, that if love is strong enough, physical death cannot destroy it, and however platitudinous that may sound to others, it is platitudinous no longer when you have discovered it by actual experience for yourself.

That moment in that fire-lit room, when I felt that spiritual heart beating with mine, is and always will be enough for me.

One more thing. Next day I left for London, and my wife was delighted to find me so completely recovered – happier, she said, than I had ever been before.

Two days afterwards, I received a parcel from Mrs. Baldwin. In the note that accompanied it, she said:

> *I think that you must have left this by mistake behind you. It was found in the small drawer in your dressing-table.*

I opened the parcel and discovered an old blue silk handkerchief, wrapped round a long, thin wooden box. The cover of the box lifted very easily, and I saw inside it an old, painted wooden doll, dressed in the period, I should think, of Queen Anne. The dress was very complete, even down to the little shoes, and the little grey mittens on the hands. Inside the silk skirt there was sewn a little tape, and on the tape, in very faded letters, "Ann Trelawney, 1710."

# The Patter of Tiny Feet

## Nigel Kneale

### Prospectus

**Address:** 47, The Street, London Suburb, England.

**Property:** Twentieth-century detached villa. Three bedrooms, lounge, dining room and kitchen with bordered gardens to the front and rear.

**Viewing Date:** Autumn, 1955.

**Agent:** Nigel Kneale (1922–) was born in Lancaster, Lancashire and trained to be an actor at the Royal Academy of Dramatic Art. He worked for a while on the stage before turning to scriptwriting and has become one of the most challenging of modern television playwrights. Kneale came to public attention with the *Quatermass* science fiction serials in the Fifties, and was also highly praised for his supernatural dramas, *The Chopper* (1971) about a biker's ghost and *The Stone Tape* (1972), with ghosts being seen as apparitions of twentieth-century technology. "The Patter of Tiny Feet", one of his rare short stories, features a poltergeist in the most everyday of settings.

"Hold on a moment. Don't knock," Joe Banner said. "Let me get a shot of the outside before the light goes."

So I waited while he backed into the road with his Leica. No traffic, nobody about but an old man walking a dog in the distance. Joe stuck his cigarette behind one ear and prowled quickly to find the best angle on Number 47. It was what the address had suggested: a narrow suburban villa in a forgotten road, an old maid of a house with a skirt of garden drawn round it, keeping itself to itself among all its sad neighbours. The flower beds were full of dead stems and grass.

Joe's camera clicked twice. "House of Usher's in the bag," he said, and resumed the cigarette. "Think the garden has any possibilities?"

"Come on! We can waste time later."

Weather had bleached the green front door. There was a big iron knocker and I used it.

"It echoed hollowly through the empty house!" said Banner. He enjoys talking like that, though it bores everybody. In addition he acts character – aping the sort of small-town photographer who wears his hat on the back of his head and stinks out the local Rotarians with damp flash-powder – but he's one of the finest in the profession.

We heard rapid footsteps inside, the lock clicked and the door swung open, all in a hurry. And there appeared – yes, remembering those comic letters to the office, it could only be – our man.

"Mr. Hutchinson?"

"At your service, gentlemen!" He shot a look over Joe's camera and the suitcase full of equipment, and seemed pleased. A small pudding-face and a long nose that didn't match it, trimmed with a narrow line of moustache. He had the style of a shop-walker, I thought. "Come inside, please. Can I lend you a hand with that? No? That's it – right along inside!" It sounded as if the word "sir" was trembling to join each phrase.

We went into the front room, where a fire was burning. The furniture was a familiar mixture: flimsy modern veneer jostling old pieces built like Noah's Ark and handed down from in-laws. Gilt plaster dancers posed on the sideboard and the rug was worn through.

"My name is Staines," I said, "and this is Joe Banner, who's going to handle the pictures. I believe you've had a letter?"

"Yes, indeed," said Hutchinson, shaking hands. "Please take a seat, both of you – I know what a tiring journey it can be, all the way from London! Yes. I must say how extremely gratified I am that your paper has shown this interest!" His voice sounded distorted by years of ingratiating; it bubbled out of the front of his mouth like a comic radio character's. "Have you . . . that is, I understand you have special experience in this field, Mr. Staines?" He seemed almost worried about it.

"Not exactly a trained investigator," I admitted, "but I've knocked out a few articles on the subject."

"Oh . . . yes, indeed. I've read them with great interest." He hadn't, of course, but he made it sound very respectful. He asked if we had eaten, and when we reassured him he produced drinks from grandmother's sideboard. Banner settled down to his performance of the "Hicks-in-the-Stick Journal" photographer out on a blind.

"You – you seem to have brought a lot of equipment." Hutchinson said quickly. "I hope I made it clear there's no guarantee of anything . . . visible."

"Guarantee? Why, then you *have* seen something?"

He sat forward on his chair, but immediately seemed to restrain himself and an artfully stiff smile appeared. "Mr. Staines, let's understand each other: I am most anxious not to give you preconceived ideas. This is your investigation, not mine." He administered this like a police caution, invitingly.

Joe put down his empty glass. "We're not easily corrupted, Mr. Hutchinson."

To scotch the mock-modesty I said: "We've read your letters and the local press-clipping. So what about the whole story, in your own way?" I took out my notebook, to encourage him.

Hutchinson blinked nervously and rose. He snapped the two standard lamps on, went to the window with hands clasped behind him. The sky was darkening. He drew the curtains and came back as if he had taken deep thought. His sigh was full of responsibility.

"I'm trying to take an impersonal view. This case is so unusual that I feel it must be examined . . . *pro bono publico*, as it were . . ." He gave a tight little laugh, all part of the act. "I don't want you to get the idea I'm a seeker after publicity."

This was too much. "No, no" I said, "you don't have to explain yourself: we're interested. Facts, Mr. Hutchinson, please. Just facts."

"For instance, what time do the noises start?" said Joe.

Hutchinson relaxed, too obviously gratified for the purity of his motives. He glanced at his watch brightly.

"Oh, it varies, Mr. Banner. After dark – any time at all after dark." He frowned like an honest witness. "I'm trying to think of any instance during daylight, but no. Sometimes it comes early, often near midnight, occasionally towards dawn: no rule about it, absolutely none. It can continue all night through."

I caught him watching my pencil as I stopped writing; his eyes came up on me and Joe, alert as a confident examination-candidate's.

"Footsteps?"

Again the arch smile. "Mr. Staines, that's for you to judge. To me it sounds like footsteps."

"The witness knows the rules of evidence, boy!" Joe said, and winked at us both. Hutchinson took his glass.

"Fill it up for you, Mr. Banner? I'm far from an ideal observer, I fear; bar Sundays, I'm out every evening."

"Business?"

"Yes, I'm assistant headwaiter in a restaurant. To-night I was able to be excused." He handed us refilled glasses. "A strange feeling, you know, to come into the house late at night, and hear those sounds going on inside, in the dark."

"Scare you?" Joe asked.

"Not now. Surprising, isn't it? But it seems one can get used to anything."

I asked: "Just what do you hear?"

Hutchinson considered, watching my pencil. "He's got the answer all ready," I thought. "A curious pattering, very erratic and light. A sort of . . . playing, if that conveys anything. Upstairs there's a small passage between the bedrooms, covered with linoleum: I'll show you presently. Well, it mostly occurs there, but it can travel down the stairs into the hallway below."

"Ever hear—?" Joe began.

Hutchinson went on: "It lasts between thirty and forty seconds. I've timed it. And in a single night I've known the whole thing to be repeated up to a dozen times."

"– a rat in the ceiling, Mr. Hutchinson?" Joe finished. "They can make a hell of a row."

"Yes, I've heard rats. This is not one."

I frowned at Joe: this was routine stuff. "Mr. Hutchinson, we'll agree on that. Look, in your last letter you said you had a theory – of profound significance."

"Yes."

"Why don't we get on to that, then?"

He whipped round instantly, full of it. "My idea is – well, it's a terribly unusual form of – the case – the case of a projection – how can I put it? It's more than a theory, Mr. Staines!" He had all the stops out at once. His hands trembled.

"Hold it!" Joe called, and reached for his Leica. "I'll be making an odd shot now and then, Mr. Hutchinson. Show you telling the story, see?"

Hutchinson's fingers went to his tie.

"You were saying—?" I turned over a leaf of the note-book.

"Well, I can vouch for this house, you know. I've lived here for many years, and it came to me from my mother. There's absolutely no . . . history attached to it."

I could believe that.

"Until about six years ago I lived alone – a woman came in to clean twice a week. And then . . . I married." He said this impressively, watching to see that I noted it.

"A strange person, my wife. She was only nineteen when we married, and very . . . unworldly." He drew a self-conscious breath. "Distant cousin of mine actually, very religious people. That's her photograph on the mantelpiece."

I took it down.

I had noticed it when first we entered the room; vignetted in its chromium-plated frame, too striking to be his daughter. It was a face of character, expressive beyond mere beauty: an attractive full-lipped mouth, eyes of exceptional vividness. Surprisingly, her hair was shapeless and her dress dull. I passed the portrait to Joe, who whistled.

"Mr. Hutchinson! Where are you hiding the lady? Come on, let's get a picture of—"

Then he also guessed. This was not a house with a woman in it.

"She passed away seven months ago," said Hutchinson, and held out his hand for the frame.

"I'm sorry," I said. Banner nodded and muttered something.

Hutchinson was expressionless. "Yes," he said, "I'm sorry too." Which was an odd thing to say, as there was evidently no sarcasm in it. I wondered why she could have married him. There must have been twenty-five years between them, and a world of temperament.

"She was extremely . . . passionate," Hutchinson said.

He spoke as if he were revealing something indecent. His voice was hushed, and his little moustache bristled over pursed lips. When his eyes dropped to the photograph in his hand, his face was quite blank.

Suddenly he said in an odd, curt way: "She was surprisingly faithful to me. I mean, she was never anything else. Very religious, strictest ideas of her duty." The flicker of a smile. "Unworldly, as I said."

I tried to be discreet. "Then you were happy together?"

His fingers were unconsciously worrying at the picture-frame, fidgeting with the strut.

"To be honest, we weren't. She wanted children."

Neither Banner nor I moved.

"I told her I couldn't agree. I had to tell her often, because she worked herself up, and it all became ugly. She used to lose control and say things she didn't mean, and afterwards she was sorry, but you can't play fast and loose with people's finger feelings! I did my best. I'd forgive her and say: 'I only want you, my dear. You're all I need in the world,' to comfort her, you see. And she'd sob loudly and . . . she was unnecessarily emotional."

His voice was thin, and tight. He rose and replaced the photograph on the mantelpiece. There was a long silence.

Joe fiddled with his camera. "No children, then?" Cruel, that.

Hutchinson turned, and we saw that somehow he had managed to relax. The accomodating smirk was back.

"No, none. I had definite views on the subject. All quite rational. Wide disparity in the prospective parents' ages, for instance – psychologically dangerous for all parties: I don't know if you've studied the subject? There were other considerations, too – financial, medical: do you wish me to go into those? I have nothing to hide."

It was blatant exhibitionism now: as if he were proffering a bill on a plate, with himself itemized in it.

"There's a limit even to journalists' curiosity," I said.

Hutchinson was ahead of me, solemnly explaining. "Now! This is my theory! You've heard of poltergeist phenomena, of course? Unexplainable knockings, scratchings, minor damage and so on. I've studied them in books – and they're always connected with development, violent emotional development, in young people. A sort of uncontrolled offshoot of the . . . personality. D'you follow?"

"Wait a minute," Joe said. "That's taking a lot for granted if you like!"

But I remembered reading such cases. One, investigated by psychical researchers, had involved a fifteen-year-old boy: ornaments had been thrown about by no visible agency. I took a glance at the unchipped gilt dancers on the sideboard before Hutchinson spoke again.

"No, my wife may not have been adolescent, but in some ways . . . she was . . . so to speak, retarded."

He looked as pleased as if he had just been heavily tipped. If that was pure intellectual triumph, it was not good to see.

"Then . . . the sounds began," Joe said, "while she was still alive?"

Hutchinson shook his head emphatically.

"Not till three weeks after the funeral! That's the intriguing part, don't you see? They were faint and unidentifiable at first – naturally I just put down traps for rats or mice. But by another month, they were taking on the present form."

Joe gave a back-street sniff and rubbed a hand over his chin.

"Hell, you ask us to believe your poltergeist lies low until nearly a month after the – the—"

"After the medium, shall we say, is dead!" His cold-bloodedness was fascinating.

Joe looked across at me and raised his eyebrows.

"Gentlemen, perhaps I'm asking you to accept too much? Well, we shall see. Please remember that I am only too happy that you should form your own – your own—" Hutchinson's voice dropped to a whisper. He raised his hand. His eyes caught ours as he listened.

My spine chilled.

Somewhere above us in the house were faint sounds. A scuffling.

"That's it!"

I tiptoed to the door and got it open in time to hear a last scamper overhead. Yes, it could have been a kitten, I thought; but it had come so promptly on cue. I was on the stairs when Hutchinson called out, as if he were the thing's manager: "No more for the present! You'll probably get another manifestation in forty minutes or so."

"Cue for the next performance," I thought.

I searched the staircase with my torch. At the top ran the little passage Hutchinson had described; open on one side, with banisters, and on the other, a dark papered wall. The linoleum was bare. There was nothing to be seen, nor any open doors. The very dinginess of this narrow place was eerie.

Downstairs I found Joe feverishly unpacking his apparatus. Hutchinson was watching, delighted.

"Anything I can possibly do, Mr. Banner? Threads across the passage – oh, yes? How very ingenious! You've your own drawingpins? – excellent! Can I carry that lamp for you?"

And he led the way upstairs.

We searched the shabby bedrooms first. Only one was in use, and we locked all of them and sealed the doors.

In half an hour preparations were complete. Hair-thin threads were stretched across the passage at different levels; adhesive squares lay in patterns on the linoleum. Joe had four high-powered lamps ready to flood the place at the pressure of a silent contact. I took the Leica; he himself now carried an automatic miniature camera.

"Four shots a second with this toy," he was telling Hutchinson, while I went to check a window outside the bathroom. I still favoured the idea of a cat: they so often make a habitual playground of other people's houses.

The window was secure. I was just sticking an additional seal across the join when I sniffed scent; for a moment I took it to be from soap in the bathroom. Sickly, warm, strangely familiar. Then it came almost overpoweringly.

I returned as quickly and quietly as I could to the stairhead.

"Smell it?" Joe breathed in the darkness.

"Yes, what d'you suppose—?"

"Ssh!"

There was a sound not four yards away, as I judged it: a tap on the linoleum. Huddled together, we all tensed. It came again, and then a scamper of feet – small and light, but unmistakable – feet in flat shoes. As if something had run across the far end of the passage. A pause – a slithering towards us – then that same shuffle we had heard earlier in the evening, clear now: it was the jigging, uneven stamp of an infant's attempt to dance! In that heavy, sweet darkness, the recognition of it came horribly.

Something brushed against me: Banner's elbow.

At the very next sound he switched on all his lamps. The narrow place was flung into dazzling brightness – it was completely empty! My head went suddenly numb inside. Joe's camera clicked and buzzed, cutting across the baby footsteps that came hesitating towards us over the floor. We kept our positions, eyes straining down at nothing but the brown faded pattern of the linoleum. Within inches of us, the footsteps changed their direction in a quick swerve and clattered away to the far corner. We waited. Every vein in my head was banging.

The silence continued. It was over.

Banner drew a thick raucous breath. He lowered the camera, but his sweaty face remained screwed up as if he were still looking through the viewfinder. "Not a sausage!" he whispered, panting. "Not a bloody sausage!"

The threads glistened there unbroken; none of the sticky patches was out of place.

"It *was* a kiddie," Joe said. He has two of his own. "Hutchinson!"

"Yes?" The flabby face was white, but he seemed less shaken than we others.

"How the hell did you –?" Banner sagged against the wall and his camera dangled, swinging slowly on its safety strap. "No – it was moving along the floor. I could have reached out and touched – My God, I need a drink!"

We went downstairs.

Hutchinson poured out. Joe drank three whiskies straight off but he still trembled. Desperate to reassure himself, he began to play the sceptic again immediately. As if with a personal grievance, he went for Hutchinson.

"Overdid that sickly smell, you know! Good trick – oh, yes, clever – particularly when we weren't expecting it!"

The waiter was quick with his denials: it had always accompanied the sounds, but he had wanted us to find out for ourselves; this time it had been stronger than usual.

"Take it easy, Joe – no violence!" I said. He pushed my hand off his arm.

"Oh, clever! That kind of talc, gripe-watery, general baby smell! But listen to this, Mr. Bloody Hutchinson: it should be more delicate, and you only get it quite that way with very tiny babies! Now this one was able to walk, seemingly. And the dancing – that comes at a different stage again. No, you lack experience, Mr. H.! This is no baby that ever was!"

I looked at Hutchinson.

He was nodding, evidently pleased. "My theory exactly," he said. "Could we call it . . . a poltergeisted maternal impulse?"

Joe stared. The full enormity of the idea struck him.

"Christ . . . Almighty!" he said, and what grip he still had on himself went. He grabbed at his handkerchief just in time, before he was sick.

When he felt better, I set about collecting the gear.

Hutchinson fussed and pleaded the whole time, persuasive as

any door-to-door salesman in trying to make us stay for the next incident. He even produced a chart he had made, showing the frequency of the manifestations over the past three months, and began to quote books on the subject.

"Agreed, it's all most extraordinary," I said. "A unique case. You'll be hearing from us." All I wanted was to be out of that house. "Ready, Joe?"

"Yes, I'm all right now."

Hutchinson was everywhere, like a dog wanting to be taken for a walk. "I do hope I've been of some service! Is there anything more I can possibly –? I suppose you can't tell me when the publication date is likely to be?"

Nauseating. "Not my department," I said. "You'll hear."

Over his shoulder I could see the girl's face in her chromium frame. She must have had a very great deal of life in her to look like that on a square of paper.

"Mr. Hutchinson," I said. "Just one last question."

He grinned. "Certainly, certainly. As the prosecution wishes."

"What did your wife die of?"

For the first time he seemed genuinely put out. His voice, when it came, had for the moment lost its careful placing.

"As a matter of fact," he said, "she threw herself under a train." He recovered himself. "Oh, shocking business, showed how unbalanced the poor girl must have been all along. If you like, I can show you a full press report of the inquest – I've nothing to hide – absolutely nothing–"

I reported the assignment as a washout. In any case Banner's photographs showed nothing – except one which happened to include me, in such an attitude of horror as to be recognisable only by my clothing. I burnt that.

"Our Mr. Hutchinson's going to be disappointed."

Joe's teeth set. "What a mind that type must have! Publicity mania and the chance of a nice touch too, he thinks. So he rigs a spook out of the dirty linen!"

"Sure he rigged it?"

Joe hesitated. "Positive."

"For argument's sake, suppose he didn't: suppose it's all

genuine. He manages to go on living with the thing, so he can't be afraid of it . . . and gradually . . . 'new emotional depths' . . ." The idea suddenly struck me as having a ghastly humour. "Of course, publicity's the only way he could do it!"

"What?"

"Banner, you ought to be sympathetic! Doesn't every father want to show off his child?"

# Uninvited Ghosts

## Penelope Lively

### Prospectus

**Address:** Norham Gardens, Oxford, England.

**Property:** Nineteenth-century family house in the much sought after county of Oxfordshire. Three-storey building with four bedrooms, spacious lounge and dining room, with large garden to the rear.

**Viewing Date:** Spring, 1981.

**Agent:** Penelope Lively (1933–) was born in Egypt, but settled in England after the Second World War, where she studied history at St. Anne's College, Oxford. She has proved to be a brilliant writer for both adults and children and the supernatural features strongly in her work, especially in *The Wild Hunt of Hagworthy* (1971) and the award-winning pair, *The Ghost of Thomas Kempe* (1973) and *A Stitch in Time* (1976). Penelope Lively has written several ghost short stories, including "Black Dog", "The Ghost of a Flea" and "Uninvited Ghosts", an amusing tale of some otherworldly residents in the Brown family's new home and how the children deal with them . . .

Marian and Simon were sent to bed early on the day that the Brown family moved house. By then everyone had lost their temper with everyone else; the cat had been sick on the sitting-room carpet; the dog had run away twice. If you have ever moved you will know what kind of a day it had been. Packing cases and newspaper all over the place . . . sandwiches instead of proper meals . . . the kettle lost and a wardrobe stuck on the stairs and Mrs Brown's favourite vase broken. There was bread and baked beans for supper, the television wouldn't work and the water wasn't hot so when all was said and done the children didn't object too violently to being packed off to bed. They'd had enough, too. They had one last argument about who was going to sleep by the window, put on their pyjamas, got into bed, switched the lights out . . . and it was at that point that the ghost came out of the bottom drawer of the chest of drawers.

It oozed out, a grey cloudy shape about three feet long smelling faintly of woodsmoke, sat down on a chair and began to hum to itself. It looked like a bundle of bedclothes, except that it was not solid: you could see, quite clearly, the cushion on the chair beneath it.

Marian gave a shriek. "That's a ghost!"

"Oh, be quiet, dear, do," said the ghost. "That noise goes right through my head. And it's not nice to call people names." It took out a ball of wool and some needles and began to knit.

What would you have done? Well, yes – Simon and Marian did just that and I daresay you can imagine what happened. You try telling your mother that you can't get to sleep because there's a ghost sitting in the room clacking its knitting-needles and humming. Mrs Brown said the kind of things she could be expected to say and the ghost continued sitting there knitting and humming and Mrs Brown went out, banging the door and saying threatening things about if there's so much as another word from either of you . . .

"She can't see it," said Marian to Simon.

"'Course not, dear," said the ghost. "It's the kiddies I'm here for. Love kiddies, I do. We're going to be ever such friends."

"Go away!" yelled Simon. "This is our house now!"

"No it isn't," said the ghost smugly. "Always been here, I have. A hundred years and more. Seen plenty of families come and go, I have. Go to bye-byes now, there's good children."

The children glared at it and buried themselves under the bedclothes. And, eventually, slept.

The next night it was there again. This time it was smoking a long white pipe and reading a newspaper dated 1842. Beside it was a second grey cloudy shape. "Hello, dearies," said the ghost. "Say how do you do to my Auntie Edna."

"She can't come here too," wailed Marian.

"Oh yes she can," said the ghost. "Always comes here in August, does Auntie. She likes a change."

Auntie Edna was even worse, if possible. She sucked peppermint drops that smelled so strong that Mrs Brown, when she came to kiss the children good night, looked suspiciously under their pillows. She also sang hymns in a loud squeaky voice. The children lay there groaning and the ghosts sang and rustled the newspapers and ate peppermints.

The next night there were three of them. "Meet Uncle Charlie!" said the first ghost. The children groaned.

"And Jip," said the ghost. "Here, Jip, good dog – come and say hello to the kiddies, then." A large grey dog that you could see straight through came out from under the bed, wagging its tail. The cat, who had been curled up beside Marian's feet (it was supposed to sleep in the kitchen, but there are always ways for a resourceful cat to get what it wants), gave a howl and shot on top of the wardrobe, where it sat spitting. The dog lay down in the middle of the rug and set about scratching itself vigorously; evidently it had ghost fleas, too.

Uncle Charlie was unbearable. He had a loud cough that kept going off like a machine-gun and he told the longest most pointless stories the children had ever heard. He said he too loved kiddies and he knew kiddies loved stories. In the middle of the seventh story the children went to sleep out of sheer boredom.

The following week the ghosts left the bedroom and were to be found all over the house. The children had no peace at all. They'd be quietly doing their homework and all of a sudden Auntie Edna would be breathing down their necks reciting arithmetic tables. The original ghost took to sitting on top of the television with his legs in front of the picture. Uncle Charlie told his stories all through the best programmes and the dog lay permanently at the top of the stairs. The Browns' cat became quite hysterical, refused to eat and went to live on the top shelf of the kitchen dresser.

Something had to be done. Marian and Simon also were beginning to show the effects; their mother decided they looked peaky and bought an appalling sticky brown vitamin medicine from the chemists to strengthen them. "It's the ghosts!" wailed the children. "We don't need vitamins!" Their mother said severely that she didn't want to hear another word of this silly nonsense about ghosts. Auntie Edna, who was sitting smirking on the other side of the kitchen table at that very moment, nodded vigorously and took out a packet of humbugs which she sucked noisily.

"We've got to get them to go and live somewhere else," said Marian. But where, that was the problem, and how? It was then that they had a bright idea. On Sunday the Browns were all going to see their uncle who was rather rich and lived alone in a big house with thick carpets everywhere and empty rooms and the biggest colour television you ever saw. Plenty of room for ghosts.

They were very cunning. They suggested to the ghosts that they might like a drive in the country. The ghosts said at first that they were quite comfortable where they were, thank you, and they didn't fancy these new-fangled motor-cars, not at their time of life. But then Auntie Edna remembered that she liked looking at the pretty flowers and the trees and finally they agreed to give it a try. They sat in a row on the back shelf of the car. Mrs Brown kept asking why there was such a strong smell of peppermint and Mr Brown kept roaring at Simon and Marian to keep still while he was driving. The fact was that the ghosts were shoving them; it was like being nudged by three cold damp flannels. And the ghost dog, who had come along too of course, was car-sick.

When they got to Uncle Dick's the ghosts came in and had a look round. They liked the expensive carpets and the enormous television. They slid in and out of the wardrobes and walked through the doors and the walls and sent Uncle Dick's budgerigars into a decline from which they have never recovered. Nice place, they said, nice and comfy.

"Why not stay here?" said Simon, in an offhand tone.

"Couldn't do that," said the ghosts firmly. "No kiddies. Dull. We like a place with a bit of life to it." And they piled back into the car and sang hymns all the way home to the Browns' house. They also ate toast. There were real toast-crumbs on the floor and the children got the blame.

Simon and Marian were in despair. The ruder they were to the ghosts the more the ghosts liked it. "Cheeky!" they said indulgently. "What a cheeky little pair of kiddies! There now . . . come and give uncle a kiss." The children weren't even safe in the bath. One or other of the ghosts would come and sit on the taps and talk to them. Uncle Charlie had produced a mouth organ and played the same tune over and over again; it was quite excruciating. The children went around with their hands over their ears. Mrs Brown took them to the doctor to find out if there was something wrong with their hearing. The children knew better than to say anything to the doctor about the ghosts. It was pointless saying anything to anyone.

I don't know what would have happened if Mrs Brown hadn't happened to make friends with Mrs Walker from down the road. Mrs Walker had twin babies, and one day she brought the babies along for tea.

Now one baby is bad enough. Two babies are trouble in a big way. These babies created pandemonium. When they weren't both howling they were crawling around the floor pulling the tablecloths off the tables or hitting their heads on the chairs and hauling the books out of the bookcases. They threw their food all over the kitchen and flung cups of milk on the floor. Their mother mopped up after them and every time she tried to have a conversation with Mrs Brown the babies bawled in chorus so that no one could hear a word.

In the middle of this the ghosts appeared. One baby was yelling its head off and the other was glueing pieces of chewed up bread onto the front of the television. The ghosts swooped down on them with happy cries. "Oh!" they trilled. "Bless their little hearts then, diddums, give auntie a smile then." And the babies stopped in mid-howl and gazed at the ghosts. The ghosts cooed at the babies and the babies cooed at the ghosts. The ghosts chattered to the babies and sang them songs and the babies chattered back and were as good as gold for the next hour and their mother had the first proper conversation she'd had in weeks. When they went the ghosts stood in a row at the window, waving.

Simon and Marian knew when to seize an opportunity. That evening they had a talk with the ghosts. At first the ghosts raised objections. They didn't fancy the idea of moving, they said; you got set in your ways, at their age; Auntie Edna reckoned a strange house would be the death of her.

The children talked about the babies, relentlessly.

And the next day they led the ghosts down the road, followed by the ghost dog, and into the Walkers' house. Mrs Walker doesn't know to this day why the babies, who had been screaming for the last half hour, suddenly stopped and broke into great smiles. And she has never understood why, from that day forth, the babies became the most tranquil, quiet, amiable babies in the area. The ghosts kept the babies amused from morning to night. The babies thrived; the ghosts were happy; the ghost dog, who was actually a bitch, settled down so well that she had puppies which is one of the most surprising aspects of the whole business. The Brown children heaved a sigh of relief and got back to normal life. The babies, though, I have to tell you, grew up somewhat peculiar.

# 6

# PSYCHIC PHENOMENA

## Signs from the Other Side

# Playing With Fire

## Sir Arthur Conan Doyle

### Prospectus

**Address:** 17, Badderly Gardens, London, England.

**Property:** Nineteenth century three-storey house situated on corner with Merton Park Road. Red-brick building with reception room, large lounge and dining room, plus extensive studio at the rear. Ideal property for an artist.

**Viewing Date:** April 1899.

**Agent:** Sir Arthur Conan Doyle (1859–1930) was born in Edinburgh where he trained to be a doctor and found in his teacher, Dr. Joseph Bell, the model for his immortal detective, Sherlock Holmes. Later, in an attempt to escape from the fame of Holmes, Doyle wrote a number of historical and scientific novels and became fascinated by spiritualism – devoting much of his time and wealth to investigating psychic phenomena. Several of his books reflect this interest, including *Dreamland and Ghostland* (1886), *The Parasite* (1894) and *The Edge of the Unknown* (1930), also the story "Playing With Fire", about a seance which produces a terrible manifestation . . .

I cannot pretend to say what occurred on the 14th of April last at No. 17, Badderly Gardens. Put down in black and white, my surmise might seem too crude, too grotesque, for serious consideration. And yet that something did occur, and that it was of a nature which will leave its mark upon every one of us for the rest of our lives, is as certain as the unanimous testimony of five witnesses can make it. I will not enter into any argument or speculation. I will only give a plain statement, which will be submitted to John Moir, Harvey Deacon, and Mrs. Delamere, and withheld from publication unless they are prepared to corroborate every detail. I cannot obtain the sanction of Paul Le Duc, for he appears to have left the country.

It was John Moir (the well-known senior partner of Moir, Moir, and Sanderson) who had originally turned our attention to occult subjects. He had, like many very hard and practical men of business, a mystic side to his nature, which had led him to the examination, and eventually to the acceptance, of those elusive phenomena which are grouped together with much that is foolish, and much that is fraudulent, under the common heading of spiritualism. His researches, which had begun with an open mind, ended unhappily in dogma, and he became as positive and fanatical as any other bigot. He represented in our little group the body of men who have turned these singular phenomena into a new religion.

Mrs. Delamere, our medium, was his sister, the wife of Delamere, the rising sculptor. Our experience had shown us that to work on these subjects without a medium was as futile as for an astronomer to make observations without a telescope. On the other hand, the introduction of a paid medium was hateful to all of us. Was it not obvious that he or she would feel bound to return some result for money received, and that the temptation to fraud would be an overpowering one? No phenomena could be relied upon which were produced at a guinea an hour. But, fortunately, Moir had discovered that his sister was mediumistic – in other words, that she was a battery of that animal magnetic force which is the only form of energy which is subtle enough to be acted upon from the spiritual plane as well as from our own material one. Of course, when I say this, I do not mean to beg the question; but I am simply indicating the theories upon which we were ourselves, rightly or wrongly, explaining what we saw. The lady came, not altogether with the approval of her husband, and though she never gave indications of any very great psychic force, we were able, at least, to obtain those usual phenomena of message-tilting which are at the same time so puerile and so inexplicable. Every Sunday evening we met in Harvey Deacon's studio at Badderly Gardens, the next house to the corner of Merton Park Road.

Harvey Deacon's imaginative work in art would prepare anyone to find that he was an ardent lover of everything which was *outré* and sensational. A certain picturesqueness in the study of the occult had been the quality which had originally attracted him to it, but his attention was speedily arrested by some of those phenomena to which I have referred, and he was coming rapidly to the conclusion that what he had looked upon as an amusing romance and an after-dinner entertainment was really a very formidable reality. He is a man with a remarkably clear and logical brain – a true descendant of his ancestor, the well-known Scotch professor – and he represented in our small circle the critical element, the man who has no prejudices, is prepared to follow facts as far as he can see them, and refuses to theorise in advance of his data. His caution annoyed Moir as much as the latter's robust faith amused Deacon, but each in his own way was equally keen upon the matter.

And I? What am I to say that I represented? I was not the devotee. I was not the scientific critic. Perhaps the best that I can claim for myself is that I was the dilettante man about town, anxious to be in the swim of every fresh movement, thankful for any new sensation which would take me out of myself and open up fresh possibilities of existence. I am not an enthusiast myself, but I like the company of those who are. Moir's talk, which made me feel as if we had a private pass-key through the door of death, filled me with a vague contentment. The soothing atmosphere of the séance with the darkened lights was delightful to me. In a word, the thing amused me, and so I was there.

It was, as I have said, upon the 14th of April last that the very singular event which I am about to put upon record took place. I was the first of the men to arrive at the studio, but Mrs. Delamere was already there, having had afternoon tea with Mrs. Harvey

Deacon. The two ladies and Deacon himself were standing in front of an unfinished picture of his upon the easel. I am not an expert in art, and I have never professed to understand what Harvey Deacon meant by his pictures; but I could see in this instance that it was all very clever and imaginative, fairies and animals and allegorical figures of all sorts. The ladies were loud in their praises, and indeed the colour effect was a remarkable one.

"What do you think of it, Markham?" he asked.

"Well, it's above me," said I. "These beasts – what are they?"

"Mythical monsters, imaginary creatures, heraldic emblems – a sort of weird, bizarre procession of them."

"With a white horse in front!"

"It's not a horse," said he, rather testily – which was surprising, for he was a very good-humoured fellow as a rule, and hardly ever took himself seriously.

"What is it, then?"

"Can't you see the horn in front? It's a unicorn. I told you they were heraldic beasts. Can't you recognize one?"

"Very sorry, Deacon," said I, for he really seemed to be annoyed.

He laughed at his own irritation.

"Excuse me, Markham!" said he; "the fact is that I have had an awful job over the beast. All day I have been painting him in and painting him out, and trying to imagine what a real live, ramping unicorn would look like. At last I got him, as I hoped; so when you failed to recognise it, it took me on the raw."

"Why, of course it's a unicorn," said I, for he was evidently depressed at my obtuseness. "I can see the horn quite plainly, but I never saw a unicorn except beside the Royal Arms, and so I never thought of the creature. And these others are griffins and cockatrices, and dragons of sorts?"

"Yes, I had no difficulty with them. It was the unicorn which bothered me. However, there's an end of it until to-morrow." He turned the picture round upon the easel, and we all chatted about other subjects.

Moir was late that evening, and when he did arrive he brought with him, rather to our surprise, a small, stout Frenchman, whom he introduced as Monsieur Paul Le Duc. I say to our surprise, for we held a theory that any intrusion into our spiritual circle deranged the conditions, and introduced an element of suspicion. We knew that we could trust each other, but all our results were vitiated by the presence of an outsider. However, Moir soon reconciled us to the innovation. Monsieur Paul Le Duc was a famous student of occultism, a seer, a medium, and a mystic. He was travelling in England with a letter of introduction to Moir from the President of the Parisian brothers of the Rosy Cross. What more natural than that he should bring him to our little séance, or that we should feel honoured by his presence?

He was, as I have said, a small, stout man, undistinguished in appearance, with a broad, smooth, clean-shaven face, remarkable only for a pair of large, brown, velvety eyes, staring vaguely out in front of him. He was well dressed, with the manners of a gentleman, and his curious little turns of English speech set the ladies smiling. Mrs. Deacon had a prejudice against our researches and left the room, upon which we lowered the lights, as was our custom, and drew up our chairs to the square mahogany table which stood in the centre of the studio. The light was subdued, but sufficient to allow us to see each other quite plainly. I remember that I could even observe the curious, podgy little square-topped hands which the Frenchman laid upon the table.

"What a fun!" said he. "It is many years since I have sat in this fashion, and it is to me amusing. Madame is medium. Does madame make the trance?"

"Well, hardly that," said Mrs. Delamere. "But I am always conscious of extreme sleepiness."

"It is the first stage. Then you encourage it, and there comes the trance. When the trance comes, then out jumps your little spirit and in jumps another little spirit, and so you have direct talking or writing. You leave your machine to be worked by another. *Hein?* But what have unicorns to do with it?"

Harvey Deacon started in his chair. The Frenchman was moving his head slowly round and staring into the shadows which draped the walls.

"What a fun!" said he. "Always unicorns. Who has been thinking so hard upon a subject so bizarre?"

"This is wonderful!" cried Deacon. "I have been trying to paint one all day. But how could you know it?"

"You have been thinking of them in this room."

"Certainly."

"But thoughts are things, my friend. When you imagine a thing you make a thing. You did not know it, *hein?* But I can see your unicorns because it is not only with my eye that I can see."

"Do you mean to say that I create a thing which has never existed by merely thinking of it?"

"But certainly. It is the fact which lies under all other facts. That is why an evil thought is also a danger."

"They are, I suppose, upon the astral plane?" said Moir.

"Ah, well, these are but words, my friends. They are there – somewhere – everywhere – I cannot tell myself. I see them. I could touch them."

"You could not make *us* see them."

"It is to materialise them. Hold! It is an experiment. But the power is wanting. Let us see what power we have, and then arrange what we shall do. May I place you as I wish?"

"You evidently know a great deal more about it than we do," said Harvey Deacon; "I wish that you would take complete control."

"It may be that the conditions are not good. But we will try what we can do. Madame will sit where she is, I next, and this gentleman beside me. Meester Moir will sit next to madame, because it is well to have blacks and blondes in turn. So! And now with your permission I will turn the lights all out."

"What is the advantage of the dark?" I asked.

"Because the force with which we deal is a vibration of ether and so also is light. We have the wires all for ourselves now – *hein*? You will not be frightened in the darkness, madame? What a fun is such a séance!"

At first the darkness appeared to be absolutely pitchy, but in a few minutes our eyes became so far accustomed to it that we could just make out each other's presence – very dimly and vaguely, it is true. I could see nothing else in the room – only the black loom of the motionless figures. We were all taking the matter much more seriously than we had ever done before.

"You will place your hands in front. It is hopeless that we touch, since we are so few round so large a table. You will compose yourself, madame, and if sleep should come to you you will not fight against it. And now we sit in silence and we expect – *hein?*"

So we sat in silence and expected, staring out into the blackness in front of us. A clock ticked in the passage. A dog barked intermittently far away. Once or twice a cab rattled past in the street, and the gleam of its lamps through the chink in the curtains was a cheerful break in that gloomy vigil. I felt those physical symptoms with which previous séances had made me familiar – the coldness of the feet, the tingling in the hands, the glow of the palms, the feeling of a cold wind upon the back. Strange little shooting pains came in my forearms, especially as it seemed to me in my left one, which was nearest to our visitor – due no doubt to disturbance of the vascular system, but worthy of some attention all the same. At the same time I was conscious of a strained feeling of expectancy which was almost painful. From the rigid, absolute silence of my companions I gathered that their nerves were as tense as my own.

And then suddenly a sound came out of the darkness – a low, sibilant sound, the quick, thin breathing of a woman. Quicker and thinner yet it came, as between clenched teeth, to end in a loud gasp with a dull rustle of cloth.

"What's that? Is all right?" someone asked in the darkness.

"Yes, all is right," said the Frenchman. "It is madame. She is in her trance. Now, gentlemen, if you will wait quiet you will see something, I think, which will interest you much."

Still the ticking in the hall. Still the breathing, deeper and fuller now, from the medium. Still the occasional flash, more welcome than ever, of the passing lights of the hansoms. What a gap we were bridging, the half-raised veil of the eternal on the one side and the cabs of London on the other. The table was throbbing with a mighty pulse. It swayed steadily, rhythmically, with an easy swooping, scooping motion under our fingers. Sharp little raps and cracks came from its substance, file-firing, volley-firing, the sounds of a fagot burning briskly on a frosty night.

"There is much power," said the Frenchman. "See it on the table!"

I had thought it was some delusion of my own, but all could see it now. There was a greenish-yellow phosphorescent light – or I should say a luminous vapour rather than a light – which lay over the surface of the table. It rolled and wreathed and undulated in dim glimmering folds, turning and swirling like clouds of smoke. I could see the white, square-ended hands of the French medium in this baleful light.

"What a fun!" he cried. "It is splendid!"

"Shall we call the alphabet?" asked Moir.

"But no – for we can do much better," said our visitor. "It is but a clumsy thing to tilt the table for every letter of the alphabet, and with such a medium as madame we should do better than that."

"Yes, you will do better," said a voice.

"Who was that? Who spoke? Was that you, Markham?"

"No, I did not speak."

"It was madame who spoke."

"But it was not her voice."

"Is that you, Mrs. Delamere?"

"It is not the medium, but it is the power which uses the organs of the medium," said the strange, deep voice.

"Where is Mrs. Delamere? It will not hurt her, I trust."

"The medium is happy in another plane of existence. She has taken my place, as I have taken hers."

"Who are you?"

"It cannot matter to you who I am. I am one who has lived as you are living, and who has died as you will die."

We heard the creak and grate of a cab pulling up next door. There was an argument about the fare, and the cabman grumbled hoarsely down the street. The green-yellow cloud still swirled faintly over the table, dull elsewhere, but glowing into a dim luminosity in the direction of the medium. It seemed to be piling itself up in front of her. A sense of fear and cold struck into my heart. It seemed to me that lightly and flippantly we had approached the most real and august of sacraments, that communion with the dead of which the fathers of the Church had spoken.

"Don't you think we are going too far? Should we not break up this séance?" I cried.

But the others were all earnest to see the end of it. They laughed at my scruples.

"All the powers are made for use," said Harvey Deacon. "If we *can* do this, we *should* do this. Every new departure of knowledge has been called unlawful in its inception. It is right and proper that we should inquire into the nature of death."

"It is right and proper," said the voice.

"There, what more could you ask?" cried Moir, who was much excited. "Let us have a test. Will you give us a test that you are really there?"

"What test do you demand?"

"Well, now – I have some coins in my pocket. Will you tell me how many?"

"We come back in the hope of teaching and of elevating, and not to guess childish riddles."

"Ha, ha, Meester Moir, you catch it that time," cried the Frenchman. "But surely this is very good sense what the Control is saying."

"It is a religion, not a game," said the cold, hard voice.

"Exactly – the very view I take of it," cried Moir. "I am sure I am very sorry if I have asked a foolish question. You will not tell me who you are?"

"What does it matter?"

"Have you been a spirit long?"

"Yes."

"How long?"

"We cannot reckon time as you do. Our conditions are different."

"Are you happy?"

"Yes."

"You would not wish to come back to life?"

"No – certainly not."

"Are you busy?"

"We could not be happy if we were not busy."

"What do you do?"

"I have said that the conditions are entirely different."

"Can you give us no idea of your work?"

"We labour for our own improvement and for the advancement of others."

"Do you like coming here to-night?"

"I am glad to come if I can do any good by coming."

"Then to do good is your object?"

"It is the object of all life on every plane."

"You see, Markham, that should answer your scruples."

It did, for my doubts had passed and only interest remained.

"Have you pain in your life?" I asked.

"No; pain is a thing of the body."

"Have you mental pain?"

"Yes; one may always be sad or anxious."

"Do you meet the friends whom you have known on earth?"

"Some of them."

"Why only some of them?"

"Only those who are sympathetic."

"Do husbands meet wives?"

"Those who have truly loved."

"And the others?"

"They are nothing to each other."

"There must be a spiritual connection?"

"Of course."

"Is what we are doing right?"

"If done in the right spirit."

"What is the wrong spirit?"

"Curiosity and levity."

"May harm come of that?"

"Very serious harm."

"What sort of harm?"

"You may call up forces over which you have no control."

"Evil forces?"

"Undeveloped forces."

"You say they are dangerous. Dangerous to body or mind?"

"Sometimes to both."

There was a pause, and the blackness seemed to grow blacker still, while the yellow-green fog swirled and smoked upon the table.

"Any questions you would like to ask, Moir?" said Harvey Deacon.

"Only this – do you pray in your world?"

"One should pray in every world."

"Why?"

"Because it is the acknowledgment of forces outside ourselves."

"What religion do you hold over there?"

"We differ exactly as you do."

"You have no certain knowledge?"

"We have only faith."

"These questions of religion," said the Frenchman, "they are of interest to you serious English people, but they are not so much fun. It seems to me that with this power here we might be able to have some great experience – *hein?* Something of which we could talk."

"But nothing could be more interesting than this," said Moir.

"Well, if you think so, that is very well," the Frenchman answered, peevishly. "For my part, it seems to me that I have heard all this before, and that tonight I should weesh to try some experiment with all this force which is given to us. But if you have other questions, then ask them, and when you are finish we can try something more."

But the spell was broken. We asked and asked, but the medium sat silent in her chair. Only her deep, regular breathing showed that she was there. The mist still swirled upon the table.

"You have disturbed the harmony. She will not answer."

"But we have learned already all that she can tell – *hein?* For my part I wish to see something that I have never seen before."

"What then?"

"You will let me try?"

"What would you do?"

"I have said to you that thoughts are things. Now I wish to *prove* it to you, and to show you that which is only a thought. Yes, yes, I can do it and you will see. Now I ask you only to sit still and say nothing, and keep ever your hands quiet upon the table."

The room was blacker and more silent than ever. The same feeling of apprehension which had lain heavily upon me at the beginning of the séance was back at my heart once more. The roots of my hair were tingling.

"It is working! It is working!" cried the Frenchman, and there was a crack in his voice as he spoke which told me that he also was strung to his tightest.

The luminous fog drifted slowly off the table, and wavered and flickered across the room. There in the farther and darkest corner it gathered and glowed, hardening down into a shining core – a strange, shifty, luminous, and yet non-illuminating patch of radiance, bright itself, but throwing no rays into the darkness. It had changed from a greenish-yellow to a dusky sullen red. Then round this centre there coiled a dark, smoky substance, thickening, hardening, growing denser and blacker. And then the light went out, smothered in that which had grown round it.

"It has gone."

"Hush – there's something in the room."

We heard it in the corner where the light had been, something which breathed deeply and fidgeted in the darkness.

"What is it? Le Duc, what have you done?"

"It is all right. No harm will come." The Frenchman's voice was treble with agitation.

"Good heavens, Moir, there's a large animal in the room. Here it is, close by my chair! Go away! Go away!"

It was Harvey Deacon's voice, and then came the sound of a blow upon some hard object. And then . . . And then . . . how can I tell you what happened then?

Some huge thing hurtled against us in the darkness, rearing, stamping, smashing, springing, snorting. The table was splintered. We were scattered in every direction. It clattered and scrambled amongst us, rushing with horrible energy from one corner of the room to another. We were all screaming with fear, grovelling upon our hands and knees to get away from it. Something trod upon my left hand, and I felt the bones splinter under the weight.

"A light! A light!" someone yelled.

"Moir, you have matches, matches!"

"No, I have none. Deacon, where are the matches? For God's sake, the matches!"

"I can't find them. Here, you Frenchman, stop it!"

"It is beyond me. Oh, *mon Dieu*, I cannot stop it. The door! Where is the door?"

My hand, by good luck, lit upon the handle as I groped about in the darkness. The hard-breathing, snorting, rushing creature tore past me and butted with a fearful crash against the oaken partition. The instant that it had passed I turned the handle, and next moment we were all outside, and the door shut behind us. From within came a horrible crashing and rending and stamping.

"What is it? In Heaven's name, what is it?"

"A horse. I saw it when the door opened. But Mrs. Delamere—?"

"We must fetch her out. Come on, Markham; the longer we wait the less we shall like it."

He flung open the door and we rushed in. She was there on the ground amidst the splinters of her chair. We seized her and dragged her swiftly out, and as we gained the door I looked over my shoulder into the darkness. There were two strange eyes glowing at us, a rattle of hoofs, and I had just time to slam the door when there came a crash upon it which split it from top to bottom.

"It's coming through! It's coming!"

"Run, run for your lives!" cried the Frenchman.

Another crash, and something shot through the riven door. It was a long white spike, gleaming in the lamplight. For a moment it shone before us, and then with a snap it disappeared again.

"Quick! Quick! This way!" Harvey Deacon shouted. "Carry her in! Here! Quick!"

We had taken refuge in the dining-room, and shut the heavy oak door. We laid the senseless woman upon the sofa, and as we did so, Moir, the hard man of business, drooped and fainted across the hearthrug. Harvey Deacon was as white as a corpse, jerking and twitching like an epileptic. With a crash we heard the studio door fly to pieces, and the snorting and stamping were in the passage, up and down, up and down, shaking the house with their fury. The Frenchman had sunk his face on his hands, and sobbed like a frightened child.

"What shall we do?" I shook him roughly by the shoulder. "Is a gun any use?"

"No, no. The power will pass. Then it will end."

"You might have killed us all – you unspeakable fool – with your infernal experiments."

"I did not know. How could I tell that it would be frightened? It is mad with terror. It was his fault. He struck it."

Harvey Deacon sprang up. "Good heavens!" he cried.

A terrible scream sounded through the house.

"It's my wife! Here, I'm going out. If it's the Evil One himself I am going out!"

He had thrown open the door and rushed out into the passage. At the end of it, at the foot of the stairs, Mrs. Deacon was lying senseless, struck down by the sight which she had seen. But there was nothing else.

With eyes of horror we looked about us, but all was perfectly quiet and still. I approached the black square of the studio door, expecting with every slow step that some atrocious shape would hurl itself out of it. But nothing came, and all was silent inside the room. Peeping and peering, our hearts in our mouths, we came to the very threshold, and stared into the darkness. There was still no sound, but in one direction there was also no darkness. A luminous, glowing cloud, with an incandescent centre, hovered in the corner of the room. Slowly it dimmed and faded, growing thinner and fainter, until at last the same dense, velvety blackness filled the whole studio. And with the last flickering gleam of that baleful light the Frenchman broke into a shout of joy.

"What a fun!" he cried. "No one is hurt, and only the door

broken, and the ladies frightened. But, my friends, we have done what has never been done before."

"And as far as I can help," said Harvey Deacon, "it will certainly never be done again."

And that was what befell on the 14th of April last at No. 17 Badderly Gardens. I began by saying that it would seem too grotesque to dogmatise as to what it was which actually did occur; but I give my impressions, *our* impressions (since they are corroborated by Harvey Deacon and John Moir), for what they are worth. You may, if it pleases you, imagine that we were the victims of an elaborate and extraordinary hoax. Or you may think with us that we underwent a very real and a very terrible experience. Or perhaps you may know more than we do of such occult matters, and can inform us of some similar occurrence. In this latter case a letter to William Markham, 146M, The Albany, would help to throw a light upon that which is very dark to us.

# The Whistling Room

## William Hope Hodgson

### Prospectus

**Address:** Iastrae Castle, near Galway, Ireland.

**Property:** Medieval castellated building with later additions. The property has two wings, extensive living accommodation, a fine gallery and library. The maze of corridors are decorated with oak-panels throughout.

**Viewing Date:** Summer, 1909.

**Agent:** William Hope Hodgson (1877–1918) was born in Blackmore End, Essex, and after running away to sea as a teenager, used his experiences afloat as the basis for his early stories and best-selling novel, *The Boats of the Glen Carrig* (1907). He also became fascinated with the supernatural and wrote a series of stories about an occult detective known simply as Carnacki, who relates his cases as a ghost hunter to a circle of friends. Three of these cases feature haunted houses, "The Searcher of the End House", "The House Among The Laurels" and "The Whistling Room", which is set in an Irish castle where *something* truly horrifying lies in wait for the unwary.

Carnacki shook a friendly fist at me as I entered, late. Then he opened the door into the dining room and ushered the four of us – Jessop, Arkright, Taylor and myself – in to dinner.

We dined well, as usual, and equally as usual Carnacki was pretty silent during the meal. At the end we took our wine and cigars to our accustomed positions and Carnacki – having got himself comfortable in his big chair – began without any preliminary:-

"I have just got back from Ireland, again," he said. "And I thought you chaps would be interested to hear my news. Besides, I fancy I shall see the thing clearer after I have told it all out straight. I must tell you this, though, at the beginning – up to the present moment I have been utterly and completely 'stumped.' I have tumbled upon one of the most peculiar cases of 'haunting' – or devilment of some sort – that I have come against. Now listen.

"I have been spending the last few weeks at Iastrae Castle, about twenty miles north east of Galway. I got a letter about a month ago from a Mr. Sid K. Tassoc, who it seemed had bought the place lately and moved in, only to find that he had got a very peculiar piece of property.

"When I reached there he met me at the station, driving a jaunting-car and drove me up to the castle, which by the way, he called a 'house-shanty.' I found that he was 'pigging it' there with his boy brother and another American who seemed to be half-servant and half-companion. It appears that all the servants had left the place, in a body, as you might say, and now they were managing among themselves, assisted by some day-help.

"The three of them got together a scratch feed and Tassoc told me all about the trouble whilst we were at table. It is most extraordinary and different from anything that I have had to do with, though that Buzzing Case was very queer too.

"Tassoc began right in the middle of his story. 'We've got a room in this shanty,' he said, 'which has got a most infernal whistling in it, sort of haunting it. The thing starts any time, you never know when, and it goes on until it frightens you. It's not ordinary whistling and it isn't the wind. Wait till you hear it."

" 'We're all carrying guns,' said the boy, and slapped his coat pocket.

" 'As bad as that?' I said, and the older brother nodded. 'I may be soft,' he replied, 'but wait till you've heard it. Sometimes I think it's some infernal thing and the next moment I'm just as sure that someone's playing a trick on us."

"'Why?' I asked. 'What is to be gained?'

"'You mean,' he said, 'that people usually have some good reason for playing tricks as elaborate as this. Well, I'll tell you. There's a lady in this province by the name of Miss Donnehue who's going to be my wife, this day two months. She's more beautiful than they make them, and so far as I can see, I've just stuck my head into an Irish hornet's nest. There's about a score of hot young Irishmen been courting her these two years gone and now that I've come along and cut them out they feel raw against me. Do you begin to understand the possibilities?"

"'Yes,' I said. 'Perhaps I do in a vague sort of way, but I don't see how all this affects the room?'

"'Like this,' he said. 'When I'd fixed it up with Miss Donnehue I looked out for a place and bought this little house-shanty. Afterwards I told her – one evening during dinner – that I'd decided to tie up here. And then she asked me whether I wasn't afraid of the whistling room. I told her it must have been thrown in gratis, as I'd heard nothing about it. There were some of her men friends present and I saw a smile go round. I found out after a bit of questioning that several people have bought this place during the last twenty odd years. And it was always on the market again, after a trial.

"'Well, the chaps started to bait me a bit and offered to take bets after dinner that I'd not stay six months in this shanty. I looked once or twice at Miss Donnehue so as to be sure I was "getting the note" of the talkee-talkee, but I could see that she didn't take it as a joke at all. Partly, I think, because there was a bit of a sneer in the way the men were tackling me and partly because she really believes there is something in this yarn of the whistling room.

"'However, after dinner I did what I could to even things up with the others. I nailed all their bets and screwed them down good and safe. I guess some of them are going to be hard hit, unless I lose; which I don't mean to. Well, there you have practically the whole yarn.'

" 'Not quite,' I told him. 'All that I know is that you have bought a castle with a room in it that is in some way "queer," and that you've been doing some betting. Also, I know that your servants have got frightened and run away. Tell me something about the whistling?'

" 'O, that!' said Tassoc. 'That started the second night we were in. I'd had a good look round the room in the daytime, as you can understand; for the talk up at Arlestrae – Miss Donnehue's place – had me wonder a bit. But it seems just as usual as some of the other rooms in the old wing only perhaps a bit more lonesome feeling. But that may be only because of the talk about it, you know.

" 'The whistling started about ten o'clock on the second night, as I said. Tom and I were in the library when we heard an awfully queer whistling coming along the East Corridor – the room is in the East Wing, you know.

" ' "That's that blessed ghost!" I said to Tom and we collared the lamps off the table and went up to have a look. I tell you, even as we dug along the corridor it took me a bit in the throat, it was so beastly queer. It was a sort of tune in a way, but more as if a devil or some rotten thing were laughing at you and going to get round at your back. That's how it makes you feel.

" 'When we got to the door we didn't wait, but rushed it open, and then I tell you the sound of the thing fairly hit me in the face. Tom said he got it the same way – sort of felt stunned and bewildered. We looked all round and soon got so nervous, we just cleared out and I locked the door.

" 'We came down here and had a stiff peg each. Then we landed fit again and began to feel we'd been nicely had. So we took sticks and went out into the grounds, thinking after all it must be some of these confounded Irishmen working the ghost-trick on us. But there was not a leg stirring.

" 'We went back into the house and walked over it and then paid another visit to the room. But we simply couldn't stand it. We fairly ran out and locked the door again. I don't know how to put it into words, but I had a feeling of being up against something that was rottenly dangerous. You know! We've carried our guns ever since.

" 'Of course we had a real turn-out of the room next day and the whole house-place, and we even hunted round the grounds but there was nothing queer. And now I don't know what to think, except that the sensible part of me tells me that it's some plan of these Wild Irishmen to try to take a rise out of me.'

" 'Done anything since?' I asked him.

" 'Yes,' he said. 'Watched outside of the door of the room at night and chased round the grounds and sounded the walls and floor of the room. We've done everything we could think of and it's beginning to get on our nerves, so we sent for you.'

"By this we had finished eating. As we rose from the table Tassoc suddenly called out: – 'Ssh! Hark!'

"We were instantly silent, listening. Then I heard it, an extraordinary hooning whistle, monstrous and inhuman, coming from far away through corridors to my right.

" 'By God!' said Tassoc, 'and it's scarcely dark yet! Collar those candles, both of you and come along.'

"In a few moments we were all out of the door and racing up the stairs. Tassoc turned into a long corridor and we followed, shielding our candles as we ran. The sound seemed to fill all the passage as we drew near, until I had the feeling that the whole air throbbed under the power of some wanton Immense Force – a sense of an actual taint, as you might say, of monstrosity all about us.

"Tassoc unlocked the door then, giving it a push with his foot, jumped back and drew his revolver. As the door flew open the sound beat out at us with an effect impossible to explain to one who has not heard it – with a certain, horrible personal note in it, as if in there in the darkness you could picture the room rocking and creaking in a mad, vile glee to its own filthy piping and whistling and hooning, and yet all the time aware of you in particular. To stand there and listen was to be stunned by Realisation. It was as if someone showed you the mouth of a vast pit suddenly and said: – That's Hell. And you *knew* that they had spoken the truth. Do you get it, even a little bit?

"I stepped a pace into the room and held the candle over my head and looked quickly round. Tassoc and his brother joined me and the man came up at the back and we all held our candles high. I was deafened with the shrill, piping hoon of the whistling and then, clear in my ear something seemed to be saying to me: – 'Get out of here – quick! Quick! Quick!'

"As you chaps know, I never neglect that sort of thing. Sometimes it may be nothing but nerves, but as you will remember, it was just such a warning that saved me in the 'Grey Dog' Case and in the 'Yellow Finger' Experiments, as well as other times. Well, I turned sharp round to the others: 'Out!' I said. 'For God's sake, *out* quick!' And in an instant I had them into the passage.

"There came an extraordinary yelling scream into the hideous whistling and then, like a clap of thunder, an utter silence. I slammed the door, and locked it. Then, taking the key, I looked round at the others. They were pretty white and I imagine I must have looked that way too. And there we stood a moment, silent.

" 'Come down out of this and have some whisky,' said Tassoc, at last, in a voice he tried to make ordinary; and he led the way. I was the back man and I knew we all kept looking over our shoulders. When we got downstairs Tassoc passed the bottle round. He took a drink himself and slapped his glass on to the table. Then sat down with a thud.

" 'That's a lovely thing to have in the house with you, isn't it!' he said. And directly afterwards:– 'What on earth made you hustle us all out like that, Carnacki?'

" 'Something seemed to be telling me to get out, *quick*,' I said. 'Sounds a bit silly – superstitious, I know, but when you are meddling with this sort of thing you've got to take notice of queer fancies and risk being laughed at.'

"I told him then about the 'Grey Dog' business and he nodded a lot to that. 'Of course,' I said, 'this may be nothing more than those would-be rivals of yours playing some funny game, but personally, though I'm going to keep an open mind, I feel that there is something beastly and dangerous about this thing.'

"We talked for a while longer and then Tassoc suggested billiards, which we played in a pretty half-hearted fashion, and all the time cocking an ear to the door as you might say, for sounds; but none came, and later after coffee he suggested early bed and a thorough overhaul of the room on the morrow.

"My bedroom was in the newer part of the castle and the door opened into the picture gallery. At the East end of the gallery was the entrance to the corridor of the East Wing; this was shut off from the gallery by two old and heavy oak doors which looked rather odd and quaint beside the more modern doors of the various rooms.

"When I reached my room I did not go to bed, but began to unpack my instrument-trunk, of which I had retained the key. I intended to take one or two preliminary steps at once in my investigation of the extraordinary whistling.

"Presently, when the castle had settled into quietness, I slipped out of my room and across to the entrance of the great corridor. I opened one of the low, squat doors and threw the beam of my pocket search-light down the passage. It was empty and I went through the doorway and pushed-to the oak behind me. Then along the great passage-way, throwing my light before and behind and keeping my revolver handy.

"I had hung a 'protection belt' of garlic round my neck and the smell of it seemed to fill the corridor and give me assurance; for as you all know, it is a wonderful 'protection' against the more usual Aeiirii forms of semi-materialisation by which I supposed the whistling might be produced, though at that period of my investigation I was still quite prepared to find it due to some perfectly natural cause, for it is astonishing the enormous number of cases that prove to have nothing abnormal in them.

"In addition to wearing the necklet I had plugged my ears loosely with garlic and as I did not intend to stay more than a few minutes in the room, I hoped to be safe.

"When I reached the door and put my hand into my pocket for the key I had a sudden feeling of sickening funk. But I was not going to back out if I could help it. I unlocked the door and turned the handle. Then I gave the door a sharp push with my foot, as Tassoc had done, and drew my revolver, though I did not expect to have any use for it, really.

"I shone the searchlight all round the room and then stepped inside with a disgustingly horrible feeling of walking slap into a waiting Danger. I stood a few seconds, expectant, and nothing happened and the empty room showed bare from corner to corner. And then, you know, I realised that the room was full of an abominable silence – can you understand that? A sort of purposeful silence, just as sickening as any of the filthy noises the Things have power to make. Do you remember what I told you about that 'Silent Garden' business? Well this room had just that same *malevolent* silence – the beastly quietness of a thing that is looking at you and not seeable itself, and thinks that it has got you. O, I recognised it instantly and I shipped the top off my lantern so as to have light over the *whole* room.

"Then I set-to working like fury and keeping my glance all about me. I sealed the two windows with lengths of human hair, right across, and sealed them at every frame. As I worked a queer, scarcely perceptible tenseness stole into the air of the place and the silence seemed, if you can understand me, to grow more solid. I knew then that I had no business there without 'full protection,' for I was practically certain that this was no mere Aeiirii development, but one of the worse forms as the Saiitii, that 'Grunting Man' case – you know.

"I finished the window and hurried over to the great fireplace. This is a huge affair and has a queer gallows-iron, I think they are called, projecting from the back of the arch. I sealed the opening with seven human hairs – the seventh crossing the six others.

"Then just as I was making an end, a low, mocking whistle grew in the room. A cold, nervous prickling went up my spine and round my forehead from the back. The hideous sound filled all the room with an extraordinary, grotesque parody of human whistling, too gigantic to be human – as if something gargantuan and monstrous made the sounds softly. As I stood there a last moment, pressing down the final seal, I had little doubt but that I had come across one of those rare and horrible cases of the *Inanimate* reproducing the functions of the *Animate*. I made a grab for my lamp and went quickly to the door, looking over my shoulder and listening for the thing that I expected. It came just as I got my hand upon the handle – a squeal of incredible, malevolent anger, piercing through the low hooning of the whistling. I dashed out, slamming the door and locking it.

"I leant a little against the opposite wall of the corridor, feeling rather funny for it had been a hideously narrow squeak . . . 'thyr be noe sayfetie to be gained bye gayrds of holieness when the monyster hath pow'r to speak throe woode and stoene.' So runs the passage in the Sigsand MS. and I proved it in that 'Nodding Door' business. There is no protection against this particular form of monster, except possibly for a fractional period of time; for it can reproduce itself in or take to its purposes the very protective material which you may use and has power to '*forme* wythine the pentycle', though not immediately. There is, of course, the possibility of the Unknown Last Line of the Saaamaaa Ritual being uttered but it is too uncertain to count upon and the danger is too hideous and even then it has no power to protect for more than 'maybe fyve beats of the harte' as the Sigsand has it.

"Inside of the room there was now a constant, meditative, hooning whistling, but presently this ceased and the silence seemed worse for there is such a sense of hidden mischief in a silence.

"After a little I sealed the door with crossed hairs and then cleared off down the great passage and so to bed.

"For a long time I lay awake, but managed eventually to get some sleep. Yet, about two o'clock I was waked by the hooning whistling of the room coming to me, even through the closed doors. The sound was tremendous and seemed to beat through the whole house with a presiding sense of terror. As if (I remember thinking) some monstrous giant had been holding mad carnival with itself at the end of that great passage.

"I got up and sat on the edge of the bed, wondering whether to go along and have a look at the seal and suddenly there came a thump on my door and Tassoc walked in with his dressing-gown over his pyjamas.

" 'I thought it would have waked you so I came along to have a talk,' he said. '*I* can't sleep. Beautiful! Isn't it?'

" 'Extraordinary!' I said, and tossed him my case.

"He lit a cigarette and we sat and talked for about an hour, and all the time that noise went on down at the end of the big corridor.

"Suddenly Tassoc stood up: –

" 'Let's take our guns and go and examine the brute,' he said, and turned towards the door.

" 'No!' I said. 'By Jove – NO! I can't say anything definite yet but I believe that room is about as dangerous at it well can be.'

" 'Haunted – *really* haunted?' he asked, keenly and without any of his frequent banter.

"I told him, of course, that I could not say a definite *yes* or *no* to such a question, but that I hoped to be able to make a statement soon. Then I gave him a little lecture on the False Re-Materialisation of the Animate-Force through the Inanimate-Inert. He began then to understand the particular way in which the room might be dangerous, if it were really the subject of a manifestation.

"About an hour later the whistling ceased quite suddenly and Tassoç went off again to bed. I went back to mine also, and eventually got another spell of sleep.

"In the morning I walked along to the room. I found the seals on the door intact. Then I went in. The window seals and the hair were all right, but the seventh hair across the great fireplace was broken. This set me thinking. I knew that it might, very possibly have snapped, through my having tensioned it too highly; but then, again, it might have been broken by something else. Yet it was scarcely possible that a man, for instance, could have passed between the six unbroken hairs for no one would ever have noticed them, entering the room that way, you see; but just walked through them, ignorant of their very existence.

"I removed the other hairs and the seals. Then I looked up the chimney. It went up straight and I could see blue sky at the top. It was a big, open flue and free from any suggestion of hiding places or corners. Yet, of course, I did not trust to any such casual examination and after breakfast I put on my overalls and climbed to the very top, sounding all the way, but I found nothing.

"Then I came down and went over the whole of the room – floor, ceiling and the walls, mapping them out in six-inch squares and sounding with both hammer and probe. But there was nothing unusual.

"Afterwards I made a three-weeks' search of the whole castle in the same thorough way, but found nothing. I went even further then for at night, when the whistling commenced I made a microphone test. You see, if the whistling were mechanically produced this test would have made evident to me the working of the machinery if there were any such concealed within the walls. It certainly was an up-to-date method of examination, as you must allow.

"Of course I did not think that any of Tassoc's rivals had fixed up any mechanical contrivance, but I thought it just possible that there had been some such thing for producing the whistling made away back in the years, perhaps with the intention of giving the room a reputation that would insure its being free of inquisitive folk. You see what I mean? Well of course it was just possible, if this were the case, that someone knew the secret of the machinery and was utilizing the knowledge to play this devil of a prank on Tassoc. The microphone test of the walls would certainly have made this known to me, as I have said, but there was nothing of the sort in the castle so that I had practically no doubt at all now but that it was a genuine case of what is popularly termed 'haunting.'

"All this time, every night, and sometimes most of each night the hooning whistling of the Room was intolerable. It was as if an Intelligence there knew that steps were being taken against it and piped and hooned in a sort of mad, mocking contempt. I tell you, it was as extraordinary as it was horrible. Time after time I went along – tiptoeing noiselessly on stockinged feet – to the sealed floor (for I always kept the Room sealed). I went at all hours of the night and often the whistling inside would seem to change to a brutally jeering note, as though the half-animate monster saw me plainly through the shut door. And all the time as I would stand, watching, the hooning of the whistling would seem to fill the whole corridor so that I used to feel a precious lonely chap messing about there with one of Hell's mysteries.

"And every morning I would enter the room and examine the different hairs and seals. You see, after the first week, I had stretched parallel hairs all along the walls of the room and along the ceiling, but over the floor which was of polished stone I had set out little colourless wafers, tacky-side uppermost. Each wafer was numbered and they were arranged after a definite plan so that I should be able to trace the exact movements of any living thing that went across.

"You will see that no material being or creature could possibly have entered that room without leaving many signs to tell me about it. But nothing was ever disturbed and I began to think that I should have to risk an attempt to stay a night in the room in the Electric Pentacle. Mind you, I *knew* that it would be a crazy thing to do, but I was getting stumped and ready to try anything.

"Once, about midnight, I did break the seal on the door and have a quick look in, but I tell you, the whole Room gave one mad yell and seemed to come towards me in a great belly of shadows as if the walls had bellied in towards me. Of course, that must have been fancy. Anyway, the yell was sufficient and I slammed the door and locked it, feeling a bit weak down my spine. I wonder whether you know the feeling.

"And then when I had got to that state of readiness for anything I made what, at first, I thought was something of a discovery:

" 'Twas about one in the morning and I was walking slowly round the castle, keeping in the soft grass. I had come under the shadow of the East Front and far above me I could hear the vile, hooning whistling of the Room up in the darkness of the unlit wing. Then suddenly, a little in front of me, I heard a man's voice speaking low, but evidently in glee: –

" 'By George! You chaps, but I wouldn't care to bring a wife home to that!' it said, in the tone of the cultured Irish.

"Someone started to reply, but there came a sharp exclamation and then a rush and I heard footsteps running in all directions. Evidently the men had spotted me.

"For a few seconds I stood there feeling an awful ass. After all, *they* were at the bottom of the haunting! Do you see what a big fool it made me seem? I had no doubt but that they were some of Tassoc's rivals and here I had been feeling in every bone that I had hit a genuine Case! And then, you know, there came the memory of hundreds of details that made me just as much in doubt again. Anyway, whether it was natural or abnatural, there was a great deal yet to be cleared up.

"I told Tassoc next morning what I had discovered and through the whole of every night for five nights we kept a close watch round the East Wing, but there was never a sign of anyone prowling about and all this time, almost from evening to dawn, that grotesque whistling would hoon incredibly, far above us in the darkness.

"On the morning after the fifth night I received a wire from here which brought me home by the next boat. I explained to Tassoc that I was simply bound to come away for a few days, but told him to keep up the watch round the castle. One thing I was very careful to do and that was to make him absolutely promise never to go into the Room between sunset and sunrise. I made it clear to him that we knew nothing definite yet, one way or the other, and if the room were what I had first thought it to be, it might be a lot better for him to die first than enter it after dark.

"When I got here and had finished my business I thought you chaps would be interested and also I wanted to get it all spread out clear in my mind, so I rang you up. I am going over again tomorrow and when I get back I ought to have something pretty extraordinary to tell you. By the way, there is a curious thing I forgot to tell you. I tried to get a phonographic record of the whistling, but it simply produced no impression on the wax at all. That is one of the things that has made me feel queer.

"Another extraordinary thing is that the microphone will not magnify the sound – will not even transmit it, seems to take not account of it and acts as if it were nonexistent. I am absolutely and utterly stumped up to the present. I am a wee bit curious to see whether any of you dear clever heads can make daylight of it. *I* cannot – not yet."

He rose to his feet.

"Good-night, all," he said, and began to usher us out abruptly, but without offence, into the night.

A fortnight later he dropped us each a card and you can imagine that I was not late this time. When we arrived Carnacki took us straight into dinner and when we had finished and all made ourselves comfortable he began again, where he had left off:-

"Now just listen quietly, for I have got something very queer to tell you. I got back late at night and I had to walk up to the castle as I had not warned them that I was coming. It was bright moonlight, so that the walk was rather a pleasure than otherwise. When I got there the whole place was in darkness and I thought I would go round outside to see whether Tassoc or his brother was keeping watch. But I could not find them anywhere and concluded that they had got tired of it and gone off to bed.

"As I returned across the lawn that lies below the front of the East Wing I caught the hooning whistling of the Room coming down strangely clear through the stillness of the night. It had a peculiar note in it I remember – low and constant, queerly meditative. I looked up at the window, bright in the moonlight, and got a sudden thought to bring a ladder from the stable-yard and try to get a look into the Room from the outside.

"With this notion I hunted round at the back of the castle among the straggle of the office and presently found a long, fairly light ladder, though it was heavy enough for one, goodness knows! I thought at first that I should never get it reared. I managed at last and let the ends rest very quietly against the wall a little below the sill of the larger window. Then, going silently, I went up the ladder. Presently I had my face above the sill and was looking in, alone with the moonlight.

"Of course the queer whistling sounded louder up there, but it still conveyed that peculiar sense of something whistling quietly to itself – can you understand? Though for all the meditative lowness of the note, the horrible, gargantuan quality was distinct – a mighty parody of the human, as if I stood there and listened to the whistling from the lips of a monster with a man's soul.

"And then, you know, I saw something. The floor in the middle of the huge, empty room was puckered upwards in the centre into a strange, soft-looking mound parted at the top into an everchanging hole that pulsated to that great, gentle hooning. At times, as I watched, I saw the heaving of the indented mound gap across with a queer, inward suction as with the drawing of an enormous breath, then the thing would dilate and pout once more to the incredible melody. And suddenly as I stared, dumb, it came to me that the thing was living. I was looking at two enormous, blackened lips, blistered and brutal, there in the pale moonlight . . .

"Abruptly they bulged out to a vast pouting mound of force and sound, stiffened and swollen and hugely massive and clean-cut in the moonbeams. And a great sweat lay heavy on the vast upper-lip. In the same moment of time the whistling had burst into a mad screaming note that seemed to stun me, even where I stood, outside of the window. And then the following moment I was staring blankly at the solid, undisturbed floor of the room – smooth, polished stone flooring from wall to wall. And there was an absolute silence.

"You can picture me staring into the quiet Room and knowing what I knew. I felt like a sick, frightened child and I wanted to slide *quietly* down the ladder and run away. But in that very instant I heard Tassoc's voice calling to me from within the Room for help, *help*. My God! but I got such an awful dazed feeling and I had a vague, bewildered notion that after all, it was the Irishmen who had got him in there and were taking it out of him. And then the call came again and I burst the window and jumped in to help him. I had a confused idea that the call had come from within the shadow of the great fireplace and I raced across to it, but there was no one there.

"'Tassoc!' I shouted, and my voice went empty-sounding round the great apartment, and then in a flash *I knew that Tassoc had never called.* I whirled round, sick with fear, towards the window and as I did so a frightful, exultant whistling scream burst through the Room. On my left the end wall had bellied-in towards me in a pair of gargantuan lips, black and utterly monstrous, to within a yard of my face. I fumbled for a mad instant at my revolver; not for *it*, but myself, for the danger was a thousand times worse than death. And then suddenly the Unknown Last Line of the Saaamaaa Ritual was whispered quite audibly in the room. Instantly the thing happened that I have known once before. There came a sense as of dust falling continually and monotonously and I knew that my life hung uncertain and suspended for a flash in a brief, reeling vertigo of unseeable things. Then *that* ended and I knew that I might live. My soul and body blended again and life and power came to me. I dashed furiously at the window and hurled myself out headforemost, for I can tell you that I had stopped being afraid of death. I crashed down on to the ladder and slithered, grabbing and grabbing and so came some way or other alive to the bottom. And there I sat in the soft, wet grass with the moonlight all about me and far above through the broken window of the Room, there was a low whistling.

"That is the chief of it. I was not hurt and I went round to the front and knocked Tassoc up. When they let me in we had a long yarn over some good whisky – for I was shaken to pieces – and I explained things as much as I could. I told Tassoc that the room would have to come down and every fragment of it be burned in a blast-furnace erected within a pentacle. He nodded. There was nothing to say. Then I went to bed.

"We turned a small army on to the work and within ten days that lovely thing had gone up in smoke and what was left was calcined and clean.

"It was when the workmen were stripping the panelling that I got hold of a sound notion of the beginnings of that beastly development. Over the great fireplace, after the great oak panels had been torn down, I found that there was let into the masonry a scrollwork of stone with on it an old inscription in ancient Celtic, that here in this room was burned Dian Tiansay, Jester of King Alzof, who made the Song of Foolishness upon King Ernore of the Seventh Castle.

"When I got the translation clear I gave it to Tassoc. He was tremendously excited for he knew the old tale and took me down to the library to look at an old parchment that gave the story in detail. Afterwards I found that the incident was well-known about the countryside, but always regarded more as a legend, than as history. And no one seemed ever to have dreamt that the old East Wing of Iastrae Castle was the remains of the ancient Seventh Castle.

"From the old parchment I gathered that there had been a pretty dirty job done, away back in the years. It seems that King Alzof and King Ernore had been enemies by birthright, as you might say truly, but that nothing more than a little raiding had occurred on either side for years until Dian Tiansay made the Song of Foolishness upon King Ernore and sang it before King Alzof, and so greatly was it appreciated that King Alzof gave the jester one of his ladies to wife.

"Presently all the people of the land had come to know the song and so it came at last to King Ernore who was so angered that he made war upon his old enemy and took and burned him and his castle; but Dian Tiansay, the jester, he brought with him to his own place and having torn his tongue out because of the song which he had made and sung, he imprisoned him in the Room in the East Wing (which was evidently used for unpleasant purposes), and the jester's wife he kept for himself, having a fancy for her prettiness.

"But one night Dian Tiansay's wife was not to be found and in the morning they discovered her lying dead in her husband's arms and he sitting, whistling the Song of Foolishness, for he had no longer the power to sing it.

"Then they roasted Dian Tiansay in the great fireplace – probably from that self-same 'gallows-iron' which I have already mentioned. And until he died Dian Tiansay 'ceased not to whistle' the Song of Foolishness which he could no longer sing. But afterwards 'in that room' there was often heard at night the sound of something whistling and there 'grew a power in that room' so that none dared to sleep in it. And presently, it would seem, the King went to another castle for the whistling troubled him.

"There you have it all. Of course, that is only a rough rendering of the translation from the parchment. It's a bit quaint! Don't you think so?"

"Yes," I said, answering for the lot. "But how did the thing grow to such a tremendous manifestation?"

"One of those cases of continuity of thought producing a positive action upon the immediate surrounding material," replied Carnacki. "The development must have been going forward through centuries, to have produced such a monstrosity. It was a true instance of Saiitii manifestation which I can best explain by likening it to a living spiritual fungus which involves the very structure of the aether-fibre itself and, of course, in so doing acquires an essential control over the 'material-substance' involved in it. It is impossible to make it plainer in a few words."

"What broke the seventh hair?" asked Taylor.

But Carnacki did not know. He thought it was probably nothing but being too severely tensioned. He also explained that they found out that the men who had run away had not been up to mischief, but had come over secretly merely to hear the whistling which, indeed, had suddenly become the talk of the whole countryside.

"One other thing," said Arkright, "have you any idea what governs the use of the Unknown Last Line of the Saaamaaa Ritual? I know, of course, that it was used by the Ab-human Priests in the Incantation of the Raaaee, but what used it on your behalf and what made it?"

"You had better read Harzam's Monograph and my Addenda to it, on Astral and 'Astarral' Co-ordination and Interference," said Carnacki. "It is an extraordinary subject and I can only say here that the human-vibration may not be insulated from the 'astarral' (as is always believed to be the case in interferences by the Ab-human), without immediate action being taken by those Forces which govern the spinning of the outer circle. In other words, it is being proved, time after time, that there is some inscrutable Protective Force constantly intervening between the human-soul (not the body, mind you) and the Outer Monstrosities. Am I clear?"

"Yes, I think so," I replied. "And you believe that the Room had become the material expression of the ancient Jester – that his soul, rotted with hatred had bred into a monster – eh?" I asked.

"Yes," said Carnacki, nodding. "I think you've put my thought rather neatly. It is a queer coincidence that Miss Donnehue is supposed to be descended (so I heard since) from the same King Ernore. It makes one think some rather curious thoughts, doesn't it? The marriage coming on and the Room waking to fresh life. If she had gone into that room, ever . . . eh? It had waited a long time. Sins of the fathers. Yes, I've thought of that. They're to be married next week and I am to be best man, which is a thing I hate. And he won his bets, rather! Just think, *if* ever she had gone into that room. Pretty horrible, eh?"

He nodded his head, grimly, and we four nodded back. Then he rose and took us collectively to the door and presently thrust us forth in friendly fashion on to the Embankment and into the fresh night air.

"Good night," we all called back and went to our various homes.

If she had, eh? If she had? That is what I kept thinking.

# Bagnell Terrace

## E. F. Benson

### Prospectus

**Address:** Bagnell Terrace, South London, England.

**Property:** Nineteenth-century terraced house. Situated in a quiet cul-de-sac, the building is small and compact, though the rooms are spacious. An additional room joined by a covered passageway has been erected in the garden.

**Viewing Date:** Winter, 1928.

**Agent:** Edward Frederic Benson (1867–1940) was born in Wokingham, Berkshire, and after pursuing an interest in archaeology by spending three years in Greece and Egypt, turned instead to writing and enjoyed a huge success with his society novel, *Dodo* (1893), following this with the popular *Lucia* series. He also became fascinated by the supernatural – particularly psychic phenomena – as his novel, *Across The Stream* (1919), and collections of short stories, *Visible and Invisible* (1923) and *Spook Stories* (1928), clearly show. "Bagnell Terrace" combines both of his interests, in the story of a small house which is haunted by the power of a very ancient evil spirit.

I had been for ten years an inhabitant of Bagnell Terrace, and, like all those who have been so fortunate as to secure a footing there, was convinced that for amenity, convenience, and tranquillity it is unrivalled in the length and breadth of London. The houses are small; we could, none of us, give an evening party or a dance, but we who live in Bagnell Terrace do not desire to do anything of the kind. We do not go in for sounds of revelry at night, nor, indeed, is there much revelry during the day, for we have gone to Bagnell Terrace in order to be anchored in a quiet little backwater. There is no traffic through it, for the terrace is a cul-de-sac, closed at the far end by a high brick wall, along which, on summer nights, cats trip lightly on visits to their friends. Even the cats of Bagnell Terrace have caught something of its discretion and tranquillity, for they do not hail each other with long-drawn yells of mortal agony like their cousins in less well-conducted places, but sit and have quiet little parties like the owners of the houses in which they condescend to be lodged and boarded.

But, though I was more content to be in Bagnell Terrace than anywhere else, I had not got, and was beginning to be afraid I never should get the particular house which I coveted above all others. This was at the top end of the terrace adjoining the wall that closed it, and in one respect it was unlike the other houses, which so much resemble each other. The others have little square gardens in front of them, where we have our bulbs abloom in the spring, when they present a very gay appearance, but the gardens are too small, and London too sunless to allow of any very effective horticulture. The house, however, to which I had so long turned envious eyes, had no garden in front of it; instead, the space had been used for the erection of a big, square room (for a small garden will make a very well-sized room) connected with the house by a covered passage. Rooms in Bagnell Terrace, though sunny and cheerful, are not large, and just one big room, so it occurred to me, would give the final touch of perfection to those delightful little residences.

Now, the inhabitants of this desirable abode were something of a mystery to our neighbourly little circle; though we knew that a man lived there (for he was occasionally seen leaving or entering his house), he was personally unknown to us. A curious point was that, though we had all (though rarely) encountered him on the pavements, there was a considerable discrepancy in the impression he had made on us. He certainly walked briskly, as if the vigour of life was still his, but while I believed that he was a young man, Hugh Abbot, who lived in the house next his, was convinced that, in spite of his briskness, he was not only old, but very old. Hugh and I, lifelong bachelor friends, often discussed him in the ramble of conversation when he had dropped in for an after-dinner pipe, or I had gone across for a game of chess. His name was not known to us, so, by reason of my desire for his house, we called him Naboth. We both agreed that there was something odd about him, something baffling and elusive.

I had been away for a couple of months one winter in Egypt; the night after my return Hugh dined with me, and after dinner I produced those trophies which the strongest-minded are unable to refrain from purchasing, when they are offered by an engaging burnoused ruffian in the Valley of the Tombs of the Kings. There were some beads (not quite so blue as they had appeared there), a scarab or two, and for the last I kept the piece of which I was really proud, namely, a small lapis-lazuli statuette, a few inches high, of a cat. It sat square and stiff on its haunches, with upright forelegs, and, in spite of the small scale, so good were the proportions and so accurate the observation of the artist, that it gave the impression of being much bigger. As it stood on Hugh's palm it was certainly small, but if, without the sight of it, I pictured it to myself, it represented itself as far larger than it really was.

"And the odd thing is," I said, "that though it is far and away the best thing I picked up, I cannot for the life of me remember where I bought it. Somehow I feel that I've always had it."

He had been looking very intently at it. Then he jumped up from his chair and put it down on the chimney-piece.

"I don't think I quite like it," he said, "and I can't tell you why. Oh, a jolly bit of workmanship; I don't mean that. And you can't remember where you got it, did you say? That's odd . . . Well, what about a game of chess?"

We played a couple of games, without much concentration or fervour, and more than once I saw him glance with a puzzled look at my little image on the chimney-piece. But he said nothing more about it, and when our games were over he gave me the discursive news of the Terrace. A house had fallen vacant and been instantly snapped up.

"Not Naboth's?" I asked.

"No, not Naboth's. Naboth is in possession still. Very much in possession; going strong."

"Anything new?" I asked.

"Oh, just bits of things. I've seen him a good many times lately, and yet I can't get any clear idea of him. I met him three days ago, as I was coming out of my gate, and had a good look at him, and for a moment I agreed with you and thought he was a young man. Then he turned and stared me in the face for a second, and I thought I had never seen anyone so old. Frightfully alive, but more than old – antique, primeval."

"And then?" I asked.

"He passed on, and I found myself, as has so often happened before, quite unable to remember what his face was like. Was he old or young? I didn't know. What was his mouth like, or his nose? But it was the question of his age which was the most baffling."

Hugh stretched his feet out towards the blaze, and sank back in his chair, with one more frowning look at my lapis lazuli cat.

"Though after all, what is age?" he said. "We measure age by time, we say 'so many years', and forget that we're in eternity here and now, just as we say we're in a room or in Bagnell Terrace, though we're much more truly in infinity."

"What has that got to do with Naboth?" I asked.

Hugh beat his pipe out against the bars of the grate before he answered.

"Well, it will probably sound quite cracked to you," he said, "unless Egypt, the land of ancient mystery, has softened your rind of materialism, but it struck me then that Naboth belonged to eternity much more obviously than we do. We belong to it, of course; we can't help that; but he's less involved in this error or illusion of time than we are. Dear me, it sounds amazing nonsense when I put it into words."

I laughed.

"I'm afraid my rind of materialism isn't soft enough yet," I said. "What you say implies that you think Naboth is a sort of apparition, a ghost, a spirit of the dead that manifests itself as a human being, though it isn't one!"

He drew his legs up to him again.

"Yes; it must be nonsense," he said. "Besides, he has been so much in evidence lately, and we can't all be seeing a ghost. It doesn't happen. And there have been noises coming from his house, loud and cheerful noises, which I've never heard before. Somebody plays an instrument like a flute in that big, square room you envy so much, and somebody beats an accompaniment as if with drums. Odd sort of music; it goes on often now at night . . . Well, it's time to go to bed."

Again he glanced up at the chimney-piece.

"Why, it's quite a little cat," he said.

This rather interested me, for I had said nothing to him about the impression left on my mind that it was bigger than its actual dimensions.

"Just the same size as ever," I said.

"Naturally. But I had been thinking of it as lifesize for some reason," said he.

I went with him to the door, and strolled out with him into the darkness of an overcast night. As we neared his house I saw that big patches of light shone into the road from the windows of the square room next door. Suddenly Hugh laid his hand on my arm.

"There!" he said. "The flutes and drums are at it to-night."

The night was very still, but, listen as I would, I could hear nothing but the rumble of traffic in the street beyond the terrace.

"I can't hear it," I said.

Even as I spoke, I heard it, and the wailing noise whisked me back to Egypt again. The boom of the traffic became for me the beat of the drum, and upon it floated just that squeal and wail of the little reed-pipes which accompany the Arab dances, tuneless and rhythmless, and as old as the temples of the Nile.

"It's like the Arab music that you hear in Egypt," I said.

As we stood listening it ceased to his ears as well as mine, as suddenly as it had begun, and simultaneously the lights in the windows of the square room were extinguished.

We waited a moment in the roadway opposite Hugh's house, but from next door came no sound at all, nor glimmer of illumination from any of its windows . . .

I turned; it was rather chilly to one lately arrived from the south.

"Good night," I said; "we'll meet tomorrow sometime."

I went straight to bed, slept at once, and woke with the impress of a very vivid dream on my mind. There was music in it, familiar Arab music, and there was an immense cat somewhere. Even as I tried to recall it, it faded, and I had but time to recognize it as a hash-up of the happenings of the evening before I went to sleep again.

The normal habits of life quickly reasserted themselves. I had work to do, and there were friends to see; all the minute events of each day stitched themselves into the tapestry of life. But somehow a new thread began to be woven into it, though at the time I did not recognize it as such. It seemed trivial and extraneous that I should so often hear a few staves of that odd music from Naboth's house, or that as often as it fixed my attention it was silent again, as if I had imagined, rather than actually heard it. It was trivial, too, that I should so often see Naboth entering or leaving his house. And then one day I had a sight of him which was unlike any previous experience of mine.

I was standing one morning in the window of my front room. I had idly picked up my lapis lazuli cat, and was holding it in the splash of sunlight that poured in, admiring the texture of its surface which, though it was of hard stone, somehow suggested fur. Then, quite casually, I looked up, and there, a few yards in front of me, leaning on the railings of my garden, and intently observing not me, but what I held, was Naboth. His eyes, fixed on it, blinked in the April sunshine with some purring sensuous content, and Hugh was right on the question of his age; he was neither old nor young, but timeless.

The moment of perception passed; it flashed on and off my mind like the revolving beam of some distant lighthouse. It was just a ray of illumination, and was instantly shut off again, so that it appeared to my conscious mind like some hallucination. He suddenly seemed aware of me, and, turning, walked briskly off down the pavement.

I remember being rather startled, but the effect soon faded, and the incident became to me one of those trivial little things that make a momentary impression and vanish. It was odd, too, but in no way remarkable, that more than once I saw one of those discreet cats of which I have spoken sitting on the little balcony outside my front room, and gravely regarding the interior. I am devoted to cats, and several times I got up in order to open the window and invite it to enter; but each time on my movement it jumped down and slunk away. And April passed into May.

I came back after dining out one night in this month, and found a telephone message from Hugh that I should ring him up on my return. A rather excited voice answered me.

"I thought you would like to know at once," he said. "An hour ago a board was put up on Naboth's house to say that the freehold was for sale. Martin and Smith are the agents. Good night; I'm in bed already."

"You're a true friend," I said.

Early next morning, of course, I presented myself at the house-agent's. The price asked was very moderate, the title perfectly satisfactory. He could give me the keys at once, for the house was empty, and he promised that I could have a couple of days to make up my mind, during which time I was to have the prior right of purchase if I was disposed to pay the full price asked. If, however, I only made an offer, he could not guarantee that the trustees would accept it . . . Hot-foot, with the keys in my pocket, I sped back up the Terrace again.

I found the house completely empty, not of inhabitants only, but of all else. There was not a blind, not a strip of drugget, not a curtain-rod in it from garret to cellar. So much the better, thought I, for there would be no tenants' fixtures to take on. Nor was there any debris of removal, of straw and waste-paper; the house looked as if it was prepared for an occupant instead of just rid of one. All was in apple-pie order, the windows clean, the floors swept, the paint and woodwork bright; it was a clean and polished shell ready for its occupier. My first inspection, of course, was of the big built-out room, which was its chief attraction, and my heart leaped at the sight of its plain spaciousness. On one side was an open fireplace, on the other a coil of pipes for central heating, and at the end, between the windows, a niche let into the wall, as if a statue had once stood there; it might have been designed expressly for my bronze Perseus. The rest of the house presented no particular features; it was on the same plan as my own, and my builder, who inspected it that afternoon, pronounced it to be in excellent condition.

"It looks as if it had been newly done up, and never lived in," he said, "and at the price you mention is a decided bargain."

The same thing struck Hugh when, on his return from his office, I dragged him over to see it.

"Why, it all looks new," he said, "and yet we know that Naboth has been here for years, and was certainly here a week ago. And then there's another thing. When did he remove his furniture? There have been no vans at the house that I have seen."

I was much too pleased at getting my heart's desire to consider anything except that I had got it.

"Oh, I can't bother about little things like that," I said. "Look at my beautiful big room. Piano there, bookcases all along the wall, sofa in front of the fire, Perseus in the niche. Why, it was made for me."

Within the specified two days the house was mine, and within a month papering and distempering, electric fittings, and blinds and curtain-rods were finished, and my move began. Two days were sufficient for the transport of my goods, and at the close of the second my old house was dismantled, except for my bedroom, the contents of which would be moved next day. My servants were installed in the new abode, and that night, after a hurried dinner with Hugh, I went back for a couple more hours' work of hauling and tugging and arranging books in the large room, which it was my purpose to finish first. It was a chilly night for May, and I had had a log-fire lit on the hearth, which from time to time I replenished, in intervals of dusting and arranging. Eventually, when the two hours had lengthened themselves into three, I determined to give over for the present, and, much tired, sat down for a recuperative pause on the edge of my sofa and contemplated with satisfaction the result of my labours. At that moment I was conscious that there was a stale, but aromatic, smell in the room that reminded me of the curious odour that hangs about an Egyptian temple. But I put it down to the dust from my books and the smouldering logs.

The move was completed next day, and after another week I was installed as firmly as if I had been there for years. May slipped by, and June, and my new house never ceased to give me a vivid pleasure; it was always a treat to return to it. Then came a certain afternoon when a strange thing happened.

The day had been wet, but towards evening it cleared up; the pavements soon dried, but the road remained moist and miry. I was close to my house on my way home when I saw form itself on the paving-stones a few yards in front of me the mark of a wet shoe, as if someone invisible to the eye had just stepped off the road. Another and yet another briskly imprinted themselves, going up towards my house. For the moment I stood stockstill, and then, with a thumping heart I followed. The marks of these strange footsteps preceded me right up to my door; there was one on the very threshold faintly visible.

I let myself in, closing the door, I confess, very quickly behind me. As I stood there I heard a resounding crash from my room, which so to speak, startled my fright from me, and I ran down the little passage and burst in. There, at the far end of the room was my bronze Perseus fallen from its niche and lying on the floor. And I knew, by what sixth sense I cannot tell, that I was not alone in the room and that the presence there was no human presence.

Now fear is a very odd thing; unless it is overmastering and overwhelming it always produces its own reaction. Whatever courage we have rises to meet it, and with courage comes anger that we have given entrance to this unnerving intruder. That, at any rate, was my case now, and I made an effective emotional resistance. My servant came running in to see what the noise was, and we set Perseus on his feet again and examined into the cause of his fall. It was clear enough; a big piece of plaster had broken away from the niche, and that must be repaired and strengthened before we reinstated him. Simultaneously my fear and the sense of an unaccountable presence in the room slipped from me. The footsteps outside were still unexplained and I told myself that if I was to shudder at everything I did not understand there would be an end to tranquil existence for ever.

I was dining with Hugh that night; he had been away for the last week, only returning to-day, and he had come in before these slightly agitating events happened to announce his arrival and suggest dinner. I noticed that as he stood chatting for a few minutes, he had once or twice sniffed the air, but he had made no comment, nor had I asked him if he perceived the strange faint odour that every now and then manifested itself to me. I knew it was a great relief to some secretly quaking piece of my mind that he was back, for I was convinced that there was some psychic disturbance going on, either subjectively in my mind, or a real invasion from without. In either case his presence was comforting, not because he is of that stalward breed which believes in nothing beyond the material facts of life, and pooh-poohs these mysterious forces which surround and so strangely interpenetrate existence, but because, while thoroughly believing in them, he has the firm confidence that the deadly and evil powers which occasionally break through into the seeming security of existence are not really to be feared, since they are held in check by forces stronger yet, ready to assist all who realize their protective care. Whether I meant to tell him what had occurred to-day I had not fully determined.

It was not till after dinner that such subjects came up at all, but I had seen there was something on his mind of which he had not spoken yet.

"And your new house," he said at length, "does it still remain as all your fancy painted?"

"I wonder why you ask that," I said.

He gave me a quick glance.

"Mayn't I take any interest in your well-being?" he said.

I knew that something was coming, if I chose to let it.

"I don't think you've ever liked my house from the first," I said. "I believe you think there's something queer about it. I allow that the manner in which I found it empty was odd."

"It was rather," he said. "But so long as it remains empty, except for what you've put in it, it is all right."

I wanted now to press him further.

"What was it you smelt this afternoon in the big room?" I said. "I saw you nosing and sniffing. I have smelt something too. Let's see if we smelt the same thing."

"An odd smell," he said. "Something dusty and stale, but aromatic."

"And what else have you noticed?" I asked.

He paused a moment.

"I think I'll tell you," he said. "This evening from my window I saw you coming up the pavement, and simultaneously I saw, or thought I saw, Naboth cross the road and walk on in front of you. I wondered if you saw him too, for you paused as he stepped on to the pavement in front of you, and then you followed him."

I felt my hands grow suddenly cold, as if the warm current of my blood had been chilled.

"No, I didn't see him," I said, "but I saw his step."

"What do you mean?"

"Just what I say. I saw footprints in front of me, which continued on to my threshold."

"And then?"

"I went in, and a terrific crash startled me. My bronze Perseus had fallen from his niche. And there was something in the room."

There was a scratching noise at the window. Without answering, Hugh jumped up and drew aside the curtain. On the sill was seated a large grey cat, blinking in the light. He advanced to the window, and on his approach the cat jumped down into the garden. The light shone out into the road, and we both saw, standing on the pavement just outside, the figure of a man. He turned and looked at me, and then moved away towards my house next door.

"It's he," said Hugh.

He opened the window and leaned out to see what had become of him. There was no sign of him anywhere, but I saw that light shone from behind the blinds of my room.

"Come on," I said. "Let's see what is happening. Why is my room lit?"

I opened the door of my house with my latchkey, and followed by Hugh went down the short passage to the room. It was perfectly dark, and when I turned the switch, we saw that it was empty. I rang the bell, but no answer came, for it was already late, and doubtless my servants had gone to bed.

"But I saw a strong light from the windows two minutes ago," I said, "and there has been no-one here since."

Hugh was standing by me in the middle of the room. Suddenly he threw out his arm as if striking at something. That thoroughly alarmed me.

"What's the matter?" I asked. "What are you hitting at?"

He shook his head.

"I don't know," he said. "I thought I saw . . . But I'm not sure. But we're in for something if we stop here. Something is coming, though I don't know what."

The light seemed to me to be burning dim; shadows began to collect in the corner of the room, and though outside the night had been clear, the air here was growing thick with a foggy vapour, which smelt dusty and stale and aromatic. Faintly, but getting louder as we waited there in silence, I heard the throb of drums and the wail of flutes. As yet I had no feeling that there were other presences in the place beyond ours, but in the growing dimness I knew that something was coming nearer. Just in front of me was the empty niche from which my bronze had fallen, and looking at it, I saw that something was astir. The shadow within it began to shape itself into a form, and out of it there gleamed two points of greenish light. A moment more and I saw that they were eyes of antique and infinite malignity.

I heard Hugh's voice in a sort of hoarse whisper.

"Look there!" he said. "It's coming! Oh, my God, it's coming!"

Sudden as the lightning that leaps from the heart of the night it came. But it came not with blaze and flash of light, but, as it were, with a stroke of blinding darkness, that fell not on the eye, or on any material sense, but on the spirit, so that I cowered under it in some abandonment of terror. It came from those eyes which gleamed in the niche, and which now I saw to be set in the face of the figure that stood there. The form of it, naked but for a loin-cloth, was that of a man, the head seemed now human, now to be that of some monstrous cat. And as I looked I knew that if I continued looking there I should be submerged and drowned in that flood of evil that poured from it. As in some catalepsy of nightmare I struggled to tear my eyes from it, but still they were riveted there, gazing on incarnate hate.

Again I heard Hugh's whisper.

"Defy it," he said. "Don't yield an inch."

A swarm of disordered and hellish images were buzzing in my brain, and now I knew as surely as if actual words had been spoken to us that the presence there told me to come to it.

"I've got to go to it," I said. "It's making me go."

I felt his hand tighten on my arm.

"Not a step," he said. "I'm stronger than it is. It will know that soon. Just pray – pray."

Suddenly his arm shot out in front of me, pointing at the presence.

"By the power of God!" he shouted. "By the power of God!"

There was dead silence. The light of those eyes faded, and then came dawn on the darkness of the room. It was quiet and orderly, the niche was empty, and there on the sofa by me was Hugh, his face white and streaming with sweat.

"It's over," he said, and without pause fell fast asleep.

Now we have often talked over together what happened that evening. Of what seemed to happen I have already given the account, which anyone may believe or not, precisely as they please. He, as I, was conscious of a presence wholly evil, and he tells me that all the time that those eyes gleamed from the niche, he was trying to realize what he believed, namely, that only one power in the world is Omnipotent, and that the moment he gained that realization the presence collapsed. What exactly that presence was it is impossible to say. It looks as if it was the essence or spirit of one of those mysterious Egyptian cults, of which the force survived, and was seen and felt in this quiet Terrace. That it was embodied in Naboth seems (among all these incredibilities) possible, and Naboth certainly has never been seen again. Whether or not it was connected with the worship and cult of cats might occur to the mythological mind, and it is perhaps worthy of record that I found next morning my little lapis lazuli image, which stood on the chimney-piece, broken into fragments. It was too badly damaged to mend, and I am not sure that, in any case, I should have attempted to have it restored.

Finally, there is no more tranquil and pleasant room in London than the one built out in front of my house in Bagnell Terrace.

# The Companion

## Joan Aiken

### Prospectus

**Address:** 3, Vascoe's Cottages, Talland, Cornwall, England.

**Property:** Nineteenth-century addition to two pairs of semi-detached labourers' dwellings. Constructed of plain red brick and embellished with ornamental woodwork, the property is secluded by a privet hedge and is to be let fully furnished.

**Viewing Date:** Autumn, 1978.

**Agent:** Joan Aiken (1924–) was born in Rye, Sussex, the daughter of the famous American writer, Conrad Aiken, and for a time wrote for BBC Radio, before beginning the career which has established her as one of today's most inventive writers of fantasy fiction. Haunted houses feature extensively in her work – notably *The Shadow Guests* (1980) and *The Haunting of Lamb House* (1999), in which two former real-life residents, E. F. Benson and Henry James, meet the tragic ghost of a child – and short stories like "Aunt Jezebel's House", "Lodging For The Night" and "The Companion", in which an exorcist attempts to remove an unwilling ghost . . .

The ugliness of her rented cottage was a constant source of perverse satisfaction to Mrs Clyrard. To have travelled, in the course of her seventy-odd years, over most of the civilised world, to have lived in several of its most elegant capitals, and finally to have come to roost in Number Three, Vascoe's Cottages, had an incongruity that pleased her tart, ironic spirit. Mrs Clyrard indulged in a constant battle against life's unreasonablenesses and inequities. Her private hobby was finding fault – with the British government, the world's so-called leaders, with her bank, with her friends, with the young, the old, the stupid, the BBC Third Programme, the weather and the cakes from the village shop.

It gave her intense, not wholly masochistic gratification to survey her hideous rented furniture, to go into her dark little unfunctional kitchen and discover that the gas-pilot had gone out again, that before putting a kettle on to boil she must laboriously poke a long-stemmed match into the dirty interstices of the stove, turn, at the same time, a small, gritty, and inconveniently-placed wheel, and wait for the resulting muffled explosion; this ritual, which often had to be enacted several times a day due to the fluctuations of gas pressure, filled her with a dour amusement, confirming, as it did, all her most pessimistic feelings about the world. The aged recalcitrant plastic ice-trays, which were more likely to split in half under the pressure of an angry thumb than to eject a single cube of ice, the front gate that refused to latch properly, the wayward taps turning in improbable directions, emitting a thin thread of lukewarm water, the varying levels of the cottage, which had steps up or steps down between all its rooms, even one in the middle of the bathroom – these things fulfilled her expectation that life was intended to be a series of cynical booby-traps.

Nevertheless Mrs Clyrard could have lived in comfort if she had chosen. She was rich, had been married, had had a successful career as a painter, had had children, even, now satisfactorily grown and disposed of; she was a handsome, intelligent, and cultivated woman. Death had removed her husband, it was true, but otherwise she need have had little to complain about; yet all possible amenities had been, it seemed, wantonly jettisoned in favour of retreat into the exile of a Cornish village. Not even romantic exile, for Talland was far from picturesque: it was a small, random conglomeration of ill-assorted, mostly granite buildings, established on a treeless hillside as if they had been dropped there.

Vascoe's Cottages, of which Mrs Clyrard occupied Number Three, had been a nineteenth-century addition; two pairs of plain red-brick semi-detached labourers' dwellings, which some hopeful later landlord's hand had embellished with heavy chalet-type ornamental woodwork, thereby further darkening the already inadequately-lit interiors.

"Oh, that will do for me very nicely," Mrs Clyrard had remarked with her usual brief smile, on first observing Number Three, over its stout enclosing privet hedge.

"Are you certain?" her friend and prospective landlady Mrs Helena Soames doubtfully inquired. "Are you sure it will be big enough for you – *light* enough? The furniture is rather a job lot, I'm afraid – I could have it taken out, if you would like to put in your own things—"

"No, no, let them stay in store. I can't be bothered with them. This is admirable. And the furniture will last my time."

Mrs Clyrard was in excellent health, but she always spoke and acted as if in expectation of imminent death.

She moved herself into the cottage with a minimum of fuss or added impedimenta: a typewriter, some books; quickly learned the names and ways of the local tradespeople and had soon established herself on terms of remarkable cordiality with all her neighbours – the terms being that she listened to – indeed, drew out by some unique osmosis of her own – all their dissatisfactions and complaints, meanwhile herself maintaining a considerable reticence. Complaint is addictive: people came back eagerly, again and again, for more; Mrs Clyrard had all the company she could have wished for. She listened, she made her own dry comments and never disbursed advice; this was the secret of her popularity. She never offered information about herself, or divulged her own feelings. If asked what she did with herself all day – for it was plain that she was neither house-proud nor a dedicated gardener – she replied, "I am writing my memoirs. I have known any number of famous people –"

and it was true, she had – "plenty of reputations will have the rug pulled from under them if I don't die before I have finished."

Although she frequently and drily referred to her possible death, she manifested no anxiety about the prospect, and seemed not particularly troubled as to whether she finished her memoirs first or not. Very few things appeared to trouble Mrs Clyrard particularly, she found a sour pleasure in her occupations. Meanwhile the years rolled by, bestowing on her no signs of age or infirmity; nor did she manifest any disposition to seek more comfortable quarters than Number Three, Vascoe's.

"I don't know how you can endure the poky little place," Miss Morgan frequently remarked, when she dropped in to complain about Mrs Soames. "It's so dark and cold. When I was living here with the old lady I thought I should go mad with the inconvenience. It must be the most awkward house in the world. Even with that lift installed—"

The old lady had been Helena Soames's mother, Mrs Musgrave. For ten years prior to her death from heart disease she had occupied Number Three, Vascoe's, and Miss Morgan had been her companion. The lift had been installed for Mrs Musgrave's benefit; it consisted of a metal chair, with a counter-balance, in the stairwell, operated by a small electric motor. Mrs Musgrave's son, an engineer, had installed it himself. The old lady had sat herself in the chair, been buckled in with a seat-belt; then she pressed a button and was conveyed slowly up or slowly down. The lift, with its ugly metalwork, still remained; but Mrs Clyrard, who had a rooted mistrust of all machinery, saw no occasion to make use of it.

After ten years Mrs Musgrave had died, and Miss Morgan, lacking a function, was removed to the manor to housekeep for the daughter, Mrs Soames – an arrangement which gave little satisfaction to either party.

Almost every day, at teatime, Miss Morgan called in on Mrs Clyrard with some grievance to relate about Mrs Soames's fault-finding, heartlessness, inconsistency, or sarcasm, to which Mrs Clyrard listened with her usual acute impassivity.

"I do wish *you* would have me for your companion, dear Mrs Clyrard," Miss Morgan, who had a slight stammer, often sighed out. "I am s-sure we should get on so well! I would be so h-happy to look after everything for you while you wrote your memoirs and would not dream of asking for a s-salary; all I want is a home."

"My dear woman, what possible use would I have for a companion in this tiny box of a house? I am almost too much company for myself."

Wispy, myopic little Miss Morgan would take herself off, pleading, "Think it over, dear Mrs Clyrard – do think it over!"

In the evenings Mrs Clyrard often heard the other side of the case: her friend Helena generally dropped in for a glass of sherry and a grumble about Miss Morgan's self-pity, inefficiency, forgetfulness, untidiness, tendency to martyrdom, and general inadequacy. Mrs Clyrard made no comment on that either. Nor did she see fit to intervene when Mrs Soames's patience finally ran out and she dismissed the unsatisfactory housekeeper, who, being far too old by now to secure another post, went lamenting away to live with her married sister in Lanlivery, after a final and unavailing plea to Mrs Clyrard to take her in.

More time went by. Mrs Clyrard lent a non-committal ear to the outpourings of other neighbours: of harassed parents who could not deal with their young; of rebellious teenagers who could not endure their parents; of betrayed husbands; of frustrated wives and of disillusioned friends who had fallen out. Her own private life remained as apparently tranquil as ever; her excellently coiffed iron-grey hair turned a shade paler, her hawklike profile was unchanged. She wrote a few pages a day at the desk in her upstairs study, cooked light meals for herself, waged her usual guerilla war against the inconveniences of her house and continued in her customary state of sardonic composure.

But presently – and how it happened Mrs Clyrard was not precisely aware, for the change came by such gradual degrees – her equable daily routine became disrupted; not seriously, but just enough to be noticeable.

The form taken by the disturbance was this: Mrs Clyrard,

seated upstairs in a state of recollected tranquillity at her typewriter, would suddenly find her concentration broken by an odd urge to go below and perform some slight unnecessary task in the kitchen. Sometimes her more rational self was able to withstand the trivial impulse; but sometimes it was not and almost before she was aware of the process she would find herself at the kitchen sink washing teacloths, or cleaning the leaded glass panes in the front door (which made no difference to the light, for the untrimmed privet hedge grew within six feet of it), or polishing shoes, or defrosting the refrigerator.

This was very annoying, but Mrs Clyrard had no intention of submitting to it. She was a woman of total practicality. If she felt a twinge in a tooth, she consulted her dentist; if she detected a rattle in her car, she referred it to the garage. Possible psychic phenomena weighed no more and no less in her estimation than failures in the electrical system or mice in the pantry: as she would call in an electrician or a cat for the latter inconveniences, for the former she had recourse to an exorcist. Fortunately she was acquainted with one: an old friend of hers, a rural Dean, living in semi-retirement in Bath, still took an active interest in paranormal occurences, and occasionally officiated at a ceremony to remove some unwelcome or disturbed spirit.

Mrs Clyrard wrote and invited him for a visit, arranging to have him accommodated at a nearby guest-house, since she detested having people staying in the cottage.

When he arrived she lost no time explaining the nuisance to him.

"Somebody is trying to occupy my mind – or my house," she said matter-of-factly, though with a considerable degree of irritation. "I should be very much obliged if you could deal with it for me, Roger."

The Dean, delighted with the odd problem, promised to see what he could do. To assist him, he fetched over a medium from Bath – a city much plagued by psychic phenomena, possibly due to its enclosed, low-lying and damp situation.

The medium, Mrs Hannah Huxley, a portly, blind lady, acquiesced with the Dean in taking the problem as a most serious challenge. They turned back the carpets, they inscribed formulae and diagrams repellent to invading spirits on the floors of all the rooms, they recited incantations, they lit candles and sprinkled water, they performed various rituals involving the doors, the windows, the curtains, the mirrors, the stairs, the fireplace, the lights. At one point during the proceedings, which were long, and to Mrs Clyrard somewhat tediously repetitious, Mrs Huxley went into a trance.

"Did your husband," she suddenly inquired, emerging from this condition as abruptly as she had gone into it, "did your husband die of a head injury, Mrs Clyrard?"

"Certainly not," said Mrs Clyrard with asperity, startled, and not best pleased at this intrusion into her private affairs. "He died of intestinal carcinoma."

"That's odd. I have distinct evidence of a presence quite close to you who has at some time suffered from a head injury. Are you quite sure that you can think of no such person?"

Mrs Clyrard moved a step or two aside, distastefully, before replying again, "Absolutely not."

Her faith by now somewhat diminished, she watched in ironic silence as the Dean and Mrs Huxley came to the conclusion of their ritual, having now apparently located the intrusive entity.

Kindly, cajolingly, uttering mellifluous Latin phrases formed for the purpose of coaxing such undesired visitants from their lodgings, the Dean walked slowly, backwards, beckoning, to the front door, opened it, waited, and recited a final prohibiting admonition, before closing the door and returning to the fireside.

"There, it's gone!" he said with a beaming smile. "It can't come back inside now."

*It*? thought Mrs Clyrard, on an impulse of strong protest; how can that vague, unhappy, intrusive, indefinable emanation be compressed into and pinned down by such a brusque, particular little monosyllable as *it*?

"Poor thing, it simply hated to leave," the Dean went on. "No, I'm afraid it didn't want to go in the very least. Did you hear it whimpering?"

Mrs Clyrard had not.

Stifling her scepticism, however, she civilly thanked the Dean and his colleague, refreshed them after their exertions with tea and cakes from the village shop, conversed for a polite hour, and finally, with relief, saw them to the door and said goodbye. Still sceptical, but in a cool spirit of scientific investigation, she went upstairs for an experimental hour's writing. – And the Dean had been completely right, perfectly justified in his confidence: there was nothing to disturb her concentration; she found she could work in untroubled peace for the whole hour. Not a single thought of the tea-things waiting unwashed downstairs so much as slipped over the edge of her consciousness.

When Helena Soames presently arrived for a glass of sherry, at half-past six, Mrs Clyrard was in a highly self-congratulatory state of mind and, contrary to her usual reticent habit, related the story.

"But I still can't imagine who the person suffering from a head injury can be," she concluded.

"Oh, can't you?" said Mrs Soames, who had listened with the greatest interest. "But it's perfectly obvious, my dear. It must be poor Miss Morgan."

"Miss *Morgan*? Did she have a head injury? I never knew of it."

"It was over before you came to the village, of course. In fact it happened while Miss Morgan was looking after my mother in this cottage; after Edward had installed the chairlift. Miss Morgan had strapped Mother in and then – stupid woman – stuck her head over the banister to say, 'Is there anything you want me to bring you, Mrs Musgrave?' Of course the counter-balance came down, hit her on the head and knocked her silly. She was never quite the same after that, but then she hadn't been too bright to start with. Luckily Mother died not long afterwards."

"Miss Morgan – yes, of course," said Mrs Clyrard reflectively, remembering the doleful little woman's plea to be allowed to return to the inconveniences of Number Three, Vascoe's – "I'd be so happy to look after the house for you while you wrote your memoirs. I wouldn't *dream* of asking for a salary. All I want is a home."

"It simply hated to leave," Roger had said. "It didn't want to go in the very least."

Looked at through those eyes the dark and poky sitting-room with its Tottenham Court Road furnishings momentarily took on the appearance of a warm and happy haven.

"Miss Morgan," Mrs Clyrard said again. "What became of her?"

"Oh, she went to live with that married sister in Lanlivery. The sister had always despised her. Miss Morgan didn't want to go, but what could she do? At her age she couldn't get another job. Anyway, evidently it was a disastrous arrangement, for about six months later I heard that she drowned herself in a brook. All for the best, really; as I said, she'd never been quite with it after that accident. Well, *you* must have noticed it – she used to come wailing round to you often enough."

"Yes. So she did," Mrs Clyrard said in the same thoughtful manner.

Miss Morgan: that melancholy, ineffectual little woman; ineffectual in death as in life, apparently.

Or was she?

Seeing Helena to the door, half an hour later, closing it briskly behind her, Mrs Clyrard was aware for the first time that the previous trivial though irritating mental distractions which had assailed her might have been exchanged for something even more unaccustomed: a sensation of discomposure, disquiet; perhaps even – to analyse it closely – fear?

For although the Dean and Mrs Huxley had led the whimpering reluctant whatever-it-was along to the front door and out of the house, that was *all* they had done; they did not claim to have annihilated it, or driven it any farther than the threshold.

Mrs Clyrard allowed herself an uneasy glance at the door which framed its glass-paned square of dark.

Might not her visitor – out there in the little privet-enclosed garden – out there behind the glass-paned door in the rainy night – might it not feel, now, perhaps, a certain degree of *resentment* at its exclusion?

Mrs Clyrard heard the garden gate – which as usual had failed to latch properly – begin to creak and clatter as it swung to and fro in the rising wind.

She knew that she ought to go and fasten the gate before the hinges were damaged. And yet she lingered in the dreary little hallway, strangely reluctant to set foot outside the security of her house.

# The Ghost Hunter

## James Herbert

### Prospectus

**Address:** Edbrook, near Ravenmoor, England.

**Property:** Nineteenth-century country mansion with swelling apses and bay windows. A tall, imposing building set amidst terrace garden, lawns and bordering woodland. Suitable for large family with its attics, library and cellars.

**Viewing Date:** Late autumn, 1988.

**Agent:** James Herbert (1943–) was born in Bethnal Green, London, and after several years working in advertising, achieved popular success with his first novel, *The Rats* (1974). His successive books have all become bestsellers and he is today rated as one of the world's most popular authors of horror fiction, alongside his American counterpart, Stephen King. Herbert has written two major novels featuring haunted houses, *Haunted* (1988) and *The Ghosts of Sleath* (1994), both cases of the resourceful but troubled David Ash of the Psychical Research Institute. The dangers facing a ghost hunter investigating a haunted building are explained in this chilling episode from *Haunted*.

Ash spent the rest of the evening setting up equipment around the house. Four thermometers, whose lowest reading during the night would be registered, were placed against walls or rested on furniture; tape recorders with noise-actuation devices were located in the library and kitchen; cameras linked to capacitance change detectors, so that any movement in the vicinity would trigger off shutters, were set up in the drawing room and study; at certain points, both upstairs and down, he sprinkled a fine layer of powder on the floor, and across one or two doorways he stretched black cotton.

Later, by lamplight, he sat in his room and studied rough plans he had drawn up of Edbrook, with its labyrinth of rooms and corridors, occasionally taking a nip from the vodka bottle standing within hand's reach on the bureau. He smoked one cigarette after another as he made notes in a pad and now and again he would glance towards the window where the night seemed to press against the glass.

Eventually he left the room to roam the house, treading warily around powder patches, not entering those places containing detection instruments, nor disturbing doors with cotton stretched across.

Edbrook was quiet. And it was still.

Somewhere in the house a clock chimed the late hour. Ash, using a flashlight for guidance, walked the length of the corridor, passing his own room, heading for the window at the far end. Even though he was tired physically, his senses were acutely alert, as if his mind were a restless passenger inside a rundown vehicle. Kate McCarrick's considered diagnosis of his usual condition was always clear-cut: "You drink too much, and smoke too much. And one day – it may be some time in coming, David, but it'll happen – your brain will be dulled as your body often is." Might be no bad thing, Kate, he thought. No bad thing at all.

He reached the window and switched off the flashlight, standing close to the glass to see beyond. The blanket clouds had finally given way, although not entirely: milky-edged cumuli remained, almost motionless, tumbled in the night sky like frozen avalanches. The moon had a space all of its own, as though its white-silver had eaten away the surrounding clutter, and deep shadows were cast across the lawns and gardens below the window. There were forms down there other than those arboreal, statues whose clearly-defined shadows pointed towards Edbrook like accusing fingers. From a distant place amidst the wooded areas came the hollow shriek of a night creature, a sound no less disturbing for its faintness.

Ash looked on, but his gaze did not rove, for his thoughts were directed inwards at that moment. The piteous, animal cry had stirred a memory, one more distant in his own mind than its catalyst from the trees. He remembered the sharp, human screech that had once skited across rushing water and possibly the vision would have emerged as a whole had not a noise from behind caused him to turn.

He flicked on the flashlight and shone it along the corridor, the beam swift to repel the blackness. The light caught a vague movement by the stairway.

Without hesitation, Ash hurried towards it and as he approached he realized that the fine powder he had laid earlier that evening was swirling in the air as though caught by a wind.

He stopped at the edge of the billowing, torchlight catching a million tiny motes in its glare, and stared in astonishment. There was no breeze that could flurry the dust so, and no person who might have caused the disturbance was on the stairs. He quickly checked a thermometer hanging nearby from a light-fitting on the wall and was alarmed to find the temperature was close to zero. Yet he felt no chill himself.

More sounds. From below. Like bare feet on wood.

Ash went to the balcony and peered over, shining the light into the hallway there. He glimpsed something grey or white disappearing round a corner.

Quietly, no more than a loud whisper, he called: "Christina?"

He moved to the stairs, brushing the still-swirling powder away from his face as he passed through. Descending hastily, he swung the beam around the hall until satisfied that all doors were closed, his attention then caught by further sounds. He pointed the light down the hallway towards the rear of the house, certain that the noises had come from the kitchen area.

As he went off in that direction he noticed the door beneath the stairs – the cellar door – was slightly ajar. He stopped, aware that he had shut it earlier, but another sound from ahead sped him onwards.

Ash entered the darkened kitchen, the flashlight darting from table to cupboards, sink to old iron ovens and grate, dresser to window. The low snarling seemed terribly close.

He turned too quickly, the torch catching the doorframe, the light instantly snuffed. With less control than he would have liked, Ash scrabbled on the wall by the door for the lightswitch, his fumbling fingers finding and striking down. The light was dull, but enough for him to see that the kitchen was empty. And that a door opposite, which he knew led to the terrace and gardens, was open.

He heard someone outside, a muffled giggle.

Leaving the broken flashlight on the table, Ash went through the kitchen and out into the night.

Bright though the moon was, it was several moments before his eyes adjusted to the contrast, and a second or two longer before he could be sure of what he was seeing. A figure dressed in flowing white was flitting across the terrace. It suddenly vanished from view.

Ash's eyes narrowed, his face washed in moonlight. Again, almost under his breath, the question: "Christina?"

He followed, breaking into a slow run, reaching the steps that led down from the terrace into the gardens. He searched for the figure in white, certain that he had lost sight of it at this point. Yet nothing moved among the flowers and shrubbery below.

Ash descended and took the centre path towards the pond, eyes seeking left and right. He reached the low crumbling wall and looked down on the water, its still surface shiny with moonlight, the silver sheen somehow compelling.

His fascination was broken by the sound he had heard before – the soft padding of footsteps. Only this time they were hurried, and the bare feet were against flagstones.

He whirled around to face whatever it was rushing towards

him, but was struck by a powerful force so that he hurtled backwards, the wall catching his legs, sending him toppling.

Stagnant water closed over his head, its grip cold and slimy. Ash struggled in panic as weed tendrils clutched him. He twisted frantically, their grip tightening. Clouds of mud stirred and swelled sluggishly so that the moonlight ceiling above was smeared.

As he fought to free his arm of syrupy fronds he saw, sinking towards him through those eddying clouds, a silhouette, a shape whose arms were outstretched, as if crucified, whose flimsy robe billowed and swayed with the currents, whose black hair spread outwards in Gorgonian tresses.

Foul-tasting water gushed in to stifle Ash's scream.

# Computer Séance

## Ruth Rendell

### Prospectus

**Address:** Kendal Street, Edgware Road, London, England.

**Property:** Nineteenth-century building converted into flats. Comfortable and intimate apartment with sitting room, kitchen, bathroom and two bedrooms. Convenient for Oxford Street and Mayfair.

**Viewing Date:** December, 1997.

**Agent:** Ruth Rendell (1930–) was born in London and began her working life as a reporter in Essex. The publication of her first novel, *From Doon with Death* (1964) featuring Chief Inspector Reginald Wexford, heralded the arrival of a major new talent in crime fiction. Ruth Rendell's subsequent books about Wexford, along with a separate series as "Barbara Vine" that deal with various *outré* subjects, have established her as arguably the leading crime writer of her generation. She has also written a number of supernatural tales, notably "The Haunting of Shawley Rectory" and "Computer Séance", which puts a completely new twist on psychic phenomena.

Sophia de Vasco (Sheila Vosper on her birth certificate) was waiting at the bus stop when she saw her brother coming out of a side turning. Her brother looked a lot younger than he had before he died seven years before, but any doubts she might have had as to his identity were dispelled when he came up to her and asked her for money.

"Price of a cup of tea, missus?"

"You haven't changed, Jimmy," said Sophia with a little laugh.

He didn't reply but continued to hold out his hand.

Sophia said roguishly, "Now how would I know the price of a cup of tea, eh?"

"Fifty pee," said Jimmy's ghost. "A couple of quid for a cuppa and a butty."

"I think you've been following my career from the Other Side, Jimmy. You know I've done rather well for myself since you passed over. You've seen how I've been responsible for London's spiritualist renaissance, haven't you? But you have to realise that I am no more made of money than I have ever been. If you're thinking Mother and Father left me anything you're quite wrong."

"You some sort of loony tune?" He was looking at her fake fur, her high-heeled boots, the two large carriers and small leather case she carried. "What's in the bag?"

"That is my computer. An indispensable tool of my trade, Jimmy. You could call it a symbol of the electronic advances spiritualism has made in recent years. My bus is coming now so I'll say goodbye."

She went upstairs. She thought he might follow her but when she was sitting down she looked behind her and he was nowhere to be seen. Encounters with her dead relatives were not unusual events in Sophia's life. Only last week her aunt Lily had walked into her bedroom at midnight – she had always been a nocturnal type – and brought her a lot of messages from her mother, mostly warnings to Sophia to be on her guard in matters of men and money. Then, two evenings ago, an old woman came through the wall while Sophia was eating her supper. They manifested themselves so confidently, Sophia thought, because she never showed fear, she absolutely wasn't frightened. The old woman didn't stay long but flitted about the flat, peering at everything, and disappeared after telling Sophia that she was her maternal grandmother who had died in the Spanish Flu epidemic of 1919.

So it was no great surprise to have seen Jimmy. In life he had always been feckless, unable to hold down a job, chronically short of money, with a talent for nothing but sponging off his relations. Few tears had been shed when his body was found floating in the Grand Union Canal, into which he had fallen after two or three too many in the Hero of Maida. Sophia devoutly hoped he wouldn't embarrass her by manifesting himself at the séance she was about to hold in half an hour's time at Mrs Paget-Brown's.

But, in fact, he was to make a more positive, almost concrete, appearance before that. As she descended the stairs from the top of the bus she saw him waiting for her at the stop. A less sensitive woman than Sophia might have assumed that he too had come on the bus and had sat downstairs, but she knew better. Why go on a bus when, in the manner of spirits, he could travel through space in no time and be wherever he wished in the twinkling of an eye?

Sophia decided that the only wise course was to ignore him. She shook her head in his direction and set off at a brisk pace along Kendal Street. Outside the butcher's she looked round and saw him following her. There was nothing to be done about it, she could only hope he wasn't going to attach himself to her, even take up residence in her flat, for that might mean all the trouble and expense of an exorcism.

Mrs Paget-Brown lived in Hyde Park Square. Before she rang the bell Sophia looked behind her once more. It was growing dark and she could no longer see Jimmy, but it might only be that he was already inside, in the drawing room, waiting for her. It couldn't be helped. Mrs Paget-Brown opened the door promptly. She had everything prepared, the long rectangular table covered by a dark brown chenille cloth, Sophia's chair, the semicircle of chairs behind it. Five guests were expected, of whom two had already arrived. They were in the dining room, having a cup of herb tea, for Sophia discouraged the consumption of alcohol before encounters with denizens of the Other Side.

When Mrs Paget-Brown had gone back to her guests, Sophia

took her laptop out of its case and set it on the table. She raised its lid so that the keyboard and screen could be seen. Then she took a large screen out of one her carriers and plugged its cable into one of the computer ports. Glancing over her shoulder to check that Mrs Paget-Brown was really gone and the door shut, she took a big keyboard out of the other carrier and plugged its cable into a second port.

The doorbell rang and rang again five minutes afterwards. That probably meant everyone had arrived for two of the expected guests were a husband and wife, a Mr. and Mrs Jameson, hoping for an encounter with their dead daughter. Mrs Paget-Brown had told her a lot about this daughter, how she had been called Deirdre, had had a husband and two small children and had been a harpist. Sophia sometimes felt a warm glow of happiness when she reflected how often she was able to bring relief and hope to such people as the Jamesons by putting them in touch with those who had gone before.

The computer was switched on, the small screen dark, the big screen alight but blank. She had settled herself into the big chair with the keyboard on her lap, and it and her hands covered by the overhang of the chenille cloth, when someone tapped on the door and asked if she was ready. In a fluting voice Sophia asked them to come in.

She wouldn't have been at all surprised if Jimmy had been among them. They wouldn't have been able to see him, of course, but she would. Still, only six people entered the room, including Mrs Paget-Brown herself, the couple called Jameson who had the dead daughter, a very fat man who wheezed, and two elderly women, one very smartly dressed in a turquoise suit, the other dowdy with untidy hair.

Sophia said a gracious "Good evening", and then, "Please take a seat behind me where you can see the screen. In a moment we shall turn out the lights but before that I want to explain what will happen. What may happen. I can guarantee nothing if the spirits are unwilling."

They sat down. The asthmatic man breathed noisily. Turquoise suit took her hat off. Sophia could see their faces reflected in the screen, Mrs Jameson's eyes bright with hope and yearning. The dowdy woman said could she ask a question and when Sophia said, certainly, my pleasure, asked if they would see anything or would it only be a matter of table raps and ectoplasm.

Sophia couldn't help laughing at the idea of ectoplasm. These people were so incredibly behind the times. But her laughter was kindly and she explained that there would be no table-rapping. The spirits, who were very advanced about such things, made their feelings and their messages known through the computer. Those seekers after truth who sat behind her would see answers appear on the screen.

Of course everyone's eyes went to the laptop's small integral keyboard. And when the lights were lowered it was possible to imagine those keys moving. Sophia kept her hands under the cloth, her fingers on the big keyboard. She was ceaselessly thankful that she had taken that touch-typing course all those years ago when she was a girl.

The asthmatic man's wife was the first spirit to present herself. Her husband asked her if she was happy and YES appeared in green letters on the screen. He asked her if she missed him and WAITING FOR YOU TO FOLLOW DEAR appeared. Very much impressed, Mrs Paget-Brown summoned up her father. She said in an awed voice that she could see the keys very faintly moving on the integral keyboard as his spirit fingers touched them. Her father answered YES when she asked if he was with her mother and NO when she inquired if death had been a painful experience. Sophia leaned back a little and closed her eyes. Communing with the spirits took it out of her.

But she supplied the dowdy woman with a fairly satisfactory dead fiancé, her dead husband's predecessor. In answer to a rather timid question he replied that he had always regretted not marrying her and his life had been a failure. When the dowdy woman reminded him that he had fathered five children, owned three houses, been a junior minister in Margaret Thatcher's administration and later on chairman of a multinational company, Sophia told herself to be more careful.

She was more successful with Deirdre Jameson. The Jamesons

were transfixed with joy when Deirdre declared her happiness on the screen and intimated that she watched over her husband and children from afar. Where she now was she had ample opportunity to play the harp and did so for all the company of heaven. For a moment Sophia wondered if she had gone too far but Mr and Mrs Jameson accepted everything and when the lights went on again, thanked her, as they put it, from the bottom of their hearts.

"Thank you, thank you, you have done a wonderful thing for us, you've transformed our lives."

As she packed everything up again, Sophia reflected on something she had occasionally thought of in the past. It wasn't possible for her to go too far, it wasn't possible for her to deceive. Although she might conceal from these seekers after truth the hidden keyboard and the busy activity of her hands, the truth must be that these spirits were present and waiting to communicate. She was a true medium and her hands were the means they entered in order to transmit their messages. The world wasn't ready yet to have the keyboard and the moving fingers exposed, there was too much ignorance and prejudice, but one day . . .

One day, Sophia believed, everyone would be attuned to seeing and speaking to the dead, as she had seen and spoken to Jimmy. One day, when the earth was filled with the glory of the supernatural.

Carrying her bags and her laptop in its case, she tapped on the dining room door, was admitted and given a small glass of sherry. Discreetly, Mrs Paget-Brown slipped an envelope containing her cheque into her hand. Turquoise suit wanted to know if she would hold a séance for herself and some personal friends in Westbourne Terrace next week and the Jamesons asked for more revelations from Deirdre. Sophia graciously accepted both invitations.

She was always the first to leave. It was wiser not to engage in too much conversation with the guests but to preserve the vague air of mystery that surrounded her. By now it was very dark and there were so many trees in this neighbourhood that the street lights failed to make much of a show. But there was enough light for her to see her brother. He was waiting for her on the corner of Hyde Park Street and Connaught Street.

No one else was about, the Edgware Road wasn't a very pleasant area for a woman to be alone in at night, and Sophia thought that, nuisance though Jimmy was, she wouldn't be altogether averse to a man's escort until her bus came. Then, of course, she realised how absurd this was. Jimmy's presence at her side would be no deterrent to a mugger who would be unable to see him.

"It's time you went back to wherever you came from, Jimmy," she said rather severely. "I must say I doubt if it's the pleasantest of places but you should have thought of that while you were on earth."

"Loony tune," said Jimmy, "I want the bag. I want all the bags. You give them to me and you'll be OK."

"Give you my computer? What an idea. You couldn't even carry it. The handle would pass right through your hand."

As if to demonstrate her error, Jimmy made a grab for the laptop in its case. Sophia snatched it back and held it above her head. She didn't cry out. It was all too absurd. She didn't see the knife either. In fact, she never saw it, only felt it like a blow that robbed her first of breath, then of life. She dropped the carriers. The secret keyboard made a little clatter when it struck the pavement.

Jimmy, or Darren Palmer, picked up the bags and retrieved the case. Next morning he sold the lot to a man he knew in Leather Lane market and spent the money on crack cocaine.

# 7

# HOUSES OF HORROR

## Terror Visions of the Stars

# In Letters of Fire

## Gaston Leroux

### Prospectus

**Address:** La Chaux-de-Fonds, Jura, France.

**Property:** Ancient mansion built on a shelf of rock previously the site of a castle. The property has two floors of large, high-ceilinged living- and bedrooms. It is surrounded by an extensive, wooded estate.

**Viewing Date:** June, 1908.

**Agent:** Gaston Leroux (1868–1927) had endured years of neglect as a writer until the worldwide success of the Andrew Lloyd Webber musical, *The Phantom of the Opera*, based on his original novel published in 1911. Born in Paris, Leroux initially earned his living as a reporter until he began producing "sensational" novels and scored a major success with *The Mystery of the Yellow Chamber* (1907), a classic "locked room" murder story. He capitalized on this with the tale of Erik, the scarred phantom of the Paris Opera House, which was filmed by Universal Pictures in 1925 starring Lon Chaney (1883–1930). Chaney, who became famous as "The Man of a Thousand Faces" for his remarkable ability to transform his features, appeared in a classic silent haunted house movie, *The Forbidden Room* (1914) before his role as the phantom. A keen reader, too, he possessed several of Gaston Leroux's works including "In Letters of Fire," which fascinated him with its story of a haunted room and an extraordinary cupboard that can apparently defy gravity.

We had been out hunting wild boars all day, when we were overtaken by a violent storm, which compelled us to seek refuge in a deep cavern. It was Makoko, our guide, who took upon himself to give utterance to the thought which haunted the minds of the four of us who had sought safety from the fury of the tempest – Mathis, Allan, Makoko, and myself.

"If the gentleman who lives in yonder house, which is said to be haunted by the devil, does not grant us the shelter of his roof tonight, we shall be compelled to sleep here."

Hardly had he uttered the words when a strange figure appeared at the entrance to the cavern.

"It is *he*!" exclaimed Makoko, grasping my arm.

I stared at the stranger.

He was tall, lanky, of bony frame, and melancholy aspect. Unconscious of our presence, he stood leaning on his fowling-piece at the entrance of the cavern, showing a strong aquiline nose, a thin moustache, a stern mouth, and lack-lustre eyes. He was bareheaded; his hair was thin, while a few grey locks fell behind his ears. His age might have been anywhere between forty and sixty. He must have been strikingly handsome in the days when the light still shone in those time-dimmed eyes and those bitter lips could still break into a smile – but handsome in a haughty and forbidding style. A kind of terrible energy still lurked beneath his features, spectral as those of an apparition.

By his side stood a hairless dog, low on its legs, which was evidently barking at us. Yet we could hear nothing! The dog, it was plain, was dumb, and *barked at us in silence*!

Suddenly the man turned towards us, and said in a voice of the most exquisite politeness:

"Gentlemen, it is out of the question for you to return to La Chaux-de-Fonds tonight. Permit me to offer you my hospitality."

Then, bending over his dog, he said:

"Stop barking, Mystère."

The dog closed his jaws at once.

Makoko emitted a grunt. During the five hours that we had been enjoying the chase, Mathis and Makoko had told Allan and myself, who were strangers to the district, some strange and startling stories about our host, whom they represented as having had, like Faust, dealings with the Evil Spirit.

It was not without some trepidation, therefore, that we all moved out of the cavern.

"Gentlemen," said the stranger, with a melancholy smile, "it is many a long year since my door was thrown open to visitors. I am not fond of society, but I must tell you that one night, six months ago, a youth who had lost his way came and knocked at that door and begged for shelter till the morning. I refused him his request. Next day a body was found at the bottom of the big marl-pit – a body partly devoured by wolves."

"Why, that must have been Petit-Leduc!" cried Makoko. "So you were heartless enough to turn the poor lad away, at night and in the midst of winter! You are his murderer!"

"Truly spoken," replied the man, simply. "It was I who killed him. And now you see, gentlemen, that the incident has rendered me hospitable."

"Would you tell us why you drove him from your door?" growled Makoko.

"Because," he replied, quietly, "my house brings misfortune."

"I would rather risk meeting the powers of darkness than catching a cold in the head," I retorted, laughing, and without further parley we set off, and in a short while had reached the door of the ancient mansion, which stood among the most desolate surroundings, on a shelf of barren rock, swept by all the winds of heaven.

The huge door, antique, iron-barred, and studded with enormous nails, revolved slowly on its hinges, and opened noiselessly. A shrunken little old dame was there to welcome us.

From the threshold we could see a large, high room, somewhat similar to the room formerly styled the retainers' hall. It certainly constituted a part of what remained of the castle, on the ruins of which the mansion had been erected some centuries before. It was fully lighted by the fire on the enormous hearth, where a huge log was burning, and by two petrol lamps hanging by chains from the stone roof. There was no furniture except a heavy table of white wood, a large armchair upholstered in leather, a few stools, and a rude sideboard.

We walked the length of the room. The old woman opened a door. We found ourselves at the foot of a worm-eaten staircase with sunken steps. This staircase, a spiral one, led to the second storey of the building, where the old woman showed us to our rooms.

To this day I can recall our host – were I to live a hundred years I could not forget that figure such as it appeared to me, as if framed by the fireplace – when I went into the hall where Mother Appenzel had spread our supper.

He was standing in front of my friends, on the stone hearth of that enormous fireplace. He was in evening dress – but such evening dress! It was in the pink of fashion, but a fashion long since vanished. The high collar of the coat, the broad lapels, the velvet waistcoat, the silken knee-breeches and stockings, the cravat, all seemed to possess the elegance of days gone by.

By his side lay his dog Mystère, his massive jaws parted in a yawn – yawning, just as he had barked, *in silence*.

"Has your dog been dumb for long?" I ventured to ask. "What strange accident has happened to him?"

"He has been dumb from his birth," replied my host, after a slight pause, as if this topic of conversation did not please him.

Still, I persisted in my questions.

"Was his father dumb – or perhaps his mother?"

"His mother, and his mother's mother," he replied, still coldly, "and *her* mother also."

"So you were the master of Mystère's great-grandmother?"

"I was, sir. She was indeed a faithful creature, and one who loved me well. A marvellous watch-dog," added my host, displaying sudden signs of emotion which surprised me.

"And she also was dumb from her birth?"

"No, sir. No, she was not born dumb – *but she became so one night when she had barked too much*!"

There was a world of meaning in the tone with which he spoke these words that at the moment I did not understand.

Supper was served. During the meal the conversation did not languish. Our host inquired whether we liked our rooms.

"I have a favour to beg of you," I ventured to say. "I should like to sleep in the haunted room!"

No sooner had I uttered the sentence than our host's pale face became still paler.

"Who has told you that there was a haunted room in this house?" he asked, striving with difficulty to restrain an evident irritation.

Mother Appenzel, who had just entered, trembled violently.

"It was you, Mother Appenzel?"

"Pray do not scold the good woman," I said; "my indiscreet behaviour alone must bear the blame. I was attempting to enter a room, the door of which was closed, when your servant forbade me to do so. 'Do not go into the haunted chamber,' she said."

"And you naturally did not do so?"

"Well, yes; I did go in."

"Heaven protect us!" wailed Mother Appenzel, letting fall a tumbler, which broke into pieces.

"Begone!" cried her master. Then, turning to us, he added, "You are indeed full of curiosity, gentlemen!"

"Pray pardon us if we are so," I said. "Moreover, permit me to remind you that it was you yourself who alluded to the rumours current on the mountainside. Well, it would afford me much pleasure if your generous hospitality should be the occasion of dispersing them. When I have slept in the room which enjoys so evil a reputation, and have rested there peacefully, it will no longer be said that, to use your own expression, 'your house brings misfortune.' "

Our host interrupted me: "You shall not sleep in that room; it is no longer used as a bedroom. No one has slept there for fifty years past."

"Who, then, was the last one to sleep in it?"

"I myself – and I should not advise anyone to sleep in it after me!"

"Fifty years ago, you say! You could only be a child at the time, at an age when one is still afraid at nights—"

"Fifty years ago I was twenty-eight!"

"Am I committing an indiscretion when asking you what

happened to you in that room? I have just come from visiting it, and nothing whatever happened to me. The room seems to me the most natural of rooms. I even attempted to prop up a wardrobe which seemed as if it were about to fall forward on its face."

"You laid hands on the wardrobe!" cried the man, throwing down his table-napkin, and coming towards me with the gleam of madness in his eyes. "You actually laid hands on the wardrobe?"

"Yes," was my quiet answer; "as I say, it seemed about to fall."

"But it cannot fall! It will never fall! Never again will it stand upright! It is its nature to be in that position for all time to come, trembling with fear for all eternity!"

We had all risen. The man's voice was harsh as he spoke these most mysterious words. Heavy drops of perspiration trickled down his face. Those eyes of his, which we had thought dimmed for ever, flashed with fury. He was indeed awful to contemplate. He grasped my wrist and wrung it with a strength of which I would have deemed him incapable.

"You did not open it?"

"No."

"Then you do not know what is in it? No? Well, all the better! By Heaven, I tell you, sir, it is all the better for *you*!"

Turning towards his dog, he shouted:

"To your kennel! When will you find your voice again, Mystère? Or are you going to die like the others – *in silence*?"

He had opened the door leading to a tower, and went out, driving the dog before him.

We were deeply moved at this unexpected scene. The man had disappeared in the darkness of the tower, still pursuing his dog.

"What did I tell you?" remarked Makoko, in a scarcely audible tone. "You may all please yourselves, but, as for me, I do not intend to sleep here tonight. I shall sit up here in this hall until daybreak."

"And so shall I," added Mathis.

Makoko, bending over us, his eyes staring out of their sockets, continued: "Do you not see that he is a madman?"

"You two fellows with your death-mask faces," exclaimed Allan, "are not going to prevent us from enjoying ourselves.

Supposing we start a game of écarté. We will ask our host to take a hand; it will divert his thoughts."

An extraordinary fellow was Allan. His fondness for card-playing amounted to a mania. He pulled out a pack of cards, and had hardly done so when our host re-entered the hall. He was now comparatively calm, but no sooner had he perceived the pack of cards on the table than his features became transformed, and assumed such an expression of fear and fury that I myself was terrified.

"Cards!" he cried. "You have cards!"

Allan rose and said, pleasantly:

"We have decided not to retire for the night. We are about to have a friendly little game of écarté. Do you know the game?"

Allan stopped. He also had been struck with the fearful expression on our host's face. His eyes were bloodshot, the sparse hairs of his moustache stood out bristling, his teeth gleamed, while his lips hissed out the words:

"Cards! Cards!"

The words escaped with difficulty from his throat, as if some invisible hand were clutching it.

"Who sent you here with cards? What do you want with me? The cards must be burnt – they must be burnt!"

Of a sudden he grasped the pack and was about to cast it into the flames, but he stopped just on the point of doing so, his trembling fingers let drop the cards, and he sank into the armchair, exclaiming hoarsely:

"I am suffocating; I am suffocating!"

We rushed to his succour, but with a single effort of his bony fingers he had already torn off his collar and his cravat; and now, motionless, holding his head erect, and settling down in the huge armchair, he burst into tears.

"You are good fellows," he said at last, in milder tones. "You shall know everything. You shall not leave this house in ignorance, taking me for a madman – for a poor, miserable, melancholy madman.

"Yes, indeed," he continued; "yes, you shall know everything. It may be of use to you."

He rose, paced up and down, then halted in front of us, staring at us with the dimmed look that had given way to the momentary flash.

"Sixty years ago I was entering upon my eighteenth year. With all the overweening presumption of youth, I was sceptical of everything. Nature had fashioned me strong and handsome. Fate had endowed me with enormous wealth. I became the most fashionable youth of my day. Paris, gentlemen, with all its pleasures, was for ten years at my feet. When I had reached the age of twenty-eight I was on the brink of ruin. There remained to me between two and three hundred thousand francs and this manor, with the land surrounding it.

"Just at that time, gentlemen, I fell madly in love with an angelic creature. I could never have dreamt of the existence of such beauty and purity. The girl whom I adored was ignorant of the passionate love which was consuming me, and she remained so. Her family was one of the wealthiest in all Europe. For nothing in this world would I have had her suspect that I aspired to the honour of her hand in order to replenish my empty coffers with her dowry. So I went the way of the gambling-dens, in the vain hope of recovering my vanished millions. I lost all, and one fine evening I left Paris to come and bury myself in this old mansion, my sole refuge.

"I found here an old man, Father Appenzel; his granddaughter, of whom later on I made a servant; and his grandson, a child of tender years, who grew up to manhood on the estate, and who is now my steward. I fell prey, on the very evening of my arrival, to despair and ennui. The astounding events that followed took place that very evening.

"When I went up to my room – the room which one of you has asked to be allowed to occupy tonight – I had made up my mind to take my own life. A brace of pistols lay on the chest of drawers. Suddenly, as I was putting my hand on one of the pistols, my dog began to howl in the courtyard – to howl as I have never heard the wind howl, unless it be tonight.

" 'So,' thought I, 'here is Mystère raising a death-howl. She must know that I am going to kill myself tonight.'

"I toyed with the pistol, recalling of a sudden what my past life had been, and wondering for the first time what my death would be like. Suddenly my eye lighted on the titles of a few old books which stood on a shelf hanging above the chest of drawers. I was surprised to see that all of them dealt with sorcerers and matters appertaining to the powers of evil. I took up a book, *The Sorcerers of the Jura*, and, with the sceptical smile of the man who has defied Fate, I opened it. The first two lines, printed in red, at once caught my eye:

" '*He who seriously wishes to see the devil has but to summon him with his whole heart, and he will come.*'

"Then followed the story of an individual who, like myself, a lover in despair – like myself, a ruined man – had in all sincerity summoned to his help the Prince of Darkness, and who had been assisted by him; for, a few months later, he had once more become incredibly rich and had married his beloved. I read the story to the end.

" 'Well, here was a lucky fellow!' I exclaimed, tossing the book on to the chest of drawers. Mystère was still howling in the grounds. I parted the window-curtains, and could not help shuddering when I saw the dog's shadow dancing in the moonlight. It really seemed as if the slut was possessed of some evil spirit, for her movements were inexplicably eccentric. She seemed to be snapping at some invisible form!

"I tried to laugh over the matter, but the state of my mind, the story I had just read, the howling of the dog, her strange leaps, the sinister locality, the old room, the pistols which I myself had loaded, all had contributed to take a greater hold of my imagination than I dared confess.

"Leaving the window I strolled about the room for awhile. Of a sudden I saw myself in the mirror of the wardrobe. My pallor was such that I thought that I was dead. Alas, no! The man standing before the wardrobe was not dead. It was, on the contrary, a living man who, with all his heart, was summoning the King of Lost Souls.

"Yes, with all my heart. I was too young to die; I wished to enjoy life for a while yet; to be rich once more; for her, for her sake, for the one who was an angel. Yes, yes, I, I myself summoned the devil!

"And then, in the mirror, side by side with my form, something appeared – something superhuman – a pale object – a mist, a terrible little cloud which was soon transformed into eyes – eyes of fearful loveliness. Another form was standing resplendent beside my haggard face; a mouth – a mouth which said to me, 'Open!' At this I recoiled. But the mouth was still saying to me, 'Open, open, if you dare!'

"Then something knocked three times upon the door inside the wardrobe – and the door flew open of its own accord!"

Just at that instant the old man's narrative was interrupted by three knocks on the door, which suddenly opened, and a man entered.

"Was it you who knocked like that, Guillaume?" asked our host, striving in vain to regain his composure.

"Yes, master."

"I had given you up for tonight. You saw the notary?"

"Yes; and I did not care to keep so great a sum of money about my person."

We gathered that Guillaume was the gentleman's steward. He advanced to the table, took a little bag from the folds of his cloak, extracted some documents from it, and laid them on the table. Then he drew an envelope from his bag, emptied its contents on the table, and counted out twelve one-thousand-franc notes.

"There's the purchase-money for Misery Wood."

"Good, Guillaume," said our host, picking up the banknotes and replacing them in the envelope. "You must be hungry. Are you going to sleep here tonight?"

"No; it is impossible. I have to call on the farmer. We have some business to transact together early in the morning. However, I do not mind having a bit of supper."

"Go to Mother Appenzel, my good fellow; she will take good care of you," adding, as the steward strode towards the kitchen, "Take away all those rubbishy papers."

The man picked up the documents, while the gentleman, taking a pocket-book out of his pocket, placed the envelope containing the twelve notes into it and returned the book to his pocket.

Then, resuming his narrative, in reply to a request from Makoko, he continued:

"You wish to know what the wardrobe contained? Well, I am going to tell you. There was something which I saw – something which scorched my eyes. There shone within the recess of the wardrobe, written in letters of fire, three words:

" 'THOU SHALT WIN!'

"Yes," he continued, in a gloomy tone, "the devil had, in three words, expressed, in characters of fire, in the depths of the wardrobe, the fate that awaited me. He had left behind him his sign-manual, the irrefutable proof of the hideous pact into which I had entered with him on that tragic night. 'Thou shalt win!' A ruined gamester, I sought to become rich, and he told me: 'Thou shalt win!' In three short words he granted me the world's wealth. 'Thou shalt win!'

"Next morning old Appenzel found me lying unconscious at the foot of the wardrobe. Alas! when I had recovered my senses I had forgotten nothing. I was fated never to forget what I had seen. Wherever I go, wherever I wend my steps, be it night, be it day, I read the fiery phrase, 'Thou shalt win!' – on the walls of darkness, on the resplendent orb of the sun, on the earth and in the skies, within myself when I close my eyes, on your faces when I look at you!"

The old man, exhausted, ceased speaking, and fell back, moaning, into the armchair.

"I must tell you," he resumed, after a few moments, "that my experience had had so terrifying an effect on me that I had been compelled to stay in bed, where Father Appenzel brought me a soothing potion of herbs. Addressing me, he said: 'Something incredible has happened, sir. Your dog has become dumb. *She barks in silence!*'

" 'Oh, I know, I understand!' I exclaimed. 'She will not recover her voice until *he* shall have returned!'

"Father Appenzel looked at me in amazement and fright, for my hair was standing on end. In spite of myself, my gaze was straying towards the wardrobe. Father Appenzel, as alarmed and agitated as myself, went on to say:

" 'When I found you, sir, on the floor this morning the wardrobe was inclined as it is now, while its door was open. I closed it, but I was unable to get it to stand upright. It seems always on the point of falling forward.'

"I begged old Appenzel to leave me to myself. I got out of bed, went to the wardrobe and opened its door. Conceive, I pray you, my feelings when I had done so. The sentence, that sentence written in characters of fire, was still there! It was graven in the boards at the back; it had burnt the boards with its imprint; and by day I read what I had read by night – the words: 'Thou shalt win.'

"I flew out of the room. I called for help. Father Appenzel returned. I said to him: 'Look into the depths of that wardrobe, and tell me what you see there!'

"My servant did as I bid him, and said to me: 'Thou shalt win!'

"I dressed myself. I fled like a madman from the accursed house, and wandered in the mountains. The mountain air did me good. When I came home in the evening I was perfectly calm; I had thought matters over; my dog might have become dumb through some perfectly natural physiological phenomenon. With regard to the sentence in the wardrobe, it had not come there of itself, and, as I had not had any previous acquaintance with that piece of furniture, it was probable that the three fatal words had been there for countless years, inscribed by someone addicted to the black art, following upon some gambling affair which was no concern of mine.

"I ate my supper, and went to bed in the same room. The night passed without incident.

"Next day I went to La Chaux-de-Fonds, to call on a notary. All that this adventure with the wardrobe had succeeded in doing was to imbue me with the idea of tempting fate in the shape of cards, one last time, ere putting into execution my idea about suicide. I borrowed a few one-thousand-franc notes on the security of the estate, and I took train for Paris. As I ascended the staircase of the club I recalled my nightmare, and remarked to myself ironically, for I placed no faith in the success of this supreme attempt: 'We shall now see whether, if the devil helps me—' I did not finish the sentence.

"The bank was being put up to auction when I entered the salon. I secured it for two hundred louis. I had not reached the middle of my deal when I had already won two hundred and fifty thousand francs! But no longer would any of the players stake against me. *I was winning every game!*

"I was jubilant; I had never dreamt that such luck would be mine. I threw up the bank – i.e., what remained of it for me to hold. I next amused myself at throwing away chances, just to see what would happen. In spite of this I continued winning. Exclamations were heard on all sides. The players vowed I had the devil's own luck. I collected my winnings and left.

"No sooner had I reached the street when I began to think and to become alarmed. The coincidence between the scene of the wardrobe and of my extraordinary success as a banker troubled me. Of a sudden, and to my surprise, I found myself wending my way back to the club. I was resolved to probe the matter to the bottom. My short-lived joy was disturbed by the fact that I had not lost once. So it was that I was anxious to lose just once.

"When I left the club for the second time, at six o'clock in the morning, I had won, in money and on parole, no less than a couple of millions. But I had not once lost – not a single, solitary time. I felt myself becoming a raving madman. When I say that I had not lost once, I speak with regard to money, for when I had played for nothing, without stakes, to see, just for the fun of the matter, I lost inexorably. But no sooner had a punter staked even as low as half a franc against me, I won his money. It mattered little, a sou or a million francs. I could no longer lose. 'Thou shalt win!' Oh, that terrible curse! That curse! For a whole week did I try. I went into the worst gambling-hells. I sat down to card-tables presided over by card-sharpers; I won even from them; I won from one and all against whom I played. I did nothing but win!

"So, you no longer laugh, gentlemen! You scoff no more! You

see now, good sirs, that one should never be in a hurry to laugh! I told you I had seen the devil! Do you believe me now? I possessed then the certainty, the palpable proof, visible to one and all, the natural and terrestrial proof of my revolting compact with the devil. The law of probabilities no longer existed as far as I was concerned. There were not even any probabilities. There remained only the supernatural certainty of winning eternally – until the day of death. Death! I could no longer dream of it as a desire. For the first time in my life I dreaded it. The terrors of death haunted me, because of what awaited me at the end!

"My uppermost thought was to redeem my soul – my wretched soul, my lost soul. I frequented the churches. I saw priests. I prostrated myself at the foot of the church steps. I beat my delirious head on the sacred flagstones! I prayed to God that I might lose, just as I had prayed to the devil that I might win. On leaving the holy place I was wont to hurry to some low gambling-den and stake a few louis on a card. But I continued winning for ever and ever! 'Thou shalt win!'

"Not for a single second did I entertain the idea of owing my happiness to those accursed millions. I offered up my heart to God as a burnt-offering, I distributed the millions I had won to the poor, and I came here, gentlemen, to await the death which spurns me – the death I dread!"

"You have never played since those days?" I asked.

"I have never played from that time until now."

Allan had read my thoughts. He too was dreaming that it might be possible to rescue from his monomania the man whom we both persisted in considering insane.

"I feel sure," he said, "that so great a sacrifice has won you pardon. Your despair has been undoubtedly sincere, and your punishment a terrible one. What more could Heaven require of you? In your place *I should try*—"

"You would try – what?" exclaimed the man, springing from his seat.

"I should try whether I were still doomed to win!"

The man struck the table a violent blow with his clenched fist.

"And so this is all the remedy you can suggest! So this is all the narrative of a curse transcending all things earthly has inspired you with? You seek to induce an old lunatic to play, with the object or demonstrating to him that he is not insane! For I read full well in your eyes what you think of me: 'He is mad, mad, mad!' You do not believe a single word of all I have told you. You think I am insane, young man! And you, too," he added, addressing Allan, "you think I am insane – mad, mad, mad! I tell you that I have seen the devil! Yes, your old madman has seen the devil! And he is going to prove it to you. The cards! Where are the cards?"

Espying them on the edge of the table, he sprang on them.

"It is you who have so willed it. I had harboured a supreme hope that I should die without having again made the infernal attempt, so that when my hour had come I might imagine that Heaven had forgiven me. Here are your cards! I will not touch them. They are yours. Shuffle them – deal me which you please – 'stack' them as you will. I tell you that I shall win. Do you believe me now?"

Allan had quietly picked up the cards.

The man, placing his hand on his shoulder, asked, "You do not believe me?"

"We shall see," replied Allan.

"What shall the stakes be?" I inquired.

"I do not know, gentlemen, whether you are well off or not, but I feel bound to inform you – you who have come to destroy my last hope – that you are ruined men."

Thereupon he took out his pocket-book and laid it on the table, saying:

"I will play you five straight points at écarté for the contents of this pocket-book. This just by way of a beginning. After that, I am willing to play you as many games as you see fit, until I cast you out of doors picked clean, your friends and yourself, ruined for the rest of your lives – yes, picked bare."

"Picked bare?" repeated Allan, who was far less moved than myself. "Do you want even our shirts?"

"Even your souls," cried the man, "which I intend to present to the devil in exchange for my own."

Allan winked at me, and asked:

"Shall we say 'Done,' and go halves in this?"

I agreed, shuffled the pack, and handed it to my opponent.

He cut. I dealt. I turned up the knave of hearts. Our host looked at his hand and led. Clearly he ought not to have played the hand he held – three small clubs, the queen of diamonds, and the seven of spades. He took a trick with his queen, I took the four others, and, as he had led, I marked two points. I entertained not the slightest doubt that he was doing his utmost to lose.

It was his turn to deal. He turned up the king of spades. He could not restrain a shudder when he beheld that black-faced card, which, in spite of himself, gave him a trick.

He scanned his hand anxiously. It was my turn to call for cards. He refused them, evidently believing that he held a very poor hand; but my own was as bad as his, and he had a ten of hearts, which took my nine – I held the nine, eight, and seven of hearts.

He then played diamonds, to which I could not respond and two clubs higher than mine. Neither of us held a single trump. He scored a point, which, with the one secured to him by his king, gave him two. We were "evens," either of us being in a position to end matters at once if we made three points.

The deal was mine. I turned up the eight of diamonds. This time both of us called for cards. He asked for one, and showed me the one he had discarded – the seven of diamonds. He was anxious not to hold any trumps. His wish was gratified, and he succeeded in making me score another two points, which gave me four.

In spite of ourselves, Allan and I glanced towards the pocket-book. Our thoughts ran: "There lies a small fortune which is shortly to be ours, one which, in all conscience, we shall not have had much trouble in winning."

Our host dealt in his turn, and when I saw the cards he had given me I considered the matter as good as settled. This time he had not turned up a king, but the seven of clubs. I held two hearts and three trumps – the ace and king of hearts, the ace, ten, and nine of clubs. I led the king, my opponent followed with the queen; I flung the ace on the table, my opponent being compelled to take it with the knave of hearts, and he then played a diamond, which I trumped. I played the ace of trumps; he took it with the queen, but I was ready for him with my last card, the ten of clubs. He had the knave of trumps! As I had led he scored two, making "four all." Our host smothered a curse which was hovering on his lips.

"No need for you to worry," I remarked, "no one has won yet."

"We are about to prove to you," said Allan, in the midst of a deathly silence, "that you can lose just like any ordinary mortal."

Our host groaned, "I cannot lose."

The interest in the game was now at its height. A point on either side, and either of us would be the winner. If I turned up the king the game was ended, and I won twelve thousand francs from a man who claimed that he could not lose. I had dealt. I turned up the king – the king of hearts. I had won!

My opponent uttered a cry of joy. He bent over the card, picked it up, considered it attentively, fingered it, raised it to his eyes, and we thought that he was about to press it to his lips. He murmured:

"Great heavens, can it be? Then – then I have lost!"

"So it would seem," I remarked.

Allan added, "You now see full well that one should not place any faith in what the devil says."

The gentleman took his pocket-book and opened it.

"Gentlemen," he sighed, "bless you for having won all that is in this book. Would that it contained a million! I should gladly have handed it over to you."

With trembling hands he searched the pocket-book, emptying it of all its contents, with a look of surprise at not finding at once the twelve thousand francs he had deposited in its folds. They were not there!

The pocket-book, searched with feverish hands, lay empty on the table. *There was nothing in the pocket-book! Nothing!*

We sat dumbfounded at this inexplicable phenomenon – the empty pocket-book! We picked it up and fingered it. We searched it carefully, only to find it empty. Our host, livid and as one possessed, was searching himself, and begging us to search him.

We searched him – we searched him, because it was beyond our power to resist his delirious will; but we found nothing – nothing!

"Hark!" exclaimed our host. "Hark, hark! Does it not seem to you tonight that the wind sounds like the voice of a dog?"

We listened, and Makoko answered, "It is true! The wind really seems to be barking – there, behind the door!"

The door was shaking strangely, and we heard a voice calling, "Open!"

I drew the bolts and opened the door. A human form rushed into the room.

"It is the steward," I said.

"Sir, sir!" he ejaculated.

"What is it?" we all exclaimed, breathlessly, wondering what was about to follow.

"Sir, I thought I had handed you your twelve thousand francs. Indeed, I am positive I did so. Those gentlemen doubtless saw me."

"Yes, indeed," from all of us.

"Well, I have just discovered them in my bag. I cannot understand how it has happened. I have returned to bring them back to you – *once more*. Here they are."

The steward again pulled out the identical envelope, and a second time counted the twelve one-thousand-franc notes, adding:

"I know not what ails the mountainside tonight, but it terrifies me. I shall sleep here."

The twelve thousand francs were now lying on the table. Our host cried:

"This time we see them there, there before us! Where are the cards? Deal them. The twelve thousand in five straight points, to see, to know for certain. I tell you that I wish to know – *to know*."

I dealt. My opponent called for cards; I refused them. He had five trumps. He scored two points. He dealt the cards. He turned up the king. I led. He again had five trumps. Three and two are five! He had won!

Then he howled; yes, howled like the wind which had the voice of a dog. He snatched the cards from the table and cast them into the flames. "Into the fire with the cards Let the fire consume them!" he shrieked.

Suddenly he strode towards the door. Outside a dog barked – a dog raising a death-howl.

The man reached the door, and speaking through it asked:

"Is that you, Mystère?"

To what phenomenon was it due that both wind and dog were silent simultaneously?

The man softly drew the bolts and half opened the door. No sooner was the door ajar than the infernal yelping broke out so prolonged and so lugubrious that it made us shiver to our very marrow. Our host had now flung himself upon the door with such force that we could almost think he had smashed it. Not content with having pushed back the bolts, he pressed with his knees and arms against the door, without uttering a sound. All we heard was his panting respiration.

Then, when the death-like yelping had ceased, and both within and without silence reigned supreme, the man, turning towards us and tottering forward, said:

"*He has returned! Beware!*"

Midnight. We have gone our respective ways. Makoko and Mathis have remained below beside the dying embers. Allan has sought his bedroom, while, driven by some unknown inner force controlling me absolutely, I find myself in the haunted room. I am repeating the doings of the man whose story we had heard that night; I select the same book, open it at the same page; I go to the same window; I pull the curtain aside; I gaze upon the same moonlit landscape, for the wind has long since driven off the tempest-clouds and the fog. I only see bare rocks, shining like steel under the rays of the bright moon, and – on the desolate plateau – a weirdly dancing shadow – the shadow of Mystère, with her formidable jaws wide apart – jaws that I can see barking. Do I hear the barking? Yes; it seems to me that I hear it. I let the curtain drop. I take my candlestick from the chest of drawers. I step towards the wardrobe. I look at myself in its mirrored panel. I dream of *him* who wrote the words which lie concealed within.

Whose face is it that I see in the mirror? It is my own! But is it possible that the face of our host on the fatal night could have been more pallid than mine is now? In all truth, my face is that of a dead man. On one side – there – there – that little cloud – that misty cloudlet in the mirror – cheek by jowl with my face – those fearful eyes – those lips! Oh, if I could but scream! I cannot. I am powerless to cry out, *when suddenly I hear three knocks*. And – and my hand strays of its own accord towards the door of the wardrobe – my inquisitive hand – my accursed hand.

Of a sudden my hand is gripped in the vice I know so well. I look round. I am face to face with our host, who says to me in a voice which seems to come from another world:

"*Do not open it!*"

## Epilogue

Next morning we did not ask our host to give us the opportunity of winning back our money. We fled from his roof without even taking leave of him. Twelve thousand francs were sent that evening to our strange host through Makoko's father, to whom we had told our adventure. He returned them to us, with the following note:

"We are quits. When we played, both the first game, which you won, and the second one, which you lost, we *believed*, you and I, that we were staking twelve thousand francs. That must be sufficient for us. The devil has my soul, but he shall not posses my honour."

We were not at all anxious to keep the twelve thousand francs, so we presented them to a hospital in La Chaux-de-Fonds which was in sore need of money. Following upon urgent repairs, to which our donation was applied, the hospital, one winter's night, was so thoroughly burned to the ground that at noon of the following day nothing but ashes remained of it.

# The Judge's House

## Bram Stoker

### Prospectus

**Address:** Judge's House, Benchurch, Hampshire, England.

**Property:** Jacobean-style house with heavy gables and beautiful oak-panelled rooms. Secluded location with high brick walls. Former residence of a notorious hanging judge.

**Viewing Date:** December, 1891.

**Agent:** Bram Stoker (1847–1912) is, of course, famous for *Dracula* (1897), which he was originally going to entitle *The Un-Dead*, and for which he had no name for the central character other than the term "old dead man made alive" until he had almost completed the first draft of the manuscript. Born in Ireland, Stoker studied briefly for the bar before becoming manager to the demanding English actor, Sir Henry Irving. Stoker used what little spare time he had to write, but apart from the enduring success of *Dracula*, most of his other novels are now forgotten. The performance of Hungarian-born Bela Lugosi (1882–1956) in the Universal Pictures' 1931 adaptation of the book began the transformation of the Transylvanian count into an icon of screen horror. The actor was a great admirer of Stoker's work, especially "The Judge's House", which – he liked to recall in his heavy mid-European accent – had a particularly memorable line, "Bogies is rats – and rats is bogies!"

When the time for his examination drew near Malcolm Malcolmson made up his mind to go somewhere to read by himself. He feared the attractions of the seaside, and also he feared completely rural isolation, for of old he knew its charms, and so he determined to find some unpretentious little town where there would be nothing to distract him. He refrained from asking suggestions from any of his friends, for he argued that each would recommend some place of which he had knowledge, and where he had already acquaintances. As Malcolmson wished to avoid friends he had no wish to encumber himself with the attention of friends' friends, and so he determined to look out for a place for himself. He packed a portmanteau with some clothes and all the books he required, and then took ticket for the first name on the local timetable which he did not know.

When at the end of three hours' journey he alighted at Benchurch, he felt satisfied that he had so far obliterated his tracks as to be sure of having a peaceful opportunity of pursuing his studies. He went straight to the one inn which the sleepy little place contained, and put up for the night. Benchurch was a market town, and once in three weeks was crowded to excess, but for the remainder of the twenty-one days it was as attractive as a desert. Malcolmson looked around the day after his arrival to try to find quarters more isolated than even so quiet an inn as "The Good Traveller" afforded. There was only one place which took his fancy, and it certainly satisfied his wildest ideas regarding quiet; in fact, quiet was not the proper word to apply to it – desolation was the only term conveying any suitable idea of its isolation. It was an old rambling, heavy-built house of the Jacobean style, with heavy gables and windows, unusually small, and set higher than was customary in such houses, and was surrounded with a high brick wall massively built. Indeed, on examination, it looked more like a fortified house than an ordinary dwelling. But all these things pleased Malcolmson. "Here," he thought, "is the very spot I have been looking for, and if I can only get opportunity of using it I shall be happy." His joy was increased when he realised beyond doubt that it was not at present inhabited.

From the post-office he got the name of the agent, who was

rarely surprised at the application to rent a part of the old house. Mr. Carnford, the local lawyer and agent, was a genial old gentleman, and frankly confessed his delight at anyone being willing to live in the house.

"To tell you the truth," said he, "I should be only too happy, on behalf of the owners, to let anyone have the house rent-free for a term of years if only to accustom the people here to see it inhabited. It has been so long empty that some kind of absurd prejudice has grown up about it, and this can be best put down by its occupation – if only," he added with a sly glance at Malcolmson, "by a scholar like yourself, who wants its quiet for a time."

Malcolmson thought it needless to ask the agent about the "absurd prejudice"; he knew he would get more information, if he should require it, on that subject from other quarters. He paid his three months' rent, got a receipt, and the name of an old woman who would probably undertake to "do" for him, and came away with the keys in his pocket. He then went to the landlady of the inn, who was a cheerful and most kindly person, and asked her advice as to such stores and provisions as he would be likely to require. She threw up her hands in amazement when he told her where he was going to settle himself.

"Not in the Judge's House!" she said, and grew pale as she spoke. He explained the locality of the house, saying that he did not know its name. When he had finished she answered:

"Aye, sure enough – sure enough the very place! It is the Judge's House sure enough." He asked her to tell him about the place, why so called, and what there was against it. She told him that it was so called locally because it had been many years before – how long she could not say, as she was herself from another part of the country, but she thought it must have been a hundred years or more – the abode of a judge who was held in great terror on account of his harsh sentences and his hostility to prisoners at Assizes. As to what there was against the house itself she could not tell. She had often asked, but no one could inform her; but there was a general feeling that there was *something*, and for her own part she would not take all the money in Drinkwater's Bank and stay in the house an hour by herself. Then she apologised to Malcolmson for her disturbing talk.

"It is too bad of me, sir, and you – and a young gentleman, too – if you will pardon me saying it, going to live there all alone. If you were my boy – and you'll excuse me for saying it – you wouldn't sleep there a night, not if I had to go there myself and pull the big alarm bell that's on the roof!" The good creature was so manifestly in earnest, and was so kindly in her intentions, that Malcomson, although amused, was touched. He told her kindly how much he appreciated her interested in him, and added:

"But, my dear Mrs. Witham, indeed you need not be concerned about me! A man who is reading for the Mathematical Tripos has too much to think of to be disturbed by any of these mysterious 'somethings,' and his work is of too exact and prosaic a kind to allow of his having any corner in his mind for mysteries of any kind. Harmonical Progression, Permutations and Combinations, and Elliptic Functions have sufficient mysteries for me!"

Mrs. Witham kindly undertook to see after his commissions, and he went himself to look for the old woman who had been recommended to him.

When he returned to the Judge's House with her, after an interval of a couple of hours, he found Mrs. Witham herself waiting with several men and boys carrying parcels, and an upholsterer's man with a bed in a cart, for she said, though tables and chairs might be all very well, a bed that hadn't been aired for mayhap fifty years was not proper for young bones to lie on. She was evidently curious to see the inside of the house; and though manifestly so afraid of the "somethings" that at the slightest sound she clutched on to Malcomson, whom she never left for a moment, went over the whole place.

After his examination of the house, Malcomson decided to take up his abode in the great dining-room, which was big enough to serve for all his requirements; and Mrs. Witham, with the aid of the charwoman, Mrs. Dempster, proceeded to arrange matters. When the hampers were brought in and unpacked, Malcomson saw that with much kind forethought she had sent from her own kitchen sufficient provisions to last for a few days. Before going she expressed all sorts of kind wishes; and at the door turned and said:

"And perhaps, sir, as the room is big and draughty it might be well to have one of those big screens put round your bed at night – though, truth to tell, I would die myself if I were to be so shut in with all kinds of – of 'things,' that put their heads round the sides, or over the top, and look on me!" The image which she had called up was too much for her nerves, and she fled incontinently.

Mrs. Dempster sniffed in a superior manner as the landlady disappeared, and remarked that for her own part she wasn't afraid of all the bogies in the kingdom.

"I'll tell you what it is, sir," she said; "bogies is all kinds and sorts of things – except bogies! Rats and mice, and beetles; and creaky doors, and loose slates, and broken panes, and stiff drawer handles, that stay out when you pull them and then fall down in the middle of the night. Look at the wainscot of the room! It is old – hundreds of years old! Do you think there's no rats and beetles there! And do you imagine, sir, that you wont see none of them? Rats is bogies, I tell you, and bogies is rats; and don't you get to think anything else!"

"Mrs. Dempster," said Malcomson gravely, making her a polite bow, "you know more than a Senior Wrangler! And let me say, that, as a mark of esteem for your indubitable soundness of head and heart, I shall, when I go, give you possession of this house, and let you stay here by yourself for the last two months of my tenancy, for four weeks will serve my purpose."

"Thank you kindly, sir!" she answered, "but I couldn't sleep away from home a night. I am in Greenhow's Charity, and if I slept a night away from my rooms I should lose all I have got to live on. The rules is very strict; and there's too many watching for a vacancy for me to run any risks in the matter. Only for that, sir, I'd gladly come here and attend on you altogether during your stay."

"My good woman," said Malcomson hastily, "I have come here on purpose to obtain solitude; and believe me that I am grateful to the late Greenhow for having so organised his admirable charity – whatever it is – that I am perforce denied the opportunity of suffering from such a form of temptation! Saint Anthony himself could not be more rigid on the point!"

The old woman laughed harshly. "Ah, you young gentlemen," she said, "you don't fear for naught; and belike you'll get all the solitude you want here." She set to work with her cleaning; and by nightfall, when Malcomson returned from his walk – he always had one of his books to study as he walked – he found the room swept and tidied, a fire burning in the old hearth, the lamp lit, and the table spread for supper with Mrs. Witham's excellent fare. "This is comfort, indeed," he said, as he rubbed his hands.

When he had finished his supper, and lifted the tray to the other end of the great oak dining table, he got out his books again, put fresh wood on the fire, trimmed his lamp, and set himself down to a spell of real hard work. He went on without pause till about eleven o'clock, when he knocked off for a bit to fix his fire and lamp, and to make himself a cup of tea. He had always been a tea-drinker, and during his college life had sat late at work and had taken tea late. The rest was a great luxury to him, and he enjoyed it with a sense of delicious, voluptuous ease. The renewed fire leaped and sparkled, and threw quaint shadows through the great old room; and as he sipped his hot tea he revelled in the sense of isolation from his kind. Then it was that he began to notice for the first time what a noise the rats were making.

"Surely," he thought, "they cannot have been at it all the time I was reading. Had they been, I must have noticed it!" Presently, when the noise increased, he satisfied himself that it was really new. It was evident that at first the rats had been frightened at the presence of a stranger, and the light of fire and lamp; but that as the time went on they had grown bolder and were now disporting themselves as was their wont.

How busy they were! And hark to the strange noises! Up and down behind the old wainscot, over the ceiling and under the floor they raced, and gnawed, and scratched! Malcomson smiled to himself as he recalled to mind the saying of Mrs. Dempster, "Bogies is rats, and rats is bogies!" The tea began to have its effect of intellectual and nervous stimulus, he saw with joy another long spell of work to be done before the night was past, and in the sense of security which it gave him, he allowed himself the luxury of a good look round the room. He took his lamp in one hand, and went all around, wondering that so quaint and beautiful an old house had been so long neglected. The carving of the oak on the panels of the wainscot was fine, and on and round the doors and windows it was beautiful and of rare merit. There were some old pictures on the walls, but they were coated so thick with dust and dirt that he could not distinguish any detail of them, though he held his lamp as high as he could over his head. Here and there as he went round he saw some crack or hole blocked for a moment by the face of a rat with its bright eyes glittering in the light, but in an instant it was gone, and a squeak and a scamper followed. The thing that most struck him, however, was the rope of the great alarm bell on the roof, which hung down in a corner of the room on the right-hand side of the fireplace.

He pulled up close to the hearth a great high-backed carved oak chair, and sat down to his last cup of tea. When this was done he made up the fire, and went back to his work, sitting at the corner of the table, having the fire to his left. For a little while the rats disturbed him somewhat with their perpetual scampering, but he got accustomed to the noise as one does to the ticking of a clock or to the roar of moving water; and he became so immersed in his work that everything in the world, except the problem which he was trying to solve, passed away from him.

He suddenly looked up, his problem was still unsolved, and there was in the air that sense of the hour before the dawn, which is so dread to doubtful life. The noise of the rats had ceased. Indeed it seemed to him that it must have ceased but lately and that it was the sudden cessation which had disturbed him. The fire had fallen low, but still it threw out a deep red glow. As he looked he started in spite of his *sang froid*.

There on the great high-backed carved oak chair by the right side of the fireplace sat an enormous rat, steadily glaring at him with baleful eyes. He made a motion to it as though to hunt it away, but it did not stir. Then he made the motion of throwing something. Still it did not stir, but showed its great white teeth angrily, and its cruel eyes shone in the lamplight with an added vindictiveness.

Malcomson felt amazed, and seizing the poker from the hearth ran at it to kill it. Before, however, he could strike it, the rat, with a squeak that sounded like the concentration of hate, jumped upon the floor, and, running up the rope of the alarm bell, disappeared in the darkness beyond the range of the green-shaded lamp. Instantly, strange to say, the noisy scampering of the rats in the wainscot began again.

By this time Malcomson's mind was quite off the problem; and as a shrill cock-crow outside told him of the approach of morning, he went to bed and to sleep.

He slept so sound that he was not even waked by Mrs. Dempster coming in to make up his room. It was only when she had tidied up the place and got his breakfast ready and tapped on the screen which closed in his bed that he woke. He was a little tired still after his night's hard work, but a strong cup of tea soon freshened him up and, taking his book, he went out for his morning walk, bringing with him a few sandwiches lest he should not care to return till dinner time. He found a quiet walk between high elms some way outside the town, and here he spent the greater part of the day studying his Laplace. On his return he looked in to see Mrs. Witham and to thank her for her kindness. When she saw him coming through the diamond-paned bay window of her sanctum she came out to meet him and asked him in. She looked at him searchingly and shook her head as she said:

"You must not overdo it, sir. You are paler this morning than you should be. Too late hours and too hard work on the brain isn't good for any man! But tell me, sir, how did you pass the night? Well, I hope? But, my heart! Sir, I was glad when Mrs. Dempster told me this morning that you were all right and sleeping sound when she went in."

"Oh, I was all right," he answered smiling, "the 'somethings' didn't worry me, as yet. Only the rats; and they had a circus, I tell you, all over the place. There was one wicked looking old devil that sat up on my own chair by the fire, and wouldn't go till I took the poker to him, and then he ran up the rope of the alarm bell and got to somewhere up the wall or the ceiling – I couldn't see where, it was so dark."

"Mercy on us," said Mrs. Witham, "an old devil, and sitting on a chair by the fireside! Take care, sir! Take care! There's many a true word spoken in jest."

"How do you mean? 'Pon my word I don't understand."

"An old devil! The old devil, perhaps. There! sir, you needn't laugh," for Malcomson had broken into a hearty peal. "You young folks thinks it easy to laugh at things that makes older ones shudder. Never mind, sir! Never mind! Please God, you'll laugh all the time. It's what I wish you myself!" and the good lady beamed all over in sympathy with his enjoyment, her fears gone for a moment.

"Oh, forgive me!" said Malcomson presently. "Don't think me rude; but the idea was too much for me – that the old devil himself was on the chair last night!" And at the thought he laughed again. Then he went home to dinner.

This evening the scampering of the rats began earlier; indeed it had been going on before his arrival, and only ceased whilst his presence by its freshness disturbed them. After dinner he sat by the fire for a while and had a smoke; and then, having cleared his table, began to work as before. Tonight the rats disturbed him more than they had done on the previous night. How they scampered up and down and under and over! How they squeaked, and scratched, and gnawed! How they, getting bolder by degrees, came to the mouths of their holes and to the chinks and cracks and crannies in the wainscoting till their eyes shone like tiny lamps as the firelight rose and fell. But to him, now doubtless accustomed to them, their eyes were not wicked; only their playfulness touched him. Sometimes the boldest of them made sallies out on the floor or along the mouldings of the wainscot. Now and again as they disturbed him Malcomson made a sound to frighten them, smiting the table with his hand or giving a fierce "Hsh, hsh," so that they fled straightway to their holes.

And so the early part of the night wore on; and despite the noise Malcomson got more and more immersed in his work.

All at once he stopped, as on the previous night, being overcome by a sudden sense of silence. There was not the faintest sound of gnaw, or scratch, or squeak. The silence was as of the grave. He remembered the odd occurrence of the previous night, and instinctively he looked at the chair standing close by the fireside. And then a very odd sensation thrilled through him.

There, on the great old high-backed carved oak chair beside the fireplace sat the same enormous rat, steadily glaring at him with baleful eyes.

Instinctively he took the nearest thing to his hand, a book of logarithms, and flung it at it. The book was badly aimed and the rat did not stir, so again the poker performance of the previous night was repeated; and again the rat, being closely pursued, fled up the rope of the alarm bell. Strangely too, the departure of this rat was instantly followed by the renewal of the noise made by the general rat community. On this occasion, as on the previous one, Malcomson could not see at what part of the room the rat disappeared, for the green shade of his lamp left the upper part of the room in darkness, and the fire had burned low.

On looking at his watch he found it was close on midnight; and, not sorry for the *divertissement*, he made up his fire and made himself his nightly pot of tea. He had got through a good spell of work, and thought himself entitled to a cigarette; and so he sat on the great carved oak chair before the fire and enjoyed it. Whilst smoking he began to think that he would like to know where the rat disappeared to, for he had certain ideas for the morrow not entirely disconnected with a rat-trap.

Accordingly he lit another lamp and placed it so that it would shine well into the right-hand corner of the wall by the fireplace. Then he got all the books he had with him, and placed them handy to throw at the vermin. Finally he lifted the rope of the alarm bell and placed the end of it on the table, fixing the extreme end under the lamp. As he handled it he could not help noticing how pliable it was, especially for so strong a rope, and one not in use. "You could hang a man with it," be thought to himself.

When his preparations were made he looked around, and said complacently:

"There now, my friend, I think we shall learn something of you this time!" He began his work again, and though as before somewhat disturbed at first by the noise of the rats, soon lost himself in his propositions and problems.

Again he was called to his immediate surroundings suddenly. This time it might not have been the sudden silence only which took his attention; there was a slight movement of the rope, and the lamp moved. Without stirring, he looked to see if his pile of books was within range, and then cast his eye along the rope. As he looked he saw the great rat drop from the rope on the oak armchair and sit there glaring at him. He raised a book in his right hand, and taking careful aim, flung it at the rat. The latter, with a quick movement, sprang aside and dodged the missile. He then took another book, and a third, and flung them one after another at the rat, but each time unsuccessfully. At last, as he stood with a book poised in his hand to throw, the rat squeaked and seemed afraid. This made Malcomson more than ever eager to strike, and the book flew and struck the rat a resounding blow. It gave a terrified squeak, and turning on his pursuer a look of terrible malevolence, ran up the chair-back and made a great jump to the rope of the alarm bell and ran up it like lightning. The lamp rocked under the sudden strain, but it was a heavy one and did not topple over. Malcomson kept his eyes on the rat, and saw it by the light of the second lamp leap to a moulding of the wainscot and disappear through a hole in one of the great pictures which hung on the wall, obscured and invisible through its coating of dirt and dust.

"I shall look up my friend's habitation in the morning," said the student, as he went over to collect his books. The third picture from the fireplace; I shall not forget." He picked up the books one by one, commenting on them as he lifted them. "*Conic Sections* he does not mind, nor *Cycloidal Oscillations*, nor the *Principia*, nor *Quaternions*, nor *Thermodynamics*. Now for the book that fetched him!" Malcomson took it up and looked at it. As he did so he started, and a sudden pallor overspread his face.

He looked round uneasily and shivered slightly, as he murmured to himself:

"The Bible my mother gave me! What an odd coincidence." He sat down to work again, and the rats in the wainscot renewed their gambols. They did not disturb him, however; somehow their presence gave him a sense of companionship. But he could not attend to his work, and after striving to master the subject on which he was engaged gave it up in despair, and went to bed as the first streak of dawn stole in through the eastern window.

He slept heavily but uneasily, and dreamed much; and when Mrs. Dempster woke him late in the morning he seemed ill at ease, and for a few minutes did not seem to realise exactly where he was. His first request rather surprised the servant.

"Mrs. Dempster, when I am out today I wish you would get the steps and dust or wash those pictures – specially that one the third from the fireplace – I want to see what they are."

Late in the afternoon Malcomson worked at his books in the shaded walk, and the cheerfulness of the previous day came back to him as the day wore on, and he found that his reading was progressing well. He had worked out to a satisfactory conclusion all the problems which had as yet baffled him, and it was in a state of jubilation that he paid a visit to Mrs. Witham at "The Good Traveller." He found a stranger in the cosy sitting room with the landlady, who was introduced to him as Dr. Thornhill. She was not quite at ease, and this, combined with the doctor's plunging at once into a series of questions, made Malcomson come to the conclusion that his presence was not an accident, so without preliminary he said:

"Dr. Thornhill, I shall with pleasure answer you any question you may choose to ask me if you will answer me one question first."

The doctor seemed surprised, but he smiled and answered at once, "Done! What is it?"

"Did Mrs. Witham ask you to come here and see me and advise me?"

Dr. Thornhill for a moment was taken aback, and Mrs. Witham got fiery red and turned away; but the doctor was a frank and ready man, and he answered at once and openly:

"She did: but she didn't intend you to know it. I suppose it was my clumsy haste that made you suspect. She told me that she did not like the idea of your being in that house all by yourself, and that she thought you took too much strong tea. In fact, she wants me to advise you if possible to give up the tea and the very late hours. I was a keen student in my time, so I suppose I may take the liberty of a college man, and without offence, advise you not quite as a stranger."

Malcomson with a bright smile held out his hand. "Shake! as they say in America," he said. "I must thank you for your kindness and Mrs. Witham too, and your kindness deserves a return on my part. I promise to take no more strong tea – no tea at all till you let me – and I shall go to bed tonight at one o'clock at latest. Will that do?"

"Capital," said the doctor. "Now tell us all that you noticed in the old house." And so Malcomson then and there told in minute detail all that had happened in the last two nights. He was interrupted every now and then by some exclamation from Mrs. Witham, till finally, when he told of the episode of the Bible the landlady's pent-up emotions found vent in a shriek; and it was not till a stiff glass of brandy and water had been administered that she grew composed again. Dr. Thornhill listened with a face of growing gravity, and when the narrative was complete and Mrs. Witham had been restored he asked:

"The rat always went up the rope of the alarm bell?"

"Always."

"I suppose you know," said the Doctor after a pause, "what the rope is?"

"No!"

"It is," said the Doctor slowly, "the very rope which the hangman used for all the victims of the Judge's judicial rancour!" Here he was interrupted by another scream from Mrs. Witham, and steps had to be taken for her recovery. Malcomson having looked at his watch, and found that it was close to his dinner hour, had gone home before her complete recovery.

When Mrs. Witham was herself again she almost assailed the Doctor with angry questions as to what he meant by putting such horrible ideas into the poor young man's mind. "He has quite enough there already to upset him," she added. Dr. Thornhill replied.

"My dear madam, I had a distinct purpose in it! I wanted to draw his attention to the bell rope, and to fix it there. It may be that he is in a highly over-wrought state, and has been studying too much, although I am bound to say that he seems as sound and healthy a young man, mentally and bodily, as ever I saw – but then the rats – and that suggestion of the devil." The doctor shook his head and went on. "I would have offered to go and stay the first night with him but that I felt sure it would have been a cause of offence. He may get in the night some strange fright or hallucination; and if he does I want him to pull that rope. All alone as he is it will give us warning, and we may reach him in time to be of service. I shall be sitting up pretty late tonight and shall keep my ears open. Do not be alarmed if Benchurch gets a surprise before morning."

"Oh, Doctor, what do you mean? What do you mean?"

"I mean this; that possibly – nay, more probably – we shall hear the great alarm bell from the Judge's House tonight," and the Doctor made about as effective an exit as could be thought of.

When Malcomson arrived home he found that it was a little after his usual time, and Mrs. Dempster had gone away – the rules of Greenhow's Charity were not to be neglected. He was glad to see that the place was bright and tidy with a cheerful fire and a well-trimmed lamp. The evening was colder than might have been expected in April, and a heavy wind was blowing with such rapidly increasing strength that there was every promise of a storm during the night.

For a few minutes after his entrance the noise of the rats ceased; but so soon as they became accustomed to his presence they began again. He was glad to hear them, for he felt once more the feeling of companionship in their noise, and his mind ran back to the strange fact that they only ceased to manifest themselves when that other – the great rat with the baleful eyes – came upon the scene. The reading-lamp only was lit and its green shade kept the ceiling and the upper part of the room in darkness, so that the cheerful light from the hearth spreading over the floor and shining on the white cloth laid over the end of the table was warm and cheery. Malcomson sat down to his dinner with a good appetite and a buoyant spirit. After his dinner and a cigarette he sat steadily down to work, determined not to let anything disturb him, for he remembered his promise to the doctor, and made up his mind to make the best of the time at his disposal.

For an hour or so he worked all right, and then his thoughts began to wander from his books. The actual circumstances around him, the calls on his physical attention, and his nervous susceptibility were not to be denied. By this time the wind had become a gale, and the gale a storm. The old house, solid though it was, seemed to shake to its foundations, and the storm roared and raged through its many chimneys and its queer old gables, producing strange, unearthly sounds in the empty rooms and corridors. Even the great alarm bell on the roof must have felt the force of the wind, for the rope rose and fell slightly, as though the bell were moved a little from time to time, and the limber rope fell on the oak floor with a hard and hollow sound.

As Malcomson listened to it he bethought himself of the doctor's words, "It is the rope which the hangman used for the victims of the Judge's judicial rancour," and he went over to the corner of the fireplace and took it in his hand to look at it. There seemed a sort of deadly interest in it, and as he stood there he lost himself for a moment in speculation as to who these victims were, and the grim wish of the Judge to have such a ghastly relic ever under his eyes. As he stood there the swaying of the bell on the roof still lifted the rope now and again; but presently there came a new sensation – a sort of tremor in the rope, as though something was moving along it.

Looking up instinctively Malcomson saw the great rat coming slowly down towards him, glaring at him steadily. He dropped the rope and started back with a muttered curse, and the rat turning ran up the rope again and disappeared, and at the same instant Malcomson became conscious that the noise of the rats, which had ceased for a while, began again.

All this set him thinking, and it occurred to him that he had not investigated the lair of the rat or looked at the pictures, as he had intended. He lit the other lamp without the shade, and, holding it up, went and stood opposite the third picture from the fireplace on the right-hand side where he had seen the rat disappear on the previous night.

At the first glance he started back so suddenly that he almost dropped the lamp, and a deadly pallor overspread his face. His knees shook, and heavy drops of sweat came on his forehead, and he trembled like an aspen. But he was young and plucky, and pulled himself together, and after the pause of a few seconds stepped forward again, raised the lamp, and examined the picture which had been dusted and washed, and now stood out clearly.

It was of a judge dressed in his robes of scarlet and ermine. His face was strong and merciless, evil, crafty, and vindictive, with a sensual mouth, hooked nose of ruddy colour, and shaped like the beak of a bird of prey. The rest of the face was of a cadaverous colour. The eyes were of peculiar brilliance and with a terribly malignant expression. As he looked at them, Malcomson grew cold, for he saw there the very counterpart of the eyes of the great rat. The lamp almost fell from his hand, he saw the rat with its baleful eyes peering out through the hole in the corner of the picture, and noted the sudden cessation of the noise of the other rats. However, he pulled himself together, and went on with his examination of the picture.

The Judge was seated in a great high-backed carved oak chair, on the right-hand side of a great stone fireplace where, in the corner, a rope hung down from the ceiling, its end lying coiled on the floor. With a feeling of something like horror, Malcomson recognised the scene of the room as it stood, and gazed around him in an awestruck manner as though he expected to find some strange presence behind him. Then he looked over to the corner of the fireplace – and with a loud cry he let the lamp fall from his hand.

There, in the Judge's armchair, with the rope hanging behind, sat the rat with the Judge's baleful eyes, now intensified and with a fiendish leer. Save for the howling of the storm without there was silence.

The fallen lamp recalled Malcomson to himself. Fortunately it was of metal, and so the oil was not spilt. However, the practical need of attending to it settled at once his nervous apprehensions. When he had turned it out, he wiped his brow and thought for a moment.

"This will not do," he said to himself. "If I go on like this I shall become a crazy fool. This must stop! I promised the doctor I would not take tea. Faith, he was pretty right! My nerves must have been getting into a queer state. Funny I did not notice it. I never felt better in my life. However, it is all right now, and I shall not be such a fool again."

Then he mixed himself a good stiff glass of brandy and water and resolutely sat down to his work.

It was nearly an hour when he looked up from his book, disturbed by the sudden stillness. Without, the wind howled and roared louder than ever, and the rain drove in sheets against the windows, beating like hail on the glass; but within there was no sound whatever save the echo of the wind as it roared in the great chimney, and now and then a hiss as a few raindrops found their way down the chimney in a lull of the storm. The fire had fallen low and had ceased to flame, though it threw out a red glow. Malcomson listened attentively, and presently heard a thin, squeaking noise, very faint. It came from the corner of the room where the rope hung down, and he thought it was the creaking of the rope on the floor as the swaying of the bell raised and lowered it. Looking up, however, he saw in the dim light the great rat clinging to the rope and gnawing it. The rope was already nearly gnawed through – he could see the lighter colour where the strands were laid bare. As he looked the job was completed, and the severed end of the rope fell clattering on the oaken floor, whilst for an instant the great rat remained like a knob or tassel at the end of the rope, which now began to sway to and fro.

Malcomson felt for a moment another pang of terror as he thought that now the possibility of calling the outer world to his assistance was cut off, but an intense anger took its place, and seizing the book he was reading he hurled it at the rat. The blow was well aimed, but before the missile could reach him the rat dropped off and struck the floor with a soft thud. Malcomson instantly rushed over towards him, but it darted away and disappeared in the darkness of the shadows of the room. Malcomson felt that his work was over for the night, and determined then and there to vary the monotony of the proceedings by a hunt for the rat, and took off the green shade of the lamp so as to insure a wider spreading light. As he did so the gloom of the upper part of the room was relieved, and in the new flood of light, great by comparison with the previous darkness, the pictures on the wall stood out boldly. From where he stood, Malcomson saw right opposite to him the third picture on the wall from the right of the fireplace. He rubbed his eyes in surprise, and then a great fear began to come upon him.

In the centre of the picture was a great irregular patch of brown canvas, as fresh as when it was stretched on the frame. The background was as before, with chair and chimney-corner and rope, but the figure of the Judge had disappeared.

Malcomson, almost in a chill of horror, turned slowly round, and then he began to shake and tremble like a man in a palsy. His strength seemed to have left him, and he was incapable of action or movement, hardly even of thought. He could only see and hear.

There, on the great high-backed carved oak chair sat the Judge in his robes of scarlet and ermine, with his baleful eyes glaring vindictively, and a smile of triumph on, the resolute, cruel mouth, as he lifted with his hands a *black cap*. Malcomson felt as if the blood was running from his heart, as one does in moments of prolonged suspense. There was a singing in his ears. Without, he could hear the roar and howl of the tempest, and through it, swept on the storm, came the striking of midnight by the great chimes in the market place. He stood for a space of time that seemed to him endless still as a statue, and with wide-open, horror-struck eyes, breathless. As the clock struck, so the smile of triumph on the Judge's face intensified, and at the last stroke of mid-night he placed the black cap on his head.

Slowly and deliberately the Judge rose from his chair and picked up the piece of the rope of the alarm bell which lay on the floor, drew it through his hands as if he enjoyed its touch, and then deliberately began to knot one end of it, fashioning it into a noose. This he tightened and tested with his foot, pulling hard at it till he was satisfied and then making a running noose of it, which he held in his hand. Then he began to move along the table on the opposite side to Malcomson keeping his eyes on him until he had passed him, when with a quick movement he stood in front of the door. Malcomson then began to feel that he was trapped, and tried to think of what he should do. There was some fascination in the Judge's eyes, which he never took off him, and he had, perforce, to look. He saw the Judge approach – still keeping between him and the door – and raise the noose and throw it towards him as if to entangle him. With a great effort he made a quick movement to one side, and saw the rope fall beside him, and heard it strike the oaken floor. Again the Judge raised the noose and tried to ensnare him, ever keeping his baleful eyes fixed on him, and each time by a mighty effort the student just managed to evade it. So this went on for many times, the Judge seeming never discouraged nor discomposed at failure, but playing as a cat does with a mouse. At last in despair, which had reached its climax, Malcomson cast a quick glance round him. The lamp seemed to have blazed up, and there was a fairly good light in the room. At the many rat-holes and in the chinks and crannies of the wainscot he saw the rats' eyes; and this aspect, that was purely physical, gave him a gleam of comfort. He looked around and saw that the rope of the great alarm bell was laden with rats. Every inch of it was covered with them, and more and more were pouring through the small circular hole in the ceiling whence it emerged, so that with their weight the bell was beginning to sway.

Hark! it had swayed till the clapper had touched the bell. The sound was but a tiny one, but the bell was only beginning to sway, and it would increase.

At the sound the Judge, who had been keeping his eyes fixed on Malcolmson, looked up, and a scowl of diabolical anger overspread his face. His eyes fairly glowed like hot coals, and he stamped his foot with a sound that seemed to make the house shake. A dreadful peal of thunder broke overhead as he raised the rope again, whilst the rats kept running up and down the rope as though working against time. This time, instead of throwing it, he drew close to his victim, and held open the noose as he approached. As he came closer there seemed something paralysing in his very presence, and Malcolmson stood rigid as a corpse. He felt the Judge's icy fingers touch his throat as he adjusted the rope. The noose tightened – tightened. Then the Judge, taking the rigid form of the student in his arms, carried him over and placed him standing in the oak chair, and stepping up beside him, put his hand up and caught the end of the swaying rope of the alarm bell. As he raised his hand the rats fled squeaking, and disappeared through the hole in the ceiling. Taking the end of the noose which was round Malcolmson's neck he tied it to the hanging-bell rope, and then descending pulled away the chair.

When the alarm bell of the Judge's House began to sound a crowd soon assembled. Lights and torches of various kinds appeared, and soon a silent crowd was hurrying to the spot. They knocked loudly at the door, but there was no reply. Then they burst in the door, and poured into the great dining-room, the doctor at the head.

There at the end of the rope of the great alarm bell hung the body of the student, and on the face of the Judge in the picture was a malignant smile.

# The Storm

## McKnight Malmar

### Prospectus

**Address:** Wildwood Road, Fairport, Conn., USA.

**Property:** Comfortable suburban home with fine views over nearby farmland. Well-appointed rooms on two floors with cellar for oil burner and wood storage.

**Viewing Date:** February, 1944.

**Agent:** McKnight Malmar (1916–1988) became a bestseller with her first book, a "gargoyle mystery," *Never Say Die*, in 1943. However, she resisted attempts to be turned into a celebrity by denying details of her background. "Some day," she said, "I shall sit down and write a red-hot account of how I was born on a raft in the South Pacific, raised by head hunters in Melanesia and upon maturity worked my way around the world." In fact, she grew up in New York, started writing at university, was published by *Good Housekeeping* and produced a string of mystery novels including *The Past Won't Die* (1948) and *Fog Is A Shroud* (1950). Boris Karloff (1887–1969) born William Henry Pratt in London, is forever associated with his benchmark performance as the monster in Universal's 1931 *Frankenstein*, a role that Lugosi refused. "The Storm" was one of Karloff's favourites stories, of which he said, "it builds through magnificent suspense to a climax comparable to the last act of Frank Vosper's grisly play, *Love From A Stranger*."

She inserted her key in the lock and turned the knob. The March wind snatched the door out of her hand and slammed it back against the wall. It took strength to close it against the pressure of the gale, and she had no sooner closed it than the rain came in a pounding downpour, beating noisily against the windows as if trying to follow her in. She could not hear the taxi as it started up and went back down the road.

She breathed a sigh of thankfulness at being home again and in time. In rain like this, the crossroads always were flooded. Half an hour later her cab could not have got through the rising water, and there was no alternative route.

There was no light anywhere in the house. Ben was not home, then. As she turned on the lamp by the sofa she had a sense of anticlimax. All the way home – she had been visiting her sister – she had seen herself going into a lighted house, to Ben, who would be sitting by the fire with his paper. She had taken delight in picturing his happy surprise at seeing her, home a week earlier than he had expected her. She had known just how his round face would light up, how his eyes would twinkle behind his glasses, how he would catch her by the shoulders and look down into her face to see the changes a month had made in her, and then kiss her resoundingly on both cheeks, like a French general bestowing a decoration. Then she would make coffee and find a piece of cake, and they would sit together by the fire and talk.

But Ben wasn't here. She looked at the clock on the mantel and saw it was nearly ten. Perhaps he had not planned to come home tonight, as he was not expecting her; even before she had left he frequently was in the city all night because business kept him too late to catch the last train. If he did not come soon, he would not be able to make it at all.

She did not like the thought. The storm was growing worse. She could hear the wild lash of the trees, the whistle of the wind around the corners of the little house. For the first time she regretted this move to the far suburbs. There had been neighbours at first, a quarter-mile down the road; but they moved away several months ago, and now their house stood empty.

She had thought nothing of the lonesomeness. It was perfect

here – for two. She had taken such pleasure in fixing up her house – her very own house – and caring for it that she had not missed company other than Ben. But now, alone and with the storm trying to batter its way in, she found it frightening to be so far away from other people. There was no one this side of the crossroads; the road that passed the house wandered past farmland into nothingness in the thick woods a mile farther on.

She hung her hat and her coat in the closet and went to stand before the hall mirror to pin up the soft strands of hair that the wind had loosened. She did not really see the pale face with its blunt little nose, the slender, almost childish figure in its grown-up black dress, or the big brown eyes that looked back at her.

She fastened the last strand into the pompadour and turned away from the mirror. Her shoulders drooped a little. There was something childlike about her, like a small girl craving protection, something immature and yet appealing, in spite of her plainness. She was thirty-one and had been married for fifteen months. The fact that she had married at all still seemed a miracle to her.

Now she began to walk through the house, turning on lights as she went. Ben had left it in fairly good order. There was very little trace of an untidy masculine presence; but then, he was a tidy man. She began to realize that the house was cold. Of course, Ben would have lowered the thermostat. He was very careful about things like that. He would not tolerate waste.

No wonder it was cold; the thermostat was set at fifty-eight. She pushed the little needle up to seventy, and the motor in the cellar started so suddenly and noisily that it frightened her for a moment.

She went into the kitchen and made some coffee. While she waited for it to drip she began to prowl around the lower floor. She was curiously restless and could not relax. Yet it was good to be back again among her own things, in her own home. She studied the living room with fresh eyes. Yes, it was a pleasant room even though it was small. The bright, flowered chintzes on the furniture and at the windows were cheerful and pretty, and the lowboy she had bought three months ago was just right for the middle of the long wall. But her plants, set so bravely along the window sill, had died. Ben had forgotten to water them, in spite of all her admonitions, and now they drooped, shrunken and pale, in whitened, powdery soil. The sight of them added to the depression that was beginning to blot out all the pleasure of home coming.

She returned to the kitchen and poured herself a cup of coffee, wishing that Ben would come home to share it with her. She carried her cup into the living room and set it on the small, round table beside Ben's special big chair. The furnace was still mumbling busily, sending up heat, but she was colder than ever. She shivered and got an old jacket of Ben's from the closet and wrapped it around her before she sat down.

The wind hammered at the door and the windows, and the air was full of the sound of water, racing in the gutters, pouring from the leaders, thudding on the roof. Listening, she wished for Ben almost feverishly. She never had felt so alone. And he was such a comfort. He had been so good about her going for this long visit, made because her sister was ill. He had seen to everything and had put her on the train with her arms loaded with books and candy and fruit. She knew those farewell gifts had meant a lot to him – he didn't spend money easily. To be quite honest, he was a little close.

But he was a good husband. She sighed unconsciously, not knowing it was because of youth and romance missed. She repeated it to herself, firmly, as she sipped her coffee. He was a good husband. Suppose he was ten years older than she, and a little set in his ways; a little – perhaps – dictatorial at times, and moody. He had given her what she thought she wanted, security and a home of her own; if security were not enough, she could not blame him for it.

Her eye caught a shred of white protruding under a magazine on the table beside her. She put out a hand toward it, yet her fingers were almost reluctant to grasp it. She pulled it out nevertheless and saw that it was, as she had known instinctively, another of the white envelopes. It was empty, and it bore, as usual, the neat, typewritten address:

"Benj. T. Willsom, Esq.
Wildwood Road
Fairport, Conn."

The postmark was New York City. It never varied.

She felt the familiar constriction about the heart as she held it in her hands. What these envelopes contained she never had known. What she did know was their effect on Ben. After receiving one – one came every month or two – he was irritable, at times almost ugly. Their peaceful life together fell apart. At first she had questioned him, had striven to soothe and comfort him; but she soon had learned that this only made him angry and of late she had avoided any mention of them. For a week after one came they shared the same room and the same table like two strangers, in a silence that was morose on his part and a little frightened on hers.

This one was postmarked three days before. If Ben got home tonight he would probably be cross, and the storm would not help his mood. Just the same she wished he would come.

She tore the envelope into tiny pieces and tossed them into the fireplace. The wind shook the house in its giant grip, and a branch crashed on the roof. As she straightened, a movement at the window caught her eye.

She froze there, not breathing, still half-bent toward the cold fireplace, her hand still extended. The glimmer of white at the window behind the sheeting blur of rain had been – she was sure of it – a human face. There had been eyes. She was certain there had been eyes staring in at her.

The wind's shout took on a personal, threatening note. She was rigid for a long time, never taking her eyes from the window. But nothing moved there now except the water on the window pane; beyond it there was blackness, and that was all. The only sounds were the thrashing of the trees, the roar of water, and the ominous howl of the wind.

She began to breathe again, at last found courage to turn out the light and go to the window. The darkness was a wall, impenetrable and secret, and the blackness within the house made the storm close in, as if it were a pack of wolves besieging the house. She hastened to put on the light again.

She must have imagined those staring eyes. Nobody could be out on a night like this. Nobody. Yet she found herself terribly shaken.

If only Ben would come home. If only she were not so alone.

She shivered and pulled Ben's coat tighter about her and told herself she was becoming a morbid fool. Nevertheless, she found the aloneness intolerable. Her ears strained to hear prowling footsteps outside the windows. She became convinced that she did hear them, slow and heavy.

Perhaps Ben could be reached at the hotel where he sometimes stayed. She no longer cared whether her home coming was a surprise to him. She wanted to hear his voice. She went to the telephone and lifted the receiver.

The line was quite dead.

The wires were down, of course.

She fought panic. The face at the window had been an illusion, a trick of the light reflected on the sluicing pane; and the sound of footsteps was an illusion, too. Actual ones would be inaudible in the noise made by the wild storm. Nobody would be out tonight. Nothing threatened her, really. The storm was held at bay beyond these walls, and in the morning the sun would shine again.

The thing to do was to make herself as comfortable as possible and settle down with a book. There was no use going to bed – she couldn't possibly sleep. She would only lie there wide awake and think of that face at the window, hear those footsteps.

She would get some wood for a fire in the fireplace. She hesitated at the top of the cellar stairs. The light, as she switched it on, seemed insufficient; the concrete wall at the foot of the stairs was dank with moisture and somehow gruesome. And wind was chilling her ankles. Rain was beating in through the outside door to the cellar, because that door was standing open.

The inner bolt sometimes did not hold, she knew very well. If it had not been carefully closed, the wind could have loosened it. Yet the open door increased her panic. It seemed to argue the presence of something less impersonal than the gale. It took her a long minute to nerve herself to go down the steps and reach out into the darkness for the doorknob.

In just that instant she was soaked; but her darting eyes could find nothing outdoors but the black, wavering shapes of the maples at the side of the house. The wind helped her and slammed the door resoundingly. She jammed the bolt home with all her strength and then tested it to make sure it would hold. She almost sobbed with the relief of knowing it to be firm against any intruder.

She stood with her wet clothes clinging to her while the thought came that turned her bones to water. Suppose – suppose the face at the window had been real, after all. Suppose its owner had found shelter in the only shelter to be had within a quarter-mile – this cellar.

She almost flew up the stairs again, but then she took herself firmly in hand. She must not let herself go. There had been many storms before; just because she was alone in this one, she must not let morbid fancy run away with her. But she could not throw off the reasonless fear that oppressed her, although she forced it back a little. She began to hear again the tread of the prowler outside the house. Although she knew it to be imagination, it was fearfully real – the crunch of feet on gravel, slow, persistent, heavy, like the patrol of a sentinel.

She had only to get an armful of wood. Then she could have a fire, she would have light and warmth and comfort. She would forget these terrors.

The cellar smelled of dust and old moisture. The beams were fuzzed with cobwebs. There was only one light, a dim one in the corner. A little rivulet was running darkly down the wall and already had formed a foot-square pool on the floor.

The woodpile was in the far corner away from the light. She stopped and peered around. Nobody could hide here. The cellar was too open, the supporting stanchions too slender to hide a man.

The oil burner went off with a sharp click. Its mutter, she suddenly realized, had had something human and companionable about it. Nothing was down here with her now but the snarl of the storm.

She almost ran to the woodpile. Then something made her pause and turn before she bent to gather the split logs.

What was it? Not a noise. Something she had seen as she had hurried across that dusty floor. Something odd.

She searched with her eyes. It was a spark of light she had seen, where no spark should be.

An inexplicable dread clutched at her heart. Her eyes widened, round and dark as a frightened deer's. Her old trunk that stood against the wall was open just a crack; from the crack came this tiny pin-point of reflected light to prick the cellar's gloom.

She went toward it like a woman hypnotized. It was only one more insignificant thing, like the envelope on the table, the vision of the face at the window, the open door. There was no reason for her to feel smothered in terror.

Yet she was sure she had not only closed, but clamped the lid on the trunk; she was sure because she kept two or three old coats in it, wrapped in newspapers and tightly shut away from moths.

Now the lid was raised perhaps an inch. And the twinkle of light was still there.

She threw back the lid.

For a long moment she stood looking down into the trunk, while each detail of its contents imprinted itself on her brain like an image on a film. Each tiny detail was indelibly clear and never to be forgotten.

She could not have stirred a muscle in that moment. Horror was a black cloak thrown around her, stopping her breath, hobbling her limbs.

Then her face dissolved into formlessness. She slammed down the lid and ran up the stairs like a mad thing. She was breathing again, in deep, sobbing breaths that tore at her lungs. She shut the door at the top of the stairs with a crash that shook the house; then she turned the key. Gasping, she clutched one of the sturdy maple chairs by the kitchen table and wedged it under the knob with hands she could barely control.

The wind took the house in its teeth and shook it as a dog shakes a rat.

Her first impulse was to get out of the house. But in the time it took her to get to the front door she remembered the face at the window.

Perhaps she had not imagined it. Perhaps it was the face of a murderer – a murderer waiting for her out there in the storm; ready to spring on her out of the dark and the rain.

She fell into the big chair, her huddled body shaken by great tremors. She could not stay here – not with that thing in her trunk. Yet she dared not leave. Her whole being cried out for Ben. He would know what to do. She closed her eyes, opened them again, rubbed them hard. The picture still burned into her brain as if it had been etched with acid. Her hair, loosened, fell in soft, straight wisps about her forehead, and her mouth was slack with terror.

Her old trunk had held the curled-up body of a woman.

She had not seen the face; the head had been tucked down into the hollow of the shoulder, and a shower of fair hair had fallen over it. The woman had worn a red dress. One hand had rested near the edge of the trunk, and on its third finger there had been a man's ring, a signet bearing the raised figure of a rampant lion with a small diamond between its paws. It had been the diamond that caught the light. The little bulb in the corner of the cellar had picked out this ring from the semidarkness and made it stand out like a beacon.

She never would be able to forget it. Never forget how the woman looked: the pale, luminous flesh of her arms; her doubled-up knees against the side of the trunk, with their silken covering shining softly in the gloom; the strands of hair that covered her face. . . .

Shudders continued to shake her. She bit her tongue and pressed her hand against her jaw to stop the chattering of her teeth. The salty taste of blood in her mouth steadied her. She tried to force herself to be rational, to plan; yet all the time the knowledge that she was imprisoned with the body of a murdered woman kept beating at her nerves like a flail.

She drew the coat closer about her, trying to dispel the mortal cold that held her. Slowly something beyond the mere fact of murder, of death, began to penetrate her mind. Slowly she realized that beyond this fact there would be consequences. That body in the cellar was not an isolated phenomenon; some train of events had led to its being there and would follow its discovery there.

There would be policemen.

At first the thought of policemen was a comforting one; big, brawny men in blue, who would take the thing out of her cellar, take it away so she never need think of it again.

Then she realized it was *her* cellar – hers and Ben's; and policemen are suspicious and prying. Would they think *she* had killed the woman? Could they be made to believe she never had seen her before?

Or would they think Ben had done it? Would they take the letters in the white envelopes, and Ben's absences on business, and her own visit to her sister, about which Ben had been so helpful, and out of them build a double life for him? Would they insist that the woman had been a discarded mistress, who had hounded him with letters until out of desperation he had killed her? That was a fantastic theory, really; but the police might do that.

They might.

Now a sudden new panic invaded her. The dead woman must be taken out of the cellar, must be hidden. The police must never connect her with this house.

Yet the dead woman was bigger than she herself was; she never could move her.

Her craving for Ben became a frantic need. If only he would come home! Come home and take that body away, hide it somewhere so the police could not connect it with this house. He was strong enough to do it.

Even with the strength to move the body by herself she would not dare to do it, because there was the prowler – real or imaginary – outside the house. Perhaps the cellar door had not been open by chance. Or perhaps it had been, and the murderer, seeing it so welcoming, had seized the opportunity to plant the evidence of his crime upon the Willsoms' innocent shoulders.

She crouched there, shaking. It was as if the jaws of a great trap had closed on her: on one side the storm and the silence of the telephone, on the other the presence of the prowler and of that still, cramped figure in her trunk. She was caught between them, helpless.

As if to accent her helplessness, the wind stepped up its shriek and a tree crashed thunderously out in the road. She heard glass shatter.

Her quivering body stiffened like a drawn bow. Was it the prowler attempting to get in? She forced herself to her feet and made a round of the windows on the first floor and the one above. All the glass was intact, staunchly resisting the pounding of the rain.

Nothing could have made her go into the cellar to see if anything had happened there.

The voice of the storm drowned out all other sounds, yet she could not rid herself of the fancy that she heard footsteps going round and round the house, that eyes sought an opening and spied upon her.

She pulled the shades down over the shiny black windows. It helped a little to make her feel more secure, more sheltered; but only a very little. She told herself sternly that the crash of glass had been nothing more than a branch blown through a cellar window.

The thought brought her no comfort – just the knowledge that it would not disturb that other woman. Nothing could comfort her now but Ben's plump shoulder and his arms around her and his neat, capable mind planning to remove the dead woman from this house.

A kind of numbness began to come over her, as if her capacity for fear were exhausted. She went back to the chair and curled up in it. She prayed mutely for Ben and for daylight.

The clock said half-past twelve.

She huddled there, not moving and not thinking, not even afraid, only numb, for another hour. Then the storm held its breath for a moment, and in the brief space of silence she heard footsteps on the walk – actual footsteps, firm and quick and loud. A key turned in the lock. The door opened and Ben came in.

He was dripping, dirty, and white with exhaustion. But it was Ben. Once she was sure of it she flung herself on him, babbling incoherently of what she had found.

He kissed her lightly on the cheek and took her arms down from around his neck. "Here, here, my dear. You'll get soaked. I'm drenched to thc skin." He removed his glasses and handed them to her, and she began to dry them for him. His eyes squinted at the light. "I had to walk in from the crossroads. What a night!" He began to strip off rubbers and coat and shoes. "You'll never know what a difference it made, finding the place lighted. Lord, but it's good to be home."

She tried again to tell him of the past hours, but again he cut her short. "Now, wait a minute, my dear. I can see you're bothered about something. Just wait until I get into some dry things; then I'll come down and we'll straighten it out. Suppose you rustle up some coffee and toast. I'm done up – the whole trip out was a nightmare, and I didn't know if I'd ever make it from the crossing. I've been hours."

He did look tired, she thought with concern. Now that he was back, she could wait. The past hours had taken on the quality of a nightmare, horrifying but curiously unreal. With Ben here, so solid and commonplace and cheerful, she began to wonder if the hours *were* a nightmare. She even began to doubt the reality of the woman in the trunk, although she could see her as vividly as ever. Perhaps only the storm was real.

She went to the kitchen and began to make fresh coffee. The chair, still wedged against the kitchen door, was a reminder of her terror. Now that Ben was home it seemed silly, and she put it back in its place by the table.

He came down very soon, before the coffee was ready. How good it was to see him in that old gray bathrobe of his, his hands thrust into its pockets. How normal and wholesome he looked with his round face rubbed pink by a rough towel and his hair standing up in damp little spikes around his bald spot. She was almost shamefaced when she told him of the face at the window, the open door, and finally of the body in the trunk. None of it, she saw quite clearly now, could possibly have happened.

Ben said so, without hesitation. But he came to put an arm around her. "You poor child. The storm scared you to death, and I don't wonder. It's given you the horrors."

She smiled dubiously. "Yes. I'm almost, beginning to think so. Now that you're back, it seems so safe. But – but you will *look* in the trunk, Ben? I've got to *know*. I can see her so plainly. How could I imagine a thing like that?"

He said indulgently: "Of course I'll look, if it will make you feel better. I'll do it now. Then I can have my coffee in peace."

He went to the cellar door and opened it and snapped on the light. Her heart began to pound once more, a deafening roar in her ears. The opening of the cellar door opened, again, the whole vista of fear: the body, the police, the suspicions that would cluster about her and Ben. The need to hide this evidence of somebody's crime.

She could not have imagined it; it was incredible that she could have believed, for a minute, that her mind had played such tricks on her. In another moment Ben would know it, too.

She heard the thud as he threw back the lid of the trunk. She clutched at the back of a chair, waiting for his voice. It came in an instant.

She could not believe it. It was as cheerful and reassuring as before. He said: "There's nothing here but a couple of bundles. Come take a look."

Nothing!

Her knees were weak as she went down the stairs, down into the cellar again.

It was still musty and damp and draped with cobwebs. The rivulet was still running down the wall, but the pool was larger now. The light was still dim.

It was just as she remembered it except that the wind was whistling through a broken window and rain was splattering in on the bits of shattered glass on the floor. The branch lying across the sill had removed every scrap of glass from the frame and left not a single jagged edge.

Ben was standing by the open trunk, waiting for her. His stocky body was a bulwark. "See," he said, "there's nothing. Just some old clothes of yours, I guess."

She went to stand beside him. Was she losing her mind? Would she, now, see that crushed figure in there, see the red dress and the smooth, shining knees, when Ben could not? And the ring with the diamond between the lion's paws?

Her eyes looked, almost reluctantly, into the trunk. "It *is* empty!"

There were the neat, newspaper-wrapped packages she had put away so carefully, just as she had left them deep in the bottom of the trunk. And nothing else.

She must have imagined the body. She was light with the relief the knowledge brought her, and yet confused and frightened, too. If her mind could play such tricks, if she could imagine anything so gruesome in the complete detail with which she had seen the dead woman in the trunk, the thought of the future was terrifying. When might she not have another such hallucination?

The actual, physical danger did not exist, however, and never had existed. The threat of the law hanging over Ben had been based on a dream.

"I— dreamed it all. I must have," she admitted. "Yet it was so horribly clear and I wasn't asleep." Her voice broke. "I thought— oh, Ben, I thought—"

"What did you think, my dear?" His voice was odd, not like Ben's at all. It had a cold, cutting edge to it.

He stood looking down at her with an immobility that chilled her more than the cold wind that swept in through the broken window. She tried to read his face, but the light from the little bulb was too weak. It left his features shadowed in broad, dark planes that made him look like a stranger, and somehow sinister.

She said, "I—" and faltered.

He still did not move, but his voice hardened. "What was it you thought?"

She backed away from him.

He moved, then. It was only to take his hands from his pockets, to stretch his arms toward her; but she stood for an instant staring at the thing that left her stricken, with a voiceless scream forming in her throat.

She was never to know whether his arms had been outstretched to take her within their shelter or to clutch at her white neck. For she turned and fled, stumbling up the stairs in a mad panic of escape.

He shouted: "Janet! Janet!" His steps were heavy behind her. He tripped on the bottom step and fell on one knee and cursed.

Terror lent her strength and speed. She could not be mistaken. Although she had seen it only once, she knew that on the little finger of his left hand there had been the same, the unmistakable ring the dead woman had worn.

The blessed wind snatched the front door from her and flung it wide, and she was out in the safe, dark shelter of the storm.

# The Waxwork

## A. M. Burrage

### Prospectus

**Address:** Marriner's Waxworks, Marylebone, London.

**Property:** Converted town house in a small square with a vaulted roof and glass double doors. Contains a dozen rooms of public figures and "Murderers' Den" in the basement.

**Viewing Date:** April, 1931

**Agent:** Alfred McClelland Burrage (1889–1956) began selling stories while he was still at school and made his name in 1925 with *Poor Dear Esme*, the extraordinary tale of a schoolboy who masquerades as a girl in a female-only public school. He was also responsible for a series of controversial supernatural tales under the pseudonym "Ex-Private X". Vincent Price (1911–1993) obtained a master's degree in fine art, but was drawn to the movies where he became a leading horror actor in the 1950s. Warner Brothers' 3-D film, *The House of Wax* (1953), made him an international star and among his best horror pictures are *House on Haunted Hill* (1959) and *The Haunted Palace* (1964). Commenting on "The Waxwork," Price said: "It is a good example of a new twist on an old theme – spending the night in a cemetery or haunted house. What makes Burrage's tale more frightening, though, is the introduction of a famous murderer. Is he *really* only a waxwork?"

While the uniformed attendants of Marriner's Waxworks were ushering the last stragglers through the great glass-panelled double doors, the manager sat in his office interviewing Raymond Hewson.

The manager was a youngish man, stout, blond and of medium height. He wore his clothes well and contrived to look extremely smart without appearing over-dressed. Raymond Hewson looked neither. His clothes, which had been good when new and which were still carefully brushed and pressed, were beginning to show signs of their owner's losing battle with the world. He was a small, spare, pale man, with lank, errant brown hair, and although he spoke plausibly and even forcibly he had the defensive and somewhat furtive air of a man who was used to rebuffs. He looked what he was, a man gifted somewhat above the ordinary who was a failure through his lack of self-assertion.

The manager was speaking.

"There is nothing new in your request," he said. "In fact we refuse it to different people – mostly young bloods who have tried to make bets – about three times a week. We have nothing to gain and something to lose by letting people spend the night in our Murderers' Den. If I allowed it, and some young idiot lost his senses, what would be my position? But your being a journalist somewhat alters the case."

Hewson smiled.

"I suppose you mean that journalists have no senses to lose."

"No, no," laughed the manager, "but one imagines them to be reasonable people. Besides, here we have something to gain; publicity and advertisement."

"Exactly," said Hewson, "and there I thought we might come to terms."

The manager laughed again.

"Oh," he exclaimed, "I know what's coming. You want to be paid twice, do you? It used to be said years ago that Madame Tussaud's would give a man a hundred pounds for sleeping alone in the Chamber of Horrors. I hope you don't think that we have made any such offer. Er – what is your paper, Mr Hewson?"

"I am freelancing at present," Hewson confessed, "working on space for several papers. However, I should find no difficulty in getting the story printed. The *Morning Echo* would use it like a shot. 'A night with Marriner's Murderers.' No live paper could turn it down."

The manager rubbed his chin.

"Ah! And how do you propose to treat it?"

"I shall make it gruesome, of course; gruesome with just a saving touch of humour."

The other nodded and offered Hewson his cigarette-case.

"Very well, Mr. Hewson," he said. "Get your story printed in the *Morning Echo*, and there will be a five-pound note waiting for you here when you care to come and call for it. But first of all, it's no small ordeal that you're proposing to undertake. I'd like to be quite sure about you, and I'd like you to be quite sure about yourself. I own I shouldn't care to take it on. I've seen those figures dressed and undressed, I know all about the process of their manufacture, I can walk about in company downstairs as unmoved as if I were walking among so many skittles, but I should hate having to sleep down there alone among them."

"Why?" asked Hewson.

"I don't know. There isn't any reason. I don't believe in ghosts. If I did I should expect them to haunt the scene of their crimes or the spot where their bodies were laid, instead of a cellar which happens to contain their waxwork effigies. It's just that I couldn't sit alone among them at night, with their seeming to stare at me the way they do. After all, they represent the lowest and most appalling types of humanity, and – although I would not own it publicly – the people who come to see them are not generally charged with the very highest motives. The whole atmosphere of the place is unpleasant, and if you are susceptible to atmosphere I warn you that you are in for a very uncomfortable night."

Hewson had known that from the moment when the idea had first occurred to him. His soul sickened at the prospect, even while he smiled casually upon the manager. But he had a wife and family to keep, and for the past month he had been living on paragraphs, eked out by his rapidly dwindling store of savings.

Here was a chance not to be missed – the price of a special story in the *Morning Echo*, with a five-pound note to add to it. It meant comparative wealth and luxury for a week, and freedom from the worst anxieties for a fortnight. Besides, if he wrote the story well, it might lead to an offer of regular employment.

"The way of transgressors – and newspaper men – is hard," he said. "I have already promised myself an uncomfortable night because your Murderers' Den is obviously not fitted up as an hotel bedroom. But I don't think your wax-works will worry me much."

"You're not superstitious?"

"Not a bit," Hewson laughed.

"But you're a journalist; you must have a strong imagination."

"The news editors for whom I've worked have always complained that I haven't any. Plain facts are not considered sufficient in our trade, and the papers don't like offering their readers unbuttered bread."

The manager smiled and rose.

"Right," he said. "I think the last of the people have gone. Wait a moment. I'll give orders for the figures downstairs not to be draped, and let the night people know that you'll be here. Then I'll take you down and show you round."

He picked up the receiver of a house telephone, spoke into it and presently replaced it.

"One condition I'm afraid I must impose on you," he remarked. "I must ask you not to smoke. We had a fire scare down in the Murderers' Den this evening. I don't know who gave the alarm, but whoever it was it was a false one. Fortunately there were very few people down there at the time, or there might have been a panic. And now, if you're ready, we'll make a move."

Hewson followed the manager through half a dozen rooms where attendants were busy shrouding the kings and queens of England, the generals and prominent statesmen of this and other generations, all the mixed herd of humanity whose fame or notoriety had rendered them eligible for this kind of immortality. The manager stopped once and spoke to a man in uniform, saying something about an arm-chair in the Murderers' Den.

"It's the best we can do for you, I'm afraid," he said to Hewson. "I hope you'll be able to get some sleep."

He led the way through an open barrier and down ill-lit stone stairs which conveyed a sinister impression of giving access to a dungeon. In a passage at the bottom were a few preliminary horrors, such as relics of the Inquisition, a rack taken from a mediaeval castle, branding irons, thumbscrews, and other mementoes of man's one-time cruelty to man. Beyond the passage was the Murderers' Den.

It was a room of irregular shape with vaulted roof, and dimly lit by electric lights burning behind inverted bowls of frosted glass. It was, by design, an eerie and uncomfortable chamber – a chamber whose atmosphere invited its visitors to speak in whispers. There was something of the air of a chapel about it, but a chapel no longer devoted to the practice of piety and given over now for base and impious worship.

The waxwork murderers stood on low pedestals with numbered tickets at their feet. Seeing them elsewhere, and without knowing whom they represented, one would have thought them a dull-looking crew, chiefly remarkable for the shabbiness of their clothes, and as evidence of the changes of fashion even among the unfashionable.

Recent notorieties rubbed dusty shoulders with the old "favourites". Thurtell, the murderer of Weir, stood as if frozen in the act of making a shop-window gesture to young Bywaters. There was Lefroy the poor half-baked little snob who killed for gain so that he might ape the gentleman. Within five yards of him sat Mrs. Thompson, that erotic romanticist, hanged to propitiate British middle-class matronhood. Charles Peace, the only member of that vile company who looked uncompromisingly and entirely evil, sneered across a gangway at Norman Thorne. Browne and Kennedy, the two most recent additions stood between Mrs. Dyer and Patrick Mahon.

The manager, walking around with Hewson, pointed out several of the more interesting of these unholy notabilities.

"That's Crippen; I expect you recognise him. Insignificant little beast who looks as if he couldn't tread on a worm. That's

Armstrong. Looks like a decent, harmless country gentleman, doesn't he? There's old Vaquier; you can't miss him because of his beard. And of course this—"

"Who's that?" Hewson interrupted in a whisper, pointing.

"Oh, I was coming to him," said the manager in a light undertone. "Come and have a good look at him. This is our star turn. He's the only one of the bunch that hasn't been hanged."

The figure which Hewson had indicated was that of a small, slight man not much more than five feet in height. It wore little waxed moustaches, large spectacles, and a caped coat. There was something so exaggeratedly French in its appearance that it reminded Hewson of a stage caricature. He could not have said precisely why the mild-looking face seemed to him so repellent, but he had already recoiled a step and, even in the manager's company, it cost him an effort to look again.

"But who is he?" he asked.

"That," said the manager, "is Dr. Bourdette."

Hewson shook his head doubtfully.

"I think I've heard the name," he said, "but I forget in connection with what."

The manager smiled.

"You'd remember better if you were a Frenchman," he said. "For some long while that man was the terror of Paris. He carried on his work of healing by day, and of throat-cutting by night, when the fit was on him. He killed for the sheer devilish pleasure it gave him to kill, and always in the same way – with a razor. After his last crime he left a clue behind him which set the police upon his track. One clue led to another, and before very long they knew that they were on the track of the Parisian equivalent of our Jack the Ripper, and had enough evidence to send him to the mad-house or the guillotine on a dozen capital charges.

"But even then our friend here was too clever for them. When he realised that the toils were closing about him he mysteriously disappeared and ever since the police of every civilised country have been looking for him. There is no doubt that he managed to make away with himself, and by some means which has prevented his body coming to light. One or two crimes of a similar nature have taken place since his disappearance, but he is believed almost for certain to be dead, and the experts believe these recrude-scences to be the work of an imitator. It's queer, isn't it, how every notorious murderer has imitators?"

Hewson shuddered and fidgetted with his feet.

"I don't like him at all," he confessed. "Ugh! What eyes he's got!"

"Yes, this figure's a little masterpiece. You find the eyes bite into you? Well, that's excellent realism, then, for Bourdette practised mesmerism, and was supposed to mesmerise his victims before dispatching them. Indeed, had he not done so, it is impossible to see how so small a man could have done his ghastly work. There was never any signs of a struggle."

"I thought I saw him move," said Hewson with a catch in his voice.

The manager smiled.

"You'll have more than one optical illusion before the night's out, I expect. You shan't be locked in. You can come upstairs when you've had enough of it. There are watchmen on the premises, so you'll find company. Don't be alarmed if you hear them moving about. I'm sorry I can't give you any more light, because all the lights are on. For obvious reasons we keep this place as gloomy as possible. And now I think you had better return with me to the office and have a tot of whisky before beginning your night's vigil."

The member of the night staff who placed the arm-chair for Hewson was inclined to be facetious.

"Where will you have it, sir?" he asked, grinning. "Just 'ere, so as you can 'ave a little talk with Crippen when you're tired of sitting still? Or there's old Mother Dyer over there, making eyes and looking as if she could do with a bit of company. Say where, sir."

Hewson smiled. The man's chaff pleased him if only because, for the moment at least, it lent the proceedings a much-desired air of the commonplace.

"I'll place it myself, thanks," he said. "I'll find out where the draughts come from first."

"You won't find any down here. Well, good night, sir. I'm upstairs if you want me. Don't let 'em sneak up be'ind you and touch your neck with their cold and clammy 'ands. And you look out for that old Mrs. Dyer; I b'lieve she's taken a fancy to you."

Hewson laughed and wished the man good-night. It was easier than he had expected. He wheeled the arm-chair – a heavy one upholstered in plush – a little way down the central gangway, and deliberately turned it so that its back was towards the effigy of Dr. Bourdette. For some undefined reason he liked Dr. Bourdette a great deal less than his companions. Busying himself with arranging the chair he was almost light-hearted, but when the attendant's footfalls had died away and a deep hush stole over the chamber he realised that he had no slight ordeal before him.

The dim unwavering light fell on the rows of figures which were so uncannily like human beings that the silence and the stillness seemed unnatural and even ghastly. He missed the sound of breathing, the rustling of clothes, the hundred and one minute noises one hears when even the deepest silence has fallen upon a crowd. But the air was as stagnant as water at the bottom of a standing pond. There was not a breath in the chamber to stir a curtain or rustle a hanging drapery or start a shadow. His own shadow, moving in response to a shifted arm or leg, was all that could be coaxed into motion. All was still to the gaze and silent to the ear. "It must be like this at the bottom of the sea," he thought and wondered how to work the phrase into his story on the morrow.

He faced the sinister figures boldly enough. They were only waxworks. So long as he let that thought dominate all others he promised himself that all would be well. It did not, however, save him long from the discomfort occasioned by the waxen stare of Dr. Bourdette, which, he knew, was directed upon him from behind. The eyes of the little Frenchman's effigy haunted and tormented him, and he itched with the desire to turn and look.

"Come!" he thought, "my nerves have started already. If I turn and look at that dressed-up dummy it will be an admission of funk."

And then another voice in his brain spoke to him.

"It's because you're afraid that you won't turn and look at him."

The two voices quarrelled silently for a moment or two, and at last Hewson slewed his chair round a little and looked behind him.

Among the many figures standing in stiff, unnatural poses, the effigy of the dreadful little doctor stood out with a queer prominence, perhaps because a steady beam of light beat straight down upon it. Hewson flinched before the parody of mildness which some fiendishly skilled craftsman had managed to convey in wax, met the eyes for one agonised second, and turned again to face the other direction.

"He's only a waxwork like the rest of you," Hewson muttered defiantly. "You're all only waxworks."

They were only waxworks, yes, but waxworks don't move. Not that he had seen the least movement anywhere, but it struck him that, in the moment or two while he had looked behind him, there had been the least subtle change in the grouping of the figures in front. Crippen, for instance, seemed to have turned at least one degree to the left. Or, thought Hewson, perhaps the illusion was due to the fact that he had not slewed his chair back into its exact original position. And there were Field and Grey, too; surely one of them had moved his hands. Hewson held his breath for a moment, and then drew his courage back to him as a man lifts a weight. He remembered the words of more than one news editor and laughed savagely to himself.

"And they tell me I've no imagination!" he said beneath his breath.

He took a notebook from his pocket and wrote quickly.

"Deathly silence and unearthly stillness of figures. Like being bottom of sea. Hypnotic eyes of Dr. Bourdette. Figures seem to move when not being watched."

He closed the book suddenly over his fingers and looked round quickly and awfully over his right shoulder. He had neither seen nor heard a movement, but it was as if some sixth sense had made him aware of one. He looked straight into the vapid countenance of Lefroy which smiled vacantly back as if to say, "It wasn't I!"

Of course it wasn't he, or any of them; it was his own nerves. Or was it? Hadn't Crippen moved again during that moment when his attention was directed elsewhere. You couldn't trust that little man! Once you took your eyes off him he took advantage of it to shift his position. That was what they were all doing, if he only knew it, he told himself; and half rose out of his chair. This was not quite good enough! He was going. He wasn't going to spend the night with a lot of waxworks which moved while he wasn't looking.

Hewson sat down again. This was very cowardly and very absurd. They *were* only waxworks, and they *couldn't* move; let him hold that thought and all would yet be well. Then why all that silent unrest about him? – a subtle something in the air which did not quite break the silence and happened, whichever way he looked, just beyond the boundaries of his vision.

He swung round quickly to encounter the mild but baleful stare of Dr. Bourdette. Then, without warning, he jerked his head back to stare straight at Crippen. Ha! He'd nearly caught Crippen that time! "You'd better be careful, Crippen – and all the rest of you! If I do see one of you move I'll smash you to pieces! Do you hear?"

He ought to go, he told himself. Already he had experienced enough to write his story, or ten stories, for the matter of that. Well, then, why not go? The *Morning Echo* would be none the wiser as to how long he had stayed, nor would it care so long as his story was a good one. Yes, but that night-watchman upstairs would chaff him. And the manager – one never knew – perhaps the manager would quibble over that five-pound note which he needed so badly. He wondered if Rose were asleep or if she were lying awake and thinking of him. She'd laugh when he told her that he had imagined . . .

This was a little too much. It was bad enough that the waxwork effigies of murderers should move when they weren't being watched, but it was intolerable that they should *breathe*. Somebody was breathing. Or was it his own breath which sounded to him as if it came from a distance? He sat rigid, listening and straining until he exhaled with a long sigh. His own breath after all, or – if not, something had divined that he was listening and had ceased breathing simultaneously.

Hewson jerked his head swiftly around and looked all about him out of haggard and hunted eyes. Everywhere his gaze encountered the vacant waxen faces, and everywhere he felt that by just some least fraction of a second had he missed seeing a movement of hand or foot, a silent opening or compression of lips, a flicker of eyelids, a look of human intelligence now smoothed out. They were like naughty children in a class, whispering, fidgeting and laughing behind their teacher's back, but blandly innocent when his gaze was turned upon them.

This would not do! This distinctly would not do! He must clutch at something, grip with his mind upon something which belonged essentially to the workaday world, to the daylight London streets. He was Raymond Hewson, an unsuccessful journalist, a living and breathing man, and these figures grouped around him were only dummies, so they could neither move nor whisper. What did it matter if they were supposed to be lifelike effigies of murderers? They were only made of wax and sawdust, and stood there for the entertainment of morbid sightseers and orange-sucking trippers. That was better! Now what was that funny story which somebody had told him in the Falstaff yesterday . . .?

He recalled part of it, but not all, for the gaze of Dr. Bourdette, urged, challenged, and finally compelled him to turn.

Hewson half-turned, and then swung his chair so as to bring him face to face with the wearer of those dreadful hypnotic eyes. His own eyes were dilated, and his mouth, at first set in a grin of terror, lifted at the corners in a snarl. Then Hewson spoke and woke a hundred sinister echoes.

"You moved, damn you!" he cried. "Yes, you did, damn you! I saw you!"

Then he sat quite still, staring straight before him, like a man frozen in the Arctic snows.

Dr. Bourdette's movements were leisurely. He stepped off his pedestal with the mincing care of a lady alighting from a bus. The platform stood about two feet from the ground, and above the edge of it a plush-covered rope hung in arclike curves. Dr. Bourdette lifted up the rope until it formed an arch for him to pass under, stepped off the platform and sat down on the edge facing Hewson. Then he nodded and smiled and said, "Good evening."

"I need hardly tell you," he continued in perfect English in which was traceable only the least foreign accent, "that not until I overheard the conversation between you and the worthy manager of this establishment, did I suspect that I should have the pleasure of a companion here for the night. You cannot move or speak without my bidding, but you can hear me perfectly well. Something tells me that you are – shall I say nervous? My dear sir, have no illusions. I am not one of these contemptible effigies miraculously come to life: I am Dr. Bourdette himself."

He paused, coughed and shifted his legs.

"Pardon me," he resumed, "but I am a little stiff. And let me explain. Circumstances with which I need not fatigue you, have made it desirable that I should live in England. I was close to this building this evening when I saw a policeman regarding me a thought too curiously. I guessed that he intended to follow and perhaps ask me embarrassing questions, so I mingled with the crowd and came in here. An extra coin bought my admission to the chamber in which we now meet, and an inspiration showed me a certain means of escape.

"I raised a cry of fire, and when all the fools had rushed to the stairs I stripped my effigy of the caped coat which you behold me wearing, donned it, hid my effigy under the platform at the back, and took its place on the pedestal.

"I own that I have since spent a very fatiguing evening, but fortunately I was not always being watched and had opportunities to draw an occasional deep breath and ease the rigidity of my pose. One small boy screamed and exclaimed that he saw me moving. I understood that he was to be whipped and put straight to bed on his return home, and I can only hope that the threat has been executed to the letter.

"The manager's description of me, which I had the embarrassment of being compelled to overhear, was biased but not altogether inaccurate. Clearly I am not dead, although it is as well that the world thinks otherwise. His account of my hobby, which I have indulged for years, although, through necessity, less frequently of late, was in the main true although not intelligently expressed. The world is divided between collectors and non-collectors. With the non-collectors we are not concerned. The collectors collect anything, according to their individual tastes, from money to cigarette cards, from moths to match boxes. I collect throats."

He paused again and regarded Hewson's throat with interest mingled with disfavour.

"I am obliged to the chance which brought us together to-night," he continued, "and perhaps it would seem ungrateful to complain. From motives of personal safety my activities have been somewhat curtailed of late years, and I am glad of this opportunity of gratifying my somewhat unusual whim. But you have a skinny neck, sir, if you will overlook a personal remark. I should never have selected you from choice. I like men with thick necks . . . thick red necks. . . ."

He fumbled in an inside pocket and took out something which he tested against a wet forefinger and then proceeded to pass gently to and fro across the palm of his left hand.

"This is a little French razor," he remarked blandly. "They are not much used in England, but perhaps you know them? One strops them on wood. The blade, you will observe, is very narrow. They do not cut very deep, but deep enough. In just one little moment you shall see for yourself. I shall ask you the little civil question of all the polite barbers: 'Does the razor suit you, sir?' "

He rose up, a diminutive but menacing figure of evil, and approached Hewson with the silent furtive step of a hunting panther.

"You will have the goodness," he said, "to raise your chin a little. Thank you, and a little more. Just a little more. Ah, thank you! . . . *Merci, m'sieur . . . Ah, merci . . . merci. . . .*"

Over one end of the chamber was a thick skylight of frosted glass which, by day, let in a few sickly and filtered rays from the floor above. After sunrise these began to mingle with the subdued light from the electric bulbs, and this mingled illumination added a certain ghastliness to the scene which needed no additional touch of horror.

The waxwork figures stood apathetically in their places, waiting to be admired or execrated by the crowds who would presently wander fearfully among them. In their midst, in the centre gangway, Hewson sat still, leaning far back in his arm-chair. His chin was uptilted as if he were waiting to receive attention from a barber, and although there was not a scratch upon his throat, nor anywhere upon his body, he was cold and dead. His previous employers were wrong in having him credited with no imagination.

Dr. Bourdette on his pedestal watched the dead man unemotionally. He did not move, nor was he capable of motion. But then, after all, he was only a waxwork.

# The Inexperienced Ghost

## H. G. Wells

### Prospectus

**Address:** Mermaid Club, Bromley, Kent, England.

**Property:** Private club adjacent to a Golf course. Formerly an inn, several rooms have been refurbished to provide sleeping and leisure accommodation for members.

**Viewing Date:** March, 1902.

**Agent:** Herbert George Wells (1866–1946) is regarded as the "Founding Father" of modern Science Fiction and the author of several classics, including *The Time Machine* (1895), *The Invisible Man* (1897) and *War of the Worlds* (1898), all of which have been repeatedly filmed. Born in Bromley, he was also an influential writer of supernatural stories, notably "The Red Room" (1896) about a room that is haunted, not by a ghost, but the residue of fear, and "The Presence by the Fire" (1897) in which a haunting is rationalised. Christopher Lee (1922– ) is one of Britain's most distinguished character actors and has played a variety of roles from Sherlock Holmes to Fu Manchu and, of course, Dracula. He has also appeared in several haunted house movies, notably *Horror Hotel* (1960) and *The House that Dripped Blood* (1970). Lee has several times considered filming "The Inexperienced Ghost" which, he says, "is a brilliant and unusual mixture of humour and the supernatural with a most surprising ending."

The scene amidst which Clayton told his last story comes back very vividly to my mind. There he sat, for the greater part of the time, in the corner of the authentic settle by the spacious open fire, and Sanderson sat beside him smoking the Broseley clay that bore his name. There was Evans, and that marvel among actors, Wish, who is also a modest man. We had all come down to the Mermaid Club that Saturday morning, except Clayton, who had slept there overnight – which indeed gave him the opening of his story. We had golfed until golfing was invisible; we had dined, and we were in that mood of tranquil kindliness when men will suffer a story. When Clayton began to tell one, we naturally supposed he was lying. It may be that indeed he was lying – of that the reader will speedily be able to judge as well as I. He began, it is true, with an air of matter-of-fact anecdote, but that we thought was only the incurable artifice of the man.

"I say!" he remarked, after a long consideration of the upward rain of sparks from the log that Sanderson had thumped, "you know I was alone here last night?"

"Except for the domestics," said Wish.

"Who sleep in the other wing," said Clayton. "Yes. Well—" He pulled at his cigar for some little time as though he still hesitated about his confidence. Then he said, quite quietly, "I caught a ghost!"

"Caught a ghost, did you?" said Sanderson. "Where is it?"

And Evans, who admires Clayton immensely and has been four weeks in America, shouted, "*Caught* a ghost, did you, Clayton? I'm glad of it! Tell us all about it right now."

Clayton said he would in a minute, and asked him to shut the door.

He looked apologetically at me. "There's no eavesdropping, of course, but we don't want to upset our very excellent service with any rumours of ghosts in the place. There's too much shadow and oak panelling to trifle with that. And this, you know, wasn't a regular ghost. I don't think it will come again – ever."

"You mean to say you didn't keep it?" said Sanderson.

"I hadn't the heart to," said Clayton.

And Sanderson said he was surprised.

We laughed, and Clayton looked aggrieved. "I know," he said, with the flicker of a smile, "but the fact is it really *was* a ghost, and I'm as sure of it as I am that I am talking to you now. I'm not joking. I mean what I say."

Sanderson drew deeply at his pipe, with one reddish eye on Clayton, and then emitted a thin jet of smoke more eloquent than many words.

Clayton ignored the comment. "It is the strangest thing that has ever happened in my life. You know I never believed in ghosts or anything of the sort, before, ever; and then, you know, I bag one in a corner; and the whole business is in my hands."

He meditated still more profoundly and produced and began to pierce a second cigar with a curious little stabber he affected.

"You talked to it?" asked Wish.

"For the space, probably, of an hour."

"Chatty?" I said, joining the party of the sceptics.

"The poor devil was in trouble," said Clayton, bowed over his cigar-end and with the very faintest note of reproof.

"Sobbing?" someone asked.

Clayton heaved a realistic sight at the memory. "Good Lord!" he said, "yes." And then, "Poor fellow! Yes."

"Where did you strike it?" asked Evans, in his best American accent.

"I never realised," said Clayton, ignoring him, "the poor sort of thing a ghost might be," and he hung us up again for a time, while he sought for matches in his pocket and lit and warmed to his cigar.

"I took an advantage," he reflected at last.

We were none of us in a hurry. "A character," he said, "remains just the same character for all that it's been disembodied. That's a thing we too often forget. People with a certain strength or fixity of purpose may have ghosts of a certain strength and fixity of purpose – most haunting ghosts, you know, must be as one-idea'd as monomaniacs and as obstinate as mules to come back again and again. This poor creature wasn't." He suddenly looked up rather queerly, and his eye went round the room. "I say it," he said, "in all kindliness, but that is the plain truth of the case. Even at the first glance he struck me as weak."

He punctuated with the help of his cigar.

"I came upon him, you know, in the long passage. His back was towards me and I saw him first. Right off I knew him for a ghost. He was transparent and whitish; clean through his chest I could see the glimmer of the little window at the end. And not only his physique but his attitude struck me as being weak. He looked, you know, as though he didn't know in the slightest whatever he meant to do. One hand was on the panelling and the other fluttered to his mouth. Like – *so!*"

"What sort of physique?" said Sanderson.

"Lean. You know that sort of young man's neck that has two great flutings down the back, here and here – so! And a little, meanish head with scrubby hair and rather bad ears. Shoulders bad, narrower than the hips; turndown collar, ready-made short jacket, trousers baggy and a little frayed at the heels. That's how he took me. I came very quietly up the staircase. I did not carry a light, you know – the candles are on the landing table and there is that lamp – and I was in my list slippers, and I saw him as I came up. I stopped dead at that – taking him in. I wasn't a bit afraid. I think that in most of these affairs one is never nearly so afraid or excited as one imagines one would be. I was surprised and interested. I thought, 'Good Lord! Here's a ghost at last! And I haven't believed for a moment in ghosts during the last five-and-twenty years.' "

"Um," said Wish.

"I suppose I wasn't on the landing a moment before he found out I was there. He turned on me sharply, and I saw the face of an immature young man, a weak nose, a scrubby little moustache, a feeble chin. So for an instant we stood – he looking over his shoulder at me – and regarded one another. Then he seemed to remember his high calling. He turned round, drew himself up, projected his face, raised his arms, spread his hands in approved ghost fashion – came towards me. As he did so his little jaw dropped, and he emitted a faint, drawn-out 'Boo.' No, it wasn't – not a bit dreadful. I'd dined. I'd had a bottle of champagne, and being all alone, perhaps two or three – perhaps even four or five – whiskies, so I was as solid as rocks and no more frightened than if

I'd been assailed by a frog. 'Boo!' I said. 'Nonsense. You don't belong to *this* place. What are you doing here?'

"I could see him wince. 'Boo – oo,' he said.

" 'Boo – be hanged! Are you a member?' I said: and just to show I didn't care a pin for him I stepped through a corner of him and made to light my candle. 'Are you a member?' I repeated, looking at him sideways.

"He moved a little so as to stand clear of me, and his bearing became crestfallen. 'No,' he said, in answer to the persistent interrogation of my eye; 'I'm not a member – I'm a ghost.'

" 'Well, that doesn't give you the run of the Mermaid Club. Is there anyone you want to see, or anything of that sort?' And doing it as steadily as possible for fear that he should mistake the carelessness of whisky for the distraction of fear, I got my candle alight. I turned on him, holding it. 'What are you doing here?' I said.

"He had dropped his hands and stopped his booing, and there he stood, abashed and awkward, the ghost of a weak, silly, aimless young man. 'I'm haunting,' he said.

" 'You haven't any business to,' I said in a quiet voice.

" 'I'm a ghost,' he said, as if in defence.

" 'That may be, but you haven't any business to haunt here. This is a respectable private club; people often stop here with nursemaids and children, and, going about in the careless way you do, some poor little mite could easily come upon you and be scared out of her wits. I suppose you didn't think of that?'

" 'No, sir,' he said, 'I didn't.'

" 'You should have done. You haven't any claim on the place, have you? Weren't murdered here, or anything of that sort?"

" 'None, sir; but I thought as it was old and oak-panelled—'

" 'That's *no* excuse.' I regarded him firmly. 'Your coming here is a mistake,' I said, in a tone of friendly superiority. I feigned to see if I had my matches, and then looked up at him frankly. 'If I were you I wouldn't wait for cock-crow – I'd vanish right away.'

"He looked embarrassed. 'The fact *is*, sir—' he began.

" 'I'd vanish,' I said, driving it home.

" 'The fact is, sir, that – somehow – I can't.'

" 'You *can't*?'

" 'No, sir. There's something I've forgotten. I've been hanging about here since midnight last night, hiding in the cupboards of the empty bedrooms and things like that. I'm flurried. I've never come haunting before, and it seems to put me out.'

" 'Put you out?'

" 'Yes, sir. I've tried to do it several times, and it doesn't come off. There's some little thing has slipped me, and I can't get back.'

"That, you know, rather bowled me over. He looked at me in such an abject way that for the life of me I couldn't keep up quite the high hectoring vein I had adopted. 'That's queer,' I said, and as I spoke I fancied I heard someone moving about down below. 'Come into my room and tell me more about it,' I said. I didn't, of course, understand this, and I tried to take him by the arm. But, of course, you might as well have tried to take hold of a puff of smoke! I had forgotten my number, I think; anyhow, I remember going into several bedrooms – it was lucky I was the only soul in that wing – until I saw my traps. 'Here we are,' I said, and sat down in the armchair; 'sit down and tell me all about it. It seems to me you have got yourself into a jolly awkward position, old chap.'

"Well, he said he wouldn't sit down; he'd prefer to flit up and down the room if it was all the same to me. And so he did, and in a little while we were deep in a long and serious talk. And presently, you know, something of those whiskies and sodas evaporated out of me, and I began to realise just a little what a thundering rum and weird business it was that I was in. There he was, semi-transparent – the proper conventional phantom, and noiseless except for his ghost of a voice – flitting to and fro in that nice, clean, chintz-hung old bedroom. You could see the gleam of the copper candlesticks through him, and the lights on the brass fender, and the corners of the framed engravings on the wall, and there he was telling me all about this wretched little life of his that had recently ended on earth. He hadn't a particularly honest face, you know, but being transparent, of course, he couldn't avoid telling the truth."

"Eh?" said Wish, suddenly sitting up in his chair.

"What?" said Clayton.

"Being transparent – couldn't avoid telling the truth – I don't see it," said Wish.

"*I* don't see it," said Clayton, with inimitable assurance. "But it *is* so, I can assure you nevertheless. I don't believe he got once a nail's breadth off the Bible truth. He told me how he had been killed – he went down into a London basement with a candle to look for a leakage of gas – and described himself as a senior English master in a London private school when that release occurred."

"Poor wretch!" said I.

"That's what I thought, and the more he talked the more I thought it. There he was, purposeless in life and purposeless out of it. He talked of his father and mother and his school-master, and all who had ever been anything to him in the world, meanly. He had been too sensitive, too nervous; none of them had ever valued him properly or understood him, he said. He had never had a real friend in the world, I think; he had never had a success. He had shirked games and failed examinations. 'It's like that with some people,' he said; 'whenever I got into the examination-room or anywhere everything seemed to go.' Engaged to be married, of course – to another over-sensitive person, I suppose – when the indiscretion with the gas escape ended his affairs. 'And where are you now?' I asked. 'Not in—?'

"He wasn't clear on that point at all. The impression he gave me was of a sort of vague, intermediate state, a special reserve for souls too non-existent for anything so positive as either sin or virtue. *I* don't know. He was much too egotistical and unobservant to give me any clear idea of the kind of place, kind of country, there is on the Other Side of Things. Wherever he was, he seems to have fallen in with a set of kindred spirits: ghosts of weak Cockney young men, who were on a footing of Christian names, and among these there was certainly a lot of talk about 'going haunting' and things like that. Yes – going haunting! They seemed to think 'haunting' a tremendous adventure, and most of them funked it all the time. And so primed, you know, he had come."

"But really!" said Wish to the fire.

"These are the impressions he gave me, anyhow," said Clayton, modestly. "I may, of course, have been in a rather uncritical state, but that was the sort of background he gave to himself. He kept flitting up and down, with his thin voice going – talking, talking about his wretched self, and never a word of clear, firm statement from first to last. He was thinner and sillier and more pointless than if he had been real and alive. Only then, you know, he would not have been in my bedroom here – if he *had* been alive. I should have kicked him out."

"Of course," said Evans, "there *are* poor mortals like that."

"And there's just as much chance of their having ghosts as the rest of us," I admitted.

"What gave a sort of point to him, you know, was the fact that he did seem within limits to have found himself out. The mess he had made of haunting had depressed him terribly. He had been told it would be a 'lark': he had come expecting it to be a 'lark,' and here it was, nothing but another failure added to his record! He proclaimed himself an utter out-and-out failure. He said, and I can quite believe it, that he had never tried to do anything all his life that he hadn't made a perfect mess of – and through all the wastes of eternity he never would. If he had had sympathy, perhaps—. He paused at that, and stood regarding me. He remarked that, strange as it might seem to me, nobody, not anyone, ever, had given him the amount of sympathy I was doing now. I could see what he wanted straight away, and I determined to head him off at once. I may be a brute, you know, but being the Only Real Friend, the recipient of the confidences of one of these egotistical weaklings, ghost or body, is beyond my physical endurance. I got up briskly. 'Don't you brood on these things too much,' I said. 'The thing you've got to do is to get out of this – get out of this sharp. You pull yourself together and *try*.' 'I can't,' he said. 'You try,' I said, and try he did."

"Try!" said Sanderson. "*How?*"

"Passes," said Clayton.

"Passes?"

"Complicated series of gestures and passes with the hands.

That's how he had come in and that's how he had to get out again. Lord, what a business I had!"

"But how could *any* series of passes—" I began.

"My dear man," said Clayton, turning on me and putting a great emphasis on certain words, "you want *everything* clear. I don't know *how*. All I know is that you *do* – that *he* did, anyhow, at least. After a fearful time, you know, he got his passes right and suddenly disappeared."

"Did you," said Sanderson slowly, "observe the passes?"

"Yes," said Clayton, and seemed to think. "It was tremendously queer," he said. "There we were, I and this thin, vague ghost, in that silent room, in this silent, empty inn, in this silent little Friday-night town. Not a sound except our voices and a faint panting he made when he swung. There was the bedroom candle, and one candle on the dressing-table alight, that was all – sometimes one or other would flare up into a tall, lean, astonished flame for a space. And queer things happened. 'I can't,' he said; 'I shall never—!' And suddenly he sat down on a little chair at the foot of the bed and began to sob and sob. Lord! what a harrowing, whimpering thing he seemed!

" 'You pull yourself together,' I said, and tried to pat him on the back, and . . . my confounded hand went through him! By that time, you know, I wasn't nearly so – massive as I had been on the landing. I got the queerness of it in full. I remember snatching back my hand out of him, as it were, with a little thrill, and walking over to the dressing-table. 'You pull yourself together,' I said to him, 'and try.' And in order to encourage and help him I began to try as well."

"What!" said Sanderson, "the passes?"

"Yes, the passes."

"But—" I said, moved by an idea that eluded me for a space.

"This is interesting," said Sanderson, with his finger in his pipe-bowl. "You mean to say this ghost of yours gave way—"

"Did his level best to give away the whole confounded barrier? *Yes*."

"He didn't," said Wish; "he couldn't. Or you'd have gone there, too."

"That's precisely it," I said, finding my elusive idea put into words for me.

"That *is* precisely it," said Clayton, with thoughtful eyes upon the fire.

For just a little while there was silence.

"And at last he did it?" said Sanderson.

"At last he did it. I had to keep him up to it hard, but he did it at last – rather suddenly. He despaired, we had a scene, and then he got up abruptly and asked me to go through the whole performance, slowly, so that he might see. 'I believe,' he said, 'if I could *see* I should spot what was wrong at once.' And he did. '*I* know,' he said. 'What do you know?' said I. '*I* know,' he repeated. Then he said, peevishly, 'I *can't* do it, if you look at me – I really *can't*; it's been that, partly, all along. I'm such a nervous fellow that you put me out.' Well, we had a bit of an argument. Naturally I wanted to see; but he was as obstinate as a mule, and suddenly I had come over as tired as a dog – he tired me out. 'All right,' I said, '*I* won't look at you,' and turned towards the mirror, on the wardrobe, by the bed.

"He started off very fast. I tried to follow him by looking in the looking-glass, to see just what it was had hung. Round went his arms and his hands, so, and so, and so, and then with a rush came to the last gesture of all – you stand erect and open out your arms – and so, don't you know, he stood. And then he didn't! He didn't! He wasn't! I wheeled round from the looking-glass to him. There was nothing! I was alone, with the flaring candles and a staggering mind. What had happened? Had anything happened? Had I been dreaming? . . . And then, with an absurd note of finality about it, the clock upon the landing discovered the moment was ripe for striking *one*. So! – Ping! And I was as grave and sober as a judge, with all my champagne and whisky gone into the vast serene. Feeling queer, you know – confoundedly *queer!* Queer! Good Lord!"

He regarded his cigar-ash for a moment. "That's all that happened," he said.

"And then you went to bed?" asked Evans.

"What else was there to do?"

I looked Wish in the eye. We wanted to scoff, and there was something, something perhaps in Clayton's voice and manner, that hampered our desire.

"And about these passes?" said Sanderson.

"I believe I could do them now."

"Oh!" said Sanderson, and produced a pen-knife and set himself to grub the dottel out of the bowl of his clay.

"Why don't you do them now?" said Sanderson, shutting his pen-knife with a click.

"That's what I'm going to do," said Clayton.

"They won't work," said Evans.

"If they do—" I suggested.

"You know, I'd rather you didn't," said Wish, stretching out his legs.

"Why?" asked Evans.

"I'd rather he didn't," said Wish.

"But he hasn't got 'em right," said Sanderson, plugging too much tobacco into his pipe.

"All the same, I'd rather he didn't," said Wish.

We argued with Wish. He said that for Clayton to go through those gestures was like mocking a serious matter. "But you don't believe—?" I said. Wish glanced at Clayton, who was staring into the fire, weighing something in his mind. "I do – more than half, anyhow, I do," said Wish.

"Clayton," said I, "you're too good a liar for us. Most of it was all right. But that disappearance . . . happened to be convincing. Tell us, it's a tale of cock and bull."

He stood up without heeding me, took the middle of the hearthrug, and faced me. For a moment he regarded his feet thoughtfully, and then for all the rest of the time his eyes were on the opposite wall, with an intent expression. He raised his two hands slowly to the level of his eyes and so began. . . .

Now, Sanderson is a Freemason, a member of the lodge of the Four Kings, which devotes itself so ably to the study and elucidation of all the mysteries of Masonry past and present, and among the students of this lodge Sanderson is by no means the least. He followed Clayton's motions with a singular interest in his reddish eye. "That's not bad," he said, when it was done. "You really do, you know, put things together, Clayton, in a most amazing fashion. But there's one little detail out."

"I know," said Clayton. "I believe I could tell you which."

"Well?"

"This," said Clayton, and did a queer little twist and writhing and thrust of the hands.

"Yes."

"That, you know, was what *he* couldn't get right," said Clayton. "But how do *you*—?"

"Most of this business, and particularly how you invented it, I don't understand at all," said Sanderson, "but just that phase – I do." He reflected. "These happen to be a series of gestures – connected with a certain branch of esoteric Masonry. Probably you know. Or else—*How?*" He reflected still further. "I do not see I can do any harm in telling you just the proper twist. After all, if you know, you know; if you don't, you don't."

"I know nothing," said Clayton, "except what the poor devil let out last night."

"Well, anyhow," said Sanderson, and placed his church-warden very carefully upon the shelf over the fireplace. Then very rapidly he gesticulated with his hands.

"So?" said Clayton, repeating.

"So," said Sanderson, and took his pipe in hand again.

"Ah, *now*," said Clayton, "I can do the whole thing – right."

He stood up before the waning fire and smiled at us all. But I think there was just a little hesitation in his smile. "If I begin—" he said.

"I wouldn't begin," said Wish.

"It's all right!" said Evans. "Matter is indestructible. You don't think any jiggery-pokery of this sort is going to snatch Clayton into the world of shades. Not it! You may try, Clayton, so far as I'm concerned, until your arms drop off at the wrists."

"I don't believe that," said Wish, and stood up and put his arm on Clayton's shoulder. "You've made me half-believe in that story somehow, and I don't want to see the thing done."

"Goodness!" said I, "here's Wish frightened!"

"I am," said Wish, with real or admirably feigned intensity. "I believe that if he goes through these motions right he'll *go*."

"He'll not do anything of the sort," I cried. "There's only one way out of this world for men, and Clayton is thirty years from that. Besides . . . And such a ghost! Do you think—?"

Wish interrupted me by moving. He walked out from among our chairs and stopped beside the table and stood there. "Clayton," he said, "you're a fool."

Clayton, with a humorous light in his eyes, smiled back to him. "Wish," he said, "is right and all you others are wrong. I shall go. I shall get to the end of these passes, and as the last swish whistles through the air, Presto! – this hearthrug will be vacant, the room will be blank amazement, and a respectably dressed gentleman of fifteen stone will plump into the world of shades. I'm certain. So will you be. I decline to argue further. Let the thing be tried."

"*No*," said Wish, and made a step and ceased, and Clayton raised his hands once more to repeat the spirit's passing.

By that time, you know, we were all in a state of tension – largely because of the behaviour of Wish. We sat all of us with our eyes on Clayton – I, at least, with a sort of tight, stiff feeling about me as though from the back of my skull to the middle of my thighs my body had been changed to steel. And there, with a gravity that was imperturbably serene, Clayton bowed and swayed and waved his hands and arms before us. As he drew towards the end one piled up, one tingled in one's teeth. The last gesture, I have said, was to swing the arms out wide open, with the face held up. And when at last he swung out to this closing gesture I ceased even to breathe. It was ridiculous, of course, but you know that ghost-story feeling. It was after dinner, in a queer old shadowy house. Would he, after all—?

There he stood for one stupendous moment, with his arms open and his upturned face, assured and bright, in the glare of the hanging lamp. We hung through that moment as if it were an age, and then came from all of us something that was half a sigh of infinite relief and half a reassuring "*No!*" For visibly – he wasn't going. It was all nonsense. He had told an idle story, and carried it almost to conviction, that was all! . . . And then in that moment the face of Clayton changed.

It changed. It changed as a lit house changes when its lights are suddenly extinguished. His eyes were suddenly eyes that were fixed, his smile was frozen on his lips, and he stood there still. He stood there, very gently swaying.

That moment, too, was an age. And then, you know, chairs were scraping, things were falling, and we were all moving. His knees seemed to give, and he fell forward, and Evans rose and caught him in his arms. . . .

It stunned us all. For a minute I suppose no one said a coherent thing. We believed it, yet could not believe it. . . . I came out of a muddled stupefaction to find myself kneeling beside him, and his vest and shirt were torn open, and Sanderson's hand lay on his heart. . . .

Well – the simple fact before us could very well wait our convenience; there was no hurry for us to comprehend. It lay there for an hour; it lies athwart my memory, black and amazing still, to this day. Clayton had, indeed, passed into the world that lies so near to and so far from our own, and he had gone thither by the only road that mortal man may take. But whether he did indeed pass there by that poor ghost's incantation, or whether he was stricken suddenly by apoplexy in the midst of an idle tale – as the coroner's jury would have us believe – is no matter for my judging; it is just one of those inexplicable riddles that must remain unsolved until the final solution of all things shall come. All I certainly know is that, in the very moment, in the very instant, of concluding those passes, he changed, and staggered, and fell down before us – dead!

# Sophy Mason Comes Back

## E. M. Delafield

### Prospectus

**Address:** Les Moineaux, near Aix en Provence, France.

**Property:** Fashionable summer house in the midi region. A tall, narrow, elegant property with blue shutters. Formerly owned by a small community of monks.

**Viewing Date:** July, 1930.

**Agent:** Edmee Monica Delafield (1890–1943) was the author of *Diary of a Provincial Lady* (1930), the story of a disaster-prone woman that earned her the accolade of "a successor to Jane Austen." Born in Sussex, she was, for a time, a member of a French religious order before returning to England and becoming a prolific writer of magazine stories, books, plays and film scripts. She later added to the success of *Provincial Lady* with three sequels set in London, America and wartime Britain. Peter Cushing (1913–1994) was the son of a Surrey surveyor's clerk who took himself to Hollywood to make a career in films, and from the mid-1950s was one of Britain's most popular horror film stars. A gentle and softly spoken man off-screen, Cushing was a devotee of Delafield's work. "Her style, her fascinating characters and her wonderful ability to tell a good tale makes 'Sophy Mason Comes Back' one of my favourite short stories," he wrote a few years before his death.

"Have you ever, actually, seen a ghost?"

It wasn't, as it is so often, a flippant enquiry. One was serious, on that particular subject, with Fenwick. He was keen on psychical research, although it was understood that he took a line of his own, and neither accepted, nor promulgated, arbitrary interpretations of any kind.

He answered cautiously:

"I've seen what the French call a *revenant*, undoubtedly."

"Was it frightening?" asked one of the women, timidly.

Fenwick shook his head:

"I wasn't frightened," he admitted. "Not by the ghost or spirit – whichever you like to call it. Still less have I been so by so-called 'haunted rooms' with mysterious noises and unexplained openings of doors, and so on. But once, in the house where I saw the *revenant* – I was frightened."

"Do you mean – wasn't it the ghost that frightened you, then?"

"No," said Fenwick, and his serious, clever face wore a look of gravity and horror.

We asked if he would tell us about it.

"I'll try, but I may have to tell the story backwards. You see, when I came into it, everything was over – far away in the forgotten past, not just on the other side of the war, but right back in the late eighties. You know – horse-drawn carriages, and oil-lamps, and the women wearing bonnets, and long, tight skirts, all bunched up at the back . . . In a French provincial town, naturally, things were as much behind the times then, as they are now. (This happened in France by the way – did I tell you?) It isn't necessary to give you the name of the town. It was somewhere in the midi, where the Latins are – very Latin indeed.

"Well, there was a house – call it Les Moineaux. One of those tall, narrow French houses, white, with blue shutters, and a straight avenue of trees leading to the front steps, and a formal arrangement of standard rose-bushes on either side of the blue frontdoor.

"It was quite a little house, you understand – not a château. It had once belonged to a very small community of contemplative monks – they'd made the garden and the avenue, I believe. When the monks became so few in number that they were absorbed into another Order, the house stayed empty for a bit. Then it was bought by a wine merchant, as a gift for his wife, who used it as a country villa for herself and her children every summer. This family lived at – well, in a town about twenty kilometres away. They could either drive out to Les Moineaux, or come by the diligence, that stopped in the village about half a mile away from the house. Most of the year, the house remained empty, and no one seems to have thought that a caretaker was necessary. Either the peasants round there were very honest, or there was nothing worth taking in the house. Probably the thrifty madame of the wine merchant brought down whatever they required for their summer visits, and took it all away again when they left. There were big cupboards in the house, too – built into the wall – and she could have locked anything away in those, and taken the key.

"The family consisted of monsieur and madame, three or four children, and an English girl, whom they all called 'mees,' who was supposed to look after the children, and make herself generally useful.

"Her name was Sophy Mason; she was about twenty when she came to them, and is said to have been very pretty.

"One imagines that she was kept fully occupied. Madame would certainly have seen to it that she earned her small salary, and her keep; and, as is customary in the French middle-class, each member of the household was prepared to do any job that needed doing, without reference to 'my work' or 'your work.' Sophy Mason, however, was principally engaged with the children. Quite often, in the spring and early summer, she was sent down with them to Les Moineaux for a few days' country air, while monsieur and madame remained with the business. They must have been go-ahead people, by the way, far in advance of their time, for 'the mees' seems to have been allowed to keep the children out of doors, quite in accordance with the English traditions, and entirely contrary to the usual French fashion of that date and that class.

"The peasants, working in the fields, used to see the English girl, with the children, running races up and down the avenue, or going out into the woods to pick wild strawberries. Sophy Mason could speak French quite well, but she was naturally expected to talk English with the children, and, except for a word or two with the people at the farm, from which milk and butter and eggs were supplied to Les Moineaux, there was in point of fact no one for her to talk to, when monsieur and madame were not there.

"Until Alcide Lamotte came on the scene.

"All I can tell you about him is that he was the son of a farmer – a big, red-headed fellow, of an unusual type, and certainly possessing brains, and a compelling personality.

When he and Sophy Mason met first, he was in the middle of his compulsory three years' military service, and home at the farm *en permission*.

"One can imagine it – this English girl, who'd been in France over a year without, probably, exchanging a word with anyone but her employers, their children, and perhaps an occasional old *curé* coming in for a game of cards in the evening – left to her own devices in the more or less isolated villa in the late spring, or early summer, in the vine country. What happened was, of course, inevitable. No one knows when or how their first meetings took place, but passions move quickly in that country. By the time monsieur and madame did appear, to inaugurate their usual summer *vie de campagne*, the neighbouring peasantry were perfectly aware that *le roux*, as they called him, was Sophy Mason's lover.

"Whether they betrayed her to her employers or not, one doesn't know. Personally, I imagine they didn't. In that country, and to that race, neither love nor passion appears as a crime, even when marital infidelity is involved, and in this case the question, for the girl merely of deceiving her mistress, and Lamotte – also a free agent – was one of themselves. Almost certainly, madame found out for herself what was going on.

"There must have been a crisis – *une scène de première classe*. Perhaps madame kept watch – was peeping through the crack of a door just left ajar, when 'the mees' stole in – noiselessly, as she hoped – from a moonlight tryst in the woods where the wild strawberries had grown a few weeks earlier.

"'What! Depraved, deceitful creature, to whom I have entrusted my innocent children! . . .'

"The French are nothing if not dramatic.

"I suspect that madame enjoyed herself, making the most of the scene, whilst poor Sophy Mason, ashamed and guilty, was frightened out of her wits. Perhaps she saw herself sent back to the Bloomsbury boarding-house of the aunt who was her only living relation, disgraced, and with no hope of ever getting another situation.

"As a matter of fact, madame forgave her. Sophy Mason was useful, the children liked her, she was very cheap – and perhaps, at the bottom of her heart, madame was not very seriously shocked at Sophy's lapse from virtue.

"At all events, after extracting a promise that she would never meet Alcide again, except for one farewell interview, madame told Sophy that she might stay.

"The farewell interview, I believe, took place in madame's presence – she'd stipulated for that. Something – one can only guess that it may have been some pathetic, scarcely disguised hint from the girl – indicated to madame's acute perceptions that if Alcide had proposed marriage Sophy would have been ready, and more than ready, to have him. But Alcide, of course, did nothing of the kind. He accepted his dismissal with a sulky acquiescence that he would certainly not have shown if Sophy Mason – more astute and less passionate – had not so readily yielded to him every privilege that he chose to demand.

"There was an unpleasant and humiliating moral to be drawn from his attitude, and it may safely be presumed that madame did not hesitate to draw it, probably in forcible language. Sophy Mason, poor child, was left to her tears and her disgrace.

"But those pangs of shame and disappointment were to give place to a much more real cause for distress.

"In the autumn, Sophy Mason discovered that she was going to have a baby.

"It is, given her youth and probable upbringing, quite likely that the possibility of such a thing had never presented itself to her. But that madame had apparently not foreseen such a contingency is much more difficult to explain.

"It may, of course, be that she attributed more sophistication to the girl than poor Sophy Mason actually possessed, and that she asked a leading question or two that Sophy answered without really understanding.

"One thing is certain: that Sophy Mason did not dare to tell her employer of her condition. She had recourse, instead, to a far more hopeless alternative.

"She appealed to her lover.

"At first, by letter. She must have written several times, if one draws the obvious inference from the only reply of his that was seen by anyone but the recipient. It is an illiterate, ugly scrawl, evidently written in haste, telling her not to write again, and concluding with a perfunctory endearment. It was probably those few, meaningless last words that gave the unfortunate Sophy courage for her final imprudence. It seems fairly certain that she was, actually, imaginatively in love with Alcide, whereas with him, of course, the attraction had been purely sensual, and had not outlasted physical gratification. In fact, I have no doubt, personally, that the usual reaction had set in, and that the mere thought of her was probably as repellent to him as it had once been alluring. Sophy, however, could not, or would not, believe that everything was over, and that she was to be left to confront disgrace and disaster alone. Under the pretext of meeting some imaginary English friends, she obtained leave of absence from madame, and went down to Les Moineaux on a day in late October.

"Either she had made an assignation beforehand with Alcide, or, as seems a good deal more probable, she had learnt that he was home again, on the termination of his military service, and counted on taking him by surprise. She must have made up her mind that if only she could see him again, and plead with him, he would, in the phrase of the time, 'make an honest woman of her.'

"The interview between them took place. What actually occurred can only be a matter of conjecture.

"That it took place at Les Moineaux is a proved fact, and I – who have seen the house – can visualise the setting of it. They would have gone into the living-room, where only the bare minimum of furniture had been left, but from the ceiling of which dangled, magnificently, a huge candelabra of pale pink glass, swinging from gilt chains. The gaudy beauty, and tinkling light music of the candelabra have always seemed to me to add that touch of incongruity that sharpens horror to the unbearable pitch. Beneath its huddled glitter, Sophy Mason must have wept, and trembled, and pleaded, in an increasing terror and despair.

"Lamotte was a southerner, a coarse, brutal fellow, with the strong animal passions of his years, and of his race. Whether what followed then was a premeditated crime, or a sudden impulse born of violent rage and exasperation, will never be known. With apparently no other weapon than his own powerful hands, Alcide Lamotte, probably by strangulation, murdered Sophy Mason.

"When the girl failed to return home, her employer, apparently, neglected to make any serious enquiry into her fate. Madame, who had perhaps suspected her condition, affected to believe that the girl had run away to England, in spite of the fact that her few belongings had been left behind.

"Possibly they were afraid of a scandalous discovery, but more probably, with the thriftiness of their class, they dreaded being put to expense that would, they well knew, never be made good by Sophy's only relation, in distant England.

"The aunt, in point of fact, behaved quite as callously as the French couple, and with even less excuse. Sophy Mason was the illegitimate child of her dead sister, and when, eventually, she learnt of the girl's disappearance, she is said to have taken up the attitude of asserting: 'Like mother, like daughter,' and declaring that Sophy had certainly gone off with a lover, like her mother before her.

"Conveniently for madame, if she wanted to convince herself and other people of the truth of that theory, Alcide Lamotte suddenly made off, towards the end of the same month, and was reported to have gone to America. Of course, said madame, they had gone together. Sophy had been traced as far as Les Moineaux without the slightest difficulty, and where she had spent the intervening weeks, between that visit and her alleged departure to America with her lover, no one seems to have enquired.

"The only clue to the mystery was that last letter, written by Lamotte, that Sophy had left behind her, and that was found and read by her employers, and in the fact that when, in the summer following her disappearance, the wine merchant and his family went as usual to Les Moineaux, they found unmistakable evidence that the house had been entered by a backdoor, of which the lock had been picked.

"Nothing else seemed to have been tampered with, or disturbed in any way, and the whole affair was allowed to drop in a fashion that, in this country and at this date, appeared almost incredible."

Fenwick paused for a while, before resuming.

"My own connection with the story, came more than forty years later. All that I have told you, was conjectured, or found out many years after it happened. I warned you that I might have to tell the story backwards.

"The wine merchant of Sophy Mason's story was the connecting link. During the war, I came to know his son – a middle-aged man, once the youngest of the children in the avenue of Les Moineaux.

"I need not trouble you with any account of how we had come to know one another well – it was no stranger than the story of many other relationships established during the war years.

"We met from time to time, long after the Armistice had taken place, and in the summer of 1925, when I was in France, Amédé, my friend, invited me to pay him a visit, in the midi. He had quite recently married a girl many years younger than himself, and in accordance with French provincial custom, was living with her in the house of his parents – or rather, of his father, for the mother had been dead for some time.

"The wine merchant himself was over seventy – a hale and hearty old man, well looked after by an unmarried daughter, and still in perfect possession of all his faculties.

"Whilst I was with them, an observation on my part as to the facility with which all the family spoke English, occasioned an allusion to Sophy Mason – the English 'mees' of forty-five years earlier.

"The old man, I remember, referred to her mysterious disappearance, but without giving any great importance to the story, and attaching to it, as a mere matter of course, the old explanation of the flight to America with Lamotte.

"In that light one would doubtless have accepted, and then forgotten it, but for two things. One of these was something that was told me by Amédé, and the other the coincidence – if you like to call it so – that forms the whole point of the story. Amédé's revelation, that was purposely not made in the presence of his father, was as follows:

"About fifteen years previously, shortly before the death of his mother, she had made over to him Les Moineaux, the little country villa that had belonged to her.

"Amédé was fond of the place, although he had no intention of ever living there, and long after the other brothers and sisters had scattered, when their mother was dead, and their father no longer cared to move from home, he continued to visit it periodically.

"It was, therefore, to Amédé that some peasants one day came, with an account of a gruesome discovery made in the wood near the house – that very wood where Sophy Mason used to take the children of her employers to pick wild strawberries.

"In a deep ditch, under the leaf-mould of more than a quarter of a century, had been uncovered, by the merest chance, the skeleton of a woman. Curiously enough – or perhaps not so curiously, taking into account the mentality of the uneducated – the older generation of villagers viewed the discovery with more horror than surprise, and displayed little hesitation in identifying the protagonists of the tragedy. The story of Sophy Mason's disappearance had survived the years, and Amédé's enquiries brought to light a singular piece of evidence.

"A woman was found who remembered, many years before, a revelation made by a servant-girl on her deathbed. This girl – a disreputable creature – had declared that on a certain October afternoon she had been in the wood, with her lover, and that, from their place of concealment, they had seen something terrible – a gigantic youth, with red hair, half-carrying and half-dragging the body of a woman, whom he had subsequently flung into the ditch, and covered with earth and stones from the hedge.

"Neither the girl, nor the man with her – who was, incidentally, married to another woman – had dared reveal their horrible discovery, fearing lest their own guilty connection should thereby come to light. This girl, in point of fact, died shortly afterwards, and her story, told on her deathbed, had actually been disbelieved at the time by her hearers, because the narrator was known to have the worst possible reputation and to be a notorious liar.

"The woman to whom it was told swore that she had never actually repeated the story, but that rumours of it had long been rife and that the wood, in consequence, had been shunned for years.

"The name of Alcide Lamotte, curiously enough, seems not to have been directly mentioned. The Lamotte family were the chief land-owners in the place, and were accounted rich and powerful, and *le roux* himself had never been heard of since his disappearance to America.

"My friend Amédé, hearing this strange echo of the past, doubted greatly what course to adopt. It is easy to say that an Englishman, in his place, would have doubted not at all. The Englishman has a natural respect for the law that is certainly lacking in the Latin. Remember, too, that it had all happened so long ago – that the only known witness of the crime was a woman of ill-repute, long since dead – that poor Sophy Mason – if it was indeed she who had been done to death – had no one to demand a tardy investigation into her fate – and finally, that by the law of France, a man cannot be brought to trial for a crime that is only discovered after the lapse of a certain number of years. Amédé, contenting himself with giving the minimum of the information in his possession – all of which, it must be taken into account, depended upon hearsay – to the authorities, saw to the burial of the unidentified remains.

"There the story would have ended, so far as such things can ever be said to end, but for the coincidence of which I spoke.

"Fifteen years later, whilst I was on my visit to Amédé's old father, and just after Amédé had told me of this strange and hidden postscript to the mystery of Sophy Mason, after an absence of close on forty-one years, Alcide Lamotte returned to the neighbourhood.

"And here, at last, is where such first-hand knowledge as I possess, begins. It is here that I, so to speak, come into the story.

"For I met Alcide Lamotte.

"He had come back – but, of course, he was not the wild, half-civilised lout – *le roux* – of a lifetime ago. He was, actually, a naturalised American, and a rich and successful man.

"There was no one left to recognise him, and, indeed, he now even called himself by a different name, and was Al Mott, from Pittsburg.

"You understand – I am not telling you a detective story, and trying to make a mystery. It *was* Alcide Lamotte, but when he came to the old wine merchant's house, Amédé and his father didn't know it. That is to say, the old man certainly didn't – and Mr. Mott called, the first time, with a business introduction, in regard to a sale of land. Amédé, when he found that, in spite of his Americanised appearance, the visitor was not only a Frenchman, but also conversant with the immediate neighbourhood, connected him with the district of Les Moineaux, but only in that vague, unemphatic fashion that just fails to put two and two together until, or unless, something happens that produces a sudden, blinding flash of illumination.

"There was certainly nothing about Al Mott, from Pittsburg, to recall the half-legendary figure of *le roux*.

"He was a big corpulent man, perfectly bald, with a hard, heavy face, and great pouches below his eyes.

"His manners were not polished, but noisy and genial.

"Neither Amédé nor his father took a fancy to him, but they were *hommes d'affaires*, there was a transaction to be concluded, and one evening he was asked to supper, and came.

"It was an evening in late October.

"The old man, of course, was there, and Amédé and his young, newly married wife. The aunt – the one that lived with them – had gone away for a few days.

"The evening, from the beginning, did not go very well. Madame Amédé, the bride, was an inexperienced hostess, and the guest was not of a type to put her at her ease.

"Amédé, who was madly in love with his wife, kept on watching her.

"For my part, I felt an extraordinary uneasiness. You all know, I believe, what is usually meant by the word 'psychic' applied to an individual, and you know, too, that it has often been applied to me. I can only tell you that, in the course of that evening, I knew, beyond any possibility of doubt, certain things not conveyed to me through the normal channels of the senses. I knew that the other guest, the man sitting opposite to me, had, somehow, some intimate connection with tragedy and violence, and I knew, too, that he was evil. At the same time I was aware, more and more as the evening went on, that something which I can only describe as a wave, or vibration, of misery, was in the atmosphere and steadily increasing in intensity.

"Afterwards, Madame Amédé told me that she had felt the same thing.

"She and her husband, it is worth remembering, were in the keyed-up, highly wrought state of people still in the midst of an overwhelming emotional experience. That is equal to saying that they were far more susceptible than usual to atmospheric influence.

"The old wine merchant, Amédé's father, was the only person, beside Mott himself, unaware of tension.

"He made a casual allusion to the countryside, and then to Les Moineaux – but not referring to it directly by name.

"Mott replied, and the conversation went on.

"But in that instant, without any conscious process of reasoning or induction, the connection was made in my mind.

"I knew him for Alcide Lamotte, and I saw that Amédé did too. My eyes, and those of Amédé met, for one terrible second, the knowledge flashing from one to the other.

"Both of us, I know, became utterly silent from that moment. Alcide, of course, went on talking. He was very talkative, and under the influence of wine, was becoming loud and boastful. He began to tell the old man, who was alone in paying attention to him, about his early struggles in America, and then his increasing successes there.

"He spoke in French, of course, the characteristic, twanging drawl of the midi, and with, actually, a queer kind of American intonation, noticeable every now and then. I can remember very vividly the effect of relentlessness that his loud tones, going on and on, made in the small room.

"He was still talking when – the thing happened.

"You can, of course, call it what you like. An apparition – a collective hallucination – or the result produced by certain psychological conditions that are perhaps not to be found once in a hundred years – but that were present that night.

"The feeling of unease that had been with me all the evening was intensified, and then – it suddenly left me altogether, as though some expected calamity had taken place, and had proved more endurable than the suspense of awaiting it. In its place, I experienced only a feeling of profound sadness and compassion.

"I *knew*, with complete certainty, that some emanation of extreme unhappiness was surrounding us. Then Madame Amédé, who sat next me, spoke, just above her breath:

"'*What is it?*'

"There were two sounds in the room. . . . One was the excited, confident voice of Alcide, now in the midst of his triumphant story, the other was a succession of sobs and stifled, despairing wails.

"The second sound came from the corner, exactly facing the place where Lamotte was sitting.

"There was a door there, and it opened slowly. Framed in the doorway, I saw her – a young girl, in the dress of the late eighties, with a scared, pitiful face, sobbing and wringing her hands.

"That was my *revenant* – Sophy Mason come back.

"I told you, when I began the story, that the – the apparition had not frightened me. That was true.

"Perhaps it was because I knew the story of the poor betrayed girl, perhaps because I have, as you know, been interested for years in psychic manifestations of all kinds. To me, it seemed apparent, even at that moment, that the emotional vibrations of the past, sent out by an anguished spirit all those years ago, had become perceptible to us because we were momentarily attuned to receive them.

"In my own case, the attunement was so complete that, for an instant or two, I could actually catch a glimpse of the very form from which those emotional disturbances had proceeded.

"Amédé and his wife – both of them, as I said before, in an unusually receptive condition – heard what I did. Amédé, however, saw nothing – only an indistinct blur, as he afterwards described it. His wife saw the outlines of a girl's figure. . . .

"It all happened you understand, within a few minutes. First, that sound of bitter crying, and then the apparition, and my own realisation that the Amédés were terror-struck. The old man, Amédé's father, had turned abruptly in his chair with a curious, strained look upon his face – uneasy, rather than frightened. He told us afterwards that he had seen and heard nothing, but had been suddenly conscious of tension in the room, and that then the expression on his son's face had frightened him. But he admitted, too, that sweat had broken out upon his forehead, although it was not hot in the room."

"But Alcide Lamotte?"

"Alcide Lamotte," said the narrator slowly, "went on talking loudly – without pause, without a tremor. He perceived nothing until Madame Amédé, with a groan, fell back on her chair in a dead faint. That of course, broke up the evening abruptly. . . .

"You remember, what I told you at the beginning? It wasn't the poor little *revenant* that frightened me – but I *was* afraid, that evening. I was afraid, with the worst terror that I have ever known, of that man who had lived a crowded lifetime away from the passionate, evil episode of his youth – who had changed his very identity, and had left the past so far behind him that no echo from it could reach him. Whatever the link had been once, between him and Sophy Mason – and who can doubt that, with her, it had survived death itself – to him, it now all meant nothing – had perished beneath the weight of the years.

"It was indeed that which frightened me – not the gentle, anguished spirit of Sophy Mason – but the eyes that saw nothing, the ears that heard nothing, the loud, confident voice that, whilst those of us who had never known her were yet tremblingly aware of her, talked on – of success, and of money, and of life in Pittsburg."

# The Boogeyman

## Stephen King

### Prospectus

**Address:** Waterbury, Connecticut, USA.

**Property:** Small family house in quiet back street. Two-storey building with well laid out ground floor living rooms and kitchen. Fitted bedrooms with spacious closet.

**Viewing Date:** March, 1973

**Agent:** Stephen King (1947– ) is the bestselling horror writer who began writing in his college newspaper and then a number of pulp magazines before bursting on to the world scene with his novel of possession, *Carrie*, in 1974. This was followed by *The Shining* (1977), a brilliant tale of a couple and their little boy who are snowed in for the winter in a Colorado resort hotel full of ghosts. In that book, and subsequent short stories such as "The Boogeyman" (1973), King has taken the old "haunted house" tradition as presented in the pages of this collection and moved it on for the new century. Robert Englund (1949– ) is the actor who created Freddy Kruger, the most popular screen monster since Dracula and Frankenstein. In seven movies that began with *Nightmare On Elm Street* in 1984, he has brought to life the fiend with razor fingernails who haunts a typical American street just like the one the one in this last story. "I am a great admirer of King's books," Englund says, "and his story, 'The Boogeyman' scared the hell out of me when I first read it!"

"I came to you because I want to tell my story," the man on. Dr. Harper's couch was saying. The man was Lester Billings from Waterbury, Connecticut. According to the history taken from Nurse Vickers, he was twenty-eight, employed by an industrial firm in New York, divorced, and the father of three children. All deceased.

"I can't go to a priest because I'm not Catholic. I can't go to a lawyer because I haven't done anything to consult a lawyer about. All I did was kill my kids. One at a time. Killed them all."

Dr. Harper turned on the tape recorder.

Billings lay straight as a yardstick on the couch, not giving it an inch of himself. His feet protruded stiffly over the end – picture of a man enduring necessary humiliation. His hands were folded corpselike on his chest. His face was carefully set. He looked at the plain white composition ceiling as if seeing scenes and pictures played out there.

"Do you mean you actually killed them, or—"

"No." Impatient flick of the hand. "But I was responsible. Denny in 1967. Shirl in 1971. And Andy this year. I want to tell you about it."

Dr. Harper said nothing. He thought that Billings looked haggard and old. His hair was thinning, his complexion sallow. His eyes held all the miserable secrets of whiskey.

"They were murdered, see? Only no one believes that. If they would, things would be all right."

"Why is that?"

"Because . . ."

Billings broke off and darted up on his elbows, staring across the room. "What's that?" he barked. His eyes had narrowed to black slots.

"What's what?"

"That door."

"The closet," Dr. Harper said. "Where I hang my coat and leave my overshoes."

"Open it. I want to see."

Dr. Harper got up wordlessly, crossed the room, and opened the closet. Inside, a tan raincoat hung on one of four or five hangers. Beneath that was a pair of shiny galoshes. The *New York Times* had been carefully tucked into one of them. That was all.

"All right?" Dr. Harper said.

"All right." Billings removed the props of his elbows and returned to his previous position.

"You were saying," Dr. Harper said as he went back to his chair, "that if the murder of your three children could be proved, all your troubles would be over. Why is that?"

"I'd go to jail," Billings said immediately. "For life. And you can see into all the rooms in a jail. All the rooms." He smiled at nothing.

"How were your children murdered?"

"Don't try to jerk it out of me!"

Billings twitched around and stared balefully at Harper.

"I'll tell you, don't worry. I'm not one of your freaks strutting around and pretending to be Napoleon or explaining that I got hooked on heroin because my mother didn't love me. I know you won't believe me. I don't care. It doesn't matter. Just to tell will be enough."

"All right." Dr. Harper got out his pipe.

"I married Rita in 1965 – I was twenty-one and she was eighteen. She was pregnant. That was Denny." His lips twisted in a rubbery, frightening grin that was gone in a wink. "I had to leave college and get a job, but I didn't mind. I loved both of them. We were very happy.

"Rita got pregnant just a little while after Denny was born, and Shirl came along in December of 1966. Andy came in the summer of 1969, and Denny was already dead by then. Andy was an accident. That's what Rita said. She said sometimes that birth-control stuff doesn't work. I think that it was more than an accident. Children tie a man down, you know. Women like that, especially when the man is brighter than they. Don't you find that's true?"

Harper grunted noncommittally.

"It doesn't matter, though. I loved him anyway." He said it almost vengefully, as it he had loved the child to spite his wife.

"Who killed the children?" Harper asked.

"The boogeyman," Lester Billings answered immediately. "The boogeyman killed them all. Just came out of the closet and killed them." He twisted around and grinned. "You think I'm crazy, all right. It's written all over you. But I don't care. All I want to do is tell you and then get lost."

"I'm listening," Harper said.

"It started when Denny was almost two and Shirl was just an infant. He started crying when Rita put him to bed. We had a two-bedroom place, see. Shirl slept in a crib in our room. At first I thought he was crying because he didn't have a bottle to take to bed anymore. Rita said don't make an issue of it, let it go, let him have it and he'll drop it on his own. But that's the way kids start off bad. You get permissive with them, spoil them. Then they break your heart. Get some girl knocked up, you know, or start shooting dope. Or they get to be sissies. Can you imagine waking up some morning and finding your kid – your *son* – is a sissy?

"After a while, though, when he didn't stop, I started putting him to bed myself. And if he didn't stop crying I'd give him a whack. Then Rita said he was saying 'light' over and over again. Well, I didn't know. Kids that little, how can you tell what they're saying. Only a mother can tell.

"Rita wanted to put in a nightlight. One of those wall-plug things with Mickey Mouse or Huckleberry Hound or something on it. I wouldn't let her. If a kid doesn't get over being afraid of the dark when he's little, he never gets over it.

"Anyway, he died the summer after Shirl was born. I put him to bed that night and he started to cry right off. I heard what he said that time. He pointed right at the closet when he said it. 'Boogeyman,' the kid says. 'Boogeyman, Daddy.'

"I turned off the light and went into our room and asked Rita why she wanted to teach the kid a word like that. I was tempted to slap her around a little, but I didn't. She said she never taught him to say that. I called her a goddamn liar.

"That was a bad summer for me, see. The only job I could get was loading Pepsi-Cola trucks in a warehouse, and I was tired all the time. Shirl would wake up and cry every night and Rita would pick her up and sniffle. I tell you, sometimes I felt like throwing them both out a window. Christ, kids drive you crazy sometimes. You could kill them.

"Well, the kid woke me at three in the morning, right on schedule. I went to the bathroom, only a quarter awake, you know, and Rita asked me if I'd check on Denny. I told her to do it herself and went back to bed. I was almost asleep when she started to scream.

"I got up and went in. The kid was dead on his back. Just as white as flour except for where the blood had . . . had sunk. Back of the legs, the head, the a – the buttocks. His eyes were open. That was the worst, you know. Wide open and glassy, like the eyes you see on a moosehead some guy put over his mantel. Like pictures you see of those gook kids over in 'Nam. But an American kid shouldn't look like that. Dead on his back. Wearing diapers and rubber pants because he'd been wetting himself again the last couple of weeks. Awful, I loved that kid."

Billings shook his head slowly, then offered the rubbery, frightening grin again. "Rita was screaming her head off. She tried to pick Denny up and rock him, but I wouldn't let her. The cops don't like you to touch any of the evidence. I know that—"

"Did you know it was the boogeyman then?" Harper asked quietly.

"Oh, no. Not then. But I did see one thing. It didn't mean anything to me then, but my mind stored it away."

"What was that?"

"The closet door was open. Not much. Just a crack. But I knew I left it shut, see. There's dry-cleaning bags in there. A kid messes around with one of those and bango. Asphyxiation. You know that?"

"Yes. What happened then?"

Billings shrugged. "We planted him." He looked morbidly at his hands, which had thrown dirt on three tiny coffins.

"Was there an inquest?"

"Sure." Billings eyes flashed with sardonic brilliance. "Some back-country fuckhead with a stethoscope and a black bag full of Junior Mints and a sheepskin from some cow college. Crib death, he called it! You ever hear such a pile of yellow manure? The kid was three years old!"

"Crib death is most common during the first year," Harper said carefully, "but that diagnosis has gone on death certificates for children up to age five for want of a better—"

"*Bullshit!*" Billings spat out violently.

Harper relit his pipe.

"We moved Shirl into Denny's old room a month after the funeral. Rita fought it tooth and nail, but I had the last word. It hurt me, of course it did. Jesus, I loved having the kid in with us. But you can't get overprotective. You make a kid a cripple that way. When I was a kid my mom used to take me to the beach and then scream herself hoarse. 'Don't go out so far! Don't go there! It's got an undertow! You only ate an hour ago! Don't go over your head!' Even to watch out for sharks, before God. So what happens? I can't even go near the water now. It's the truth. I get the cramps if I go near a beach. Rita got me to take her and the kids to Savin Rock once when Denny was alive. I got sick as a dog. I know, see? You can't overprotect kids. And you can't coddle yourself either. Life goes on. Shirl went right into Denny's crib. We sent the old mattress to the dump, though. I didn't want my girl to get any germs.

"So a year goes by. And one night when I'm putting Shirl into her crib she starts to yowl and scream and cry. 'Boogeyman, Daddy, boogeyman, boogeyman!'

"That threw a jump into me. It was just like Denny. And I started to remember about that closet door, open just a crack when we found him. I wanted to take her into our room for the night."

"Did you?"

"No." Billings regarded his hands and his face twitched. "How could I go to Rita and admit I was wrong? I *had* to be strong. She was always such a jellyfish . . . look how easy she went to bed with me when we weren't married."

Harper said, "On the other hand, look how easily *you* went to bed with *her*."

Billings froze in the act of rearranging his hands and slowly turned his head to look at Harper. "Are you trying to be a wise guy?"

"No, indeed," Harper said.

"Then let me tell it my way," Billings snapped. "I came here to get this off my chest. To tell my story. I'm not going to talk about my sex life, if that's what you expect. Rita and I had a very normal sex life, with none of that dirty stuff. I know it gives some people a charge to talk about that, but I'm not one of them."

"Okay," Harper said.

"Okay," Billings echoed with uneasy arrogance. He seemed to have lost the thread of his thought, and his eyes wandered uneasily to the closet door, which was firmly shut.

"Would you like that open?" Harper asked.

"No!" Billings said quickly. He gave a nervous little laugh. "What do I want to look at your overshoes for?

"The boogeyman got her, too," Billings said. He brushed at his forehead, as if sketching memories. "A month later. But something happened before that. I heard a noise in there one night. And then she screamed. I opened the door real quick – the hall light was on – and . . . she was sitting up in the crib crying and . . . something *moved*. Back in the shadows, by the closet. Something *slithered*."

"Was the closet door open?"

"A little. Just a crack." Billings licked his lips. "Shirl was screaming about the boogeyman. And something else that sounded like 'claws.' Only she said 'craws,' you know. Little kids have trouble with that 'l' sound. Rita ran upstairs and asked what the matter was. I said she got scared by the shadows of the branches moving on the ceiling."

"Crawset?" Harper said.

"Huh?"

"Crawset . . . closet. Maybe she was trying to say 'closet.' "

"Maybe," Billings said. "Maybe that was it. But I don't think so. I think it was 'claws.' " His eyes began seeking the closet door again. "Claws, long claws." His voice had sunk to a whisper.

"Did you look in the closet?"

"Y-yes." Billings' hands were laced tightly across his chest, laced tightly enough to show a white moon at each knuckle.

"Was there anything in there? Did you see the—"

"*I didn't see anything!*" Billings screamed suddenly. And the words poured out, as if a black cork had been pulled from the bottom of his soul: "When she died I found her, see. And she was black. All black. She swallowed her own tongue and she was just as black as a nigger in a minstrel show and she was staring at me. Her eyes, they looked like those eyes you see on stuffed animals, all shiny and awful, like live marbles, and they were saying it got me, Daddy, you let it get me, you killed me, you helped it kill me . . ." His words trailed off. One single tear very large and silent, ran down the side of his cheek.

"It was a brain convulsion, see? Kids get those sometimes. A bad signal from the brain. They had an autopsy at Hartford Receiving and they told us she choked on her tongue from the convulsion. And I had to go home alone because they kept Rita under sedation. She was out of her mind. I had to go back to that house all alone, and I know a kid don't just get convulsions because their brain frigged up. You can scare a kid into convulsions. And I had to go back to the house where *it* was."

He whispered, "I slept on the couch. With the light on."

"Did anything happen?"

"I had a dream," Billings said. "I was in a dark room and there was something I couldn't . . . couldn't quite see, in the closet. It made a noise . . . a squishy noise. It reminded me of a comic book I read when I was a kid. *Tales from the Crypt*, you remember that? Christ! They had a guy named Graham Ingles; he could draw every god-awful thing in the world – and some out of it. Anyway, in this story this woman drowned her husband, see? Put cement blocks on his feet and dropped him into a quarry. Only he came back. He was all rotted and black-green and the fish had eaten away one of his eyes and there was seaweed in his hair. He came back and killed her. And when I woke up in the middle of the night, I thought that would be leaning over me. With claws . . . long claws . . ."

Dr. Harper looked at the digital clock inset into his desk. Lester Billings had been speaking for nearly half an hour. He said, "When your wife came back home, what was her attitude toward you?"

"She still loved me," Billings said with pride. "She still wanted to do what I told her. That's the wife's place, right? This women's lib only makes sick people. The most important thing in life is for a person to know his place. His . . . his . . . uh . . ."

"Station in life?"

"That's it!" Billings snapped his fingers. "That's it exactly. And a wife should follow her husband. Oh, she was sort of colourless the first four or five months after – dragged around the house, didn't sing, didn't watch the TV, didn't laugh. I knew she'd get over it. When they're that little, you don't get so attached to them. After a while you have to go to the bureau drawer and look at a picture to even remember exactly what they looked like.

"She wanted another baby," he added darkly. "I told her it was a bad idea. Oh, not forever, but for a while. I told her it was a time for us to get over things and begin to enjoy each other. We never had a chance to do that before. If you wanted to go to a movie, you had to hassle around for a babysitter. You couldn't go into town to see the Mets unless her folks would take the kids, because my mom wouldn't have anything to do with us. Denny was born too soon after we were married, see? She said Rita was just a tramp, a common little corner-walker. Corner-walker is what my mom always called them. Isn't that a sketch? She sat me down once and told me diseases you can get if you went to a cor . . . to a prostitute. How your pri . . . your penis has just a little tiny sore on it one day and the next day it's rotting right off. She wouldn't even come to the wedding."

Billings drummed his chest with his fingers.

"Rita's gynaecologist sold her on this thing called an IUD – interuterine device. Foolproof, the doctor said. He just sticks it up the woman's . . . her place, and that's it. If there's anything in there, the egg can't fertilize. You don't even know it's there." He smiled at the ceiling with dark sweetness. "No one knows if it's there or not. And next year she's pregnant again. Some foolproof.

"No birth-control method is perfect," Harper said. "The pill is only ninety-eight percent. The IUD may be ejected by cramps, strong menstrual flow, and, in exceptional cases, by evacuation."

"Yeah. Or you can take it out."

"That's possible."

"So what's next? She's knitting little things, singing in the shower, and eating pickles like crazy. Sitting on my lap and saying things about how it must have been God's will. *Piss*."

"The baby came at the end of the year after Shirl's death?"

"That's right. A boy. She named it Andrew Lester Billings. I didn't want anything to do with it, at least at first. My motto was she screwed up, so let her take care of it. I know how that sounds but you have to remember that I'd been through a lot.

"But I warmed up to him, you know it? He was the only one of the litter that looked like me, for one thing. Denny looked like his mother, and Shirl didn't look like anybody, except maybe my Grammy Ann. But Andy was the spitting image of me.

"I'd get to playing around with him in his playpen when I got home from work. He'd grab only my finger and smile and gurgle. Nine weeks old and the kid was grinning up at his old dad. You believe that?

"Then one night, here I am coming out of a drugstore with a mobile to hang over the kid's crib. Me! Kids don't appreciate presents until they're old enough to say thank you, that was always my motto. But there I was, buying him silly crap and all at once I realize I love him the most of all. I had another job by then, a pretty good one, selling drill bits for Cluett and Sons. I did real well, and when Andy was one, we moved to Waterbury. The old place had too many bad memories.

"And too many closets.

"That next year was the best one for us. I'd give every finger on my right hand to have it back again. Oh, the war in Vietnam was still going on, and the hippies were still running around with no clothes on, and the niggers were yelling a lot, but none of that touched us. We were on a quiet street with nice neighbours. We were happy," he summed up simply. "I asked Rita once if she wasn't worried. You know, bad luck comes in threes and all that. She said not for us. She said Andy was special. She said God had drawn a ring around him."

Billings looked morbidly at the ceiling.

"Last year wasn't so good. Something about the house changed. I started keeping my boots in the hall because I didn't like to open the closet door anymore. I kept thinking: Well, what if it's in there? All crouched down and ready to spring the second I open the door? And I'd started thinking I could hear squishy noises, as if something black and green and wet was moving around in there just a little.

"Rita asked me if I was working too hard, and I started to snap at her, just like the old days. I got sick to my stomach leaving them alone to go to work, but I was glad to get out. God help me, I was glad to get out. I started to think, see, that it lost us for a while when we moved. It had to hunt around, slinking through the streets at night and maybe creeping in the sewers. Smelling for us. It took a year, but it found us. It's back. It wants Andy and it wants me. I started to think, maybe if you think of a thing long enough, and believe in it, it gets real. Maybe all the monsters we were scared of when we were kids, Frankenstein and Wolfman and Mummy, maybe they were real. Real enough to kill the kids that were supposed to have fallen into gravel pits or drowned in lakes or were just never found. Maybe . . ."

"Are you backing away from something, Mr. Billings?"

Billings was silent for a long time – two minutes clicked off the digital clock. Then he said abruptly; "Andy died in February. Rita wasn't there. She got a call from her father. Her mother had been in a car crash the day after New Year's and wasn't expected to live. She took a bus back that night.

"Her mother didn't die, but she was on the critical list for a long time – two months. I had a very good woman who stayed with Andy days. We kept house nights. And closet doors kept coming open."

Billings licked his lips. "The kid was sleeping in the room with me. It's funny, too. Rita asked me once when he was two if I wanted to move him into another room. Spock or one of those other quacks claims its bad for kids to sleep with their parents, see? Supposed to give them traumas about sex and all that. But we never did it unless the kid was asleep. And I didn't want to move him. I was afraid to, after Denny and Shirl."

"But you did move him, didn't you?" Dr. Harper asked.

"Yeah," Billings said. He smiled a sick, yellow smile. "I did." Silence again. Billings wrestled with it.

"I had to!" he barked finally. "I had to! It was all right when Rita was there, but when she was gone, it started to get bolder. It started . . ." He rolled his eyes at Harper and bared his teeth in a savage grin. "Oh, you won't believe it. I know what you think, just another goofy for your casebook, I now that, but you weren't there, you lousy smug head-peeper.

"One night every door in the house blew wide open. One morning I got up and found a trail of mud and filth across the hall between the coat closet and the front door. Was it going out? Coming in? I don't know! Before Jesus, I just don't know! Records all scratched up and covered with slime, mirrors broken . . . and the sounds . . . the sounds . . ."

He ran a hand through his hair. "You'd wake up at three in the morning and look into the dark and at first you'd say, 'It's only the clock.' But underneath it you could hear something moving in a stealthy way. But not too stealthy, because it wanted you to hear it. A slimy sliding sound like something from the kitchen drain. Or a clicking sound, like claws being dragged lightly over the staircase banister. And you'd close your eyes, knowing that hearing it was bad, but if you *saw* it . . .

"And always you'd be afraid that the noises might stop for a little while, and then there would be a laugh right over your face and a breath of air like stale cabbage on your face, and then hands on your throat."

Billings was pallid and trembling.

"So I moved him. I knew it would go for him, see. Because he was weaker. And it did. That very first night he screamed in the middle of the night and finally, when I got up the cojones to go in, he was standing up in bed and screaming. 'The boogeyman, Daddy . . . boogeyman . . . wanna go wif Daddy, go wif Daddy.' " Billings' voice had become a high treble, like a child's. His eyes seemed to fill his entire face; he almost seemed to shrink on the couch.

"But I couldn't," the childish breaking treble continued, "I couldn't. And an hour later there was a scream. An awful, gurgling scream. And I knew how much I loved him because I ran in, I didn't even turn on the light, I ran, ran, *ran*, oh, Jesus God Mary, it had him; it was shaking him, shaking him just like a terrier shakes a piece of cloth and I could see something with awful slumped shoulders and a scarecrow head and I could smell something like a dead mouse in a pop bottle and I heard . . ." He trailed off, and then his voice clicked back into an adult range. "I heard it when Andy's neck broke." Billings' voice was cool and dead. "It made a sound like ice cracking when you're skating on a country pond in winter."

"Then what happened?"

"Oh, I ran," Billings said in the same cool, dead voice. "I went to an all-night diner. How's that for complete cowardice? Ran to an all-night diner and drank six cups of coffee. Then I went home. It was already dawn. I called the police even before I went upstairs. He was lying on the floor and staring at me. Accusing me. A tiny bit of blood had run out of one ear. Only a drop, really. And the closet door was open – but just a crack."

The voice stopped. Harper looked at the digital clock. Fifty minutes had passed.

"Make an appointment with the nurse," he said. "In fact, several of them. Tuesdays and Thursdays?"

"I only came to tell my story," Billings said. "To get it off my chest. I lied to the police, see? Told them the kid must have tried to get out of his crib in the night and . . . they swallowed it. Course they did. That's just what it looked like. Accidental, like the others. But Rita knew. Rita . . . finally . . . knew . . ."

He covered his eyes with his right arm and began to weep.

"Mr. Billings, there is a great deal to talk about," Dr. Harper said after a pause. "I believe we can remove some of the guilt you've been carrying, but first you have to want to get rid of it."

"Don't you believe I *do?*" Billings cried, removing his arm from his eyes. They were red, raw, wounded.

"Not yet," Harper said quietly. "Tuesdays and Thursdays?"

After a long silence, Billings muttered, "Goddamn shrink. All right. All right."

"Make an appointment with the nurse, Mr. Billings. And have a good day."

Billings laughed emptily and walked out of the office quickly, without looking back.

The nurse's station was empty. A small sign on the desk blotter said: "Back in a Minute."

Billings turned and went back into the office. "Doctor, your nurse is—"

The room was empty.

But the closet door was open. Just a crack.

"So nice," the voice from the closet said. "So nice." The words sounded as if they might have come through a mouthful of rotted seaweed.

Billings stood rooted to the spot as the closet door swung open. He dimly felt warmth at his crotch as he wet himself.

"So nice," the boogeyman said as it shambled out.

It still held its Dr. Harper mask in one rotted, spade-claw hand.

# Appendix

## Haunted House Novels: A Listing

Anson, Jay *The Amityville Horror* (1978)
Based on a true story about a family of five including three children, who move into a new house on Long Island and are subjected to a terrifying plague of strange voices, extreme cold and green slime issuing from the walls.

Bangs, John Kendrick *Toppleton's Client, Or A Spirit in Exile* (1893)
A young American lawyer takes over an apartment in London which is haunted by a ghost who induces him to act as his attorney in a long-running dispute.

Barker, Clive *Coldheart Canyon* (2002)
When ageing actor Todd Pickett has a facelift that goes wrong, he retreats to a house on the outskirts of Hollywood. The owner is Katya Lupi, a film star of the 1920s who has not aged a day, and Pickett is soon surrounded by a plethora of ghosts of past stars and creatures from the dark realms of hell.

Bessand-Massenet, Pierre *Amorous Ghost* (1957)
Amusing story of a haunted building where a female ghost establishes a conversational and ultimately sexual relationship with a young writer.

Blackwood, Algernon *Jimbo* (1909)
Young James Stone, nicknamed Jimbo, is terrified of an empty house near where he lives, believing it to be haunted, and when he unwittingly finds himself inside, requires all the assistance of his former governess to escape a terrible fate.

Blatty, William Peter *The Exorcist* (1971)
Horror story inspired by a haunted plot in Washington and focusing on a young girl whose personality and actions are drastically affected by the weird sensations occurring in the family home.

Bradbury, Ray *From The Dust Returned* (2001)
Dwelling in an ancient, legend-haunted mansion in the heart of the American Midwest are a family destined to live forever. But a sense of doom is slowly gathering around the house and its inhabitants as they prepare for a grand gala reunion.

Crompton, Richmal *The House* (1926) [*USA: Dread Dwelling*]
Weird novel by the British author famous for the "Just William" children's series, about an old Tudor mansion which evokes madness and death among its inhabitants.

Danielewski, Mark Z. *House of Leaves* (2000)
Ostensibly a many-layered critique of a documentary film, *The Navidson Record*, about a house in Virginia inhabited by the family of photographer Will Navidson. The humdrum place is supposed to be his haven from danger-filled shoots in the Third World, but instead proves to be very far from normal.

De Morgan, William *Alice For Short* (1907)
The ghosts of a beautiful woman dressed in eighteenth-century costume and a man carrying a sword haunt an old house in Soho, regularly re-enacting a murder until the mystery is solved by the discovery of some bones in the cellar below.

Dick, R. A. *The Ghost and Mrs Muir* (1945)
Coastal house haunted by the ghost of an old sea Captain who does not take kindly to the strong-willed widow who moves in, but is ultimately won over by her charm.

Falconer, Lanoe *Cecilia De Noel* (1891)
Novel, highly regarded by M. R. James, about a ghost who materialises at a house party in Weald Manor and influences all the guests in different ways.

Hall, Leland *Sinister House* (1919)
A lone ancient house amidst a new development in Boston is haunted by the ghost of a man and woman, its former owners, who prey on the new residents.

Herbert, James *The Ghosts of Sleath* (1994)
Psychic investigator David Ash risks his sanity when he delves into the mysterious events terrorising a small community in the Chiltern Hills.

Herbert, James *Haunted* (1988)
Another case for ghost hunter David Ash, when he spends three nights in the terror-ridden house called Edbrook trying to solve its nightmare past.

Heyse, Paul *The House of The Unbelieving Thomas* (1894)
Two ghosts haunt a German town house, appear at séances and also intervene in the affairs of the residents to prove their actuality.

Horsnell, Horace *Castle Cottage* (1940)
The maid in a beautiful Regency home learns the secret of two ghosts – a young man and woman – and tries to help them escape their fate.

Jackson, Shirley *The Haunting of Hill House* (1959)
Acclaimed as the most famous haunted house story in literature, it recounts how a psychic researcher invites a group of people to help solve the mystery which seems to lie in the character of the original builder of Hill House.

James, Henry *The Turn of The Screw* (1898)
Another of the great landmarks of supernatural fiction – allegedly based on a true story told to the author – about a pair of dead, evil servants who return to haunt a house and gain control over the two small children living there.

King, Stephen *The Shining* (1977)
Author Jack Torrance agrees to look after an old hotel while it is shut up and snowed in for the winter. Soon he and his wife and small son are experiencing strange sights, sounds and inexplicable occurrences as the building takes on a life of its own.

Lindsay, David *The Haunted Woman* (1922)
Runhill Court is built over the site of an ancient Saxon building and is the focus of supernatural forces which provide the occupants with vivid pictures of the past, as well as putting them in danger of their lives.

Lovecraft, H. P. *The Shunned House* (1928)
Classic novel of an old house on Rhode Island which destroys the sanity and health of all those who live in it until its terrible secret is revealed.

Lytle, Andrew *A Name for Evil* (1947)
A run-down rural plantation in the American south is haunted by the ghost of a tyrannical former owner, who returns to prey on his descendants and tries to abduct the wife of one of them.

McGrath, Patrick *Asylum* (1996)
Set in a top-security mental hospital, this is the story of Stella Raphael, the beautiful wife of the new deputy superintendent, who sets out to possess Edgar Stark, an artist, sculptor and the perpetrator of an unspeakably brutal crime.

Macardle, Dorothy *Uneasy Freehold* (1941) [USA: *The Uninvited*]
Famous novel of a young playwright and his sister, who take over a remote house near Bristol where two women died in mysterious circumstances and return to haunt the new occupiers.

Malet, Lucas *The Tall Villa* (1919)
Romantic story by a member of the Henry James circle about a lonely woman in a villa haunted by the ghost of a nobleman who protects her from an unscrupulous seducer.

Marsh, Richard *Tom Ossington's Ghost* (1898)
A young teacher who rents a cottage discovers it is haunted by a restless ghost, but he returns her kindness by showing her the way to a lost fortune.

Matheson, Richard *Hell House* (1971)
The house has terrible supernatural powers that have defied the investigations of a number of psychic researchers. When a new team arrives to find the source of the phenomena, they are soon confronting the terror that slaughtered their predecessors.

Mills, Weymer Jay *The Ghosts of Their Ancestors* (1906)
Set in an old New York mansion, the ghost of the owner's great-grandmother returns to put a wayward daughter in her place with unexpected results.

Nicolson, John Urban *Fingers of Fear* (1937)
While studying the influence of Elizabethan literature on the American colonies, a professor visits an ancient haunted mansion in Berkshire full of unimaginable horrors and there meets a terrible fate.

Norton, Frank *The Malachite Cross* (1894)
Occult thriller about a spectacularly haunted house in New York and a curious religious cross, which holds the key to solving the supernatural events.

Pargeter, Edith *The City Lies Four-Square* (1939)
Gothic novel by the mystery writer better-known as Ellis Peters about a young doctor living in a fine house in the middle of a slum and the interventions of a ghostly victim of a riding accident.

Peck, Richard *The Ghost Belonged To Me* (1997)
The Armsworth family have pretensions to be among the social elite in a small Illinois town. Alexander, the son, is uneasy about this situation, but things begin to change when he discovers the ghost of a young Creole girl from the Civil War era haunting the barn.

Peeke, Margaret *Born of Flame* (1892)
The house at Lone Lake is haunted by the ghost of a woman of great paranormal powers as well as her possessions just as she left them – together providing clues about the ancient inhabitants of America.

Priestley, J.B *Night Sequence* (1932)
A quarrelling husband and wife lose their way while on a night drive and are forced to seek shelter in an old, decaying house inhabited by a weird family and their servants. Filmed as *The Old Dark House* starring Boris Karloff.

Reid, Forrest *Pender Among the Residents* (1922)
A man recovering from illness in a haunted house in rural England solves the mystery of the tortured spirit in the living room when he discovers a cache of old letters.

Riddell, Charlotte *The Haunted House at Latchford* (1872)
The ghost of Crow Hall is a woman whose presence effects the health of the residents, but ultimately leads to the discovery of a skeleton and some hidden jewellery.

Riddell, Charlotte *The Haunted River* (1877)
When two half-sisters rent semi-decayed Mill House, they are confronted by various supernatural manifestations including the reenactment of a crime which they ultimately solve.

Riddell, Charlotte *The Uninhabited House* (1875)
River Hall is so badly haunted that no one will live there – until the ghost finally appears to confront its murderer and thereby lifts a terrible curse.

Rives, Amelia *The Ghost Garden* (1918)
The ghost of a colonial beauty who haunts a Virginia mansion, "vampirises" the suitor of a young woman living on the adjacent estate.

Sampson, Ashley *The Ghost of Mr. Brown* (1941)
Novel told from the point of a view of a ghost who is trying to discover why he is condemned to haunt a house by making contact with its residents – with fatal results.

Stone, Mary *A Riddle of Luck* (1893)
A would-be author who stays in a haunted house is invited by the ghost to tell its remarkable story and does so with great success – until the young man refuses to fulfil his part of the bargain with the spirit.

Thorndyke, Russell *The Master of The Macabre* (1947)
The ghost of a lewd and wicked monk who haunts an old palace is laid to rest by a visitor forced to spend a night in the old man's cell.

Toye, Nina *The Shadow of Fear* (1921)
An old abbey where black magic was once practised works its evil on a couple, in particular the neurotic wife.

Wilde, Oscar *The Canterville Ghost* (1887)
Classic farce about an American family who take up residence in haunted Canterville Chase in Berkshire where the sympathetic young daughter helps the tormented ghost to gain release from his punishment.

Wood, Mrs. Henry *The Shadow of Ashlydyat* (1863)
The ghosts of two mourners carrying a coffin haunt the ancient family estate of Ashlydyat – their appearance said to herald a death in the family – until the discovery of a skeleton brings events to a dramatic climax.

Young, Francis Brett *Cold Harbour* (1924)
A famous surgeon and his wife holidaying in Worcestershire learn about the ill-repute of Cold Harbour House and come to suspect that its reputation for being haunted originated from an ancient evil that dates back to Roman times.